P9-DUI-672

LORD PETER AND HARRIET: PART II

A Mystery Guild Lost Classics Omnibus

LORD PETER AND HARRIET: PART II

GAUDY NIGHT

BUSMAN'S HONEYMOON

Dorothy L. Sayers

Mystery Guild
Garden City, New York

ISBN 978-0-7394-7650-5

Manufactured in the United States of America.

Dorothy L. Sayers

Dorothy L. Sayers is the author of novels, short stories, poetry collections, essays, reviews, and translations. Although she was a noted Christian scholar, she is most known for her detective fiction. Born in 1893, she was one of the first women to be awarded a degree from Oxford University. Her first book featuring Lord Peter Wimsey, *Whose Body?*, was published in 1923 and over the next twenty years more novels and short stories about the aristocratic amateur sleuth appeared. Dorothy L. Sayers is recognized as one of the greatest mystery writers of the twentieth century. She died in 1957, but her books continue to enthrall readers today.

Mysteries by
Dorothy L. Sayers

BUSMAN'S HONEYMOON
CLOUDS OF WITNESS
THE DOCUMENTS IN THE CASE
THE FIVE RED HERRINGS
GAUDY NIGHT
HANGMAN'S HOLIDAY
HAVE HIS CARCASE
IN THE TEETH OF THE EVIDENCE
LORD PETER: *A Collection of All the Lord Peter Wimsey Stories*
LORD PETER VIEWS THE BODY
MURDER MUST ADVERTISE
STRONG POISON
UNNATURAL DEATH
THE UNPLEASANTNESS AT THE BELLONA CLUB
WHOSE BODY?

Contents

GAUDY NIGHT

The University is a Paradise, Rivers of Knowledge are there, Arts and Sciences flow from thence. Counsell Tables are *Horti conclusi*, (as it is said in the Canticles) *Gardens that are walled in*, and they are *Fontes signati, Wells that are sealed up*; bottomless depths of unsearchable Counsels there.

JOHN DONNE

AUTHOR'S NOTE

It would be idle to deny that the City and University of Oxford (*in aeternum floreant*) do actually exist, and contain a number of colleges and other buildings, some of which are mentioned by name in this book. It is therefore the more necessary to affirm emphatically that none of the characters which I have placed upon this public stage has any counterpart in real life. In particular, Shrewsbury College, with its dons, students and scouts, is entirely imaginary; nor are the distressing events described as taking place within its walls founded upon any events that have occurred anywhere. Detective-story writers are obliged by their disagreeable profession to invent startling and unpleasant incidents and people, and are (I presume) at liberty to imagine what might happen if such incidents and people were to intrude upon the life of an innocent and well-ordered community; but in so doing they must not be supposed to suggest that any such disturbance ever has occurred or is ever likely to occur in any community in real life.

Certain apologies are, however, due from me: first, to the University of Oxford, for having presented it with a Chancellor and Vice-Chancellor of my own manufacture and with a college of 150 women students, in excess of the limit ordained by statute. Next, and with deep humility, to Balliol College—not only for having saddled it with so wayward an alumnus as Peter Wimsey, but also for my monstrous impertinence in having erected Shrewsbury College upon its spacious and sacred cricket-ground. To

New College, also to Christ Church, and especially to Queen's, I apologize for the follies of certain young gentlemen, to Brasenose for the facetiousness of a middle-aged one, and to Magdalen for the embarrassing situation in which I have placed an imaginary pro-Proctor. The corporation Dump, on the other hand, is, or was, a fact, and no apology for it is due from me.

To the Principal and Fellows of my own college of Somerville, I tender my thanks for help generously given in questions of proctorial rules and general college discipline —though they are not to be held responsible for details of discipline in Shrewsbury College, many of which I have invented to suit my own purpose.

Persons curious in chronology may, if they like, work out from what they already know of the Wimsey family that the action of the book takes place in 1935; but if they do, they must not be querulously indignant because the King's Jubilee is not mentioned, or because I have arranged the weather and the moon's changes to suit my own fancy. For, however realistic the background, the novelist's only native country is Cloud-Cuckooland, where they do but jest, poison in jest: no offense in the world.

CHAPTER 1

Thou blind man's mark, thou fool's self-chosen snare,
Fond fancy's scum, and dregs of scattered thought,
Band of all evils; cradle of causeless care;
Thou web of will, whose end is never wrought:
Desire! Desire! I have too dearly bought
With price of mangled mind, thy worthless ware.
SIR PHILIP SIDNEY

Harriet Vane sat at her writing-table and stared out into Mecklenburg Square. The late tulips made a brave show in the Square garden, and a quartet of early tennis-players were energetically calling the score of a rather erratic and unpracticed game. But Harriet saw neither tulips nor tennis-players. A letter lay open on the blotting-pad before her, but its image had faded from her mind to make way for another picture. She saw a stone quadrangle, built by a modern architect in a style neither new nor old, but stretching out reconciling hands to past and present. Folded within its walls lay a trim grass plot, with flower-beds splashed at the angles, and surrounded by a wide stone plinth. Behind the level roofs of Cotswold slate rose the brick chimneys of an older and less formal pile of buildings—a quadrangle also of a kind, but still keeping a domestic remembrance of the original Victorian dwelling-houses that had sheltered the first shy students of Shrewsbury College. In front were the trees of Jowett Walk, and beyond them, a jumble of ancient gables and the tower of New College, with its jackdaws wheeling against a windy sky.

Memory peopled the quad with moving figures. Students sauntering in pairs. Students dashing to lectures, their gowns hitched hurriedly over light summer frocks, the wind jerking their flat caps into the absurd likeness of so many jesters' cockscombs. Bicycles stacked in the porter's lodge, their carriers piled with books and gowns twisted about their handle-bars. A grizzled woman don crossing the turf with vague eyes, her thoughts riveted upon aspects of sixteenth-century philosophy, her sleeves floating, her shoulders cocked to the academic angle that automatically compensated the backward drag of the pleated poplin. Two male commoners in search of a coach, bareheaded, hands in their trousers-pockets, talking loudly about boats. The Warden—grey and stately—and the Dean—stocky, brisk, birdlike, a Lesser Redpoll—in animated conference under the archway leading to the Old Quadrangle. Tall spikes of delphinium against the grey, quiveringly blue like flames, if flame were ever so blue. The college cat, preoccupied and remote, stalking with tail erect in the direction of the buttery.

It was all so long ago; so closely encompassed and complete; so cut off as by swords from the bitter years that lay between. Could one face it now? What would those women say to her, to Harriet Vane, who had taken her First in English and gone to London to write mystery fiction, to live with a man who was not married to her, and to be tried for his murder amid a roar of notoriety? That was not the kind of career that Shrewsbury expected of its old students.

She had never gone back; at first, because she had loved the place too well, and a clean break seemed better than a slow wrenching-away; and also because, when her parents had died and left her penniless, the struggle to earn a livelihood had absorbed all her time and thought. And afterwards, the stark shadow of the gallows had fallen between her and that sundrenched quadrangle of grey and green. But now—?

She picked up the letter again. It was an urgent entreaty

that she should attend the Shrewsbury Gaudy—an entreaty of the kind that it is difficult to disregard. A friend whom she had not seen since they went down together; married now and remote from her, but fallen sick, and eager to see Harriet once again before going abroad for a delicate and dangerous operation.

Mary Stokes, so pretty and dainty as Miss Patty in the Second-Year play; so charming and finished in manner; so much the social center of her year. It had seemed strange that she should take such a fancy to Harriet Vane, rough and gawky and anything but generally popular. Mary had led and Harriet had followed; when they punted up the Cher with strawberries and thermos flasks; when they climbed Magdalen tower together before sunrise on May-Day and felt it swing beneath them with the swing of the reeling bells; when they sat up late at night over the fire with coffee and parkin, it was always Mary who took the lead in all the long discussions about love and art, religion and citizenship. Mary, said all her friends, was marked for a First; only the dim, inscrutable dons had not been surprised when the lists came out with Harriet's name in the First Class and Mary's in the Second. And since then, Mary had married and scarcely been heard of; except that she haunted the College with a sick persistence, never missing an Old Students' Meeting or a Gaudy. But Harriet had broken all her old ties and half the commandments, dragged her reputation in the dust and made money, had the rich and amusing Lord Peter Wimsey at her feet, to marry him if she chose, and was full of energy and bitterness and the uncertain rewards of fame. Prometheus and Epimetheus had changed their parts, it seemed; but for one there was the box of troubles and for the other the bare rock and the vulture; and never, it seemed to Harriet, could they meet on any common ground again.

"But, by God!" said Harriet, "I won't be a coward. I'll go and be damned to it. Nothing can hurt me worse than I've been hurt already. And what does it matter after all?"

She filled up her invitation form, addressed it, stamped

it with a sharp thump and ran quickly down to drop it in the pillar-box before she changed her mind.

She came back slowly across the Square garden, mounted the Adam stone stair to her flat and, after a fruitless rummage in a cupboard, came out and climbed up slowly again to a landing at the top of the house. She dragged out an ancient trunk, unlocked it and flung back the lid. A close, cold odor. Books. Discarded garments. Old shoes. Old manuscripts. A faded tie that had belonged to her dead lover—how horrible that that should still be hanging about! She burrowed to the bottom of the pile and dragged a thick, black bundle out into the dusty sunlight. The gown, worn only once at the taking of her M.A. degree, had suffered nothing from its long seclusion: the stiff folds shook loose with hardly a crease. The crimson silk of the hood gleamed bravely. Only the flat cap showed a little touch of the moth's tooth. As she beat the loose fluff from it, a tortoise-shell butterfly, disturbed from its hibernation beneath the flap of the trunk-lid, fluttered out into the brightness of the window, where it was caught and held by a cobweb.

Harriet was glad that in these days she could afford her own little car. Her entry into Oxford would bear no resemblance to those earlier arrivals by train. For a few hours longer she could ignore the whimpering ghost of her dead youth and tell herself that she was a stranger and a sojourner, a well-to-do woman with a position in the world. The hot road span away behind her; towns rose from the green landscape, crowded close about her with their inn-signs and petrol-pumps, their shops and police and perambulators, then reeled back and were forgotten. June was dying among the roses, the hedges were darkening to a duller green; the blatancy of red brick sprawled along the highway was a reminder that the present builds inexorably over the empty fields of the past. She lunched in High Wycombe, solidly, comfortably, ordering a half-bottle of white wine and tipping the waitress generously. She was eager to distinguish herself as sharply as possible from that former undergraduate who would have had to be content with a packet of sandwiches and a flask of coffee beneath the bough in a by-lane. As one grew older, as one established one's self, one gained a new delight in formality. Her dress for the Garden-party, chosen to combine suitably with full academicals, lay, neatly folded, inside her suitcase. It was long and severe, of plain black georgette, wholly and unimpeachably correct. Beneath it was an evening dress for the Gaudy Dinner, of a rich petunia color, excellently cut on restrained lines, with no unbecoming display of back or breast; it would not affront the portraits of dead Wardens, gazing down from the slowly mellowing oak of the Hall.

Headington. She was very near now, and in spite of herself a chill qualm cramped her stomach. Headington Hill, up which one had toiled so often, pushing a decrepit bicycle. It seemed less steep now, as one made decorous descent behind four rhythmically pulsating cylinders; but every leaf and stone hailed one with the intrusive familiarity of an old schoolfellow. Then the narrow street, with its cramped, untidy shops, like the main street of a village; one or two stretches had been widened and improved, but there was little real change to take refuge in.

Magdalen Bridge. Magdalen Tower. And here, no change at all—only the heartless and indifferent persistence of man's handiwork. Here one must begin to steel one's self in earnest. Long Wall Street. St. Cross Road. The iron hand of the past gripping at one's entrails. The college gates; and now one must go through with it.

There was a new porter at the St. Cross lodge, who heard Harriet's name unmoved and checked it off upon a list. She handed him her bag, took her car round to a garage in Mansfield Lane,* and then, with her gown over

* For the purposes of this book, Mansfield Lane is deemed to run from Mansfield Road to St. Cross Road, behind Shrewsbury College and somewhere about the junction between the Balliol and Merton Cricket grounds as they stand at present.

her arm, passed through the New Quad into the Old, and so, by way of an ugly brick doorway, into Burleigh Building.

She met nobody of her year in the corridors or on the staircase. Three contemporaries of a far senior generation were greeting one another with effusive and belated girlishness at the door of the Junior Common Room; but she knew none of them, and went by unspeaking and unspoken to, like a ghost. The room allotted to her she recognized, after a little calculation, as one that had been occupied in her day by a woman she particularly disliked, who had married a missionary and gone to China. The present owner's short gown hung behind the door; judging by the bookshelves, she was reading History; judging by her personal belongings, she was a Fresher with an urge for modernity and very little natural taste. The narrow bed, on which Harriet flung down her belongings, was covered with drapery of a crude green color and ill-considered Futuristic pattern; a bad picture in the neo-archaic manner hung above it; a chromium-plated lamp of angular and inconvenient design swore acidly at the table and wardrobe provided by the college, which were of a style usually associated with the Tottenham Court Road; while the disharmony was crowned and accentuated by the presence, on the chest of drawers, of a curious statuette or three-dimensional diagram carried out in aluminum, which resembled a gigantic and contorted corkscrew, and was labelled upon its base: ASPIRATION. It was with surprise and relief that Harriet discovered three practicable dress-hangers in the wardrobe. The looking glass, in conformity with established college use, was about a foot square, and hung in the darkest corner of the room.

She unpacked her bag, took off her coat and skirt, slipped on a dressing-gown and set out in search of a bathroom. She had allowed herself three-quarters of an hour for changing, and Shrewsbury's hot-water system had always been one of its most admirable minor efficiencies. She had forgotten exactly where the bathrooms were on this floor, but surely they were round here to the left. A pantry, two pantries, with notices on the doors: NO WASHING-UP TO BE DONE AFTER 11 P.M.; three lavatories, with notices on the doors: KINDLY EXTINGUISH THE LIGHT WHEN LEAVING; yes, here she was—four bathrooms, with notices on the doors: NO BATHS TO BE TAKEN AFTER 11 P.M., and, underneath, an exasperated addendum to each: IF STUDENTS PERSIST IN TAKING BATHS AFTER 11 P.M. THE BATHROOMS WILL BE LOCKED AT 10:30 P.M. *SOME* CONSIDERATION FOR OTHERS IS NECESSARY IN COMMUNITY LIFE. Signed: L. MARTIN, DEAN. Harriet selected the largest bathroom. It contained a notice: REGULATIONS IN CASE OF FIRE, and a card printed in large capitals: THE SUPPLY OF HOT WATER IS LIMITED. PLEASE AVOID UNDUE WASTE. With a familiar sensation of being under authority, Harriet pushed down the waste-plug and turned on the tap. The water was boiling, though the bath badly needed a new coat of enamel and the cork mat had seen better days.

Once bathed, Harriet felt better. She was lucky again in returning to her room to meet no one whom she knew. She was in no mood for reminiscent gossipings in dressing-gowns. She saw the name "Mrs. H. Attwood" on the door next but one to hers. The door was shut, and she was grateful. The next door bore no name, but as she went by, someone turned the handle from within, and it began to open slowly. Harriet leapt quickly past it and into shelter. She found her heart beating absurdly fast.

The black frock fitted her like a glove. It was made with a small square yoke and long, close sleeves, softened by a wristfrill falling nearly to the knuckles. It outlined her figure to the waist and fell full-skirted to the ground, with a suggestion of the medieval robe. Its dull surface effaced itself, not outshining the dull gleam of the academic poplin. She pulled the gown's heavy folds forward upon her shoulders, so that the straight fronts fell stole-wise, serene. The hood cost her a small struggle, before she remembered the right twist at the throat which turned the bright silk outwards. She pinned it invisibly on her breast, so that it sat poised and balanced—one black shoulder and one crimson. Standing and stooping before the inadequate looking-glass (the present student who owned the room was obviously a very short woman), she adjusted the soft cap to lie flat and straight, peak down in the center of the forehead. The glass showed her her own face, rather pale, with black brows fronting squarely either side of a strong nose, a little too broad for beauty. Her own eyes looked back at her—rather tired, rather defiant—eyes that had looked upon fear and were still wary. The mouth was the mouth of one who has been generous and repented of generosity; its wide corners were tucked back to give nothing away. With the thick, waving hair folded beneath the black cloth, the face seemed somehow stripped for action. She frowned at herself and moved her hands a little up and down upon the stuff of her gown; then, becoming impatient with the looking-glass, she turned to the window, which looked out into the Inner or Old Quad. This, indeed, was less a quad than an oblong garden, with the college buildings grouped about it. At one end, tables and chairs were set out upon the grass beneath the shade of the trees. At the far side, the new Library wing, now almost complete, showed its bare rafters in a forest of scaffolding. A few groups of women crossed the lawn; Harriet observed with irritation that most of them wore their caps badly, and one had had the folly to put on a pale lemon frock with muslin frills, which looked incongruous beneath a gown.

"Though, after all," she thought, "the bright colors are medieval enough. And at any rate, the women are no worse than the men. I once saw old Hammond walk in the Encaenia procession in a Mus. Doc. gown, a grey flannel suit, brown boots and a blue spotted tie, and nobody said anything to him."

She laughed suddenly, and for the first time felt confident.

"They can't take this away, at any rate. Whatever I may have done since, this remains. Scholar; Master of Arts;

Domina; Senior Member of this University (*statutum est quod Juniores Senioribus debitam et congruam reverentiam tum in privato tum in publico exhibeant*); a place achieved, inalienable, worthy of reverence.

She walked firmly from the room and knocked upon the door next but one to her own.

The four women walked down to the garden together—slowly, because Mary was ill and could not move fast. And as they went, Harriet was thinking:

"It's a mistake—it's a great mistake—I shouldn't have come. Mary is a dear, as she always was, and she is pathetically pleased to see me, but we have nothing to say to one another. And I shall always remember her, *now*, as she is today, with that haggard face and look of defeat. And she will remember me as I am—hardened. She told me I looked successful. I know what that means."

She was glad that Betty Armstrong and Dorothy Collins were doing all the talking. One of them was a hardworking dog-breeder; the other ran a bookshop in Manchester. They had evidently kept in touch with one another, for they were discussing things and not people, as those do who have lively interests in common. Mary Stokes (now Mary Attwood) seemed cut off from them, by sickness, by marriage, by—it was no use to blink the truth—by a kind of mental stagnation that had nothing to do with either illness or marriage. "I suppose," thought Harriet, "she had one of those small, summery brains, that flower early and run to seed. Here she is—my intimate friend—talking to me with a painful kind of admiring politeness about my books. And I am talking with a painful kind of admiring politeness about her children. We ought *not* to have met again. It's awful."

Dorothy Collins broke in upon her thoughts by asking her a question about publishers' contracts, and the reply to this tided them over till they emerged into the quad. A brisk figure came bustling along the path, and stopped with a cry of welcome.

"Why, it's Miss Vane! How nice to see you after all this long time."

Harriet thankfully allowed herself to be scooped up by the Dean, for whom she had always had a very great affection, and who had written kindly to her in the days when a cheerful kindliness had been the most helpful thing on earth. The other three, mindful of reverence toward authority, passed on; they had paid their respects to the Dean earlier in the afternoon.

"It was splendid that you were able to come."

"Rather brave of me, don't you think?" said Harriet.

"Oh, nonsense!" said the Dean. She put her head on one side and fixed Harriet with a bright and birdlike eye. "You mustn't think about all that. Nobody bothers about it at all. We're not nearly such dried-up mummies as you think. After all, it's the work you are doing that really counts, isn't it? By the way, the Warden is longing to see you. She simply loved *The Sands of Crime*. Let's see if we can catch her before the Vice-Chancellor arrives. . . . How did you think Stokes was looking—Attwood, I mean? I never *can* remember all their married names."

"Pretty rotten, I'm afraid," said Harriet. "I came here to see her, really, you know—but I'm afraid it's not going to be much of a success."

"Ah!" said the Dean. "She's stopped growing, I expect. She was a friend of yours—but I always thought she had a head like a day-old chick. Very precocious, but no staying power. However, I hope they'll put her right. . . . Bother this wind—I can't keep my cap down. You manage yours remarkably well; how do you do it? And I notice that we are both decently sub-fusc. *Have* you seen Trimmer in that frightful frock like a canary lampshade?"

"That was Trimmer, was it? What's *she* doing?"

"Oh, lord! my dear, she's gone in for mental healing. Brightness and love and all that. . . . Ah! I thought we should find the Warden here."

Shrewsbury College had been fortunate in its wardens. In the early days, it had been dignified by a woman of position; in the difficult period when it fought for Women's degrees it had been guided by a diplomat; and now that it was received into the University, its behavior was made acceptable by a personality. Dr. Margaret Baring wore her scarlet and French grey with an air. She was a magnificent figure-head on all public occasions, and she could soothe with tact the wounded breasts of crusty and affronted male dons. She greeted Harriet graciously, and asked what she thought of the new Library Wing, which would complete the North side of the Old Quad. Harriet duly admired what could be seen of its proportions, said it would be a great improvement, and asked when it would be finished.

"By Easter, we hope. Perhaps we shall see you at the Opening."

Harriet said politely that she should look forward to it, and, seeing the Vice-Chancellor's gown flutter into sight in the distance, drifted tactfully away to join the main throng of old students.

Gowns, gowns, gowns. It was difficult sometimes to recognize people after ten years or more. That in the blue-and-rabbit-skin hood must be Sylvia Drake—she had taken that B.Litt. at last, then. Miss Drake's B.Litt. had been the joke of the college; it had taken her so long; she was continually rewriting her thesis and despairing over it. She would hardly remember Harriet, who was so much her junior, but Harriet remembered her well—always popping in and out of the J.C.R. during her year of residence, and chattering away about medieval Courts of Love. Heavens! Here was that awful woman, Muriel Campshott, coming up to claim acquaintance. Campshott had always simpered. She still simpered. And she was dressed in a shocking shade of green. She was going to say, "How *do* you think of all your plots?" She did say it. Curse the woman. And Vera Mollison. She was asking: "Are you writing anything now?"

"Yes, certainly," said Harriet. "Are you still teaching?"

"Yes—still in the same place," said Miss Mollison. "I'm afraid my doings are very small beer compared with yours."

As there was no possible answer to this but a deprecating laugh, Harriet laughed deprecatingly. A movement took place. People were drifting into the New Quad, where a Presentation Clock was to be unveiled, and taking up their positions upon the stone plinth that ran round behind the flower-beds. An official voice was heard exhorting the guests to leave a path for the procession. Harriet used this excuse to disentangle herself from Vera Mollison and establish herself at the back of a group, all of whose faces were strange to her. On the opposite side of the Quad she could see Mary Attwood and her friends. They were waving. She waved back. She was *not* going to cross the grass and join them. She would remain detached, a unit in an official crowd.

From behind a drapery of bunting the clock, anticipating its official appearance in public, chimed and struck three. Footsteps crunched along the gravel. The procession came into sight beneath the archway; a small crocodile-walk of elderly people, dressed with the incongruous brilliance of a more sumptuous era, and moving with the slovenly dignity characteristic of university functions in England. They crossed the quad; they mounted the plinth beneath the clock; the male dons removed their Tudor bonnets and mortar-boards in deference to the Vice-Chancellor; the female dons adopted a reverential attitude suggestive of a prayer-meeting. In a thin, delicate voice, the Vice-Chancellor began to speak. He spoke of the history of the college; he made a graceful allusion to achievements which could not be measured by the mere passing of time; he cracked a dry and nutty little jest about relativity and adorned it with a classical tag; he referred to the generosity of the donor and the beloved personality of the deceased Member of Council in whose memory the clock was presented; he expressed himself happy to unveil this handsome clock, which would add so greatly to the beauty of the quadrangle—a quadrangle, he would add, which, although a newcomer in point of time, was fully worthy to take its place among those ancient and noble buildings which were the glory of our University. In the name of the Chancellor and University of Oxford, he now unveiled the clock. His hand went out to the rope; an agitated expression came over the face of the Dean, resolving itself into a wide smile of triumph when the drapery fell away without any unseemly hitch or disaster; the clock was revealed, a few bold spirits started a round of applause; the Warden, in a short, neat speech, thanked the Vice-Chancellor for his kindness in coming and his friendly expressions; the golden hand of the clock moved on, and the quarter-chime rang out mellowly. The assembly heaved a sigh of satisfaction; the procession collected itself and made the return journey through the archway, and the ceremony was happily over.

Harriet, following with the throng, discovered to her horror that Vera Mollison had bobbed up again beside her, and was saying she supposed all mystery-writers must feel a strong personal interest in clocks, as so many alibis turned upon clocks and time-signals. There had been a curious incident one day at the school where she taught; it would, she thought, make a splendid plot for a detective-story, for anybody who was clever enough to work such things out. She had been longing to see Harriet and tell her all about it. Planting herself firmly on the lawn of the Old Quad, at a considerable distance from the refreshment-tables, she began to retail the curious incident, which required a good deal of preliminary explanation. A scout advanced, carrying cups of tea. Harriet secured one, and instantly wished she hadn't; it prevented swift movement, and seemed to nail her to Miss Mollison's side to all eternity. Then, with a heart-lifting surge of thankfulness, she saw Phoebe Tucker. Good old Phoebe, looking exactly the same as ever. She excused herself hurriedly to Miss Mollison, begging that she might hear the clock incident at a more leisured moment, made her way through a bunch of gowns and said, "Hullo!"

"Hullo?" said Phoebe. "Oh, it's you. Thank God! I was beginning to think there wasn't a soul of our year here, except Trimmer and that ghastly Mollison female. Come and get some sandwiches; they're quite good, strange to say. How are you these days; flourishing?"

"Not too bad."

"You're doing good stuff, anyhow."

"So are you. Let's find something to sit upon. I want to hear all about the digging."

Phoebe Tucker was a History student, who had married an archaeologist, and the combination seemed to work remarkably well. They dug up bones and stones and pottery in forgotten corners of the globe, and wrote pamphlets and lectured to learned societies. At odd moments they had produced a trio of cheerful youngsters, whom they dumped casually upon delighted grandparents before hastening back to the bones and stones.

"Well, we've only just got back from Ithaca. Bob is fearfully excited about a new set of burial-places, and has evolved an entirely original and revolutionary theory about funerary rites. He's writing a paper that contradicts all old Lambard's conclusions, and I'm helping by toning down his adjectives and putting in deprecatory footnotes. I mean, Lambard may be a perverse old idiot, but it's more dignified not to say so in so many words. A bland and deadly courtesy is more devastating, don't you think?"

"Infinitely."

Here at any rate was somebody who had not altered by a hair's-breadth, in spite of added years and marriage. Harriet was in a mood to be glad of that. After an exhaustive inquiry into the matter of funerary rites, she asked after the family.

"Oh, they're getting to be rather fun. Richard—that's the eldest—is thrilled by the burial-places. His grandmother was horrified the other day to find him very patiently and correctly excavating the gardener's rubbish-heap and making a collection of bones. Her generation always get so agitated about germs and dirt. I suppose they're quite right, but the offspring doesn't seem any the worse. So his father gave him a cabinet to keep the bones in. Simply encouraging him, Mother said. I think we shall have to take Richard out with us next time, only Mother would be so worried, thinking about no drainage and what he might pick up from the Greeks. All the children seem to be coming out quite intelligent, thank goodness. It would have been such a bore to be the mother of morons, and it's an absolute toss-up, isn't it? If one could only invent them, like characters in books, it would be much more satisfactory to a well-regulated mind."

From this the conversation naturally passed to biology, Mendelian factors and *Brave New World*. It was cut short by the emergence of Harriet's former tutor from a crowd of old students. Harriet and Phoebe made a concerted rush to greet her. Miss Lydgate's manner was exactly what it had always been. To the innocent and candid eyes of that great scholar, no moral problem seemed ever to present itself. Of a scrupulous personal integrity, she embraced the irregularities of other people in a wide, unquestioning charity. As any student of literature must, she knew all the sins of the world by name, but it was doubtful whether she recognized them when she met them in real life. It was as though a misdemeanor committed by a person she knew was disarmed and disinfected by the contact. So many young people had passed through her hands, and she had found so much good in all of them; it was impossible to think that they could be deliberately wicked, like Richard III or Iago. Unhappy, yes; misguided, yes; exposed to difficult and complicated temptations which Miss Lydgate herself had been mercifully spared, yes. If she heard of a theft, a divorce, even worse things, she would knit puzzled brows and think how utterly wretched the offenders must have been before they could do so dreadful a thing. Only once had Harriet ever heard her speak with unqualified disapproval of anyone she knew, and that was of a former pupil of her own who had written a popular book about Carlyle. "No research at all," had been Miss Lydgate's verdict, "and no effort at critical judgment. She has reproduced all the old gossip without troubling to verify anything. Slipshod, showy, and catchpenny. I am really ashamed of her." And even then she had added: "But I believe, poor thing, she is very hard up."

Miss Lydgate showed no signs of being ashamed of Miss Vane. On the contrary, she greeted her warmly, begged her to come and see her on Sunday morning, spoke appreciatively of her work, and commended her for keeping up a scholarly standard of English, even in mystery fiction.

"You give a lot of pleasure in the S.C.R.," she added, "and I believe Miss de Vine is also a fervent admirer of yours."

"Miss de Vine?"

"Ah, of course, you don't know her. Our new Research Fellow. She's such a nice person, and I know she wants to talk to you about your books. You must come and make her acquaintance. We've got her for three years, you know. That is, she only comes into residence next term, but she's been living in Oxford for the last few weeks, working in Bodley. She's doing a great work on National Finance under the Tudors, and makes it perfectly fascinating, even for people like me, who are stupid about money. We are all so glad that the College decided to offer her the Jane Barraclough Fellowship, because she is a most distinguished scholar, and has had rather a hard time."

"I think I've heard of her. Wasn't she Head of one of the big provincial colleges?"

"Yes; she was Provost of Flamborough for three years; but it wasn't really her job; too much administration, though of course she was marvelous on the financial side. But she was doing too much, what with her own work, and examining for doctorates and so on, and coping with students—the University and the College between them wore her out. She's one of those people who always *will* give of her best; but I think she found all the personal contacts uncongenial. She got ill, and had to go abroad for a couple of years. In fact, she has only just got back to England. Of course, having to give up Flamborough made a good deal of difference from the financial point of view; so it's nice to think that for the next three years she'll be able to get on with her book and not worry about that side of things."

"I remember about it now," said Harriet; "I saw the election announced somewhere or other, last Christmas or thereabouts."

"I expect you saw it in the Shrewsbury Year-Book. We are naturally very proud to have her here. She ought really to have a professorship, but I doubt if she could stand the tutorial side of it. The fewer distractions she has, the better, because she's one of the *real* scholars. There she is, over there—and, oh, dear! I'm afraid she's been caught by Miss Gubbins. You remember Miss Gubbins?"

"Vaguely," said Phoebe. "She was Third Year when we were freshers. An excellent soul, but rather earnest, and an appalling bore at College Meetings."

"She is a very conscientious person," said Miss Lydgate, "but she has rather an unfortunate knack of making any subject sound dull. It's a great pity, because she is exceptionally sound and dependable. However, that doesn't greatly matter in her present appointment; she holds a librarianship somewhere—Miss Hillyard would remember where—and I believe she's researching on the Bacon family. She's such a hard worker. But I'm afraid she's putting poor Miss de Vine through a cross-examination, which doesn't seem quite fair on an occasion like this. Shall we go to the rescue?"

As Harriet followed Miss Lydgate across the lawn, she was visited by an enormous nostalgia. If only one could come back to this quiet place, where only intellectual achievement counted; if one could work here steadily and obscurely at some close-knit piece of reasoning, undistracted and uncorrupted by agents, contracts, publishers, blurb-writers, interviewers, fan-mail, autograph-hunters, notoriety-hunters, and competitors; abolishing personal contacts, personal spites, personal jealousies; getting one's teeth into something dull and durable; maturing into solidity like the Shrewsbury beeches—then, one might be able to forget the wreck and chaos of the past, or see it, at any rate, in a truer proportion. Because, in a sense, it was not important. The fact that one had loved and sinned and suffered and escaped death was of far less ultimate moment than a single footnote in a dim academic journal establishing the priority of a manuscript or restoring a lost iota subscript. It was the hand-to-hand struggle with the insistent personalities of other people, all pushing for a place in the limelight, that made the accidents of one's own personal adventure bulk so large in the scheme of things.

But she doubted whether she were now capable of any such withdrawal. She had long ago taken the step that put the grey-walled paradise of Oxford behind her. No one can bathe in the same river twice, not even in the Isis. She would be impatient of that narrow serenity—or so she told herself.

Pulling her wandering thoughts together, she found herself being introduced to Miss de Vine. And, looking at her, she saw at once that here was a scholar of a kind very unlike Miss Lydgate, for example, and still more grotesquely unlike anything that Harriet Vane could ever become. Here was a fighter, indeed; but one to whom the quadrangle of Shrewsbury was a native and proper arena: a soldier knowing no personal loyalties, whose sole allegiance was to the fact. A Miss Lydgate, standing serenely untouched by the world, could enfold it in a genial warmth of charity; this woman, with infinitely more knowledge of the world, would rate it at a just value and set it out of her path if it incommoded her. The thin, eager face, with its large grey eyes deeply set and luminous behind thick glasses, was sensitive to impressions; but behind that sensitiveness was a mind as hard and immovable as granite. As the Head of a woman's college she must, thought Harriet, have had a distasteful task; for she looked as though the word "compromise" had been omitted from her vocabulary; and all statesmanship is compromise. She would not be likely to tolerate any waverings of purpose or woolliness of judgment. If anything came between her and the service of truth, she would walk over it without rancour and without pity—even if it were her own reputation. A formidable woman when pursuing the end in view—and the more so, for the deceptive moderation and modesty she would display in dealing with any subject of which she was not master. As they came up, she was saying to Miss Gubbins:

"I entirely agree that a historian ought to be precise in detail; but unless you take all the characters and circumstances concerned into account, you are reckoning without the facts. The proportions and relations of things are just as much facts as the things themselves; and if you get those wrong, you falsify the picture really seriously."

Here, just as Miss Gubbins, with a mulish look in her eye, was preparing to expostulate, Miss de Vine caught sight of the English tutor and excused herself. Miss Gubbins was obliged to withdraw; Harriet observed with regret that she had untidy hair, an ill-kept skin and a large white safety-pin securing her hood to her dress.

"Dear me!" said Miss de Vine, "who is that very uninspired young woman? She seems very much annoyed with my review of Mr. Winterlake's book on Essex. She seems to think I ought to have torn the poor man to pieces because of a trifling error of a few months made in dealing, quite incidentally, with the early history of the Bacon family. She attaches no importance to the fact that the book is the most illuminating and scholarly handling to date of the interactions of two most enigmatic characters."

"Bacon family history is her subject," said Miss Lydgate, "so I've no doubt she feels strongly about it."

"It's a great mistake to see one's own subject out of proportion to its background. The error should be corrected, of course; I did correct it—in a private letter to the author, which is the proper medium for trifling corrections. But the man has, I feel sure, got hold of the master-key to the situation between those two men, and in so doing he has got hold of a fact of genuine importance."

"Well," said Miss Lydgate, showing her strong teeth in a genial grin, "you seem to have taken a strong line with Miss Gubbins. Now I've brought along somebody I know you're anxious to meet. This is Miss Harriet Vane—also an artist in the relating of details."

"Miss Vane?" The historian bent her brilliant, short-sighted eyes on Harriet, and her face lit up. "This is delightful. Do let me say how much I enjoyed your last book. I thought it quite the best thing you'd done—though of course I'm not competent to form an opinion from the scientific point of view. I was discussing it with Professor Higgins, who is quite a devotee of yours, and he said it suggested a most interesting possibility, which had not before occurred to him. He wasn't quite sure whether it would work, but he would do his best to find out. Tell me, what did you have to go upon?"

"Well, I got a pretty good opinion," said Harriet, feeling a hideous qualm of uncertainty, and cursing Professor Higgins from the bottom of her heart. "But of course—"

At this point, Miss Lydgate espied another old pupil in the distance and ran away. Phoebe Tucker had already been lost on the way across the lawn. Harriet was left to her fate. After ten minutes, during which Miss de Vine ruthlessly turned her victim's brain inside out, shook the facts out of it like a vigorous housemaid shaking dust from a carpet, beat it, refreshed it, rubbed up the surface of it, relaid it in a new position and tacked it into place with a firm hand, the Dean mercifully came up and burst into the conversation.

"Thank *goodness*, the Vice-Chancellor's taking himself off. Now we can get rid of this filthy old bombazine and show off our party frocks. *Why* did we ever clamor for degrees and the fun of stewing in full academicals on a hot day? There! he's gone! Give me those anything-but-glad-rags and I'll shove them into the S.C.R. with mine. Has yours got a name on it, Miss Vane? Oh, good girl! I've got three unknown gowns sitting in my office already. Found lying about at the end of term. No clue to owners, of course. The untidy little beasts seem to think it's our job to sort out their miserable belongings. They strew them everywhere, regardless, and then borrow each other's; and if anybody's fined for being out without a gown, it's always because somebody pinched it. And the wretched things are always as dirty as dishclouts. They use them for dusters and drawing the fire up. When I think how our devoted generation *sweated* to get the right to these garments—and these young things don't care *that* for them! They go about looking all bits and pieces, like illustrations to *Pendennis—so* out of date of them! But their idea of being modern is to imitate what male undergraduates were like half a century ago."

"Some of us old students aren't much to write home about," said Harriet. "Look at Gubbins, for instance."

"Oh, my dear! That crashing bore. And *all* held together with safety-pins. And I wish she'd wash her neck."

"I think," said Miss de Vine, with painstaking readiness to set the facts in a just light, "that the color is natural to her skin."

"Then she should eat carrots and clear her system," retorted the Dean, snatching Harriet's gown from her. "No, don't you bother. It won't take me a minute to chuck them through the S.C.R. window. And don't you dare to run away, or I shall *never* find you again."

"Is my hair tidy?" inquired Miss de Vine, becoming suddenly human and hesitating with the loss of her cap and gown.

"Well," said Harriet, surveying the thick, iron-grey coils from which a quantity of overworked hair-pins stood out like croquet-hoops, "it's coming down just a trifle."

"It always does," said Miss de Vine, making vague dabs at the pins. "I think I shall have to cut it short. It must be much less trouble that way."

"I like it as it is. That big coil suits you. Let me have a go at it, shall I?"

"I wish you would," said the historian, thankfully submitting to having the pins thrust into place. "I am very stupid with my fingers. I do possess a hat somewhere," she added, with an irresolute glance round the quad, as though she expected to see the hat growing on a tree, "but the

Dean said we'd better stay here. Oh, thank you. That feels much better—a marvelous sense of security. Ah! here's Miss Martin. Miss Vane has kindly been acting as hairdresser to the White Queen—but oughtn't I to put on a hat?"

"Not now," said Miss Martin emphatically. "I'm going to have some proper tea, and so are you. I'm *ravenous*. I've been tagging after old Professor Boniface who's ninety-seven and practically gaga, and screaming in his deaf ear till I'm almost *dead*. What's the time? Well, I'm like Marjory Fleming's turkey—I do not give a single damn for the Old Students' Meeting; I simply must eat and drink. Let's swoop down upon the table before Miss Shaw and Miss Stevens collar the last ices."

CHAPTER II

'Tis proper to all melancholy men, saith Mercurialis, *what conceit they have once entertained, to be most intent, violent and continually about it.* Invitis occurrit, *do what they may, they cannot be rid of it, against their wills they must think of it a thousand times over,* perpetuo molestantur, nec oblivisci possunt, *they are continually troubled with it, in company, out of company; at meat, at exercise, at all times and places,* non desinunt ea, quae minime volunt, cogitare; *if it be offensive especially, they cannot forget it.*

ROBERT BURTON

So far, so good, thought Harriet, changing for dinner. There had been baddish moments, like trying to renew contact with Mary Stokes. There had also been a brief encounter with Miss Hillyard, the History tutor, who had never liked her, and who had said, with wry mouth and acidulated tongue, "Well, Miss Vane, you have had some very *varied* experiences since we saw you last." But there had been good moments too, carrying with them the promise of permanence in a Heraclitean universe. She felt it might be possible to survive the Gaudy Dinner, though Mary Stokes had dutifully bagged for her a place next herself, which was trying. Fortunately, she had contrived to get Phoebe Tucker on her other side. (In these surroundings, she thought of them still as Stokes and Tucker.)

The first thing to strike her, when the procession had slowly filed up to the High Table, and grace had been said, was the appalling noise in Hall. "Strike" was the right word. It fell upon one like the rush and weight of a shouting waterfall; it beat on the ear like the hammer-clang of some infernal smithy; it savaged the air like the metallic clatter of fifty thousand monotype machines casting type. Two hundred female tongues, released as though by a spring, burst into high, clamorous speech. She had forgotten what it was like, but it came back to her tonight how, at the beginning of every term, she had felt that if the noise were to go on like that for one minute more, she would go quite mad. Within a week, the effect of it had always worn off. Use had made her immune. But now it shattered her unaccustomed nerves with all and more than all its original violence. People screamed in her ear, and she found herself screaming back. She looked rather anxiously at Mary; could any invalid bear it? Mary seemed not to notice; she was more animated than she had been earlier in the day and was screaming quite cheerfully at Dorothy Collins. Harriet turned to Phoebe.

"Gosh! I'd forgotten what this row was like. If I scream I shall be as hoarse as a crow. I'm going to bellow at you in a fog-horn kind of voice. Do you mind?"

"Not a bit. I can hear you quite well. Why on earth did God give women such shrill voices? Though I don't mind frightfully. It reminds me of native workmen quarreling. They're doing us rather well, don't you think? Much better soup than we ever got."

"They've made a special effort for Gaudy. Besides, the new Bursar's rather good, I believe; she was something to do with Domestic Economy. Dear old Straddles had a mind above food."

"Yes; but I liked Straddles. She was awfully decent to me when I got ill just before Schools. Do you remember?"

"What happened to Straddles when she left?"

"Oh, she's Treasurer at Brontë College. Finance was really her line, you know. She had a real genius for figures."

"And what became of that woman—what's her name? —Peabody? Freebody?—you know—the one who always said solemnly that her great ambition in life was to become Bursar of Shrewsbury?"

"Oh, my dear! She went absolutely potty on some new kind of religion and joined an extraordinary sect somewhere or other where they go about in loin-cloths and have agapemones of nuts and grape-fruit. That is, if you mean Brodribb?"

"Brodribb—I knew it was something like Peabody. Fancy her of all people! So intensely practical and subfusc."

"Reaction, I expect. Repressed emotional instincts and all that. She was frightfully sentimental inside, you know."

"I know. She wormed round rather. Had a sort of G.P. for Miss Shaw. Perhaps we were all rather inhibited in those days."

"Well, the present generation doesn't suffer from that, I'm told. *No* inhibitions of any kind."

"Oh, come, Phoebe. We had a good bit of liberty. Not like before Women's Degrees. We weren't monastic."

"No, but we were born long enough before the War to feel a few restrictions. We inherited some sense of responsibility. And Brodribb came from a fearfully rigid sort of household—Positivists, or Unitarians or Presbyterians or something. The present lot are the real War-time generation, you know."

"So they are. Well, I don't know that I've any right to throw stones at Brodribb."

"Oh, my dear! That's entirely different. One thing's natural; the other's—I don't know, but it seems to me like complete degeneration of the grey matter. She even wrote a book."

"About agapemones?"

"Yes. And the Higher Wisdom. And Beautiful Thought. That sort of thing. Full of bad syntax."

"Oh, lord! Yes—that's pretty awful, isn't it? I can't think why fancy religions should have such a ghastly effect on one's grammar."

"It's a kind of intellectual rot that sets in, I'm afraid. But which of them causes the other, or whether they're both symptoms of something else, I don't know. What with Trimmer's mental healing, and Henderson going nudist—"

"No!"

"Fact. There she is, at the next table. That's why she's so brown."

"And her frock so badly cut. If you can't be naked, be as ill-dressed as possible, I suppose."

"I sometimes wonder whether a little normal, hearty wickedness wouldn't be good for a great many of us."

At this moment, Miss Mollison, from three places away on the same side of the table, leaned across her neighbors and screamed something.

"What?" screamed Phoebe.

Miss Mollison leaned still further, compressing Dorothy Collins, Betty Armstrong and Mary Stokes almost to suffocation.

"I hope Miss Vane isn't telling you anything *too* bloodcurdling!"

"No," said Harriet, loudly. "Mrs. Bancroft is curdling *my* blood."

"How?"

"Telling me the life-histories of our year."

"Oh!" screamed Miss Mollison, disconcerted. The service of a dish of lamb and green peas intervened and broke up the formation, and her neighbors breathed again. But to Harriet's intense horror, the question and reply seemed to have opened up an avenue for a dark, determined woman with large spectacles and rigidly groomed hair, who sat opposite to her, and who now bent over and said, in piercingly American accents:

"I don't suppose you remember me, Miss Vane? I was only in college for one term, but I would know you anywhere. I'm always recommending your books to my friends in America who are keen to study the British detective story, because I think they are just terribly good."

"Very kind of you," said Harriet, feebly.

"And we have a very dear mutooal acquaintance," went on the spectacled lady.

Heavens! thought Harriet. What social nuisance is going to be dragged out of obscurity now? And who is this frightful female?

"Really?" she said, aloud, trying to gain time while she ransacked her memory. "Who's that, Miss—"

"Schuster-Slatt," prompted Phoebe's voice in her ear.

"Schuster-Slatt." (Of course. Arrived in Harriet's first summer term. Supposed to read Law. Left after one term because the conditions at Shrewsbury were too restrictive of liberty. Joined the Home Students, and passed mercifully out of one's life.)

"How clever of you to know my name. Yes, well, you'll be surprised when I tell you, but in my work I see so many of your British aristocracy."

Hell! thought Harriet. Miss Schuster-Slatt's strident tones dominated even the surrounding uproar.

"Your marvelous Lord Peter. He was so kind to me, and terribly interested when I told him I was at college with you. I think he's just a lovely man."

"He has very nice manners," said Harriet. But the implication was too subtle. Miss Schuster-Slatt proceeded:

"He was just wonderful to me when I told him all about my work." (I wonder what it is, thought Harriet.) "And of course I wanted to hear all about his thrilling detective cases, but he was much too modest to say anything. Do tell me, Miss Vane, does he wear that cute little eyeglass because of his sight, or is it part of an old English tradition?"

"I have never had the impertinence to ask him," said Harriet.

"Now isn't that just like your British reticence!" exclaimed Miss Schuster-Slatt; when Mary Stokes struck in with:

"Oh, Harriet, do tell us about Lord Peter! He must be perfectly charming, if he's at all like his photographs. Of course you know him very well, don't you?"

"I worked with him over one case."

"It must have been frightfully exciting. Do tell us what he's like."

"Seeing," said Harriet, in angry and desperate tones, "seeing that he got me out of prison and probably saved me from being hanged, I am naturally bound to find him delightful."

"Oh!" said Mary Stokes, flushing scarlet, and shrinking from Harriet's furious eyes as if she had received a blow. "I'm sorry—I didn't think—"

"Well, there," said Miss Schuster-Slatt, "I'm afraid I've been very, very tactless. My mother always said to me, 'Sadie, you're the most tactless girl I ever had the bad luck to meet.' But I am enthusiastic. I get carried away. I don't stop to think. I'm just the same with my work. I don't consider my own feelings; I don't consider other people's feelings. I just wade right in and ask for what I want, and I mostly get it."

After which, Miss Schuster-Slatt, with more sensitive feeling than one might have credited her with, carried the conversation triumphantly away to the subject of her own work, which turned out to have something to do with the sterilization of the unfit, and the encouragement of matrimony among the intelligentsia.

Harriet, meanwhile, sat miserably wondering what devil possessed her to display every disagreeable trait in her character at the mere mention of Wimsey's name. He had done her no harm; he had only saved her from a shameful death and offered her an unswerving personal devotion; and for neither benefit had he ever claimed or expected her gratitude. It was not pretty that her only return should be a snarl of resentment. The fact is, thought Harriet, I have got a bad inferiority complex; unfortunately, the fact that I know it doesn't help me to get rid of it. I could have liked him so much if I could have met him on an equal footing. . . .

The Warden rapped upon the table. A welcome silence fell upon the Hall. A speaker was rising to propose the toast of the university.

She spoke gravely, unrolling the great scroll of history, pleading for the Humanities, proclaiming the Pax Academica to a world terrified with unrest. "Oxford has been called the home of lost causes: if the love of learning for its own sake is a lost cause everywhere else in the world, let us see to it that here at least, it finds its abiding home." Magnificent, thought Harriet, but it is not war. And then, her imagination weaving in and out of the spoken words, she saw it as a Holy War, and that whole wildly heterogeneous, that even slightly absurd collection of chattering women fused into a corporate unity with one another and with every man and woman to whom integrity of mind meant more than material gain—defenders in the central keep of Man-soul, their personal differences forgotten in face of a common foe. To be true to one's calling, whatever follies one might commit in one's emotional life, that was the way to spiritual peace. How could one feel fettered, being the freeman of so great a city, or humiliated, where all enjoyed equal citizenship? The eminent professor who rose to reply spoke of a diversity of gifts but the same spirit. The note, once struck, vibrated on the lips of every speaker and the ear of every hearer. Nor was the Warden's review of the Academic year out of key with it: appointments, degrees, fellowships—all these were the domestic details of the discipline without which the community could not function. In the glamour of one Gaudy night, one could realize that one was a citizen of no mean city. It might be an old and an old-fashioned city, with inconvenient buildings and narrow streets where the passersby squabbled foolishly about the right of way; but her foundations were set upon the holy hills and her spires touched heaven.

Leaving the Hall in this rather exalted mood, Harriet found herself invited to take coffee with the Dean.

She accepted, after ascertaining that Mary Stokes was bound for bed by doctor's orders and had therefore no claim upon her company. She therefore made her way along to the New Quad and tapped upon Miss Martin's door. Gathered together in the sitting-room she found

Betty Armstrong, Phoebe Tucker, Miss de Vine, Miss Stevens the Bursar, another of the Fellows who answered to the name of Barton, and a couple of old students a few years senior to herself. The Dean, who was dispensing coffee, hailed her arrival cheerfully.

"Come along! Here's coffee that is coffee. Can *nothing* be done about the Hall coffee, Steve?"

"Yes, if you'll start a coffee-fund," replied the Bursar. "I don't know if you've ever worked out the finance of really first-class coffee for two hundred people."

"I know," said the Dean. "It's so trying to be grovellingly poor. I think I'd better mention it to Flackett. You remember Flackett, the rich one, who was always rather odd. She was in your year, Miss Fortescue. She has been following me round, trying to present the College with a tankful of tropical fish. Said she thought it would brighten the Science Lecture-Room."

"If it would brighten some of the lectures," said Miss Fortescue, "it might be a good thing. Miss Hillyard's Constitutional Developments were a bit gruesome in our day."

"Oh, my *dear!* Those Constitutional Developments! Dear me, yes—they still go on. She starts every year with about thirty students and ends up with two or three earnest black men, who take every word down solemnly in notebooks. Exactly the same lectures; I don't think even fish would help them. Anyway, I said, 'It's very good of you, Miss Flackett, but I really don't think they'd thrive. It would mean putting in a special heating system, wouldn't it? And it would make extra work for the gardeners.' She looked so disappointed, poor thing; so I said she'd better consult the Bursar."

"All right," said Miss Stevens, "I'll tackle Flackett, and suggest the endowment of a coffee-fund."

"*Much* more useful than tropical fish," agreed the Dean. "I'm afraid we do turn out some oddities. And yet, you know, I believe Flackett is extremely sound upon the life-history of the liver-fluke. Would anybody like a Benedictine with the coffee? Come along, Miss Vane. Alcohol loosens the tongue, and we want to hear all about your latest mysteries."

Harriet obliged with a brief résumé of the plot she was working on.

"Forgive me, Miss Vane, for speaking frankly," said Miss Barton, leaning earnestly forward, "but after your own terrible experience, I wonder that you care about writing that kind of book."

The Dean looked a little shocked.

"Well," said Harriet, "for one thing, writers can't pick and choose until they've made money. If you've made your name for one kind of book and then switch over to another, your sales are apt to go down, and that's the brutal fact." She paused. "I know what you're thinking—that anybody with proper sensitive feeling would rather scrub floors for a living. But I should scrub floors very badly, and I write detective stories rather well. I don't see why proper feeling should prevent me from doing my proper job."

"Quite right," said Miss de Vine.

"But surely," persisted Miss Barton, "you must feel that terrible crimes and the sufferings of innocent suspects ought to be taken seriously, and not just made into an intellectual game."

"I do take them seriously in real life. Everybody must. But should you say that anybody who had tragic experience of sex, for example, should never write an artificial drawing-room comedy?"

"But isn't that different?" said Miss Barton, frowning. "There is a lighter side to love; whereas there's no lighter side to murder."

"Perhaps not, in the sense of a comic side. But there is a purely intellectual side to the detection."

"You did investigate a case in real life, didn't you? How did you feel about that?"

"It was very interesting."

"And, in the light of what you knew, did you like the idea of sending a man to the dock and the gallows?"

"I don't think it's quite fair to ask Miss Vane that," said

the Dean. "Miss Barton," she added, a little apologetically, to Harriet, "is interested in the sociological aspects of crime, and very eager for the reform of the penal code."

"I am," said Miss Barton. "Our attitude to the whole thing seems to me completely savage and brutal. I have met so many murderers when visiting prisons; and most of them are very harmless, stupid people, poor creatures, when they aren't definitely pathological."

"You might feel differently about it," said Harriet, "if you'd happened to meet the victims. They are often still stupider and more harmless than the murderers. But *they* don't make a public appearance. Even the jury needn't see the body unless they like. But I saw the body in that Wilvercombe case—I *found* it; and it was beastlier than anything you can imagine."

"I'm quite sure you must be right about that," said the Dean. "The description in the papers was more than enough for me."

"And," went on Harriet to Miss Barton, "you don't see the murderers actively engaged in murdering. You see them when they're caught and caged and looking pathetic. But the Wilvercombe man was a cunning, avaricious brute, and quite ready to go on and do it again, if he hadn't been stopped."

"That's an unanswerable argument for stopping them," said Phoebe, "whatever the law does with them afterwards."

"All the same," said Miss Stevens, "isn't it a little cold-blooded to catch murderers as an intellectual exercise? It's all right for the police—it's their duty."

"In law," said Harriet, "it is every citizen's obligation—though most people don't know that."

"And this man Wimsey," said Miss Barton, "who seems to make a hobby of it—does he look upon it as a duty or as an intellectual exercise?"

"I'm not sure," said Harriet, "but, you know, it was just as well for me that he did make a hobby of it. The police were wrong in my case—I don't blame them, but they were —so I'm glad it wasn't left to them."

"I call that a perfectly noble speech," said the Dean. "If anyone had accused me of doing something I hadn't done, I should be foaming at the mouth."

"But it's my job to weigh evidence," said Harriet, "and I can't help seeing the strength of the police case. It's a matter of a + b, you know. Only there happened to be an unknown factor."

"Like that thing that keeps cropping up in the new kind of physics," said the Dean. "Planck's constant, or whatever they call it."

"Surely," said Miss de Vine, "whatever comes of it, and whatever anybody feels about it, the important thing is to get at the facts."

"Yes," said Harriet; "that's the point. I mean, the fact is that I *didn't* do the murder, so that my feelings are quite irrelevant. If I had done it, I should probably have thought myself thoroughly justified, and been deeply indignant about the way I was treated. As it is, I still think that to inflict the agonies of poisoning on anybody is unpardonable. The particular trouble I got let in for was as much sheer accident as falling off a roof."

"I really ought to apologize for having brought the subject up at all," said Miss Barton. "It's very good of you to discuss it so frankly."

"I don't mind—now. It would have been different just after it happened. But that awful business down at Wilvercombe shed rather a new light on the matter—showed it up from the other side."

"Tell me," said the Dean, "Lord Peter—what is he like?"

"To look at, do you mean? or to work with?"

"Well, one knows more or less what he looks like. Fair and Mayfair. I meant, to talk to."

"Rather amusing. He does a good deal of the talking himself, if it comes to that."

"A little merry and bright, when you're feeling off-color?"

"I met him once at a dog-show," put in Miss Armstrong unexpectedly. "He was giving a perfect imitation of the silly-ass-about-town."

"Then he was either frightfully bored or detecting something," said Harriet, laughing. "I know that frivolous mood, and it's mostly camouflage—but one doesn't always know for what."

"There must be something behind it," said Miss Barton, "because he's obviously very intelligent. But is it only intelligence, or is there any genuine feeling?"

"I shouldn't," said Harriet, gazing thoughtfully into her empty coffee cup, "accuse him of any lack of feeling. I've seen him very much upset, for instance, over convicting a sympathetic criminal. But he is really rather reserved, in spite of that deceptive manner."

"Perhaps he's shy," suggested Phoebe Tucker, kindly. "People who talk a lot often are. I think they are very much to be pitied."

"Shy?" said Harriet. "Well, hardly. Nervy, perhaps—that blessed word covers a lot. But he doesn't exactly seem to call for pity."

"Why should he?" said Miss Barton. "In a very pitiful world, I don't see much need to pity a young man who has everything he can possibly want."

"He must be a remarkable person if he has that," said Miss de Vine, with a gravity that her eyes belied.

"And he's not so young as all that," said Harriet. "He's forty-five." (This was Miss Barton's age.)

"I think it's rather an impertinence to pity people," said the Dean.

"Hear, hear!" said Harriet. "Nobody likes being pitied. Most of us enjoy self-pity, but that's another thing."

"Caustic," said Miss de Vine, "but painfully true."

"But what I should like to know," pursued Miss Barton, refusing to be diverted, "is whether this dilettante gentleman does anything, outside his hobbies of detecting crimes and collecting books, and, I believe, playing cricket in his off-time."

Harriet, who had been congratulating herself upon the way in which she was keeping her temper, was seized with irritation.

"I don't know," she said. "Does it matter? Why should he do anything else? Catching murderers isn't a soft job, or a sheltered job. It takes a lot of time and energy, and you may very easily get injured or killed. I dare say he does it for fun, but at any rate, he does do it. Scores of people must have as much reason to thank him as I have. You can't call that nothing."

"I absolutely agree," said the Dean. "I think one ought to be very grateful to people who do dirty jobs for nothing, whatever their reason is."

Miss Fortescue applauded this. "The drains in my weekend cottage got stopped up last Sunday, and a most helpful neighbor came and unstopped them. He got quite filthy in the process and I apologized profusely, but he said I owed him no thanks, because he was inquisitive and liked drains. He may not have been telling the truth, but even if he was, I certainly had nothing to grumble about."

"Talking of drains," said the Bursar—

The conversation took a less personal and more anecdotal turn (for there is no chance assembly of people who cannot make lively conversation about drains), and after a little time Miss Barton retired to bed. The Dean breathed a sigh of relief.

"I hope you didn't mind too much," she said. "Miss Barton is the most terribly downright person, and she was determined to get all that off her chest. She is a splendid person, but hasn't very much sense of humor. She can't bear anything to be done except from the very loftiest motives."

Harriet apologized for having spoken so vehemently.

"I thought you took it all wonderfully well. And your Lord Peter sounds a most interesting person. But I don't see why you should be forced to discuss him, poor man."

"If you ask me," observed the Bursar, "we discuss everything a great deal too much in this university. We argue about this and that and why and wherefore, instead of getting the thing done."

"But oughtn't we to ask what things we want done," objected the Dean.

Harriet grinned at Betty Armstrong, hearing the familiar academic wrangle begin. Before ten minutes had passed, somebody had introduced the word "values." An hour later they were still at it. Finally the Bursar was heard to quote:

"God made the integers; all else is the work of man."

"Oh, bother!" cried the Dean. "Do let's keep mathematics out of it. And physics. I cannot cope with them."

"Who mentioned Planck's constant a little time ago?"

"I did, and I'm sorry for it. I call it a revolting little object."

The Dean's emphatic tones reduced everybody to laughter, and, midnight striking, the party broke up.

"I am still living out of College," said Miss de Vine to Harriet. "May I walk across to your room with you?"

Harriet assented, wondering what Miss de Vine had to say to her. They stepped out together into the New Quad. The moon was up, painting the buildings with cold washes of black and silver whose austerity rebuked the yellow gleam of lighted windows behind which old friends reunited still made merry with talk and laughter.

"It might almost be term-time," said Harriet.

"Yes." Miss de Vine smiled oddly. "If you were to listen at those windows, you would find it was the middle-aged ones who were making the noise. The old have gone to bed, wondering whether they have worn as badly as their contemporaries. They have suffered some shocks, and their feet hurt them. And the younger ones are chattering soberly about life and its responsibilities. But the women of forty are pretending they are undergraduates again, and finding it rather an effort. Miss Vane—I admired you for speaking as you did tonight. Detachment is a rare virtue, and very few people find it lovable, either in themselves or in others. If you ever find a person who likes you in spite of it—still more, because of it—that liking has very great value, because it is perfectly sincere, and because, with that person, you will never need to be anything but sincere yourself."

"That is probably very true," said Harriet, "but what makes you say it?"

"Not any desire to offend you, believe me. But I imagine you come across a number of people who are disconcerted by the difference between what you do feel and what they fancy you ought to feel. It is fatal to pay the smallest attention to them."

"Yes," said Harriet, "but I am one of them. I disconcert myself very much. I never know what I do feel."

"I don't think that matters, provided one doesn't try to persuade one's self into appropriate feelings."

They had entered the Old Quad, and the ancient beeches, most venerable of all Shrewsbury institutions, cast over them a dappled and changing shadow-pattern that was more confusing than darkness.

"But one has to make some sort of choice," said Harriet. "And between one desire and another, how is one to know which things are really of overmastering importance?"

"We can only know that," said Miss de Vine, "when they have overmastered us."

The checkered shadow dropped off them, like the dropping of linked silver chains. Each after each, from all the towers of Oxford, clocks struck the quarter-chime, in a tumbling cascade of friendly disagreement. Miss de Vine bade Harriet good night at the door of Burleigh Building and vanished, with her long, stooping stride beneath the Hall archway.

An odd woman, thought Harriet, and of a penetrating shrewdness. All Harriet's own tragedy had sprung from "persuading herself into appropriate feelings" towards a man whose own feelings had not stood up to the test of sincerity either. And all her subsequent instability of purpose had sprung from the determination that never again would she mistake the will to feel for the feeling itself. "We can only know what things are of overmastering importance when they have overmastered us." Was there anything at all that had stood firm in the midst of her indecisions? Well, yes; she had stuck to her work—and that in the face of what might have seemed overwhelming reasons for abandoning it and doing something different. Indeed, though she had shown cause that evening for this particular loyalty, she had never felt it necessary to show cause to herself. She had written what she felt herself called upon to write; and, though she was beginning to feel that she might perhaps do this thing better, she had no doubt that the thing itself was the right thing for her. It had overmastered her without her knowledge or notice, and that was the proof of its mastery.

She paced for some minutes to and fro in the quad, too restless to go in and sleep. As she did so, her eye was caught by a sheet of paper, fluttering untidily across the trim turf. Mechanically she picked it up and, seeing that it was not blank, carried it into Burleigh Building with her for examination. It was a sheet of common scribbling paper, and all it bore was a childish drawing scrawled heavily in pencil. It was not in any way an agreeable drawing—not at all the kind of thing that one would expect to find in a college quadrangle. It was ugly and sadistic. It depicted a naked figure of exaggeratedly feminine outlines, inflicting savage and humiliating outrage upon some person of indeterminate gender clad in a cap and gown. It was neither sane nor healthy; it was, in fact, a nasty, dirty and lunatic scribble.

Harriet stared at it for a little time in disgust, while a number of questions formed themselves in her mind. Then she took it upstairs with her into the nearest lavatory, dropped it in and pulled the plug on it. That was the proper fate for such things, and there was an end of it; but for all that, she wished she had not seen it.

CHAPTER III

They do best who, if they cannot but admit love, yet make it keep quarter, and sever it wholly from their serious affairs and actions of life; for if it check once with business it troubleth men's fortunes, and maketh men that they can no ways be true to their own ends.

FRANCIS BACON

Sunday, as the S.C.R. always declared, was invariably the best part of a Gaudy. The official dinner and speeches were got out of the way; the old students resident in Oxford, and the immensely busy visitors with only one night to spare had all cleared off. People began to sort themselves out, and one could talk to one's friends at leisure, without being instantly collared and hauled away by a collection of bores.

Harriet paid her visit of state to the Warden, who was holding a small reception with sherry and biscuits, and then went to call upon Miss Lydgate in the New Quad. The English tutor's room was festooned with proofs of her forthcoming work on the Prosodic elements in English verse from Beowulf to Bridges. Since Miss Lydgate had perfected, or was in process of perfecting (since no work of scholarship ever attains a static perfection), an entirely new prosodic theory, demanding a novel and complicated system of notation which involved the use of twelve different varieties of type; and since Miss Lydgate's handwriting was difficult to read and her experience in dealing with printers limited, there existed at that moment five successive revises in galley form, at different stages of completion, together with two sheets in page-proof, and an appendix in typescript, while the important Introduction which afforded the key to the whole argument still remained to be written. It was only when a section had advanced to page-proof condition that Miss Lydgate became fully convinced of the necessity of transferring large paragraphs of argument from one chapter to another, each change of this kind naturally demanding expensive over-running on the page-proof, and the elimination of the corresponding portions in the five sets of revises; so that in the course of the necessary cross-reference, Miss Lydgate would be discovered by her pupils and colleagues wound into a kind of paper cocoon and helplessly searching for her fountain-pen amid the litter.

"I am afraid," said Miss Lydgate, rubbing her head, in response to Harriet's polite inquiries as to the magnum opus, "I am dreadfully ignorant about the practical side of book-making. I find it very confusing and I'm not at all clever at explaining myself to the printers. It will be a great help having Miss de Vine here. She has such an orderly mind. It's really an education to see her manuscript, and of course her work is far more intricate than mine—all sorts of little items out of Elizabethan pay-rolls and so on, all wonderfully sorted out and arranged in a beautiful clear argument. And she understands setting out footnotes properly, so that they fit in with the text. I always find that so difficult, and though Miss Harper is kindly doing all my typing for me, she really knows more about Anglo-Saxon than about compositors. I expect you remember Miss Harper. She was two years junior to you and took a second in English and lives in the Woodstock Road."

Harriet said she thought footnotes were always very tiresome, and might she see some of the book.

"Well, if you're really interested," said Miss Lydgate, "but I don't want to bore you." She extracted a couple of paged sheets from a desk stuffed with papers. "Don't prick your fingers on that bit of manuscript that's pinned on. I'm afraid it's rather full of marginal balloons and interlineations, but you see, I suddenly realized that I could work out a big improvement in my notation, so I've had to alter it all through. I expect," she added wistfully, "the printers will be rather angry with me."

Harriet privately agreed with her, but said comfortingly that the Oxford University Press was no doubt accustomed to deciphering the manuscripts of scholars.

"I sometimes wonder whether I am a scholar at all," said Miss Lydgate. "It's all quite clear in my head, you know, but I get muddled when I put it down on paper. How do you manage about your plots? All that time-table work with the alibis and so on must be terribly hard to bear in mind."

"I'm always getting mixed up myself," admitted Harriet. "I've never yet succeeded in producing a plot without at least six major howlers. Fortunately, nine readers out of ten get mixed up too, so it doesn't matter. The tenth writes me a letter, and I promise to make the correction in the second edition, but I never do. After all, my books are only meant for fun; it's not like a work of scholarship."

"You always had a scholarly mind, though," said Miss Lydgate, "and I expect you find your training a help in some ways, don't you? I used to think you might take up an academic career."

"Are you disappointed that I didn't?"

"No, indeed. I think it's so nice that our students go out and do such varied and interesting things, provided they do them well. And I must say, most of our students do do exceedingly good work along their own lines."

"What are the present lot like?"

"Well," said Miss Lydgate, "we've got some *very* good people up, and they work surprisingly hard, when you think of all the outside activities they manage to carry on at the same time. Only sometimes I'm afraid they rather overdo it, and don't get enough sleep at night. What with young men and motor-cars and parties, their lives are so much fuller than they were before the War—even more so than in your day, I think. I'm afraid our old Warden would be very greatly disconcerted if she saw the college as it is today. I must say that I am occasionally a little startled myself, and even the Dean, who is so broad-minded, thinks a brassière and a pair of drawers rather unsuitable for sun-bathing in the quad. It isn't so much the male undergraduates—they're used to it—but after all, when the Heads of the men's colleges come to call on the Warden, they really ought to be able to get through the grounds without blushing. Miss Martin has really had to insist on bathing dresses—backless if they like, but proper bathing dresses made for the purpose, and not ordinary underwear."

Harriet agreed that this seemed only reasonable.

"I am so glad you think so," said Miss Lydgate. "It is rather difficult for us of the older generation to hold the balance between tradition and progress—if it is progress. Authority as such commands very little respect nowadays, and I expect that is a good thing on the whole, though it makes the work of running any kind of institution more difficult. I am sure you would like a cup of coffee. No, really—I always have one myself about this time. Annie!—I think I hear my scout in the pantry—Annie! Would you please bring in a second cup for Miss Vane."

Harriet was fairly well satisfied already with eatables and drinkables, but politely accepted the refreshment brought in by the smartly uniformed maid. She made some remark, when the door was shut again, as to the great improvements made since her own day in the staff and service at Shrewsbury, and again heard the praise awarded to the new bursar.

"Though I am afraid," added Miss Lydgate, "we may have to lose Annie from this staircase. Miss Hillyard finds her too independent; and perhaps she *is* a little absent-minded. But then, poor thing, she is a widow with two children, and really ought not to have to be in service at all. Her husband was in quite a good position, I believe, but he went out of his mind, or something, poor man, and died or shot himself, or something tragic of that kind, leaving her very badly off, so she was glad to take what she could. The little girls are boarded out with Mrs. Jukes—you remember the Jukeses, they were at the St. Cross Lodge in your time. They live down in St. Aldate's now, so Annie is able to go and see them at weekends. It is nice for her and brings in a trifle extra for Mrs. Jukes."

"Did Jukes retire? He wasn't very old, was he?"

"Poor Jukes," said Miss Lydgate, her kind face clouding. "He got into sad trouble and we were obliged to dismiss him. He turned out to be not quite honest, I am sorry to say. But we found him work as a jobbing gardener," she went on more cheerfully, "where he wouldn't be exposed to so much temptation in the matter of parcels and so on. He was a most hardworking man, but he would put money on horse-races, and so, naturally, he found himself in difficulties. It was so unfortunate for his wife."

"She was a good soul," agreed Harriet.

"She was terribly upset about it all," went on Miss Lydgate. "And so, to do him justice, was Jukes. He quite broke down, and there was a sad scene with the Bursar when she told him he must go."

"Ye-es," said Harriet. "Jukes always had a pretty glib tongue."

"Oh, but I'm sure he was really very sorry for what he'd done. He explained how he'd slipped into it, and one thing led to another. We were all very much distressed about it. Except, perhaps, the Dean—but then she never did like Jukes very much. However, we made a small loan to his wife, to pay off his debts, and they certainly repaid it most honestly, a few shillings each week. Now that he's *put* straight I feel sure he will *keep* straight. But of course, it was impossible to keep him on here. One could never feel absolutely easy, and one must have entire confidence in the porter. The present man, Padgett, is most reliable and a very amusing character. You must get the Dean to tell you some of Padgett's quaint sayings."

"He looks a monument of integrity," said Harriet. "He

may be less popular, on that account. Jukes took bribes, you know—if one came in late, and that sort of thing."

"We were afraid he did," said Miss Lydgate. "Of course, it's a responsible post for a man who isn't of very strong character. He'll do much better where he is."

"You've lost Agnes, too, I see."

"Yes—she was Head-Scout in your time; yes, she has left. She began to find the work too much for her and had to retire. I'm glad to say we were able to squeeze out a tiny pension for her—only a trifle, but as you know, our income has to be stretched very carefully to cover everything. And we arranged a little scheme by which she takes in odd jobs of mending and so on for the students and attends to the College linen. It all helps; and she's especially glad because that crippled sister of hers can do part of the work and contribute something to their small income. Agnes says the poor soul is so much happier now that she need not feel herself a burden."

Harriet marveled, not for the first time, at the untiring conscientiousness of administrative women. Nobody's interests ever seemed to be overlooked or forgotten, and an endless goodwill made up for a perennial scarcity of funds.

After a little more talk about the doings of past dons and students, the conversation turned upon the new Library. The books had long outgrown their old home in Tudor Building, and were at last to be adequately housed.

"And when that is finished," said Miss Lydgate, "we shall feel that our College Buildings are substantially complete. It does seem rather wonderful to those of us who remember the early days when we only had the one funny old house with ten students, and were chaperoned to lectures in a donkey-carriage. I must say we rather wept to see the dear old place pulled down to make way for the Library. It held so many memories."

"Yes, indeed," said Harriet, sympathetically. She supposed that there was no moment of the past upon which this experienced and yet innocent soul could not dwell with unaffected pleasure. The entrance of another old pupil cut short her interview with Miss Lydgate, and she went out, vaguely envious, to encounter the persistent Miss Mollison, primed with every remorseless detail of the clock incident. It gave her pleasure to inform Miss Mollison that Mr. A. E. W. Mason had hit on the same idea earlier. Unquenchable, Miss Mollison proceeded to question her victim eagerly about Lord Peter Wimsey, his manners, customs and appearance; and when Miss Mollison was driven away by Miss Schuster-Slatt, the irritation was little relieved, for Harriet was subjected to a long harangue about the sterilization of the unfit, to which (it appeared) a campaign to encourage the marriage of the fit was a necessary corollary. Harriet agreed that intellectual women should marry and reproduce their kind; but she pointed out that the English husband had something to say in the matter and that, very often, he did not care for an intellectual wife.

Miss Schuster-Slatt said she thought English husbands were lovely, and that she was preparing a questionnaire to be circulated to the young men of the United Kingdom, with a view to finding out their matrimonial preferences.

"But English people won't fill up questionnaires," said Harriet.

"Won't fill up questionnaires?" cried Miss Schuster-Slatt, taken aback.

"No," said Harriet, "they won't. As a nation we are not questionnaire-conscious."

"Well, that's too bad," said Miss Schuster-Slatt. "But I do hope you will join the British Branch of our League for the Encouragement of Matrimonial Fitness. Our President, Mrs. J. Poppelhinken, is a wonderful woman. You would so much like to meet her. She will be coming to Europe next year. In the meantime I am here to do propaganda and study the whole question from the angle of British mentality."

"I'm afraid you will find it a very difficult job. I wonder," added Harriet (for she felt she owed Miss Schuster-Slatt a riposte for her unfortunate observations of the night before), "whether your intentions are as disinterested as you make out. Perhaps you are thinking of investigating the loveliness of English husbands in a personal and practical way."

"Now you're making fun of me," said Miss Schuster-Slatt, with perfect good-humor. "No. I'm just the little worker-bee, gathering honey for the queens to eat."

"How all occasions do inform against me!" muttered Harriet to herself. One would have thought that Oxford at least would offer a respite from Peter Wimsey and the marriage question. But although she herself was a notoriety, if not precisely a celebrity, it was an annoying fact that Peter was a still more spectacular celebrity, and that, of the two, people would rather know about him than about her. As regards marriage—well, here one certainly had a chance to find out whether it worked or not. Was it worse to be a Mary Attwood (*née* Stokes) or a Miss Schuster-Slatt? Was it better to be a Phoebe Bancroft (*née* Tucker) or a Miss Lydgate? And would all these people have turned out exactly the same, married or single?

She wandered into the J.C.R., which was empty, but for one drab and ill-dressed woman who sat desolately reading an illustrated paper. As Harriet passed, this woman looked up and said, rather tentatively, "Hullo! it's Miss Vane, isn't it?"

Harriet racked her memory hastily. This was obviously someone very much senior to herself—she looked nearer fifty than forty. Who on earth?

"I don't suppose you remember me," said the other. "Catherine Freemantle."

(Catherine Freemantle, good God! But she had been only two years senior to Harriet. Very brilliant, very smart, very lively and the outstanding scholar of her year. What in Heaven's name had happened to her?)

"Of course I remember you," said Harriet, "but I'm always so stupid about names. What have you been doing?"

Catherine Freemantle, it seemed, had married a farmer,

and everything had gone wrong. Slumps and sickness and tithe and taxes and the Milk Board and the Marketing Board, and working one's fingers to the bone for a bare living and trying to bring up children—Harriet had read and heard enough about agricultural depression to know that the story was a common one enough. She was ashamed of being and looking so prosperous. She felt she would rather be tried for life over again than walk the daily treadmill of Catherine's life. It was a saga, in its way, but it was preposterous. She broke in rather abruptly upon a complaint against the hard-heartedness of the Ecclesiastical Commissioners.

"But, Miss Freemantle—I mean, Mrs.—Mrs. Bendick—it's absurd that you should have to do this kind of thing. I mean, pick your own fruit and get up at all hours to feed poultry and slave like a navvy. Surely to goodness it would have paid far better for you to take on some kind of writing or intellectual job and get someone else to do the manual work."

"Yes, it would. But at the beginning I didn't see it like that. I came down with a lot of ideas about the dignity of labor. And besides, at that time, my husband wouldn't have liked it much if I'd separated myself from his interests. Of course, we didn't think it would turn out like this."

What damned waste! was all Harriet could say to herself. All that brilliance, all that trained intelligence, harnessed to a load that any uneducated country girl could have drawn, and drawn far better. The thing had its compensations, she supposed. She asked the question bluntly.

Worth it? said Mrs. Bendick. Oh, yes, it was certainly worth it. The job was worth doing. One was serving the land. And that, she managed to convey, was a service harsh and austere indeed, but a finer thing than spinning words on paper.

"I'm quite prepared to admit that," said Harriet. "A ploughshare is a nobler object than a razor. But if your natural talent is for barbering, wouldn't it be better to *be* a barber, and a good barber—and use the profits (if you like) to speed the plough? However grand the job may be, is it *your* job?"

"It's got to be my job now," said Mrs. Bendick. "One can't go back to things. One gets out of touch and one's brain gets rusty. If you'd spent your time washing and cooking for a family and digging potatoes and feeding cattle, you'd know that that kind of thing takes the edge off the razor. You needn't think I don't envy you people your easy life; I do. I came to the Gaudy out of sentiment, and I wish I'd stopped away. I'm two years older than you, but I look twenty. None of you care in the least for my interests, and yours all seem to me to be mere beating the air. You don't seem to have anything to do with real life. You are going about in a dream." She stopped speaking, and her angry voice softened. "But it's a beautiful dream in its way. It seems queer to me now to think that once I was a scholar . . . I don't know. You may be right after all. Learning and literature have a way of outlasting the civilization that made them."

"*The word and nought else*
in time endures.
Not you long after,
perished and mute
will last, but the defter
viol and lute,"

quoted Harriet. She stared vaguely out into the sunshine. "It's curious—because I have been thinking exactly the same thing—only in a different connection. Look here! I admire you like hell, but I believe you're all wrong. I'm sure one should do one's own job, however trivial, and not persuade one's self into doing somebody else's, however noble."

As she spoke, she remembered Miss de Vine; here was a new aspect of persuasion.

"That's all very well," replied Mrs. Bendick. "But one's rather apt to marry into somebody else's job."

True; but Harriet was offered the opportunity of marrying into a job as near her own as made no great difference. And into money enough to make any job supererogatory. Again she saw herself unfairly provided with advantages which more deserving people desired in vain.

"I suppose," she said, "marriage is the really important job, isn't it?"

"Yes, it is," said Mrs. Bendick. "My marriage is happy as marriages go. But I often wonder whether my husband wouldn't have been better off with another kind of wife. He never says so, but I wonder. I think he knows I miss—things, and resents it sometimes. I don't know why I should say this to you—I've never said it to anybody and I never knew you very well, did I?"

"No; and I haven't been very sympathetic, either. In fact, I've been disgustingly rude."

"You have, rather," said Mrs. Bendick. "But you have such a beautiful voice to be rude in."

"Good gracious!" said Harriet.

"Our farm's on the Welsh border, and the people all speak in the most hideous local sing-song. Do you know what makes me feel most homesick here? The cultured speech. The dear old much-abused Oxford accent. That's funny, isn't it?"

"I thought the noise in Hall was more like a cage full of peacocks."

"Yes; but out of Hall you can pick out the people who speak the right way. Lots of them don't, of course; but some do. You do; and you have a lovely voice into the bargain. Do you remember the old Bach Choir days?"

"Do I not. Do you manage to get any music on the Welsh border? The Welsh can sing."

"I haven't much time for music. I try to teach the children."

Harriet took advantage of this opening to make suitable domestic inquiries. She parted eventually from Mrs.

Bendick with a depressed feeling that she had seen a Derby winner making shift with a coal-cart.

Sunday lunch in Hall was a casual affair. Many people did not attend it, having engagements in the town. Those who did, dropped in as and when they liked, fetched their food from the serving-hatches and consumed it in chattering groups wherever they could find seats. Harriet, having seized a plate of cold ham for herself, looked round for a lunch partner, and was thankful to see Phoebe Tucker just come in and being helped by the attendant scout to a portion of cold roast beef. The two joined forces, and sat down at the far end of a long table which ran parallel to the High and at right angles to the other tables. From there they commanded the whole room, including the High Table itself and the row of serving-hatches. As her eye wandered from one briskly occupied luncher to the next, Harriet kept on asking herself, Which? Which of all these normal and cheerful-looking women had dropped that unpleasant paper in the quad the night before? Because you never knew; and the trouble of not knowing was that you dimly suspected everybody. Haunts of ancient peace were all very well, but very odd things could crawl and creep beneath lichen-covered stones. The Warden in her great carved chair was bending her stately head and smiling at some jest of the Dean's. Miss Lydgate was attending, with eager courtesy, to the wants of a very old student indeed, who was almost blind. She had helped her stumbling feet up the three steps of the dais, fetched her lunch from the hatch and was now putting salad on her plate for her. Miss Stevens the Bursar and Miss Shaw the Modern Language Tutor had collected about them three other old students of considerable age and attainments; their conversation was animated and apparently amusing. Miss Pyke, the Classical Tutor, was deep in a discussion with a tall, robust woman whom Phoebe Tucker had recognized and pointed out to Harriet as an eminent archaeologist, and in a momentary flash of comparative silence, the Tutor's high voice rang out unexpectedly: "The tumulus at Halos appears to be an isolated instance. The cist-graves of Theotokou . . ." Then the clamor again closed over the argument. Two other dons, whom Harriet did not recognize (they were new since her day) appeared from their gestures to be discussing millinery. Miss Hillyard, whose sarcastic tongue tended to isolate her from her colleagues, was slowly eating her lunch and glancing at a pamphlet she had brought in with her. Miss de Vine, arriving late, sat down beside Miss Hillyard and began to consume ham in a detached way with her eyes fixed on vacancy.

Then the Old Students in the body of the Hall—all types, all ages, all varieties of costume. Was it the curious round-shouldered woman in a yellow djibbah and sandals, with her hair coiled in two snail-shells over her ears? Or the sturdy, curly-headed person in tweeds, with a masculine-looking waistcoat and the face like the back of a cab? Or the tightly-corseted peroxide of sixty, whose hat would better have suited an eighteen-year-old débutante at Ascot? Or one of the innumerable women with "schoolteacher" stamped on their resolutely cheery countenances? Or the plain person of indeterminate age who sat at the head of her table with the air of a chairman of committee? Or that curious little creature dressed in unbecoming pink, who looked as though she had been carelessly packed away in a drawer all winter and put into circulation again without being ironed? Or that handsome, well-preserved business woman of fifty with the well-manicured hands, who broke into the conversation of total strangers to inform them that she had just opened a new hairdressing establishment "just off Bond Street"? Or that tall, haggard, tragedy-queen in black silk marocain who looked like Hamlet's aunt, but was actually Aunt Beatrice who ran the Household Column in the *Daily Mercury*? Or the bony woman with the long horseface who had devoted herself to Settlement work? Or even that unconquerably merry and bright little dumpling of a creature who was the highly-valued secretary of a political secretary and had secretaries under her? The faces came and went, as though in a dream, all animated, all inscrutable.

Relegated to a remote table at the lower end of the Hall were half-a-dozen present students, still lingering in Oxford for viva voce examinations. They babbled continually among themselves, rather obviously ignoring the invasion of their college by all these quaint old freaks who were what they themselves would be in ten years' time, or twenty or thirty. They were a badly-turned-out bunch, Harriet thought, with an end-of-term crumpled appearance. There was an odd, shyfaced, sandy girl with pale eyes and restless fingers, and next to her a dark, beautiful one, for whose face men might have sacked cities, if it had had any sort of animation; and there was a gawky and unfinished-looking young person, very badly made up, who had a pathetic air of seeking to win hearts and never succeeding; and, most interesting of the bunch, a girl with a face like eager flame who was dressed with a maddening perversity of wrongness, but who one day would undoubtedly hold the world in her hands for good or evil. The rest were nondescript, as yet undifferentiated—yet nondescripts, thought Harriet, were the most difficult of all human beings to analyze. You scarcely knew they were there, until—bang! Something quite unexpected blew up like a depth charge and left you marveling, to collect strange floating débris.

So the Hall seethed, and the scouts looked on impassively from the serving-hatches. "And what they think of us all, God only knows," mused Harriet.

"Are you plotting an exceptionally intricate murder?" demanded Phoebe's voice in her ear. "Or working out a difficult alibi? I've asked you three times to pass the cruet."

"I'm sorry," said Harriet, doing as she was requested. "I was meditating on the impenetrability of the human countenance." She hesitated, on the verge of telling Phoebe about the disagreeable drawing, but her friend went on to ask some other question, and the moment passed by.

But the episode had troubled and unsettled her. Passing

through the empty Hall, later in the day, she stopped to stare at the portrait of that Mary, Countess of Shrewsbury, in whose honor the college had been founded. The painting was a well-executed modern copy of the one in St. John's College, Cambridge, and the queer, strong-featured face, with its ill-tempered mouth and sidelong, secretive glance, had always exercised a curious fascination over her —even in her student days, a period when the portraits of dead and gone celebrities exposed in public places incur more sarcastic comment than reverential consideration. She did not know, and indeed had never troubled to inquire, how Shrewsbury College had come to adopt so ominous a patroness. Bess of Hardwick's daughter had been a great intellectual, indeed, but something of a holy terror; uncontrollable by her menfolk, undaunted by the Tower, contemptuously silent before the Privy Council, an obstinate recusant, a staunch friend and implacable enemy and a lady with a turn for invective remarkable even in an age when few mouths suffered from mealiness. She seemed, in fact, to be the epitome of every alarming quality which a learned woman is popularly credited with developing. Her husband, the "great and glorious Earl of Shrewsbury," had purchased domestic peace at a price; for, said Bacon, there was "a greater than he, which is my Lady of Shrewsbury." And that, of course, was a dreadful thing to have said about one. The prospect seemed discouraging for Miss Schuster-Slatt's matrimonial campaign, since the rule seemed to be that a great woman must either die unwed, to Miss Schuster-Slatt's distress, or find a still greater man to marry her. And that limited the great woman's choice considerably, since, though the world of course abounded in great men, it contained a very much larger number of middling and common-place men. The great man, on the other hand, could marry where he liked, not being restricted to great women; indeed, it was often found sweet and commendable in him to choose a woman of no sort of greatness at all.

"Though of course," Harriet reminded herself, "a

woman may achieve greatness, or at any rate great renown, by merely being a wonderful wife and mother, like the mother of the Gracchi; whereas the men who have achieved great renown by being devoted husbands and fathers might be counted on the fingers of one hand. Charles I was an unfortunate king, but an admirable family man. Still, you would scarcely class him as one of the world's great fathers, and his children were not an unqualified success. Dear me! Being a great father is either a very difficult or a very sadly unrewarded profession. Wherever you find a great man, you will find a great mother or a great wife standing behind him—or so they used to say. It would be interesting to know how many great women have had great fathers and husbands behind them. An interesting thesis for research. Elizabeth Barrett? Well, she had a great husband, but he was great in his own right, so to speak—and Mr. Barrett was not exactly—The Brontës? Well, hardly. Queen Elizabeth? She had a remarkable father, but devoted helpfulness towards his daughters was scarcely his leading characteristic. And she was so wrong-headed as to have no husband. Queen Victoria? You might make a good deal out of poor Albert, but you couldn't do much with the Duke of Kent."

Somebody passed through the Hall behind her; it was Miss Hillyard. With a mischievous determination to get some response out of this antagonistic personality, Harriet laid before her the new idea for a historical thesis.

"You have forgotten physical achievements," said Miss Hillyard. "I believe many female singers, dancers, Channel swimmers and tennis stars owe everything to their devoted fathers."

"But the fathers are not famous."

"No. Self-effacing men are not popular with either sex. I doubt whether even your literary skill would gain recognition for their virtues. Particularly if you select your women for their intellectual qualities. It will be a short thesis in that case."

"Graveled for lack of matter?"

"I'm afraid so. Do you know any man who sincerely admires a woman for her brains?"

"Well," said Harriet, "certainly not many."

"You may think you know *one*," said Miss Hillyard, with a bitter emphasis. "Most of us think at some time or other that we know *one*. But the man usually has some other little axe to grind."

"Very likely," said Harriet. "You don't seem to have a very high opinion of men—of the male character, I mean, as such."

"No," said Miss Hillyard, "not very high. But they have an admirable talent for imposing their point of view on society in general. All women are sensitive to male criticism. Men are not sensitive to female criticism. They despise the critics."

"Do you, personally, despise male criticism?"

"Heartily," said Miss Hillyard. "But it does damage. Look at this University. All the men have been amazingly kind and sympathetic about the Women's Colleges. Certainly. But you won't find them appointing women to big University posts. That would never do. The women might perform their work in a way beyond criticism. But they are quite pleased to see us playing with our little toys."

"Excellent fathers and family men," murmured Harriet.

"In that sense—yes," said Miss Hillyard, and laughed rather unpleasantly.

Something funny there, thought Harriet. A personal history, probably. How difficult it was not to be embittered by personal experience. She went down to the J.C.R. and examined herself in the mirror. There had been a look in the History Tutor's eyes that she did not wish to discover in her own.

Sunday evening prayers. The College was undenominational, but some form of Christian worship was held to be essential to community life. The chapel, with its stained glass windows, plain oak panelling and unadorned Communion Table was a kind of Lowest Common Multiple of all sects and creeds. Harriet, making her way towards it, remembered that she had not seen her gown since the previous afternoon, when the Dean had taken it to the S.C.R. Not liking to penetrate uninvited into that Holy of Holies, she went in search of Miss Martin, who had, it appeared, taken both gowns together to her own room. Harriet wriggled into the gown, one fluttering sleeve of which struck an adjacent table with a loud bang.

"Mercy!" said the Dean, "what's that?"

"My cigarette-case," said Harriet. "I thought I'd lost it. I remember now. I hadn't a pocket yesterday, so I shoved it into the sleeve of my gown. After all, that's what these sleeves are for, aren't they?"

"Oh, my dear! Mine are always a perfect dirty-clothes bag by the end of term. When I have absolutely *no* clean handkerchiefs left in the drawer, my scout turns out my gown sleeves. My best collection worked out at twenty-two —but then I'd had a bad cold one week. Dreadful insanitary garments. Here's your cap. Never mind taking your hood—you can come back here for it. What have you been doing today?—I've scarcely seen you."

Again Harriet felt an impulse to mention the unpleasant drawing, but again she refrained. She felt she was getting rather unbalanced about it. Why think about it at all? She mentioned her conversation with Miss Hillyard.

"Lor'!" said the Dean. "That's Miss Hillyard's hobby-horse. Rubbidge, as Mrs. Gamp would say. Of *course* men don't like having their poor little noses put out of joint—who does? I think it's perfectly noble of them to let us come trampling over their University at all, bless their hearts. They've been used to being lords and masters for hundreds of years and they want a bit of time to get used to the change. Why, it takes a man months and *months* to reconcile himself to a new hat. And *just* when you're preparing to send it to the jumble sale, he says, 'That's rather a nice hat you've got on, where did you get it?' And you say, 'My dear Henry, it's the one I had last year and you said made me look like an organ-grinder's monkey.' My brother-in-law says that *every* time, and it does make my sister so wild."

They mounted the steps of the chapel.

It had not, after all, been so bad. Definitely not so bad as one had expected. Though it was melancholy to find that one had grown out of Mary Stokes, and a little tiresome, in a way, that Mary Stokes refused to recognize the fact. Harriet had long ago discovered that one could not like people any the better, merely because they were ill, or dead—still less because one had once liked them very much. Some happy souls could go through life without making this discovery, and they were the men and women who were called "sincere." Still, there remained old friends whom one was glad to meet again, like the Dean and Phoebe Tucker. And really, everybody had been quite extraordinarily decent. Rather inquisitive and silly about "the man Wimsey," some of them, but no doubt with the best intentions. Miss Hillyard might be an exception, but there had always been something a little twisted and uncomfortable about Miss Hillyard.

As the car wound its way over the Chilterns, Harriet grinned to herself, thinking of her parting conversation with the Dean and Bursar.

"Be sure and write us a new book soon. And remember, if ever we get a mystery at Shrewsbury we shall call upon you to come and disentangle it."

"All right," said Harriet. "When you find a mangled corpse in the buttery, send me a wire—and be sure you let Miss Barton view the body, and then she won't so much mind my haling the murderess off to justice."

And suppose they actually did find a bloody corpse in the buttery, how surprised they would all be. The glory of a college was that nothing drastic ever happened in it. The most frightful thing that was ever likely to happen was that an undergraduate should "take the wrong turning." The purloining of a parcel or two by a porter had been enough to throw the whole Senior Common Room into consternation. Bless their hearts, how refreshing and soothing and *good* they all were, walking beneath their ancient beeches and meditating on k κÆd c k and the finance of Queen Elizabeth.

"I've broken the ice," she said aloud, "and the water wasn't so cold after all. I shall go back, from time to time. I shall go back."

She picked out a pleasant pub for lunch and ate with a good appetite. Then she remembered that her cigarette-case was still in her gown. She had brought the garment in with her on her arm, and, thrusting her hand down to the bottom of the long sleeve, she extracted the case. A piece of paper came out with it—an ordinary sheet of scribbling paper folded into four. She frowned at a disagreeable memory as she unfolded it.

There was a message pasted across it, made up of letters cut apparently from the headlines of a newspaper.

YOU DIRTY MURDERESS. AREN'T YOU
ASHAMED TO SHOW YOUR FACE?

"Hell!" said Harriet. "Oxford, thou too?" She sat very still for a few moments. Then she struck a match and set light to the paper. It burned briskly, till she was forced to drop it upon her plate. Even then, the letters showed grey upon the crackling blackness, until she pounded their spectral shapes to powder with the back of a spoon.

CHAPTER IV

Thou canst not, Love, disgrace me half so ill,
To set a form upon desirèd change,
As I'll myself disgrace: knowing thy will,
I will acquaintance strangle and look strange,
Be absent from thy walks, and in my tongue
Thy sweet beloved name no more shall dwell,
Lest I, too much profane, should do it wrong
And haply of our old acquaintance tell.

WILLIAM SHAKESPEARE

There are incidents in one's life which, through some haphazard coincidence of time and mood, acquire a symbolic value. Harriet's attendance at the Shrewsbury Gaudy was of this kind. In spite of minor incongruities and absurdities, it had shown itself to have one definite significance; it had opened up to her the vision of an old desire, long obscured by a forest of irrelevant fancies, but now standing up unmistakable, like a tower set on a hill. Two phrases rang in her ears: the Dean's, "It's the work you're doing that really counts"; and that one melancholy lament for eternal loss: "Once, I was a scholar."

"Time is," quoth the Brazen Head; "time was; time is past." Philip Boyes was dead; and the nightmares that had haunted the ghastly midnight of his passing were gradually fading away. Clinging on, by blind instinct, to the job that had to be done, she had fought her way back to an insecure stability. Was it too late to achieve wholly the clear eye and the untroubled mind? And what, in that case, was she to do with one powerful fetter which still tied her ineluctably to the bitter past? What about Peter Wimsey?

During the past three years, their relations had been peculiar. Immediately after the horrible business that they had investigated together at Wilvercombe, Harriet—feeling that something must be done to ease a situation which was fast becoming intolerable—had carried out a long-cherished scheme, now at last made practicable by her increasing reputation and income as a writer. Taking a woman friend with her as companion and secretary, she had left England, and traveled slowly about Europe, staying now here, now there, as fancy dictated or a good background presented itself for a story. Financially the trip had been a success. She had gathered material for two full-length novels, the scenes laid respectively in Madrid and Carcassonne, and written a series of short stories dealing with detective adventures in Hitlerite Berlin, and also a number of travel articles; thus more than replenishing the treasury. Before her departure, she had asked Wimsey not to write. He had taken the prohibition with unexpected meekness.

"I see. Very well. *Vade in pace*. If you ever want me, you will find the Old Firm at the usual stand."

She had occasionally seen his name in the English papers, and that was all. At the beginning of the following June, she had returned home, feeling that, after so long a break, there should be little difficulty in bringing the relationship to a cool and friendly close. By this time he was probably feeling as much settled and relieved as she was. As soon as she got back to London, she moved to a new flat in Mecklenburg Square, and settled down to work at the Carcassonne novel.

A trifling incident, soon after her return, gave her the opportunity to test her own reactions. She went down to Ascot, in company with a witty young woman writer and her barrister husband—partly for fun and partly because she wanted to get local color for a short story, in which an unhappy victim was due to fall suddenly dead in the Royal

Enclosure, just at the exciting moment when all eyes were glued upon the finish of a race. Scanning those sacred precincts, therefore, from without the pale, Harriet became aware that the local color included a pair of slim shoulders tailored to swooning-point and carrying a well-known parrot profile, thrown into prominence by the acute backward slant of a pale-grey topper. A froth of summer hats billowed about this apparition, so that it resembled a slightly grotesque but expensive orchid in a bouquet of roses. From the expressions of the parties, Harriet gathered that the summer hats were picking long-priced and impossible outsiders, and that the topper was receiving their instructions with an amusement amounting to hilarity. At any rate, his attention was well occupied.

"Excellent," thought Harriet; "nothing to trouble about there." She came home rejoicing in the exceptional tranquility of her own spirits. Three days later, while reading in the morning paper that among the guests at a literary luncheon-party had been seen "Miss Harriet Vane, the well-known detective authoress," she was interrupted by the telephone. A familiar voice said, with a curious huskiness and uncertainty:

"Miss Harriet Vane? . . . Is that you, Harriet? I saw you were back. Will you dine with me one evening?"

There were several possible answers; among them, the repressive and disconcerting "*Who* is that speaking, please?" Being unprepared and naturally honest, Harriet feebly replied:

"Oh, thank you, Peter. But I don't know whether . . ."

"What?" said the voice, with a hint of mockery. "*Every* night booked from now till the coming of the Coqcigrues?"

"Of course not," said Harriet, not at all willing to pose as the swollen-headed and much-run-after celebrity.

"Then say when."

"I'm free tonight," said Harriet, thinking that the shortness of the notice might force him to plead a previous engagement.

"Admirable," said he. "So am I. We will taste the sweets

of freedom. By the way, you have changed your telephone number."

"Yes; I've got a new flat."

"Shall I call for you? Or will you meet me at Ferrara's at 7 o'clock?"

"At Ferrara's?"

"Yes. Seven o'clock, if that's not too early. Then we can go on to a show, if you care about it. Till this evening, then. Thank you."

He hung up the receiver before she had time to protest. Ferrara's was not the place she would have chosen. It was both fashionable and conspicuous. Everybody who could get there, went there; but its charges were so high that, for the present at least, it could afford not to be crowded. That meant that if you went there you were seen. If one intended to break off a connection with anyone, it was perhaps not the best opening move to *afficher* one's self with him at Ferrara's.

Oddly enough, this would be the first time she had dined in the West End with Peter Wimsey. During the first year or so after her trial, she had not wanted to appear anywhere, even had she then been able to afford the frocks to appear in. In those days, he had taken her to the quieter and better restaurants in Soho, or, more often, carried her off, sulky and rebellious, in the car to such roadside inns as kept reliable cooks. She had been too listless to refuse these outings, which had probably done something to keep her from brooding, even though her host's imperturbable cheerfulness had often been repaid only with bitter or distressful words. Looking back, she was as much amazed by his patience as fretted by his persistence.

He received her at Ferrara's with the old, quick, sidelong smile and ready speech, but with a more formal courtesy than she remembered in him. He listened with interest, and indeed with eagerness, to the tale of her journeyings abroad; and she found (as was to be expected) that the map of Europe was familiar ground to him. He contributed a few amusing incidents from his own experience, and added some well-informed comments on the conditions of life in modern Germany. She was surprised to find him so closely acquainted with the ins-and-outs of international politics, for she had not credited him with any great interest in public affairs. She found herself arguing passionately with him about the prospects of the Ottawa Conference, of which he appeared to entertain no very great hopes; and by the time they got to the coffee she was so eager to disabuse his mind of some perverse opinions about Disarmament that she had quite forgotten with what intentions (if any) she had come to meet him. In the theater she contrived to remind herself from time to time that something decisive ought to be said; but the conversational atmosphere remained so cool that it was difficult to introduce the new subject.

The play being over, he put her into a taxi, asked what address he should give the driver, requested formal permission to see her home and took his seat beside her. This, to be sure, was the moment; but he was babbling pleasantly about the Georgian architecture of London. It was only as they were running along Guilford Street that he forestalled her by saying (after a pause, during which she had been making up her mind to take the plunge):

"I take it, Harriet, that you have no new answer to give me?"

"No, Peter. I'm sorry, but I can't say anything else."

"All right. Don't worry. I'll try not to be a nuisance. But if you could put up with me occasionally, as you have done tonight, I should be very grateful to you."

"I don't think that would be at all fair to you."

"If that's the only reason, I am the best judge of that." Then, with a return of his habitual self-mockery: "Old habits die hard. I will not promise to reform altogether. I shall, with your permission, continue to propose to you, at decently regulated intervals—as a birthday treat, and on Guy Fawkes Day and on the Anniversary of the King's Accession. But consider it, if you will, as a pure formality. You need not pay the smallest attention to it."

"Peter, it's foolish to go on like this."

"And, of course, on the Feast of All Fools."

"It would be better to forget all about it—I hoped you had."

"I have the most ill-regulated memory. It does those things which it ought not to do and leaves undone the things it ought to have done. But it has not yet gone on strike altogether."

The taxi drew up, and the driver peered round inquiringly. Wimsey handed her out and waited gravely while she disentangled her latch-key. Then he took it from her, opened the door for her, said goodnight and was gone.

Mounting the stone staircase, she knew that, as far as this situation was concerned, her flight had been useless. She was back in the old net of indecision and distress. In him, it appeared to have worked some kind of change; but it had certainly not made him any easier to deal with.

He had kept his promise, and troubled her very little. He had been out of Town a good deal, hard at work upon cases, some of which trickled through into newspaper columns, while others appeared to settle themselves in discreet obscurity. For six months he had himself been out of the country, offering no explanation except "business." One summer, he had been involved in an odd affair, which had led him to take a post in an Advertising Agency. He had found office life entertaining; but the thing had come to a strange and painful conclusion. There had been an evening when he had turned up to keep a previously-made dinner appointment, but had obviously been unfit either to eat or talk. Eventually he had confessed to a splitting headache and a temperature and suffered himself to be personally conducted home. She had been sufficiently alarmed not to leave him till he was safely in his own flat and in the capable hands of Bunter. The latter had been reassuring: the trouble was nothing but reaction—of frequent occurrence at the end of a trying case, but soon over. A day or two later, the patient had rung up, apologized, and made a fresh appointment, at which he had displayed a quite remarkable effervescence of spirits.

On no other occasion had Harriet ever passed his threshold. Nor had he ever violated the seclusion of Mecklenburg Square. Two or three times, courtesy had moved her to invite him in; but he had always made some excuse, and she understood that he was determined to leave her that place, at least, free from any awkward associations. It was clear that he had no fatuous intention of making himself more valued by withdrawal: he had rather the air of trying to make amends for something. He renewed his offer of marriage on an average once in three months, but in such a way as to afford no excuse for any outbreak of temperament on either side. One First of April, the question had arrived from Paris in a single Latin sentence, starting off dispiritedly. "Num . . . ?"—a particle which notoriously "expects the answer No." Harriet, rummaging the Grammar book for "polite negatives," replied, still more briefly, "Benigne."

Looking back upon her visit to Oxford, Harriet found that it had had an unsettling effect. She had begun to take Wimsey for granted, as one might take dynamite for granted in a munitions factory. But the discovery that the mere sound of his name still had the power to provoke such explosions in herself—that she could so passionately resent, at one and the same time, either praise or blame of him on other people's lips—awakened a misgiving that dynamite was perhaps still dynamite, however harmless it might come to look through long custom.

On the mantelpiece of her sitting-room stood a note, in Peter's small and rather difficult writing. It informed her that he had been called away by Chief-Inspector Parker, who was in difficulties over a murder in the north of England. He must therefore regretfully cancel their appointment for that week. Could she oblige him by making use of the tickets, of which he had no time to dispose otherwise?

Harriet pinched her lips over that last cautious sentence. Ever since one frightful occasion, during the first year of their acquaintance, when he had ventured to send her a Christmas present and she, in an access of mortified pride, had returned it to him with a stinging rebuke, he had been careful never to offer her anything that could possibly be looked upon as a material gift. Had he been wiped out of existence at any moment, there was nothing among her possessions to remind her of him. She now took up the tickets and hesitated over them. She could give them away, or she could go herself and take a friend. On the whole, she thought she would rather not sit through the performance with a kind of Banquo's ghost disputing possession of the next stall with somebody else. She put the tickets in an envelope, dispatched them to the married couple who had taken her to Ascot, and then tore the note across and deposited it in the waste-paper basket. Having thus disposed of Banquo, she breathed more freely, and turned to deal with the day's next nuisance.

This was the revision of three of her books for a new edition. The re-reading of one's own works is usually a dismal matter; and when she had completed her task she felt thoroughly jaded and displeased with herself. The books were all right, as far as they went; as intellectual exercises, they were even brilliant. But there was something lacking about them; they read now to her as though they had been written with a mental reservation, a determination to keep her own opinions and personality out of view. She considered with distaste a clever and superficial discussion between two of the characters about married life. She could have made a much better thing of that, if she had not been afraid of giving herself away. What hampered her was this sense of being in the middle of things, too close to things, pressed upon and bullied by reality. If she could succeed in standing aside from herself she would achieve self-confidence and a better control. That was the great possession in which—with all his limitations—the scholar could account himself blessed: the single eye, directed to the object, not dimmed nor distracted by private motes and beams. "Private, indeed?" muttered Harriet to herself, as she smacked her proofs irritably into brown paper.

"You not alone, when you are still alone,
O God, from you that I could private be!"

She was exceedingly glad that she had got rid of the theater tickets.

So that when Wimsey eventually got back from his expedition north, she went to meet him in a belligerent spirit. He had asked her to dine with him, this time, at the Egotists' Club—an unusual venue. It was a Sunday night, and they had the room to themselves. She mentioned her Oxford visit and took the opportunity to recite to him a list of promising scholars, distinguished in their studies and subsequently extinguished by matrimony. He agreed mildly that such things did happen, far too often, and instanced a very brilliant painter who, urged on by a socially ambitious wife, had now become a slick machine for the production of Academy portraits.

"Sometimes, of course," he went on dispassionately, "the partner is merely jealous or selfish. But half the time it's sheer stupidity. They don't mean it. It's surprisin' how few people ever mean anything definite from one year's end to the other."

"I don't think they could help it, whatever they meant. It's the pressure of other people's personalities that does the mischief."

"Yes. Best intentions no security. They never are, of course. You may say you won't interfere with another person's soul, but you do—merely by existing. The snag about it is the practical difficulty, so to speak, of not existing. I mean, here we all are, you know, and what are we to do about it?"

"Well, I suppose some people feel themselves called to

make personal relationships their life-work. If so, it's all right for them. But what about the others?"

"Tiresome, isn't it?" he said, with a gleam of amusement that annoyed her. "Do you think they ought to cut out human contacts altogether? It's not easy. There's always the butcher or the baker or the landlady or somebody one has to wrestle with. Or should the people with brains sit tight and let the people with hearts look after them?"

"They frequently do."

"So they do." For the fifth time he summoned the waiter to pick up Harriet's napkin for her. "Why do geniuses make bad husbands, and all that? But what are you going to do about the people who are cursed with both hearts and brains?"

"I'm sorry I keep on dropping things; this silk's so slippery. Well, that's just the problem, isn't it? I'm beginning to believe they've got to choose."

"Not compromise?"

"I don't think the compromise works."

"That I should live to hear any person of English blood blaspheme against compromise!"

"Oh, I'm not all English. I've got some bits of Scotch and Irish tucked away somewhere."

"That proves you're English. No other race ever boasts of being mongrel. I'm quite offensively English myself, because I'm one-sixteenth French, besides all the usual nationalities. So that compromise is in my blood. However. Should you catalogue me as a heart or a brain?"

"Nobody," said Harriet, "could deny your brain."

"Who déniges of it? And you may deny my heart, but I'm damned if you shall deny its existence."

"You argue like an Elizabethan wit—two meanings under one word."

"It was your word. You will have to deny something, if you intend to be like Caesar's sacrifice."

"Caesar's . . . ?"

"A beast without a heart. Has your napkin gone again?"

"No—it's my bag this time. It's just under your left foot."

"Oh!" He looked round, but the waiter had vanished. "Well," he went on, without moving, "it is the heart's office to wait upon the brain, but in view of—"

"Please don't trouble," said Harriet, "it doesn't matter in the least."

"In view of the fact that I've got two cracked ribs, I'd better not try; because if I once got down I should probably never get up again."

"Good gracious!" said Harriet. "I thought you seemed a little stiff in your manner. Why on earth didn't you say so before, instead of sitting there like a martyr and inveigling me into misjudging you?"

"I don't seem able to do anything right," he said plaintively.

"How did you manage to do it?"

"Fell off a wall in the most inartistic manner. I was in a bit of a hurry; there was a very plain-looking bloke on the other side with a gun. It wasn't so much the wall, as the wheelbarrow at the bottom. And it isn't really so much the ribs as the sticking-plaster. It's strapped as tight as hell and itches infernally."

"How beastly for you. I'm so sorry. What became of the bloke with the gun?"

"Ah! I'm afraid personal complications won't trouble him any longer."

"If the luck had been the other way, I suppose they wouldn't have troubled *you* any longer?"

"Probably not. And then I shouldn't have troubled *you* any longer. If my mind had been where my heart was, I might have welcomed that settlement. But my mind being momentarily on my job, I ran away with the greatest rapidity, so as to live to finish the case."

"Well, I'm glad of that, Peter."

"Are you? That shows how hard it is for even the most powerful brain to be completely heartless. Let me see. It is not my day for asking you to marry me, and a few yards of sticking-plaster are hardly enough to make it a special occasion. But we'll have coffee in the lounge, if you don't mind, because this chair is getting as hard as the wheelbarrow, and seems to be catching me in several of the same places."

He got up cautiously. The waiter arrived and restored Harriet's bag, together with some letters which she had taken from the postman as she left the house and thrust into the outer pocket of the bag without reading. Wimsey steered his guest into the lounge, established her in a chair and lowered himself with a grimace into one corner of a low couch.

"Rather a long way down, isn't it?"

"It's all right when you get there. Sorry to be always presenting myself in such a decrepit state. I do it on purpose, of course, to attract attention and awaken sympathy; but I'm afraid the maneuver's getting rather obvious. Would you like a liqueur with the coffee or a brandy? Two old brandies, James."

"Very good, my lord. This was found under the table in the dining-room, madam."

"More of your scattered belongings?" said Wimsey, as she took the postcard; then, seeing her flush and frown of disgust, "What is it?"

"Nothing," said Harriet, pushing the ugly scrawl into her bag.

He looked at her.

"Do you often get that kind of thing?"

"What kind of thing?"

"Anonymous dirt."

"Not very often now. I got one at Oxford. But they used to come by every post. Don't worry; I'm used to it. I only wish I'd looked at it before I got here. It's horrible of me to have dropped it about your club for the servants to read."

"Careless little devil, aren't you? May I see it?"

"No, Peter; please."

"Give it to me."

She handed it to him without looking up. "*Ask your boy*

friend with the title if he likes arsenic in his soup. What did you give him to get you off?" it inquired, disagreeably.

"God, what muck!" said he, bitterly. "So that's what I'm letting you in for. I might have known it. I could hardly hope that it wasn't so. But you said nothing, so I allowed myself to be selfish."

"It doesn't matter. It's just part of the consequences. You can't do anything about it."

"I might have the consideration not to expose you to it. Heaven knows you've tried hard enough to get rid of me. In fact, I think you've used every possible lever to dislodge me, except that one."

"Well, I knew you would hate it so. I didn't want to hurt you."

"Didn't want to *hurt* me?"

She realized that this, to him, must sound completely lunatic.

"I mean that, Peter. I know I've said about every damnable thing to you that I could think of. But I have my limits." A sudden wave of anger surged up in her. "My God, do you really think that of me? Do you suppose there's no meanness I wouldn't stoop to?"

"You'd have been perfectly justified in telling me that I was making things more difficult for you by hanging round."

"Should I? Did you expect me to tell you that you were compromising my reputation, when I had none to compromise? To point out that you'd saved me from the gallows, thank you very much, but left me in the pillory? To say, my name's mud, but kindly treat it as lilies? I'm not quite such a hypocrite as that."

"I see. The plain fact is, that I am doing nothing but making life a little bitterer for you. It was generous of you not to say so."

"Why did you insist on seeing that thing?"

"Because," he said, striking a match and holding the flame to a corner of the postcard, "while I am quite ready to take flight from plug-uglies with guns, I prefer to look other kinds of trouble in the face." He dropped the burning paper on to the tray and crushed the ashes together, and she was again reminded of the message she had found in her sleeve. "You have nothing to reproach yourself with—you didn't tell me this; I found it out for myself. I will admit defeat and say good-bye. Shall I?"

The club waiter set down the brandies. Harriet, with her eyes on her own hands, sat plaiting her fingers together. Peter watched her for some minutes, and then said gently:

"Don't look so tragic about it. The coffee's getting cold. After all, you know, I have the consolation that 'not you but Fate has vanquished me.' I shall emerge with my vanity intact, and that's something."

"Peter. I'm afraid I'm not very consistent. I came here tonight with the firm intention of telling you to chuck it. But I'd rather fight my own battles. I—I—" she looked up and went on rather quaveringly—"I'm *damned* if I'll have you wiped out by plug-uglies or anonymous-letter writers!"

He sat up sharply, so that his exclamation of pleasure turned half-way into an anguished grunt.

"Oh, curse this sticking-plaster! . . . Harriet, you have got guts, haven't you? Give me your hand, and we'll fight on until we drop. Here! none of that. You can't cry in this club. It's never been done, and if you disgrace me like this, I shall get into a row with the Committee. They'll probably close the Ladies' Rooms altogether."

"I'm sorry, Peter."

"And *don't* put sugar in my coffee."

Later in the evening, having lent a strong arm to extricate him, swearing loudly, from the difficult depths of the couch, and dispatched him to such rest as he might reasonably look for between the pains of love and sticking-plaster, she had leisure to reflect that if fate had vanquished either of them it was not Peter Wimsey. He knew too well the wrestler's trick of letting the adversary's own strength defeat itself. Yet she knew with certainty that if, when he had said, "Shall I go?" she had replied with firm kindness, "I'm sorry, but I think it would be better," there would have been the desired end of the matter.

"I wish," she said to the friend of the European trip, "he would take a firm line of some kind."

"But he has," replied the friend, who was a clear-headed person. "He knows what he wants. The trouble is that you don't. I know it isn't pleasant putting an end to things, but I don't see why he should do all your dirty work for you, particularly as he doesn't want it done. As for anonymous letters, it seems to me quite ridiculous to pay any attention to them."

It was easy for the friend to say this, having no vulnerable points in her brisk and hard-working life.

"Peter says I ought to get a secretary and have them weeded out."

"Well," said the friend, "that's a practical suggestion, anyway. But I suppose, since it's his advice, you'll find some ingenious reason for not taking it."

"I'm not as bad as that," said Harriet; and engaged the secretary.

So matters went on for some months. She made no further effort to discuss the conflicting claims of heart and brain. That line of talk led to a perilous exchange of personalities, in which he, with a livelier wit and better self-control, could always drive her into a corner without exposing himself. It was only by sheer brutal hacking that she could beat down his guard; and she was beginning to be afraid of those impulses to savagery.

She heard no news of Shrewsbury College in the interval, except that one day in the Michaelmas Term there was a paragraph in one of the more foolish London dailies about an "Undergraduettes' Rag," informing the world that somebody had made a bonfire of gowns in Shrewsbury Quad and that the "Lady Head" was said to be taking disciplinary measures. Women, of course, were always news. Harriet wrote a tart letter to the paper, pointing out that either "undergraduate" or "woman student" would be seemlier English than "undergraduette," and that the correct method of describing Dr. Baring was "the Warden." The only result of this was to provoke a correspondence headed "Lady Undergrads," and a reference to "sweet girl-graduates."

She informed Wimsey—who happened to be the nearest male person handy for scarifying—that this kind of vulgarity was typical of the average man's attitude to women's intellectual interests. He replied that bad manners always made him sick; but was it any worse than headlining foreign monarchs by their Christian names, untitled?

About three weeks before the end of the Easter term, however, Harriet's attention was again called to college affairs in a way that was more personal and more disquieting.

February was sobbing and blustering its lachrymose way into March, when she received a letter from the Dean.

MY DEAR MISS VANE,

I am writing to ask you whether you will be able to get up to Oxford for the opening of the New Library Wing by the Chancellor next Thursday. This, as you know, has always been the date for the official opening, though we had hoped that the buildings themselves would be ready for habitation at the beginning of this term. However, what with a dispute in the contractors' firm, and the unfortunate illness of the architect, we got badly held up, so that we shall only *just* be ready in time. In fact, the interior decoration of the ground floor isn't finished *yet*.—Still, we couldn't very well ask Lord Oakapple to change the date, as he is such a busy man; and after all, the Library is the chief thing, and not the Fellows' sets, however badly they may need a home to go to, poor dears.

We are particularly anxious—I am speaking for Dr.

Baring as well as myself—that you should come, if you *can* manage to find time (though of course you have a lot of engagements). We should be very glad to have your advice about a most unpleasant thing that has been happening here. Not that one expects a detective novelist to be a practical policeman; but I know you have taken part in one real investigation, and I feel sure you know a lot more than we do about tracking down malefactors.

Don't think we are all getting murdered in our beds! In some ways I'm not sure that a "nice, clean murder" wouldn't be easier to deal with! The fact is, we are being victimized by a cross between a Poltergeist and a Poison-Pen, and you can imagine how disgusting it is for everybody. It seems that the letters started coming some time ago, but at first nobody took much notice. I suppose everyone gets vulgar anonymous communications from time to time; and though some of the beastly things didn't come by post, there's nothing in a place like this to prevent an outsider from dropping them at the Lodge or even inside the College. But wanton destruction of property is a different matter, and the last outbreak has been so abominable that something really must be done about it. Poor Miss Lydgate's *English Prosody*—you saw that colossal work in progress—has been defaced and mutilated in the most *revolting* manner, and some important manuscript portions completely destroyed, so that they will have to be done all over again. She was almost in tears, poor dear—and the alarming thing is that it now looks as though somebody in college *must* be responsible. We suppose that some student must have a grudge against the S.C.R.—but it must be more than a grudge—it must be a very horrid kind of pottiness.

One can scarcely call in the police—if you'd seen some of the letters you'd realize that the less publicity the better, and you know how things get about. I dare say you noticed there was a wretched newspaper paragraph about that bonfire in the quad last November. We never discovered who did that, by the way; we thought, naturally, it was a stupid practical joke; but we are now beginning to wonder whether it wasn't all part of the same campaign.

So if you could possibly snatch time to give us the benefit of your experience, we should be exceedingly grateful. There must be *some* way of coping—this sort of persecution simply CAN'T GO ON. But it's an awfully difficult job to pin anything down in a place like this, with 150 students and all doors open everywhere night and day.

I am afraid this is rather an incoherent letter, but I'm feeling *that* put about, with the Opening looming ahead and *all* the entrance and scholarship papers blowing about me like leaves in Vallombrosa! Hoping very much to see you next Thursday,

Yours very sincerely,

LETITIA MARTIN

Here was a pretty thing! Just the kind of thing to do the worst possible damage to University women—not only in Oxford, but everywhere. In any community, of course, one always ran the risk of harboring somebody undesirable; but parents obviously would not care to send their young innocents to places where psychological oddities flourished unchecked. Even if the poison campaign led to no open disaster (and you never knew what people might be driven to under persecution) a washing of dirty linen in public was not calculated to do Shrewsbury any good. Because, though nine-tenths of the mud might be thrown at random, the remaining tenth might quite easily be, as it usually was, dredged from the bottom of the well of truth, and would stick.

Who should know that better than herself? She smiled wryly over the Dean's letter. "The benefit of your experience"; yes, indeed. The words had, of course, been written in the most perfect innocence, and with no suspicion that they could make the galled jade wince. Miss Martin herself would never dream of writing abusive letters to a person who had been acquitted of murder, and it had undoubtedly never occurred to her that to ask the notorious Miss Vane for advice about how to deal with that kind of thing was to talk of rope in the house of the hanged. This was merely an instance of that kind of unworldly tactlessness to which learned and cloistered women were prone. The Dean would be horrified to know that Harriet was the last person who should, in charity, have been approached in the matter; and that, even in Oxford itself, in Shrewsbury College itself—

In Shrewsbury College itself: and at the Gaudy. That was the point. The letter she had found in her sleeve had been put there in Shrewsbury College *and at the Gaudy*. Not only that; there had been the drawing she had picked up in the quad. Was either, or were both of these, part only of her own miserable quarrel with the world? Or were they rather to be connected with the subsequent outbreak in the college itself? It seemed unlikely that Shrewsbury should have to harbor *two* dirty-minded lunatics in such quick succession. But if the two lunatics were one and the same lunatic, then the implication was an alarming one, and she herself must, at all costs, interfere at least so far as to tell what she knew. There did come moments when all personal feelings had to be set aside in the interests of public service; and this looked like being one of them.

Reluctantly, she reached for the telephone and put a call through to Oxford. While she waited for it, she thought the matter over in this new light. The Dean had given no details about the poison letters, except that they suggested a grudge against the S.C.R. and that the culprit appeared to belong to the college. It was natural enough to attribute destructive ragging to the undergraduates; but then, the Dean did not know what Harriet knew. The warped and repressed mind is apt enough to turn and wound itself. "Soured virginity"—"unnatural life"—"semi-demented spinsters"—"starved appetites and suppressed impulses"—"unwholesome atmosphere"—she could think of whole sets of epithets, ready-minted for circulation. Was this what lived in the tower set on the hill? Would it turn out to be like Lady Athaliah's tower in *Frolic Wind*, the home of frustration and perversion and madness? "If thine eye be single, the whole body is full of light"—but was it physically possible to have the single eye? "What are you to do with the people who are cursed with both hearts and brains?" For them, stereoscopic vision was probably a necessity; as for whom was it not? (This was a foolish play on words, but it meant something.) Well, then, what about this business of choosing one way of life? Must one, after all, seek a compromise, merely to preserve one's sanity? Then one was doomed for ever to this miserable inner warfare, with confused noise and garments rolled in blood—and, she reflected drearily, with the usual war aftermath of a debased coinage, a lowered efficiency and unstable conditions of government.

At this point the Oxford call came through, with the Dean's voice sounding full of agitation. Harriet, after hurriedly disclaiming all pretence to detective ability in real life, expressed concern and sympathy and then asked the question that, to her, was of prime importance.

"How are the letters written?"

"That's *just* the difficulty. They're mostly done by pasting together bits out of newspapers. So, you see, there's no handwriting to identify."

That seemed to settle it; there were not two anonymous correspondents, but only one. Very well, then:

"Are they merely obscene, or are they abusive or threatening too?"

"All three. Calling people names that poor Miss Lydgate didn't know existed—the worst she knows being Restoration Drama—and threatening everything from public exposure to the gallows."

Then the tower was Lady Athaliah's tower.

"Are they sent to anybody besides the S.C.R.?"

"It's difficult to say, because people don't always come

and tell you things. But I believe one or two of the students here have had them."

"And they come sometimes by post and sometimes to the Lodge?"

"Yes. And they are beginning to come out on the walls now, and lately they've been pushed under people's doors at night. So it looks as though it *must* be somebody in college."

"When did you get the first one?"

"The first one I *definitely* know about was sent to Miss de Vine last Michaelmas Term. That was her first term here, and of course, she thought it must be somebody who had a personal grudge against her. But several people got them shortly afterwards, so we decided it couldn't be that. We'd never had anything of that sort happening before, so just at present we're inclined to check up on the First Year students."

The one set of people that it can't possibly be, thought Harriet. She only said, however:

"It doesn't do to take too much for granted. People may go on quite all right for a time, till something sets them off. The whole difficulty with these things is that the person generally behaves quite normally in other respects. It might be anybody."

"That's true. I suppose it might even be one of ourselves. That's what's so horrible. Yes, I know—elderly virgins, and all that. It's awful to know that at any minute one may be sitting cheek by jowl with somebody who feels like that. Do you think the poor creature knows that she does it herself? I've been waking up with nightmares, wondering whether I didn't perhaps prowl round in my sleep, spitting at people. And, my dear! I'm so terrified about next week! Poor Lord Oakapple, coming to open the Library, with venomous asps simply *dripping* poison over his boots! Suppose they send *him* something!"

"Well," said Harriet, "I think I'll come along next week. There's a very good reason why I'm not quite the right person to handle this, but on the other hand, I think I ought to come. I'll tell you why when we meet."

"It's terribly good of you. I'm sure you'll be able to suggest something. I suppose you'll want to see all the specimens there are. Yes? Very well. Every fragment shall be cherished next our hearts. Do we handle them with the tongs for the better preservation of finger-prints?"

Harriet doubted whether finger-prints would be of much service, but advised that precautions should be taken on principle. When she had rung off, with the Dean's reiterated thanks still echoing from the other end of the line, she sat for a few moments with the receiver in her hand. Was there any quarter to which she might usefully turn for advice? There was; but she was not eager to discuss the subject of anonymous letters, still less the question of what lived in academic towers. She hung up resolutely, and pushed the instrument away.

She woke next morning with a change of heart. She had said that personal feeling ought not to stand in the way of public utility. And it should not. If Wimsey could be made useful to Shrewsbury College, she would use him. Whether she liked it or not, whether or not she had to put up with his saying "I told you so," she would put her pride in her pocket and ask him the best way to go about the job. She had her bath and dressed, glowing all the time with a consciousness of her own disinterested devotion to the cause of truth. She came into the sitting-room and enjoyed a good breakfast, still congratulating herself. As she was finishing her toast and marmalade, the secretary arrived, bringing in the morning's post. It contained a hurried note from Peter, sent off the previous evening from Victoria.

> Hauled off abroad again at a moment's notice. Paris first, then Rome. Then God knows. If you should want me—*per impossible*—you can get me through the Embassies, or the post-office will forward letters from the Pic-

cadilly address. In any case, you will hear from me on April 1st.

P. D. B. W.

Post occasio calva. One could scarcely bombard the Embassies with letters about an obscure and complicated little affair in an Oxford college, especially when one's correspondent was urgently engaged in investigating something else all over Europe. The call must have been urgent, for the note was very ill and hastily written, and looked, in fact, as though it had been scribbled at the last moment in a taxi. Harriet amused herself with wondering whether the Prince of Ruritania had been shot, or the Master-Crook of the Continent had brought off a fresh *coup*, or whether this was the International Conspiracy to Wreck Civilization with a Death-Ray—all those situations being frequent in her kind of fiction. Whatever it was all about, she would have to carry on unaided and find consolation in a proper independence of spirit.

CHAPTER V

Virginity is a fine picture, as Bonaventure *calls it, a blessed thing in itself, and if you will believe a Papist, meritorious. And although there be some inconveniences, irksomeness, solitariness, etc., incident to such persons . . . yet they are but toys in respect, easily to be endured, if conferred to those frequent incumbrances of marriage. . . . And methinks sometime or other, amongst so many rich Bachelors, a benefactor should be found to build a monastical College for old, decayed, deformed, or discontented maids to live together in, that have lost their first loves, or otherwise miscarried, or else are willing howsoever to lead a single life. The rest, I say, are toys in respect, and sufficiently recompensed by those innumerable contents and incomparable privileges of Virginity.*

ROBERT BURTON

Harriet drove out to Oxford through a vile downpour of sleet that forced its way between the joints of the all-weather curtains and kept the windscreen-wiper hard at work. Nothing could have been less like her journey of the previous June; but the greatest change of all was in her own feelings. Then, she had been reluctant and uneasy; a prodigal daughter without the romantic appeal of husks and very uncertain of the fatted calf. Now, it was the College that had blotted its copybook and had called her in as one calls in a specialist, with little regard to private morals but a despairing faith in professional skill. Not that she cared much for the problem, or had very much hope of solving it; but she was able by now to look upon it as pure problem and a job to be done. In June, she had said to herself, at every landmark on the way:

"Plenty of time yet—thirty miles before I need begin to feel uncomfortable—twenty miles more respite—ten miles is still a good way to go." This time, she was plainly and simply anxious to reach Oxford as quickly as possible—a state of mind for which the weather was perhaps largely responsible. She slithered down Headington Hill with no concern beyond a passing thought for possible skids, crossed Magdalen Bridge with only a caustic observation addressed to a shoal of push-cyclists, muttered "Thank God!" as she reached the St. Cross Road gate, and said "Good afternoon" cheerfully to Padgett the porter.

"Good afternoon, miss. Nasty day it's been. The Dean left a message, miss, as you was to be put in the Guest Room over at Tudor and she was out at a meeting but would be back for tea. Do you know the Guest Room, miss? That would be since your time, perhaps. Well, it's on the New Bridge, miss, between Tudor Building and the North Annexe where the Cottage used to be, miss, only of course that's all done away now and you has to go up by the main staircase past the West Lecture-Room, miss, what used to be the Junior Common Room, miss, before they made the new entrance and moved the stairs, and then turn right and it's half-way along the corridor. You can't mistake it, miss. Any of the Scouts would show you, miss, if you can find one about just now."

"Thank you, Padgett. I'll find it all right. I'll just take the car round to the garage."

"Don't you trouble, miss. Raining cats and dogs, it is. I'll take her round for you later on. She won't 'urt in the street for a bit. And I'll have your bag up in half a moment, miss; only I can't leave the gate till Mrs. Padgett comes back from running over to the Buttery, or I'm sure I'd show you the way myself."

Harriet again begged him not to trouble.

"Oh, it's quite easy when you know, miss. But what with pulling down here and building up there and altering this and that, there's a many of our old ladies gets quite lost when they comes back to see us."

"I won't get lost, Padgett." And she had, in fact, no difficulty in finding the mysterious Guest Room by the shifting stair and the non-existent Cottage. She noticed that its windows gave her a commanding view over the Old Quad, though the New Quad was out of range and the greater part of the new Library Building hidden by the Annexe Wing of Tudor.

Having had tea with the Dean, Harriet found herself seated in the Senior Common Room at an informal meeting of the Fellows and Tutors, presided over by the Warden. Before her lay the documents in the case—a pitiful little heap of dirty imaginations. Fifteen or so of them had been collected for inspection. There were half-a-dozen drawings, all much of a same kind with the one she had picked up on the Gaudy night. There were a number of messages, addressed to various members of the S.C.R., and informing them, with various disagreeable epithets, that their sins would find them out, that they were not fit for decent society and that unless they left men alone, various unpleasing things would occur to them. Some of these missives had come by post; others had been found on window-sills or pushed under doors; all were made up of the same cut-out letters pasted on sheets of rough scribbling-paper. Two other messages had been sent to undergraduates: one, to the Senior Student, a very well-bred and inoffensive young woman who was reading Greats; the other to a Miss Flaxman, a brilliant Second Year scholar. The latter was rather more definite than most of the letters, in that it mentioned a name: "IF YOU DON'T LEAVE YOUNG FARRINGDON ALONE," it said, adding an abusive term, "IT WILL BE THE WORSE FOR YOU."

The remaining items in the collection consisted, first, of a small book written by Miss Barton: *The Position of Women in the Modern State*. The copy belonged to the Library, and had been discovered one Sunday morning merrily burning on the fire in the Junior Common Room in Burleigh House. Secondly, there were the proofs and manuscript of Miss Lydgate's *English Prosody*. The history of these was as follows. Miss Lydgate had at length transferred all her corrections in the text to the final page-proof and destroyed all the earlier revises. She had then handed the proofs, together with the manuscript of the Introduction, to Miss Hillyard, who had undertaken to go through them with a view to verifying certain historical allusions. Miss Hillyard stated that she had received them on a Saturday morning and taken them to her own rooms (which were on Miss Lydgate's staircase and on the floor immediately above). She had subsequently taken them into the Library (that is to say, the Library in Tudor, now about to be superseded by the New Library), and had there worked upon them for some time with the aid of some reference books. She said she had been alone in the Library at the time, except for someone, whom she had never seen, who was moving about in the bay at the far end. Miss Hillyard had then gone out to lunch in Hall, leaving the papers on the Library table. After lunch, she had gone on the river to put a group of First-Year students through a sculling-test. On her return to the Library after tea to resume work, she found that the papers had disappeared from the table. She had at first supposed that Miss Lydgate had come in and, seeing them there, carried them off to make a few more of her celebrated corrections. She went to Miss Lydgate's rooms to ask about them, but Miss Lydgate was not there. She said she had been a little surprised that Miss Lydgate should have removed them without leaving a note to say what she had done; but she was not actually alarmed until, knocking again at Miss Lydgate's door shortly before Hall, she suddenly remembered that the English Tutor had said that she was leaving before lunch to spend a couple of nights in Town. An inquiry was, of course, immediately set on foot, but nothing had come of it until, on the Monday morning, just after Chapel, the missing proofs had been found sprawled over the table and floor of the Senior Common Room. The finder had been Miss Pyke, who had been the first don to enter the room that morning. The scout responsible for dusting the S.C.R. was confident that nothing of the kind had been there before Chapel; the appearance of the papers suggested that they had been tossed into the room by somebody passing the window, which would have been an easy enough thing for anybody to do. Nobody, however, had seen anything suspicious, though the entire college, particularly late-comers to Chapel and those students whose windows overlooked the S.C.R., had been interrogated.

The proofs, when found, had been defaced throughout with thick copying-ink. All the manuscript alterations in the margins had been heavily blacked out and on certain pages offensive epithets had been written in rough block capitals. The manuscript Introduction had been burnt, and a triumphant note to this effect pasted in large printed letters across the first sheet of the proofs.

This was the news with which Miss Hillyard had had to face Miss Lydgate when the latter returned to College immediately after breakfast on the Monday. Some effort had been made to find out when, exactly, the proofs had been taken from the Library. The person in the far bay had been found, and turned out to have been Miss Burrows, the Librarian. She, however, said that she had not seen Miss Hillyard, who had come in after her and gone to lunch before her. Nor had she seen, or at any rate noticed, the proofs lying on the table. The Library had not been very much used on the Saturday afternoon; but a student who had gone in there at about 3 o'clock to consult Ducange's Late Latin Dictionary, in the bay where Miss Hillyard had been working, had said that she had taken the volume down and laid it on the table, and she *thought* that if the proofs had been there, she would have noticed them. This student was a Miss Waters, a second-year French student and a pupil of Miss Shaw's.

A slight awkwardness had been introduced into the situation by the Bursar, who had seen Miss Hillyard apparently entering the Senior Common Room just before Chapel on Monday morning. Miss Hillyard explained that she had only gone as far as the door, thinking that she had left her gown there; but remembering in time that she had hung it up in the cloakroom of Queen Elizabeth Building, had come out immediately without entering the S.C.R. She demanded, angrily, whether the Bursar suspected her of having done the damage herself. Miss Stevens said, "Of course not, but if Miss Hillyard had gone in, she could have seen whether the proofs were already in the room, and so provided a *terminus a quo*, or alternatively *ad quem*, for that part of the investigation."

This was really all the material evidence available, except that a large bottle of copying ink had disappeared from the office of the College Secretary and Treasurer, Miss Allison. The Treasurer had not had occasion to enter the office during Saturday afternoon or Sunday; she could only say that the bottle had been in its usual place at one o'clock on Saturday. She did not lock the door of her office at any time, as no money was kept there, and all important papers were locked up in a safe. Her assistant did not live in college and had not been in during the week-end.

The only other manifestation of any importance had been an outbreak of unpleasant scribbling on the walls of passages and lavatories. These inscriptions had, of course, been effaced as soon as noticed and were not available.

It had naturally been necessary to take official notice of the loss and subsequent disfigurement of Miss Lydgate's proofs. The whole college had been addressed by Dr. Baring and asked whether anybody had any evidence to bring forward. Nobody offered any; and the Warden had thereupon issued a warning against making the matter known outside the college, together with an intimation that anybody sending indiscreet communications to either the University papers or the daily press might find herself liable to severe disciplinary action. Delicate interrogation among the other Women's Colleges had made it fairly clear that the nuisance was, so far, confined to Shrewsbury.

Since nothing, so far, had come to light to show that the persecution had started before the previous October, suspicion rather naturally centered upon the First-Year students. It was when Dr. Baring had reached this point of her exposition that Harriet felt obliged to speak.

"I am afraid, Warden," she said, "that I am in a position to rule out the First Year, and in fact the majority of the present students altogether."

And she proceeded, with some discomfort, to tell the meeting about the two specimens of the anonymous writer's work that she had discovered at and after the Gaudy.

"Thank you, Miss Vane," said the Warden, when she had finished. "I am extremely sorry that you should have had so unpleasant an experience. But your information of course narrows the field a great deal. If the culprit is someone who attended the Gaudy, it must have been either one of the few present students who were then waiting up for vivas, or one of the scouts, or—one of ourselves."

"Yes. I'm afraid that is the case."

The dons looked at one another.

"It cannot, of course," went on Dr. Baring, "be an old student, since the outrages have continued in the interim; nor can it be an Oxford resident outside the college, since we know that certain papers have been pushed under people's doors during the night, to say nothing of inscriptions on the walls which have been proved to have come into existence between, say, midnight and the next morning. We therefore have to ask ourselves who, among the comparatively small number of persons in the three categories I have mentioned, can possibly be responsible."

"Surely," said Miss Burrows, "it is far more likely to be one of the scouts than one of ourselves. I can scarcely imagine that a member of this Common Room would be capable of anything so disgusting. Whereas that class of persons—"

"I think that is a very unfair observation," said Miss Barton. "I feel strongly that we ought not to allow ourselves to be blinded by any sort of class prejudice."

"The scouts are all women of excellent character, so far as I know," said the Bursar, "and you may be sure that I take very great care in engaging the staff. The scrubbing-women and others who come in by the day are, naturally, excluded from suspicion. Also, you will remember that the greater number of the scouts sleep in their own wing. The outer door of this is locked at night and the ground-floor windows have bars. Besides this, there are the iron gates which cut off the back entrance from the rest of the college buildings. The only possible communication at night would be by way of the buttery, which is also locked. The Head Scout has the keys. Carrie has been with us fifteen years, and is presumably to be trusted."

"I have never understood," said Miss Barton, acidly, "why the unfortunate servants should be locked up at night as though they were dangerous wild beasts, when everybody else is free to come and go at pleasure. However, as things are, it seems to be just as well for them."

"The reason, as you very well know," replied the Bursar, "is that there is no porter at the tradesmen's entrance, and that it would not be difficult for unauthorized persons to climb over the outer gates. And I will remind you that *all* the ground-floor windows that open directly upon the street or the kitchen yard are barred, including those belonging to the Fellows. As for the locking of the buttery, I may say that it is done to prevent the students from raiding the pantry as they frequently did in my predecessor's time, or so I am informed. The precautions are taken quite as much against the members of the college as against the scouts."

"How about the scouts in the other buildings?" asked the Treasurer.

"There are perhaps two or three occupying odd bedrooms in each building," replied the Bursar. "They are all reliable women who have been in our service since before my time. I haven't the list here at the moment; but I think there are three in Tudor, three or four in Queen Elizabeth, and one in each of the four little dormer rooms in the New Quad. Burleigh is all students' rooms. And there is, of course, the Warden's own domestic staff, besides the Infirmary maid who sleeps there with the Infirmarian."

"I will take steps," said Dr. Baring, "to make sure that no member of my own household is at fault. You, Bursar, had better do the same by the Infirmary. And, in their own interests, the scouts sleeping in College had better be subjected to some kind of supervision."

"Surely, Warden—" began Miss Barton, hotly.

"In their own interests," said the Warden, with quiet emphasis. "I entirely agree with you, Miss Barton, that there is no greater reason for suspecting them than for suspecting one of ourselves. But that is the more reason why they should be cleared completely and at once."

"By all means," said the Bursar.

"As to the method used," went on the Warden, "to keep check upon the scouts, or upon anybody else, I feel strongly that the fewer people who know anything about that, the better. Perhaps Miss Vane will be able to put forward a good suggestion, in confidence to myself, or to . . ."

"Exactly," said Miss Hillyard, grimly. "To whom? So far as I can see, nobody among us can be taken on trust."

"That is unfortunately quite true," said the Warden, "and the same thing applies to myself. While I need not say that I have every confidence in the senior members of the College, both jointly and severally, it appears to me that, exactly as in the case of the scouts, it is of the highest importance that we should be safeguarded, in our own interests. What do you say, Sub-Warden?"

"Certainly," replied Miss Lydgate. "There should be no distinction made at all. I am perfectly willing to submit to any measures of supervision that may be recommended."

"Well, you at least can scarcely be suspected," said the Dean. "You are the greatest sufferer."

"We have nearly all suffered to some extent," said Miss Hillyard.

"I am afraid," said Miss Allison, "we shall have to allow for what I understand is the well-known practice of these unfortunate—um, ah—anonymous-letter writers, of sending letters to themselves to distract suspicion. Isn't that so, Miss Vane?"

"Yes," said Harriet, bluntly. "It seems unlikely, on the face of it, that anybody would do herself the kind of material damage Miss Lydgate has received; but if we once begin to make distinctions it is difficult to know where to stop. I don't think anything but a plain alibi ought to be accepted as evidence."

"And I have no alibi," said Miss Lydgate. "I did not leave College on the Saturday till after Miss Hillyard had gone to lunch. What is more, I went over to Tudor during lunchtime, to return a book to Miss Chilperic's room before I left; so that I might quite easily have taken the manuscript from the Library then."

"But you have an alibi for the time when the proofs were put in the S.C.R.," said Harriet.

"No," said Miss Lydgate; "not even that. I came by the early train and arrived when everybody was in Chapel. I should have had to be rather quick to run across and throw the proofs into the S.C.R. and be back in my rooms again before the discovery was made; but I suppose I *could* have done it. In any case, I would much rather be treated on the same footing as other people."

"Thank you," said the Warden. "Is there anybody who does not feel the same?"

"I am sure we must all feel the same," said the Dean. "But there is one set of people we are overlooking."

"The present students who were up at the Gaudy," said the Warden. "Yes; how about them?"

"I forget exactly who they were," said the Dean, "but I think most of them were Schools people, and have since gone down. I will look up the lists and see. Oh, and, of course, there was Miss Cattermole who was up for Responsions—for the second time of asking."

"Ah!" said the Bursar. "Yes. Cattermole."

"And that woman who was taking Mods—what's her name? Hudson, isn't it? Wasn't she still up?"

"Yes," said Miss Hillyard, "she was."

"They will be in their Second and Third Years now, I suppose," said Harriet. "By the way, is it known who 'young Farringdon' is, in this note addressed to Miss Flaxman?"

"There's the point," said the Dean. "Young Farringdon is an undergraduate of—New College, I think it is—who was engaged to Cattermole when they both came up, but is now engaged to Flaxman."

"Is he, indeed?"

"Mainly, I understand, or partly, in consequence of that letter. I am told that Miss Flaxman accused Miss Cattermole of sending it and showed it to Mr. Farringdon; with the result that the gentleman broke off the engagement and transferred his affections to Flaxman."

"Not pretty," said Harriet.

"No. But I don't think the Cattermole engagement was ever anything much more than a family arrangement, and that the new deal was not much more than an open recognition of the *fait accompli*. I gather there has been some feeling in the Second Year about the whole thing."

"I see," said Harriet.

"The question remains," said Miss Pyke, "what steps do we propose to take in the matter? We have asked Miss Vane's advice, and personally I am prepared to agree—particularly in view of what we have heard this evening—that it is abundantly necessary that some outside person should lend us assistance. To call in the police authorities is clearly undesirable. But may I ask whether, at this stage, it is suggested that Miss Vane should personally undertake an investigation? Or alternatively, would she propose our placing the matter in the hands of a private inquiry agent? Or what?"

"I feel I am in a very awkward position," said Harriet. "I am willing to give any help I can; but you do realize, don't you, that this kind of inquiry is apt to take a long time, especially if the investigator has to tackle it single-handed. A place like this, where people run in and out everywhere at all hours, is almost impossible to police or patrol efficiently. It would need quite a little squad of inquiry agents—and even if you disguised them as scouts or students a good deal of awkwardness might arise."

"Is there no material evidence to be obtained from an examination of the documents themselves?" asked Miss Pyke. "Speaking for myself, I am quite ready to have my fingerprints taken or to undergo any other kind of precautionary measure that may be considered necessary."

"I'm afraid," said Harriet, "the evidence of finger-prints isn't quite so easy a matter as we make it appear in books. I mean, we could take finger-prints, naturally, from the S.C.R. and, possibly, from the scouts—though they wouldn't like it much. But I should doubt very much whether rough scribbling-paper like this would show distinguishable prints. And besides—"

"Besides," said the Dean, "every malefactor nowadays knows enough about finger-prints to wear gloves."

"And," said Miss de Vine, speaking for the first time, and with a slightly grim emphasis, "if we didn't know it before, we know it now."

"Great Scott!" cried the Dean, impulsively, "I'd forgotten all about its being us."

"You see what I meant," said the Warden, "when I said that it was better not to discuss methods of investigation too freely."

"How many people have handled all these documents already?" inquired Harriet.

"Ever so many, I should think," said the Dean.

"But could not a search be made for—" began Miss Chilperic. She was the most junior of the dons; a small, fair and timid young woman, assistant-tutor in English Language and Literature, and remarkable chiefly for being engaged to be married to a junior don at another college. The Warden interrupted her.

"Please, Miss Chilperic. That is the kind of suggestion that ought not to be made here. It might convey a warning."

"This," said Miss Hillyard, "is an intolerable position." She looked angrily at Harriet, as though she were responsible for the position; which, in a sense, she was.

"It seems to me," said the Treasurer, "that, now that we have asked Miss Vane to come and give us her advice, it is impossible for us to take it, or even to hear what it is. The situation is rather Gilbertian."

"We shall have to be frank up to a point," said the Warden. "Do you advise the private inquiry agent, Miss Vane?"

"Not the ordinary sort," said Harriet; "you wouldn't like them at all. But I do know of an organization where you could get the right type of person and the greatest possible discretion."

For she had remembered that there was a Miss Katherine Climpson, who ran what was ostensibly a Typing Bureau but was in fact a useful organization of women engaged in handling odd little investigations. The Bureau was self-supporting, though it had, she knew, Peter Wimsey's money behind it. She was one of the very few people in the Kingdom who did know it.

The Treasurer coughed.

"Fees paid to a Detective Agency," she observed, "will have an odd appearance in the Annual Audit."

"I think that might be arranged," said Harriet. "I know the organization personally. A fee might not be necessary."

"That," said the Warden, "would not be right. The fees would, of course, have to be paid. I would gladly be personally responsible."

"That would not be right either," said Miss Lydgate. "We certainly should not like that."

"Perhaps," suggested Harriet, "I could find out what the fees were likely to be." She had, in fact, no idea how this part of the business was worked.

"There would be no harm in inquiring," said the Warden. "In the meantime—"

"If I may make the suggestion," said the Dean, "I should propose, Warden, that the evidence should be handed over to Miss Vane, as she is the only person in this room who cannot possibly come under suspicion. Perhaps she would like to sleep upon the matter and make a report to you in the morning. At least, not in the morning, because of Lord Oakapple and the Opening; but at some time during to-morrow."

"Very well," said Harriet, in response to an inquiring look from the Warden. "I will do that. And if I can think of any way in which I can be helpful, I'll do my best."

The Warden thanked her. "We all appreciate," she added, "the extreme awkwardness of the situation, and I am sure we shall all do what we can to co-operate in getting the matter cleared up. And I should like to say this: Whatever any of us may think or feel, it is of the very greatest importance that we should dismiss, as far as possible, all vague suspicions from our minds, and be particularly careful how we may say anything that might be construed as an accusation against anybody at all. In a close community of this kind, nothing can be more harmful than an atmosphere of mutual distrust. I repeat that I have the very greatest confidence in every Senior Member of the College. I shall endeavour to keep an entirely open mind, and I shall look to all my colleagues to do the same."

The dons assented; and the meeting broke up.

"*Well!*" said the Dean, as she and Harriet turned into the New Quad, "that is the most uncomfortable meeting I have ever had to sit through. My dear, you *have* thrown a bombshell into our midst!"

"I'm afraid so. But what could I do?"

"You couldn't possibly have done anything else. Oh, dear! It's all very well for the Warden to talk about an open mind, but we shall all feel perfectly ghastly wondering what other people are thinking about us, and whether our own conversation doesn't sound a little potty. It's the pottiness, you know, that's so awful."

"I know. By the way, Dean, I do absolutely refuse to suspect *you*. You're quite the sanest person I ever met."

"I don't think that's keeping an open mind, but thank you all the same for those few kind words. And one can't possibly suspect the Warden or Miss Lydgate, can one? But I'd better not say even that, I suppose. Otherwise, by a process of elimination—oh, lord! For Heaven's sake can't we find some handy outsider with a cast-iron alibi ready for busting?"

"We'll hope so. And of course there are those two students and the scouts to be disposed of." They turned in at the Dean's door. Miss Martin savagely poked up the fire in the sitting-room, sat down in an armchair and stared at the leaping flames. Harriet coiled herself on a couch and contemplated Miss Martin.

"Look here," said the Dean; "you had better not tell me too much about what *you* think, but there's no reason why any of us shouldn't tell *you* what *we* think, is there? No. Well. Here's the point. What is the object of all this persecution? It doesn't look like a personal grudge against anybody in particular. It's a kind of blind malevolence, directed against everybody in College. What's at the back of it?"

"Well, it might be somebody who thought the College as a body had injured her. Or it might be a personal grudge masking itself under a general attack. Or it might be just somebody with a mania for creating disturbance in order to enjoy the fun; that's the usual reason for this kind of outbreak, if you can call it a reason."

"That's sheer pottiness, in that case. Like those tiresome children who throw furniture about and the servants who pretend to be ghosts. And, talking of servants, do you think there's anything in that idea that it's more likely to be somebody of that class? Of course, Miss Barton wouldn't agree; but after all, some of the words used are very coarse."

"Yes," said Harriet; "but actually there isn't one that I, for example, don't know the meaning of. I believe, when you get even the primmest people under an anaesthetic, they are liable to bring the strangest vocabulary out of the subconscious—in fact, the primmer the coarser."

"True. Did you notice that there wasn't a single spelling mistake in the whole bunch of messages?"

"I noticed that. It probably points to a fairly well educated person; though the converse isn't necessarily true. I mean, educated people often put in mistakes on purpose, so that spelling mistakes don't prove much. But an absence of mistakes is a more difficult thing to manage, if it doesn't come natural. I'm not putting this very clearly."

"Yes, you are. A good speller could pretend to be a bad one; but a bad speller can't pretend to be a good one, any more than I could pretend to be a mathematician."

"She could use a dictionary."

"But then she would have to know enough to be dictionary-conscious—as the new slang would call it. Isn't our poison-pen rather silly to get all her spelling right?"

"I don't know. The educated person often fakes bad spelling rather badly; misspells easy words and gets quite difficult ones right. It's not so hard to tell when people are putting it on. I think it's probably cleverer to make no pretence about it."

"I see. Does this tend to exclude the scouts? . . . But probably they spell far better than we do. They so often *are* better educated. And I'm sure they dress better. But that's rather off the point. Stop me when I dither."

"You're not dithering," said Harriet. "Everything you say is perfectly true. At present I don't see how anybody is to be excluded."

"And *what,*" demanded the Dean, "becomes of the mutilated newspapers?"

"This won't do," said Harriet; "you're being a great deal too sharp about this. That's just one of the things I was wondering about."

"Well, we've been into that," said the Dean, in a tone of satisfaction. "We've checked up on all the S.C.R. and J.C.R. papers ever since this business came to our notice—that is, more or less, since the beginning of this term. Before anything goes to be pulped, the whole lot are checked up with the list and examined to see that nothing has been cut out."

"Who has been doing that?"

"My secretary, Mrs. Goodwin. I don't think you've met her yet. She lives in College during term. Such a nice girl —or woman, rather. She was left a widow, you know, very hard up, and she's got a little boy of ten at a prep. school. When her husband died—he was a schoolmaster—she set to work to train as a secretary and really did splendidly. She's simply invaluable to me, and most careful and reliable."

"Was she here at Gaudy?"

"Of course she was. She—good gracious! You surely don't think—my dear, that's *absurd!* The *most* straightforward and sane person. And she's very grateful to the College for having found her the job, and she certainly wouldn't want to run the risk of losing it."

"All the same, she's got to go on the list of possibles. How long has she been here?"

"Let me see. Nearly two years. Nothing at all happened till the Gaudy, you know, and she'd been here a year before that."

"But the S.C.R. and the scouts who live in College have been here still longer, most of them. We can't make exceptions along those lines. How about the other secretaries?"

"The Warden's secretary—Miss Parsons—lives at the Warden's Lodgings. The Bursar's and the Treasurer's secretaries both live out, so they can be crossed off."

"Miss Parsons been here long?"

"Four years."

Harriet noted down the names of Mrs. Goodwin and Miss Parsons.

"I think," she said, "for Mrs. Goodwin's own sake we'd better have a second check on those newspapers. Not that it really matters; because, if the poison-pen knows that the papers are being checked, she won't use those papers. And

I suppose she must know, because of the care taken to collect them."

"Very likely. That's just the trouble, isn't it?"

"How about people's private newspapers?"

"Well, naturally, we couldn't check them. We've kept an eye on the waste-paper baskets as well as we can. Nothing is ever destroyed, you know. It's all thriftily collected in sacks and sent to the paper-makers or whoever it is that gives pence for old papers. The worthy Padgett is instructed to examine the sacks—but it's a terrific job. And then, of course, since there are fires in all the rooms, why *should* anybody leave evidence in the W.P.B.?"

"How about the gowns that were burnt in the quad? That must have taken some doing. Surely more than one person would have been needed to work that."

"We don't know whether that was part of the same business or not. About ten or a dozen people had left their gowns in various places—as they do, you know—before Sunday supper. Some were in the Queen Elizabeth portico, and some at the foot of the Hall stairs and so on. People bring them over and dump them, ready for evening Chapel." (Harriet nodded; Sunday evening Chapel was held at a quarter to eight, and was compulsory; being also a kind of College Meeting for the giving-out of notices.) "Well, when the bell started, these people couldn't find their gowns and so couldn't go in to Chapel. Everybody thought it was just a rag. But in the middle of the night somebody saw a blaze in the quad, and it turned out to be a merry little bonfire of bombazine. The gowns had all been soaked in petrol and they went up beautifully."

"Where did the petrol come from?"

"It was a can Mullins keeps for his motor-cycle. You remember Mullins—the Jowett Lodge porter. His machine lies in a little outhouse in the Lodge garden. He didn't lock it up—why should he? He does *now*, but that doesn't help. Anybody could have gone and fetched it. He and his wife heard nothing, having retired to their virtuous rest. The bonfire happened bang in the middle of the Old Quad and burnt a nasty patch in the turf. Lots of people rushed out when the flare went up, and whoever did it probably mingled with the crowd. The victims were four M.A. gowns, two scholars' gowns and the rest commoners' gowns; but I don't suppose there was any selection; they just happened to be lying about."

"I wonder where they were put in the interval between supper and the bonfire. Anybody carrying a whole bunch of gowns round College would be a bit conspicuous."

"No; it was at the end of November, and it would be pretty dark. They could easily have been bundled into a lecture room to be left till called for. There wasn't a proper organized search over College, you see. The poor victims who were left gownless thought somebody was having a joke; they were very angry, but not very efficient. Most of them rushed round to accuse their friends."

"Yes; I don't suppose we can get much out of that episode at this time of day. Well—I suppose I'd better go and wash-and-brush-up for Hall."

Hall was an embarrassed meal at the High Table. The conversation was valiantly kept to matters of academic and world interest. The undergraduates babbled noisily and cheerfully; the shadow that rested upon the college did not seem to have affected their spirits. Harriet's eye roamed over them.

"Is that Miss Cattermole at the table on the right? In a green frock, with a badly made-up face?"

"That's the young lady," replied the Dean. "How did you know?"

"I remember seeing her at Gaudy. Where is the all-conquering Miss Flaxman?"

"I don't see her. She may not be dining in Hall. Lots of them prefer to boil an egg in their rooms, so as to avoid the bother of changing. Slack little beasts. And that's Miss Hudson, in a red jumper, at the middle table. Black hair and horn rims."

"She looks quite normal."

"So far as I know, she is. So far as I know, we all are."

"I suppose," said Miss Pyke, who had overheard the last remark, "even murderers look much like other people, Miss Vane. Or do you hold any opinions about the theories put forward by Lombroso? I understand that they are now to a considerable extent exploded."

Harriet was quite thankful to be allowed to discuss murderers.

After Hall, Harriet felt herself rather at a loose end. She felt she ought to be doing something or interviewing somebody; but it was hard to know where to begin. The Dean had announced that she would be busy with some lists, but would be open to receive visitors later on. Miss Burrows the Librarian was to be engaged in putting the final touches to the Library before the Chancellor's visit; she had been carting and arranging books the greater part of the day and had roped in a small band of students to assist her with the shelving of them. Various other dons mentioned that they had work to do; Harriet thought they seemed a little shy of one another's company.

Catching hold of the Bursar, Harriet asked whether it was possible to get hold of a plan of the College and a list of the various rooms and their occupants. Miss Stevens offered to supply the list and said she thought there was a plan in the Treasurer's office. She took Harriet across into the New Quad to get these things.

"I hope," said the Bursar, "you will not pay too much attention to that unfortunate remark of Miss Burrows' about the scouts. Nothing would please me more, personally, than to transfer all the maids to the Scouts' Wing out of reach of suspicion, if that were practicable; but there is no room for them there. Certainly I do not mind giving you the names of those who sleep in College, and I agree, certainly, that precautions should be taken. But to my mind, the episode of Miss Lydgate's proofs definitely rules out the scouts. Very few of them would be likely to know or care anything about proofsheets; nor would the idea of mutilating manuscripts be likely to come into their heads. Vulgar letters—yes, possibly. But damaging those proofs was an educated person's crime. Don't you think so?"

"I'd better not say what I think," said Harriet.

"No; quite right. But I can say what *I* think. I wouldn't say it to anybody but you. Still, I do not like this haste to make scapegoats of the scouts."

"The thing that seems so extraordinary," said Harriet, "is that Miss Lydgate, of all people, should have been chosen as a victim. How could *anybody*—particularly one of her own colleagues—have any grudge against *her*? Doesn't it look rather as though the culprit knew nothing about the value of the proofs, and was merely making a random gesture of defiance to the world in general?"

"That's possible, certainly. I must say, Miss Vane, that your evidence today has made matters very complicated. I would rather suspect the scouts than the S.C.R., I admit; but when these hasty accusations are made by the last person known to have been in the same room with the manuscript, I can only say that—well, that it appears to me injudicious."

Harriet said nothing to this. The Bursar, apparently feeling that she had gone a little too far, added:

"I have no suspicions of anybody. All I say is, that statements ought not to be made without proof."

Harriet agreed, and, after marking off the relevant names upon the Bursar's list, went to find the Treasurer.

Miss Allison produced a plan of the College, and showed the positions of the rooms occupied by various people.

"I hope this means," she said, "that you intend to undertake the investigation yourself. Not, I suppose, that we ought to ask you to spare the time for any such thing. But I do most strongly feel that the presence of paid detectives in this college would be *most* unpleasant, however discreet they might be. I have served the College for a considerable number of years and I have its interests very much at heart.

You know how undesirable it is that any outsider should be brought into a matter of this kind."

"It is; very," said Harriet. "All the same, a spiteful or mentally deficient servant is a misfortune that might occur anywhere. Surely the important thing is to get to the bottom of the mystery as quickly as possible; and a trained detective or two would be very much more efficient than I should be."

Miss Allison looked thoughtfully at her, and swayed her glasses to and fro slowly on their gold chain.

"I see you incline to the most comfortable theory. Probably we all do. But there is the other possibility. Mind you, I quite see that from your own point of view, you would not wish to take part in an exposure of a member of the Senior Common Room. But if it came to the point, I would put more faith in your tact than in that of an outside professional detective. And you start with a knowledge of the workings of the collegiate system, which is a great advantage."

Harriet said that she thought she would know better what to suggest when she had made a preliminary review of all the circumstances.

"If," said Miss Allison, "you do undertake an inquiry, it is probably only fair to warn you that you may meet with some opposition. It has already been said—but perhaps I ought not to tell you this."

"That is for you to judge."

"It has already been said that the narrowing-down of the suspects within the limits mentioned at today's meeting rests only upon your assertion. I refer, of course, to the two papers you found at the Gaudy."

"I see. Am I supposed to have invented those?"

"I don't think anybody would go as far as that. But you have said that you sometimes received similar letters on your own account. And the suggestion is that—"

"That if I found anything of the sort I must have brought it with me? That would be quite likely, only that the style of the things was so like the style of these others. However, I admit you have only my word for that."

"*I'm* not doubting it for a moment. What is being said is that your experience in these affairs is—if anything—a disadvantage. Forgive me. That is not what *I* say."

"That is the thing that made me very unwilling to have anything to do with the inquiry. It is absolutely true. I haven't lived a perfectly blameless life, and you can't get over it."

"If you ask me," said Miss Allison, "some people's blameless lives are to blame for a good deal. I am not a fool, Miss Vane. No doubt my own life has been blameless as far as the more generous sins are concerned. But there are points upon which I should expect you to hold more balanced opinions than certain people here. I don't think I need say more than that, need I?"

Harriet's next visit was to Miss Lydgate; her excuse being to inquire what she should do with the mutilated proofs in her possession. She found the English Tutor patiently correcting a small pile of students' essays.

"Come in, come in," said Miss Lydgate, cheerfully. "I have nearly done with these. Oh, about my poor proofs? I'm afraid they're not much use to me. They're really quite undecipherable. I'm afraid the only thing is to do the whole thing again. The printers will be tearing their hair, poor souls. I shan't have very much difficulty with the greater part of it, I hope. And I have the rough notes of the Introduction, so it isn't as bad as it might have been. The worst loss is a number of manuscript footnotes and two manuscript appendices that I had to put in at the last moment to refute what seemed to me some very ill-considered statements in Mr. Elkbottom's new book on *Modern Verse-Forms*. I stupidly wrote those in on the blank pages of the proofs and they are quite irrecoverable. I shall have to verify all the references again in Elkbottom. It's so tiresome, especially as one is always so busy towards the end of term. But it's all my own fault for not keeping a proper record of everything."

"I wonder," said Harriet, "if I could be of any help to you in getting the proofs put together. I'd gladly stay up for a week or so if it would do any good. I'm quite used to juggling with proof-sheets, and I think I can remember enough of my Schools work to be reasonably intelligent about the Anglo-Saxon and Early English."

"That would be a tremendous help!" exclaimed Miss Lydgate, her face lighting up. "But wouldn't it be trespassing far too much on your time?"

Harriet said, No; she was well ahead with her own work and would enjoy putting in a little time on English Prosody. It was in her mind that, if she really meant to pursue inquiries at Shrewsbury, Miss Lydgate's proofs would offer a convenient excuse for her presence in College.

The suggestion was left there for the moment. As regards the author of the outrages, Miss Lydgate could make no suggestion; except that, whoever it was, the poor creature must be mentally afflicted.

As she left Miss Lydgate's room, Harriet encountered Miss Hillyard, who was descending the staircase from her own abode.

"Well," said Miss Hillyard, "how is the investigation progressing? But I ought not to ask that. You have contrived to cast the Apple of Discord among us with a vengeance. However, as you are so well accustomed to the receipt of anonymous communications, you are no doubt the fittest person to handle the situation."

"In my case," said Harriet, "I only got what was to some extent deserved. But this is a very different matter. It's not the same problem at all. Miss Lydgate's book could offend nobody."

"Except some of the men whose theories she has attacked," replied Miss Hillyard. "However, circumstances seem to exclude the male sex from the scope of the inquiry. Otherwise, this mass-attack on a woman's college would suggest to me the usual masculine spite against educated women. But you, of course, would consider that ridiculous."

"Not in the least. Plenty of men are very spiteful. But surely there are no men running about the college at night."

"I wouldn't be too sure of that," said Miss Hillyard, smiling sarcastically. "It is quite ridiculous for the Bursar to talk about locked gates. What is to prevent a man from concealing himself about the grounds before the gates are locked and escaping again when they are opened in the morning? Or climbing the walls, if it comes to that?"

Harriet thought the theory far-fetched; but it interested her, as evidence of the speaker's prejudice, which amounted almost to obsession.

"The thing that in my opinion points to a man," went on Miss Hillyard, "is the destruction of Miss Barton's book, which is strongly pro-feminist. I don't suppose you have read it; probably it would not interest you. But why else should that book be picked out?"

Harriet parted from Miss Hillyard at the corner of the quad and went over to Tudor Building. She had not very much doubt who it was that was likely to offer opposition to her inquiries. If one was looking for a twisted mind, Miss Hillyard's was certainly a little warped. And, when one came to think of it, there was no evidence whatever that Miss Lydgate's proofs had ever been taken to the Library or ever left Miss Hillyard's hands at all. Also, she had undoubtedly been seen on the threshold of the S.C.R. before Chapel on the Monday morning. If Miss Hillyard was sufficiently demented to inflict a blow of this kind on Miss Lydgate, then she was fit for a lunatic asylum. But, indeed, this would apply to whoever it was.

She went into Tudor and tapped on Miss Barton's door, asking, when she was admitted, whether she might borrow a copy of *Woman's Place in the Modern State*.

"The sleuth at work?" said Miss Barton. "Well, Miss Vane, here it is. By the way, I should like to apologize to you for some of the things I said when you were here last. I shall be very glad to see you handle this most unpleasant business, which can scarcely be an agreeable thing for you.

I admire exceedingly anyone who can subordinate her own feelings to the common advantage. The case is obviously pathological—as all anti-social behavior is, in my opinion. But here there is no question of legal proceedings, I imagine. At least, I hope not. I feel extremely anxious that it should *not* be brought into court; and on that account I am against hiring detectives of any kind. If you are able to get to the bottom of it, I am ready to give you any help I can."

Harriet thanked the Fellow for her good opinion and for the book.

"You are probably the best psychologist here," said Harriet. "What do you think of it?"

"Probably the usual thing: a morbid desire to attract attention and create a public uproar. The adolescent and the middle-aged are the most likely suspects. I should very much doubt whether there is much more to it than that. Beyond, I mean, that the incidental obscenities point to some kind of sexual disturbance. But that is a commonplace in cases of this kind. But whether you ought to look for a man-hater or a man-trap," added Miss Barton, with the first glimmer of humour Harriet had ever seen in her, "I can't tell you."

Having put away her various acquisitions in her own room, Harriet thought it was time to go and see the Dean. She found Miss Burrows with her, very tired and dusty after coping with the Library, and being refreshed with a glass of hot milk, to which Miss Martin insisted on adding just a dash of whisky to induce slumber.

"What new light one gets on the habits of the S.C.R. when one's an old student," said Harriet. "I always imagined that there was only one bottle of ardent spirits in the college, kept under lock and key by the Bursar for life-and-death emergencies."

"It used to be so," said the Dean, "but I'm getting frivolous in my old age. Even Miss Lydgate cherishes a small stock of cherry brandy, for high-days and holidays. The

Bursar is even thinking of laying down a little port for the College."

"Great Scott!" said Harriet.

"The students are not supposed to imbibe alcohol," said the Dean, "but I shouldn't like to go bail for the contents of all the cupboards in College."

"After all," said Miss Burrows, "their tiresome parents bring them up to have cocktails and things at home, so it probably seems ridiculous to them that they shouldn't do the same thing here."

"And what can one do about it? Make a police search through their belongings? Well, I flatly refuse. We can't keep the place like a gaol."

"The trouble is," said the Librarian, "that everybody sneers at restrictions and demands freedom, till something annoying happens; then they demand angrily what has become of the discipline."

"You can't exercise the old kind of discipline in these days," said the Dean; "it's too bitterly resented."

"The modern idea is that young people should discipline themselves," said the Librarian. "But do they?"

"No; they won't. Responsibility bores 'em. Before the War they passionately had College Meetings about everything. Now, they won't be bothered. Half the old institutions, like the College debates and the Third Year Play, are dead or moribund. They don't want responsibility."

"They're all taken up with their young men," said Miss Burrows.

"Drat their young men," said the Dean. "In my day, we simply thirsted for responsibility. We'd all been sat on at school for the good of our souls, and came up bursting to show how brilliantly we could organize things when we were put in charge."

"If you ask me," said Harriet, "it's the fault of the schools. Free discipline and so on. Children are sick to death of running things and doing prefect duty; and when they get up to Oxford they're tired out and only want to sit back and let somebody else run the show. Even in my time, the people from the up-to-date republican schools were shy of taking office, poor brutes."

"It's all very difficult," said Miss Burrows with a yawn. "However, I did get my Library volunteers to do a job of work today. We've got most of the shelves decently filled, and the pictures hung and the curtains up. It looks very well. I hope the Chancellor will be impressed. They haven't finished painting the radiators downstairs, but I've bundled the paintpots and things into a cupboard and hoped for the best. And I borrowed a squad of scouts to clean up, so as not to leave anything to be done tomorrow."

"What times does the Chancellor arrive?" asked Harriet.

"Twelve o'clock; reception in the S.C.R. and show him round the College. Then lunch in Hall, and I hope he enjoys it. Ceremony at 2:30. And then push him off to catch the 3:45. Delightful man; but I am getting fed up with Openings. We've opened the New Quad, the Chapel (with choral service), the S.C.R. Dining Room (with lunch to Former Tutors and Fellows), the Tudor Annexe (with Old Students' Tea), the Kitchens and Scouts' Wing (with Royalty), the Sanatorium (with address by the Lister Professor of Medicine), the Council Chamber and the Warden's Lodgings, and we've unveiled the late Warden's Portrait, the Willett Memorial Sundial and the New Clock. And now it's the Library. Padgett said to me last term, when we were making those alterations in Queen Elizabeth, 'Excuse me, madam Dean, miss, but could you tell me, miss, the date of the Opening?' 'What Opening, Padgett?' said I. 'We aren't opening anything this term. What is there to open?' 'Well, miss,' says Padgett, 'I was thinking of these here new lavatories, if you'll excuse me, madam Dean, miss. We've opened everything there was to open up to the present, miss, and if there was to be a Ceremony, miss, it would be convenient if I was to know in good time, on account of arranging for taxis and parking accommodation.' "

"Dear Padgett!" said Miss Burrows. "He's the brightest spot in this academy." She yawned again. "I'm dead."

"Take her away to bed, Miss Vane," said the Dean, "and we'll call it a day."

CHAPTER VI

Often when they were gone to Bed, the inner doors were flung open, as also the Doors of a Cupboard which stood in the Hall; and this with a great deal of Violence and Noise. And one Night the Chairs, which when they went to Bed stood all in the Chimney-corner, were all removed and placed in the middle of the Room in very good order, and a Meal-sieve hung upon one cut full of Holes, and a Key of an inner Door upon another. And in the Day-time, as they sate in the House spinning, they could see the Barn-doors often flung open, but not by whom. Once, as Alice *sate spinning the Rock or Distaff leapt several times out of the Wheel into the middle of the room . . . with much more such ridiculous stuff as this is, which would be tedious to relate.*

WILLIAM TURNER

Peter," said Harriet. And with the sound of her own voice she came drowsing and floating up out of the strong circle of his arms, through a green sea of sun-dappled beechleaves into darkness.

"Oh, damn," said Harriet softly to herself. "Oh, damn. And I didn't want to wake up."

The clock in the New Quad struck three musically.

"This won't do," said Harriet. "This really will not do. My sub-conscious has a most treacherous imagination." She groped for the switch of her bedside lamp. "It's disquieting to reflect that one's dreams never symbolize one's real wishes, but always something Much Worse." She turned the light on and sat up.

"If I really wanted to be passionately embraced by Peter, I should dream of something like dentists or gardening. I wonder what are the unthinkable depths of awfulness that can only be expressed by the polite symbol of Peter's embraces. Damn Peter! I wonder what he would do about a case like this."

This brought her mind back to the evening in the Egotists' Club and the anonymous letter; and thence back to his absurd fury with the sticking-plaster.

". . . but my mind being momentarily on my job . . ."

You'd think he was quite bird-witted, sometimes, she thought. But he does keep his mind on the job, when he's doing it. One's mind on the job. Yes. What am I doing, letting my mind stray all over the place. Is this a job, or isn't it? . . . Suppose the Poison-Pen is on its rounds now, dropping letters at people's doors . . . Whose door, though? One can't watch all the doors . . . I ought to be sitting up at the window, keeping an eye open for creeping figures in the quad . . . Somebody ought to do it—but who's to be trusted? Besides, dons have their jobs to do; they can't sit up all night and work all day . . . The job . . . keeping one's mind on the job . . .

She was out of bed now and pulling the window-curtains aside. There was no moon, and nothing at all to be seen. Not even a late essay-writer seemed to be burning the midnight lamp.

Anybody could go anywhere on a dark night like this, she thought to herself. She could scarcely see even the outline of the roofs of Tudor on her right, or the dark bulk of the New Library jutting out on her left from behind the Annexe.

The Library; with not a soul in it.

She put on a dressing-gown and opened her door softly. It was bitterly cold. She found the wall-switch and went down the central corridor of the Annexe, past a row of doors behind which students were sleeping and dreaming of goodness knew what—examinations, sports, undergraduates, parties, all the queer jumble of things that are summed up as "activities." Outside their doors lay little heaps of soiled crockery for the scouts to collect and wash.

Also shoes. On the doors were cards, bearing their names: Miss H. Brown, Miss Jones, Miss Colburn, Miss Szleposky, Miss Isaacson—so many unknown quantities. So many destined wives and mothers of the race; or, alternatively, so many potential historians, scientists, schoolteachers, doctors, lawyers; as you liked to think one thing of more importance than the other. At the end of the passage was a large window, hygienically open at top and bottom. Harriet gently pushed up the bottom sash and looked out, shivering.

And suddenly she knew that whatever reason or instinct had led her to look at the Library had taken a very just view of the situation. The New Library should have been quite dark. It was not. One of the long windows was split from top to bottom by a narrow band of light.

Harriet thought rapidly. If this was Miss Burrows, carrying on legitimately (though at an unreasonable and sacrificial hour) with her preparations, why had she troubled to draw the curtains? The windows had been curtained, because a Library that faces south must have some protection against strong sunlight. But it would be absurd for the Librarian to protect herself and her proper functions from scrutiny in the middle of a dark March night. College authorities were not so secretive as all that. Something was up. Should one go and investigate on one's own, or rouse somebody else?

One thing was clear; if it was a member of the S.C.R. lurking behind those curtains, it would not be politic to bring a student to witness the discovery. What dons slept in Tudor? Without consulting the list, Harriet remembered that Miss Barton and Miss Chilperic had rooms there, but on the far side of the building. Here was an opportunity to check up on them, at any rate. With a last glance at the Library window, Harriet made her way quickly back past her own room on the Bridge and through into the main building. She cursed herself for not having a torch; she was delayed by fumbling with the switches. Along the corridor, past the stair-head and round to the left. No don on that floor; it must be on the floor below. Back, and down the stairs and along to the left again. She was leaving all the passage-lights burning behind her, and wondered whether they would arouse attention in other buildings. At last. A door on her left labelled "Miss Barton." And the door stood open.

She knocked at it sharply, and went in. The sitting-room was empty. Beyond it, the bedroom door stood open too. "Gracious!" said Harriet. "Miss Barton!" There was no reply; and, looking in, she saw that the bedroom was as empty as the sitting-room. The bed-clothes were flung back and the bed had been slept in; but the sleeper had risen and gone.

It was easy to think of an innocent explanation. Harriet stood for a moment, considering; and then called to mind that the window of the room overlooked the quad. The curtains were drawn back; she looked out into the darkness. The light still shone in the Library window; but while she looked, it went out.

She ran back to the foot of the stair and through the entrance-hall. The front door of the building was ajar. She pulled it open and ran out and across the quad. As she ran, something seemed to loom up ahead of her. She made for it and closed with it. It caught her in a muscular grip.

"Who's that?" demanded Harriet, fiercely.

"And who's *that?*"

The grip of one hand was released and a torch was switched on into Harriet's face.

"Miss Vane! What are you doing here?"

"Is that Miss Barton? I was looking for you. I saw a light in the New Library."

"So did I. I've just been over to investigate. The door's locked."

"Locked?"

"And the key inside."

"Isn't there another way up?" asked Harriet.

"Yes, of course there is. I ought to have thought of that.

Up through the Hall passage and the Fiction Library. Come along!"

"Wait a minute," said Harriet. "Whoever it is may be still there. You watch the main door, to see they don't get out that way. I'll go up through the Hall."

"Very well. Good idea. Here! haven't you got a torch? You'd better take mine. You'll waste time turning on lights."

Harriet snatched the torch and ran, thinking hard. Miss Barton's story sounded plausible enough. She had woken up (why?), seen the light (very likely she slept with her curtains drawn open) and gone out to investigate while Harriet was running about the upper floors hunting for the right room. In the meantime, the person in the Library had either finished what she was doing or, possibly, peeped out and been alarmed by seeing the lights go up in Tudor. She had switched out the light. She had not gone out by the main door; she was either still somewhere in the Hall-Library Wing, or she had crept out by the Hall stair while Miss Barton and Harriet were grappling with one another in the quad.

Harriet found the Hall stair and started up it, using her torch as little as possible and keeping the light low. It came forcibly into her mind that the person she was hunting was —must be—unbalanced, if not mad, and might possibly deliver a nasty swipe out of a dark corner. She arrived at the head of the stair, and pushed back the swinging glass double door that led to the passage between the Hall and the Buttery. As she did so, she fancied she heard a slight scuffling sound ahead, and almost simultaneously she saw the gleam of a torch. There ought to be a two-way switch just on the right, behind the door. She found it, and pressed it down. There was a quick flicker, and then darkness. A fuse? Then she laughed at herself. Of course not. The person at the other end of the passage had flicked the switch at the same moment as herself. She pushed the switch up again, and the lights flooded the passage.

On her left she saw the three doorways, with the

serving-hatches between, that led into the Hall. On the right was the long blank wall between the passage and the kitchens. And ahead of her, at the far end of the passage, close to the Buttery door, stood somebody clutching a dressing-gown about her with one hand and a large jug in the other.

Harriet advanced swiftly upon this apparition, which came meekly enough to meet her. Its features seemed familiar, and in a moment she identified them. It was Miss Hudson, the Third Year student who had been up at Gaudy.

"What in the world are you doing here at this time of night?" demanded Harriet, severely. Not that she had any particular right to question students about their movements. Nor did she feel that her own appearance, in pyjamas and a jaeger dressing-gown, suggested dignity or authority. Miss Hudson, indeed, seemed quite flabbergasted at being thus accosted by a total stranger at three in the morning. She stared, speechless.

"Why shouldn't I be here?" said Miss Hudson, at last, defiantly. "I don't know who you are. I've as much right to walk about as you have . . . Oh, gosh!" she added, and burst out laughing. "I suppose you're one of the scouts. I didn't recognize you without your uniform."

"No," said Harriet, "I'm an old student. You're Miss Hudson, aren't you? But your room isn't here. Have you been along to the Buttery?" Her eyes were on the jug; Miss Hudson blushed.

"Yes—I wanted some milk. I've got an essay."

She spoke of it as though it were a disease. Harriet chuckled.

"So that still goes on, does it? Carrie's just as softhearted as Agnes was in my day." She went up to the Buttery hatch and shook it, but it was locked. "No, apparently she isn't."

"I asked her to leave it open," said Miss Hudson, "but I expect she forgot. I say—don't give Carrie away. She's awfully decent."

"You know quite well that Carrie isn't supposed to leave the hatch open. You ought to get your milk before ten o'clock."

"I know. But one doesn't always know if one will want it. You've done the same thing in your time, I expect."

"Yes," said Harriet. "Well, you'd better cut along. Wait a second. When did you come up here?"

"Just now. Just a few seconds before you did."

"Did you meet anybody?"

"No." Miss Hudson looked alarmed. "Why? Has anything happened?"

"Not that I know of. Get along to bed."

Miss Hudson escaped and Harriet tried the Buttery door which was as firmly locked as the hatch. Then she went on, through the Fiction Library, which was empty, and put her hand on the handle of the oak door that led to the New Library.

The door was immovable. There was no key in the lock. Harriet looked round the Fiction Library. On the window-sill lay a thin pencil, beside a book and a few papers. She pushed the pencil into the key-hole; it encountered no resistance.

She went to the window of the Fiction Library and pushed it up. It looked on to the roof of a small loggia. Two people were not enough for this game of hide-and-seek. She pulled a table across the Library door, so that if anybody tried to come out that way behind her back she should have notice of it; then she climbed out on to the loggia roof and leaned over the balcony. She could see nothing distinctly beneath her, but she pulled her torch from her pocket and signalled with it.

"Hullo!" said Miss Barton's voice, cautiously, from below.

"The other door's locked, and the key gone."

"That's awkward. If either of us goes, somebody may come out. And if we yell for help there'll be an uproar."

"That's about the size of it," said Harriet.

"Well, listen; I'll try and get in through one of the

groundfloor windows. They all seem to be latched, but I might break a pane of glass."

Harriet waited. Presently she heard a faint tinkle. Then there was a pause, and presently the sound of a moving sash. There was a longer pause. Harriet came back into the Fiction Library and pulled the table away from the door. In about six or seven minutes' time she saw the door handle move and heard a tap on the other side of the oak. She stooped to the key-hole, and called: "What's up?" and bent her ear to listen.

"Nobody here," said Miss Barton's voice on the other side. "Key's gone. And the most ghastly mess-up."

"I'll come round."

She hurried back through the Hall and round to the front of the Library. Here she found the window that Miss Barton had opened, climbed through and ran on up the stairs into the Library.

"Well!" said Harriet.

The New Library was a handsome, lofty room, with six bays on the South side, lit by as many windows running nearly from the floor to the ceiling. On the North side, the wall was windowless, and shelved to a height of ten feet. Above this was a space of blank wall, along which it would be possible, at some future time, to run an extra gallery when the books should become too many for the existent shelving. This blank space had been adorned by Miss Burrows and her party with a series of engravings, such as every academic community possesses, representing the Parthenon, the Colosseum, Trajan's Column and other topographical and classical subjects.

All the books in the room had been dragged out and flung on the floor, by the simple expedient of removing the shelves bodily. The pictures had been thrown down. And the blank wall-space thus exposed had been adorned with a frieze of drawings, roughly executed in brown paint, and with inscriptions in letters a foot high, all of the most unseemly sort. A pair of library steps and a pot of paint with a wide brush in it stood triumphantly in the midst of the wreckage, to show how the transformation had been accomplished.

"That's torn it," said Harriet.

"Yes," said Miss Barton. "A very nice reception for Lord Oakapple."

There was an odd note in her voice—almost of satisfaction. Harriet looked sharply at her.

"What are you going to do? What does one do? Go over the place with a magnifying glass? or send for the police?"

"Neither," said Harriet. She considered for a moment.

"The first thing," she said, "is to send for the Dean. The next is to find either the original keys or a spare set. The third, is to clean off these filthy inscriptions before anybody sees them. And the fourth is to get the room straight before twelve o'clock. There's plenty of time. Will you be good enough to wake the Dean and bring her with you. In the meantime, I'll have a look round for clues. We can discuss afterwards who did the job and how she got out. Please make haste."

"H'm!" said the Fellow. "I like people who know their own minds."

She went with surprising promptness.

"Her dressing-gown is all over paint," said Harriet aloud to herself. "But she may have got it climbing in." She went downstairs and examined the open window. "Yes, here's where she scrambled over the wet radiator. I expect I'm marked too. Yes, I am. Nothing to show whether it all came from there. Damp footmarks—hers and mine, no doubt. Wait a moment."

She traced the damp marks up to the top of the stairs, where they grew faint and ceased. She could find no third set; but the footmarks of the intruder would probably have had time to dry. Whoever it was must have begun operations very soon after midnight at latest. The paint had splashed about a good deal; if it were possible to search the whole college for paint-stained clothing, well and good. But it would cause a terrific scandal. Miss Hudson—had she shown any marks of paint anywhere? Harriet thought not.

She looked about her again, and realized unexpectedly that she had the lights full on, and that the curtains were drawn open. If anybody was looking across from one of the other buildings, the interior of the room would show up like a lighted stage. She snapped the lights off, and drew the curtains again carefully before putting them on again.

"Yes," she said. "I see. That was the idea. The curtains were drawn while the job was done. Then the lights were turned off and the curtains opened. Then the artist escaped, leaving the doors locked. In the morning, everything would look quite ordinary from the outside. Who would have been the first to try and come in? An early scout, to do a final clean-round? She would find the door locked, think Miss Burrows had left it like that, and probably do nothing about it. Miss Burrows would probably have come up first. When? A little after Chapel, or a little before. She would not have been able to get in. Time would have been wasted hunting for the keys. When anybody did get in, it would have been too late to straighten things up. Everybody would have been about. The Chancellor—?

Miss Burrows would have been the first to come up. She had also been the last to leave, and was the person who knew best where the paint pots had been put. Would she have wrecked her own job, any more than Miss Lydgate would have wrecked her own proofs? How far was that psychological premise sound? One would surely damage anything in the world, *except* one's own work. But on the other hand, if one were cunning enough to see that people would think exactly that, then one would promptly take the precaution of seeing that one's own work did suffer.

Harriet moved slowly about the Library. There was a big splash of paint on the parquet. And at the edge of it—oh, yes! it would be very useful to hunt the place over for paint-stained clothes. But here was evidence that the culprit had worn no slippers. Why should she have worn anything? The radiators on this floor were working at full blast, and a complete absence of clothing would be not merely politic but comfortable.

And how had the person got away? Neither Miss Hudson (if she was to be trusted) nor Harriet had met anyone on the way up. But there had been plenty of time for escape, after the lights were put out. A stealthy figure creeping away under the Hall archway could not have been seen from the far side of the Old Quad. Or, if it came to that, there might quite well have been somebody lurking in the Hall while Harriet and Miss Hudson were talking in the passage.

"I've mucked it a bit," said Harriet. "I ought to have turned on the Hall lights to make sure."

Miss Barton re-entered with the Dean, who took one look round and said "Mercy!" She looked like a stout little mandarin, with her long red pigtail and quilted blue dressing-gown sprawled over with green-and-scarlet dragons. "What *idiots* we were not to expect it. Of course, the *obvious* thing! If we'd only thought about it, Miss Burrows could have locked up before she went. And *what* do we do now?"

"My first reaction," said Harriet, "is turpentine. And the second is Padgett."

"My dear, you are perfectly right. Padgett will cope. He always does. Like charity, he never fails. What a mercy you people spotted what was going on. As soon as we get these disgusting inscriptions cleaned off, we can put on a coat of quick-drying distemper or something, or paper the wall over, and—goodness! I don't know where the turpentine will come from, unless the painters have left a lot. It'll need a young bath. But Padgett will manage."

"I'll run over and get him," said Harriet, "and at the same time I'll collar Miss Burrows. We'll have to get these books back into place. What's the time? Five to four. I think it can be done all right. Will you hold the fort till I come back?"

"Yes. Oh, and you'll find the main door open now. I had an extra key, fortunately. A beautiful *plated* key—all ready for Lord Oakapple. But we'll have to get a locksmith to the other door, unless the builders have a spare."

The most remarkable thing about that remarkable morning was the imperturbability of Padgett. He answered Harriet's summons attired in a handsome pair of striped pyjamas, and received her instructions with monumental stolidity.

"The Dean is sorry to say, Padgett, that somebody has been playing some very disagreeable tricks in the New Library."

"Have they indeed, miss?"

"The whole place has been turned upside down, and some very vulgar words and pictures scrawled on the wall."

"Very unfortunate, miss, that is."

"In brown paint."

"That's awkward, miss."

"It will have to be cleaned at once, before anybody sees it."

"Very good, miss."

"And then we shall have to get hold of the decorators or somebody to paper or wash it over before the Chancellor arrives."

"Very good, miss."

"Do you think you can manage it, Padgett?"

"Just you leave it to me, miss."

Harriet's next job was to collect Miss Burrows, who received the news with loud expressions of annoyance.

"How loathsome! And do you mean to say all those books have got to be done *again?* Now? Oh, lord, yes—I suppose there's no help for it. What a blessing I hadn't put the Folio Chaucer and the other valuables in the showcases. Lord!"

The Librarian scrambled out of bed. Harriet looked at her feet. They were quite clean. But there was an odd smell in the bedroom. She traced it after a moment or two to the neighbourhood of the permanent basin.

"I say—is that turps?"

"Yes," replied Miss Burrows, struggling into her stockings. "I brought it across from the library. I got paint on my hands when I moved those pots and things."

"I wish you'd lend it me. We had to scramble in through the window over a wet radiator."

"Yes, rather."

Harriet went out, puzzled. Why should Miss Burrows have bothered to bring the can over to the New Quad, when she could have cleaned off the paint on the spot? But she could well understand that if anyone had wanted to remove paint from her feet, after being disturbed in the middle of a piece of dirty work, there might have been nothing for it but to snatch up the can and bolt for it.

Then she had another idea. The culprit could not have left the Library with her feet bare. She would have put on her slippers again. If you put paint-stained feet into slippers, the slippers ought to show signs of it.

She went back to her own room and dressed. Then she returned to the New Quad. Miss Burrows had gone. Her bedroom slippers lay by the bed. Harriet examined them minutely, inside and out, but they were quite free from paint.

On her way back again, Harriet overtook Padgett. He was walking sedately across the lawn, carrying a large can of turpentine in each hand.

"Where did you rake that up, Padgett, so early in the morning?"

"Well, miss, Mullins went on his motor-bike and knocked up a chap he knows what lives over his own oil-shop, miss."

As simple as that.

Some time later, Harriet and the Dean, decorously robed and gowned, found themselves passing along the East side of Queen Elizabeth Building in the wake of Padgett and the decorators' foreman.

"Young ladies," Padgett was heard to say, "will 'ave their larks, same as young gentlemen."

"When I was a lad," replied the foreman, "young ladies was young ladies. And young gentlemen was young gentlemen. If you get my meaning."

"Wot this country wants," said Padgett, "is a 'Itler."

"That's right," said the foreman. "Keep the girls at 'ome. Funny kind o' job you got 'ere, mate. Wot was you, afore you took to keepin' a 'en 'ouse?"

"Assistant camel 'and at the Zoo. Very interesting job it was, too."

"Wot made you chuck it?"

"Blood-poison. I was bit in the arm," said Padgett, "by a female."

"Ah!" said the foreman decorator.

By the time Lord Oakapple arrived, the Library presented nothing unseemly to the eye, beyond a certain dampness and streakiness in its upper parts, where the new paper was drying unevenly. The glass had been swept up and the paint stains cleaned from the floor; twenty photographs of classical statuary had been unearthed from a store-cupboard to replace the Colosseum and the Parthenon; the books were back on their shelves, and the showcases duly displayed the Chaucer Folio, the Shakespeare First Quarto, the three Kelmscott Morrises, the autographed copy of *The Man of Property*, and the embroidered glove belonging to the Countess of Shrewsbury.

The Dean hovered about the Chancellor like a hen with one chick, in a martyrdom of nervous apprehension lest some indelicate missive should drop from his table-napkin or flutter out unexpectedly from the folds of his robes; and when, in the Senior Common Room after lunch, he took out a bunch of notes from his pocket and riffled them over with a puzzled frown, the tension became so acute that she nearly dropped the sugar-basin. It turned out, however, that he had merely mislaid a Greek quotation. The Warden, though the history of the Library was known to her, displayed her usual serene poise.

Harriet saw nothing of all this. She spent the whole

interval, after the decorators had done their part, in the Library, watching the movements of everyone who came in or out, and seeing that they left nothing undesirable behind them.

Apparently, however, the College Poltergeist had shot its bolt. A cold lunch was brought up to the self-appointed invigilator. A napkin covered it; but nothing lurked beneath its folds beyond a plate of ham sandwiches and other such harmless matter. Harriet recognized the scout.

"It's Annie, isn't it? Are you on the kitchen staff now?"

"No, madam. I wait upon the Hall and Senior Common Room."

"How are your little girls getting on? I think Miss Lydgate said you had two little girls?"

"Yes, madam. How kind of you to ask." Annie's face beamed with pleasure. "They're splendid. Oxford suits them, after living in a manufacturing town, where we were before. Are you fond of children, madam?"

"Oh, yes," said Harriet. Actually, she did not care much about children; but one can scarcely say so, bluntly, to those possessed of these blessings.

"You ought to be married and have some of your own, madam. There! I oughtn't to have said that—it's not my place. But it seems to me a dreadful thing to see all these unmarried ladies living together. It isn't natural, is it?"

"Well, Annie, it's all according to taste. And one has to wait for the right person to come along."

"That's very true, madam." Harriet suddenly recollected that Annie's husband had been queer, or committed suicide, or something unfortunate, and wondered whether her commonplace had been a tactful one. But Annie seemed quite pleased with it. She smiled again; she had large, light blue eyes, and Harriet thought she must have been a good-looking woman before she got so thin and worried-looking. "I'm sure I hope he'll come along for you—or perhaps you are engaged to be married?"

Harriet frowned. She had no particular liking for the question, and did not want to discuss her private affairs with the college servants. But there seemed to be no impertinent intention behind the inquiry, so she answered pleasantly, "Not just yet; but you never know. How do you like the new Library?"

"It's a very handsome room, isn't it, madam? But it seems a great shame to keep up this big place just for women to study books in. I can't see what girls want with books. Books won't teach them to be good wives."

"What dreadful opinions!" said Harriet. "Whatever made you take a job in a women's college, Annie?"

The scout's face clouded. "Well, madam, I've had my misfortunes. I was glad to take what I could get."

"Yes, of course; I was only joking. Do you like the work?"

"It's quite all right. But some of these clever ladies are a bit queer, don't you think, madam? Funny, I mean. No heart in them."

Harriet remembered that there had been misunderstandings with Miss Hillyard.

"Oh, no," she said briskly. "Of course they are very busy people, and haven't much time for outside interests. But they are all very kind."

"Yes, madam; I'm sure they mean to be. But I always think of what it says in the Bible, about 'much learning hath made thee mad.' It isn't a right thing."

Harriet looked up sharply and caught an odd look in the scout's eyes.

"What do you mean by that, Annie?"

"Nothing at all, madam. Only funny things go on sometimes, but of course, being a visitor, you wouldn't know, and it's not my place to mention them—being only a servant, nowadays."

"I certainly," said Harriet, rather alarmed, "wouldn't mention anything of the kind you suggest to outside people or visitors. If you have any complaint to make, you should speak to the Bursar, or the Warden."

"I haven't any complaint, madam. But you may have heard about rude words being written up on the walls, and about the things that were burnt in the Quad—why, there was a bit in the papers about that. Well, you'll find, madam, they all happened since a certain person came into the college."

"What person?" said Harriet sternly.

"One of these learned ladies, madam. Well, perhaps I'd better not say anything more about that. You write detective books, don't you, madam? Well, you'll find something in that lady's past, you may be sure of it. At least, that's what a good many people are saying. And it isn't a nice thing for anybody to be in the same place with a woman like that."

"I feel quite sure you must be mistaken, Annie; I should be very careful how you spread about a tale of that kind. You'd better run along back to the Hall, now; I expect they'll be needing you."

So that was what the servants were saying. Miss de Vine, of course; she was the "learned lady" whose arrival had coincided with the beginning of the disturbances—coincided more exactly than Annie could know, unless she too had seen that drawing in the quad at the Gaudy. A curious woman, Miss de Vine, and undoubtedly with a varied experience behind those disconcerting eyes. But Harriet was inclined to like her, and she certainly did not look mad in the way that the "Poison-Pen" was mad; though it would not be surprising to learn that she had a streak of fanaticism somewhere. What, by the way, had she been doing the previous night? She had rooms at the moment in Queen Elizabeth; there was probably little likelihood of proving an alibi for her now. Miss de Vine—well! she would have to be put on the same footing as everybody else.

The opening of the Library took place without a hitch. The Chancellor unlocked the main door with the plated key, unaware that the same key had opened it, under curious circumstances, the night before. Harriet watched carefully the faces of the assembled dons and scouts; none of them showed any sign of surprise, anger or disappointment at the decorous appearance of the Library. Miss Hudson was present, looking cheerfully unconcerned; Miss Cattermole, too, was there. She looked as though she had been crying; and Harriet noticed that she stood in a corner by herself and talked to nobody until, at the conclusion of the ceremony, a dark girl in spectacles made her way through the crowd to her and they walked away together.

Later in the day, Harriet went to the Warden to make her promised report. She pointed out the difficulty of dealing with an outbreak like that of the previous night single-handed. A careful patrol of the quads and passages by a number of helpers would probably have resulted in the capture of the culprit; and the whole of the suspects could in any case have been checked up at an early moment. She strongly advised enlisting some women from Miss Climpson's Agency, the nature of which she explained.

"I see the point," replied the Warden; "but I find that at least two members of the Senior Common Room feel very strong objections to that course of action."

"I know," said Harriet. "Miss Allison and Miss Barton. Why?"

"I think, too," pursued the Warden, without answering this question, "that the matter presents certain difficulties. What would the students think of these strangers prowling about the college at night? They will wonder why police duties cannot be undertaken by ourselves, and we can hardly inform them that we ourselves are particularly under suspicion. And to perform such duties as you suggest, properly, quite a large number would be required—if all the strategic points are to be held. Then these persons would be quite ignorant of the conditions of college life, and might easily make unfortunate mistakes by following and questioning the wrong people. I do not see how we could avoid a very unpleasant scandal and some complaints."

"I see all that, Warden. But all the same, that is the quickest solution."

The Warden bent her head over a handsome piece of tapestry-work on which she was engaged.

"I cannot feel it to be very desirable. I know you will say that the whole situation is undesirable. I quite agree with you." She looked up. "I suppose, Miss Vane, you could not yourself spare the time to assist us?"

"I could spare the time," said Harriet, slowly. "But without help it is going to be very difficult. If there were only one or two people who were exonerated without a shadow of doubt, it would be very much easier."

"Miss Barton assisted you very ably last night."

"Yes," said Harriet; "but—how shall I put it? If I were writing a story about this, the person first on the spot would be the first person to be suspected."

The Warden selected an orange skein from her basket and threaded her needle deliberately.

"Will you explain that, please?"

Harriet explained carefully.

"That is very clearly put," said Dr. Baring. "I understand perfectly. Now, about this student, Miss Hudson. Her explanation does not seem to be satisfactory. She could not possibly have expected to get food from the Buttery at that hour; and in fact, she did not."

"No," said Harriet; "but I know quite well that in my day it wasn't too difficult to get round the right side of the Head Scout to leave the hatch open all night. Then, if one had a late essay or anything and felt hungry, one went down and got what one wanted."

"Dear me," said the Warden.

"We were always quite honourable about it," said Harriet, "and entered it all on the slate, so that it figured in our battels at the end of term. Though," she added thoughtfully, "there were some items of cold meat and dripping that must have been camouflaged a bit. Still—I think Miss Hudson's explanation will pass muster."

"Actually, the hatch was locked."

"Actually, it was. As a matter of fact, I have seen Carrie, and she assures me that it was locked at 10:30 last night as usual. She admits that Miss Hudson asked her to leave it open, but says she didn't do so, because, only last night, the Bursar had given special instructions about the locking of the hatch and Buttery. That would be after the meeting, no doubt. She also says she has been more particular this term than she used to be, because of a little trouble there was over the same thing last term."

"Well—I see there is no proof against Miss Hudson. I believe she is rather a lively young woman, however; so it may be as well to keep an eye on her. She is very able; but her antecedents are not particularly refined, and I dare say, it is possible that she might look upon even the disagreeable expressions found in the—er—the communications in the light of a joke. I tell you this, not to create any prejudice against the girl, but merely for whatever evidential value it may possess."

"Thank you. Well, then, Warden; if you feel it is impossible to call in outside help, I suggest that I should stay in College for a week or so, ostensibly to help Miss Lydgate with her book and to do some research on my own account in Bodley. I could then make a few more investigations. If nothing decisive results by the end of the term, I really think the question of engaging professionals will have to be faced."

"That is a very generous offer," said the Warden. "We shall all be exceedingly grateful to you."

"I ought to warn you," said Harriet, "that one or two of the Senior Members do not approve of me."

"That may make it a little more difficult. But if you are ready to put up with that unpleasantness in the interests of the College, it can only increase our sense of gratitude. I cannot too strongly emphasize how exceedingly important it is to avoid publicity. Nothing is more prejudicial to the College in particular and to University women in general than spiteful and ill-informed gossip in the press. The students, so far, seem to have been very loyal. If any of them had been indiscreet we should certainly have heard of it by now."

"How about Miss Flaxman's young man at New College?"

"Both he and Miss Flaxman have behaved quite well. At first, naturally, it was taken to be a purely personal matter. When the situation developed, I spoke to Miss Flaxman, and received her assurance that she and her fiancé would keep the whole thing to themselves until it could be properly cleared up."

"I see," said Harriet. "Well, we must do what we can. One thing I should like to suggest, and that is that some of the passage-lights should be left on at night. It is difficult enough to patrol a large set of buildings in the light: in the dark, it is impossible."

"That is reasonable," replied Dr. Baring. "I will speak to the Bursar about it."

And with this unsatisfactory arrangement, Harriet was obliged to be content.

CHAPTER VII

O my deare Cloris *be not sad,*
Nor with these Furies daunted,
But let these female fooles be mad,
With Hellish pride inchanted;
Let not thy noble thoughts descend
So low as their affections,
Whom neither counsell can amend,
Nor yet the Gods corrections.

MICHAEL DRAYTON

It was a matter of mild public interest at Shrewsbury College that Miss Harriet Vane, the well-known detective novelist, was spending a couple of weeks in College, while engaged in research at the Bodleian upon the life and works of Sheridan Le Fanu. The excuse was good enough; Harriet really was gathering material, in a leisurely way, for a study of Le Fanu, though the Bodleian was not, perhaps, the ideal source for it. But there must be some reason given for her presence, and Oxford is willing enough to believe that the Bodleian is the hub of the scholar's universe. She was able to find enough references among the Periodical Publications to justify an optimistic answer to kindly inquiries about her progress; and if, in fact, she snoozed a good deal in the arms of Duke Humphrey by day, to make up for those hours of the night spent in snooping about the corridors, she was probably not the only person in Oxford to find the atmosphere of old leather and central heating favorable to slumber.

At the same time, she devoted a good many hours to

establishing order among Miss Lydgate's chaotic proofs. The introduction was re-written, and the obliterated passages restored, from the author's capacious memory; the disfigured pages were replaced from fresh proof-sheets; fifty-nine errors and obscurities in the cross-references were eliminated; the rejoinder to Mr. Elkbottom was incorporated in the text and made more vigorous and conclusive; and the authorities at the Press began to speak quite hopefully about the date of publication.

Whether because Harriet's night prowlings, or because the mere knowledge that the circle of suspects was so greatly narrowed, had intimidated the Poison-Pen, or from whatever cause, there were few outbreaks during the next few days. One tiresome episode was the complete stopping-up of the lavatory basin drain in the S.C.R. cloak-room. This was found to be due to some torn fragments of material, which had been rammed firmly down through the grid with the help of a fine rod, and which, when the plumber had got them out, proved to be the remains of a pair of fabric gloves, stained with brown paint and quite unidentifiable as anybody's property. Another was the noisy emergence of the missing Library keys from the interior of a roll of photographs which Miss Pyke had left for half an hour in one of the lecture-rooms before using them to illustrate some remarks about the Parthenon Frieze. Neither of these episodes led to any discovery.

The Senior Common Room behaved to Harriet with that scrupulous and impersonal respect for a person's mission in life which the scholarly tradition imposes. It was clear to them that, once established as the official investigator, she must be allowed to investigate without interference. Nor did they hasten to her with protestations of innocence or cries of indignation. They treated the situation with a fine detachment, making little reference to it, and confining the conversation in Common Room to matters of general and University interest. In solemn and ritual order, they invited her to consume sherry or coffee in their rooms, and refrained from comment upon one another.

Miss Barton, indeed, went out of her way to invite Harriet's opinions upon *Women in the Modern State* and to consult her on the subject of conditions in Germany. It is true that she flatly disagreed with many of the opinions expressed, but only objectively and without personal rancor; the vexed subject of the amateur's right to investigate crimes was decently shelved. Miss Hillyard also, setting aside animosity, took pains to interrogate Harriet about the technical aspect of such historical crimes as the murder of Sir Edmund Berry Godfrey and the alleged poisoning of Sir Thomas Overbury by the Countess of Essex. Such overtures might, of course, be policy; but Harriet was inclined to attribute them to a careful instinct for propriety.

With Miss de Vine she had many interesting conversations. The Fellow's personality attracted and puzzled her very much. More than with any other of the dons, she felt that with Miss de Vine the devotion to the intellectual life was the result, not of the untroubled following of a natural or acquired bias, but of a powerful spiritual call, over-riding other possible tendencies and desires. She felt inquisitive enough, without any prompting, about Miss de Vine's past life; but inquiry was difficult, and she always emerged from an encounter with the feeling that she had told more than she had learnt. She could guess at a history of conflict; but she found it difficult to believe that Miss de Vine was unaware of her own repressions or unable to control them.

With a view to establishing friendly relations with the Junior Common Room, Harriet further steeled herself to compose and deliver a "talk" on "Detection in Fact and Fiction" for a College literary society. This was perilous work. To the unfortunate case in which she had herself figured as the suspected party she naturally made no allusion; nor in the ensuing discussion was anybody so tactless as to mention it. The Wilvercombe murder was a different matter. There was no obvious reason why she should not tell the students about that, and it seemed unkind to deprive them of a legitimate thrill on the purely personal grounds that it was a bore to have to mention Peter Wimsey in every second sentence. Her exposition, though perhaps erring slightly on the dry and academic side, was received with hearty applause, and at the end of the meeting the Senior Student, one Miss Millbanks, invited her to coffee.

Miss Millbanks had her room in Queen Elizabeth, and had furnished it with a good deal of taste. She was a tall, elegant girl, obviously well-to-do, much better dressed than the majority of the students, and carrying her intellectual attainments easily. She held a minor scholarship without emoluments, declaring publicly that she was only a scholar because she would not be seen dead in the ridiculous short gown of a commoner. As alternatives to coffee, she offered Harriet the choice of madeira or a cocktail, politely regretting that the inadequacy of college arrangements made it impossible to provide ice for the shaker. Harriet, who disliked cocktails after dinner, and had consumed madeira and sherry on an almost wearisome number of occasions since her arrival in Oxford, accepted the coffee, and chuckled as cups and glasses were filled. Miss Millbanks inquired courteously what the joke was.

"Only," said Harriet, "that I gathered the other day from an article in the *Morning Star* that 'undergraduettes,' in the journalist's disgusting phrase, lived entirely on cocoa."

"Journalists," said Miss Millbanks, condescendingly, "are always thirty years behind the times. Have you ever seen cocoa in College, Miss Fowler?"

"Oh, yes," said Miss Fowler. She was a dark, thick-set Third Year, dressed in a very grubby sweater which, as she had previously explained, she had not had time to change, having been afflicted with an essay up to the moment of attending Harriet's talk. "Yes, I've seen it in dons' rooms. Occasionally. But I've always looked on that as a kind of infantilism."

"Isn't it a re-living of the heroic past?" suggested Miss Millbanks. "*O les beaux jours que ce siècle de fer*. And so on."

"Groupists drink cocoa," added another Third Year. She was thin, with an eager, scornful face, and made no apology for her sweater, apparently thinking such matters beneath her notice.

"But they are oh! so tender to the failings of others," said Miss Millbanks. "Miss Layton was 'changed' once, but she has now changed back. It was good while it lasted."

Miss Layton, curled on a pouffe by the fire, lifted a wicked little heart-shaped face alight with mischief.

"I did enjoy telling people what I thought of them. Too rapturous. Especially confessing in public the evil, evil thoughts I had had about that woman Flaxman."

"Bother Flaxman," said the dark girl, shortly. Her name was Haydock, and she was, as Harriet presently discovered, considered to be a safe History First. "She's setting the whole Second Year by the ears. I don't like her influence at all. And if you ask me, there's something very wrong with Cattermole. Goodness knows, I don't want any of this business of being my brother's keeper—we had quite enough of that at school—but it'll be awkward if Cattermole is driven into doing something drastic. As Senior Student, Lilian, don't you think you could do something about it?"

"My dear," protested Miss Millbanks, "what can anybody do? I can't forbid Flaxman to make people's lives a burden to them. If I could, I wouldn't. You don't surely expect me to exercise authority? It's bad enough hounding people to College Meetings. The S.C.R. don't understand our sad lack of enthusiasm."

"In their day," said Harriet, "I think people had a passion for meetings and organization."

"There are plenty of inter-collegiate meetings," said Miss Layton. "We discuss things a great deal, and are indignant about the Proctorial Rules for Mixed Parties. But our enthusiasm for internal affairs is more restrained."

"Well, I think," said Miss Haydock bluntly, "we sometimes overdo the *laisser-aller* side of it. If there's a big blow-up, it won't pay anybody."

"Do you mean about Flaxman's cutting-out expeditions?

Or about the ragging affair? By the way, Miss Vane, I suppose you have heard about the College Mystery."

"I've heard something," replied Harriet, cautiously. "It seems to be all very tiresome."

"It will be extremely tiresome if it isn't stopped," said Miss Haydock. "I say we ought to do a spot of private investigation ourselves. The S.C.R. don't seem to be making much progress."

"Well, the last effort at investigation wasn't very satisfactory," said Miss Millbanks.

"Meaning Cattermole? I don't believe it's Cattermole. She's too obvious. And she hasn't the guts. She could and does make an ass of herself, but she wouldn't go about it so secretively."

"There's nothing against Cattermole," said Miss Fowler, "except that somebody wrote Flaxman an offensive letter on the occasion of her swiping Cattermole's young man. Cattermole was the obvious suspect then, but why should she do all these other things?"

"Surely," Miss Layton appealed to Harriet, "surely the obvious suspect is always innocent."

Harriet laughed; and Miss Millbanks said:

"Yes; but I do think Cattermole is getting to the stage when she'd do almost anything to attract attention."

"Well, I don't believe it's Cattermole," said Miss Haydock. "Why should she write letters to *me?*"

"Did you have one?"

"Yes; but it was only a kind of wish that I should plough in Schools. The usual silly thing made of pasted-up letters. I burnt it, and took Cattermole in to dinner on the strength of it."

"Good for you," said Miss Fowler.

"I had one too," said Miss Layton. "A beauty—about there being a reward in hell for women who went my way. So, acting on the suggestion given, I forwarded it to my future address by way of the fireplace."

"All the same," said Miss Millbanks, "it is rather disgusting. I don't mind the letters so much. It's the rags, and the writing on the wall. If any snoopy person from outside happened to get hold of it, there'd be a public stink, and that would be a bore. I don't pretend to much public spirit, but I admit to some. We don't want to get the whole College gated by way of reprisals. And I'd rather not have it said that we were living in a madhouse."

"Too shame-making," agreed Miss Layton; "though of course, you may get an isolated queer specimen anywhere."

"There are some oddities in the First Year all right," said Miss Fowler. "Why is it that every year seems to get shriller and scrubbier than the last?"

"They always did," said Harriet.

"Yes," said Miss Haydock, "I expect the Third Year said the same about us when we first came up. But it's a fact that we had none of this trouble before we had this bunch of freshers in."

Harriet did not contradict this, not wishing to focus suspicion on either the S.C.R. or on the unfortunate Cattermole who (as everybody would remember) was up during the Gaudy, waging simultaneous war against despised love and Responsions. She did ask, however, whether any suspicion had fallen upon other students besides Miss Cattermole.

"Not definitely, no," replied Miss Millbanks. "There's Hudson, of course—she came up from school with a bit of a reputation for ragging, but in my opinion she's quite sound. I should call the whole of our year pretty sound. And Cattermole really has only herself to thank. I mean, she's asking for trouble."

"How?" asked Harriet.

"Various ways," said Miss Millbanks, with a caution which suggested that Harriet was too much in the confidence of the S.C.R. to be trusted with details. "She is rather inclined to break rules for the sake of it—which is all right if you get a kick out of it; but she doesn't."

"Cattermole's going in off the deep end," said Miss Haydock. "Wants to show young what's-his-name—Farringdon—he isn't the only pebble on the beach. All very well. But she's being a bit blatant. She's simply pursuing that lad Pomfret."

"That fair-faced goop at Queen's?" said Miss Fowler. "Well, she's going to be unlucky again, because Flaxman is steadily hauling him off."

"Curse Flaxman!" said Miss Haydock. "Can't she leave other people's men alone? She's bagged Farringdon; I do think she might leave Pomfret for Cattermole."

"She hates to leave anybody anything," said Miss Layton.

"I hope," said Miss Millbanks, "she has not been trying to collect your Geoffrey."

"I'm not giving her the opportunity," said Miss Layton, with an impish grin. "Geoffrey's sound—yes, darlings, definitely sound—but I'm taking no chances. Last time we had him to tea in the J.C.R., Flaxman came undulating in—*so* sorry, she had no idea anybody was there, and she'd left a book behind. With the Engaged Label on the door as large as life. I did not introduce Geoffrey."

"Did he want you to?" inquired Miss Haydock.

"Asked who she was. I said she was the Templeton Scholar and the world's heavyweight in the way of learning. That put him off."

"What'll Geoffrey do when you pull off your First, my child?" demanded Miss Haydock.

"Well, Eve—it *will* be awkward if I do that. Poor lamb! I shall have to make him believe I only did it by looking fragile and pathetic at the viva."

And Miss Layton did, indeed, contrive to look fragile and pathetic, and anything but learned. Nevertheless, on inquiry from Miss Lydgate, Harriet discovered that she was an exceptionally well-fancied favorite for the English School, and was taking, of all things, a Language Special. If the dry bones of Philology could be made to live by Miss Layton, then she was a very dark horse indeed. Harriet felt a respect for her brains; so unexpected a personality might be capable of anything.

• • • • •

So much for Third-Year opinion. Harriet's first personal encounter with the Second Year was more dramatic.

The College had been so quiet for the last week that Harriet gave herself a holiday from police-duty and went to a private dance given by a contemporary of her own, who had married and settled in North Oxford. Returning between twelve and one, she garaged the car in the Dean's private garage, let herself quietly through the grille dividing the Traffic Entrance from the rest of College and began to cross the Old Quad towards Tudor. The weather had turned finer, and there was a pale glimmer of cloudy moonlight. Against that glimmer, Harriet, skirting the corner of Burleigh Building, observed something humped and strange about the outline of the eastern wall, close to where the Principal's private postern led out into St. Cross Road. It seemed clear that here, in the words of the old song, was "a man where nae man should be."

If she shouted at him, he would drop over on the outer side and be lost. She had the key of the postern with her—having been trusted with a complete set of keys for patrol purposes. Pulling her black evening cloak about her face and stepping softly, Harriet ran quickly down the grass path between the Warden's House and the Fellows' Garden, let herself silently out into St. Cross Road and stood beneath the wall. As she emerged, a second dark form stepped out from the shadows and said urgently, "Oy!"

The gentleman on the wall looked round, exclaimed, "Oh, hell!" and scrambled down in a hurry. His friend made off at a smart pace, but the wall-climber seemed to have damaged himself in his descent, and made but poor speed. Harriet, who was nimble enough, for all she was over nine years down from Oxford, gave chase and came up with him a few yards from the corner of Jowett Walk. The accomplice, now well away, looked back, hesitating.

"Clear out, old boy!" yelled the captive; and then, turning to Harriet, remarked with a sheepish grin, "Well, it's a fair cop. I've bust my ankle or something."

"And what were you doing on our wall, sir?" demanded Harriet. In the moonlight she beheld a fresh, fair and ingenuous face, youthfully rounded and, at the moment, disturbed by an expression of mingled apprehension and amusement. He was a very tall and very large young man; but Harriet had clasped him in a wiry grip that he could scarcely shake off without hurting her, and he showed no disposition to use violence.

"Just having a beano," said the young man, promptly. "A bet, you know, and all that. Hang my cap on the tiptop branch of the Shrewsbury beeches. My friend there was the witness. I seem to have lost, don't I?"

"In that case," said Harriet, severely, "where's your cap? And your gown, if it comes to that? And, sir, your name and college?"

"Well," said the young man, impudently, "if it comes to that, where and what are yours?"

When one's thirty-second birthday is no more than a matter of months away, such a question is flattering. Harriet laughed.

"My dear young man, do you take me for an undergraduate?"

"A don—a female don, God help us!" exclaimed the young man, whose spirits appeared to be sustained, though not unduly exalted, by spirituous liquors.

"Well?" said Harriet.

"I don't believe it," said the young man, scanning her face as closely as he could in the feeble light. "Not possible. Too young. Too charming. Too much sense of humor."

"A great deal too much sense of humor to let you get away with that, my lad. And no sense of humor at all about this intrusion."

"I say," said the young man, "I'm really most frightfully sorry. Mere light-heartedness and all that kind of thing. Honestly, we weren't doing any harm. Quite definitely not. I mean, we were just winning the bet and going away quietly. I say, do be a sport. I mean, you're not the Warden or the Dean or anything. I know them. Couldn't you overlook it?"

"It's all very well," said Harriet. "But we can't have this kind of thing. It doesn't do. You must see that it doesn't do."

"Oh, I do see," agreed the young man. "Absolutely. Definitely. Dashed silly thing to do. Open to misinterpretation." He winced, and drew up one leg to rub his injured ankle. "But when you do see a tempting bit of wall like that—"

"Ah, yes," said Harriet, "what *is* the temptation? Just come and show me, will you?" She led him firmly, despite his protests, towards the postern. "Oh, I see, yes. A brick or two out of that buttress. Excellent foothold. You'd almost think they'd been knocked out on purpose, wouldn't you? And a handy tree in the Fellows' Garden. The Bursar will have to see to it. Are you well acquainted with that buttress, young man?"

"It's known to exist," admitted her captive. "But, look here, we weren't—we weren't calling on anybody or anything of that kind, you know, if you know what I mean."

"I hope not," said Harriet.

"No, we were all on our own," explained the young man, eagerly. "Nobody else involved. Good Heavens, no. And, look here, I've bust my ankle and we shall be gated anyhow, and, dear, kind lady—"

At this moment, a loud groan resounded from within the College wall. The young man's face became filled with agonized alarm.

"What's that?" asked Harriet.

"I really couldn't say," said the young man.

The groan was repeated. Harriet grasped the undergraduate tightly by the arm and led him along to the postern.

"But look here," said the gentleman, limping dolefully beside her, "you mustn't—please don't think—"

"I'm going to see what's the matter," said Harriet.

She unlocked the postern, drew her captive in with her, and relocked the gate. Under the wall, just beneath the spot where the young man had been perched, lay a huddled figure, which was apparently suffering acute internal agonies of some kind.

"Look here," said the young man, abandoning all pretence, "I'm most frightfully sorry about this. I'm afraid we were a bit thoughtless. I mean, we didn't notice. I mean, I'm afraid she isn't very well, and we didn't notice how it was, you know."

"The girl's drunk," said Harriet, uncompromisingly.

She had, in the bad old days, seen too many young poets similarly afflicted to make any mistake about the symptoms.

"Well, I'm afraid—yes, that's about it," said the young man. "Rogers *will* mix 'em so strong. But look here, honestly, there's no harm done, and I mean—"

"H'm!" said Harriet. "Well, don't shout. That house is the Warden's Lodgings."

"Hell!" said the young man, for the second time. "I say—are you going to be sporting?"

"That depends," said Harriet. "As a matter of fact, you've been extraordinarily lucky. I'm not one of the dons. I'm only staying in College. So I'm a free agent."

"Bless you!" exclaimed the young man, fervently.

"Don't be in a hurry. You'll have to tell me about this. Who's the girl, by the way?"

The patient here gave another groan.

"Oh, dear!" said the undergraduate.

"Don't worry," said Harriet. "She'll be sick in a minute." She walked over and inspected the sufferer. "It's all right. You can preserve a gentlemanly reticence. I know her. Her name's Cattermole. What's yours?"

"My name's Pomfret—of Queen's."

"Ah!" said Harriet.

"We threw a party round in my friend's rooms," explained Mr. Pomfret. "At least, it started as a meeting, but it ended as a party. Nothing wrong whatever. Miss Cattermole came along for a joke. All clean fun. Only there were a lot of us, and what with one thing and another we had a few too many, and then we found Miss Cattermole was rather under the weather. So we got her collected up, and Rogers and I—"

"Yes, I see," said Harriet. "Not very creditable, was it?"

"No, it's rotten," admitted Mr. Pomfret.

"Had she got leave to attend the meeting? And late leave?"

"I don't know," said Mr. Pomfret, disturbed. "I'm afraid —look here! It's all rather tiresome. I mean, she doesn't belong to the Society—"

"What Society?"

"The Society that was meeting. I think she pushed in for a joke."

"Gate-crashed you? H'm. That probably means no late leave."

"Sounds serious," said Mr. Pomfret.

"It's serious for *her*," said Harriet. "You'll get off with a fine or a gating, I suppose; but we have to be more particular. It's a nasty-minded world, and our rules have to remember that fact."

"I know," said Mr. Pomfret. "As a matter of fact we were dashed worried. We had a devil of a job getting her along," he burst out confidentially. "Fortunately it was only from this end of Long Wall. Phew!"

He pulled out his handkerchief and wiped his forehead.

"Anyhow," he went on, "I'm thankful you aren't a don."

"That's all very well," said Harriet austerely; "but I'm a Senior Member of College and I must feel responsibility. This isn't the kind of thing one wants."

She turned a cold glance on the unfortunate Miss Cattermole, to whom the worst was happening.

"I'm sure *we* didn't want it," said Mr. Pomfret, averting his eyes; "but what could we do? It's no good trying to corrupt your porter," he added ingenuously; "it's been tried."

"Indeed?" said Harriet. "No; you wouldn't get much

change out of Padgett. Was anybody else there from Shrewsbury?"

"Yes—Miss Flaxman and Miss Blake. But they had ordinary leave to come and went off at about eleven. So they're all right."

"They ought to have taken Miss Cattermole with them."

"Of course," said Mr. Pomfret. He looked gloomier than ever. Obviously, thought Harriet, Miss Flaxman would not mind at all if Miss Cattermole got into trouble. Miss Blake's motives were more obscure; but she was probably only weakminded. Harriet was fired with a quite unscrupulous determination that Miss Cattermole should not get into trouble if she could prevent it. She went across to the limp form and hauled it to its feet. Miss Cattermole groaned dismally. "She'll do now," said Harriet. "I wonder where the little fool's room is. Do *you* know?"

"Well, as a matter of fact, I do," replied Mr. Pomfret. "Sounds bad, but there—people do show people their rooms, you know, all regulations notwithstanding and all that. It's somewhere over there, through that archway."

He waved a vague hand towards the New Quad at the other end of nowhere.

"Heavens!" said Harriet, "it would be. I'm afraid you'll have to give me a hand with her. She's a bit too much for me, and she can't stay here in the damp. If anybody sees us, you'll have to go through with it. How's the ankle?"

"Better, thanks," said Mr. Pomfret. "I think I can make shift to stagger a bit. I say, you're being very decent."

"Get on with the job," said Harriet, grimly, "and don't waste time in speeches."

Miss Cattermole was a thickly-built young woman, and no inconsiderable weight. She had also reached the stage of complete inertia. For Harriet, hampered by high-heeled shoes, and to Mr. Pomfret, afflicted with a game ankle, the progress across the quads was anything but triumphal. It was also rather noisy, what with the squeak of stone and gravel under their feet, and the grunts and shufflings of the limp figure between them. At every moment, Harriet expected to hear a window thrust up, or to see the shape of an agitated don come rushing out to demand some explanation of Mr. Pomfret's presence at that early hour of the morning. It was with very great relief that she at last found the right doorway and propelled Miss Cattermole's helpless form through it.

"What next?" inquired Mr. Pomfret in a hoarse whisper.

"I must let you out. I don't know where her room is, but I can't have you wandering all over College. Wait a minute. We'll deposit her in the nearest bathroom. Here you are. Round the corner. Easy does it."

Mr. Pomfret again bent obligingly to the task.

"There!" said Harriet. She laid Miss Cattermole on her back on the bathroom floor, took the key from the lock and came out, securing the door behind her. "She must stay there for the moment. Now we'll get rid of you. I don't think anybody saw us. If we're met on the way back, you were at Mrs. Hemans' dance and saw me home. Get that? It's not very convincing, because you ought not to have done any such thing, but it's better than the truth."

"I only wish I *had* been at Mrs. Hemans' dance," said the grateful Mr. Pomfret. "I'd have danced every dance with you and all the extras. Do you mind telling me who you are?"

"My name's Vane. And you'd better not start being enthusiastic too soon. I'm not considering *your* welfare particularly. Do you know Miss Cattermole well?"

"Rather well. Oh, yes. Naturally. I mean, we know some of the same people and that sort of thing. As a matter of fact, she used to be engaged to an old schoolfellow of mine —New College man—only that fell through and all that. No affair of mine; but you know how it is. One knows people and one kind of goes on knowing them. And there you are."

"Yes, I see. Well, Mr. Pomfret, I am not anxious to get either you or Miss Cattermole into a row—"

"I knew you were a sport!" cried Mr. Pomfret.

"(Don't *shout*)—but this sort of thing cannot go on. There must be no more late parties and no more climbing over walls. You understand. Not with anybody. It's not fair. If I go to the Dean with this story, nothing much will happen to *you*, but Miss Cattermole will be lucky if she's not sent down. For God's sake, stop being an ass. There are much better ways of enjoying Oxford than fooling round at midnight with the women students."

"I know there are. I think it's all rather rot, really."

"Then why do it?"

"I don't know. Why does one do idiotic things?"

"Why?" said Harriet. They were passing the end of the Chapel, and Harriet stood still to give emphasis to what she was saying. "I'll tell you why, Mr. Pomfret. Because you haven't the guts to say No when somebody asks you to be a sport. That tom-fool word has got more people in trouble than all the rest of the dictionary put together. If it's sporting to encourage girls to break rules and drink more than they can carry and get themselves into a mess on your account, then I'd stop being a sport and try being a gentleman."

"Oh, I say," said Mr. Pomfret, hurt.

"I mean it," said Harriet.

"Well, I see your point," said Mr. Pomfret, shifting his feet uneasily. "I'll do my best about it. You've been dashed spor— I mean you've behaved like a perfect gentleman about all this—" he grinned—"and I'll try to—good Lord! here's somebody coming."

A quick patter of slippered feet along the passage between the Hall and Queen Elizabeth was approaching rapidly.

On an impulse, Harriet stepped back and pushed open the Chapel door.

"Get in," she said.

Mr. Pomfret slipped hastily in behind her. Harriet shut the door on him and stood quietly in front of it. The footsteps came nearer, came opposite the porch and stopped suddenly. The night-walker uttered a little squeak.

"Ooh!"

"What is it?" said Harriet.

"Oh, miss, it's you! You gave me such a start. Did you see anything?"

"See what? Who is it, by the way?"

"Emily, miss. I sleep in the New Quad, miss, and I woke up, and I made sure I heard a man's voice in the quadrangle, and I looked out and there he was, miss, as plain as plain, coming this way with one of the young ladies. So I slipped on my slippers, miss. . . ."

"Damn!" said Harriet to herself. Better tell part of the truth, though.

"It's all right, Emily. It was a friend of mine. He came in with me and wanted very much to see the New Quad by moonlight. So we just walked across and back again."

(A poor excuse, but probably less suspicious than a flat denial.)

"Oh, I see, miss. I beg your pardon. But I get that nervous, with one thing and another. And it's unusual, if you'll excuse me saying so, miss. . . ."

"Yes, very," said Harriet, strolling gently away in the direction of the New Quad, so that the scout was bound to follow her. "It was stupid of me not to think that it might disturb people. I'll mention it to the Dean in the morning. You did quite right to come down."

"Well, miss, of course I didn't know who it was. And the Dean is so particular. And with all these queer things happening. . . ."

"Yes, absolutely. Of course. I'm really very sorry to have been so thoughtless. The gentleman has gone now, so you won't get woken up again."

Emily seemed doubtful. She was one of those people who never feel they have said a thing till they have said it three times over. She paused at the foot of her staircase to say everything again. Harriet listened impatiently, thinking of Mr. Pomfret, fuming in the Chapel. At last she got rid of the scout and turned back.

Complicated, thought Harriet; silly situation, like a

farce. Emily thinks she's caught a student: I think I've caught a poltergeist. We catch each other. Young Pomfret parked in the Chapel. He thinks I'm kindly shielding him and Cattermole. Having carefully hidden Pomfret, I have to admit he was there. But if Emily *had* been the Poltergeist —and perhaps she is—then I couldn't have had Pomfret helping to chase her. This kind of sleuthing is very confusion-making.

She pushed open the Chapel door. The porch was empty.

"Damn!" said Harriet, irreverently. "The idiot's gone. Perhaps he's gone inside, though."

She looked in through the inner door and was relieved to see a dark figure faintly outlined against the pale oak of the stalls. Then, with a sudden, violent shock, she became aware of a second dark figure, poised strangely, it seemed, in midair.

"Hullo!" said Harriet. In the thin light of the South windows she saw the flash of a white shirt-front as Mr. Pomfret turned. "It's only me. *What's that?*"

She took a torch from her handbag and recklessly switched it on. The beam showed a dismal shape dangling from the canopy above the stalls. It was swinging a little to and fro and turning slowly as it swung. Harriet darted forward.

"Morbid kind of imagination these girls have got, haven't they?" said Mr. Pomfret.

Harriet contemplated the M.A. cap and gown, arranged over a dress and bolster hitched by a thin cord to one of the terminals with which the architect had decorated the canopies.

"Bread-knife stuck through the tummy, too," pursued Mr. Pomfret. "Gave me quite a turn, as my aunt would say. Did you catch the young woman?"

"No. Was she in here?"

"Oh, definitely," said Mr. Pomfret. "Thought I'd retreat a bit further, you know. So in I came. Then I saw that. So I came along to investigate and heard somebody scrambling out by the other door—over there."

He pointed vaguely towards the north side of the building, where a door led into the vestry. Harriet hastened to look. The door was open, and the outer vestry door, though shut, had been unlocked from within. She peered out. All was quiet.

"Bother them and their rags," said Harriet, returning. "No, I didn't meet the lady. She must have got away while I was taking Emily back to the New Quad. Just my luck!" She muttered the last exclamation under her breath. It was really sickening to have had the Poltergeist under her hand like that, and to have been distracted by Emily. She went up to the dummy again, and saw that a paper was pinned to its middle by the bread-knife.

"Quotation from the classics," said Mr. Pomfret, easily. "Looks as though somebody had a grouse against your dons."

"Silly young fools!" said Harriet. "Very convincing bit of work, though, come to look at it. If we hadn't found it first, it would have created quite a sensation when we all filed into prayers. A little investigation is indicated. Well, now, it's time you went quietly home and were gated for the good of your soul."

She led him down to the postern and let him out.

"By the way, Mr. Pomfret, I'd be obliged if you didn't mention this rag to anybody. It's not in the best of taste. One good turn deserves another."

"Just as you say," replied Mr. Pomfret. "And, look here —may I push round tomorrow—at least, it's this morning, isn't it?—and make inquiries and all that? Only proper, you know. When shall you be in? Please!"

"No visitors in the morning," said Harriet, promptly. "I don't know what I shall be doing in the afternoon. But you can always ask at the Lodge."

"Oh, I may? That's top-hole. I'll call—and if you're not there I'll leave a note. I mean, you must come round and have tea or a cocktail or something. And I do honestly promise it shan't happen again, if I can help it."

"All right. By the way—what time did Miss Cattermole arrive at your friend's place?"

"Oh—about half-past nine, I think. Couldn't be sure. Why?"

"I only wondered whether her initials were in the porter's book. But I'll see to it. Good-night."

"Good-night," said Mr. Pomfret, "and thanks frightfully."

Harriet locked the postern behind him and returned across the quadrangle, feeling that, out of all this absurd tiresomeness, something had been most definitely gained. The dummy could scarcely have been put in position before 9:30; so that Miss Cattermole, through sheer folly, had contrived to give herself a cast-iron alibi. Harriet was so grateful to her for advancing the inquiry by even this small step that she determined the girl should, if possible, be let off the consequences of her escapade.

This reminded her that Miss Cattermole still lay on the bathroom floor, waiting to be dealt with. It would be awkward if she had come to her senses in the interval and started to make a noise. But on reaching the New Quad and unlocking the door, Harriet found her prisoner in the somnolent stage of her rake's progress. A little research along the corridors revealed that Miss Cattermole slept on the first floor. Harriet opened the door of the room, and as she did so the door next it opened also, and a head popped out.

"Is that you, Cattermole?" whispered the head. "Oh, I'm sorry." It popped in again.

Harriet recognized the girl who had gone up and spoken to Miss Cattermole after the Opening of the Library. She went to her door, which bore the name of "C. I. Briggs," and knocked gently. The head reappeared.

"Were you expecting to see Miss Cattermole come in?"

"Well," said Miss Briggs, "I heard somebody at her door —oh! it's Miss Vane, isn't it?"

"Yes. What made you sit up and wait for Miss Cattermole?"

Miss Briggs, who was wearing a woolly coat over her pyjamas, looked a little alarmed.

"I had some work to do. I was sitting up in any case. Why?"

Harriet looked at the girl. She was short and sturdily built, with a plain, strong, sensible face. She appeared trustworthy.

"If you're a friend of Miss Cattermole's," said Harriet, "you'd better come and help me upstairs with her. She's down in the bathroom. I found her being helped over the wall by a young man, and she's rather under the weather."

"Oh, dear!" said Miss Briggs. "Tight?"

"I'm afraid so."

"She *is* a fool," said Miss Briggs. "I knew there'd be trouble some day. All right, I'll come."

Between them they lugged Miss Cattermole up the noisy, polished stairs and dumped her upon her bed. In grim silence they undressed her and put her between the sheets.

"She'll sleep it off now," said Harriet. "I think, by the way, a little explanation wouldn't be a bad idea. How about it?"

"Come into my room," said Miss Briggs. "Would you like any hot milk or Ovaltine or coffee, or anything?"

Harriet accepted hot milk. Miss Briggs put a kettle on the ring in the pantry opposite, came in, stirred up the fire and sat down on a pouffe.

"Please tell me," said Miss Briggs, "what has happened."

Harriet told her, omitting the names of the gentlemen concerned. But Miss Briggs promptly supplied the omission.

"That was Reggie Pomfret, of course," she observed. "Poor blighter. He *always* gets left with the baby. After all, what is the lad to do, if people go chasing him?"

"It's awkward," said Harriet. "I mean, you need some knowledge of the world to get out of it gracefully. Does the girl really care for him?"

"No," said Miss Briggs. "Not really. She just wants somebody or something. You know. She got a nasty knock when her engagement was broken. You see, she and Lionel Farringdon had been childhood friends and so on, and it was all settled before she came up. Then Farringdon got collared by our Miss Flaxman, and there was a frightful bust-up. And there were complications. And Violet Cattermole has gone all unnerved."

"I know," said Harriet. "Sort of desperate feeling—I must have a man of my own—that kind of thing."

"Yes. Doesn't matter who he is. I think it's a sort of inferiority complex, or something. One must do idiotic things and assert one's self. Am I making myself clear?"

"Oh, yes. I understand that perfectly. It happens so often. One just has to make one's self out no end of a little devil. . . . Has this kind of thing happened often?"

"Well," confessed Miss Briggs, "more often than I like. I've tried to keep Violet reasonable, but what's the good of preaching to people? When they get into that worked-up state you might as well talk to the man in the moon. And though it's very tiresome for young Pomfret, he's awfully decent and safe. If he were strong-minded, of course he'd get out of it. But I'm rather thankful he's not, because, if it wasn't for him it might be some frightful tick or other."

"Is anything likely to come of it?"

"Marriage, do you mean? No-o. I think he has enough sense of self-protection to avoid that. And besides— Look here, Miss Vane, it really is an awful shame. Miss Flaxman simply cannot leave anybody alone, and she's trying to get Pomfret away too, though she doesn't want him. If only she'd leave poor Violet alone, the whole thing would probably work itself out quite quietly. Mind you, I'm very fond of Violet. She's a decent sort, and she'd be absolutely all right with the right kind of man. She's no business to be up at Oxford at all, really. A nice domestic life with a man to be devoted to is what she really wants. But he'd have to be a solid, decided kind of man, and frightfully affectionate in a firm kind of way. But not Reggie Pomfret, who is a chivalrous young idiot."

Miss Briggs poked the fire savagely.

"Well," said Harriet, "something has got to be done about all this. I don't want to go to the Dean, but—"

"Of course, something must be done," said Miss Briggs. "It's extraordinarily lucky it should have been you who spotted it and not one of the dons. I've been almost wishing that *something* might happen. I've been frightfully worried about it. It isn't the kind of thing I know how to cope with at all. But I had to stand by Violet more or less—otherwise I should simply have lost her confidence altogether and goodness knows what stupid thing she'd have done then."

"I think you're quite right," said Harriet. "But now, perhaps, I can have a word with her and tell her to mind her step. After all, she has got to give some guarantee of sensible behavior if I'm not to report her to the Dean. A spot of benevolent blackmail is indicated, I fancy."

"Yes," agreed Miss Briggs. "You can do it. It's exceedingly decent of you. I'll be thankful to be relieved of the responsibility. It's all rather wearing—and it does upset one's work. After all, work's what one's here for. I've got Honor Mods. next term, and it's frightfully upsetting, never knowing what's going to happen next."

"I expect Miss Cattermole relies on you a lot."

"Yes," said Miss Briggs, "but listening to people's confidences does take such a time, and I'm not awfully good at wrestling with fits of temperament."

"The confidante has a very heavy and thankless task," said Harriet. "It's not surprising if she goes mad in white linen. It's more surprising if she keeps sane and sensible like you. But I agree that you ought to have the burden taken off your shoulders. Are you the only one?"

"Pretty well. Poor old Violet lost a lot of friends over the uproar."

"And the business of the anonymous letters?"

"Oh, you've heard about that? Well, of course, it wasn't Violet. That's ridiculous. But Flaxman spread the story all over the college, and once you've started an accusation like that, it takes a lot of killing."

"It does. Well, Miss Briggs, you and I had better get to bed. I'll come along and see Miss Cattermole after breakfast. Don't worry too much. I dare say this upset will be a blessing in disguise. Well, I'll be going now. Can you lend me a strong knife?"

Miss Briggs, rather astonished, produced a stout penknife and said good-night. On her way over to Tudor, Harriet cut down the dangling dummy and carried it away with her for scrutiny and action at a later hour. She felt she badly needed to sleep on the situation.

She must have been weary, for she dropped off as soon as she was in bed, and dreamed neither of Peter Wimsey nor of anything else.

CHAPTER VIII

Tho marking him with melting eyes
A thrilling throbbe from her hart did aryse,
And interrupted all her other speache
With some old sorowe that made a newe breache:
Seemed shee sawe in the younglings face
The old lineaments of his fathers grace.
EDMUND SPENSER

"The fact remains," said Miss Pyke, "that I have to lecture at nine. Can anybody lend me a gown?"

A number of the dons were breakfasting in the S.C.R. dining-room. Harriet entered in time to hear the request, formulated in a high and rather indignant tone.

"Have you lost your gown, Miss Pyke?"

"You could have mine with pleasure, Miss Pyke," said little Miss Chilperic, mildly, "but I'm afraid it wouldn't be nearly long enough."

"It isn't safe to leave *anything* in the S.C.R. cloakroom these days," said Miss Pyke. "I *know* it was there after dinner, because I saw it."

"Sorry," said Miss Hillyard, "but I've got a 9 o'clock lecture myself."

"You can have mine," suggested Miss Burrows, "if you can get it back to me by 10 o'clock."

"Ask Miss de Vine or Miss Barton," said the Dean. "They have no lectures. Or Miss Vane—hers would fit you."

"Certainly," said Harriet, carelessly. "Do you want a cap as well?"

"The cap has *gone* as well," replied Miss Pyke. "I don't need it for the lecture; but it would be convenient to know where my property has gone to."

"It's surprising the way things disappear," said Harriet, helping herself to scrambled eggs. "People are very thoughtless. Who, by the way, owns a black semi-evening crêpe de Chine, figured with bunches of red and green poppies, with a draped cross-over front, deep hip-yoke and flared skirt and sleeves about three years out of date?"

She looked round the dining-room, which was by now fairly well filled with dons. "Miss Shaw—you have a very good eye for a frock. Can you identify it?"

"I might if I saw it," said Miss Shaw. "I don't recollect one like it from your description."

"Have you found one?" asked the Bursar.

"Another chapter in the mystery?" suggested Miss Barton.

"I'm sure none of my students has one like it," said Miss Shaw. "They like to come and show me their frocks. I think it's a good thing to take an interest in them."

"I don't remember a frock like that in the Senior Common Room," said the Bursar.

"Didn't Miss Wrigley have a black figured crêpe de Chine?" asked Mrs. Goodwin.

"Yes," said Miss Shaw. "But she's left. And anyhow, hers had a square neck and no hip-yoke. I remember it very well."

"Can't you tell us what the mystery is, Miss Vane?" inquired Miss Lydgate. "Or is it better that you shouldn't say anything?"

"Well," said Harriet, "I don't see any reason why I shouldn't tell you. When I came in last night after my dance I—er—went the rounds a bit—"

"Ah!" said the Dean. "I thought I heard somebody going to and fro outside my window. And whispering."

"Yes—Emily came out and caught me. I think she

thought I was the Practical Joker. Well—I happened to go into the Chapel."

She told her story, omitting all mention of Mr. Pomfret, and merely saying that the culprit had apparently left by the vestry door.

"And," she concluded, "as a matter of fact, the cap and gown were yours, Miss Pyke, and you can have them any time. The bread-knife was taken from the Hall, presumably, or from here. And the bolster—I can't say where they got that."

"I think I can guess," said the Bursar. "Miss Trotman is away. She lives on the ground floor of Burleigh. It would be easy to nip in and bag her bolster."

"Why is Trotman away?" asked Miss Shaw. "She never told me."

"Father taken ill," said the Dean. "She went off in a hurry yesterday afternoon."

"I can't think why she shouldn't have told me," said Miss Shaw. "My students always come to me with their troubles. It's rather upsetting, when you think your pupils value your sympathy—"

"But you were out to tea," said the Treasurer, practically.

"I put a note in your pigeon-hole," said the Dean.

"Oh," said Miss Shaw. "Well, I didn't see it. I knew nothing about it. It's very odd that nobody should have mentioned it."

"Who *did* know it?" asked Harriet.

There was a pause; during which everybody had time to think it strange and improbable that Miss Shaw should not have received the note or heard of Miss Trotman's departure.

"It was mentioned at the High last night, I think," said Miss Allison.

"I was out to dinner," said Miss Shaw. "I shall go and see if that note's there."

Harriet followed her out; the note was there—a sheet of paper folded together and not sealed in an envelope.

"Well," said Miss Shaw; "I never saw it."

"Anybody might have read that and put it back," said Harriet.

"Yes—including myself, you mean."

"I didn't say that, Miss Shaw. Anybody."

They returned gloomily to the Common Room.

"The—er—the joke was perpetrated between dinner-time, when Miss Pyke lost her gown, and about a quarter to one, when I found it out," said Harriet. "It would be convenient if anybody could produce a water-tight alibi for the whole of that time. Particularly for the time after 11:15. I suppose I can find out whether any students had late leave till midnight. Anybody coming in then might have seen something."

"I have a list," said the Dean. "And the porter could show you the names of those who came in after nine."

"That will be a help."

"In the meantime," said Miss Pyke, pushing away her plate and rolling her napkin, "the ordinary duties of the day must be proceeded with. Could I have my gown—or *a* gown?"

She went over to Tudor with Harriet, who restored the gown and displayed the crêpe de Chine frock.

"I have never seen that dress to my knowledge before," said Miss Pyke; "but I cannot pretend to be observant in these matters. It appears to be made for a slender person of medium height."

"There's no reason to suppose it belongs to the person who put it there," said Harriet, "any more than your gown."

"Of course not," said Miss Pyke; "no." She gave Harriet an odd, swift glance from her sharp, black eyes. "But the owner might provide some clue to the thief. Would it not —pardon me if I am trespassing upon your province— would it not be possible to draw some deduction from the name of the shop where it was bought?"

"Obviously it would have been," said Harriet; "the tab has been removed."

"Oh," said Miss Pyke. "Well; I must go to my lecture. As soon as I can find leisure I will endeavour to provide you with a time-table of my movements last night. I fear, however, it will scarcely be illuminating. I was in my room after dinner and in bed by half-past ten."

She stalked out, carrying her cap and gown. Harriet watched her go, and then took out a piece of paper from a drawer. The message upon it was pasted up in the usual way, and ran:

tristius haud illis monstrum nec saevior ulla
pestis et ira deum Stygiis sese extulit undis.
Virginei volucrum vultus foedissima ventris
proluvies uncaeque manus et pallida semper
ora fame.

"Harpies," said Harriet aloud. "Harpies. That seems to suggest a train of thought. But I'm afraid we can't suspect Emily or any of the scouts of expressing their feelings in Virgilian hexameters."

She frowned. Matters were looking rather bad for the Senior Common Room.

Harriet tapped on Miss Cattermole's door, regardless of the fact that it bore a large notice: HEADACHE—DO NOT DISTURB. It was opened by Miss Briggs, whose brow was anxious, but cleared when she saw who the visitor was.

"I was afraid it might be the Dean," said Miss Briggs.

"No," said Harriet, "so far I have held my hand. How is the patient?"

"Not too good," said Miss Briggs.

"Ah! 'His lordship has drunk his bath and gone to bed again.' That's about it, I suppose." She strode across to the bed and looked down at Miss Cattermole, who opened her eyes with a groan. They were large, light, hazel eyes, set in a plump face that ought to have been of a pleasant rose-leaf pink. A quantity of fluffy brown hair tumbled damply about her brow, adding to the general impression of an

Angora rabbit that had gone on the loose and was astonished at the result.

"Feeling bloody?" inquired Harriet, with sympathy.

"Horrible," said Miss Cattermole.

"Serve you right," said Harriet. "If you must take your drink like a man, the least you can do is to carry it like a gentleman. It's a great thing to know your own limitations."

Miss Cattermole looked so woebegone that Harriet began to laugh. "You don't seem to be a very practised hand at this kind of thing. Look here; I'll get you something to pull you together and then I'm going to talk to you."

She went out briskly and nearly fell over Mr. Pomfret in the outer doorway.

"You here?" said Harriet. "I told you, no visitors in the morning. It makes a noise in the quad and is contrary to regulations."

"I'm not a visitor," said Mr. Pomfret, grinning. "I've been attending Miss Hillyard's lecture on Constitutional Developments."

"God help you!"

"And seeing you cross the quad in this direction, I turned in that direction like the needle to the North. Dark," said Mr. Pomfret, with animation, "and true and tender is the North. That's a quotation. It's very nearly the only one I know, so it's a good thing it fits."

"It does not fit. I am not feeling tender."

"Oh! . . . how's Miss Cattermole?"

"Bad hang-over. As you might expect."

"Oh! . . . sorry . . . No row, I hope?"

"No."

"Bless you!" said Mr. Pomfret. "I was lucky too. Friend of mine has a dashed good window. All quiet on the Western Front. So—look here! I wish there was something I could do to—"

"You shall," said Harriet. She twitched his lecture notebook from under his arm and scribbled in it.

"Get that made up at the chemist's and bring it back.

I'm damned if I want to go myself and ask for a recipe for hobnailed liver."

Mr. Pomfret looked at her with respect.

"Where did you learn that one?" said he.

"Not at Oxford. I may say I have never had occasion to taste it; I hope it's nasty. The quicker you can get it made up, the better, by the way."

"I know, I know," said Mr. Pomfret, disconsolately. "You're fed up with the sight of me, and no wonder. But I do wish you'd come round some time and meet old Rogers. He's incredibly penitent. Come and have tea. Or a drink or something. Come this afternoon. Do. Just to show there's no ill-feeling."

Harriet was opening her mouth to say No, when she looked at Mr. Pomfret, and her heart softened. He had the appeal of a very young dog of a very large breed—a kind of amiable absurdity.

"All right," said Harriet. "I will. Thank you very much."

Mr. Pomfret exhausted himself in expressions of delight, and, still vocal, allowed himself to be shepherded to the gate, where, almost in the act of stepping out, he had to step back to allow the entrance of a tall, dark student wheeling a bicycle.

"Hullo, Reggie!" cried the young woman, "looking for me?"

"Oh, good morning," said Mr. Pomfret, rather taken aback. Then, catching sight of a handsome leonine head over the student's shoulder, he added with more assurance, "Hullo, Farringdon!"

"Hullo, Pomfret!" replied Mr. Farringdon. The adjective "Byronic" fitted him well enough, thought Harriet. He had an arrogant profile, a mass of close chestnut curls, hot brown eyes and a sulky mouth, and looked less pleased to see Mr. Pomfret than Mr. Pomfret to see him.

Mr. Pomfret presented Mr. Farringdon of New College to Harriet, and murmured that of course Miss Flaxman was known to her. Miss Flaxman stared coolly at Harriet and said how much she had enjoyed her detective talk the other night.

"We're throwing a party at 6 o'clock," went on Miss Flaxman to Mr. Pomfret. She pulled off her scholar's gown and stuffed it unceremoniously into her bicycle-basket. "Care to come? In Leo's room. Six o'clock. I think we've room for Reggie, haven't we, Leo?"

"I suppose so," said Mr. Farringdon, rather ungraciously. "There'll be an awful crowd anyway."

"Then we can always stuff in one more," said Miss Flaxman. "Don't mind Leo, Reggie; he's mislaid his manners this morning."

Mr. Pomfret appeared to think that somebody else's manners had also been mislaid, for he replied with more spirit than Harriet had expected of him:

"I'm sorry; I'm afraid I'm engaged. Miss Vane is coming to tea with me."

"Another time will do for that," said Harriet.

"Oh, no," said Mr. Pomfret.

"Couldn't you both come along, then, afterwards?" said Mr. Farringdon. "Always room for one more, as Catherine says." He turned to Harriet. "I hope you will come, Miss Vane. We should be delighted."

"Well—" said Harriet. It was Miss Flaxman's turn to look sulky.

"I say," said Mr. Farringdon, suddenly putting two and two together, "are you *the* Miss Vane? the novelist . . . You *are!* Then, look here, you simply *must* come. I shall be the most envied man in New College. We're all detective fans there."

"What about it?" said Harriet, deferring to Mr. Pomfret.

It was so abundantly clear that Miss Flaxman did not want Harriet, that Mr. Farringdon did not want Mr. Pomfret, and that Mr. Pomfret did not want to go, that she felt the novelist's malicious enjoyment in a foolish situation. Since none of the party could now very well get out of the situation without open rudeness, the invitation was eventually accepted. Mr. Pomfret stepped into the street to join Mr. Farringdon; Miss Flaxman could scarcely get out of accompanying Miss Vane back through the quadrangle.

"I didn't know you knew Reggie Pomfret," said Miss Flaxman.

"Yes, we have met," said Harriet. "Why didn't you bring Miss Cattermole home with you last night? Especially as you must have seen she was unwell."

Miss Flaxman looked startled.

"It was nothing to do with me," she said. "Was there a row?"

"No; but did you do anything to prevent it? You might have done, mightn't you?"

"I can't be Violet Cattermole's guardian."

"Anyway," said Harriet, "you may be glad to know that some good has come of this stupid business. Miss Cattermole is now definitely cleared of all suspicion about the anonymous letters and other disturbances. So it would be quite a good idea to behave decently to her, don't you think?"

"I tell you," said Miss Flaxman, "that I don't care one way or the other about it."

"No; but you started the rumours about her; it's up to you to stop them, now you know. I think it would be only fair to tell Mr. Farringdon the truth. If you do not, I shall."

"You seem to be very much interested in my affairs, Miss Vane."

"They seem to have aroused a good deal of general interest," said Harriet, bluntly. "I don't blame you for the original misunderstanding, but now it is cleared up—and you can take my word for it that it is—I am sure you will see it is unfair that Miss Cattermole should be made a scapegoat. You can do a lot with your own year. Will you do what you can?"

Miss Flaxman, perplexed and annoyed, and obviously not quite clear what status she was to accord to Harriet, said, rather grudgingly:

"Of course, if she didn't do it, I'm glad. Very well. I'll tell Leo."

"Thank you very much," said Harriet.

Mr. Pomfret must have run very fast both ways, for the prescription appeared in a remarkably short space of time, along with a large bunch of roses. The draught was a potent one, and enabled Miss Cattermole not only to appear in Hall, but to eat her lunch. Harriet pursued her as she was leaving and carried her off to her own room.

"Well," said Harriet, "you are a young idiot, aren't you?"

Miss Cattermole dismally agreed.

"What's the sense of it?" said Harriet. "You have contrived to commit every crime in the calendar and got dashed little fun out of it, haven't you? You've attended a meeting in a man's rooms after Hall without leave, and you oughtn't to have got leave, because you gate-crashed the meeting. That's a social crime as well as a breach of rules. In any case, you were out after nine, without putting your initials in the book. That would cost you two bob. You came back to College after 11:15 without extra late leave—which would be five shillings. You returned, in fact, after midnight, which would be ten shillings, even if you had had leave. You climbed the wall, for which you ought to be gated; and finally, you came in blotto, for which you ought to be sent down. Incidentally, that's another social crime. What have you got to say, prisoner at the bar? Is there any reason why sentence should not be passed upon you? Have a cigarette."

"Thank you," said Miss Cattermole, faintly.

"If," said Harriet, "you hadn't, by this silly piece of work, contrived to clear yourself of the suspicion of being the College lunatic, I should go to the Dean. As it is, the episode has had its usefulness, and I'm inclined to be merciful."

Miss Cattermole looked up.

"Did something happen while I was out?"

"Yes, it did."

"Oh-h-h!" said Miss Cattermole, and burst into tears.

Harriet watched her for a few minutes and then brought out a large clean handkerchief from a drawer and silently handed it over.

"You can forget all that," said Harriet, when the victim's sobs had died down a little. "But do chuck all this nonsense. Oxford isn't the place for it. You can run after young men any time—God knows the world's full of them. But to waste three years which are unlike anything else in one's lifetime is ridiculous. And it isn't fair to College. It's not fair to other Oxford women. Be a fool if you like—I've been a fool in my time and so have most people—but for Heaven's sake do it somewhere where you won't let other people down."

Miss Cattermole was understood to say, rather incoherently, that she hated College and loathed Oxford, and felt no responsibility towards those institutions.

"Then why," said Harriet, "are you here?"

"I don't want to be here; I never did. Only my parents were so keen. My mother's one of those people who work to get things open to women—you know—professions and things. And father's a lecturer in a small provincial University. And they've made a lot of sacrifices and things."

Harriet thought Miss Cattermole was probably the sacrificial victim.

"I didn't mind coming up, so much," went on Miss Cattermole; "because I was engaged to somebody, and he was up, too, and I thought it would be fun and the silly old Schools wouldn't matter much. But I'm not engaged to him any more and how on earth can I be expected to bother about all this dead-and-gone History?"

"I wonder they bothered to send you to Oxford, if you didn't want to go, and were engaged."

"Oh! but they said that didn't make any difference. Every woman ought to have a University education, even if she married. And *now*, of course, they say what a good thing it is I still have my College career. And I can't make them understand that I *hate* it! They can't see that being brought up with everybody talking education all round one is enough to make one loathe the sound of it. I'm sick of education."

Harriet was not surprised.

"What should you have liked to do? I mean, supposing the complication about your engagement hadn't happened?"

"I think," said Miss Cattermole, blowing her nose in a final manner and taking another cigarette, "I think I should have liked to be a cook. Or possibly a hospital nurse, but I think I should have been better at cooking. Only, you see, those are two of the things Mother's always trying to get people out of the way of thinking women's sphere ought to be restricted to."

"There's a lot of money in good cooking," said Harriet.

"Yes—but it's not an educational advance. Besides, there's no school of Cookery at Oxford, and it had to be Oxford, you see, or Cambridge, because of the opportunity of making the right kind of friends. Only I haven't made any friends. They all hate me. Perhaps they won't so much, now that the beastly letters—"

"Quite so," said Harriet, hastily, fearing a fresh outburst. "How about Miss Briggs? She seems to be a very good sort."

"She's awfully kind. But I'm always having to be grateful to her. It's very depressing. It makes me want to bite."

"How right you are," said Harriet, to whom this was a direct hit over the solar plexus. "I know. Gratitude is simply damnable."

"And now," said Miss Cattermole, with devastating candor, "I've got to be grateful to *you*."

"You needn't be. I was serving my own ends as much as yours. But I'll tell you what I'd do. I'd stop trying to do sensational things, because it's apt to get you into positions where you have to be grateful. And I'd stop chasing undergraduates, because it bores them to tears and interrupts their work. I'd tackle the History and get through Schools.

And then I'd turn round and say, 'Now I've done what you want me to, and I'm going to be a cook.' And stick to it."

"Would you?"

"I expect you want to be very truly run after, like Old Man Kangaroo. Well, good cooks are. Still, as you've started here on History, you'd better worry on at it. It won't hurt you, you know. If you learn how to tackle one subject—any subject—you've learnt how to tackle all subjects."

"Well," said Miss Cattermole, in rather an unconvinced tone, "I'll try."

Harriet went away in a rage and tackled the Dean.

"Why do they send these people here? Making themselves miserable and taking up the place of people who *would* enjoy Oxford. *We* haven't got room for women who aren't and never will be scholars. It's all right for the men's colleges to have hearty passmen who gambol round and learn to play games, so that they can gambol and game in Prep. Schools. But this dreary little devil isn't even hearty. She's a wet mess."

"I *know*," said the Dean, impatiently. "But schoolmistresses and parents are such jugginses. We do our best, but we can't always weed our their mistakes. And here's my secretary—called away, just when we're all so busy, because her tiresome little boy's got chicken-pox at his infuriating school. Oh, dear! I oughtn't to talk like that, because he's a delicate child and naturally children must come first, but it is *too* crushing!"

"I'll be off," said Harriet. "It's a shame you should have to be working of an afternoon and a shame of me to interrupt. By the way, I may as well tell you that Cattermole had an alibi for last night's affair."

"Had she? Good! That's something. Though I suppose it means *more* suspicion on our miserable selves. Still, facts are facts. Miss Vane, what *was* the noise in the quad last night? And who was the young man you were bear-leading?

I didn't ask this morning in Common-Room, because I had an idea you didn't want me to."

"I didn't," said Harriet.

"And you don't?"

"As Sherlock Holmes said on another occasion: 'I think we must ask for an amnesty in that direction.' "

The Dean twinkled shrewdly at her.

"Two and two make four. Well, I trust you."

"But I was going to suggest a row of revolving spikes on the wall of the Fellows' Garden."

"Ah!" said the Dean. "Well, I don't *want* to know things. And most of it's sheer cussedness. They want to make heroes and heroines of themselves. Last week of term's the worst for wall-climbing. They make bets. Have to work 'em off before the end of term. Tiresome little cuckoos. All the same, it can't be allowed."

"It won't happen again, I fancy, with this particular lot."

"Very well. I'll speak to the Bursar—in a general way—about spikes."

Harriet changed her frock, pondering on the social absurdities of the party to which she was invited. Clearly, Mr. Pomfret clung to her as a protection against Miss Flaxman, and Mr. Farringdon, as a protection against Mr. Pomfret, while Miss Flaxman, who was apparently her hostess, did not want her at all. It was a pity that she could not embark on the adventure of annexing Mr. Farringdon, to complete a neat little tail-chasing circle. But she was both too old and too young to feel any thrill over the Byronic profile of Mr. Farringdon; there was more amusement to be had out of remaining a buffer state. She did, however, feel sufficient resentment against Miss Flaxman for her handling of the Cattermole affair, to put on an exceedingly well-cut coat and skirt and a hat of unexceptionable smartness, before starting out for the first item in her afternoon's program.

She had little difficulty in finding Mr. Pomfret's staircase, and none whatever in finding Mr. Pomfret. As she wound her way up the dark and ancient stair, past the shut door of one, Mr. Smith, the sported oak of one, Mr. Banerjee, and the open door of one, Mr. Hodges, who seemed to be entertaining a large and noisy party of male friends, she became aware of an altercation going on upon the landing above, and presently Mr. Pomfret himself came into view, standing in his own doorway and arguing with a man whose back was turned towards the stair.

"You can go to the devil," said Mr. Pomfret.

"Very good, sir," said the back; "but how about me going to the young lady? If I was to go and tell her that I seen you a-pushing of her over the wall—"

"Blast you!" exclaimed Mr. Pomfret. "*Will* you shut up?"

At this point, Harriet set her foot upon the top stair, and encountered the eye of Mr. Pomfret.

"Oh!" said Mr. Pomfret, taken aback. Then, to the man, "Clear off now; I'm busy. You'd better come again."

"Quite a man for the ladies, ain't you, sir?" said the man, disagreeably.

At these words, he turned, and, to her amazement, Harriet recognized a familiar face.

"Dear me, Jukes," said she. "Fancy seeing you here!"

"Do you know this blighter?" said Mr. Pomfret.

"Of course I do," said Harriet. "He was a porter at Shrewsbury, and was sacked for petty pilfering. I hope you're going straight now, Jukes. How's your wife?"

"All right," said Jukes, silkily. "I'll come again."

He made a move to slip down the staircase, but Harriet had set her umbrella so awkwardly across it as to bar the way pretty effectively.

"Hi!" said Mr. Pomfret. "Let's hear about this. Just come back here a minute, will you?" He stretched out a powerful arm, and yanked the reluctant Jukes over the threshold.

"You can't get me on that old business," said Jukes, scornfully, as Harriet followed them in, shutting oak and door after her with a bang. "That's over and done with. It ain't got nothing to do with that other little affair what I mentioned."

"What's that?" asked Harriet.

"This nasty piece of work," said Mr. Pomfret, "has had the blasted neck to come here and say that if I don't pay him to keep his mouth shut, he'll lay an information about what happened last night."

"Blackmail," said Harriet, much interested. "That's a serious offense."

"I didn't mention no money," said Jukes, injured. "I only told this gentleman as I seen something as didn't ought to have happened and was uneasy in my mind about it. He says I can go to the devil, so I says in that case I'll go to the lady, being troubled in my conscience, don't you see."

"Very well," said Harriet. "I'm here. Go ahead."

Mr. Jukes stared at her.

"I take it," said Harriet, "you saw Mr. Pomfret help me in over the Shrewsbury wall last night when I'd forgotten my key. What were you doing out there, by the way? Loitering with intent? You then probably saw me come out again, thank Mr. Pomfret and ask him to come in and see the College Buildings by moonlight. If you waited long enough, you saw me let him out again. What about it?"

"Nice goings-on, I don't think," said Jukes, disconcerted.

"Possibly," said Harriet. "But if Senior Members choose to enter their own college in an unorthodox way, I don't see who's to prevent them. Certainly not you."

"I don't believe a word of it," said Jukes.

"I can't help that," said Harriet. "The Dean saw Mr. Pomfret and me, so she will. Nobody's likely to believe you. Why didn't you tell this man the whole story at once, Mr. Pomfret, and relieve his conscience? By the way, Jukes, I've just told the Dean she ought to have that wall spiked. It was handy for us, but it really isn't high enough to keep out burglars and other undesirables. So it's not much good your loitering about there any more. One or two things have been missed from people's rooms lately," she added, with some truth, "it might be as well to have that road specially policed."

"None of that," said Jukes. "I ain't a-going to have my character took away. If it's as you say, then I'm sure I'd be the last to want to make trouble for a lady like yourself."

"I hope you'll bear that in mind," said Mr. Pomfret. "Perhaps you'd like to have something to remember it by."

"No assault!" cried Jukes, backing towards the door. "No assault! Don't you go to lay 'ands on me!"

"If ever you show your dirty face here again," said Mr. Pomfret, opening the door, "I'll kick you downstairs and right through the quad. Get that? Then get out!"

He flung the oak back with one hand and propelled Jukes vigorously through it with the other. A crash and a curse proclaimed that the swiftness of Jukes's exit had carried him over the head of the stairs.

"Whew!" exclaimed Mr. Pomfret, returning. "By jove! that was great! That was marvelous of you. How did you come to think of it?"

"It was fairly obvious. I expect it was all bluff, really. I don't see how he could have known who Miss Cattermole was. I wonder how he got on to you."

"He must have followed me back when I came out. But I didn't get in through this window—obviously—so how did he—? Oh! yes, when I knocked Brown up I believe he stuck his head out and said, 'That you, Pomfret?' Careless blighter. I'll talk to him. . . . I say, you do seem to be everybody's guardian angel, don't you? It's marvelous, being able to keep your wits about you like that."

He gazed at her with dog-like eyes. Harriet laughed, as Mr. Rogers and the tea entered the room together.

Mr. Rogers was in his third year—tall, dark, lively and full of an easy kind of penitence.

"All this running round and busting rules is rot," said Mr. Rogers. "Why do we do it? Because somebody says it is fun, and one believes it. Why should one believe it? I can't imagine. One should look at these things more objectively.

Is the thing beautiful in itself? No. Then let us not do it. By the way, Pomfret, have you been approached about debagging Culpepper?"

"I am all for it," said Mr. Pomfret.

"True, Culpepper is a wart. He is a disgusting object. But would he look any better debagged? No, Socrates, he would not. He would look much worse. If anybody is to be debagged, it shall be somebody with legs that will stand exposure —your own, Pomfret, for example."

"You try, that's all," said Mr. Pomfret.

"In any case," pursued Mr. Rogers, "debagging is otiose and out of date. The modern craze for exposing unaesthetic legs needs no encouragement from me. I shall not be a party to it. I intend to be a reformed character. From now on, I shall consider nothing but the value of the Thing-in-Itself, unmoved by any pressure of public opinion."

Having, in this pleasant manner, confessed his sins and promised amendment, Mr. Rogers gracefully led the conversation to topics of general interest, and, about 5 o'clock, departed, murmuring something in an apologetic way about work and his tutor, as though they were rather indelicate necessities. At this point, Mr. Pomfret suddenly went all solemn, as a very young man occasionally does when alone with a woman older than himself, and told Harriet a good deal about his own view of the meaning of life. Harriet listened with as much intelligent sympathy as she could command; but was slightly relieved when three young men burst in to borrow Mr. Pomfret's beer and remained to argue over their host's head about Komisarjevsky. Mr. Pomfret seemed faintly annoyed, and eventually asserted his right to his own guest by announcing that it was time to pop round to New College for old Farringdon's party. His friends let him go with mild regret and, before Harriet and her escort were well out of the room, took possession of their armchairs and continued the argument.

"Very able fellow, Marston," said Mr. Pomfret, amiably enough. "Great noise on O.U.D.S. and spends his vacations in Germany. I don't know how they contrive to get so worked up about plays. I like a good play, but I don't understand all this stuff about stylistic treatment and planes of vision. I expect you do, though."

"Now a word," said Harriet, cheerfully. "I dare say they don't, either. Anyhow, I know I don't like plays in which all the actors have to keep on tumbling up and down flights of steps, or where the lighting's so artistically done that you can't see anything, or where you keep on wondering all the time what the symbolical whirligig in the center of the stage is going to be used for, if anything. It distracts me. I'd rather go to the Holborn Empire and have my fun vulgar."

"Would you?" said Mr. Pomfret, wistfully. "You wouldn't come and do a show with me in Town in the vac, would you?"

Harriet made a vague kind of promise, which seemed to delight Mr. Pomfret very much, and they presently found themselves in Mr. Farringdon's sitting-room, packed like sardines among a mixed crowd of undergraduates and struggling to consume sherry and biscuits without moving their elbows.

The crowd was such that Harriet never set eyes on Miss Flaxman from first to last. Mr. Farringdon did, however, struggle through to them, bringing with him a bunch of young men and women who wanted to talk about detective fiction. They appeared to have read a good deal of this kind of literature, though very little of anything else. A School of Detective Fiction would, Harriet thought, have a fair chance of producing a goodly crop of Firsts. The fashion for psychological analysis had, she decided, rather gone out since her day: she was instinctively aware that a yearning for action and the concrete was taking its place. The pre-War solemnity and the post-War exhaustion were both gone; the desire now was for an energetic doing of something definite, though the definitions differed. The detective story, no doubt, was acceptable, because in it something definite was done, the "what" being comfortably decided beforehand by the author. It was borne in upon

Harriet that all these young men and women were starting out to hoe a hardish kind of row in a very stony ground. She felt rather sorry for them.

Something definite done. Yes, indeed. Harriet, reviewing the situation next morning, felt deeply dissatisfied. She did not like this Jukes business at all. He could scarcely, she supposed, have anything to do with the anonymous letters: where could he have got hold of that passage from the *Aeneid?* But he was a man with a grudge, a nasty-minded man, and a thief; it was not pleasant that he should make a habit of hanging round the College walls after dark.

Harriet was alone in the Senior Common Room, everybody else having departed to her work. The S.C.R. scout came in, carrying a pile of clean ash-trays, and Harriet suddenly remembered that her children lodged with the Jukeses.

"Annie," she said, impulsively, "what does Jukes come down into Oxford for, after dark?"

The woman looked startled. "Does he, madam? For no good, I should think."

"I found him loitering in St. Cross Road last night, in a place where he might easily get over. Is he keeping honest, do you know?"

"I couldn't say, I'm sure, madam, but I have my doubts. I like Mrs. Jukes very much, and I'd be sorry to add to her troubles. But I never have trusted Jukes. I've been thinking I ought to put my little girls somewhere else. He might be a bad influence on them, don't you think?"

"I certainly do think so."

"I'm the last person to wish to put difficulties into the way of a respectable married woman," went on Annie, slapping an ash-tray smartly down, "and naturally she's right to stick by her husband. But one's own children must come first, mustn't they?"

"Of course," said Harriet, rather inattentively. "Oh, yes. I should find somewhere else for them. I suppose you haven't ever heard either Jukes or his wife say anything to suggest that he—well, that he was stealing from the College or cherishing bad feelings against the dons."

"I don't have much to say to Jukes, madam, and if Mrs. Jukes knew anything, she wouldn't tell me. It wouldn't be right if she did. He's her husband, and she has to take his part. I quite see that. But if Jukes is behaving dishonestly, I shall have to find somewhere else for the children. I'm much obliged to you for mentioning it, madam. I shall be going round there on Wednesday, which is my free afternoon, and I'll take the opportunity to give notice. May I ask if you have said anything to Jukes, madam?"

"I have spoken to him, and told him that if he hangs round here any more he will have to do with the police."

"I'm very glad to hear that, madam. It isn't right at all that he should come here like that. If I'd known about it, I really shouldn't have been able to sleep. I feel sure it ought to be put a stop to."

"Yes, it ought. By the way, Annie, have you ever seen anybody in the College in a dress of this description?"

Harriet picked up the black figured crêpe de Chine from the chair beside her. Annie examined it carefully.

"No, madam, not to my recollection. Perhaps one of the maids that been here longer than me might know. There's Gertrude in the dining-room; should you like to ask her?"

Gertrude, however, could give no help. Harriet asked them to take the dress and catechize the rest of the staff. This was done, but with no result. An inquiry among the students produced no identification, either. The dress was brought back, still unclaimed and unrecognized. One more puzzle. Harriet concluded that it must actually be the property of the Poison-Pen; but if so, it must have been brought to College and kept in hiding till the moment of its dramatic appearance in Chapel; for if it had ever been worn in College, it was almost inconceivable that no one should be able to recognize it.

The alibis produced, meekly enough, by the members of the S.C.R. were none of them water-tight. That was not surprising; it would have been more surprising if they had been. Harriet (and Mr. Pomfret, of course) alone knew the exact time for which the alibi was required; and though many people were able to show themselves covered up to midnight or thereabouts, all had been, or claimed to have been, virtuously in their own rooms and beds by a quarter to one. Nor, though the porter's book and late-leave tickets had been examined, and all students interrogated who might have been about the quad at midnight, had anybody seen any suspicious behavior with gowns or bolsters or bread-knives. Crime was too easy in a place like this. The College was too big, too open. Even if a form had been seen crossing the quad with a bolster, or indeed for that matter a complete set of bedding and a mattress, nobody would ever think anything of it. Some hardy fresh-air fiend sleeping out; that would be the natural conclusion.

Harriet, exasperated, went over to Bodley and plunged into her researches upon Lefanu. There, at least, one did know what one was investigating.

She felt so much the need of a soothing influence that, in the afternoon, she went down to Christ Church to hear service at the Cathedral. She had been shopping—purchasing, among other things, a bag of meringues for the entertainment of some students she had asked to a small party in her room that evening—and it was only when her arms were already full of parcels that the idea of Cathedral suggested itself. It was rather out of her way; but the parcels were not heavy. She dodged across Carfax, angrily resenting its modern bustle of cars and complication of stop-and-go lights, and joined the little sprinkling of foot-passengers who were tripping down St. Aldate's and through Wolsey's great unfinished quadrangle, bound on the same pious errand as herself.

It was quiet and pleasant in Cathedral. She lingered in her seat for some little time after the nave had emptied and until the organist had finished the voluntary. Then she came slowly out, turning left along the plinth with a vague idea of once more admiring the great staircase and the Hall, when a slim figure in a grey suit shot with such velocity from a dark doorway that he cannoned full tilt against her, nearly knocking her down, and sending her bag and parcels flying in disorder along the plinth.

"Hell!" said a voice which set her heart beating by its unexpected familiarity, "have I hurt you? Me all over—bargin' and bumpin' about like a bumble-bee in a bottle. Clumsy lout! I say, do say I haven't hurt you. Because, if I have, I'll run straight across and drown myself in Mercury."

He extended the arm that was not supporting Harriet in a vague gesture towards the pond.

"Not in the least, thank you," said Harriet, recovering herself.

"Thank God for that. This is my unlucky day. I've just had a most unpleasant interview with the Junior Censor. Was there anything breakable in the parcels? Oh, look! your bag's opened itself wide and all the little oojahs have gone down the steps. Please don't move. You stand there, thinkin' up things to call me, and I'll pick 'em all up one by one on my knees sayin' 'meâ culpâ' to every one of 'em."

He suited the action to the words.

"I'm afraid it hasn't improved the meringues." He looked up apologetically. "But if you'll say you forgive me, we'll go and get some new ones from the kitchen—the real kind—*you* know—speciality of the House, and all that."

"Please don't bother," said Harriet.

It wasn't he, of course. This was a lad of twenty-one or two at the most, with a mop of wavy hair tumbling over his forehead and a handsome, petulant face, full of charm, though ominously weak about the curved lips and upward-slanting brows. But the color of the hair was right—the pale yellow of ripe barley; and the light drawling voice, with its clipped syllables and ready babble of speech; and the quick, sidelong smile; and above all, the beautiful, sensitive hands that were gathering the "oojahs" deftly up into their native bag.

"You haven't called me any names yet," said the young man.

"I believe I could almost put a name to you," said Harriet. "Isn't it—are you any relation of Peter Wimsey's?"

"Why, of course," said the young man, sitting up on his heels. "He's my uncle; and a dashed sight more accommodating than the Jewish kind," he added, as though struck by a melancholy association of ideas. "Have I met you somewhere? Or was it pure guesswork? You don't think I'm like him, do you?"

"When you spoke, I thought you were your uncle for the moment. Yes, you're very like him, in some ways."

"That'll break my mater's heart, all right," said the young man, with a grin. "Uncle Peter's not approved. I wish to God he was here, though. He'd come in uncommonly handy at the moment. But he seems to have beetled off somewhere as usual. Mysterious old tom-cat, isn't he? I take it you know him—I forgot the proper bromide about how small the world is, but we'll take it as read. Where *is* the old blighter?"

"I believe he's in Rome."

"He *would* be. That means a letter. It's awfully hard to be persuasive in a letter, don't you think? I mean, it all takes so much explaining, and the famous family charm doesn't seem to go over so well in black and white."

He smiled at her with engaging frankness as he recaptured a last straying copper.

"Do I gather," said Harriet, with some amusement, "that you anticipate an appeal to Uncle Peter's better feelings?"

"That's about it," said the young man. "He's quite human, really, you know, if you go about him the right way. Besides, you see, I've got the bulge on Uncle Peter. If the worst comes to the worst, I can always threaten to cut my throat and land him with the strawberry leaves."

"With the what?" said Harriet, fancying that this must be the latest Oxford version of giving the raspberry.

"The strawberry leaves," said the young man. "The

balm, the scepter, and the ball. Four rows of moth-eaten ermine. To say nothing of that dashed great barracks down at Denver, eating its moldy head off." Seeing that Harriet still looked blankly at him, he explained further: "I'm sorry; I forgot. My name's Saint-George and the Governor forgot to provide me with any brothers. So the minute they write d.s.p. after me, Uncle Peter's for it. Of course, my father might outlive him; but I don't believe Uncle Peter's the sort to die young, unless one of his pet criminals manages to bump him off."

"That might easily happen," said Harriet, thinking of the plug-ugly.

"Well, that makes it all the worse for him," said Lord Saint-George, shaking his head. "The more risks he takes, the quicker he's got to toe the line for the matrimonial stakes. No more bachelor freedom with old Bunter in a Piccadilly flat. *And* no more spectacular Viennese singers. So you see, it's as much as his life's worth to let anything happen to me."

"Obviously," said Harriet, fascinated by this new light on the subject.

"Uncle Peter's weakness," went on Lord Saint-George, carefully disentangling the squashed meringues from their paper, "is his strong sense of public duty. You mightn't think it to look at him, but it's there. (Shall we try these on the carp? I don't think they're really fit for human consumption.) He's kept out of it so far—he's an obstinate old devil. Says he'll have the right wife or none."

"But suppose the right one says No."

"That's the story he puts up. I don't believe a word of it. Why should anybody object to Uncle Peter? He's no beauty and he'd talk the hind leg off a donkey; but he's dashed well-off and he's got good manners and he's in the stud-book." He balanced himself on the edge of Mercury and peered into its tranquil waters. "Look! there's the big old one. Been here since the foundation, by the looks of him—see him go? Cardinal Wolsey's particular pet." He tossed a crumb to the great fish, which took it with a quick snap and submerged again.

"I don't know how well you know my uncle," he proceeded, "but if you do get a chance, you might let him know that when you saw me I was looking rather unwell and hag-ridden and hinted darkly at felo-de-se."

"I'll make a point of it," said Harriet. "I will say you seemed scarcely able to crawl and, in fact, fainted into my arms, accidentally crushing all my parcels. He won't believe me, but I'll do my best."

"No—he isn't good at believing things, confound him. I'm afraid I shall have to write, after all, and produce the evidence. Still, I don't know why I should bore you with my personal affairs. Come on down to the kitchen."

The Christ Church cook was well pleased to produce meringues from the ancient and famous College oven; and when Harriet had duly admired the vast fireplace with its shining spits and heard statistics of the number of joints roasted and the quantity of fuel consumed per week in term-time, she followed her guide out into the quadrangle again with all proper expressions of gratitude.

"Not at all," said the viscount. "Not much return, I'm afraid, after banging you all over the place and throwing your property about. May I know, by the way, whom I have had the honor of inconveniencing?"

"My name's Harriet Vane."

Lord Saint-George stood still, and smote himself heavily over the forehead.

"My God, what have I done? Miss Vane, I do beg your pardon—and throw myself abjectly on your mercy. If my uncle hears about this he'll never forgive me, and I *shall* cut my throat. It is borne in upon me that I have said every possible thing I should not."

"It's my fault," said Harriet, seeing that he looked really alarmed, "I ought to have warned you."

"As a matter of fact, I've no business to say things like that to anybody. I'm afraid I've inherited my uncle's tongue and my mother's want of tact. Look here, for God's sake forget all that rot. Uncle Peter's a dashed good sort, and as decent as they come."

"I've reason to know it," said Harriet.

"I suppose so. By the way—hell! I seem to be putting my foot in it all round, but I ought to explain that I've never heard him talk about you. I mean, he's not that sort. It's my mother. She says all kinds of things. Sorry. I'm making things worse and worse."

"Don't worry," said Harriet. "After all, I *do* know your uncle, you know—well enough, anyhow, to know what sort he is. And I certainly won't give you away."

"For Heaven's sake, don't. It isn't only that I'd never get anything more out of him—and I'm in a devil of a mess—but he makes one feel such an appalling tick. I don't suppose you've ever been given the wrong side of my uncle's tongue—naturally not. But of the two, I recommend skinning."

"We're both in the same boat. I'd no business to listen. Good-bye—and many thanks for the meringues."

She was half-way up St. Aldate's when the viscount caught her up.

"I say—I've just remembered. That old story I was ass enough to rake up—"

"The Viennese dancer?"

"Singer—music's his line. Please forget that. I mean, it's got whiskers on it—it's six years old, anyway. I was a kid at school and I dare say it's all rot."

Harriet laughed, and promised faithfully to forget the Viennese singer.

CHAPTER IX

Come hether freind, I am ashamed to hear that what I hear of you. . . . You have almost attayned to the age of nyne yeeres, at least to eight and a halfe, and seeing that you knowe your dutie, if you neglect it you deserve greater punishment then he which through ignorance doth it not. Think not that the nobilitie of your Ancestors doth free you to doe all that you list, contrarywise, it bindeth you more to followe vertue.

PIERRE ERONDELL

"So," said the Bursar, coming briskly up to the High Table for lunch on the following Thursday; "Jukes has come to grief once more. . . ."

"Has he been stealing again?" asked Miss Lydgate. "Dear me, how disappointing!"

"Annie tells me she's had her suspicions for some time, and yesterday being her half-day she went down to tell Mrs. Jukes she would have to place the children somewhere else—when lo, and behold! in walked the police and discovered a whole lot of things that had been stolen a fortnight ago from an undergraduate's rooms in Holywell. It was most unpleasant for her—for Annie, I mean. They asked her a lot of questions."

"I always thought it was a mistake to put those children there," said the Dean.

"So that's what Jukes did with himself at night," said Harriet. "I heard he'd been seen outside the College here. As a matter of fact, I gave Annie the tip. It's a pity she couldn't have removed the children earlier."

"I thought he was doing quite well," said Miss Lydgate.

"He had a job—and I know he kept chickens—and there was the money for the little Wilsons, Annie's children, I mean—so he ought not to have needed to steal, poor man. Perhaps Mrs. Jukes is a bad manager."

"Jukes is a bad lot," said Harriet. "A nasty bit of business altogether. He's much best out of the way."

"Had he taken much?" inquired the Dean.

"I gather from Annie," said the Bursar, "that they rather think they can trace a lot of petty thieving to Jukes. I understand it's a question of finding out where he sold the things."

"He'd dispose of them through a fence, I suppose," said Harriet; "some pawnbroker or somebody of that kind. Has he been inside—in prison—before?"

"Not that I know of," said the Dean, "though he *ought* to have been."

"Then I suppose he'll get off lightly as a first offender."

"Miss Barton will know all about that. We'll ask her. I do hope poor Mrs. Jukes isn't involved," said the Bursar.

"Surely not," cried Miss Lydgate, "she's such a nice woman."

"She must have known about it," said Harriet, "unless she was a perfect imbecile."

"What a dreadful thing, to know your husband was a thief!"

"Yes," said the Dean. "It would be very uncomfortable to have to live on the proceeds."

"Terrible," said Miss Lydgate. "I can't imagine anything more dreadful to an honest person's feelings."

"Then," said Harriet, "we must hope, for Mrs. Jukes's sake, she was as guilty as he was."

"What a terrible hope!" exclaimed Miss Lydgate.

"Well, she's got to be either guilty or unhappy," said Harriet, passing the bread to the Dean with a twinkle in her eye.

"I dissent altogether," said Miss Lydgate. "She must either be innocent and unhappy or guilty and unhappy—I don't see how she can be happy, poor creature."

"Let us ask the Warden next time we see her," said Miss Martin, "whether it is possible for a guilty person to be happy. And if so, whether it is better to be happy or virtuous."

"Come, Dean," said the Bursar, "we can't allow this sort of thing. Miss Vane, a bowl of hemlock for the Dean, if you please. To return to the subject under discussion, the police have not, so far, taken up Mrs. Jukes, so I suppose there's nothing against her."

"I'm very glad of that," said Miss Lydgate; and, Miss Shaw arriving at that moment, full of woe about one of her pupils who was suffering from perpetual headache, and an incapacity to work, the conversation wandered into other channels.

Term was drawing to a close, and the investigation seemed little farther advanced; but it appeared possible that Harriet's nightly perambulations and the frustration of the Library and Chapel scandals had exercised a restraining influence on the Poltergeist, for there was no further outbreak of any kind, not so much as an inscription in a lavatory or an anonymous letter, for three days. The Dean, exceedingly busy, was relieved by the respite, and also cheered by the news that Mrs. Goodwin the secretary would be back on the Monday to cope with the end-of-term rush. Miss Cattermole was seen to be more cheerful, and wrote a quite respectable paper for Miss Hillyard about the naval policy of Henry VIII. Harriet asked the enigmatic Miss de Vine to coffee. As usual, she had intended to lay bare Miss de Vine's soul, and, as usual, found herself laying bare her own.

"I quite agree with you," said Miss de Vine, "about the difficulty of combining intellectual and emotional interests. I don't think it affects women only; it affects men as well. But when men put their public lives before their private lives, it causes less outcry than when a woman does the same thing, because women put up with neglect better than men, having been brought up to expect it."

"But suppose one doesn't quite know which one wants to put first. Suppose," said Harriet, falling back on words which were not her own, "suppose one is cursed with both a heart and a brain?"

"You can usually tell," said Miss de Vine, "by seeing what kind of mistakes you make. I'm quite sure that one never makes *fundamental* mistakes about the thing one really wants to do. Fundamental mistakes arise out of lack of genuine interest. In my opinion, that is."

"I made a very big mistake once," said Harriet, "as I expect you know. I don't think that arose out of lack of interest. It seemed at the time the most important thing in the world."

"And yet you made the mistake. Were you really giving all your mind to it, do you think? Your *mind?* Were you really being as cautious and exacting about it as you would be about writing a passage of fine prose?"

"That's rather a difficult sort of comparison. One can't, surely, deal with emotional excitements in that detached spirit."

"Isn't the writing of good prose an emotional excitement?"

"Yes, of course it is. At least, when you get the thing dead right and know it's dead right, there's no excitement like it. It's marvelous. It makes you feel like God on the Seventh Day—for a bit, anyhow."

"Well, that's what I mean. You expend the trouble and you don't make any mistakes—and *then* you experience the ecstasy. But if there's any subject in which you're content with the second-rate, then it isn't really your subject."

"You're dead right," said Harriet, after a pause. "If one's genuinely interested one knows how to be patient, and let time pass, as Queen Elizabeth said. Perhaps that's the meaning of the phrase about genius being eternal patience, which I always thought rather absurd. If you truly want a thing, you don't snatch; if you snatch, you don't really want it. Do you suppose that, if you find yourself taking pains about a thing, it's a proof of its importance to you?"

"I think it is, to a large extent. But the big proof is that the thing comes right, without those fundamental errors. One always makes surface errors, of course. But a fundamental error is a sure sign of not caring. I wish one could teach people nowadays that the doctrine of snatching what one thinks one wants is unsound."

"I saw six plays this winter in London," said Harriet, "all preaching the doctrine of snatch. I agree that they left me with the feeling that none of the characters knew what they wanted."

"No," said Miss de Vine. "If you are once sure what you do want, you find that everything else goes down before it like grass under a roller—all other interests, your own and other people's. Miss Lydgate wouldn't like my saying that, but it's as true of her as of anybody else. She's the kindest soul in the world, in things she's indifferent about, like the peculations of Jukes. But she hasn't the slightest mercy on the prosodical theories of Mr. Elkbottom. She wouldn't countenance those to save Mr. Elkbottom from hanging. She'd say she couldn't. And she couldn't, of course. If she actually *saw* Mr. Elkbottom writhing in humiliation, she'd be sorry, but she wouldn't alter a paragraph. That would be treason. One can't be pitiful where one's own job is concerned. You'd lie cheerfully, I expect, about anything except—what?"

"Oh, anything!" said Harriet, laughing. "Except saying that somebody's beastly book is good when it isn't. I can't do that. It makes me a lot of enemies, but I can't do it."

"No, one can't," said Miss de Vine. "However painful it is, there's always one thing one has to deal with sincerely, if there's any root to one's mind at all. I ought to know, from my own experience. Of course, the one thing may be an emotional thing; I don't say it mayn't. One may commit all the sins in the calendar, and still be faithful and honest towards one person. If so, then that one person is probably one's appointed job. I'm not despising that kind of loyalty; it doesn't happen to be mine, that is all."

"Did you discover that by making a fundamental mistake?" asked Harriet, a little nervously.

"Yes," said Miss de Vine. "I once got engaged to somebody. But I found I was always blundering—hurting his feelings, doing stupid things, making quite elementary mistakes about him. In the end I realized that I simply wasn't taking as much trouble with him as I should have done over a disputed reading. So I decided he wasn't my job." She smiled. "For all that, I was fonder of him than he was of me. He married an excellent woman who is devoted to him and does make him her job. I should think he was a full-time job. He is a painter and usually on the verge of bankruptcy; but he paints very well."

"I suppose one oughtn't to marry anybody, unless one's prepared to make him a full-time job."

"Probably not; though there are a few rare people, I believe, who don't look on themselves as jobs but as fellow-creatures."

"I should think Phoebe Tucker and her husband were like that," said Harriet. "You met her at the Gaudy. That collaboration seems to work. But what with the wives who are jealous of their husbands' work and the husbands who are jealous of their wives' interests, it looks as though most of us imagined ourselves to be jobs."

"The worst of being a job," said Miss de Vine, "is the devastating effect it has on one's character. I'm very sorry for the person who is somebody else's job; he (or she, of course) ends by devouring or being devoured, either of which is bad for one. My painter has devoured his wife, though neither of them knows it; and poor Miss Cattermole is in great danger of being identified with her parents' job and being devoured."

"Then you're all for the impersonal job?"

"I am," said Miss de Vine.

"But you say you don't despise those who make some other person their job?"

"Far from despising them," said Miss de Vine; "I think they are dangerous."

CHRIST CHURCH,
FRIDAY.

DEAR MISS VANE,

If you can forgive my idiotic behavior the other day, will you come and lunch with me on Monday at 1 o'clock? Please do. I am still feeling suicidal, so it would really be a work of charity all round. I hope the meringues got home safely.

Very sincerely yours,
SAINT-GEORGE

My dear young man, thought Harriet, as she wrote an acceptance of this naïve invitation, if you think I can't see through that, you're mightily mistaken. This is not for me, but for *les beaux yeux de la cassette de l'oncle Pierre*. But there are worse meals than those that come out of the House kitchen, and I will go. I should like to know how much money you're managing to get through, by the way. The heir of Denver should be rich enough in his own right without appealing to Uncle Peter. Gracious! when I think that I was given my college fees and my clothes and five pounds a term to make whoopee on! You won't get much sympathy or support from me, my lord.

Still in this severe mood, she drove down St. Aldate's on Monday and inquired of the porter beneath Tom Tower for Lord Saint-George; only to be told that Lord Saint-George was not in College.

"Oh!" said Harriet, disconcerted, "but he asked me to lunch."

"What a pity you weren't let know, miss. Lord Saint-George was in a nasty motor-accident on Friday night. He's in the Infirmary. Didn't you see it in the papers?"

"No, I missed it. Is he badly hurt?"

"Injured his shoulder and cut his head open pretty badly, so we hear," said the porter, with regret, and yet with a slight relish at the imparting of bad news. "He was unconscious for twenty-four hours; but we are informed that his condition is now improving. The Duke and Duchess have left for the country again."

"Dear me!" said Harriet. "I'm very sorry to hear this. I'd better go round and inquire. Do you know whether he is allowed to see anybody yet?"

The porter looked her over with a paternal eye, which somehow suggested to her that if she had been an undergraduate the answer would have been No.

"I believe, miss," said the porter, "that Mr. Danvers and Lord Warboys were permitted to visit his lordship this morning. I couldn't say further than that. Excuse me—there is Mr. Danvers just crossing the quadrangle. I will ascertain."

He emerged from his glass case and pursued Mr. Danvers, who immediately came running to the lodge.

"I say," said Mr. Danvers, "are you Miss Vane? Because poor old Saint-George has only just remembered about you. He's terribly sorry, and I was to catch you and give you some grub. No trouble at all—a great pleasure. We ought to have let you know, but he was knocked clean out, poor old chap. And then, what with the family fussing round—do you know the Duchess?—No?—Ah! Well, she went off this morning, and then I was allowed to go round and got my instructions. Terrific apologies and all that."

"How did it happen?"

"Driving a racing car to the danger of the public," said Mr. Danvers, with a grimace. "Trying to make it before the gates were shut. No police on the spot, as it happened, so we don't know exactly what *did* happen. Nobody killed, fortunately. Saint-George took a telegraph-pole in his stride, apparently, went out head first and pitched on his shoulder. Lucky he had the windscreen down, or he'd have had no face to speak of. The car's a total wreck, and I don't know why he isn't. But all those Wimseys have as many lives as cats. Come along in. These are my rooms. I hope you can eat the usual lamb cutlets—there wasn't time to think up anything special. But I had particular orders to hunt out Saint-George's Niersteiner '23 and mention Uncle Peter in connection with it. Is that right? I don't know whether Uncle Peter bought it or recommended it or merely enjoyed it, or what he had to do with it, but that's what I was told to say."

Harriet laughed. "If he did any of those things, it'll be all right."

The Niersteiner was excellent, and Harriet heartlessly enjoyed her lunch, finding Mr. Danvers a pleasant host.

"And do go up and see the patient," said Mr. Danvers, as he escorted her at length to the gate. "He's quite fit to receive company, and it'll cheer him up no end. He's in a private ward, so you can get in any time."

"I'll go straight away," said Harriet.

"Do," said Mr. Danvers. "What's that?" he added, turning to the porter, who had come out with a letter in his hand. "Oh, something for Saint-George. Right. Yes. I expect the lady will take it up, if she's going now. If not, it can wait for the messenger."

Harriet looked at the inscription. "The Viscount Saint-George, Christ Church, Oxford, Inghilterra." Even without the Italian stamp, there was no mistaking where that came from. "I'll take it," she said—"it might be urgent."

Lord Saint-George, with his right arm in a sling, his forehead and one eye obscured by bandages and the other eye black and bloodshot, was profuse in welcome and apology.

"I hope Danvers looked after you all right. It's frightfully decent of you to come along."

Harriet asked if he was badly hurt.

"Well, it might be worse. I fancy Uncle Peter had a near squeak of it this time, but it's worked out at a cut head and a busted shoulder. And shock and bruises and all that. Much less than I deserve. Stay and talk to me. It's dashed dull being all alone, and I've only got one eye and can't see out of that."

"Won't talking make your head ache?"

"It can't ache worse than it does already. And you've got a nice voice. Do be kind and stay."

"I've brought a letter along for you from College."

"Some dashed dun or other, I suppose."

"No. It's from Rome."

"Uncle Peter. Oh, my God! I suppose I'd better know the worst."

She put it into his left hand, and watched his fingers fumble across the broad red seal.

"Ugh! Sealing-wax and the family crest. I know what that means. Uncle Peter at his stuffiest."

He struggled impatiently with the tough envelope.

"Shall I open it for you?"

"I wish you would. And, look here—be an angel and read it to me. Even with two good eyes, his fist's a bit of a strain."

Harriet drew out the letter and glanced at the opening words.

"This looks rather private."

"Better you than the nurse. Besides, I can bear it better with a spot of womanly sympathy. I say, is there any enclosure?"

"No enclosure. No."

The patient groaned.

"Uncle Peter turns to bay. That's torn it. How does it start? If it's 'Gherkins' or 'Jerry,' or even 'Gerald,' there's hope yet."

"It starts, 'My dear Saint-George,' "

"Oh, gosh! Then he's really furious. And signed with all the initials he can rake up, what?"

Harriet turned the letter over.

"Signed with all his names in full."

"Unrelenting monster! You know, I had a sort of feeling he wouldn't take it very well. I don't know what the devil I'm going to do now."

He looked so ill that Harriet said, rather anxiously:

"Hadn't we better leave it till tomorrow?"

"No. I must know where I stand. Carry on. Speak gently to your little boy. Sing it to me. It'll need it."

> MY DEAR SAINT-GEORGE,
>
> If I have rightly understood your rather incoherent statement of your affairs, you have contracted a debt of honor for a sum which you do not possess. You have settled it with a cheque which you had no money to meet. As cover for this, you have borrowed from a friend, giving him a post-dated cheque which you have no reason to suppose will be met either. You suggest that I should accommodate you by backing your bill at six months; failing which, you will either (a) "try Levy again," or (b) blow your brains out. The former alternative would, as you admit, increase your ultimate liability; the second, as I will myself venture to point out, would not reimburse your friend but merely add disgrace to insolvency.

Lord Saint-George shifted restlessly upon his pillows. "Nasty clear-headed way he has of putting things."

> You are good enough to say that you approach me rather than your father, because I am, in your opinion, more likely to be sympathetic to this dubious piece of finance. I cannot say I feel flattered by your opinion.

"I didn't mean that, exactly," groaned the viscount. "He knows quite well what I mean. The Governor would fly right off the handle. Damn it, it's his own fault! He oughtn't to keep me so short. What does he expect? Considering the money *he* got through in his giddy youth, he should know something about it. And Uncle Peter's rolling—it wouldn't hurt him to cough up a bit."

"I don't think it's the money so much as the dud cheques, is it?"

"That's the trouble. Well, why the devil does he go barging off to Rome just when he's wanted? He knows I wouldn't have given a dud if I could have got cover for it. But I couldn't get at him if he wasn't there. Well, read on. Let's hear the worst."

> I am quite aware that your premature decease would leave me heir-presumptive to the title—

"Heir-presumptive? . . . Oh, I see. My mother might peg out and my father marry again. Calculating brute."

> —heir-presumptive to the title and estate. Tedious as such an inheritance might be, you will forgive me for suggesting that I might prove a more honest steward than yourself.

"Hell! That's one in the eye," said the viscount. "If that line of defense has gone, it's all up."

> You remind me that when you attain your majority next July, you will receive an increased allowance. Since, however, even the sum you have mentioned amounts to about a year's income on the higher scale of payment, your prospect of redeeming your bill in six months' time seems to be remote; nor do I understand what you propose to live on when you have anticipated your income to this extent. Further, I do not for one moment suppose that the sum in question represents the whole of your liabilities.

"Damned thought-reader!" growled his lordship. "Of course it doesn't. But how does *he* know?"

> Under the circumstances, I must decline to back your bill or to lend you money.

"Well, that's flat. Why didn't he say so at once?"

Since, however, you have put your name to a cheque, and that name must not be dishonored, I have instructed my bankers—

"Come! that sounds a bit better. Good old Uncle Peter! You can always get him on the family name."

—instructed my bankers to arrange to cover your cheques—

"Cheque, or cheques?"

"Cheques, in the plural; quite distinctly."

—cover your cheques from now until the time of my return to England, when I shall come and see you. This will probably be before the end of the Trinity Term. I will ask you to see to it that the whole of your liabilities are discharged by that time, including your outstanding Oxford debts and your obligations to the children of Israel.

"First gleam of humanity," said the viscount.

May I offer you, in addition, a little advice? Bear in mind that the amateur professional is peculiarly rapacious. This applies both to women and to people who play cards. If you must back horses, back them at a reasonable price and both ways. And, if you insist on blowing out your brains, do it in some place where you will not cause mess and inconvenience.

Your affectionate Uncle,

PETER DEATH BREDON WIMSEY

"Whew!" said Lord Saint-George, "that's a stinker! I fancy I detect a little softening in the last paragraph. Otherwise, I should say that a nastier kind of letter never came to soothe the sufferer's aching brow. What do you think?"

Harriet privately agreed that it was not the kind of letter she should care to receive. It displayed, in fact, almost everything that she resented most in Peter; the condescending superiority, the arrogance of caste and the generosity that was like a blow in the face. However:—

"He's done far more than you asked him," she pointed out. "So far as I can see, there's nothing to prevent you from drawing a cheque for fifty thousand and blueing the lot."

"That's the devil of it. He's got me by the short hairs. He's trusted me with the whole dashed outfit. I did think he might offer to settle up for me, but he's left me to do it and hasn't even asked for an account. That means it'll have to be done. I don't see how I can get out of it. He has the most ingenious ways of making a fellow feel a sweep. Oh, hell! my head's splitting."

"You'd better keep quiet and try to go to sleep. You've nothing to worry about now."

"No. Wait a minute. Don't go away. The cheque's all right, that's the chief thing. Just as well, because I'd have had a job to raise the wind elsewhere, laid up like this. There's one thing about it—I can't use this arm, so I shan't have to write a long screed full of grateful penitence."

"Does he know about your accident?"

"Not unless Aunt Mary's written to him. My grandmother's on the Riviera, and I don't suppose it would occur to my sister. She's at school. The Governor never writes to anybody, and my mother certainly wouldn't bother with Uncle Peter. Look here, I must do something. I mean, the old boy's been thoroughly decent, really. Couldn't you write a line for me, explaining all about it! I don't want to let my family in on this."

"I'll do that, certainly."

"Tell him I'll settle the blasted debts as soon as I can produce a recognizable signature. I say! think of having a free hand with Uncle Peter's pile and not being able to sign a cheque. Enough to make a cat laugh, isn't it? Say I—what's the phrase?—appreciate his confidence and won't let him down. Here! you might give me a spot of the stuff in that jug, would you? I feel like Dives in what's-his-name."

He gulped the iced drink down gratefully.

"No, damn it! I must do something. The old boy's really worried. I think I can work these fingers after a fashion. Find me a pencil and paper and I'll have a shot."

"I don't think you'd better."

"Yes, I had better. And I will if it kills me. Find me something, there's a darling."

She found writing materials, and held the paper in place while he scrawled a few staggering words. The pain made him sweat; a shoulder joint which has been dislocated and returned to position is no cushion of ease the day after; but he set his teeth and went through with it gamely.

"There," he said, with a faint grin, "that looks dashed pathetic. Now it's up to you. Do your best for me, won't you?"

Perhaps, thought Harriet, Peter knew the right way with his nephew. The boy was unblushingly ready to consider other people's money his own; and probably, if Peter had simply backed his bill, he would have thought his uncle easy game and proceeded to issue more paper on the same terms. As it was, he seemed inclined to stop and think. And he had, what she herself lacked, the grace of gratitude. His facile acceptance of favors might be a sign of shallowness; still, it had cost him something to scribble that painful note.

It was only when, in her own room after Hall, she set about writing to Peter, that she realized how awkward her own task was going to be. To put down a brief explanation of her own acquaintance with Lord Saint-George and a reassuring account of his accident was child's play. The difficulties began with the matter of the young man's finances. Her first draft ran easily; it was slightly humorous and rather gave the benefactor to understand that his precious balms were calculated to break the recipient's head, where other agents had not already broken it. She rather enjoyed writing this one. On reading it over, she was disappointed to find that it had an air of officious impertinence. She tore it up.

The students were making a vast noise of trampling and laughter in the corridor. Harriet briefly cursed them and tried again.

The second draft began stiffly: "Dear Peter—I am writing on behalf of your nephew, who has unfortunately—"

This one, when finished, conveyed the impression that she disapproved strongly of uncle and nephew alike, and was anxious to dissociate herself as far as possible from their affairs.

She tore it up, cursed the students again and made a third draft.

This, when completed, turned out to be a moving, and indeed, powerful piece of special pleading on the young sinner's behalf, but contained remarkably little of the gratitude and repentance which she had been instructed to convey. The fourth draft, erring in the opposite direction, was merely fulsome.

"What the devil is the matter with me?" she said aloud. "(Damn those noisy brats!) Why can't I write a straightforward piece of English on a set subject?"

When she had once formulated the difficulty in this plain question, the detached intellect bent meekly to its academic task and produced the answer.

"Because, however you put it, all this is going to hurt his pride damnably."

Answer adjudged correct.

What she had to say, stripped of its verbiage, was: Your nephew has been behaving foolishly and dishonestly, and I know it; he gets on badly with his parents, and I know that, too; he has taken me into his confidence and, what is more, into yours, where I have no right to be; in fact, I know a great many things you would rather I did not know, and you can't lift a hand to prevent it.

In fact, for the first time in their acquaintance, she had the upper hand of Peter Wimsey, and could rub his aristocratic nose in the dirt if she wanted to. Since she had been looking for such an opportunity for five years, it would be odd if she did not hasten to take advantage of it.

Slowly and with extreme pains, she started on Draft No. 5.

> DEAR PETER,
>
> I don't know whether you know that your nephew is in the Infirmary, recovering from what might have been a nasty motor accident. His right shoulder is dislocated and his head badly cut; but he is getting on all right and is lucky not to have been killed. Apparently he skidded into a telegraph pole. I don't know the details; perhaps you have already heard from his people. I met him by chance a few days ago, and only heard of the accident today, when I went round to see him.

So far, so good; now for the awkward bit.

> One of his eyes was bandaged up and the other badly swollen, so he asked me to read him the letter he had just that moment received from you. (Please don't think his sight is damaged—I asked the nurse, and it's only cuts and bruises.) There was nobody else to read it to him, as his parents left Oxford this morning. As he can't write much himself, he asks me to send you the enclosed and to say he thanks you very much and is sorry. He appreciates your confidence and will do exactly as you ask him, as soon as he is well enough.

She hoped there was nothing there that could offend. She had started to write "honorably do as you ask," and then erased the first word: to mention honor was to suggest its opposite. Her consciousness seemed to have become all one exposed nerve-center, sensitive to the lightest breath of innuendo in her own words.

> I didn't stay long, as he was really a good bit under the weather, but they assure me he is doing very well. He insisted on writing this note himself, though I suppose I oughtn't to have let him. I'll look him up again before I leave Oxford—entirely for my own sake, because he is perfectly charming. I hope you don't mind my saying so, though I'm sure you don't need to be told it.
>
> Yours,
> HARRIET D. VANE

I seem to be taking a lot of trouble about this, she thought, as she carefully re-read it. If I believed Miss de Vine, I might begin to imagine—*damn* those students!—Would anybody believe it could take one two hours to write a simple letter?

She put the letter resolutely into an envelope, and addressed and stamped it. Nobody, having put on a two-penny-half-penny stamp, was ever known to open the envelope again. That was *done*. For a couple of hours now she would devote herself to the affairs of Sheridan Le Fanu.

She worked away happily till half-past ten; the racket in the passage calmed down; words flowed smoothly. From time to time, she looked up from her paper, hesitating for a word, and saw through the window the lights of Burleigh and Queen Elizabeth burning back across the quad, counterparts of her own. Many of them, no doubt, illumined cheerful parties, like the one in the Annexe; others lent their aid to people who, like herself, were engaged in the elusive pursuit of knowledge, covering paper with ink and hesitating now and again over a word. She felt herself to be a living part of a community engaged in a common purpose. "Wilkie Collins," wrote Harriet, "was always handicapped in his treatment of the supernatural by the fatal itch" (could one be handicapped by an itch? Yes, why not?

Let it go, anyway, for the moment)—"the fatal itch to explain everything. His legal training—" Bother! Too long. ". . . was handicapped by the lawyer's fatal habit of explaining everything. His ghaisties and ghoulies"—no; worn-out humor—"His dream-phantasies and apparitions are too careful to tuck their shrouds neatly about them and leave no loose ends to trouble us. It is in Le Fanu that we find the natural maker of—natural master of—the master of the uncanny whose mastery comes by nature. If we compare—"

Before the comparison could be instituted, the lamp went suddenly out.

"Curse!" said Harriet. She rose and pressed down the wall-switch. Nothing happened. "Fused!" said Harriet, opening the door to investigate. The corridor was in darkness, and a lamentable outcry on either side proclaimed that the lights were out in the whole of Tudor.

Harriet snatched her torch from the table and turned right towards the main block of the building. She was soon swept into a crowd of students, some with torches and some clinging to those that had them, all clamoring and wanting to know what was wrong with the lights.

"Shut *up!*" said Harriet, peering behind the barrier of the torch-lights to find anybody she recognized. "The main fuse must have gone. Where's the fuse-box?"

"I think it's under the stairs," said somebody.

"Stay where you are," said Harriet. "I'll go and see."

Nobody, naturally, stayed where she was. Everybody came helpfully and angrily downstairs.

"It's the Poltergeist," said somebody.

"Let's catch her this time," said somebody else.

"Perhaps it's only blown," suggested a timid voice out of the darkness.

"Blown be blowed!" exclaimed a louder voice, scornfully. "How often does a main fuse blow?" Then, in an agitated whisper, "Hellup, it's the Chilperic. Sorry I spoke."

"Is that you, Miss Chilperic?" said Harriet, glad to round

up one member of the Senior Common Room. "Have you met Miss Barton anywhere?"

"No, I've only just got out of bed."

"Miss Barton isn't there," said a voice from the hall below, and then another voice chimed in:

"Somebody's pulled out the main fuse and taken it away!"

And then, in a shrill cry from someone at the end of the lower corridor: "There she goes! Look! running across the quad!"

Harriet was carried down the stairs with a rush of twenty or thirty students into the midst of those already milling in the hall. There was a cram in the doorway. She lost Miss Chilperic and was left behind in the struggle. Then, as she thrust her way through on to the terrace, she saw under the dim sky a string of runners stretched across the quad. Voices were calling shrilly. Then, as the first half-dozen or so of the pursuers were outlined against the blazing lower windows of Burleigh, those lights too were blacked out.

She ran, desperately—not to Burleigh, where the uproar was repeating itself, but to Queen Elizabeth, which, she judged, would be the next point of attack. The side-door would, she knew, be locked. She dashed past the hall stair and through to the portico, where she flung herself upon the main door. That was locked also. She stepped back and shouted through the nearest window: "Look out! There's somebody in here playing tricks. I'm coming in." A student put out a tousled head. Other heads appeared. "Let me get past," said Harriet, flinging the sash up, and hauling herself up over the sill. "They're putting out all the lights in College. Where's your fuse-box?"

"I'm sure I don't know," said the student, as Harriet plunged across the room.

"Of course you wouldn't!" said Harriet, unreasonably. She flung the door open and burst out—into Stygian blackness. By this time the hue-and-cry outside had reached Queen Elizabeth. Somebody found the front door and unlocked it, and the tumult increased, those within surging out and those outside surging in. A voice said: "Somebody came through my room and went out of the window, just after the lights went out." Torches appeared. Here and there a face—mostly unfamiliar—was momentarily lit up. Then the lights in the New Quad began to go out also, beginning on the South side. Everybody was running aimlessly. Harriet, dashing along the plinth, cannoned full tilt into somebody and flashed the torch in her face. It was the Dean.

"Thank God!" said Harriet. "Here's somebody in the right place." She held on to her.

"What's happening?" said the Dean.

"Stand still," said Harriet: "I'll have an alibi for you if I die for it." As she spoke, the lights on the North-East angle went out. "You're all right," said Harriet. "Now then! make for the West Staircase and we'll catch her."

The same idea seemed to have occurred to a number of other people, for the entrance to the West Staircase was blocked with a crowd of students, while a crowd of scouts, released by Carrie from their own Wing, added to the congestion. Harriet and the Dean forced a pathway through them, and found Miss Lydgate standing bewildered, and clasping her proof-sheets to her bosom, being determined that this time nothing should happen to them. They scooped her up with them—"like playing 'Staggie,'" thought Harriet—and made their way to the fuse-boxes under the stair. There they found Padgett, grimly on guard, with his trousers hastily pulled on over his pajamas and a rolling-pin in his hand.

"They don't get this," said Padgett. "You leave it to me, madam Dean, miss. Just turning into my bed, I was, all the late-leave ladies being in. My wife's telephoning across to Jackson to fetch over some new fuses. Have you seen the boxes, miss? Wrenched open with a chisel; they was, or summat of that. A nice thing to happen. But they won't get this."

Nor did "they." In the West side of the New Quad, the

Warden's House, the Infirmary, and the Scouts' Wing entrenched behind its relocked grille, the lights burned on steadily. But when Jackson arrived with the new fuses, every darkened building showed its trail of damage. While Padgett had sat by the mouse-hole, waiting for the mouse that did not come, the Poltergeist had passed through the college, breaking ink-bottles, flinging papers into the fire, smashing lamps and crockery and throwing books through the windowpanes. In the Hall, where the main fuse had also been taken, the silver cups on the High Table had been hurled at the portraits, breaking the glass, and the plaster bust of a Victorian benefactor pitched down the stone stair, to end in a fragmentary trail of detached side-whiskers and disintegrated features.

"*Well!*" said the Dean, surveying the wreckage. "That's *one* thing to be grateful for. We've seen the last of the Reverend Melchisedek Entwistle. But, oh, *lord!*"

CHAPTER X

Some say thy fault is youth, some wantonness,
Some say thy grace is youth and gentle sport;
Both grace and faults are loved of more and less;
Thou makst faults graces that to thee resort.
WILLIAM SHAKESPEARE

It would seem, at first sight, as though, in an episode witnessed by so many people and lasting altogether about an hour (counting, that is, from the first alarm in Tudor to the refitting of the final fuse) it should have been easy to find alibis for all the innocent. In practice, it was not so at all, chiefly owing to the stubborn refusal of human beings to stay where they are put. It was the very multiplicity of witnesses that made the difficulty; for it seemed likely that the culprit had mixed with the crowd over and over again in the dark. Some alibis were established for certain: Harriet and the Dean had been standing together when the lights were extinguished on the North-east angle of the New Quad; the Warden had not left her own house till after the uproar had started, as her household staff could attest; the two porters were vouched for by their respective wives, and had, in fact, never been suspected, since on various earlier occasions disturbances had occurred while they were at their posts; the Infirmarian and the Infirmary maid had also been together the whole time. Miss Hudson, the student who had been considered a "possible," had been at a coffee-party when the trouble began, and was clear; Miss Lydgate also, to Harriet's great relief, had been in Queen Elizabeth, enjoying the hospitality of a party of Third Years; she had just risen to say good night, remarking that it was past her usual time, when the lights had gone out. She had then been caught up in the throng and, as soon as she could free herself, had run hastily up to her own room to rescue her proofs.

Other members of the S.C.R. were less fortunately placed. The case of Miss Barton was exciting and mysterious. According to her own account, she had been sitting working when the fuse was pulled out in Tudor. After trying the wall-switch, she had looked out of the window, seen the figure hastening across the quad, and gone immediately in pursuit. The figure had dodged her round Burleigh twice, and had then suddenly come upon her from behind, flung her against the wall "with extraordinary strength" and knocked her torch from her hand. Before she could recover herself, the evil-doer had extinguished the Burleigh lights and gone again. Miss Barton could give no description of this person, except that it wore "something dark" and ran very fast. She had not seen its face. The only proof of this story was that Miss Barton certainly had received a heavy bruise on the side of the face where, so she said, she had been flung against an angle of the building. She had remained where she lay for a few minutes after receiving the blow; by that time the excitement had spread to the New Quad. Here she had certainly been seen for a few seconds together by a pair of students. She had then run to look for the Dean, found her room empty, run out again and joined Harriet and the rest in the West Staircase.

Miss Chilperic's story was equally difficult of proof. When the cry of "There she goes!" had been raised at Tudor, she had been among the first to run out, but, having no torch, and being too much excited to notice where she was going, she had tripped and fallen down the steps of the terrace, twisting her foot slightly. This had made her late in arriving on the scene. She had come up with the crowd at Queen Elizabeth, been carried in with it through the portico and run straight into the New Quadrangle Buildings. She had thought she heard footsteps scurrying along to her right, and had followed them, when the lights had gone out and, not knowing the building at all well, she had wandered about in some confusion, till at last she found the way out into the Quad. Nobody seemed able to remember seeing Miss Chilperic at all after she left Tudor; she was that kind of person.

The Treasurer had been sitting up at work on the term's accounts. The lights in her building had been the last to go out, and her windows looked outward upon the road and not upon the quad, so that she had known nothing about the affair till a late stage in the proceedings. When the darkness fell on her she went (so she said) to the Bursar's set opposite, electrical replacements being in the Bursar's department. The Bursar was not in her bedroom or office; but as Miss Allison came out from looking for her, she emerged from the place where the fuse-boxes were, to announce the disappearance of the main fuse. Treasurer and Bursar had then joined the crowd in the quadrangle.

The account given by Miss Pyke of her movements seemed to be the most incredible of all. She lived above the Treasurer and had been working at an article for a learned Society's transactions. When her lights had gone out, she had said, "Bother!", taken a pair of candles from a stock which she kept for such emergencies, and gone quietly on working.

Miss Burrows asserted that she had been having a bath when the Burleigh Building Lights failed, and, by an extraordinary coincidence, had found, on getting hastily out of it, that she had left her towel in her bedroom. She did not possess a self-contained set with a private bathroom, and so was obliged to grope, with her dressing-gown clutched about her dripping body, along the passage to her bedroom, and there dry and dress herself in the dark. This had taken a surprisingly long time and, when she came up with the main party, most of the fun was over. No proof, except the undoubted presence of soapy water in a bathroom on her floor.

Miss Shaw's set was over the Bursar's, and her bedroom looked out on St. Cross Road. She had gone to bed and to sleep, being very tired, and knew nothing about it till it was all over. The same story was told by Mrs. Goodwin, who had returned to College only that day, rather exhausted by sick-nursing. As for Miss Hillyard and Miss de Vine, living above Miss Lydgate; their lights had never gone out at all, and, their windows facing on the road, they had never known that anything was wrong, putting down a vague noise in the quad to the natural cussedness of undergraduates.

It had only been after Padgett had sat for about five minutes in vain at the mousehole, that Harriet had done what she should have done earlier, and attempted to make a count of the Senior Common Room. She had then found them all in the places where, by their subsequent accounts of themselves, they should have been. But to collect them all into one lighted room and keep them there was not so easy. She established Miss Lydgate in her own room and went to look for the rest, asking them to go straight down to Miss Lydgate's room and stay there. The Warden, meanwhile, had arrived and was addressing the students, imploring them also to stay where they were and keep quiet. Unfortunately, just as it began to seem possible to make sure of everybody's whereabouts, some inquisitive person, who had broken away from the rest, had gone roaming through the Old Quad, arrived, breathless, to announce the tale of damage in the Hall. Instantly, pandemonium broke loose again. Dons who were trotting like lambs into the sheep-fold suddenly lost their heads and raced with the students into the darkness. Miss Burrows screamed "The Library!" and tore away, and the Bursar, with an anguished cry for the College property, dashed after her. The Dean called, "Stop them!" and Miss Pyke and Miss Hillyard, taking the command to themselves, rushed out and disappeared. In the resulting confusion, everybody got lost twenty times over; and by the time the fuses were replaced and the community at last gathered and numbered, the damage had all been done.

It is surprising how much can be done in a very few minutes. Harriet calculated that the Hall had probably been wrecked first of all, being in a detached wing, where noise was not likely to attract much attention; all that was done there could have been done in a couple of minutes. From the extinguishing of the first lights in Tudor to that of the last lights in the New Quad, rather less than ten minutes had elapsed. The third, and longest part of the business—the wrecking of the rooms in the darkened buildings, had taken anything from a quarter to half an hour.

The Warden addressed the College after Chapel, again enjoining discretion, begging the culprit to come forward, and promising that all possible measures should be taken to identify her in case she did not confess.

"I have no intention," said Dr. Baring, "of inflicting any restriction or punishment upon the college in general for the act of one irresponsible person. I will ask anyone who has any suggestion to make or any evidence to offer with regard to the identity of this foolish practical joker to come privately, either to the Dean or myself, and make the communication in strict confidence."

She added a few words about the solidarity of the College and departed with a grave face, her gown flowing behind her.

The glaziers were already at work restoring damaged window-panes. In the Hall, the Bursar was affixing neat cards in the places of portraits whose glass had been broken: "Portrait of Miss Matheson: Warden 1899–1912. Removed for cleaning." Broken crockery was being swept from the grass of the Old Quad. The College was engaged in presenting a serene face to the world.

• • • • •

It did not improve anybody's temper to discover a printed message, consisting of "HA! HA!" and a vulgar epithet, pasted across the mirror in the Senior Common Room, shortly before lunch. The Common Room had been empty from 9 o'clock onwards, so far as was known. The Common Room maid, going in at lunch-time with the coffee-cups, had been the first to see the notice; and it had by then dried hard. The Bursar, who had missed her pot of Gloy after the night's excitement, found it placed neatly in the center of the S.C.R. mantelpiece.

The feeling in the Senior Common Room after this episode underwent a subtle alteration. Tongues were sharpened; the veneer of detachment began to wear thin; the uneasiness of suspicion began to make itself felt; only Miss Lydgate and the Dean, being proved innocent, remained unmoved.

"Your bad luck seems to have repeated itself, Miss Barton," observed Miss Pyke, acidly. "Both in the Library affair and in this last outbreak, you seem to have been first on the spot and yet unhappily prevented from securing the culprit."

"Yes," said Miss Barton. "It's very unfortunate. If next time my gown gets taken as well, the College sleuth will begin to smell a rat."

"Very trying for you, Mrs. Goodwin," said Miss Hillyard, "to come back to all this upset, just when you needed a rest. I trust your little boy is better. It is particularly tiresome, because all the time you were away we had no disturbance at all."

"It's most annoying," said Mrs. Goodwin. "The poor creature who does these things must be quite demented. Of course these disorders do tend to occur in celibate, or chiefly celibate communities. It is a kind of compensation, I suppose, for the lack of other excitements."

• • • • •

"The great mistake," said Miss Burrows, "was, of course, our not keeping together. Naturally I wanted to see if any damage had been done in the Library—but why so many people should have come pelting after me—"

"The Hall was my concern," said the Bursar.

"Oh! you *did* get to the Hall? I completely lost sight of you in the quad."

"That," said Miss Hillyard, "was exactly the catastrophe I was trying to avoid when I pursued you. I called loudly to you to stop. You *must* have heard me."

"There was too much noise to hear anything," said Miss Stevens.

"I came to Miss Lydgate's room," said Miss Shaw, "the moment I could get dressed, understanding that everybody was to be there. But there was really nobody. I thought I must have misunderstood, so I tried to find Miss Vane, but she seemed to have gone off into the Ewigkeit."

"It must have taken you a remarkably long time to dress," said Miss Burrows. "Anybody could run three times round College in the time it takes you to pull your stockings on."

"Somebody," said Miss Shaw, "apparently *did*."

"They're beginning to get fractious," said Harriet to the Dean.

"What *can* you expect? The silly cuckoos! If they'd *only* sat tight on their little behinds last night, we could have cleared the whole business up. It's not *your* fault. You couldn't be everywhere at once. *How* we can expect discipline from the students, when a whole bunch of middle-aged seniors behave like a flock of *hens* in a crisis, I can't think. Who's that out there, conducting that strident conversation with a top window? Oh! I think it's Baker's young man. Well, discipline must be observed, I suppose. Give me the house-telephone, would you? Thanks. I don't see how we're to prevent this last outbreak from getting— Oh! Martha! The Dean's compliments, if you please, to Miss Baker, and will she kindly bear in mind the rule about morning visitors—And the students are getting rather annoyed about the destruction of their property. I think they're actually getting worked up to calling a J.C.R. meeting, and it's very unfair on them, poor lambs, to let *them* go on suspecting one another, but what *can* we do about it? Thank God, it's the last week of term! I suppose we're not making a ghastly mistake? It must be one of us, and not a student or a scout."

"We seem to have eliminated the students—unless it's a conspiracy between two of them. It might be that. Hudson and Cattermole together. But as for the scouts—I can show you this, now, I suppose. Would any of the scouts quote Virgil?"

"No," said the Dean, examining the "Harpy" passage. "No; it doesn't seem likely. Oh, dear!"

The reply to Harriet's letter arrived by return.

MY DEAR HARRIET,

It is exceedingly good of you to be bothered with my graceless nephew. I am afraid the episode must have left you with an unfortunate impression of both of us.

I am very fond of the boy, and he is, as you say, attractive; but he is rather easily led, and my brother is not, in my opinion, handling him in the wisest way. Considering his expectations, Gerald is kept absurdly short of money, and naturally he feels he has a right to anything he can lay hands on. Still, he must learn to draw the line between carelessness and dishonesty. I have offered to augment his allowance myself, but the suggestion was not well received at home. His parents, I know, feel that I am stealing his confidence from them; but if I refused to help him, he would go elsewhere and get himself into worse trouble. Though I do not like the position into which I am forced of "Codlin is the friend, not Short," I still think it better that he should turn to me than to an outsider. I call this family pride; it may be mere vanity; I know it is vexation of spirit.

Let me assure you that so far, when I have trusted

Gerald with anything, he has not let me down. He is amenable to some of the shibboleths. But he is not amenable to a discipline of alternate indulgence and severity; and indeed I do not know who is.

I must again apologize for troubling you with our family affairs. What on earth are you doing in Oxford? Have you retired from the world to pursue the contemplative life? I will not attempt to dissuade you now, but shall address you on the subject in the usual form on the 1st April next.

Yours in all gratitude,
P.D.B.W.

I had forgotten to say, thank you for telling me about the accident and reassuring me as to its results. It was the first I had heard of it—as old James Forsyte says, "Nobody ever tells me anything." I will oblige with a few kind words.

"Poor old Peter!" said Harriet.

The remark probably deserves to be included in an anthology of Great First Occasions.

Lord Saint-George, when she went to pay him a parting visit, was considerably improved in appearance; but his expression was worried. His bed strewn with untidy papers, he seemed to be trying to cope with his affairs and to be making but heavy weather of it. He brightened up considerably at sight of Harriet.

"Oh, look! You're just the person I've been praying for. I've no head for this kind of thing, and all the beastly bills keep sliding off the bed. I can write my name pretty well, but I can't keep track of things. I'm sure I've paid some of these brutes twice over."

"Let me help; can I?"

"I hoped you'd say that. It's so nice of you to spoil me, isn't it? I can't think how things mount up so. They rook one shockingly at these places. But one must have something to eat, mustn't one? And belong to a few clubs. And play a game or two. Of course polo comes a bit expensive, but it's rather done just now. It's nothing, really. Of course, the mistake was going round with that bunch in Town last vac. Mother imagines they're O.K. because they're in the stud-book, but they're pretty hot, really. She'll be no end surprised if they end up in gaol, and her white-headed boy with them. Sad degeneracy of old landed families, and that kind of thing. Solemn rebuke by learned judge. I somehow got behindhand with things about the New Year, and never caught up again. It looks to me as though Uncle Peter was going to get a bit of a shock. He's written, by the way. Much more like himself."

He tossed the letter over.

DEAR JERRY,

Of all the thundering nuisances that ever embittered the lives of their long-suffering relatives, you are the worst. For God's sake put down that racing car before you kill yourself; strange as it may appear, I still retain some lingering remnants of affection for you. I hope they take your license away for life, and I hope you feel like hell. You probably do. Don't worry any more about the money.

I am writing to thank Miss Vane for her kindness to you. She is a person whose good opinion I value, so be merciful to my feelings as a man and an uncle.

Bunter has just found three silver threads among the gold. He is incredibly shocked. He begs to tender you his respectful commiseration, and advises scalp-massage (for me, I mean).

When you can manage it, send a line to report progress to your querulous and rapidly-decaying uncle.

P.W.

"He'll get a whole crop of silver threads when he realizes that I hadn't paid up the insurance," said the viscount, callously, as he took the letter back.

"What!"

"Fortunately there was nobody else involved, and the police weren't on the spot. But I suppose I shall hear from the Post Office about their blasted telegraph pole. If I have to go before the magistrates and the Governor hears of it, he'll be annoyed. It'll cost a bit to get the car put right. I'd throw the damned thing away, only Dad gave it to me in one of his generous fits. And of course, about the first thing he asked when I came out from under was whether the insurance was all right. And being in no state to argue, I said Yes. If only it doesn't get into the papers about the insurance, we're all right—only the repairs will make a nice little item in Uncle Peter's total."

"Is it fair to make him pay for that?"

"Damned unfair," said Lord Saint-George, cheerfully. "The Governor ought to pay the insurance himself. He's like the Old Man of Thermopylae—never does anything properly. If you come to that, it isn't fair to make Uncle Peter pay for all the horses that fall down when one backs them. Or for all the rotten little gold-diggers one carts round, either—I shall have to lump *them* together under 'Sundries.' And he'll say, 'Ah, yes! Postage stamps, telephone calls and live wires.' And then I shall lose my head and say, 'Well, Uncle—' I hate those sentences that start with 'Well, Uncle.' They always seem to go on and on and lead anywhere."

"I don't suppose he'll ask for details, if you don't volunteer them. Look! I've got all these bills sorted. Shall I write out the cheques for you to sign?"

"I wish you would. No, he won't ask. He'll only sit looking harmless till I tell him. I suppose that's the way he gets criminals to come across with it. It's not a nice characteristic. Have you got that note from Levy? That's the main thing. And there's a letter from a chap called Cartwright that's rather important. I borrowed a bit from him up in Town once or twice. What's he make it come to? . . . Oh, rot! It can't be as much as that . . . Let's see . . . Well, I suppose he's right . . . And Archie Campbell—he's my bookmaker—God! what a lot of screws! they oughtn't to allow the poor beasts out. And the odds-and-ends here? What a marvelously neat way you have with these things, haven't you? Shall we tot them all up and see where we get to? Then if I faint, you can ring the bell for Nurse."

"I'm not very good at arithmetic. You'd better check this up. It looks a bit unlikely, but I can't make it come any less."

"Add on, say a hundred and fifty, estimated repairs to car, and then we'll see. Oh, hell! what have we here?"

"The portrait of a blinking idiot," said Harriet, irresistibly.

"Amazin' fellow, Shakespeare. The apt word for all occasions. Yes; there's a 'Well, Uncle' look about this, all right. Of course, I get my quarter's allowance at the end of the month, but there's the vac. to get through and all next term. One thing, I'll have to go home and be good; can't get about the place much like this. The Governor more or less hinted that I ought to pay my own doctor's bill, but I wasn't taking the hint. Mother blames Uncle Peter for the whole thing."

"Why on earth?"

"Setting me a bad example of furious driving. He is a bit hot, of course, but he never seems to get my foul luck."

"Can he possibly be a better driver?"

"Darling Harriet, that's unkind. You don't mind my calling you Harriet?"

"As a matter of fact, I do, rather."

"But I can't keep on saying 'Miss Vane' to a person who knows all my hideous secrets. Perhaps I'd better accustom myself to saying 'Aunt Harriet' . . . What's wrong with that? You simply can't refuse to be an adopted aunt to me. My Aunt Mary has gone all domestic and hasn't time for me, and my mother's sisters are the original gorgons. I'm dreadfully unappreciated and quite auntless for all practical purposes."

"You deserve neither aunts nor uncles, considering how

you treat them. Do you mean to finish these cheques today? Because, if not, I have other things to do."

"Very well. We will continue to rob Peter to pay all. It's wonderful what a good influence you have over me. Unbending devotion to duty. If you'd only take me in hand I might turn out quite well after all."

"Sign, please."

"But you don't seem very susceptible. Poor Uncle Peter!"

"It will be poor Uncle Peter by the time you've finished."

"That's what I mean. Fifty-three, nineteen, four—it's shocking the way other people smoke one's fags, and I'm sure my scout bags half of them. Twenty-six, twelve, eight. Nineteen, seven, two. A hundred quid gone before you've time to look at it. Thirty-one, fourteen. Twelve, nine, six. Five, fifteen, three. What's all this tale about ghosts playing merry hell in Shrewsbury?"

Harriet jumped. "Damn! which of our little beasts told you about that?"

"None of 'em told *me*. I don't encourage women students. Nice girls, no doubt, but too grubby. There's a chap on my staircase who came up today with a story. . . . I forget, he told me not to mention it. What's it all about? and why the hush-hush?"

"Oh, dear! and they were implored not to talk. They never think of the harm this kind of thing does to the College."

"Well, but it's only a rag, isn't it?"

"I'm afraid it's a bit more than that. Look here, if I tell you why it's hush-hush, will you promise not to pass it on?"

"Well," said Lord Saint-George, candidly, "you know how my tongue runs away with me. I'm not very dependable."

"Your uncle says you are."

"Uncle Peter? Good lord! he must be potty. Sad to see a fine brain going to rack and ruin. Of course, he's not as young as he was. . . . You're looking very sober about it."

"It is rather grim, really. We're afraid the trouble's caused by somebody who's not quite right in her head. Not a student—but of course we can't very well tell the students that, especially when we don't know who it is."

The viscount stared. "Good lord! How beastly for you! I quite see your point. Naturally you don't want a thing like that to get about. Well, I'll not say a word—honestly, I won't. And if anybody mentions it I'll register a concentrated expression of no enthusiasm. I say! Do you know, I wonder if I've met your ghost."

"Met her?"

"Yes. I certainly met somebody who didn't seem quite all there. It scared me a bit. You'll be the first person I've told about it."

"When was this? Tell me about it."

"End of last term. I was awfully short of cash, and I'd had a bet with a man that I'd get into Shrewsbury and—" He stopped and looked up at her with the smile that was so uncannily not his own. "What do you know about that?"

"If you mean that bit of the wall by the private gate, it's having a set of spikes put on it. The revolving sort."

"Ah! all is known. Well, it wasn't an awfully good night for it—full moon and all that—but it seemed about the last chance to get that ten quid, so I hopped over. There's a bit of a garden there."

"The Fellows' Garden. Yes."

"Yes. Well, I was just pushing along there, when somebody hopped out from behind a bush and grabbed me. My heart nearly shot right out of my mouth on to the lawn. I wanted to do a bunk."

"What was the person like?"

"It was in black and had a bit of black stuff sort of twisted round its head. I couldn't see anything but its eyes, and they looked beastly. So I said, 'Oh, gosh!' and she said, 'Which of 'em do you want?' in a horrid voice, like glue. Well, that wasn't nice and not what I expected. I don't pretend to be a good boy, but such were not my intentions at the time. So I said, 'Nothing of that sort; I only made a bet I wouldn't be caught, and I have been caught, so I'll go away and I'm sorry.' So she said, 'Yes, go away. We murder beautiful boys like you and eat their hearts out.' So I said, 'Good God! how very unpleasant!' I didn't like it a bit."

"Are you making all this up?"

"Honestly, I'm not. Then she said, 'The other one had fair hair, too.' And I said, 'No, did he really?' And she said something, I forget what—it seemed to me she had a kind of hungry look about her, if you know what I mean—and anyhow, it was all most uncomfortable, and I said, 'Excuse me, I think I'd better be getting along,' and I pulled free (she was uncommonly strong in the wrists) and legged it over the wall like one, John Smith."

Harriet looked at him, but he appeared to be perfectly serious.

"How tall was she?"

"About your height, I should think, or a bit less. Honestly, I was too scared to notice much. I couldn't recognize her again, I don't think. She didn't give me the impression of being a young thing, and that's about all I can tell you."

"And you say you've kept this remarkable story to yourself?"

"Yes. Doesn't sound like me, does it? But there was something about it—I don't know. If I'd told any of the men, they'd have thought it howlingly funny. But it wasn't. So I didn't mention it. It didn't seem the right thing, somehow."

"I'm glad you didn't want it laughed at."

"No. The boy has quite nice instincts. Well, that's all. Twenty-five, eleven, nine; that blasted car simply eats oil and petrol—all those big engines do. It's going to be awfully awkward about that insurance. Please, dear Aunt Harriet, need I do any more of these? They depress me."

"You can leave them till I've gone, and write all the cheques and envelopes yourself."

"Slave-driver. I shall burst into tears."

"I'll fetch you a handkerchief."

"You are the most unwomanly woman I ever met. Uncle

Peter has my sincere sympathy. Look at this! Sixty-nine, fifteen—account rendered; I wonder what it was all about."

Harriet said nothing but continued to make out the cheques.

"One thing, there doesn't seem to be much at Blackwell's. A mere trifle of six pounds twelve."

"One halfpennyworth of bread to this intolerable deal of sack."

"Did you catch that habit of quotation from Uncle Peter?"

"You needn't lay any *more* burdens on your uncle's shoulders."

"Must you rub it in? There's practically nothing at the wine-merchant's either. Hard drinking has quite gone out. Isn't that satisfactory? Of course, the Governor obliges with a bottle or two from time to time. Did you like that Niersteiner the other day? Uncle Peter obliged with that. How many more of these things are there?"

"Quite a few."

"Oh! My arm aches horribly."

"If you're really too tired—"

"No, I can manage."

Half an hour later, Harriet said. "That's the lot."

"Thank God! Now talk prettily to me."

"No; I must get back now. I'll post these on my way."

"You're not really going? Right away?"

"Yes; right away to London."

"Wish I was you. Shall you be up next term?"

"I don't know."

"Oh, dear, oh, dear! Well, kiss me good-bye nicely."

Since she could think of no form of refusal that might not provoke some nerve-shattering comment, Harriet sedately complied. She was turning to go, when the nurse arrived to announce another visitor. This was a young woman, dressed in the more foolish extreme of the current fashion, with an intoxicated-looking hat and bright purple fingernails, who advanced, crying sympathetically:

"Oh, darling Jerry! How too ruinously shattering!"

"Good lord, Gillian!" said the viscount, without very much enthusiasm. "How did you—?"

"My lamb! You don't sound very pleased to see me."

Harriet escaped, and found the nurse in the passage, putting an armful of roses in a bowl.

"I hope I haven't tired your patient too much with all that business."

"I'm glad you came to help him out with it; it was on his mind. Aren't these roses beautiful? The young lady brought them from London. He gets a lot of visitors. But you can't wonder, can you? He's a dear boy, and the things he says to Sister! It's as much as one can do to keep a straight face. He's looking a lot better now, don't you think? Mr. Whybrow's made a beautiful job of the cut on his head. He's got his stitches out now—oh, yes! it'll hardly show at all. It *is* a mercy, isn't it? Because he's ever so handsome."

"Yes; he's a very good-looking young man."

"He takes after his father. Do you know the Duke of Denver? He's ever so handsome, too. I shouldn't call the Duchess good-looking; more distinguished. She was terribly afraid he might be disfigured for life, and it *would* have been a pity. But Mr. Whybrow's a splendid surgeon. You'll see he'll be quite all right. Sister's ever so pleased—we tell her she's quite lost her heart to Number Fifteen. I'm sure we shall all be sorry to say good-bye to him; he keeps us all lively."

"I expect he does."

"And the way he pulls Matron's leg. Impudent young monkey, she calls him, but she can't help laughing at his ways. Oh, dear! there's Number Seventeen ringing again. I expect she wants a bed-pan. You know your way out, don't you?"

Harriet departed; feeling that it might be rather an onerous position to be aunt to Lord Saint-George.

"Of course," said the Dean, "if anything should happen in vacation—"

"I rather doubt if it will," said Harriet. "Not a big enough audience. A public scandal is the thing aimed at, I imagine. But if another episode should occur, it will narrow the field."

"Yes; most of the S.C.R. will be away. Next term, what with the Warden, Miss Lydgate and myself definitely clear of suspicion, we ought to be able to patrol the place better. What are you going to do?"

"I don't know. I've been rather thinking of coming back to Oxford altogether for a time, to do some work. This place gets you. It's so completely uncommercial. I think I'm getting a little shrill in my mind. I need mellowing."

"Why not work for a B.Litt.?"

"That would be rather fun. I'm afraid they wouldn't accept Le Fanu, would they? It would have to be somebody duller. I should enjoy a little dullness. One would have to go on writing novels for bread and butter, but I'd like an academic and meaty egg to my tea for a change."

"Well, I hope you'll come back for part of next term, anyway. You can't leave Miss Lydgate now till those proofs are in the printer's hands."

"I'm almost afraid to set her loose this vac. She is dissatisfied with her chapter on Gerard Manley Hopkins; she feels she may have attacked him from the wrong angle altogether."

"Oh, *no!*"

"I'm afraid it's Oh, yes! . . . Well, I'll cope with that, anyway. And the rest—well, we shall see what happens."

Harriet left Oxford just after lunch. As she was putting her suitcase in the car, Padgett came up to her.

"Excuse me, miss, but the Dean thinks you would like to see this, miss. In Miss de Vine's fireplace it was found this morning, miss."

Harriet looked at the half-burnt sheet of crumpled newspaper. Letters had been cut out from the advertising columns.

"Is Miss de Vine still in College?"

"She left by the 10:10, miss."

"I'll keep this, Padgett, thank you. Does Miss de Vine usually read the *Daily Trumpet?*"

"I shouldn't think so, miss. It would be more likely the *Times* or *Telegraph*. But you could easy find out."

"Of course, anybody might have dropped this in the fireplace. It proves nothing. But I'm very glad to have seen it. Good morning, Padgett."

"Good morning, miss."

CHAPTER XI

Leave me, O Love, which reachest but to dust;
And thou, my mind, aspire to higher things;
Grow rich in that which never taketh rust,
Whatever fades, but fading pleasures brings.
Draw in thy beams, and humble all thy might
To that sweet yoke where lasting freedoms be;
Which breaks the clouds, and opens forth the light
That doth both shine and give us sight to see.

SIR PHILIP SIDNEY

Town seemed remarkably empty and uninteresting. Yet a lot of things were going on. Harriet saw her agent and publisher, signed a contract for serial rights, heard the inner history of the quarrel between Lord Gobbersleigh, the newspaper proprietor, and Mr. Adrian Cloot, the reviewer, entered warmly into the triangular dispute raging among Gargantua Colour-Talkies Ltd., Mr. Garrick Drury, the actor, and Mrs. Snell-Wilmington, author of *Passion-flower Pie*, and into the details of Miss Sugar Toobin's monstrous libel action against the *Daily Headline*, and was, of course, passionately interested to learn that Jacqueline Squills had made a malicious exposé of her second divorced husband's habits and character in her new novel, *Gas-Filled Bulbs*.

Yet, somehow, these distractions failed to keep her amused. To make matters worse, her new mystery novel had got somehow stuck. She had five suspects, neatly confined in an old water-mill with no means of entrance or egress except by a plank bridge, and all provided with motives and alibis for a pleasantly original kind of murder. There seemed to be nothing fundamentally wrong with the thing. But the permutations and combinations of the five people's relationships were beginning to take on an unnatural, an incredible symmetry. Human beings were not like that; human problems were not like that; what you really got was two hundred or so people running like rabbits in and out of a college, doing their work, living their lives, and actuated all the time by motives unfathomable even to themselves, and then, in the midst of it all—not a plain, understandable murder, but an unmeaning and inexplicable lunacy.

How could one, in any case, understand other people's motives and feelings, when one's own remained mysterious? Why did one look forward with irritation to the receipt of a letter on April 1st, and then feel alarmed and affronted when it did not arrive by the first post? Very likely the letter had been sent to Oxford. There was no possible urgency about it, since one knew what it would contain and how it had to be answered; but it was annoying to sit about, expecting it.

Ring. Enter secretary with telegram (this was probably it). Wordy and unnecessary cable from American magazine representative to say she was shortly arriving in England and very anxious to talk to Miss Harriet Vane about a story for their publication. Cordially. What on earth did these people want to talk about? You did not write stories by talking about them.

Ring. Second post. Letter with Italian stamp. (Slight delay in sorting, no doubt.) Oh, thank you, Miss Bracey. Imbecile, writing very bad English, was eager to translate Miss Vane's works into Italian. Could Miss Vane inform the writer of what books she had composed? Translators were all like that—no English, no sense, no backing. Harriet said briefly what she thought of them, told Miss Bracey to refer the matter to the agent and returned to her dictation.

"Wilfrid stared at the handkerchief. What was it doing

there in Winchester's bedroom? With a curious feeling of . . ."

Telephone. Hold on a moment, please. (It couldn't very well be that; it would be ridiculous to put through an expensive foreign call.) Hullo! Yes. Speaking. Oh?

She might have known it. There was a kind of mild determination about Reggie Pomfret. Would Miss Vane, could Miss Vane put up with his company for dinner and the new show at the Palladium? That night? the next night? Any night? That very night? Mr. Pomfret was inarticulate with pleasure. Thank you. Ring off. Where were we, Miss Bracey?

"With a curious feeling of—Oh, yes, Wilfrid. Very distressing for Wilfrid to find his young woman's handkerchief in the murdered man's bedroom. Agonizing. A curious feeling of—What should you feel like under the circumstances, Miss Bracey?"

"I should think the laundry had made a mistake, I expect."

"Oh, Miss Bracey! Well—we'd better say it was a lace handkerchief. *Winchester* couldn't have mistaken a lace handkerchief for one of his own, whatever the laundry sent him."

"But would Ada have used a lace handkerchief, Miss Vane? Because she's been made rather a boyish, out-door person. And it's not as if she was in evening dress, because it was so important she should turn up in a tweed costume."

"That's true. Well—well, better make the handkerchief small, but not lace. Plain but good. Turn back to the description of the handkerchief. . . . Oh, dear! No, I'll answer it. Yes? *Yes?* YES! . . . No, I'm afraid I can't possibly. No, really. Oh? Well, you had better ask my agents. Yes, that's right. Good-bye. . . . Some club wanting a debate on 'Should Genius Marry?' The question's not likely to concern any of their members personally, so why do they bother? . . . Yes, Miss Bracey? Oh, yes, Wilfrid. Bother Wilfrid! I'm taking quite a dislike to the man."

By tea-time, Wilfrid was behaving so tiresomely that Harriet put him away in a rage and sallied out to attend a literary cocktail party. The room in which it was held was exceedingly hot and crowded, and all the assembled authors were discussing (*a*) publishers, (*b*) agents, (*c*) their own sales, (*d*) other people's sales, and (*e*) the extraordinary behavior of the Book of the Moment selectors in awarding their ephemeral crown to Tasker Hepplewater's *Mock Turtle*. "I finished this book," one distinguished adjudicator had said, "with the tears running down my face." The author of *Serpent's Fang* confided to Harriet over a *petite saucisse* and a glass of sherry that they must have been tears of pure boredom; but the author of *Dust and Shiver* said, No—they were probably tears of merriment, called forth by the unintentional humor of the book; had she ever met Hepplewater? A very angry young woman, whose book had been passed over, declared that the whole thing was a notorious farce. The Book of the Moment was selected from each publisher's list in turn, so that her own *Ariadne Adams* was automatically excluded from benefit, owing to the mere fact that her publisher's imprint had been honored in the previous January. She had, however, received private assurance that the critic of the *Morning Star* had sobbed like a child over the last hundred pages of *Ariadne*, and would probably make it his Book of the Fortnight, if only the publisher could be persuaded to take advertising space in the paper. The author of *The Squeezed Lemon* agreed that advertising was at the bottom of it: had they heard how the *Daily Flashlight* had tried to blackmail Humphrey Quint into advertising with them? And how, on his refusal, they had said darkly, "Well, you know what will happen, Mr. Quint?" And how no single Quint book had received so much as a review from the *Flashlight* ever since? And how Quint had advertised that fact in the *Morning Star* and sent up his net sales 50 per cent. in consequence? Well, by some fantastic figure, anyhow. But the author of *Primrose Dalliance* said that with the Book of the Moment crowd, what counted was Personal Pull—surely they remembered that Hepplewater had married Walton Strawberry's latest wife's sister. The author of *Jocund Day* agreed about the Pull, but thought that in this instance it was political, because there was some powerful anti-Fascist propaganda in *Mock Turtle* and it was well known that you could always get old Sneep Fortescue with a good smack at the Blackshirts.

"But what's *Mock Turtle* about?" inquired Harriet.

On this point the authors were for the most part vague; but a young man who wrote humorous magazine stories, and could therefore afford to be wide-minded about novels, said he had read it and thought it rather interesting, only a bit long. It was about a swimming instructor at a watering-place, who had contracted such an unfortunate anti-nudity complex through watching so many bathing-beauties that it completely inhibited all his natural emotions. So he got a job on a whaler and fell in love at first sight with an Eskimo, because she was such a beautiful bundle of garments. So he married her and brought her back to live in a suburb, where she fell in love with a vegetarian nudist. So then the husband went slightly mad and contracted a complex about giant turtles, and spent all his spare time staring into the turtle-tank at the Aquarium, and watching the strange, slow monsters swimming significantly round in their encasing shells. But of course a lot of things came into it—it was one of those books that reflect the author's reactions to Things in General. Altogether, significant was, he thought, the word to describe it.

Harriet began to feel that there might be something to be said even for the plot of *Death 'twixt Wind and Water*. It was, at least, significant of nothing in particular.

Harriet went back, irritated, to Mecklenburg Square. As she entered the house, she could hear her telephone ringing apoplectically on the first floor. She ran upstairs hastily —one never knew with telephone calls. As she thrust her key into the lock, the telephone stopped dead.

"Damn!" said Harriet. There was an envelope lying inside the door. It contained press cuttings. One referred to her as Miss Vines and said she had taken her degree at Cambridge; a second compared her work unfavorably with that of an American thriller-writer; a third was a belated review of her last book, which gave away the plot; a fourth attributed somebody else's thriller to her and stated that she "adopted a sporting outlook on life" (whatever that might mean). "This," said Harriet, much put out, "is one of those days! April the First, indeed! And now I've got to dine with this dashed undergraduate, and be made to feel the burden of incalculable age."

To her surprise, however, she enjoyed both the dinner and the show. There was a refreshing lack of complication about Reggie Pomfret. He knew nothing about literary jealousies; he had no views about the comparative importance of personal and professional loyalties; he laughed heartily at obvious jokes; he did not expose your nerve-centers or his own; he did not use words with double meanings; he did not challenge you to attack him and then suddenly roll himself into an armadillo-like ball, presenting a smooth, defensive surface of ironical quotations; he had no overtones of any kind; he was a good-natured, not very clever, young man, eager to give pleasure to someone who had shown him a kindness. Harriet found him quite extraordinarily restful.

"Will you come up for a moment and have a drink or anything?" said Harriet, on her own doorstep.

"Thanks awfully," said Mr. Pomfret, "if it isn't too late."

He instructed the taxi to wait and galumphed happily up. Harriet opened the door of the flat and switched the light on. Mr. Pomfret stooped courteously to pick up the letter lying on the mat.

"Oh, thank you," said Harriet.

She preceded him into the sitting-room and let him remove her cloak for her. A moment or two later, she became aware that she was still holding the letter in her hand and that her guest and she were still standing.

"I beg your pardon. Do sit down."

"Please—" said Mr. Pomfret, with a gesture that indicated, "Read it and don't mind me."

"It's nothing," said Harriet, tossing the envelope on the table. "I know what's in it. What will you have? Will you help yourself?"

Mr. Pomfret surveyed such refreshments as offered themselves and asked what he might mix for her. The drink question being settled, there was a pause.

"Er—by the way," said Mr. Pomfret, "is Miss Cattermole all right? I haven't seen very much of her since—since that night when I made your acquaintance, you know. Last time we met she said she was working rather hard."

"Oh, yes. I believe she is. She's got Mods next term."

"Oh, poor girl! She has a great admiration for you."

"Has she? I don't know why. I seem to remember ticking her off rather brutally."

"Well, you were fairly firm with me. But I agree with Miss Cattermole. Absolutely. I mean, we agree about having a great admiration for you."

"How nice of you," said Harriet, inattentively.

"Yes, really. Rather. I'll never forget the way you tackled that fellow Jukes. Did you see he got himself into trouble only a week or so later?"

"Yes. I'm not surprised."

"No. A most unpleasant wart. Thoroughly scaly."

"He always was."

"Well, here's to a long stretch for comrade Jukes. Not a bad show tonight, don't you think?"

Harriet pulled herself together. She was all at once tired of Mr. Pomfret and wished he would go; but it was monstrous of her not to behave politely to him. She exerted herself to talk with bright interest of the entertainment to which he had kindly taken her and succeeded so well that it was nearly fifteen minutes before Mr. Pomfret remembered his waiting taxi, and took himself off in high spirits.

Harriet took up the letter. Now that she was free to

open it, she did not want to. It had spoilt the evening for her.

Dear Harriet,

I send in my demand notes with the brutal regularity of the income-tax commissioners; and probably you say when you see the envelopes, 'Oh, God! I know what this is.' The only difference is that, some time or other, one *has* to take notice of the income-tax.

Will you marry me?—It's beginning to look like one of those lines in a farce—merely boring till it's said often enough; and after that, you get a bigger laugh every time it comes.

I should like to write you the kind of words that burn the paper they are written on—but words like that have a way of being not only unforgettable and unforgivable. You will burn the paper in any case; and I would rather there should be nothing in it that you cannot forget if you want to.

Well, that's over. Don't worry about it.

My nephew (whom you seem, by the way, to have stimulated to the most extraordinary diligence) is cheering my exile by dark hints that you are involved in some disagreeable and dangerous job of work at Oxford about which he is in honor bound to say nothing. I hope he is mistaken. But I know that, if you have put anything in hand, disagreeableness and danger will not turn you back, and God forbid they should. Whatever it is, you have my best wishes for it.

I am not my own master at the moment, and do not know where I shall be sent next or when I shall be back —soon, I trust. In the meantime may I hope to hear from time to time that all is well with you?

Yours, more than my own,

Peter Wimsey

After reading that letter, Harriet knew that she could not rest till it was answered. The bitter unhappiness of its opening paragraphs was readily explained by the last two. He probably thought—he could not possibly help thinking—that she had known him all these years, only to confide in the end, not in him, but in a boy less than half his age and his own nephew, whom she had known only a couple of weeks and had little reason to trust. He had made no comment and asked no questions—that made it worse. More generously still, he had not only refrained from offers of help and advice which she might have resented; he had deliberately acknowledged that she had the right to run her own risks. "Do be careful of yourself"; "I hate to think of your being exposed to unpleasantness"; "If only I could be there to protect you"; any such phrase would express the normal male reaction. Not one man in ten thousand would say to the woman he loved, or to any woman: "Disagreeableness and danger will not turn you back, and God forbid they should." That was an admission of equality, and she had not expected it of him. If he conceived of marriage along those lines, then the whole problem would have to be reviewed in that new light; but that seemed scarcely possible. To take such a line and stick to it, he would have to be, not a man but a miracle. But the business about Saint-George must be cleared up immediately. She wrote quickly, without stopping to think too much.

DEAR PETER,

No. I can't see my way to it. But thank you all the same. About the Oxford business—I would have told you all about it long ago, only that it is not my secret. I wouldn't have told your nephew, only that he had stumbled on part of it and I had to trust him with the rest to keep from making unintentional mischief. I wish I could tell you; I should be very glad of your help; if ever I get leave to, I will. It is rather disagreeable but not dangerous, I hope. Thank you for not telling me to run away and play—that's the best compliment you ever paid me.

I hope your case, or whatever it is, is getting on all right. It must be a tough one to take so long.

HARRIET

Lord Peter Wimsey read this letter while seated upon the terrace of an hotel overlooking the Pincian Gardens, which were bathed in brilliant sunshine. It astonished him so much that he was reading it for the fourth time, when he became aware that the person standing beside him was not the waiter.

"My dear Count! I beg your pardon. What manners! My head was in the clouds. Do me the favor to sit down and join me. *Servitore!*"

"I beg you will not apologize. It is my fault for interrupting you. But fearing that last night might have somewhat entangled the situation—"

"It is foolish to talk so long and so late. Grown men behave like tired children who are allowed to sit up till midnight. I admit that we were all very fractious, myself not least."

"You are always the soul of amiability. That is why I thought that a word with you alone—We are both reasonable men."

"Count, Count, I hope you have not come to persuade me to anything. I should find it too difficult to refuse you." Wimsey folded the letter away in his pocketbook. "The sun is shining, and I am in the mood to make mistakes through overconfidence."

"Then, I must take advantage of the good moment." The Count set his elbows on the table and leaned forward, thumb-tip to thumb-tip and little-finger-tip to little-finger-tip, smiling, irresistible. Forty minutes later, he took his leave, still smiling, having ceded, without noticing it, rather more than he had gained, and told in ten words more than he had learned in a thousand.

But of this interlude Harriet naturally knew nothing. On the evening of the same day, she was dining alone, a little depressed, at Romano's. She had nearly finished, when she saw a man, just leaving the restaurant, who was sketching a vague gesture of recognition. He was in the forties, going a little bald, with a smooth, vacant face and a dark mustache. For a moment she could not place him; then something about his languid walk and impeccable tailoring brought back an afternoon at Lord's. She smiled at him, and he came up to her table.

"Hullo—ullo! Hope I'm not bargin' in. How's all the doings and all that?"

"Very well, thanks."

"That's grand. Thought I must just ooze over and pass the time of day. Or night. Only I was afraid you wouldn't remember me, and might think I was bein' a nuisance."

"Of course I remember you. You're Mr. Arbuthnot—the Honorable Frederick Arbuthnot—and you're a friend of Peter Wimsey's, and I met you at the Eton and Harrow match two years ago, and you're married and have two children. How are they?"

"Fair to middlin', thanks. What a brain you've got! Yes, ghastly hot afternoon that was, too. Can't think why harmless women should be dragged along to be bored while a lot of little boys play off their Old School Ties. (That's meant for a joke.) You were frightfully well-behaved, I remember."

Harriet said sedately that she always enjoyed a good cricket match.

"Do you? I thought it was politeness. It's pretty slow work, if you ask me. But I was never any good at it myself. It's all right for old Peter. He can always work himself into a stew thinking how much better he'd have done it himself."

Harriet offered him coffee.

"I didn't know anybody ever got into a stew at Lord's. I thought it wasn't done."

"Well, the atmosphere doesn't exactly remind one of the Cup Final; but mild old gentlemen do sometimes break out into a spot of tut-tuttery. How about a brandy? Waiter, two liqueur brandies. Are you writing any more books?"

Suppressing the rage that this question always rouses in a professional writer, Harriet admitted that she was.

"It must be splendid to be able to write," said Mr. Arbuthnot. "I often think I could spin a good yarn myself if I had the brains. About the odd things that happen, you know. Queer deals, and that kind of thing."

A dim recollection of something Wimsey had once said lit up the labyrinth of Harriet's mind. Money. That was the connection between the two men. Mr. Arbuthnot, moron as he might be in other respects, had a flair for money. He knew what that mysterious commodity was going to do; it was the one thing he did know, and he only knew that by instinct. When things were preparing to go up or down, they rang a little warning bell in what Freddy Arbuthnot called his mind, and he acted on the warning without being able to explain why. Peter had money, and Freddy understood money; that must be the common interest and bond of mutual confidence that explained an otherwise inexplicable friendship. She admired the strange nexus of interests that unites the male half of mankind into a close honeycomb of cells, each touching the other on one side only, and yet constituting a tough and closely adhering fabric.

"Funny kind of story popped up the other day," went on Mr. Arbuthnot. "Mysterious business. Couldn't make head or tail of it. It would have amused old Peter. How is old Peter, by the way?"

"I haven't seen him for some time. He's in Rome. I don't know what he's doing there, but I suppose he's on a case of some kind."

"No. I expect he's left his country for his country's good. It's usually that. I hope they manage to keep things quiet. The exchanges are a bit nervy."

Mr. Arbuthnot looked almost intelligent.

"What's Peter got to do with the exchange?"

"Nothing. But if anything blows up, it's bound to affect the exchange."

"This is Greek to me. What is Peter's job out there?"

"Foreign Office. Didn't you know?"

"I hadn't the slightest idea. He's not permanently attached there, is he?"

"In Rome, do you mean?"

"To the Foreign Office."

"No; but they sometimes push him out when they think he's wanted. He gets on with people."

"I see. I wonder why he never mentioned it."

"Oh, everybody knows; it's not a secret. He probably thought it wouldn't interest you." Mr. Arbuthnot balanced his spoon across his coffee-cup in an abstracted way. "I'm damned fond of old Peter," was his next, rather irrelevant, contribution. "He's a dashed good sort. Last time I saw him, I thought he seemed a bit under the weather. . . . Well, I'd better be toddling."

He got up, a little abruptly, and said good-night.

Harriet thought how humiliating it was to have one's ignorance exposed.

Ten days before the beginning of term, Harriet could bear London no longer. The final touch was put to her disgust by the sight of an advance notice of *Death 'twixt Wind and Water*, embodying an exceptionally fulsome blurb. She developed an acute homesickness for Oxford and for the *Study of Le Fanu*—a book which would never have any advertising value, but of which some scholar might some day moderately observe, "Miss Vane has handled her subject with insight and accuracy." She rang up the Bursar, discovered that she could be accommodated at Shrewsbury, and fled back to Academe.

College was empty, but for herself, the Bursar and Treasurer, and Miss Barton, who vanished daily into the Radcliffe Camera and was only seen at meals. The Warden was up, but remained in her own house.

April was running out, chilly and fickle, but with the promise of good things to come; and the city wore the withdrawn and secretive beauty that wraps her about in vacation. No clamor of young voices echoed along her ancient stones; the tumult of flying bicycles was stilled in the narrow strait of the Turl; in Radcliffe Square the Camera slept like a cat in the sunshine, disturbed only by the occasional visit of a slow-footed don; even in the High, the roar of car and charabanc seemed minished and brought low, for the holiday season was not yet; punts and canoes, new-fettled for the summer term, began to put forth upon the Cherwell like the varnished buds upon the horse-chestnut tree, but as yet there was no press of traffic upon the shining reaches; the mellow bells, soaring and singing in tower and steeple, told of time's flight through an eternity of peace; and Great Tom, tolling his nightly hundred-and-one, called home only the rooks from off Christ Church Meadow.

Mornings in Bodley, drowsing among the worn browns and tarnished gilding of Duke Humphrey, snuffing the faint, musty odor of slowly perishing leather, hearing only the discreet tippety-tap of Agag-feet along the padded floor; long afternoons, taking an outrigger up the Cher, feeling the rough kiss of the sculls on unaccustomed palms, listening to the rhythmical and satisfying ker-klunk of the rowlocks, watching the play of muscle on the Bursar's sturdy shoulders at stroke, as the sharp spring wind flattened the thin silk shirt against them; or, if the day were warmer, flicking swiftly in a canoe under Magdalen walls and so by the twisting race at King's Mill by Mesopotamia to Parson's Pleasure; then back, with mind relaxed and body stretched and vigorous, to make toast by the fire; and then, at night, the lit lamp and the drawn curtain, with the flutter of the turned page and soft scrape of pen on paper the only sounds to break the utter silence between quarter and quarter chime. Now and again, Harriet took out the dossier of the poison-pen and looked it over; yet, viewed by that solitary lamp, even the ugly, printed scrawls looked harmless and impersonal, and the whole dismal problem less important than the determining of a first edition date or the settlement of a disputed reading.

In that melodious silence, something came back to her

that had lain dumb and dead ever since the old, innocent undergraduate days. The singing voice, stifled long ago by the pressure of the struggle for existence, and throttled into dumbness by that queer, unhappy contact with physical passion, began to stammer a few uncertain notes. Great golden phrases, rising from nothing and leading to nothing, swam up out of her dreaming mind like the huge, sluggish carp in the cool waters of Mercury. One day she climbed up Shotover and sat looking over the spires of the city, deep-down, fathom-drowned, striking from the round bowl of the river-basin, improbably remote and lovely as the towers of Tir-nan-Og beneath the green sea-rollers. She held on her knee the looseleaf notebook that contained her notes upon the Shrewsbury scandal; but her heart was not in that sordid inquiry. A detached pentameter, echoing out of nowhere, was beating in her ears—seven marching feet—a pentameter and a half:—

To that still center where the spinning world
Sleeps on its axis—

Had she made it or remembered it? It sounded familiar, but in her heart she knew certainly that it was her own, and seemed familiar only because it was inevitable and right.

She opened the notebook at another page and wrote the words down. She felt like the man in the *Punch* story: "Nice little barf-room, Liza—what shall we do with it?" Blank verse? . . . No . . . it was part of the octave of a sonnet . . . it had the feel of a sonnet. But what a rhyme-sound! Curled? furled? . . . she fumbled over rhyme and meter, like an unpracticed musician fingering the keys of a disused instrument.

Then, with many false starts and blank feet, returning and filling and erasing painfully as she went, she began to write again, knowing with a deep inner certainty that somehow, after long and bitter wandering, she was once more in her own place.

Here, then, at home . . .

the center, the middle sea, the heart of the labyrinth . . .

Here, then, at home, by no more storms distrest,
Stay we our steps—course—flight—hands folded and
wings furled.

Here, then, at home, by no more storms distrest,
Folding laborious hands we sit, wings furled;
Here in close perfume lies the rose-leaf curled,
Here the sun stands and knows not east nor west,
Here no tide runs; we have come, last and best,
From the wide zone through dizzying circles hurled,
To that still center where the spinning world
Sleeps on its axis, to the heart of rest.

Yes; there was something there, though the meter halted monotonously, lacking a free stress-shift, and the chime "dizzying-spinning" was unsatisfactory. The lines swayed and lurched in her clumsy hands, uncontrollable. Still, such as it was, she had an octave.

And there it seemed to end. She had reached the full close, and had nothing more to say. She could find no turn for the sestet to take, no epigram, no change of mood. She put down a tentative line or two and crossed them out. If the right twist would not come of itself, it was useless to manufacture it. She had her image—the world sleeping like a great top on its everlasting spindle—and anything added to that would be mere verse-making. Something might come of it some day. In the meanwhile she had got her mood on to paper—and this is the release that all writers, even the feeblest, seek for as men seek for love; and, having found it, they doze off happily into dreams and trouble their hearts no further.

She shut up the notebook, scandal and sonnet together, and began to make her way slowly down the steep path. Halfway down, she met a small party coming up: two small, flaxen-haired girls in charge of a woman whose face seemed at first only vaguely familiar. Then, as they came close, she realized that it was Annie, looking strange without her cap and apron, taking the children for a walk.

As in duty bound, Harriet greeted them and asked where they were living now.

"We've found a very nice place in Headington, madam, thank you. I'm stopping there myself for my holiday. These are my little girls. This one's Beatrice and this is Carola. Say how do you do to Miss Vane."

Harriet shook hands gravely with the children and asked their ages and how they were getting on.

"It's nice for you having them so close."

"Yes, madam. I don't know what I should do without them." The look of quick pride and joy was almost fiercely possessive. Harriet got a glimpse of a fundamental passion that she had, as it were, forgotten when she made her reckoning; it blazed across the serenity of her sonnet-mood like an ominous meteor.

"They're all I have—now that I've lost their father."

"Oh, dear, yes," said Harriet, a little uncomfortably. "Has he—how long ago was that, Annie?"

"Three years, madam. He was driven to it. They said he did what he ought not, and it preyed on his mind. But I didn't care. He never did any harm to anybody, and a man's first duty is to his wife and family, isn't it? I'd have starved with him gladly, and worked my fingers to the bone to keep the children. But he couldn't get over it. It's a cruel world for anyone with his way to make and so much competition."

"Yes, indeed," said Harriet. The elder child, Beatrice, was looking up at her mother with eyes that were too intelligent for her eight years. It would be better to get off the subject of the husband's wrongs and iniquities, whatever they might be. She murmured that the children must be a great comfort.

"Yes, madam. There's nothing like having children of your own. They make life worth living. Beatrice here is her father's living image, aren't you, darling? I was sorry not to have a boy; but now I'm glad. It's difficult to bring up boys without a father."

"And what are Beatrice and Carola going to be when they grow up?"

"I hope they'll be good girls, madam, and good wives and mothers—that's what I'll bring them up to be."

"I want to ride a motorcycle when I'm bigger," said Beatrice, shaking her curls assertively.

"Oh, no, darling. What things they say, don't they, madam?"

"Yes, I do," said Beatrice. "I'm going to have a motorcycle and keep a garage."

"Nonsense," said her mother, a little sharply. "You mustn't talk so. That's a boy's job."

"But lots of girls do boys' jobs nowadays," said Harriet.

"But they ought not, madam. It isn't fair. The boys have hard enough work to get jobs of their own. Please don't put such things into her head, madam. You'll never get a husband, Beatrice, if you mess about in a garage, getting all ugly and dirty."

"I don't want one," said Beatrice, firmly. "I'd rather have a motorcycle."

Annie looked annoyed; but laughed when Harriet laughed.

"She'll find out some day, won't she, madam?"

"Very likely she will," said Harriet. If the woman took the view that any husband was better than none at all, it was useless to argue. And she had rather got into the habit of shying at all discussion that turned upon men and marriage. She said good-afternoon pleasantly and strode on, a little shaken in her mood, but not unduly so. Either one liked discussing these matters or one did not. And when there were ugly phantoms lurking in the corners of one's mind, skeletons that one dared not show to anybody, even to Peter—

Well, of course not to Peter; he was the last person. And he, at any rate, had no niche in the gray stones of Oxford.

He stood for London, for the swift, rattling, chattering, excitable and devilishly upsetting world of strain and uproar. Here, at the still center (yes, that line was definitely good), he had no place. For a whole week, she had scarcely given him a thought.

And then the dons began to arrive, full of their vacation activities and ready to take up the burden of the most exacting, yet most lovable term of the academic year. Harriet watched them come, wondering which of those cheerful and determined faces concealed a secret. Miss de Vine had been consulting a library in some ancient Flemish town, where was preserved a remarkable family correspondence dealing with trade conditions between England and Flanders under Elizabeth. Her mind was full of statistics about wool and pepper, and it was difficult to get her to think back to what she had done on the last day of the Hilary Term. She had undoubtedly burnt some old papers —there might have been newspapers among them—certainly she never read the *Daily Trumpet*—she could throw no light on the mutilated newspaper found in the fireplace.

Miss Lydgate—as Harriet had expected—had contrived in a few short weeks to make havoc of her proofs. She was apologetic. She had spent a most interesting long weekend with Professor Somebody, who was a great authority upon Greek quantitative measures; and he had discovered several passages that contained inaccuracies and thrown an entirely fresh light upon the argument of Chapter Seven. Harriet groaned dismally.

Miss Shaw had taken five of her students for a reading-party, had seen four new plays and bought a rather exciting summer outfit. Miss Pyke had spent an enthralling time assisting the curator of a local museum to put together the fragments of three figured pots and a quantity of burial-urns that had been dug up in a field in Essex. Miss Hillyard was really glad to be back in Oxford; she had had to spend a month at her sister's house while the sister was having a baby; looking after her brother-in-law seemed to have soured her temper. The Dean, on the other hand, had been helping to get a niece married and had found the whole business full of humor. "One of the bridesmaids went to the wrong church and only turned up when it was all over, and there were at *least* two hundred of us squeezed into a room that would only hold fifty, and I only got half a glass of champagne and no wedding-cake, my tummy was flapping against my spine; and the bridegroom lost his hat at the last moment, and, my *dear!* would you believe it? people *still* give plated biscuit-barrels!" Miss Chilperic had gone with her fiancé and his sister to a number of interesting places to study medieval domestic sculpture. Miss Burrows had spent most of her time playing golf. There arrived also a reinforcement in the person of Miss Edwards, the Science tutor, just returned from taking a term's leave. She was a young and active woman, square in face and shoulder, with bobbed hair and a stand-no-nonsense manner. The only member missing from the Senior Common Room was Mrs. Goodwin, whose small son (a most unfortunate child) had come out with measles immediately upon his return to school and again required his mother's nursing.

"Of course she can't help it," said the Dean, "but it's a very great nuisance, just at the beginning of the Summer Term. If I'd only known, I could have come back earlier."

"I don't see," observed Miss Hillyard, grimly, "what else you can expect, if you give jobs to widows with children. You have to be prepared for these perpetual interruptions. And for some reason, these domestic preoccupations always have to be put before the work."

"Well," said the Dean, "one must put work aside in a case of serious illness."

"But all children get measles."

"Yes; but he's not a very strong child, you know. His father was tubercular, poor man—in fact, that's what he died of—and if measles should turn to pneumonia, as it so often does, the consequences might be serious."

"But *has* it turned to pneumonia?"

"They're afraid it may. He's got it very badly. And, as he's a nervous little creature, he naturally likes to have his mother with him. And in any case, she'd be in quarantine."

"The longer she stays with him, the longer she'll *be* in quarantine."

"It's very tiresome of course," put in Miss Lydgate, mildly. "But if Mrs. Goodwin had isolated herself and come back at the earliest possible moment—as she very bravely offered to do—she would have been suffering a great deal of anxiety."

"A great many of us have to suffer from anxiety in one way or another," said Miss Hillyard, sharply. "I have been very anxious about my sister. It is always an anxious business to have a first baby at thirty-five. But if the event had happened to occur in term-time, it would have had to take place without my assistance."

"It is always difficult to say which duty one should put first," said Miss Pyke. "Each case must be decided individually. I presume that, in bringing children into the world, one accepts a certain responsibility towards them."

"I'm not denying it," said Miss Hillyard. "But if the domestic responsibility is to take precedence of the public responsibility, then the work should be handed over to someone else to do."

"But the children must be fed and clothed," said Miss Edwards.

"Quite so. But the mother should not take a resident post."

"Mrs. Goodwin is an excellent secretary," said the Dean. "I should be very sorry to lose her. And it's nice to think that we are able to help her in her very difficult position."

Miss Hillyard lost patience.

"The fact is, though you will never admit it, that everybody in this place has an inferiority complex about married women and children. For all your talk about careers and independence, you all believe in your hearts that we ought to abase ourselves before any woman who has fulfilled her animal functions."

"That is absolute nonsense," said the Bursar.

"It is natural, I suppose, to feel that married women lead a fuller life," began Miss Lydgate.

"And a more useful one," retorted Miss Hillyard. "Look at the fuss that's made over 'Shrewsbury grandchildren'! Look how delighted you all are when old students get married! As if you were saying 'Aha! education doesn't unfit us for real life after all!' And when a really brilliant scholar throws away all her prospects to marry a curate, you say perfunctorily, 'What a pity! But of course her own life must come first.' "

"I've *never* said such a thing," cried the Dean indignantly. "I always say they're perfect *fools* to marry."

"I shouldn't mind," said Miss Hillyard, unheeding, "if you said openly that intellectual interests were only a second-best; but you pretend to put them first in theory and are ashamed of them in practice."

"There's no need to get so heated about it," said Miss Barton, breaking in upon the angry protest of Miss Pyke. "After all, *some* of us may have deliberately chosen not to marry. And, if you will forgive my saying so—"

At this ominous phrase, always the prelude to something quite unforgivable, Harriet and the Dean broke hastily into the discussion.

"Considering that we are devoting our whole lives—"

"Even for a man, it is not always easy to say—"

Their common readiness confounded their good intention. Each broke off and begged the other's pardon, and Miss Barton went on unchecked:

"It is not altogether wise—or convincing—to show so much animus against married women. It was the same unreasonable prejudice that made you get that scout removed from your staircase—"

"I object," said Miss Hillyard, with a heightened color, "to this preferential treatment. I do not see why we should put up with slackness on duty because a servant or a secretary happens to be a widow with children. I do not see why Annie should be given a room to herself in the Scouts'

Wing, and charge over a corridor, when servants who have been here for longer than she has have to be content to share a room. I do not—"

"Well," said Miss Stevens, "I think she is entitled to a little consideration. A woman who has been accustomed to a nice home of her own—"

"Very likely," said Miss Hillyard. "At any rate, it was not *my* lack of consideration that led to her precious children being placed in the charge of a common thief."

"I was always against that," said the Dean.

"And why did you give in? Because poor Mrs. Jukes was such a nice woman and had a family to keep. She *must* be considered and rewarded for being fool enough to marry a scoundrel. What's the good of pretending that you put the interests of the College first, when you hesitate for two whole terms about getting rid of a dishonest porter, because you're so sorry for his family?"

"There," said Miss Allison, "I entirely agree with you. The College ought to come first in a case like that."

"It ought always to come first. Mrs. Goodwin ought to see it, and resign her post if she can't carry out her duties properly." She stood up. "Perhaps, however, it is as well that she should be away and stay away. You may remember that, *last* time she was away, we had no trouble from anonymous letters or monkey-tricks."

Miss Hillyard put down her coffee-cup and stalked out of the room. Everybody looked uncomfortable.

"Bless my heart!" said the Dean.

"Something very wrong there," said Miss Edwards, bluntly.

"She's so prejudiced," said Miss Lydgate. "I always think it's a very great pity she never married."

Miss Lydgate had a way of putting into language that a child could understand things which other people did not say, or said otherwise.

"I should be sorry for the man, I must say," observed Miss Shaw; "but perhaps I am showing an undue consideration for the male sex. One is almost afraid to open one's mouth."

"Poor Mrs. Goodwin!" exclaimed the Bursar. "The very last person!"

She got up angrily and went out. Miss Lydgate followed her. Miss Chilperic, who had said nothing, but looked quite alarmed, murmured that she must get along to work. The Common Room slowly cleared, and Harriet was left with the Dean.

"Miss Lydgate has the most terrifying way of hitting the nail on the head," said Miss Martin; "because it is obviously much more likely that—"

"A great deal more likely," said Harriet.

Mr. Jenkyn was a youngish and agreeable don whom Harriet had met the previous term at a party in North Oxford—the same party, in fact, which had led to her acquaintance with Mr. Reginald Pomfret. He resided at Magdalen, and was incidentally one of the pro-Proctors. Harriet had happened to say something to him about the Magdalen Mayday ceremony, and he had promised to send her a ticket for the Tower. Being a scientist and a man of scrupulously exact mind, he remembered his promise; and the ticket duly arrived.

None of the Shrewsbury S.C.R. was going. Most of them had been up on May mornings before. Miss de Vine had not; but though she had been offered tickets, her heart would not stand the stairs. There were students who had received invitations; but they were not students whom Harriet knew. She therefore set off alone, well before sunrise, having made an appointment to meet Miss Edwards when she came down and take an outrigger down to the Isis for a pipe-opener before having breakfast on the river.

The choristers had sung their hymn. The sun had risen, rather red and angry, casting a faint flush over the roofs and spires of the waking city. Harriet leaned over the parapet, looking down upon the heart-breaking beauty of the curved High Street, scarcely disturbed as yet by the roar of petrol-driven traffic. Under her feet, the tower began to swing to the swinging of the bells. The little group of bicyclists and pedestrians far below began to break up and move away. Mr. Jenkyn came up, said a few pleasant words, remarked that he had to hurry off to go bathing with a friend at Parson's Pleasure; there was no need for her to hurry—could she get down the stairs all right alone?

Harriet laughed and thanked him, and he took leave of her at the stair-head. She moved to the East side of the tower. There lay the river and Magdalen Bridge, with its pack of punts and canoes. Among them, she distinguished the sturdy figure of Miss Edwards, in a bright orange jumper. It was wonderful to stand so above the world, with a sea of sound below and an ocean of air above, all mankind shrunk to the proportions of an ant-heap. True, a cluster of people still lingered upon the tower itself—her companions in this airy hermitage. They too, spell-bound with beauty—

Great Scott! What was that girl trying to do?

Harriet made a dive at the young woman who was just placing one knee on the stonework and drawing herself up between two crenellations of the parapet.

"Here!" she said, "you mustn't do that. It's dangerous."

The girl, a thin, fair, frightened-looking child, desisted at once.

"I only wanted to look over."

"Well, that's very silly of you. You might get giddy. You'd better come along down. It would be very unpleasant for the Magdalen authorities if anyone fell over. They might have to stop letting people come up."

"I'm so sorry. I didn't think."

"Well, you should think. Is anybody with you?"

"No."

"I'm going down now; you'd better come too."

"Very well."

Harriet shepherded the girl down the dark spiral. She had no proof of anything but rash curiosity, but she wondered. The girl spoke with a slightly common accent, and Harriet would have put her down for a shop-assistant, but for the fact that tickets for the Tower were more likely to be restricted to University people and their friends. She might be an undergraduate, come up with a County Scholarship. In any case, one was perhaps attaching too much importance to the incident.

They were passing the bell-chamber now, and the brazen clamor was loud and insistent. It reminded her of a story that Peter Wimsey had told her, years ago now, one day when only a resolute determination to talk on and on had enabled him to prevent a most unfortunate outing from ending in a quarrel. Something about a body in a belfry, and a flood, and the great bells bawling the alarm across three counties.

The noise of the bells died down behind her as she passed, and the recollection with it; but she had paused for a moment in the awkward descent, and the girl, whoever she was, had got ahead of her. When she reached the foot of the stair and came out into clear daylight, she saw the slight figure scurrying off through the passage into the quad. She was doubtful whether to pursue it or not. She followed at a distance, watched it turn downwards up the High, and suddenly found herself almost in the arms of Mr. Pomfret, coming down from Queen's in a very untidy grey flannel suit, with a towel over his arm.

"Hullo!" said Mr. Pomfret. "You been saluting the sunrise?"

"Yes. Not a very good sunrise, but quite a good salute."

"I think it's going to rain," said Mr. Pomfret. "But I said I would bathe and I am bathing."

"Much the same here," said Harriet. "I said I'd scull, and I'm sculling."

"Aren't we a pair of heroes?" said Mr. Pomfret. He accompanied her to Magdalen Bridge, was hailed by an irritable friend in a canoe, who said he had been waiting for half an hour, and went off upriver, grumbling that nobody loved him and that he knew it was going to rain.

Harriet joined Miss Edwards, who said, on hearing about the girl:

"Well, you might have got her name, I suppose. But I don't see what one could do about it. It wasn't one of our people, I suppose?"

"I didn't recognize her. And she didn't seem to recognize me."

"Then it probably wasn't. Pity you didn't get the name, all the same. People oughtn't to do that kind of thing. Inconsiderate. Will you take bow or stroke?"

CHAPTER XII

As a Tulipant to the Sun (which our herbalists call Narcissus) *when it shines,* is admirandus flos ad radios solis se pandens, *a glorious Flower exposing itself; but when the Sun sets, or a tempest comes, it hides itself, pines away, and hath no pleasure left . . . do all Enamoratoes to their Mistress.*

ROBERT BURTON

The mind most effectually works upon the body, producing by his passions and perturbations miraculous alterations, as melancholy, despair, cruel diseases, and sometimes death itself. . . . They that live in fear are never free, resolute, secure, never merry, but in continual pain. . . . It causeth oft-times sudden madness.

ID.

The arrival of Miss Edwards, together with the rearrangements of residences due to the completion of the Library Building, greatly strengthened the hands of authority at the opening of the Trinity Term. Miss Barton, Miss Burrows and Miss de Vine moved into the three new sets on the ground floor of the Library; Miss Chilperic was transferred to the New Quad, and a general redistribution took place; so that Tudor and Burleigh Buildings were left entirely denuded of dons. Miss Martin, Harriet, Miss Edwards and Miss Lydgate established a system of patrols, by which the New Quad, Queen Elizabeth and the Library Building could be visited nightly at irregular intervals and an eye kept on all suspicious movements.

Thanks to this arrangement, the more violent demonstrations of the Poison-Pen received a check. It is true that a few anonymous letters continued to arrive by post, containing scurrilous insinuations and threats of revenge against various persons. Harriet was carefully docketing as many of these as she could hear of or lay hands on—she noticed that by this time every member of the S.C.R. had been persecuted, with the exception of Mrs. Goodwin and Miss Chilperic; in addition, the Third Year taking Schools began to receive sinister prognostications about their prospects, while Miss Flaxman was presented with an ill-executed picture of a harpy tearing the flesh of a gentleman in a mortar-board. Harriet had tried to eliminate Miss Pyke and Miss Burrows from suspicion, on the ground that they were both fairly skillful with a pencil, and would therefore be incapable of producing such bad drawings, even by taking thought; she discovered, however, that, though both were dexterous, neither of them was ambidexterous, and that their left-handed efforts were quite as bad as anything produced by the Poison-Pen, if not worse. Miss Pyke, indeed, on being shown the Harpy picture, pointed out that it was, in several respects, inconsistent with the classical conception of this monster; but there again it was clearly easy enough for the expert to assume ignorance; and perhaps the eagerness with which she drew attention to the incidental errors told as much against her as in her favor.

Another trifling but curious episode, occurring on the third Monday in term, was the complaint of an agitated and conscientious First-Year that she had left a harmless modern novel open upon the table in the Fiction Library, and that on her return to fetch it after an afternoon on the river, she had found several pages from the middle of the book—just where she was reading—ripped out and strewn about the room. The First-Year, who was a County Council Scholar, and as poor as a church mouse, was almost in tears; it really wasn't her fault; should she have to replace the book? The Dean, to whom the question was addressed, said, No; it certainly didn't seem to be the First-Year's fault. She made a note of the outrage: "*The Search* by C. P. Snow, pp. 327 to 340 removed and mutilated, May 13th," and passed the information on to Harriet, who incorporated it in her diary of the case, together with such items as: "March 7—abusive letter by post to Miss de Vine," "March 11, do. to Miss Hillyard and Miss Layton," "April 29—Harpy drawing to Miss Flaxman," of which she had now quite a formidable list.

So the Summer Term set in, sun-flecked and lovely, a departing April whirled on wind-spurred feet towards a splendor of May. Tulips danced in the Fellows' Garden; a fringe of golden green shimmered and deepened upon the secular beeches; the boats put out upon the Cher between the budding banks, and the wide reaches of the Isis were strenuous with practicing eights. Black gowns and summer frocks fluttered up and down the streets of the city and through the College gates, making a careless heraldry with the green of smooth turf and the silver-sable of ancient stone; motor-car and bicycle raced perilously side by side through narrow turnings and the wail of gramophones made hideous the water-ways from Magdalen Bridge to far above the new By-pass. Sun-bathers and untidy tea-parties desecrated Shrewsbury Old Quad, newly-whitened tennis-shoes broke out like strange, unwholesome flowers along plinth and window-ledge, and the Dean was forced to issue a ukase in the matter of the bathing-dresses which flapped and fluttered, flag-fashion, from every coign of vantage. Solicitous tutors began to cluck and brood tenderly over such ripening eggs of scholarship as were destined to hatch out damply in the Examination Schools after their three years' incubation; candidates, realizing with a pang that they had now fewer than eight weeks in which to make up for cut lectures and misspent working hours, went flashing from Bodley to lecture-room and from Camera to coaching; and the thin trickle of abuse from the Poison-Pen was swamped and well-nigh forgotten in that stream of genial commination always poured out from the lips of examinees elect upon examining bodies. Nor, in the onset of Schools Fever, was a lighter note lacking to the general delirium. The draw for the Schools Sweep was made in the Senior

Common Room, and Harriet found herself furnished with the names of two "horses," one of whom, a Miss Newland, was said to be well fancied. Harriet asked who she was, having never to her knowledge seen or heard of her.

"I don't suppose you have," said the Dean. "She's a shy child. But Miss Shaw thinks she's pretty safe for a First."

"She isn't looking well this term, though," said the Bursar. "I hope she isn't going to have a break-down or anything. I told her the other day she ought not to cut Hall so often."

"They *will* do it," said the Dean. "It's all very well to say they can't be bothered to change when they come off the river and prefer pajamas and an egg in their rooms; but I'm sure a boiled egg and a sardine aren't sustaining enough to do Schools on."

"And the mess it all makes for the scouts to clear up," grumbled the Bursar. "It's almost impossible to get the rooms done by eleven when they're crammed with filthy crockery."

"It isn't being out on the river that's the matter with Newland," said the Dean. "That child works."

"All the worse," said the Bursar. "I distrust the candidate who swots in her last term. I shouldn't be a bit surprised if your horse scratched, Miss Vane. She looks nervy to me."

"That's very depressing," said Harriet. "Perhaps I'd better sell half my ticket while the price is good. I agree with Edgar Wallace, 'Give me a good stupid horse who will eat his oats.' Any offers for Newland?"

"What's that about Newland?" demanded Miss Shaw, coming up to them. They were having coffee in the Fellows' Garden at the time. "By the way, Dean, couldn't you put up a notice about sitting on the grass in the New Quad? I have had to chase two parties off. We cannot have the place looking like Margate Beach."

"Certainly not. They know quite *well* it isn't allowed. *Why* are women undergraduates so sloppy?"

"They're always exceedingly anxious to be like the

men," said Miss Hillyard, sarcastically, "but I notice the likeness doesn't extend to showing respect for the College grounds."

"Even you must admit that men have some virtues," said Miss Shaw.

"More tradition and discipline, that's all," said Miss Hillyard.

"I don't know," said Miss Edwards. "I think women are messier by nature. They are naturally picnic-minded."

"It's nice to sit out in the open air in this lovely weather," suggested Miss Chilperic, almost apologetically (for her student days were not far behind her), "and they don't think how awful it looks."

"In hot weather," said Harriet, moving her chair back into the shade, "men have the common sense to stay indoors, where it's cooler."

"Men," said Miss Hillyard, "have a passion for frowst."

"Yes," said Miss Shaw, "but what were you saying about Miss Newland? You weren't offering to sell your chance, Miss Vane, were you? Because, take it from me, she's a hot favorite. She's the Latymer Scholar, and her work's brilliant."

"Somebody suggested she was off her feed and likely to be a nonstarter."

"That's very unkind," said Miss Shaw, with indignation. "Nobody's any right to say such things."

"I think she looks harassed and on edge," said the Bursar. "She's too hardworking and conscientious. She hasn't got the wind-up about Schools, has she?"

"There's nothing wrong with her work," said Miss Shaw. "She does look a little pale, but I expect it's the sudden heat."

"Possibly she's worried about things at home," suggested Mrs. Goodwin. She had returned to College on the May 9th, her boy having taken a fortunate turn for the better, though he was still not out of the wood. She looked anxious and sympathetic.

"She'd have told me if she had been," said Miss Shaw.

"I encourage my students to confide in me. Of course she's a very reserved girl, but I have done my best to draw her out, and I feel sure I should have heard if there was anything on her mind."

"Well," said Harriet, "I must see this horse of mine before I decide what to do about my sweepstake ticket. Somebody must point her out."

"She's up in the Library at this moment, I fancy," said the Dean; "I saw her stewing away there just before dinner —cutting Hall as usual. I nearly spoke to her. Come and stroll through, Miss Vane. If she's there, we'll chase her out for the good of her soul. I want to look up a reference, anyhow."

Harriet got up, laughing, and accompanied the Dean.

"I sometimes think," said Miss Martin, "that Miss Shaw would get more real confidence from her pupils if she wasn't always probing into their little insides. She likes people to be fond of her, which I think is rather a mistake. Be kind, but leave 'em alone, is my motto. The shy ones shrink into their shells when they're poked, and the egotistical ones talk a lot of rubbish to attract attention. However, we all have our methods."

She pushed open the Library door, halted in the end bay to consult a book and verify a quotation, and then led the way through the long room. At a table near the center, a thin, fair girl was working amid a pile of reference books. The Dean stopped.

"You still here, Miss Newland? Haven't you had any dinner?"

"I'll have some later, Miss Martin. It was so hot, and I want to get this language paper done."

The girl looked startled and uneasy. She pushed the damp hair back from her forehead. The whites of her eyes showed like those of a fidgety horse.

"Don't you be a little juggins," said the Dean. "All work and no play is simply silly in your Schools term. If you go on like this, we'll have to send you away for a rest-cure and forbid work altogether for a week or so. Have you got a headache? You look as if you had."

"Not very much, Miss Martin."

"For goodness' sake," said the Dean, "chuck that perishing old Ducange and Meyer-Lübke or whoever it is and go away and play. I'm always having to chase the Schools people off to the river and into the country," she added, turning to Harriet. "I wish they'd all be like Miss Camperdown—she was after your time. She frightened Miss Pyke by dividing the whole of her Schools term between the river and the tennis courts, and she ended up with a First in Greats."

Miss Newland looked more alarmed than ever.

"I don't seem able to think," she confessed. "I forget things and go blank."

"Of course you do," said the Dean, briskly. "Sure sign you're doing too much. Stop it at once. Get up now and get yourself some food and then take a nice novel or something, or find somebody to have a knock-up with you."

"Please don't bother, Miss Martin. I'd rather go on with this. I don't feel like eating and I don't care about tennis—I *wish* you wouldn't bother!" she finished, rather hysterically.

"All right," said the Dean; "bless you, *I* don't want to fuss. But do be sensible."

"I will, really, Miss Martin. I'll just finish this paper. I couldn't feel comfortable if I hadn't. I'll have something to eat then and go to bed. I promise I will."

"That's a good girl." The Dean passed on, out of the Library, and said to Harriet:

"I don't like to see them getting into that state. What do you think of your horse's chance?"

"Not much," said Harriet. "I do know her. That is, I've seen her before. I saw her last on Magdalen Tower."

"What?" said the Dean. "Oh, lord!"

Of Lord Saint-George, Harriet had not seen very much during that first fortnight of term. His arm was out of a sling; but a remaining weakness in it had curbed his sporting activities, and when she did see him, he informed her that he was working. The matter of the telegraph pole and the insurance had been safely adjusted, and the parental wrath avoided. "Uncle Peter," to be sure, had had something to say about it, but Uncle Peter, though scathing, was as safe as houses. Harriet encouraged the young gentleman to persevere with his work and refused an invitation to dine and meet "his people." She had no particular wish to meet the Denvers, and had hitherto successfully avoided doing so.

Mr. Pomfret had been assiduously polite. He and Mr. Rogers had taken her on the river, and had included Miss Cattermole in the party. They had all been on their best behavior, and a pleasant time had been enjoyed by all, the mention of previous encounters having, by common consent, been avoided. Harriet was pleased with Miss Cattermole; she seemed to have made an effort to throw off the blight that had settled upon her, and Miss Hillyard's report had been encouraging. Mr. Pomfret had also asked Harriet to lunch and to play tennis; on the former occasion she had truthfully pleaded a previous engagement and, on the second, had said, with rather less truth, that she had not played for years, was out of form and was not really keen. After all, one had one's work to do (*Le Fanu*, *'Twixt Wind and Water*, and the *History of Prosody* among them made up a fairly full program), and one could not spend all one's time idling with undergraduates.

On the evening after her formal introduction to Miss Newland, however, Harriet encountered Mr. Pomfret accidentally. She had been to see an old Shrewsburian who was attached to the Somerville Senior Common Room, and was crossing St. Giles on her way back, shortly before midnight, when she was aware of a group of young men in evening dress, standing about one of the trees which adorn that famous thoroughfare. Being naturally inquisitive, Harriet went to see what was up. The street was practically deserted, except for through traffic of the ordinary kind.

The upper branches of the tree were violently agitated, and Harriet, standing on the outskirts of the little group beneath, learned from their remarks that Mr. Somebody-or-the-other had undertaken, in consequence of an after-dinner bet, to climb every tree in St. Giles without interference from the Proctor. As the number of trees was large and the place public, Harriet felt the wager to be rather optimistic. She was just turning away to cross the street in the direction of the Lamb and Flag, when another youth, who had evidently been occupying an observation-post, arrived, breathless, to announce that the Proggins was just coming into view round the corner of Broad Street. The climber came down rather hastily, and the group promptly scattered in all directions—some running past her, some making their way down side-streets, and a few bold spirits fleeing towards the small enclosure known as the Fender, within which (since it belongs not to the Town but to St. John's) they could play at tig with the Proctor to their hearts' content. One of the young gentlemen darting in this general direction passed Harriet close, stopped with an exclamation, and brought up beside her.

"Why, it's you!" cried Mr. Pomfret, in an excited tone.

"Me again," said Harriet. "Are you always out without your gown at this time of night?"

"Practically always," said Mr. Pomfret, falling into step beside her. "Funny you should always catch me at it. Amazing luck, isn't it? . . . I say, you've been avoiding me this term. Why?"

"Oh, no," said Harriet; "only I've been rather busy."

"But you *have* been avoiding me," said Mr. Pomfret. "I know you have. I suppose it's ridiculous to expect you to take any particular interest in me. I don't suppose you ever think about me. You probably despise me."

"Don't be so absurd, Mr. Pomfret. Of course I don't do anything of the sort. I like you very much, but—"

"Do you? . . . Then why won't you let me see you? Look here, I *must* see you. There's something I've got to tell you. When can I come and talk to you?"

"What about?" said Harriet, seized with a sudden and awful qualm.

"What *about*? Hang it, don't be so unkind. Look here, Harriet—No, stop, you've got to listen. Darling, wonderful Harriet—"

"Mr. Pomfret, please—"

But Mr. Pomfret was not to be checked. His admiration had run away with him, and Harriet, cornered in the shadow of the big horse-chestnut by the Lamb and Flag, found herself listening to as eager an avowal of devotion as any young gentleman in his twenties ever lavished upon a lady considerably his senior in age and experience.

"I'm frightfully sorry, Mr. Pomfret. I never thought—No, really, it's quite impossible. I'm at least ten years older than you are. And besides—"

"What does that matter?" With a large and clumsy gesture Mr. Pomfret swept away the difference of age and plunged on in a flood of eloquence, which Harriet, exasperated with herself and him, could not stop. He loved her, he adored her, he was intensely miserable, he could neither work nor play games for thinking of her, if she refused him he didn't know what he should do with himself, she must have seen, she must have realized—he wanted to stand between her and all the world—

Mr. Pomfret was six feet three and broad and strong in proportion.

"Please don't do that," said Harriet, feeling as though she were feebly saying "Drop it, Caesar," to somebody else's large and disobedient Alsatian. "No, I mean it. I can't let you—" And then in a different tone:

"Look out, juggins! Here's the Proctor."

Mr. Pomfret, in some consternation, gathered himself together and turned as to flee. But the Proctor's bulldogs, who had been having a lively time with the tree-climbers in St. Giles, and were now out for blood, had come through the archway at a smart trot, and seeing a young gentleman not only engaged in nocturnal vagation without his gown but actually embracing a female (*mulier vel mere-*

trix, cujus consortio Christianis prorsus interdictum est) leapt gleefully upon him, as upon a lawful prey.

"Oh, blast!" said Mr. Pomfret. "Here, you—"

"The Proctor would like to speak to you, sir," said the Bulldog, grimly.

Harriet debated with herself whether it might not be more tactful to depart, leaving Mr. Pomfret to his fate. But the Proctor was close on the heels of his men; he was standing within a few yards of her and already demanding to know the offender's name and college. There seemed to be nothing for it but to face the matter out.

"Just a moment, Mr. Proctor," began Harriet, struggling, for Mr. Pomfret's sake, to control a rebellious uprush of laughter. "This gentleman is with me, and you can't—Oh! good evening, Mr. Jenkyn."

It was, indeed, that amiable pro-Proctor. He gazed at Harriet, and was struck dumb with embarrassment.

"I say," broke in Mr. Pomfret, awkwardly, but with a gentlemanly feeling that some explanation was due from him; "it was entirely my fault. I mean, I'm afraid I was annoying Miss Vane. She—I—"

"You can't very well prog him, you know," said Harriet, persuasively, "can you now?"

"Come to think of it," replied Mr. Jenkyn, "I suppose I can't. You're a Senior Member, aren't you?" He waved his bulldogs to a distance. "I beg your pardon," he added, a little stiffly.

"Not at all," said Harriet. "It's a nice night. Did you have good hunting in St. Giles?"

"Two culprits will appear before their dean tomorrow," said the pro-Proctor, rather more cheerfully. "I suppose nobody came through here?"

"Nobody but ourselves," said Harriet; "and I can assure you that we haven't been climbing trees."

A wicked facility in quotation tempted her to add "except in the Hesperides"; but she respected Mr. Pomfret's feelings and restrained herself.

"No, no," said Mr. Jenkyn. He fingered his bands nervously and hitched his gown with its velvet facings protectively about his shoulders. "I had better be away in pursuit of those that have."

"Good-night," said Harriet.

"Good-night," said Mr. Jenkyn, courteously raising his square cap. He turned sharply upon Mr. Pomfret. "Good-night, sir."

He stalked away with brisk steps between the posts into Museum Road, his long liripipe sleeves agitated and fluttering. Between Harriet and Mr. Pomfret there occurred one of those silences into which the first word spoken falls like the stroke of a gong. It seemed equally impossible to comment on the interruption or to resume the interrupted conversation. By common consent, however, they turned their backs upon the pro-Proctor and moved out once more into St. Giles. They had turned left and were passing through the now-deserted Fender before Mr. Pomfret found his tongue.

"A nice fool I look," said Mr. Pomfret, bitterly.

"It was very unfortunate," said Harriet, "but I must have looked much the more foolish. I very nearly ran away altogether. However, all's well that ends well. He's a very decent sort and I don't suppose he'll think twice about it."

She remembered, with another disconcerting interior gurgle of mirth, an expression in use among the irreverent: "to catch a Senior girling." "To boy" was presumably the feminine equivalent of the verb "to girl"; she wondered whether Mr. Jenkyn would employ it in Common Room next day. She did not grudge him his entertainment; being old enough to know that even the most crashing social bricks make but a small ripple in the ocean of time, which quickly dies away. To Mr. Pomfret, however, the ripple must inevitably appear of the dimensions of a maelstrom. He was muttering sulkily something about a laughing-stock.

"Please," said Harriet, "don't worry about it. It's of no importance. I don't mind one bit."

"Of course not," said Mr. Pomfret. "Naturally, you can't take me seriously. You're treating me like a child."

"Indeed I'm not. I'm very grateful—I'm very much honored by everything you said to me. But really and truly, it's quite impossible."

"Oh, well, never mind," said Mr. Pomfret, angrily.

It was too bad, thought Harriet. To have one's young affections trampled upon was galling enough; to have been made an object of official ridicule as well was almost unbearable. She must do something to restore the young gentleman's self-respect.

"Listen, Mr. Pomfret. I don't think I shall ever marry anybody. Please believe that my objection isn't personal at all. We have been very good friends. Can't we—?"

Mr. Pomfret greeted this fine old bromide with a dreary snort.

"I suppose," he said, in a savage tone, "there's somebody else."

"I don't know that you've any right to ask that."

"Of course not," said Mr. Pomfret, affronted. "I've no right to ask you anything. I ought to apologize for asking you to marry me. And for making a scene in front of the Proggins—in fact, for existing. I'm exceedingly sorry."

Very clearly, the only balm that could in the least soothe the wounded vanity of Mr. Pomfret would be the assurance that there *was* somebody else. But Harriet was not prepared to make any such admission; and besides, whether there was anybody else or not, nothing could make the notion of marrying Mr. Pomfret anything but preposterous. She begged him to take a reasonable view of the matter; but he continued to sulk; and indeed, nothing that could possibly be said could mitigate the essential absurdity of the situation. To offer a lady one's chivalrous protection against the world in general, and to be compelled instead to accept her senior standing as a protection for one's self against the just indignation of the Proctor is, and remains, farcical.

Their ways lay together. In resentful silence they paced

the stones, past the ugly front of Balliol and the high iron gates of Trinity, past the fourteen-fold sneer of the Caesars and the top-heavy arch of the Clarendon Building, till they stood at the junction of Cat Street and Holywell.

"Well," said Mr. Pomfret, "if you don't mind, I'd better cut along here. It's just going twelve."

"Yes. Don't bother about me. Good-night. . . . And thank you again very much."

"Good-night."

Mr. Pomfret ran hurriedly in the direction of Queen's College, pursued by a yelping chorus of chimes.

Harriet went on down Holywell. She could laugh now if she wanted to; and she did laugh. She had no fear of any permanent damage to Mr. Pomfret's heart; he was far too cross to be suffering in anything but his vanity. The incident had that rich savor of the ludicrous which neither pity nor charity can destroy. Unfortunately, she could not in decency share it with anybody; she could only enjoy it in lonely ecstasies of mirth. What Mr. Jenkyn must be thinking of her she could scarcely imagine. Did he suppose her to be an unprincipled cradle-snatcher? or a promiscuous sexual maniac? or a disappointed woman eagerly grasping at the rapidly disappearing skirts of opportunity? or what? The more she thought about her own part in the episode, the funnier it appeared to her. She wondered what she should say to Mr. Jenkyn if she ever met him again.

She was surprised to find how much Mr. Pomfret's simple-minded proposal had elated her. She ought to have been thoroughly ashamed of herself. She ought to be blaming herself for not having seen what was happening to Mr. Pomfret and taken steps to stop it. Why hadn't she? Simply, she supposed, because the possibility of such a thing had never occurred to her. She had taken it for granted that she could never again attract any man's fancy, except the eccentric fancy of Peter Wimsey. And to him she was, of course, only the creature of his making and the mirror of his own magnanimity. Reggie Pomfret's devotion, though ridiculous, was at least single-minded; *he* was no King Cophetua; she had not to be humbly obliged to *him* for kindly taking notice of her. And that reflection, after all, was pleasurable. However loudly we may assert our own unworthiness, few of us are really offended by hearing the assertion contradicted by a disinterested party.

In this unregenerate mood she reached the College, and let herself in by the postern. There were lights in the Warden's Lodgings, and somebody was standing at the gate, looking out. At the sound of Harriet's footsteps, this person called out, in the Dean's voice:

"It that you, Miss Vane. The Warden wants to see you."

"What's the matter, Dean?"

The Dean took Harriet by the arm.

"Newland hasn't come in. You haven't seen her anywhere?"

"No—I've been round at Somerville. It's only just after twelve. She'll probably turn up. You don't think—?"

"We don't know what to think. It's not like Newland to be out without leave. And we've found things."

She led Harriet into the Warden's sitting-room. Dr. Baring was seated at her desk, her handsome face stern and judicial. In front of her stood Miss Haydock, with her hands thrust into her dressing-gown pockets; she looked excited and angry. Miss Shaw, curled dismally in a corner of the big couch, was crying; while Miss Millbanks the Senior Student, half-frightened and half-defiant, hovered uneasily in the background. As Harriet came in with the Dean, everybody looked hopefully towards the door and then away again.

"Miss Vane," said the Warden, "the Dean tells me that you saw Miss Newland behaving in a peculiar manner on Magdalen Tower last May-Day. Can you give me any more exact details about that?"

Harriet told her story again.

"I am sorry," she added in conclusion, "that I didn't get her name at the time; but I didn't recognize her as one of our students. As a matter of fact, I don't remember ever noticing her at all, until she was pointed out to me yesterday by Miss Martin."

"That's quite right," said the Dean. "I'm not at all surprised you shouldn't have known her. She's very quiet and shy and seldom comes in to Hall or shows herself anywhere. I think she works nearly all day at the Radcliffe. Of course, when you told me about the May-Day business, I decided that somebody ought to keep an eye on her. I informed Dr. Baring and Miss Shaw, and I asked Miss Millbanks whether any of the Third Year had noticed that she seemed to be in any trouble."

"I can't understand it," cried Miss Shaw. "Why couldn't she have come to me about it? I always encourage my pupils to give me their full confidence. I asked her again and again. I really thought she had a real affection for me. . . ."

She sniffed hopelessly into a damp handkerchief.

"I knew something was up," said Miss Haydock, bluntly. "But I didn't know what it was. The more questions you asked, the less she'd tell you—so I didn't ask many."

"Has the girl no friends?" asked Harriet.

"I thought she looked on me as a friend," complained Miss Shaw.

"She didn't make friends," said Miss Haydock.

"She's a very reserved child," said the Dean. "I don't think anybody could make much out of her. I know I couldn't."

"But what has happened, exactly?" asked Harriet.

"When Miss Martin spoke to Miss Millbanks about her," said Miss Haydock, cutting in without respect of persons upon the Warden's reply, "Miss Millbanks mentioned the matter to me, saying she couldn't see that we could be expected to do anything."

"But I scarcely knew her . . ." began Miss Millbanks.

"Nor did I," said Miss Haydock. "But I thought something had better be done about it. I took her out on the river this afternoon. She said she ought to work, but I told her not to be an idiot, or she'd crack up. We took a punt up over the Rollers and had tea along by the Parks. She seemed all right then. I brought her back and persuaded her to come and dine properly in Hall. After that, she said she wanted to go and work at the Radder. I had an engagement, so I couldn't go with her—besides, I thought she'd think it funny if I trailed after her all day. So I told Miss Millbanks that somebody else had better carry on."

"Well, I carried on myself," said Miss Millbanks, rather defiantly. "I took my own work across there. I sat in a desk where I could see her. She was there till half-past nine. I came away at ten and found she'd gone."

"Didn't you see her go?"

"No. I was reading and I suppose she slipped out. I'm sorry; but how was I to know? I've got Schools this term. It's all very well to say I oughtn't to have taken my eyes off her, but I'm not a nurse or anything—"

Harriet noticed how Miss Millbank's self-assurance had broken down. She was defending herself angrily and clumsily like a school-girl.

"On returning," pursued the Warden, "Miss Millbanks—"

"But has anything been done about it?" interrupted Harriet, impatient with this orderly academic exposition. "I suppose you asked whether she'd been up to the gallery of the Radcliffe."

"I thought of that later on," replied the Warden, "and suggested that a search should be made there. I understand that it has been made, without result. However, a subsequent—"

"How about the river?"

"I am coming to that. Perhaps I had better continue in chronological order. I can assure you that no time has been wasted."

"Very well, Warden."

"On returning," said the Warden, taking up her tale exactly where she had left it, "Miss Millbanks told Miss Haydock about it, and they ascertained that Miss Newland was not in College. They then, very properly, informed the

Dean, who instructed Padgett to telephone through as soon as she came in. At 11:15 she had not returned, and Padgett reported that fact. He mentioned at the same time that he had himself been feeling uneasy about Miss Newland. He had noticed that she had taken to going about alone, and that she looked strained and nervous."

"Padgett is pretty shrewd," said the Dean. "I often think he knows more about the students than any of us."

"Up till tonight," wailed Miss Shaw, "I should have said I knew all my pupils intimately."

"Padgett also said he had seen several of the anonymous letters arrive at the Lodge for Miss Newland."

"He ought to have reported that," said Harriet.

"No," said the Dean. "It was after you came last term that we instructed him to report. The ones he saw came before that."

"I see."

"By that time," said the Warden, "we were beginning to feel alarmed, and Miss Martin rang up the police. In the meantime, Miss Haydock made a search in Miss Newland's room for anything that might throw light on her state of mind; and found—these."

She took a little sheaf of papers from her desk and handed them to Harriet, who said, "Good God."

The Poison-Pen, this time, had found a victim ready made to her hand. There were the letters, thirty or more of them ("and I don't suppose that's the lot, either," was the Dean's comment)—menacing, abusive, insinuating—all hammering remorselessly upon the same theme. "You needn't think you will get away with it"—"What will you do when you fail in Schools?"—"You deserve to fail and I shall see that you do"—then more horrible suggestions: "Don't you feel your brain going?"—"If they see you are going mad they will send you down"—and finally, in a sinister series: "You'd better end it now"—"Better dead than in the loony-bin"—"In your place I should throw myself out of the window"—"Try the river"—and so on;

the continuous, deadly beating on weak nerves that of all things is hardest to resist.

"If only she had shown them to me!" Miss Shaw was crying.

"She wouldn't, of course," said Harriet. "You have to be very well balanced to admit that people think you're going mad. That's what's done the mischief."

"Of all the wicked things—" said the Dean. "Think of that unfortunate child collecting all these horrors and brooding over them! I'd like to kill whoever it is!"

"It's a definite effort at murder," said Harriet. "But the point is, has it come off?"

There was a pause. Then the Warden said in an expressionless voice:

"One of the boathouse keys is missing."

"Miss Stevens and Miss Edwards have gone upstream in the Water-fly," said the Dean, "and Miss Burrows and Miss Barton have taken the other sculler down to the Isis. The police are searching too. They've been gone about three-quarters of an hour. We didn't discover till then that the key was gone."

"Then there's not much we can do," said Harriet, suppressing the angry comment that the boathouse keys should have been checked the moment Miss Newland's absence had been remarked. "Miss Haydock—did Miss Newland say anything to you—anything at all—while you were out, that might suggest where she was likely to go in case she wanted to drown herself?"

The blunt phrase, spoken openly for the first time, shook everybody. Miss Haydock put her head in her hands.

"Wait a minute," she said. "I do remember something. We were well up through the Parks— Yes— It was after tea, and we went a bit further before turning. I struck a bad bit of water and nearly lost the pole. I remember saying it would be a nasty place to go in, because of the weeds. It's a bad bottom—all mud with deep holes in it. Miss Newland asked if that wasn't the place where a man had been drowned last year. I said I didn't know, but I thought it was near there. She didn't say anything more, and I'd forgotten it till this moment."

Harriet looked at her watch.

"Half-past nine, she was last seen. She'd have to get to the boathouse. Had she a bicycle? No? Then it would take her nearly half an hour. Ten. Say another forty minutes to the Rollers, unless she was very quick—"

"She's not a quick punter. She'd take a canoe."

"She'd have the wind and stream against her. Say 10:45. And she'd have to get the canoe over the Rollers by herself. That takes time. But she would still have over an hour. We may be too late, but it's just worth trying."

"But she might have gone in anywhere."

"Of course she might. But there's just the chance. People get an idea and stick to it. And they don't always make their minds up instantly."

"If I know anything of the girl's psychology," began Miss Shaw.

"What's the good of arguing?" said Harriet. "She's either dead or alive and we've got to risk a guess. Who'll come with me? I'll get the car—we shall go quicker by road than by river. We can commandeer a boat somewhere above the Parks—if we have to break open a boathouse. Dean—"

"I'm with you," said Miss Martin.

"We want torches and blankets. Hot coffee. Brandy. Better get the police to send up a constable to meet us at Timms's. Miss Haydock, you're a better oar than I am—"

"I'll come," said Miss Haydock. "Thank God for something to do."

Lights on the river. The plash of sculls. The steady chock of the rowlocks.

The boat crept slowly downstream. The constable, crouched in the bows, swept the beam of a powerful torch from bank to bank. Harriet holding the rudder-lines, divided her attention between the dark current and the moving light ahead. The Dean, setting a slow and steady stroke, kept her eyes before her and her wits on the job.

At a word from the policeman, Harriet checked the boat and let her drift down towards a dismal shape, black and slimy on the black water. The boat lurched as the man leaned out. In the silence came the answering groan, plash, chuck of oars on the far side of the next bend.

"All right," said the policeman. "Only a bit o' sacking."

"Ready? Paddle!"

The sculls struck the water again.

"Is that the Bursar's boat coming up?" said the Dean.

"Very likely," said Harriet.

Just as she spoke, someone in the other boat gave a shout. There was a heavy splash and a cry ahead, and an answering shout from the constable:

"There she goes!"

"Pull like blazes," said Harriet. As she drew on the rudder-lines to bring their nose round the bend, she saw, across stroke's shoulder in the beam of the torch, the thing they had come to find—the shining keel of a canoe adrift in midstream, with the paddles floating beside it; and all around it the water ran, ringed and rippling with the shock of the plunge.

"Look out, ladies. Don't run her down. She can't be far off."

"Easy!" said Harriet. And then, "Back her! Hold her!"

The stream chuckled and eddied over the reversed oar-blades. The constable shouted to the upcoming sculler, and then pointed away towards the left bank.

"Over by the willow there."

The light caught the silver leaves, dripping like rain towards the river. Something swirled below them, pale and ominous.

"Easy. Paddle. One on bow. Another on bow. Another. Easy. Paddle. One. Two. Three. Easy. Paddle on stroke, backwater on bow. One. Two. Easy. Look out for your bow oars."

The boat swung across the stream and turned, following

the policeman's signal. He was kneeling and peering into the water on the bow side. A white patch glimmered up to the surface and sank again.

"Fetch her round a bit more, miss."

"Ready? One on stroke, paddle. Another. Easy. Hold her." He was leaning out, groping with both hands among the ribbonweed. "Back a little. Easy. Keep those bow oars out of the water. Trim the boat. Sit over to stroke. Have you got her?"

"I've got her—but the weeds are cruel strong."

"Mind you don't go over or there'll be two of you. Miss Haydock—ready, ship! See if you can help the constable. Dean—paddle one very gentle stroke and sit well over."

The boat rocked perilously as they heaved and tore at the clinging weeds, razor-sharp and strong as grave-bands. The Water-fly had come up now and was pulling across the stream. Harriet yelled to Miss Stevens to keep her sculls out of mischief. The boats edged together. The girl's head was out of the water, dead-white and lifeless, disfigured with black slime and dark stripes of weed. The constable was supporting the body. Miss Haydock had both hands in the stream, slashing with a knife at the ribbon-weed that was wrapped viciously about the legs. The other boat, hampered by its own lightness, was heeling over to stroke with gunwales awash, as her passengers reached and grappled.

"Trim your boat, damn you!" said Harriet, not pleased at the idea of having two fresh corpses to see to, and forgetting in her wrath to whom she was speaking. Miss Stevens paid no attention; but Miss Edwards threw her weight over; and as the boat lifted the body lifted too. Harriet, keeping her torch steady so that the rescuers could see what they were doing, watched the reluctant weeds loose their last coils and slip back.

"Better get her in here," said the constable. Their boat had the less room in it, but the stronger arms and the better balance. There was a strong heave and a violent lurch as the dead weight was hauled over the side and rolled in a dripping heap at Miss Haydock's feet.

The constable was a capable and energetic young man. He took the first-aid measures in hand with admirable promptness. The women, gathered on the bank, watched with anxious faces. Other help had now arrived from the boathouse. Harriet took it upon herself to stem the stream of questions.

"Yes. One of our students. Not a good waterman. Alarmed to think she had taken a canoe out alone. Reckless. Yes, we were afraid there might be an accident. Wind. Strong current. Yes. No. Quite against the rules." (If there was going to be an inquest, other explanations might have to be made there. But not here. Not now.) "Very unwise. High spirits. Oh, yes. Most unfortunate. Taking risks. . . ."

"She'll do now," said the constable.

He sat up and wiped the sweat from his eyes.

Brandy. Blankets. A melancholy little procession along the fields to the boathouse, but less melancholy than it might have been. Then an orgy of telephoning. Then the arrival of the doctor. Then Harriet found herself, suddenly shaking with nerves, being given whisky by some kindly person. The patient was better. The patient was quite all right. The capable policeman and Miss Haydock and Miss Stevens were having their hands dressed, where the sharp weeds had slashed them to the bone. People were talking and talking; Harriet hoped they were not talking foolishly.

"Well," said the Dean in her ear, "we *are* having a night!"

"Who's with Miss Newland?"

"Miss Edwards. I've warned her not to let the child say anything if she can help it. And I've muzzled that nice policeman. Accident, my dear, accident. It's quite all right. We've taken your cue. You kept your head wonderfully. Miss Stevens lost hers a bit, though. Started to cry and talk about suicide. I soon shut *her* up."

"Damn!" said Harriet. "What did she want to do that for?"

"What indeed? You'd think she *wanted* to make a scandal."

"Somebody obviously does."

"You don't think Miss Stevens—? She did her bit with the rescue-work, you know."

"Yes, I know. All right, Dean. I don't think. I won't try to think. I thought she and Miss Edwards would have that boat over between them."

"Don't let's discuss it now. Thank Heaven the worst hasn't happened. The girl's safe and that's all that matters. What we've got to do now is to put the best face on it."

It was nearly five in the morning when the rescuers, weary and bandaged, sat once again in the Warden's house. Everybody was praising everybody else.

"It was so clever of Miss Vane," said the Dean, "to realize that the wretched child would go up to that particular place. What a mercy that we arrived just when we did."

"I'm not so sure about that," said Harriet. "We may have done more harm than good. Do you realize that it was only when she saw us coming that she made up her mind to do it?"

"Do you mean she mightn't have done it at all if we hadn't gone after her?"

"Difficult to say. She was putting it off, I think. What really sent her in was that shout from the other boat. Who shouted, by the way?"

"I shouted," said Miss Stevens. "I looked over my shoulder and saw her. So I shouted."

"What was she doing when you saw her?"

"Standing up in the canoe."

"No, she wasn't," said Miss Edwards. "I looked round when you shouted, and she was just getting to her feet then."

"You're quite mistaken," contradicted Miss Stevens. "I say she was standing up when I saw her, and I shouted to stop her. You couldn't have seen past me."

"I saw perfectly plainly," said Miss Edwards. "Miss Vane

is quite right. It was when she heard the shout that she got up."

"I know what I saw," said the Bursar, obstinately.

"It's a pity you didn't take somebody to cox," said the Dean. "Nobody can see clearly what's going on behind her back."

"It is hardly necessary to argue about it," said the Warden, a little sharply. "The tragedy has been prevented, and that is all that matters. I am exceedingly grateful to everybody."

"I resent the suggestion," said Miss Stevens, "that I drove the unfortunate girl to destroy herself. And as for saying that we ought not to have gone in search of her—"

"I never said that," said Harriet, wearily. "I only said that *if* we had not gone it *might* not have happened. But of course we had to go."

"What does Newland say herself?" demanded the Dean.

"Says, why couldn't we leave her alone?" replied Miss Edwards. "I told her not to be an inconsiderate little ass."

"Poor child!" said Miss Shaw.

"If I were you," said Miss Edwards, "I shouldn't be too soft with these people. Bracing up is what does them good. You let them talk too much about themselves—"

"But she didn't talk to me," said Miss Shaw. "I tried very hard to make her."

"They'd talk much more if you'd only leave them alone."

"I think we'd better all go to bed," said Miss Martin.

"What a night," said Harriet, as she rolled, dog-weary, between the sheets. "What a gaudy night!" Her memory, thrashing round her brain like a cat in a sack, brought up the images of Mr. Pomfret and the pro-Proctor. They seemed to belong to another existence.

CHAPTER XIII

My sad hurt it shall releeve,
When my thoughts I shall disclose,
For thou canst not chuse but greeve,
When I shall recount my woes;
There is nothing to that friend,
To whose close uncranied breast,
We our secret thoughts may send,
And there safely let it rest;
And thy faithfull counsell may
My distressed case assist,
Sad affliction else may sway
Me a woman as it list.

MICHAEL DRAYTON

You must see," said Harriet, "that it's impossible to go on like this. You've got to call in expert help and risk the consequences. Any scandal is better than a suicide and an inquest."

"I think you are right," said the Warden.

Only Miss Lydgate, the Dean and Miss Edwards sat with Dr. Baring in the Warden's sitting-room. The brave pretense at confidence had been given up. In the Senior Common Room, members averted their eyes from one another and set a guard upon their lips. They were no longer angry and suspicious. They were afraid.

"The girl's parents are not likely to keep quiet about it," went on Harriet, remorselessly. "If she had succeeded in drowning herself, we should have the police and the reporters in at this moment. Next time, the attempt may come off."

"Next time—" began Miss Lydgate.

"There will be a next time," said Harriet. "And it may not be suicide; it may be open murder. I told you at the beginning that I did not think the measures adequate. I now say that I refuse to take any further share in the responsibility. I have tried, and I have failed, every time."

"What could the police do?" asked Miss Edwards. "We did have them in once—about those thefts, you remember, Warden. They made a great deal of fuss and arrested the wrong person. It was a very troublesome business."

"I don't think the police are the right people at all," said the Dean. "Your idea was a firm of private detectives, wasn't it?"

She turned to Harriet.

"Yes; but if anybody else has anything better to suggest—"

Nobody had any very helpful suggestion. The discussion went on. In the end:

"Miss Vane," said the Warden, "I think your idea is the best. Will you get into communication with these people?"

"Very well, Warden. I will ring up the head of the firm."

"You will use discretion."

"Of course," said Harriet. She was becoming a little impatient; the time for discretion seemed to her to be past. "If we call people in, we shall have to give them a free hand, you know," she added.

This was obviously an unpalatable reminder, though its force had to be admitted. Harriet could foresee endless hampering restrictions placed upon the investigators, and felt the difficulties that went with a divided authority. The police were answerable to nobody but themselves, but paid private detectives were compelled to do more or less as they were told. She looked at Dr. Baring, and wondered whether Miss Climpson or any of her underlings was capable of asserting herself against that formidable personality.

"And now," said the Dean, as she and Harriet crossed the quad together, "I've got to go and tackle the Newlands.

I'm *not* looking forward to it. They'll be terribly upset, poor things. He's a very minor civil servant, and their daughter's career means everything to them. Quite apart from the personal side of it, it'll be a frightful blow if this ruins her Schools. They're very poor and hardworking, and so proud of her—"

Miss Martin made a little despairing gesture, squared her shoulders and went to face her task.

Miss Hillyard, in her gown, was making for one of the lecture-rooms. She looked hollow-eyed and desperate, Harriet thought. Her glance shot from side to side, as though she were pursued.

From an open window on the ground floor of Queen Elizabeth came the voice of Miss Shaw, giving a coaching: "You might have quoted also from the essay *De la Vanité*. You remember the passage. *Je me suis couché mille fois chez moi, imaginant qu'on me trahirait et assomeroit cette nuit-là*—his morbid preoccupation with the idea of death and his—"

The academic machine was grinding on. At the entrance leading to their offices, the Bursar and Treasurer stood together, their hands full of papers. They seemed to be discussing some question of finance. Their glances were secretive and mutually hostile; they looked like sullen dogs, chained together and forced into a grumbling amity by the reprimand of their master.

Miss Pyke came down her staircase and passed them without a word. Still without a word, she passed Harriet and turned along the plinth. Her head was held high and defiantly. Harriet went in and along to Miss Lydgate's room. Miss Lydgate, as she knew, was lecturing; she could use her telephone undisturbed. She put her call through to London.

A quarter of an hour later, she hung up the receiver with a sinking heart. Why she should be surprised to learn that Miss Climpson was absent from Town "engaged on a case" she could not have said. It seemed vaguely monstrous that this should be so; but it was so. Would she like to speak to anyone else? Harriet had asked for Miss Murchison, the only other member of the firm who was personally known to her. Miss Murchison had left a year ago to be married. Harriet felt this as almost a personal affront. She did not like to pour all the details of the Shrewsbury affair into the ears of a complete stranger. She said she would write, rang off, and sat feeling curiously helpless.

It is all very well to take a firm line about things, and rush to the telephone, determined to "do something" without delay; other people do not sit with folded hands waiting upon the convenience even of our highly interesting and influential selves. Harriet laughed at her own annoyance. She had made up her mind to instant action, and now she was furious because a business firm had affairs of its own to attend to. Yet to wait any longer was impossible. The situation was becoming a nightmare. Faces had grown sly and distorted overnight; eyes fearful; the most innocent words charged with suspicion. At any moment some new terror might break bounds and carry all before it.

She was suddenly afraid of all these women: *horti conclusi*, *fontes signati*, they were walled in, sealed down, by walls and seals that shut her out. Sitting there in the clear light of morning, staring at the prosaic telephone on the desk, she knew the ancient dread of Artemis, moon-goddess, virgin-huntress, whose arrows are plagues and death.

It struck her then as a fantastic idea that she should fly for help to another brood of spinsters; even if she succeeded in getting hold of Miss Climpson, how was she to explain matters to that desiccated and elderly virgin? The very sight of some of the poison letters would probably make her sick, and the whole trouble would be beyond her comprehension. In this, Harriet did the lady less than justice; Miss Climpson had seen many strange things in sixty-odd years of boarding-house life, and was as free from repressions and complexes as any human being could very well be. But, in fact, the atmosphere of Shrewsbury was getting on Harriet's nerves. What she wanted was someone with whom she did not need to mince her words, somebody who would neither show nor feel surprise at any manifestation of human eccentricity, somebody whom she knew and could trust.

There were plenty of people in London—both men and women—to whom the discussion of sexual abnormalities was a commonplace; but most of them were very little to be trusted. They cultivated normality till it stood out of them all over in knobs, like the muscles upon professional strong men, and scarcely looked normal at all. And they talked interminably and loudly. From their bouncing mental health ordinary ill-balanced mortals shrank in alarm. She ran over various names in her mind, but found none that would do.

"The fact is," said Harriet to the telephone, "I don't know whether I want a doctor or a detective. But I've got to have somebody."

She wished—and not for the first time—that she could have got hold of Peter Wimsey. Not, of course, that this was the kind of case he could very suitably have investigated himself; but he would probably have known the right person. He at least would be surprised at nothing, shocked at nothing; he had far too wide an experience of the world. And he was completely to be trusted. But he was not there. He had vanished from view at the very moment when the Shrewsbury affair had first come to her notice; it seemed almost pointed. Like Lord Saint-George, she began to feel that Peter really had no right to disappear just when he was wanted. The fact that she had spent five years angrily refusing to contract further obligations towards Peter Wimsey had no weight with her now; she would readily have contracted obligations towards the devil himself, if she could have been sure that the prince of darkness was a gentleman of Peter's kidney. But Peter was as far beyond reach as Lucifer.

Was he? There was the telephone at her elbow. She could speak to Rome as easily as to London—though at a trifle more expense. It was probably only the financial modesty of the person whose income is all earned by work that made it seem more momentous to ring somebody up across a continent than across a city. At any rate, it could do no harm to fetch Peter's last letter and find the telephone number of his hotel. She went out quickly, and encountered Miss de Vine.

"Oh!" said the Fellow. "I was coming to look for you. I thought I had better show you this."

She held out a piece of paper; the sight of the printed letters was odiously familiar:

YOUR TURN'S COMING

"It's nice to be warned," said Harriet, with a lightness she did not feel. "Where? when? and how?"

"It fell out of one of the books I'm using," said Miss de Vine, blinking behind her glasses at the questions, "just now."

"When did you use the book last?"

"That," said Miss de Vine, blinking again, "is the odd thing about it. I didn't. Miss Hillyard borrowed it last night, and Mrs. Goodwin brought it back to me this morning."

Considering the things Miss Hillyard had said about Mrs. Goodwin, Harriet was faintly surprised that she should have chosen her to run her errands. But in certain circumstances the choice might, of course, be a wise one.

"Are you sure the paper wasn't there yesterday?"

"I don't think it could have been. I was referring to various pages, and I think I should have seen it."

"Did you give it directly into Miss Hillyard's own hands?"

"No; I put it in her pigeon-hole before Hall."

"So that anybody might have got hold of it."

"Oh, yes."

Exasperating. Harriet took possession of the paper and passed on. It was now not even clear against whom the threat was directed, much less from whom it came. She fetched Peter's letter, and discovered that in the interval she had made up her mind. She had said she would ring up the head of the firm; and so she would. If he was not technically the head, he was certainly the brains of it. She put the call through. She did not know how long it would take, but left instructions at the Lodge that when it came she was to be searched for and found without fail. She felt abominably restless.

The next piece of news was that a violent quarrel had taken place between Miss Shaw and Miss Stevens, who were normally the closest of friends. Miss Shaw, having heard the full story of the previous night's adventure, had accused Miss Stevens of frightening Miss Newland into the river; Miss Stevens had in her turn accused Miss Shaw of deliberately playing on the girl's feelings, so as to work her up into a state of nerves.

The next disturber of the peace was Miss Allison. As Harriet had discovered the previous term, Miss Allison had a way of passing on to people the things other people had said of them. In a spirit of candor she had now chosen to pass on to Mrs. Goodwin the hints thrown out by Miss Hillyard. Mrs. Goodwin had tackled Miss Hillyard about it; and there had been a most unpleasant scene, in which Miss Allison, the Dean and poor little Miss Chilperic, who had been drawn into the discussion by malignant chance, took sides with Mrs. Goodwin against Miss Pyke and Miss Burrows, who, though they thought Miss Hillyard had spoken ill-advisedly, resented any aspersions cast against the unmarried state as such. This unpleasantness took place in the Fellows' Garden.

Finally, Miss Allison had further inflamed the situation by passing on a vivid account of the matter to Miss Barton, who had gone away indignantly to tell Miss Lydgate and

Miss de Vine exactly what she thought of the psychology both of Miss Hillyard and Miss Allison.

It was not an agreeable morning.

Between the married (or about-to-be-married) and the unmarried, Harriet felt herself to be like Aesop's bat between the birds and beasts; an odd result, she felt, of having sown her wild oats in public. Lunch was a strained meal. She came into Hall rather late, to find that the High Table had sorted itself out into opposing camps, with Miss Hillyard at one end and Mrs. Goodwin at the other. She found an empty chair between Miss de Vine and Miss Stevens, and amused herself by drawing them and Miss Allison, who was next to Miss de Vine on the other side, into a discussion of currency and inflation. She knew nothing of the subject, but they, naturally, knew a great deal, and her tact was rewarded. Conversation spread; the table presented a less sullen front to the assembled students; and Miss Lydgate beamed approval. Things were moving nicely when a scout, leaning between Miss Allison and Miss de Vine, murmured a message.

"From Rome?" said Miss de Vine. "Who can that be, I wonder?"

"Telephoning from Rome?" said Miss Allison, in piercing accents. "Oh, one of your correspondents, I suppose. He must be better off than most historians."

"I think it's for me," said Harriet, and turned to the scout. "Are you sure they said de Vine and not Vane?"

The scout was not very sure.

"If you're expecting it, it must be for you," said Miss de Vine. Miss Allison made some rather sharp observation about writers of international celebrity and Harriet left the table, flushing uncomfortably and angry with herself for doing so.

As she went down to the public call-box in Queen Elizabeth, to which the call had been put through, she tried to arrange in her own mind what to say. A brief sentence of apology; another brief sentence of explanation; and a request for advice; into whose hands should the case be put? There was, surely, nothing difficult about that.

The voice from Rome spoke English very well. It did not think Lord Peter Wimsey was in the hotel, but would inquire. A pause, during which she could hear feet passing to and fro on the other side of the continent. Then the voice again, suave and apologetic.

"His lordship left Rome three days ago."

Oh! Did they know for what destination?

They would inquire. Another pause, and voices speaking Italian. Then the same voice again.

"His lordship left for Warsaw."

"Oh! Thank you very much."

And that was that.

At the thought of ringing up the British Embassy at Warsaw, her heart failed her. She replaced the receiver and went upstairs again. She did not seem to have gained very much by taking a firm line.

Friday afternoon. Crises always, thought Harriet, occurred at the weekend, when there were no posts. If she wrote now to London and they replied by return, she would still, in all probability, be able to take no action till Monday. If she wrote to Peter, there might be an Air-Mail —but suppose he wasn't at Warsaw after all. He might by now have gone on to Bucharest or Berlin. Could she possibly ring up the Foreign Office and demand to know his whereabouts? Because, if the letter got to him over the weekend and he wired a reply, she would not be losing so very much time. She was not sure if she would be very good at dealing with the Foreign Office. Was there anybody who could? How about the Hon. Freddy?

It took a little time to locate Freddy Arbuthnot, but eventually she ran him down, by phone, at an office in Throgmorton Street. He was definitely helpful. He had no idea where old Peter was, but he would take steps to find out, and if she liked to send a letter care of him (Freddy) he would see that it was forwarded on at the earliest possible moment. No trouble at all. Charmed to be of use.

So the letter was written, and dispatched so as to reach Town first post on the Saturday morning. It contained a brief outline of the case, and finished up:

> "Can you tell me whether you think Miss Climpson's people could handle it? And who, in her absence, is the most competent person there? Or, if not, can you suggest anybody else I could ask? Perhaps it should be a psychologist and not a detective. I know that anybody you recommend will be trustworthy. Would you mind wiring as soon as you get this? I should be immensely grateful. We are all getting rather worked up, and I'm afraid something drastic may happen if we don't cope with it quickly."

She hoped that last sentence did not sound as panicky as she felt.

> "I rang up your hotel in Rome and they said you had gone on to Warsaw. As I don't know where you may be by this time, I'm getting Mr. Arbuthnot to forward this through the Foreign Office."

That sounded faintly reproachful, but it couldn't be helped. What she really wanted to say was, "I wish to God you were here and could tell me what to do"; but she felt that that might make him feel uncomfortable, since he obviously couldn't be there. Still, it could do no harm to ask, "How soon do you think you will be back in England?" And with this addition, the letter was finished and posted.

"And to put the lid on things," said the Dean, "there's this man coming to dinner."

"This man" was Dr. Noel Threep, a very worthy and important man, a Fellow of a distinguished college and a member of the Council by which Shrewsbury was governed. Friends and benefactors of this kind were not infrequently entertained in College, and as a rule the High Table was glad of their presence. But the moment was scarcely auspicious. However, the engagement had been made early in the term, and it was quite impossible to put Dr. Threep off. Harriet said she thought his visit might be a good thing, and help to keep the minds of the S.C.R. off their troubles.

"We'll hope so," said the Dean. "He's a very nice man, and talks very interestingly. He's a political economist."

"Hard-boiled or soft-boiled?"

"Hard, I think."

This question had no reference to Dr. Threep's politics or economics, but only to his shirt-front. Harriet and the Dean had begun to collect shirt-fronts. Miss Chilperic's "young man" had started the collection. He was extremely tall and thin and rather hollow-chested; by way of emphasizing this latter defect, he always wore a soft pleated dress-shirt, which made him look (according to the Dean) like the scooped-out rind of a melon. By way of contrast, there had been an eminent and ample professor of chemistry—a visitor from another university—who had turned up in a front of intense rigidity, which stood out before him like the chest of a pouter pigeon, bulging out of all control and displaying a large area of the parent shirt at either side. A third variety of shirt fairly common among the learned was that which escaped from the center stud and gaped in the middle; and one never-to-be-forgotten happy day a popular poet had arrived to give a lecture on his methods of composition and the future of poetry, whereby, at every gesticulation (and he had used a great many), his waistcoat had leapt in the air, allowing a line of shirt, adorned with a little tab, to peep out, rabbit-like, over the waistline of the confining trouser. On this occasion, Harriet and the Dean had disgraced themselves badly.

Dr. Threep was a large, agreeable, talkative person, who at first sight appeared to present no loophole for sartorial criticism. But he had not been seated at table three minutes before Harriet realized that he was doomed to form one of the most notable additions to the collection. For he popped. When he bent over his plate, when he turned to pass the mustard, when he courteously inclined himself to catch what his neighbor was saying, his shirt-front exploded with a merry little report like the opening of ginger-beer. The clamor in Hall seemed louder than usual that night, so that the poppings were inaudible beyond a few places to right and left of him; but the Warden and the Dean, who sat beside him, heard them, and Harriet, sitting opposite, heard them; she dared not catch the Dean's eye. Dr. Threep was too well-bred, or perhaps too much embarrassed, to allude to the matter; he talked on imperturbably, raising his voice more and more to be heard above the din of the undergraduates. The Warden was frowning.

"—the excellent relations between the Women's Colleges and the University," said Dr. Threep. "All the same—"

The Warden summoned a scout, who presently went down to the Junior High and thence to the other tables, with the usual message:

"The Warden's compliments, and she would be obliged if there could be rather less noise."

"I beg your pardon, Dr. Threep. I didn't quite catch."

"All the same," repeated Dr. Threep, with a polite bend and pop, "it is curious to see how traces of the old prejudice linger. Only yesterday the Vice-Chancellor showed me a remarkably vulgar anonymous letter sent to him that very morning . . ."

The noise in Hall was dying down gradually; it was like a lull in the intervals of a storm.

". . . making the most absurd accusations—oddly enough against your own Senior Common Room in particular. Accusations of murder, of all things. The Vice-Chancellor . . ."

Harriet missed the next few words; she was watching how, as Dr. Threep's voice rang out in the comparative quiet, the heads at the High Table jerked towards him, as though pulled by wires.

". . . pasted on paper—quite ingenious. I said, 'My dear Mr. Vice-Chancellor, I doubt whether the police can do much; it is probably the work of some harmless crank.' But is it not curious that such peculiar delusions should exist—and *per*sist—at this day?"

"Very curious indeed," said the Warden, with stiff lips.

"So I advised against police interference—for the moment, at any rate. But I said I would put the matter before you, since Shrewsbury was particularly mentioned. I defer, of course, to your opinion."

The dons sat spellbound; and in that moment, Dr. Threep, bowing to the Warden's decision, popped—with so loud and violent an explosion that it resounded from end to end of the table, and the major embarrassment was swallowed up in the minor. Miss Chilperic suddenly broke out into a spasm of high, nervous laughter.

How dinner ended, Harriet could never properly recall. Dr. Threep went over to have coffee with the Warden, and Harriet found herself in the Dean's room, helpless between mirth and alarm.

"It's really very serious," said Miss Martin.

"Horribly. 'I said to the Vice-Chancellor—' "

"Pop!"

"No; but honestly, what are we to do about it?"

"I defer to your opinion."

"Pop!"

"I can't imagine what makes shirts do that. Can you?"

"I've no idea. And I meant to be so clever this evening. Here, said I, is a Man come among us; I will watch everybody's reactions—and then it all went Pop!"

"It's no good watching reactions to Dr. Threep," said the Dean. "Everyone's too used to him. And anyhow, he has half a dozen children. But it's going to be very awkward if the Vice-Chancellor—"

"Very."

• • • •

Saturday dawned dull and lowering.

"I believe it's going to thunder," said Miss Allison.

"Rather early in the year for that," said Miss Hillyard.

"Not at all," retorted Mrs. Goodwin; "I've known plenty of thunderstorms in May."

"There is certainly something electrical in the atmosphere," said Miss Lydgate.

"I agree with you," said Miss Barton.

Harriet had slept badly. She had, in fact, been walking about College half the night, a prey to imaginary alarms. When at length she had gone to bed, she had had the tiresome dream about trying to catch a train, hampered all the time by a quantity of luggage which she strove vainly to pack in misty and unmanageable suitcases. In the morning, she struggled desperately with the proofs of Miss Lydgate's chapter on Gerard Manley Hopkins, finding it as unmanageable as the suitcases and very nearly as misty. In the intervals of disentangling the poet's own system of sprung, counterpoint and logaoedic rhythm, with its rove-over lines and outrides, from Miss Lydgate's rival system of scansion (which required five alphabets and a series of pothooks for its expression), she wondered whether Freddy Arbuthnot had succeeded in doing what he had promised and whether she ought to leave it at that or do something else: in which case, what? In the afternoon, she could bear herself no longer and set out, under a threatening sky, to wander about Oxford, and walk herself, if possible, into exhaustion. She started up the High, pausing for a few moments to stare into the window of an Antique shop; there was a set of carved ivory chessmen there, for which she had conceived an unreasonable affection. She even played with the idea of going boldly in and buying them; but she knew they would cost too much. They were Chinese, and each piece was a complicated nest of little revolving balls, delicate as fine lace. It would be jolly to handle them, but idiotic to buy them; she was not even a good chess-player, and in any case, one couldn't play chess comfortably with pieces like that. She put temptation aside and moved on. There was a shop full of wooden objects embellished with the painted shields of colleges: bookends, matchstands, pens shaped like oars and horribly top-heavy, cigarette-boxes, ink-pots and even powder-compacts. Did it add a zest to facial repairs to have them watched over by the lions of Oriel or the martlets of Worcester? To be reminded during the process that one had a betrothed among the tripping stags of Jesus or a brother nourished by the pious pelican of Corpus? She crossed the street before she came to Queen's (for Mr. Pomfret might conceivably pop out of the gate, and she was rather avoiding an encounter with Mr. Pomfret) and went on up the other side. Books and prints—fascinating at most times, but insufficiently exciting to hold her attention. Robes and gowns, colorful, but too academic for her mood. A chemist's shop. A stationer's, with more college bric-à-brac, this time in glass and pottery. A tobacconist's, with more coats of arms, on ash-trays and tobacco-jars. A jeweler's, with college arms on spoons and brooches and napkin-rings. She grew weary of college arms and turned down a side-street into Merton Street. In this untouched and cobbled thoroughfare there should be peace, if anywhere. But peace is in the mind, and not in streets, however old and beautiful. She passed through the iron gate into Merton Grove, and so, crossing over Dead Man's Walk, into the Broad Walk of Christ Church and along this and round to the towing path where the New Cut meets the Isis. And there, to her horror, she was hailed by a well-known voice. Here, by special interposition of all the powers of evil, was Miss Schuster-Slatt, whose presence in Oxford she had till that moment mercifully forgotten, convoying a party of American visitors, all eager for information. Miss Vane was the very person to tell them everything. Did she know which of these barges belonged to which college? Were those cute little blue-and-gold heads griffins or phoenixes and were there three of them to symbolize the Trinity or was that just accident? Were those the Magdalen lilies? If so, why was there the initial "W" painted all round the barge and what did it stand for? Why did Pembroke have the English rose and the Scotch thistle at the top of the shield? Were the roses of New College English roses, too? Why was it called New when it was so old, and why mustn't you call it "New" but always "New College"? Oh! look, Sadie—are those geese flying across? Swans? How interesting! Were there many swans on the river? Was it true that all the swans in England belonged to the King? Was that a swan on that barge? Oh, an eagle. Why did some barges have figure-heads and some not? Did the boys ever have tea-parties on the barges? Could Miss Vane explain about those bumping races, because nobody had been able to understand from Sadie's description. Was that the University barge? Oh, the University *College* barge. Was the University College the place where all the classes were held?

And so forth and so on—all along the towing path, all the way up the long avenue to the Meadow Buildings and all the way round Christ Church, from Hall to Kitchen, from Cathedral to Library, from Mercury to Great Tom, while all the time the sky brooded lower and the weather became more oppressive, until Harriet, who had started out feeling as though her skull were stuffed with wool, ended up with a raging headache.

The storm held off till after Hall, except for threatenings and grumblings of thunder. At 10 o'clock the first great flash went across the sky like a searchlight, picking out roof and treetop violet-blue against the blackness, and followed by a clap that shook the walls. Harriet flung her window open and leaned out. There was a sweet smell of approaching rain. Another flash and crash; a swift gust of wind; and then the swish and rush of falling water, the gurgle of overflowing gutters, and peace.

CHAPTER XIV

Truce gentle love, a parly now I crave,
Me thinks, 'tis long since first these wars begun,
Nor thou nor I, the better yet can have:
Bad is the match where neither party won.
I offer free conditions of faire peace,
My hart for hostage, that it shall remaine,
Discharge our forces heere, let malice cease,
So for my pledge, thou give me pledge againe.

MICHAEL DRAYTON

"It was a good storm," said the Dean.

"First-class," said the Bursar, dryly, "for those that like it and don't have to cope with those that don't. The scouts' quarters were a pandemonium; I had to go over. There was Carrie in hysterics, and Cook thinking her last hour had come, and Annie shrieking to Heaven that her darling children would be terrified and wanting to rush off to Headington then and there to comfort them—"

"I wonder you didn't send her there at once in the best car available," put in Miss Hillyard in sarcastic tones.

"—and one of the kitchen-maids having an outbreak of religious blues," went on Miss Stevens, "and confessing her sins to an admiring circle. I can't think why people have so little self-control."

"I'm horribly afraid of thunder," said Miss Chilperic.

"The wretched Newland was all upset again," said the Dean. "The Infirmarian was quite frightened about her. Said the Infirmary maid was hiding in the linen-cupboard and she didn't like to be left alone with Newland. However, Miss Shaw obligingly coped."

"Who were the four students who were dancing in the quad in bathing-dresses?" inquired Miss Pyke. "They had quite a ritual appearance. I was reminded of the ceremonial dances of the—"

"I was afraid the beeches were going to be struck," said Miss Burrows. "I sometimes wonder whether it's safe to have them so near the buildings. If they came down—"

"There's a bad leak in my ceiling, Bursar," said Mrs. Goodwin. "The rain came in like a waterspout—just over my bed. I had to move all the furniture, and the carpet is quite—"

"Anyhow," repeated the Dean, "it was a good storm, and it's cleared the air. Look at it. Could anybody want a better and brighter Sunday morning?"

Harriet nodded. The sun was brilliant on the wet grass and the wind blew fresh and cool.

"It's taken my headache away, thank goodness! I'd like to do something calm and cheerful and thoroughly Oxonian. Isn't everything a lovely color? Like the blues and scarlets and greens in an illuminated missal!"

"I'll tell you what we'll do," said the Dean, brightly. "We'll toddle along like two good little people and hear the University Sermon. I can't think of anything more soothingly normal and academic than that. And Dr. Armstrong's preaching. He's always interesting."

"The University Sermon?" said Harriet, amused. "Well, that's the last thing I should have thought of for myself. But it's an idea; definitely an idea. We'll go."

Yes; the Dean was right; here was the great Anglican compromise at its most soothing and ceremonial. The solemn procession of doctors in hood and habit; the Vice-Chancellor bowing to the preacher, and the beadles tripping before them; the throng of black gowns and the decorous gaiety of the summer-frocked wives of dons; the hymn and the bidding-prayer; the gowned and hooded preacher austere in cassock and bands; the quiet discourse delivered in a thin, clear, scholarly voice, and dealing gently with the relations of the Christian philosophy to atomic physics. Here were the Universities and the Church of England kissing one another in righteousness and peace, like the angels in a Botticelli Nativity: very exquisitely robed, very cheerful in a serious kind of way, a little mannered, a little conscious of their fine mutual courtesy. Here, without heat, they could discuss their common problem, agreeing pleasantly or pleasantly agreeing to differ. Of the grotesque and ugly devil-shapes sprawling at the foot of the picture these angels had no word to say. What solution could either of them produce, if challenged, for the Shrewsbury problem? Other bodies would be bolder: the Church of Rome would have its answer, smooth, competent and experienced; the queer, bitterly-jarring sects of the New Psychology would have another, ugly, awkward, tentative and applied with a passionate experimentalism. It was entertaining to imagine a Freudian University indissolubly wedded to a Roman Establishment: they certainly would not live so harmoniously together as the Anglican Church and the School of Litterae Humaniores. But it was delightful to believe, if only for an hour, that all human difficulties could be dealt with in this detached and amiable spirit. "The University is a Paradise"—true, but—"then saw I that there was a way to hell even from the gates of Heaven . . ."

The blessing was given; the voluntary rolled out—something fugal and pre-Bach; the procession reformed and dispersed again, passing out south and north; the congregation rose to their feet and began to stream away in an orderly disorder. The Dean, who was fond of early fugues, remained quietly in her place and Harriet sat dreamily beside her, with eyes fixed on the softly-tinted saints in the rood-screen. At length they both rose and made their way to the door. A mild, clear gust of wind met them as they passed between the twisted columns of Dr. Owen's porch, making the Dean clutch at the peak of her rebellious cap and bellying out their gowns into wide arcs and volutes. The sky, between pillow and pillow of rounded cloud, was the pale and transparent blue of aquamarine.

Standing at the corner of Cat Street was a group of gowns, chatting with animation—among them, two Fellows of All Souls and a dignified figure which Harriet recognized as that of the Master of Balliol. Beside him was another M.A. who, as Harriet and the Dean went by, conversing of counterpoint, turned suddenly and lifted his mortar-board.

For a long moment, Harriet simply could not believe her eyes. Peter Wimsey. Peter, of all people. Peter, who was supposed to be in Warsaw, planted placidly in the High as though he had grown there from the beginning. Peter, wearing cap and gown like any orthodox Master of Arts, presenting every appearance of having piously attended the University Sermon, and now talking mild academic shop with two Fellows of All Souls and the Master of Balliol.

"And why not?" thought Harriet, after the first second of shock. "He is a Master of Arts. He was at Balliol. Why shouldn't he talk to the Master if he likes? But how did he get here? And why? And when did he come? And why didn't he let me know?"

She found herself confusedly receiving introductions and presenting Lord Peter to the Dean.

"I rang up yesterday from Town," Wimsey was saying, "but you were out." And then more explanations—something about flying over from Warsaw, and "my nephew at the House," and "the Master's kind hospitality," and sending a note round to College. Then, out of the jumble of polite nothings, a sentence she grasped clearly.

"If you are free and in College during the next half-hour or so, may I come round and look you up?"

"Yes, do," said Harriet, lamely, "that would be delightful." She pulled herself together. "I suppose it's no good asking you to lunch?"

It appeared that he was lunching with the Master, and that one of the All Souls men was lunching also. In fact, a little lunch-party with, she gathered, some kind of historical basis, with mention of somebody's article for the Proceedings of Something or Other, which Wimsey was going to "step into All Souls and look at—it won't take you ten minutes," and references to the printing and distribution of Reformation polemical pamphlets—to Wimsey's expert knowledge—to the other man's expert knowledge—and to the inexpert pretense at knowledge of some historian from another university.

Then the whole group broke up. The Master raised his cap and drifted away, reminding Wimsey and the historian that lunch would be at 1:15; Peter said something to Harriet about being "round in twenty minutes," and then vanished with the two Fellows into All Souls, and Harriet and the Dean were walking together again.

"Well!" said the Dean, "so that's the man."

"Yes," said Harriet weakly, "that's him."

"My dear, he's perfectly charming. You never said he was coming to Oxford."

"I didn't know. I thought he was in Warsaw. I knew he was supposed to be coming up some time this term to see his nephew, but I'd no idea he could get away so soon. As a matter of fact, I wanted to ask him—only I don't suppose he could have got my letter—"

She felt that her efforts at explanation were only darkening counsel. In the end she made a clean breast of the whole affair to the Dean.

"I don't know whether he got my letter and knows already, or whether, if he doesn't, I ought to tell him. I know he's absolutely safe. But whether the Warden and the S.C.R.—I didn't expect him to turn up like this."

"I should think it was the wisest thing you could have done," said Miss Martin. "I shouldn't say too much at College. Bring him along, if he'll come, and let him turn the whole lot of us inside out. A man with manners like that could twist the whole High Table round his little finger. What a mercy he's a historian—that will put him on the right side of Miss Hillyard."

"I never thought of him as a historian."

"Well, he took a First, anyway . . . didn't you know?"

She had not known. She had not even troubled to wonder. She had never consciously connected Wimsey and Oxford in her mind. This was the Foreign Office business all over again. If he had realized her thoughtlessness it must have hurt him. She saw herself as a monster of callous ingratitude.

"I'm told he was looked upon as one of the ablest scholars of his year," pursued the Dean. "A. L. Smith thought highly of him. It's a pity, in a way, he didn't stick to History—but naturally, his chief interests wouldn't be academic."

"No," said Harriet.

So the Dean had been making inquiries. Naturally, she would. Probably the whole S.C.R. could by now give her detailed information about Wimsey's University career. That was comprehensible enough: they thought along those lines. But she herself might surely have found the energy for two minutes' study of the Calendar.

"Where shall I put him when he comes? I suppose if I take him off to my own room it will set a bad example to the students. And it is a bit cramped."

"You can have my sitting-room. Much better than any of the public rooms, if you're going to discuss this beastly business. I wonder if he *did* get that letter. Perhaps the eager interest behind that penetrating eye was due to his suspicions of me. And I put it all down to my personal fascination! The man's dangerous, though he doesn't look it."

"That's why he's dangerous. But if he read my letter, he'll know that it isn't you."

Some minor confusions were cleared up when they reached College and found a note from Peter in Harriet's pigeonhole. It explained that he had reached London early on Saturday afternoon and found Harriet's letter waiting for him at the Foreign Office. "I tried to ring you, but left no name, as I did not know whether you wanted me to appear personally in this matter." He had been engaged in London that afternoon, motored to Oxford for dinner, been captured by some Balliol friends and kindly invited by the Master to stay the night, and would call "some time tomorrow" in the hope of finding her in.

So she waited in the Dean's room, idly watching the summer sun play through the branches of the plane-tree in the New Quad and make a dancing pattern upon the plinth, until she heard his knock. When she said "Come in!" the commonplace formula seemed to take on a startling significance. For good or evil, she had called in something explosive from the outside world to break up the ordered tranquility of the place; she had sold the breach to an alien force; she had sided with London against Oxford and with the world against the cloister.

But when he entered, she knew that the image had been a false one. He came into the quiet room as though he belonged there, and had never belonged to any other place.

"Hullo-ullo!" he said, with a faint echo of the old, flippant manner. Then he stripped off his gown and tossed it on the couch beside her own, laying his mortar-board on the table.

"I found your note when I got back. So you did get my letter?"

"Yes; I'm sorry you should have had all this bother. It seemed to me, as I was coming to Oxford in any case, I had better push along and see you. I meant to come round yesterday evening, but I got tied up with people—and I thought perhaps I had better announce myself first."

"It was good of you to come. Sit down."

She pulled an armchair forward, and he dropped into it rather heavily. She noticed, with a curious little prick of anxiety, how the clear light picked out the angles of the skull on jaw and temple.

"Peter! You look tired to death. What have you been doing with yourself?"

"Talking," he said, discontentedly. "Words, words, words. All these interminable weeks. I'm the professional funny man of the Foreign Office. You didn't know that? Well, I am. Not often, but waiting in the wings if wanted. Some turn goes wrong—some Under-Secretary's secretary with small discretion and less French uses an ill-considered phrase in an after-dinner speech, and they send on the patter-comedian to talk the house into a good humor again. I take people out to lunch and tell them funny stories and work them up to mellowing point. God! what a game!"

"I didn't know this, Peter. I've just discovered that I've been too selfish even to try and know anything. But it isn't like you to sound so dreadfully discouraged. You look—"

"Spare me, Harriet. Don't say I'm getting to look my age. That won't do. An eternal childishness is my one diplomatic asset."

"You only look as though you hadn't slept for weeks."

"I'm not sure that I have, now you mention it. I thought—at one point we all thought—something might be going to happen. All the old, filthy uproar. I got as far as saying to Bunter one night: 'It's coming; it's here; back to the Army again, sergeant.' . . . But in the end, you know, it made a noise like a hoop and rolled away—for the moment."

"Thanks to the comic cross-talk?"

"Oh, no. Great Scott, no. Mine was a very trivial affair. Slight frontier skirmish. Don't get it into your head that I'm the man who saved the Empire."

"Then who did?"

"Dunno. Nobody knows. Nobody ever does know, for certain. The old bus wobbles one way, and you think, 'That's done it!' and then it wobbles the other way and you think, 'All serene'; and then, one day, it wobbles over too far and you're in the soup and can't remember how you got there."

"That's what we're all afraid of, inside ourselves."

"Yes. It terrifies me. It's a relief to get back and find you here—and all this going on as it used to do. Here's where the real things are done, Harriet—if only those bunglers out there will keep quiet and let it go on. God! how I loathe haste and violence and all that ghastly, slippery cleverness. Unsound, unscholarly, insincere—nothing but propaganda and special pleading and 'what do we get out of this?' No time, no peace, no silence; nothing but conferences and newspapers and public speeches till one can't hear one's self think. . . . If only one could root one's self in here among the grass and stones and do something worth doing, even if it was only restoring a lost breathing for the love of the job and nothing else."

She was astonished to hear him speak with so much passion.

"But, Peter, you're saying exactly what I've been feeling all this time. But can it be done?"

"No; it can't be done. Though there are moments when one comes back and thinks it might."

" 'Ask for the old paths, where is the good way, and walk therein, and ye shall find rest for your souls.' "

"Yes," said he bitterly, "and it goes on: 'But they said: we will not walk therein.' Rest? I had forgotten there was such a word."

"So had I."

They sat silent for a few minutes. Wimsey offered her his cigarette-case and struck a match for them both.

"Peter, it's queer we should sit here and talk like this. Do you remember that horrible time at Wilvercombe when we could find nothing to throw at one another but cheap wit and spiteful remarks? At least, I was spiteful: you never were."

"It was the watering-place atmosphere," said Wimsey. "One is always vulgar at watering-places. It is the one haunting terror of my life that some day some perfectly irresistible peach of a problem will blossom out at Brighton or Blackpool, and that I shall be weak-minded enough to go and meddle with it." The laughter had come back to his voice and his eyes were tranquil. "Thank Heaven, it's extremely difficult to be cheap in Oxford—after one's second year, at any rate. Which reminds me that I haven't yet properly thanked you for being so kind to Saint-George."

"Have you seen him yet?"

"No; I have threatened to descend on him on Monday, and show him a damned disinheriting countenance. He has gone off somewhere today with a party of friends. I know what that means. He's getting thoroughly spoilt."

"Well, Peter, you can't wonder. He's terribly good-looking."

"He's a precocious little monkey," said his uncle, without enthusiasm. "Though I can't blame him for that; it runs in the blood. But it's characteristic of his impudence that he should have gate-crashed your acquaintance, after you had firmly refused to meet any of my people."

"I found him for myself, you see, Peter."

"Literally, or so he says. I gather that he nearly knocked you down, damaged your property and generally made a nuisance of himself, and that you instantly concluded he must be some relation to me."

"That's— If he said that, you know better than to believe it. But I couldn't very well miss the likeness."

"Yet people have been known to speak slightingly of my personal appearance! I congratulate you on a perception worthy of Sherlock Holmes at his keenest."

It amused and touched her to discover this childish streak of vanity in him. But she knew that he would see through her at once if she tried to pander to it by saying anything more flattering than the truth.

"I recognized the voice before I looked at him at all. And he has your hands; I shouldn't think anybody has ever spoken slightingly about those."

"Confound it, Harriet! My one really shameful weakness. My most jealously guarded bit of personal conceit. Dragged into the light of day and remorselessly exposed. I am idiotically proud of having inherited the Wimsey hands. My brother and my sister both missed them, but they go back in the family portraits for three hundred years." His face clouded for a moment. "I wonder all the strength hasn't been bred out of them by this time; our sands are running down fast. Harriet, will you come with me one day to Denver and see the place before the new civilization grows in on it like the jungle? I don't want to go all Galsworthy about it. They'll tell you I don't care a damn for the whole outfit, and I don't know that I do. But I was born there, and I shall be sorry if I live to see the land sold for ribbon-building and the Hall turned over to a Hollywood Color-Talkie king."

"Lord Saint-George wouldn't do that, would he?"

"I don't know, Harriet. Why shouldn't he? Our kind of show is dead and done for. What the hell good does it do anybody these days? But he may care more than he thinks he does."

"You care, don't you, Peter?"

"It's very easy for me to care, because I'm not called upon to do a hand's turn in the matter. I am the usual middle-aged prig, with an admirable talent for binding heavy burdens and laying them on other men's shoulders. Don't think I envy my nephew his job. I'd rather live at peace and lay my bones in the earth. Only I have a cursed hankering after certain musty old values, which I'm coward enough to deny, like my namesake of the Gospels. I never go home if I can help it, and I avoid coming here; the cocks crow too long and too loudly."

"Peter, I'd no idea you felt like that. I'd like to see your home."

"Would you? Then we'll go, one of these days. I won't inflict the family on you—though I think you'd like my mother. But we'll choose a time when they're all away—except a dozen or so harmless dukes in the family vault. All embalmed, poor devils, to linger on dustily to the Day of Judgment. Typical, isn't it, of a family tradition that it won't even let you rot."

Harriet could find nothing to say to him. She had

fought him for five years, and found out nothing but his strength; now, within half an hour, he had exposed all his weaknesses, one after the other. And she could not in honesty say: "Why didn't you tell me before?" because she knew perfectly well what the answer ought to be. Fortunately, he did not seem to expect any comment.

"Great Scott!" was his next remark, "look at the time! You've let me maunder on, and we've never said a word about your problem."

"I've been only too thankful to forget it for a bit."

"I dare say you have," he said, looking thoughtfully at her. "Listen, Harriet, couldn't we make today a holiday? You've had enough of this blasted business. Come and be bothered with me for a change. It'll be a relief for you—like getting a nice go of rheumatism in exchange for toothache. Equally damnable, but different. I've got to go to this lunch-party, but it needn't take too long. How about a punt at 3 o'clock from Magdalen Bridge?"

"There'll be an awful crowd on the river. The Cherwell's not what it was, especially on a Sunday. More like Bank Holiday at Margate, with gramophones and bathing-dresses and everybody barging into everybody else."

"Never mind. Let's go and do our bit of barging along with the happy populace. Unless you'd rather come in the car and fly with me to the world's end. But the roads will be worse than the river. And if we find a quiet spot, either I shall make a pest of myself or else we shall start on the infernal problem. There's safety in publicity."

"Very well, Peter. We'll do exactly as you like."

"Then we'll say Magdalen Bridge at three. Trust me, I'm not shirking the problem. If we can't see our way through it together, we'll find somebody who can. There are no seas innavigable nor lands unhabitable."

He got up and held out a hand.

"Peter, what a rock you are! The shadow of a great rock in a weary land. My dear, what are you thinking about? One doesn't shake hands at Oxford."

"The elephant never forgets." He kissed her fingers gently. "I have brought my formal cosmopolitan courtesy with me. My God! talk of courtesy—I'm going to be late for lunch."

He snatched up cap and gown and was gone before she had time even to think of seeing him down to the Lodge.

"But it's just as well," she thought, watching him run across the quad like an undergraduate, "he hasn't too much time as it is. Bless the man, if he hasn't taken my gown instead of his own! Oh, well, it doesn't matter. We're much of a height and mine's pretty wide on the shoulders, so it's exactly the same thing."

And then it struck her as strange that it should be the same thing.

Harriet smiled to herself as she went to change for the river. If Peter was keen on keeping up decayed traditions he would find plenty of opportunity by keeping to a pre-War standard of watermanship, manners and dress. Especially dress. A pair of grubby shorts or a faded regulation suit rolled negligently about the waist was the modern version of Cherwell fashions for men; for women, a sun-bathing costume with (for the tender-footed) a pair of gaily-colored beach-sandals. Harriet shook her head at the sunshine, which was now hot as well as bright. Even for the sake of startling Peter, she was not prepared to offer a display of grilled back and mosquito-bitten legs. She would go seemly and comfortable.

The Dean, meeting her under the beeches, gazed with exaggerated surprise at her dazzling display of white linen and pipe-clay.

"If this were twenty years ago I should say you were going on the river."

"I am. Hand in hand with a statelier past."

The Dean groaned gently. "I'm afraid you are making yourself conspicuous. That kind of thing is not done. You are clothed, clean and cool. On a Sunday afternoon, too. I am ashamed of you. I hope, at least, the parcel under your arm contains the records of crooners."

"Not even that," said Harriet.

Actually, it contained her diary of the Shrewsbury scandal. She had thought that the best thing would be to let Peter take it away and study it for himself. Then he could decide what was best to be done about it.

She was punctual at the bridge, but found Peter there before her. His obsolete politeness in this respect was emphasized by the presence of Miss Flaxman and another Shrewsburian, who were sitting on the raft, apparently waiting for their escort, and looking rather hot and irritable. It amused Harriet to let Wimsey take charge of her parcel, hand her ceremoniously into the punt and arrange the cushions for her, and to know, by his ironical eyes, that he perfectly well understood the reason of her unusual meekness.

"Is it your pleasure to go up or down?"

"Well, going up there's more riot but a better bottom; going down you're all right as far as the fork, and then you choose between thick mud and the Corporation dump."

"It appears to be altogether a choice of evils. But you have only to command. My ear is open like a greedy shark to catch the tunings of a voice divine."

"Great heavens! Where did you find that?"

"That, though you might not believe it, is the crashing conclusion of a sonnet by Keats. True, it is a youthful effort; but there are some things that even youth does not excuse."

"Let us go downstream. I need solitude to recover from the shock."

He turned the punt out into the stream and shot the bridge accurately. Then:

"Admirable woman! You have allowed me to spread the tail of vanity before that pair of deserted Ariadnes. Would you now prefer to be independent and take the pole? I admit it is better fun to punt than to be punted, and that a desire to have all the fun is nine-tenths of the law of chivalry."

"Is it possible that you have a just and generous mind? I will not be outdone in generosity. I will sit like a perfect lady and watch you do the work. It's nice to see things well done."

"If you say that, I shall get conceited and do something silly."

He was, in fact, a pretty punter to watch, easy in action and quite remarkably quick. They picked their way at surprising speed down the crowded and tortuous stream until, in the narrow reach above the ferry, they were checked by another punt, which was clumsily revolving in midstream and cramming a couple of canoes rather dangerously against the bank.

"Before you come on this water," cried Wimsey, thrusting the offenders off with his heel and staring offensively at the youth in charge (a stringy young man, naked to the waist and shrimp-pink with the sun), "you should learn the rule of the river. Those canoes have the right of way. And if you can't handle a pole better than that, I recommend you to retire up the backwater and stay there till you know what God gave you feet for."

Whereat a middle-aged man, whose punt was moored a little way further on, turned his head sharply and cried in ringing tones:

"Good lord! Wimsey of Balliol!"

"Well, well, well," said his lordship, abandoning the pink youth, and ranging up alongside the punt. "Peake of Brasenose, by all that's holy. What brings you here?"

"Dash it," said Mr. Peake, "I live here. What brings *you* here is more to the point. You haven't met my wife—Lord Peter Wimsey, my dear—the cricket blue, you know. The rest is my family."

He waved his hand vaguely over a collection of assorted offspring.

"Oh, I thought I'd look the old place up," said Peter, when the introductions were completed all round. "I've got a nephew here and all that. What are you doing? Tutor? Fellow? Lecturer?"

"Oh, I coach people. A dog's life, a dog's life. Dear me! A lot of water has flowed under Folly Bridge since we last met. But I'd have known your voice anywhere. The moment I heard those arrogant, off-hand, go-to-blazes tones I said, 'Wimsey of Balliol.' Wasn't I right?"

Wimsey shipped the pole and sat down.

"Have pity, old son, have pity! Let the dead bury their dead."

"You know," said Mr. Peake to the world at large, "when we were up together—shocking long time ago that is—never mind! If anyone got landed with a country cousin or an American visitor who asked, as these people will, 'What is this thing called the Oxford manner?' we used to take 'em round and show 'em Wimsey of Balliol. He fitted in very handily between St. John's Gardens and the Martyrs' Memorial."

"But suppose he wasn't there, or wouldn't perform?"

"That catastrophe never occurred. One never failed to find Wimsey of Balliol planted in the center of the quad and laying down the law with exquisite insolence to somebody."

Wimsey put his head between his hands.

"We were accustomed to lay bets," went on Mr. Peake, who seemed to have preserved an undergraduate taste in humor, owing, no doubt, to continuous contact with First-Year mentality, "upon what they would say about him afterwards. The Americans mostly said, 'My, but isn't he just the perfect English aristocrat!' but some of them said, 'Does he need that glass in his eye or is it just part of the costume?' "

Harriet laughed, thinking of Miss Schuster-Slatt.

"My dear—" said Mrs. Peake, who seemed to have a kindly nature.

"The country cousins," said Mr. Peake remorselessly, "invariably became speechless and had to be revived with coffee and ices at Buol's."

"Don't mind me," said Peter, whose face was invisible, except for the tip of a crimson ear.

"But you're wearing very well, Wimsey," pursued Mr. Peake, benevolently. "Kept your waistline. Still good for a sprint between the wickets? Can't say I'm much use now, except for the Parents' Match, eh, Jim? That's what marriage does for a man—makes him fat and lazy. But *you* haven't changed. Not an atom. Not a hair. Absolutely unmistakable. And you're quite right about these louts on the river. I'm sick and tired of being barged into and getting their beastly punts over my bows. They don't even know enough to apologize. Think it's dashed funny. Stupid oafs. And gramophones bawling in your ears. And look at 'em! Just look at 'em! Enough to make you sick. Like the monkey-house at the Zoo!"

"Noble and nude and antique?" suggested Harriet.

"I don't mean that. I mean the pole-climbing. Watch that girl—hand over hand, up she goes! And turning round to shove as if she was trying to clear a drain. She'll be in if she isn't careful."

"She's dressed for it," said Wimsey.

"I'll tell you what," said Mr. Peake, confidentially. "That's the real reason for the costume. They *expect* to fall in. It's all right to come out with those beautiful creases down your flannels, but if you do go in it makes it all the funnier."

"How true that is. Well, we're blocking the river. We'd better be getting on. I'll look you up one day, if Mrs. Peake will allow me. So long."

The punts parted company.

"Dear me," said Peter, when they were out of earshot; "it's pleasant to meet old friends. And very salutary."

"Yes; but don't you find it depressing when they go on making the same joke they were making about a hundred years ago?"

"Devilish depressing. It's the one great drawback to living in this place. It keeps you young. Too young."

"It's rather pathetic, isn't it?"

The river was wider here, and by way of answer he bent his knees to the stroke, making the punt curtsey and the water run chuckling under the bows.

"Would you have your youth back if you could, Harriet?"

"Not for the world."

"Nor I. Not for anything you could give me. Perhaps that's an exaggeration. For one thing you could give me I might want twenty years of my life back. But not the same twenty years. And if I went back to my twenties, I shouldn't be wanting the same thing."

"What makes you so sure of that?" said Harriet, suddenly reminded of Mr. Pomfret and the pro-Proctor.

"The vivid recollection of my own follies . . . Harriet! Are you going to tell me that all young men in their twenties are not fools?" He stood, trailing the pole, and looking down at her; his raised eyebrows lent his face a touch of caricature.

"Well, well, well. . . . I hope it is not Saint-George, by the way. That would be a most unfortunate domestic complication."

"No, not Saint-George."

"I thought not; his follies are less ingenuous. But somebody. Well, I refuse to be alarmed, since you have sent him about his business."

"I like the rapidity of your deductions."

"You are incurably honest. If you had done anything drastic you would have told me so in your letter. You would have said, 'Dear Peter, I have a case to submit to you; but before doing so I think it only right to inform you that I am engaged to Mr. Jones of Jesus.' Should you not?"

"Probably. Should you have investigated the case all the same?"

"Why not? A case is a case. What is the bottom like in the Old River?"

"Foul. You're pulled back two strokes for every stroke you make."

"Then we will stick to the New Cut. Well, Mr. Jones of

Jesus has my sincere sympathy. I hope his troubles will not affect his class."

"He is only in his Second year."

"Then he has time to get over it. I should like to meet him. He is probably the best friend I have in the world."

Harriet said nothing. Peter's intelligence could always make rings round her own more slowly-moving wits. It was quite true that the spontaneous affections of Reggie Pomfret had, somehow, made it easier to believe that Peter's own feelings might be something more than an artist's tenderness for his own achievement. But it was indecent of Peter to reach that conclusion so rapidly. She resented the way in which he walked in and out of her mind as if it was his own flat.

"Good God!" said Peter, suddenly. He peered with an air of alarm into the dark green water. A string of oily bubbles floated slowly to the surface, showing where the pole had struck a patch of mud; and at the same moment their nostrils were assaulted by a loathsome stench of decay.

"What's the matter?"

"I've struck something horrible. Can't you smell it? It's scandalous the way corpses pursue me about. Honestly, Harriet . . ."

"My dear idiot, it's only the Corporation garbage dump."

His eye followed her pointing hand to the farther bank, where a cloud of flies circled about a horrid mound of putrefaction.

"Well, of all the—! What the devil do they mean by doing a thing like that?" He passed a wet hand across his forehead. "For a moment I really thought I *had* run across Mr. Jones of Jesus. I was beginning to be sorry I had spoken so light-heartedly about the poor chap. Here! Let's get out of this!"

He drove the punt vigorously forward.

"The Isis for me. There is *no* romance left on this river."

CHAPTER XV

Do but consider what an excellent thing sleep is: it is so inestimable a jewel that, if a tyrant would give his crown for an hour's slumber, it cannot be bought: of so beautiful a shape is it, that though a man lie with an Empress, his heart cannot beat quiet till he leaves her embracements to be at rest with the other: yea, so greatly indebted are we to this kinsman of death, that we owe the better tributary, half of our life to him: and there is good cause why we should do so: for sleep is that golden chain that ties health and our bodies together. Who complains of want? of wounds? of cares? of great men's oppressions? of captivity? whilst he sleepeth? Beggars in their beds take as much pleasure as kings: can we therefore surfeit on this delicate Ambrosia? Can we drink too much of that whereof to taste too little tumbles us into a churchyard, and to use it but indifferently throws us into Bedlam? No, no, look upon Endymion, the moon's minion, who slept three score and fifteen years, and was not a hair the worse for it.

THOMAS DEKKER

"You will find the tea-basket," said Wimsey, "behind you in the bows."

They had put in under the dappled shade of an overhanging willow a little down the left bank of the Isis. Here there was less crowd, and what there was could pass at a distance. Here, if anywhere, they might hope for comparative peace. It was, therefore, with more than ordinary irritation that Harriet, with the thermos yet in her hand, observed a heavily-laden punt approaching.

"Miss Schuster-Slatt and her party. Oh, God! and she says she knows you."

The poles were firmly driven in at either end of the boat; escape was impossible. Ineluctably the American contingent advanced upon them. They were alongside. Miss Schuster-Slatt was crying out excitedly. It was Harriet's turn to blush for her friends. With incredible coyness Miss Schuster-Slatt apologized for her intrusion, effected introductions, was sure they were terribly in the way, reminded Lord Peter of their former encounter, recognized that he was far too pleasantly occupied to wish to be bothered with her, poured out a flood of alarming enthusiasm about the Propagation of the Fit, again drew strident attention to her own tactlessness, informed Lord Peter that Harriet was a lovely person and just too sympathetic, and favored each of them with an advance copy of her new questionnaire. Wimsey listened and replied with imperturable urbanity, while Harriet, wishing that the Isis would flood its banks and drown them all, envied his self-command. When at length Miss Schuster-Slatt removed herself and her party, the treacherous water wafted back her shrill voice from afar:

"Well, girls! Didn't I tell you he was just the perfect English aristocrat?"

At which point the much-tried Wimsey lay down among the tea-cups and became hysterical.

"Peter," said Harriet, when he had finished crowing like a cock, "your unconquerable sweetness of disposition is very shaming. I lose my temper with that harmless woman. Have some more tea."

"I think," said his lordship, mournfully, "I had better stop being the perfect English aristocrat and become the great detective after all. Fate seems to be turning my one-day romance into a roaring farce. If that is the dossier, let me have it. We'll see," he added with a faint chuckle, "what kind of a detective you make when you're left to yourself."

Harriet handed him the loose-leaf book and an envelope containing the various anonymous documents, all endorsed, where possible, with the date and manner of publication. He examined the documents first, separately and carefully, without manifesting surprise, disgust, or, indeed, any emotion beyond meditative interest. He then put them all back in the envelope, filled and lit a pipe, curled himself up among the cushions and devoted his attention to her manuscript. He read slowly, turning back every now and again to verify a date or a detail. At the end of the first few pages he looked up to remark:

"I'll say one thing for the writing of detective fiction: you know how to put your story together; how to arrange the evidence."

"Thank you," said Harriet drily; "praise from Sir Hubert is praise indeed."

He read on.

His next observation was:

"I see you have eliminated all the servants in the Scouts' Wing on the strength of one locked door."

"I'm not so simple-minded as that. When you come to the Chapel episode, you'll find that it eliminates them all, for another reason."

"I beg your pardon; I was committing the fatal error of theorizing ahead of my data."

Accepting rebuke, he relapsed into silence, while she studied his half-averted face. Considered generally, as a façade, it was by this time tolerably familiar to her, but now she saw details, magnified as it were by some glass in her own mind. The flat setting and fine scroll-work of the ear, and the height of the skull above it. The glitter of close-cropped hair where the neck-muscles lifted to meet the head. A minute sickle-shaped scar on the left temple. The faint laughter-lines at the corner of the eye and the droop of the lid at its outer end. The gleam of gold down on the cheekbone. The wide spring of the nostril. An almost imperceptible beading of sweat on the upper lip and a tiny muscle that twitched the sensitive corner of the mouth. The slight sun-reddening of the fair skin and its sudden whiteness below the base of the throat. The little hollow above the points of the collarbone.

He looked up; and she was instantly scarlet, as though she had been dipped in boiling water. Through the confusion of her darkened eyes and drumming ears some enormous bulk seemed to stoop over her. Then the mist cleared. His eyes were riveted upon the manuscript again, but he breathed as though he had been running.

So, thought Harriet, it has happened. But it happened long ago. The only new thing that has happened is that now I have got to admit it to myself. I have known it for some time. But does he know it? He has very little excuse, after this, for not knowing it. Apparently he refuses to see it, and that may be new. If so, it ought to be easier to do what I meant to do.

She stared out resolutely across the dimpling water. But she was conscious of his every movement, of every page he turned, of every breath he drew. She seemed to be separately conscious of every bone in his body. At length he spoke, and she wondered how she could ever have mistaken another man's voice for his.

"Well, Harriet, it's not a pretty problem."

"It's not. And it simply musn't go on, Peter. We can't have any more people frightened into the river. Publicity or no publicity, it's got to be stopped. Otherwise, even if nobody else gets hurt, we shall all go mad."

"That's the devil of it."

"Tell me what we are to do, Peter."

She had once again lost all consciousness of him except as the familiar intelligence that lived and moved so curiously behind an oddly amusing set of features.

"Well—there are two possibilities. You can plant spies all over the place and wait to pounce on this person when the next outbreak occurs."

"But you don't know what a difficult place it is to police. And it's ghastly waiting for the outbreak. And suppose we don't catch her and something horrible happens."

"I agree. The other, and I think the better, way is to do what we can to frighten this lunatic into keeping quiet while we dig out the motive behind the whole thing. I'm sure it's not mere blind malignity; there's a method in it."

"Isn't the motive only too painfully obvious?"

He stared pensively at her, and then said:

"You remind me of a charming old tutor, now dead, whose particular subject of research was the relations of the Papacy to the Church in England between certain dates which I do not precisely recall. At one time, a special subject on these lines was set for the History School, and undergraduates taking that subject were naturally sent to the old boy for coaching and did very well. But it was noticed that no man from his own college ever entered for that particular special—the reason being that the tutor's honesty was such that he would earnestly dissuade his pupils from taking his own subject for fear lest his encouragement might influence their decision."

"What a charming old gentleman! I'm flattered by the comparison, but I don't see the point."

"Don't you? Isn't it a fact that, having more or less made up your mind to a spot of celibacy you are eagerly peopling the cloister with bogies? If you want to do without personal relationships, then do without them. Don't stampede yourself into them by imagining that you've got to have them or qualify for a Freudian casebook."

"We're not talking about me and my feelings. We're talking about this beastly case in College."

"But you can't keep your feelings out of the case. It's no use saying vaguely that sex is at the bottom of all these phenomena—that's about as helpful as saying that human nature is at the bottom of them. Sex isn't a separate thing functioning away all by itself. It's usually found attached to a person of some sort."

"That's rather obvious."

"Well, let's have a look at the obvious. The biggest crime of these blasted psychologists is to have obscured the obvious. They're like a man packing for the weekend and turning everything out of his drawers and cupboards till he can't find his pajamas and toothbrush. Take a few obvious points to start with. You and Miss de Vine met at Shrewsbury for the first time at the Gaudy, and the first letter was put into your sleeve at that time; the people attacked are nearly all dons or scholars; a few days after your tea-party with young Pomfret, Jukes goes to prison; all the letters received by post come either on a Monday or a Thursday; all the communications are in English except the Harpy quotation; the dress found on the dummy was never seen in College: do all those facts taken together suggest nothing to you beyond a general notion of sex repression?"

"They suggest a lot of things separately, but I can't make anything of them taken together."

"You are usually better than that at a synthesis. I wish you could clear this personal preoccupation out of your mind. My dear, what are you afraid of? The two great dangers of the celibate life are a forced choice and a vacant mind. Energies bombinating in a vacuum breed chimaeras. But *you* are in no danger. If you want to set up your everlasting rest, you are far more likely to find it in the life of the mind than the life of the heart."

"*You* say that?"

"I say that. It is *your* needs we are considering, you know; not anybody else's. That is my opinion as an honest scholar, viewing the question academically and on its merits."

She had the old sensation of being outwitted. She grasped again at the main theme of the discussion:

"Then you think we can solve the problem by straight detection, without calling in a mental specialist?"

"I think it can be solved by a little straight and unprejudiced reasoning."

"Peter. I seem to be behaving very stupidly. But the reason why I want to—to get clear of people and feelings and go back to the intellectual side is that that is the only side of life I haven't betrayed and made a mess of."

"I know that," he said, more gently. "And it's upsetting to think that it may betray you in its turn. But why should you think that? Even if much learning makes one person mad it need not make everybody mad. All these women are beginning to look abnormal to you because you don't know which one to suspect, but actually even you don't suspect more than one."

"No; but I'm beginning to feel that almost any one of them might be capable of it."

"That, I fancy, is where your fears are distorting your judgment. If every frustrate person is heading straight for the asylum I know at least one danger to Society who ought to be shut up."

"Damn you, Peter. Will you keep to the point!"

"Meaning: what steps ought we to take? Will you give me tonight to think it over? If you will trust me to deal with it, I fancy I see one or two lines that might be followed up with profit."

"I would rather trust you than anybody."

"Thank you, Harriet. Shall we now resume our interrupted holiday? . . . Oh, my lost youth. Here are the ducks coming up for the remains of our sandwiches. Twenty-three years ago I fed these identical ducks with these identical sandwiches."

"Ten years ago, I too fed them to bursting-point."

"And ten and twenty years hence the same ducks and the same undergraduates will share the same ritual feast, and the ducks will bite the undergraduates' fingers as they have just bitten mine. How fleeting are all human passions compared with the massive continuity of ducks. . . . Be off, cullies, that's the lot."

He tossed the last crumbs of bread into the water, rolled over among the cushions and lay watching the ripples with half-shut eyes. . . . A punt went past, full of silent, sun-stupefied people, with a plop and a tinkle alternately as the pole entered and left the water; then a noisy party with a gramophone bawling "Love in Bloom"; then a young man in spectacles, by himself in a canoe, and paddling as though for dear life; then another punt, paddled at a funeral pace by a whispering man and girl; then a hot and energetic party of girls in an outrigger; then another canoe, driven swiftly by two Canadian undergraduates kneeling to their work; then a very small canoe, punted dangerously by a giggling girl in a bathing-dress, with a jeering young man crouched in the bows, costumed, and obviously prepared, for the inevitable plunge; then a very sedate and fully-clothed party in a punt—mixed undergraduates being polite to a female don; then a bunch of both sexes and all ages in an inrigger with another gramophone whining "Love in Bloom"—the Town at play; then a succession of shrill cries which announced the arrival of a hilarious party teaching a novice to punt; then, in ludicrous contrast, a very stout man in a blue suit and linen hat, solemnly propelling himself all alone in a two-pair tub, and a slim, singleted youth shooting contemptuously past him in a pair-oar skiff; then three punts side by side, in which everybody seemed to be asleep except those actually responsible for pole and paddle. One of these passed within a paddle's length of Harriet: a tousle-headed, rather paunchy young man lay with his knees cocked up, his mouth slightly open and his face flushed with the heat; a girl sprawled against his shoulder, while the man opposite, his hat over his face and his hands clasped over his chest with the thumbs beneath his braces, had also given up all interest in the outer world. The fourth passenger, a woman, was eating chocolates. The punter had a crumpled cotton frock and bare legs, much bitten. Harriet was reminded of a third-class railway compartment in an excursion train on a hot day; it was fatal to sleep in public; and how tempting to throw something at the paunchy youth. At that moment, the chocolate-eater screwed her remaining lollipops tightly in the bag and did throw it at the paunchy youth. It caught him in the midriff, and he woke with a loud snort. Harriet took a cigarette from her case and turned to ask her companion for a match. He was asleep.

It was a neat and noiseless kind of sleep; the posture might be described as the half-hedgehog, and offered neither mouth nor stomach as a target for missiles. But asleep he undoubtedly was. And here was Miss Harriet Vane, gone suddenly sympathetic, afraid to move for fear of waking him and savagely resenting the approach of a boatload of idiots whose gramophone was playing (for a change) "Love in Bloom."

"How wonderful," says the poet, "is Death, Death and his brother Sleep!" And, having asked whether Ianthe will wake again and being assured that she will, he proceeds to weave many beautiful thoughts about Ianthe's sleep. From this we may fairly deduce that he (like Henry who kneeled in silence by her couch) felt tenderly towards Ianthe. For another person's sleep is the acid test of our own sentiments. Unless we are savages, we react kindly to death, whether of friend or enemy. It does not exasperate us; it does not tempt us to throw things at it; we do not find it funny. Death is the ultimate weakness, and we dare not insult it. But sleep is only an illusion of weakness and, unless it appeals to our protective instincts, is likely to arouse in us a nasty, bullying spirit. From a height of conscious superiority we look down on the sleeper, thus exposing himself in all his frailty, and indulge in derisive comment upon his appearance, his manners and (if the occasion is a public one) the absurdity of the position in which he has placed his companion, if he has one, and particularly if we are that companion.

Harriet, thus cozened into playing Phoebe to the sleeping Endymion, had plenty of opportunity to examine herself. After careful consideration, she decided that what she most needed was a box of matches. Peter had used matches to light his pipe: where were they? He had gone to sleep on the whole outfit, confound him! But his blazer was beside him on the cushions; had anybody ever known a man to carry only *one* box of matches in his pockets?

To take possession of the blazer was ticklish work, for the punt rocked at every movement and she had to lift the garment over his knees; but his sleep was the deep sleep of physical fatigue, and she crawled back in triumph without having wakened him. With a curious sense of guilt she ransacked his pockets, finding three boxes of matches, a book and a corkscrew. With tobacco and literature one could face out any situation, provided, of course, that the book was not written in an unknown tongue. The spine was untitled, and as she turned back the worn calf cover the first thing she saw was the engraved bookplate with its achievement of arms: the three silver mice on a field sable and the "domestick Catt" couched menacingly on the helmet-wreath. Two armed Saracens supported the shield, beneath which ran the mocking and arrogant motto: "As my Whimsy takes me." She turned on to the title-page. *Religio Medici*. Well! . . . Well? Was that so very unexpected?

Why did he travel about with that? Did he fill in the spare moments of detection and diplomacy with musing upon the "strange and mystical" transmigrations of silkworms and the "legerdemain of changelings"? or with considering how "we vainly accuse the fury of guns and the new inventions of death"? "Certainly there is no happiness within this circle of flesh; nor is it in the optics of these eyes to behold felicity. The first day of our jubilee is death." She had no wish to suppose that he could find any personal application for that; she would rather have him secure and happy in order that she might resent his happy security. She flicked the pages over hurriedly. "When I am from him, I am dead till I be with him. United souls are not satisfied with embraces, but desire to be truly each other; which being impossible, these desires are infinite, and must proceed without a possibility of satisfaction." That was a most uncomfortable passage, whichever way you looked at it. She turned back to the first page and began to read steadily, with critical attention to grammar and style, so as to occupy the upper current of her mind without prying too closely into what might be going on beneath the surface.

The sun moved down the sky and the shadows lengthened upon the water. There were fewer craft on the river now; the tea-parties were hurrying home to dinner and the supper-parties had not yet put out. Endymion had the air of being settled for the night; it was really time to harden her heart and pull up the poles. She put off decision from moment to moment, till a loud shriek and a bump at her end of the punt came to spare her the trouble. The incompetent novice had returned with her crew and, having left her pole in the middle of the river, had let her craft drift across their stern. Harriet pushed the intruders off with more vigor than sympathy and turned to find her host sitting up and grinning rather sheepishly.

"Have I been asleep?"

"Getting on for two hours," said Harriet, with a pleased chuckle.

"Good lord, what disgusting behavior! I'm frightfully sorry. Why didn't you give me a shout? What time is it? My poor girl, you'll get no dinner tonight if we don't hurry up. Look here, I do apologize most abjectly."

"It doesn't matter a bit. You were awfully tired."

"That's no excuse." He was on his feet now, extricating the punt-poles from the mud. "We might make it by double-punting—if you'll forgive the infernal cheek of asking you to work to make up for my soul-destroying sloth."

"I'd love to punt. But, Peter!" She suddenly liked him enormously. "What's the hurry? I mean, is the Master expecting you, or anything?"

"No; I've removed myself to the Mitre. I can't use the Master's Lodgings as a hotel; besides, they've got people coming in."

"Then couldn't we get something to eat somewhere along the river and make a day of it? I mean, if you feel like it. Or must you have a proper dinner?"

"My dear, I would gladly eat husks for having behaved like a hog. Or thistles. Preferably thistles. You are a most forgiving woman."

"Well, give me the pole. I'll stay up in the bows and you can do the steering."

"And watch you bring the pole up in three."

"I promise to do that."

She was conscious, nevertheless, of Wimsey of Balliol's critical eye upon her handling of the heavy pole. For either you look graceful or you look ghastly; there is no middle way in punting. They set their course towards Iffley.

"On the whole," said Harriet, as they took boat again some little time later, "thistles would have been preferable."

"That kind of food is provided for very young people whose minds are elsewhere. Men of passions but no parts. I am glad to have dined on apricot flan and synthetic lemonade; it enlarges one's experience. Shall I, you or we pole? Or shall we abandon aloofness and superiority and paddle in beauty side by side?" His eyes mocked her. "I am tame; pronounce."

"Whichever you prefer."

He handed her gravely to the stern seat and coiled himself down beside her.

"What the devil am I sitting on?"

"Sir Thomas Browne, I expect. I'm afraid I rifled your pockets."

"Since I was such a bad companion, I'm glad I provided you with a good substitute."

"Is he a constant companion of yours?"

"My tastes are fairly catholic. It might easily have been *Kai Lung* or *Alice in Wonderland* or Machiavelli—"

"Or Boccaccio or the Bible?"

"Just as likely as not. Or Apuleius."

"Or John Donne?"

He was silent for a moment, and then said in a changed voice:

"Was that a bow drawn at a venture?"

"A good shot?"

"Whang in the gold. Between the joints of the harness. . . . If you would paddle a little on your side it would make it handier to steer."

"Sorry. . . . Do you find it easy to get drunk on words?"

"So easy that, to tell you the truth, I am seldom perfectly sober. Which accounts for my talking so much."

"And yet, if anybody had asked me, I should have said you had a passion for balance and order—no beauty without measure."

"One may have a passion for the unattainable."

"But you do attain it. At least, you appear to attain it."

"The perfect Augustan? No; I'm afraid it's at most a balance of opposing forces. . . . The river's filling up again."

"Lots of people come out after supper."

"Yes—well, bless their hearts, why shouldn't they? You're not feeling cold?"

"Not the least bit."

That was the second time within five minutes that he had warned her off his private ground. His mood had changed since the early hours of the afternoon and all his defenses were up once more. She could not again disregard the "No Thoroughfare" sign; so she left it to him to start a fresh subject.

He did so, courteously enough, by asking how the new novel was getting on.

"It's gone sticky."

"What's happened to it?"

This involved a full rehearsal of the plot of *Death 'twixt Wind and Water*. It was a complicated story, and the punt had covered a good deal of water before she reached the solution.

"There's nothing fundamentally wrong with that," said he; and proceeded to offer a few suggestions about detail.

"How intelligent you are, Peter. You're quite right. Of course that would be much the best way to get over the clock difficulty. But why does the whole story sound so dead and alive?"

"If you ask me," said Wimsey, "it's Wilfrid. I know he marries the girl—but must he be such a mutt? Why does he go and pocket the evidence and tell all those unnecessary lies?"

"Because he thinks the girl's done it."

"Yes—but why should he? He's dotingly in love with

her—he thinks she's absolutely the cat's pajamas—and yet, merely because he finds her handkerchief in the bedroom he is instantly convinced, on evidence that wouldn't hang a dog, that she not only is Winchester's mistress but has also murdered him in a peculiarly diabolical way. That may be one way of love, but—"

"But, you would like to point out, it isn't yours—and in fact, it wasn't yours."

There it was again—the old resentment, and the impulse to hit back savagely for the pleasure of seeing him wince.

"No," he said, "I was considering the question impersonally."

"Academically, in fact."

"Yes—please. . . . . From a purely constructional point of view, I don't feel that Wilfrid's behavior is sufficiently accounted for."

"Well," said Harriet, recovering her poise, "academically speaking, I admit that Wilfrid is the world's worst goop. But if he doesn't conceal the handkerchief, where's my plot?"

"Couldn't you make Wilfrid one of those morbidly conscientious people, who have been brought up to think that anything pleasant must be wrong—so that, if he *wants* to believe the girl an angel of light she is, for that very reason, all the more likely to be guilty. Give him a puritanical father and a hell-fire religion."

"Peter, that's an idea."

"He has, you see, a gloomy conviction that love is sinful in itself, and that he can only purge himself by taking the young woman's sins upon him and wallowing in vicarious suffering. . . . He'd still be a goop, and a pathological goop, but he would be a bit more consistent."

"Yes—he'd be interesting. But if I give Wilfrid all those violent and lifelike feelings, he'll throw the whole book out of balance."

"You would have to abandon the jigsaw kind of story and write a book about human beings for a change."

"I'm afraid to try that, Peter. It might go too near the bone."

"It might be the wisest thing you could do."

"Write it out and get rid of it?"

"Yes."

"I'll think about that. It would hurt like hell."

"What would that matter, if it made a good book?"

She was taken aback, not by what he said, but by his saying it. She had never imagined that he regarded her work very seriously, and she had certainly not expected him to take this ruthless attitude about it. The protective male? He was being about as protective as a can-opener.

"You haven't yet," he went on, "written the book you could write if you tried. Probably you couldn't write it when you were too close to things. But you could do it now, if you had the—the—"

"The guts?"

"Exactly."

"I don't think I could face it."

"Yes, you could. And you'll get no peace till you do. I've been running away from myself for twenty years, and it doesn't work. What's the good of making mistakes if you don't use them? Have a shot. Start on Wilfrid."

"Damn Wilfrid! . . . All right. I'll try. I'll knock the sawdust out of Wilfrid, anyhow."

He took his right hand from the paddle and held it out to her, deprecatingly.

" 'Always laying down the law with exquisite insolence to somebody.' I'm sorry."

She accepted the hand and the apology and they paddled on in amity. But it was true, she thought, that she had had to accept a good deal more than that. She was quite surprised by her own lack of resentment.

They parted at the postern.

"Good-night, Harriet. I'll bring back your manuscript tomorrow. Would some time in the afternoon suit you? I must lunch with young Gerald, I suppose, and play the heavy uncle."

"Come round about six, then. Good-night—and thank you very much."

"I am in your debt."

He waited politely while she shut and locked the heavy grille against him.

"And so-o-o" (in saccharine accents), "the co-onvent gates closed behind So-o-onia!"

He smote his forehead with a theatrical gesture and an anguished cry and reeled away almost into the arms of the Dean, who was coming up the road at her usual brisk trot.

"Serve him right," said Harriet, and fled up the path without waiting to see what happened.

As she got into bed she recalled the extempore prayer of a well-meaning but incoherent curate, heard once and never forgotten:

"Lord, teach us to take our hearts and look them in the face, however difficult it may be."

CHAPTER XVI

From noise of Scare-fires rest ye free,
From Murders Benedicite.
From all mischances, they may fright
Your pleasing slumbers in the night:
Mercie secure ye all, and keep
The Goblin from ye, while ye sleep.

ROBERT HERRICK

"Oh, miss!"

"We are so sorry to disturb you, madam."

"Good gracious, Carrie, what is it?"

When you have been lying awake for an hour or so wondering how to reconstruct a Wilfrid without inflicting savage mayhem upon your plot, and have just tumbled into an uneasy slumber haunted by the embalmed bodies of dukes, it is annoying to be jerked into consciousness again by two excited and partly hysterical maid-servants in dressing-gowns.

"Oh, miss, the Dean said to come and tell you. Annie and me have been so frightened. We nearly caught it."

"Caught what?"

"Whatever it is, miss. In the Science lecture-room, miss. We saw it there. It was awful."

Harriet sat up, dazed.

"And it's gone off, miss, rampaging something horrible, and nobody knows what it mayn't be up to, so we thought we ought to tell somebody."

"For goodness' sake, Carrie, *do* tell me. Sit down, both of you, and begin from the beginning."

"But, miss, didn't we ought to see what's gone with it? Out through the darkroom window, that's where it went, and it may be murdering people at this very minute. And the room locked and the key inside—there might be a dead body lying there, all blood."

"Don't be ridiculous," said Harriet. But she got out of bed, none the less, and began to hunt for her slippers. "If somebody's playing another practical joke, we must try and stop it. But don't let's have any nonsense about blood and bodies. Where did it go to?"

"We don't know, miss."

Harriet looked at the stout and agitated Carrie, whose face was puckered and twitching and her eyes bolting with imminent hysteria. She had never thought the present head scout any too dependable, and was inclined to put down her abundant energy to an excess of thyroid.

"Where is the Dean, then?"

"Waiting by the lecture-room door, miss. She said to fetch you—"

"All right."

Harriet put her torch into her dressing-gown pocket and hustled her visitors out.

"Now tell me quickly what's the matter, and don't make a noise."

"Well, miss, Annie comes to me and says—"

"When was this?"

"About a quarter of an hour ago, miss, or it might be more or less."

"About that, madam."

"I was in bed and asleep, never dreaming of nothing, and Annie says, 'Have you got the keys, Carrie? There's something funny going on in the lecture-room.' So I says to Annie—"

"Just a minute. Let Annie tell her part first."

"Well, madam, you know the Science lecture-room at the back of the New Quad, and how you can see it from our wing. I woke up about half-past one and happened to look out of my window and I saw a light in the lecture-room. So I thought, that's funny, as late as this. And I saw a shadow on the curtain, like somebody moving about."

"The curtains were drawn, then?"

"Yes, madam; but they're only buff casement-cloth, you know, so I could see the shadow as plain as plain. So I watched a bit, and the shadow went away but the light stayed on and I thought it was funny. So I went and woke Carrie and said to her to give me the keys so as I could go and look in case it was something that wasn't quite right. And she saw the light, too. And I said, 'Oh, Carrie, come with me; I don't like to go alone.' So Carrie came down with me."

"Did you go through the Hall or across the yard?"

"Across the yard, madam. We thought it would be quicker. Through the yard and the iron gate. And we tried to look through the window, but it was tight shut and the curtains pulled close."

They were out of Tudor Building now; its corridors as they passed through had seemed quiet enough. Nor did there seem to be any disturbance in the Old Quad. The Library Wing was dark, except for a lamp burning in Miss de Vine's window and the dim illumination of the passage lights.

"When we came to the lecture-room door, it was locked and the key in it, because I stooped down to look through the hole, but I couldn't see anything. And then I saw that the curtain wasn't quite drawn across the door—it has glass panels, you know, miss. So I looked through the crack and saw something all in black, madam. And I said, 'Oh, there it is!' And Carrie said, 'Let me see,' and she gave me a bit of a push and my elbow bumped against the door and that must have frightened it, because the light went out."

"Yes, miss," said Carrie, eagerly. "And I said, 'There now!' and then there was a most awful crash inside—dreadful, it was, and something bumping, and I calls out, 'Oh, it's coming out after us!' "

"And I said to Carrie, 'Run and fetch the Dean! We've got it in here.' So Carrie went for the Dean and I heard whoever it was moving about a bit, and then I didn't hear anything more."

"And the Dean came along and we waited a bit, and I said 'Ooh! do you think it's lying in there with its throat cut?' and the Dean said, 'There, now! How silly we've been. It'll have gone out through the window.' And I says, 'But all them windows are barred,' I says. And the Dean says, 'The darkroom window, that's where it's gone.' The darkroom door was locked too, so we run round outside and sure enough, there's the window wide open. So the Dean says, 'Fetch Miss Vane.' So we comes for you, miss."

By this time they had reached the east angle of the New Quad, where Miss Martin stood waiting.

"Our friend's vanished, I'm afraid," said the Dean. "We ought to have been quick enough to think of that window. I've been round this quad, but I can't find anything wrong there. Let's hope the creature's gone back to bed."

Harriet examined the door. It was certainly locked from the inside, and the curtain over the glass panel did not fit quite closely. But everything within was dark and silent.

"What does Sherlock Holmes do now?" inquired the Dean.

"I think we go in," said Harriet. "I suppose you haven't such a thing as a pair of long-nosed pliers? No. Well, it's probably just as good to break the glass."

"Don't cut yourself."

How many times, thought Harriet, had her detective, Robert Templeton, broken through doors to discover the dead body of the murdered financier! With a ludicrous feeling that she was acting a part, she laid a fold of her dressing-gown across the panel and delivered a sharp blow upon it with her closed fist. Rather to her astonishment, the panel broke inwards exactly as it should have done, to the accompaniment of a modest tinkle of glass. Now—a scarf or handkerchief wrapped round to protect the hand and wrist, and prevent leaving extra fingerprints on key and handle. The Dean obligingly fetched this needful accessory, and the door was opened.

Harriet's first glance by torchlight was for the switch. It stood in the "Off" position, and she struck it down with the handle of the torch. The room stood revealed.

It was a rather bare, uncomfortable place, furnished with a couple of long tables, a quantity of hard chairs and a blackboard. It was called the Science lecture-room partly because Miss Edwards occasionally used it for coachings that needed little in the way of apparatus, but chiefly because some dead-and-damned benefactor had left to the College a sum of money, together with a quantity of scientific books, anatomical casts, portraits of deceased scientists and glass cases filled with geological specimens; saddling this already sufficiently embarrassing bequest with the condition that all the bric-à-brac should be housed in one room together. Otherwise there was nothing that particularly fitted the room for scientific study, except that it communicated on one side with a closet containing a sink. The closet was occasionally used by photographic enthusiasts as a darkroom, and was so called.

The cause of the crash and bumping heard by the two scouts was plain enough as soon as the light was turned on. The blackboard had been flung to the ground and a few chairs displaced, as though somebody, hurriedly making her way from the room in the dark, had become entangled among the furniture. The most interesting thing about the room was the collection of things that lay on one of the tables. There was a spread sheet of newspaper, on which stood a paste-pot with a brush in it, part of a cheap scribbling block and the lid of a cardboard box, filled with cut-out letters. Also, laid out upon the table were several messages, couched in the Poison-Pen's now familiar style, and pasted together in the usual way; while a half-finished work in the same style of art had fluttered to the floor, showing that the Pen had been interrupted in the middle of her work.

"So here's where she does it!" cried the Dean.

"Yes," said Harriet. "I wonder why. It seems unnecessarily public. Why not her own room? . . . I say, Dean—

don't pick that up, if you don't mind. Better leave everything as it is."

The door into the darkroom was open. Harriet went in and examined the sink, and the open window above it. Marks in the dust showed clearly where something had scrambled over the sill.

"What's underneath this window outside?"

"It's a flagged path. I'm afraid you won't find much there."

"No; and it happens to be a spot that's overlooked by absolutely nothing except those bathroom windows in the corridor. It's very unlikely that the person should have been seen getting out. If the letters *had* to be concocted in a lecture-room, this is as good a place as any. Well! I don't see that we can do much here at the moment." Harriet turned sharply on the two scouts. "You say you saw the person, Annie."

"Not exactly saw her, madam, not to recognize. She had on something black and was sitting at the far table with her back to the door. I thought she was writing."

"Didn't you see her face when she got up and came across to turn off the light?"

"No, madam. I told Carrie what I saw and Carrie asked to look and bumped the door, and while I was telling her not to make a noise the light went out."

"Didn't you see anything, Carrie?"

"Well, I don't hardly know, miss. I was in such a fluster. I saw the light, and then I didn't see nothing."

"Perhaps she crept round the wall to get to the light," said the Dean.

"Must have, Dean. Will you go in and sit at the table on the chair that's pulled out a bit, while I see what I can see from the door. Then, when I knock on the glass, will you get up and out of sight as quickly as you can and work round to the switch and turn it off? Is the curtain much as it was, Annie, or did I disarrange it when I broke the glass?"

"I think it's much the same, madam."

The Dean went in and sat down. Harriet shut the door and put her eye to the chink in the curtain. This was at the hinge side of the door, and gave her a sight of the window, the ends of the two tables and the place where the blackboard had stood beneath the window.

"Have a look, Annie; was it like that?"

"Yes, madam. Only the blackboard was standing up then, of course."

"Now—do as you did then. Say to Carrie whatever it was you said, and Carrie, you knock on the door and then look in as you did the first time."

"Yes, madam. I said, 'There she is! we've got her.' And I jumped back like this."

"Yes, and I said, 'Oh, dear! Let's have a look!'—and then I sort of caught against Annie and knocked—like that."

"And I said, 'Look out—now you've done it.'"

"And I says, 'Coo!' or something like that, and I looked in and I didn't see nobody—"

"Can you see anybody now?"

"No, miss. And I was trying to see when the light went out all of a sudden."

The light went out.

"How did that go off?" asked the Dean, cautiously, with her mouth at the hole in the panel.

"First-rate performance," said Harriet. "Dead on time."

"The second I heard the knock, I just nipped away to the right and crept round the wall. Did you hear me?"

"Not a sound. You've got soft slippers on, haven't you?"

"We didn't hear the other one either, miss."

"She'd be wearing soft slippers, too. Well, I suppose that settles that. We'd better have a look round College to see that all's well and get back to bed. You two can be off now, Carrie—Miss Martin and I can see to things."

"Very good, miss. Come along, Annie. Though I'm sure I don't know how anybody's to get to sleep—"

"*Will* you stop making that filthy row!"

An exasperated voice heralded the appearance of an exceedingly angry student in pajamas.

"Do remember some people want to get a bit of rest at night. This corridor's a— Oh, I'm sorry, Miss Martin. Is anything wrong?"

"Nothing at all, Miss Perry. I'm so sorry we disturbed you. Somebody left the lights on in the lecture room and we came to see if it was all right."

The student vanished, with a jerk of a tousled head that showed what she thought of the matter. The two servants went their way. The Dean turned to Harriet.

"Why all that business of reconstructing the crime?"

"I wanted to find out whether Annie could really have seen what she said she saw. These people sometimes let their imagination run away with them. If you don't mind, I'm going to lock these doors and remove the keys. I'd rather like a second opinion."

"Aha!" said the Dean. "The exquisite gentleman who kissed my feet in St. Cross Road, crying, *Vera incessu patuit dean?*"

"That sounds characteristic. Well, Dean, you have got pretty feet. I've noticed them."

"They have been admired," said the Dean, complacently, "but seldom in so public a place or after five minutes' acquaintance. I said to his lordship, 'You are a foolish young man.' He said, 'A man, certainly; and sometimes foolish enough to be young.' 'Well,' I said, 'please get up; you can't be young here.' So then he said, very nicely, 'I beg your pardon for behaving like a mountebank; I have no excuse to offer, so will you forgive me?' So I asked him to dinner."

Harriet shook her head.

"I'm afraid you're susceptible to fair hair and a slim figure. That in the slender's but a humorous word which in the stout is flat impertinence."

"It might have been extremely impertinent, but actually it was not. I shall be interested to know what he makes of tonight's affair. We'd better go and see if there's been any more funny business."

Nothing unusual was, however, to be observed.

Harriet rang up the Mitre before breakfast.

"Peter, could you possibly come round this morning instead of at six o'clock?"

"Within five minutes, when and where you will. 'If she bid them, they will go barefoot to Jerusalem, to the great Cham's court, to the East Indies, to fetch her a bird to wear in her hat.' Has anything happened?"

"Nothing alarming; a little evidence *in situ*. But you may finish the bacon and eggs."

"I will be at the Jowett Walk Lodge in half an hour."

He came accompanied by Bunter and a camera. Harriet took them into the Dean's room and told them the story, with some assistance from Miss Martin, who asked whether he would like to interview the two scouts.

"Not for the moment. You seem to have asked all the necessary questions. We'll go and look at the room. There's no way to it, I take it, except along this passage. Two doors on the left—students' rooms, I suppose. And one on the right. And the rest bathrooms and things. Which is the door of the darkroom? This? In full view of the other door—so there was no escape except by the window. I see. The key of the lecture room was inside and the curtain left exactly like that? You're sure? All right. May I have the key?"

He threw the door open and glanced in.

"Get a photograph of this, Bunter. You have very nice, well-fitting doors in this building. Oak. No paint, no polish."

He took a lens from his pocket and ran it, rather perfunctorily, over the light switch and the door handle.

"Am I really going to see fingerprints discovered?" asked the Dean.

"Why, of course," said Wimsey. "It won't tell us anything, but it impresses the spectator and inspires confidence. Bunter, the insufflator. You will now see," he pumped the white powder rapidly over the frame and handle of the door, "how inveterate is the habit of catching hold of doors when you open them." An astonishing number of superimposed prints sprang into view above the lock as he blew the superfluous powder away. "Hence the excellent old-fashioned institution of the fingerplate. May I borrow a chair from the bathroom? . . . Oh, thank you, Miss Vane; I didn't mean *you* to fetch it."

He extended the blowing operations right up to the top of the door and the upper edge of the frame.

"You surely don't expect to find fingerprints up there," said the Dean.

"Nothing would surprise me more. This is merely a shop-window display of thoroughness and efficiency. All a matter of routine, as the policeman says. Your college is kept very well dusted; I congratulate you. Well, that's that. We will now direct our straining eyes to the darkroom door and do the same thing there. The key? Thank you. Fewer prints here, you see. I deduce that the room is usually approached by way of the lecture room. That probably also accounts for the presence of dust along the top of the door. Something always gets overlooked, doesn't it? The linoleum, however, has been honorably swept and polished. Must I go down on my knees and do the floor-walk for footprints? It is shockingly bad for one's trousers and seldom useful. Let us rather examine the window. Yes—somebody certainly seems to have got out here. But we knew that already. She climbed over the sink and knocked that beaker off the draining-board."

"She trod in the sink," said Harriet, "and left a damp smear on the sill. It's dried up now, of course."

"Yes; but that proves she really did get out this way and at that time. Though it scarcely needed proving. There *is* no other way out. This isn't the old problem of a hermetically-sealed chamber and a body. Have you finished in there, Bunter?"

"Yes, my lord; I have made three exposures."

"That ought to do. You might clean those doors, would you?" He turned, smiling, on the Dean. "You see, even if we did identify all those fingerprints, they would all belong to people who had a perfect right to be here. And in any case, our culprit, like everybody else these days, probably knows enough to wear gloves."

He surveyed the lecture room critically.

"Miss Vane!"

"Yes?"

"Something worried you about this room. What was it?"

"You don't need to be told."

"No; I am convinced that our two hearts beat as one. But tell Miss Martin."

"When the Poison-Pen turned off the light, she must have been close to the door. Then she went out by way of the darkroom. Why did she knock over the blackboard, which is right out of the line between the two doors?"

"Exactly."

"Oh!" cried the Dean, "but that's nothing. One often loses one's way in a dark room. My reading lamp fused one night, and I got up to try and find the wall switch and brought up with my nose against the wardrobe."

"There!" said Wimsey. "The chill voice of common sense falls on our conjectures like cold water on hot glass, and shatters them to bits. But I don't believe it. She had only to feel her way along the wall. She must have had some reason for going back into the middle of the room."

"She'd left something on one of the tables."

"That's more likely. But what? Something identifiable."

"A handkerchief or something that she'd been using to press down the letters as she pasted them on."

"We'll say it was that. These papers are just as you found them, I imagine. Did you test them to see if the paste was still wet?"

"I just felt this unfinished one on the floor. You see how it's done. She drew a line of paste right across the paper and then dabbed the letters on. The unfinished line was just tacky, but not wet. But then, you see, we didn't get in till after she'd been gone five or ten minutes."

"You didn't test any of the others?"

"I'm afraid not."

"I only wondered how long she'd been working here. She's managed to get through a good bit. But we may be able to find out another way." He took up the box lid containing the odd letters.

"Rough brown cardboard; I don't think we'll bother to look for fingerprints on this. Or to trace it; it might have come from anywhere. She'd nearly finished her job; there are only a couple of dozen letters left, and a lot of them are Q's and K's and Z's and such-like unhandy consonants. I wonder how this last message was meant to end."

He picked the paper from the floor and turned it over.

"Addressed to you, Miss Vane. Is this the first time you have been honored?"

"The first time—since the first time."

"Ah! 'You needn't think you'll get me, you make me laugh, you . . .' Well, the epithet remains to be supplied —from the letters in the box. If your vocabulary is large enough you may discover what it was going to be."

"But . . . Lord Peter—"

It was so long since she had addressed him by his title that she felt self-conscious about it. But she appreciated his formality.

"What I want to know is, why she came to this room at all."

"That is the mystery, isn't it?"

There was a shaded reading lamp on the table, and he stood idly clicking the light on and off. "Yes. Why couldn't she do it in her own room? Why invite discovery?"

"Excuse me, my lord."

"Yes, Bunter?"

"Would this be any contribution to the inquiry?"

Bunter dived beneath the table and came up, holding a long black hairpin.

"Good heavens, Bunter! This is like a leaf out of a forgotten story. How many people use these things?"

"Oh, quite a number, nowadays," said the Dean. "Little buns in the neck have come back. I use them myself, but mine are bronze ones. And some of the students. And Miss Lydgate—but I think hers are bronze, too."

"I know who uses black ones this shape," said Harriet. "I once had the pleasure of sticking them in for her."

"Miss de Vine, of course. Always the White Queen. And she *would* drop them all over the place. But I should think she was about the only person in College who would never, by any chance, come into this room. She gives no lectures or classes and never uses the darkroom or consults scientific works."

"She was working in her room when I came across last night," said Harriet.

"Did you see her?" said Wimsey, quickly.

"I'm sorry. I'm an idiot. I only meant that her reading lamp was on, close to her window."

"You can't establish an alibi on the strength of a reading lamp," said Wimsey. "I'm afraid I shall have to do the floor-walk after all."

It was the Dean who picked up a second hairpin—in the place where one might most reasonably expect to find it—in a corner near the sink in the darkroom. She was so pleased with herself as a detective that she almost forgot the implications of the discovery, till Harriet's distressed exclamation forced them upon her.

"We haven't identified the hairpins for certain," said Peter, comfortingly. "That will be a little task for Miss Vane." He gathered up the papers. "I'll take these and add them to the dossier. I suppose there's no message for us on the blackboard?"

He picked up the board, which contained only a few chemical formulae, scribbled in chalk, in Miss Edwards's handwriting, and restored the easel to an upright position, on the far side of the window.

"Look!" said Harriet, suddenly. "I know why she went

round that way. She meant to get out by the lecture room window, and had forgotten the bars. It was only when she pulled the curtain aside and saw them that she remembered the darkroom and plunged away in a hurry, knocking over the blackboard and tumbling into the chairs on the way. She must have been between the window and the easel, because the board *and* the easel fell forward into the room, and not backwards towards the wall."

Peter looked at her thoughtfully. Then he went back into the darkroom and lowered and raised the windowsash. It moved easily and almost in silence.

"If this place wasn't so well built," he said, almost accusingly, to the Dean, "somebody would have heard this window go up and run round in time to catch the lady. As it is, I wonder that Annie didn't notice the noise of the beaker falling into the sink. . . . But if she did, she probably thought it was something in the lecture room—one of those glass cases or what not. *You* didn't hear anything after you arrived, did you?"

"Not a thing."

"Then she must have got out while Carrie was fetching you out of bed. I suppose nobody saw her go."

"I've asked the only three students whose windows overlook that wall, and they saw nothing," said Harriet.

"Well, you might ask Annie about the beaker. And ask both of them whether they noticed, as they came past, if the darkroom window was open or shut. I don't suppose they noticed anything, but you never can tell."

"What does it matter?" asked the Dean.

"Not very much. But if it was shut, it rather supports Miss Vane's idea about the blackboard. If it was open, it would suggest that a retreat had been planned in that direction. It's a question of whether we're dealing with a short-sighted or a long-sighted person—mentally, I mean. And you might inquire at the same time whether any of the other women in the Scouts' Wing saw the light in the lecture room, and if so, how early."

Harriet laughed.

"I can tell you that at once. None of them. If they had, there would have been an eager rush to tell us all about it. You may be perfectly certain that Annie's and Carrie's adventure formed the staple of conversation in the servants' hall this morning."

"That," said his lordship, "is very true indeed."

There was a pause. The lecture room seemed to offer no further field for research. Harriet suggested that Wimsey might like to look round the College.

"I was about to suggest it," said he, "if you can spare the time."

"Miss Lydgate is expecting me in half an hour for a fresh attack on the *Prosody*," said Harriet. "I mustn't cut that, because her time is so precious, poor dear, and she's suddenly thought of a new appendix."

"Oh, *no!*" cried the Dean.

"Alas, yes! But we could just go round and view the more important battlefields."

"I should like particularly to see the Hall and Library and the connection between them, the entrance to Tudor Building, with Miss Barton's former room, the layout of the Chapel with reference to the postern and the place where, with the help of God, one leaps over the wall, and the way from Queen Elizabeth into the New Quad."

"Great heavens!" said Harriet. "Did you sit up all night with the dossier?"

"Hush! no, I woke rather early. But don't let Bunter hear, or he will start being solicitous. Men have died and the worms have eaten them, but not for early rising. In fact, it is said that it's the early worm that gets the bird."

"You remind me," said the Dean, "that there are half-a-dozen worms waiting in my room to get the bird this minute. Three late-without-leaves, two gramophones-out-of-hours, and an irregular motor vehicle. We shall meet again at dinner, Lord Peter."

She ran briskly away to deal with the malefactors, leaving Peter and Harriet to make their tour. From Peter's comments, Harriet could make out little of his mind; she fancied, indeed, that he was somewhat abstracted from the matter in hand.

"I fancy," he said at last, as they came to the Jowett Walk Lodge, where he had left the car, "that you will have very little more trouble at night."

"Why?"

"Well, for one thing, the nights are getting very short, and the risks very great. . . . All the same—shall you be offended if I ask you—if I suggest that you should take some personal precautions?"

"What sort of precautions?"

"I won't offer you a revolver to take to bed with you. But I have an idea that from now on you and at least one other person may be in some danger of attack. That may be imagination. But if this joker is alarmed and bottled up for a bit—and I think she has been alarmed—the next outrage may be a serious one—when it comes."

"Well," said Harriet, "we have her word for it that she finds me merely funny."

His attention seemed to be attracted by something among the dashboard fittings, and he said, looking not at her but at the car:

"Yes. But without any vanity, I wish I were your husband or your brother or your lover, or anything but what I am."

"You mean, your being here is a danger—to me?"

"I dare say I'm flattering myself."

"But it wouldn't stop *you* to damage *me*."

"She may not think very clearly about that."

"Well, I don't mind the risk, if it is one. And I don't see why it would be any less if you were a relation of mine."

"There'd be an innocent excuse for my presence, wouldn't there? . . . Don't think I'm trying to make capital out of this on my own account. I'm being careful to observe the formalities, as you may have noticed. I'm only warning you that I'm sometimes a dangerous person to know."

"Let's have this clear, Peter. You think that your being

here may make this person desperate and that she may try to take it out of me. And you are trying to tell me, very delicately, that it might be safer if we camouflaged your interest in the case as another kind of interest."

"Safer for you."

"Yes—though I can't see why you think so. But you're sure I'd rather die than make such an embarrassing pretense."

"Well, wouldn't you?"

"And on the whole you'd rather see me dead than embarrassed."

"That is probably another form of egotism. But I am entirely at your service."

"Of course, if you're such a perilous ally, I could tell you to go away."

"I can see you urging me to go away and leave a job undone."

"Well, Peter, I'd certainly rather die than make any sort of pretense to you or about you. But I think you're exaggerating the whole thing. You don't usually get the wind up like this."

"I do, though; quite often. But if it's only my own risk, I can afford to let it blow. When it comes to other people—"

"Your instinct is to clap the women and children under hatches."

"Well," he admitted, deprecatingly, "one can't suppress one's natural instincts altogether; even if one's reason and self-interest are all the other way."

"Peter, it's a shame. Let me introduce you to some nice little woman who adores being protected."

"I should be wasted on her. Besides, she would always be deceiving me, in the kindest manner, for my own good; and that I could not stand. I object to being tactfully managed by somebody who ought to be my equal. If I want tactful dependents, I can hire them. And fire them if they get too tactful. I don't mean Bunter. He braces me by a continual cold shower of silent criticism. I don't protect him; he protects me, and preserves an independent judgment. . . . However; without presuming to be protective, may I yet suggest that you should use a reasonable caution? I tell you frankly, I don't like your friend's preoccupation with knives and strangling."

"Are you serious?"

"For once."

Harriet was about to tell him not to be ridiculous; then she remembered Miss Barton's story about the strong hands that had seized her from behind. It might have been quite true. The thought of perambulating the long corridors by night was suddenly disagreeable.

"Very well; I'll be careful."

"I think it would be wise. I'd better push off now. I'll be round in time to face the High Table at dinner. Seven o'clock?"

She nodded. He had interpreted strictly her injunction to come "this morning instead of at six." She went, feeling a little blank, to cope with Miss Lydgate's proofs.

CHAPTER XVII

He that questioneth much shall learn much, and content much: but especially if he apply his questions to the skill of the persons whom he asketh; for he shall give them occasion to please themselves in speaking, and himself shall continually gather knowledge. But let his questions not be troublesome, for that is fit for a poser; and let him be sure to leave other men their turns to speak.

FRANCIS BACON

"You look," said the Dean, "like a nervous parent whose little boy is about to recite *The Wreck of the Hesperus* at a School Concert."

"I feel," said Harriet, "more like the mother of Daniel.

King Darius said to the lions:—
Bite Daniel. Bite Daniel.
Bite him. Bite him. Bite him."

"G'rrrrr!" said the Dean.

They were standing at the door of the Senior Common Room, which conveniently overlooked the Jowett Walk Lodge. The Old Quad was animated. Latecomers were hurrying over to change for dinner; others, having changed, were strolling about in groups, waiting for the bell; some were still playing tennis; Miss de Vine emerged from the Library Building, still vaguely pushing in hairpins (Harriet had checked up on those hairpins and identified them); an elegant figure paraded towards them from the direction of the New Quadrangle.

"Miss Shaw's got a new frock," said Harriet.

"So she has! How posh of her!

And she was as fine as a melon in the corn-field,
Gliding and lovely as a ship upon the sea.

That, my dear, is meant for Daniel."

"Dean, darling, you're being a cat."

"Well, aren't we all? This early arrival of everybody is exceedingly sinister. Even Miss Hillyard is arrayed in her best black gown with a train to it. We all feel there's safety in numbers."

It was not out of the way for the Senior Common Room to collect outside their own door before dinner of a fine summer's day, but Harriet, glancing round, had to admit that there were more of them there that evening than was usual before 7 o'clock. She thought they all seemed apprehensive and some, even hostile. They tended to avoid one another's eyes; yet they gathered together as though for protection against a common menace. She suddenly found it absurd that anybody should be alarmed by Peter Wimsey; she saw them as a harmless collection of nervous patients in a dentist's waiting room.

"We seem," said Miss Pyke's harsh voice in her ear, "to be preparing a somewhat formidable reception for our guest. Is he of a timid disposition?"

"I should say he was completely hard-boiled," said Harriet.

"That reminds me," said the Dean. "In the matter of shirt-fronts—"

"Hard, of course," said Harriet, indignantly. "And if he pops or bulges, I will pay you five pounds."

"I have been meaning to ask you," said Miss Pyke. "How is the popping sound occasioned? I did not like to ask Dr. Threep so personal a question, but my curiosity was very much aroused."

"You'd better ask Lord Peter," said Harriet.

"If you think he will not be offended," replied Miss Pyke, with perfect seriousness, "I will do so."

The chimes of New College, rather out of tune, played the four quarters and struck the hour.

"Punctuality," said the Dean, her eyes turned towards the Lodge, "seems to be one of the gentleman's virtues. You'd better go and meet him and settle his nerves before the ordeal."

"Do you think so?" Harriet shook her head. "Ye'll no fickle Tammas Yownie."

It may, perhaps, be embarrassing for a solitary man to walk across a wide quadrangle under a fire of glances from a collection of collegiate females; but it is child's play compared, for example, with the long trek from the pavilion at Lord's to the far end of the pitch, with five wickets down and ninety needed to save the follow-on. Thousands of people then alive might have recognized that easy and unhurried stride and confident carriage of the head. Harriet let him do three-quarters of the journey alone, and then advanced to meet him.

"Have you cleaned your teeth and said your prayers?"

"Yes, mamma; and cut my nails and washed behind the ears and got a clean handkerchief."

Looking at a bunch of students who happened to pass at the moment, Harriet wished she could have said the same of them. They were grubby and disheveled and she felt unexpectedly obliged to Miss Shaw for having made an effort in the matter of dress. As for her convoy, from his sleek yellow head to his pumps she distrusted him; his mood of the morning was gone, and he was as ready for mischief as a wilderness of monkeys.

"Come along, then, and behave prettily. Have you seen your nephew?"

"I have seen him. My bankruptcy will probably be announced tomorrow. He asked me to give you his love, no doubt thinking I can still be lavish in that commodity. It all returned from him to you, though it was mine before. That color is very becoming to you."

His tone was pleasantly detached and she hoped he was referring to her dress; but she was not sure. She was glad to relinquish him to the Dean, who came forward to claim him and to relieve her of the introductions. Harriet watched in some amusement. Miss Lydgate, far too unself-conscious to have any attitude at all, greeted him exactly as she would have greeted anybody else, and asked eagerly about the situation in Central Europe; Miss Shaw smiled with a graciousness that emphasized Miss Stevens's brusque "How-d'you do" and immediate retreat into animated discussion of college affairs with Miss Allison; Miss Pyke pounced on him with an intelligent question about the latest murder; Miss Barton, advancing with an evident determination to put him right about capital punishment, was disarmed by the blank amiability of the countenance offered for her inspection and observed instead that it had been a remarkably fine day.

"Comedian!" thought Harriet, as Miss Barton, finding she could make nothing of him, passed him on to Miss Hillyard.

"Ah!" said Wimsey instantly, smiling into the History Tutor's sulky eyes, "this is delightful. Your paper in the *Historical Review* on the diplomatic aspects of the Divorce . . ."

(Heavens! thought Harriet, I hope he knows his stuff.)

". . . really masterly. Indeed, I felt that, if anything, you had slightly underestimated the pressure brought to bear upon Clement by . . ."

". . . consulted the unedited dispatches in the possession of . . ."

". . . you might have carried the argument a trifle further. You very rightly point out that the Emperor . . ."

(Yes; he had read the article all right.)

". . . disfigured by prejudice, but a considerable authority on the Canon Law . . ."

". . . needing to be thoroughly overhauled and reedited. Innumerable mistranscriptions and at least one unscrupulous omission. . . ."

". . . if at any time you require access, I could probably put you into touch with . . . official channels . . . personal introduction . . . raise no difficulties . . ."

"Miss Hillyard," said the Dean to Harriet, "looks as though she had been given a birthday present."

"I think he's offering her access to some out-of-the-way source of information." (After all, she thought, he is Somebody, though one never seems able to remember it.)

". . . not so much political as economic."

"Ah!" said Miss Hillyard, "when it comes to a question of national finance, Miss de Vine is the real authority."

She effected the introduction herself, and the discussion continued.

"Well," said the Dean, "he has made a complete conquest of Miss Hillyard."

"And Miss de Vine is making a complete conquest of him."

"It's mutual, I fancy. At any rate, her back hair's coming down, which is a sure sign of pleasure and excitement."

"Yes," said Harriet. Wimsey was arguing with intelligence about the appropriation of monastic funds, but she had little doubt that the back of his mind was full of hairpins.

"Here comes the Warden. We shall have to separate them forcibly. He's *got* to face Dr. Baring and take her in to dinner. . . . All's well. She has collared him. That firm assertion of the Royal Prerogative! . . . Do you want to sit next him and hold his hand?"

"I don't think he needs any assistance from me. You're the person for him. Not a suspect, but full of lively information."

"All right; I'll go and prattle to him. You'd better sit opposite to us and kick me if I say anything indiscreet."

By this arrangement, Harriet found herself placed a little uncomfortably between Miss Hillyard (in whom she always felt an antagonism to herself) and Miss Barton (who was obviously still worried about Wimsey's detective hobbies), and face to face with the two people whose glances were most likely to disturb her gravity. On the other side of the Dean sat Miss Pyke; on the other side of Miss Hillyard was Miss de Vine, well under Wimsey's eye. Miss Lydgate, that secure fortress, was situated at the far end of the table, offering no kind of refuge.

Neither Miss Hillyard nor Miss Barton had much to say to Harriet, who was thus able to follow, without too much difficulty, the Warden's straightforward determination to size up Wimsey and Wimsey's diplomatically veiled but equally obstinate determination to size up the Warden; a contest carried on with unwavering courtesy on either side.

Dr. Baring began by inquiring whether Lord Peter had been conducted over the College and what he thought of it, adding, with due modesty, that architecturally, of course, it could scarcely hope to compete with the more ancient foundations.

"Considering," said his lordship plaintively, "that the architecture of my own ancient foundation is mathematically compounded of ambition, distraction, uglification and derision, that remark sounds like sarcasm."

The Warden, almost seduced into believing herself guilty of a breach of manners, earnestly assured him that she had intended no personal allusion.

"An occasional reminder is good for us," said he. "We are mortified in nineteenth-century Gothic, lest in our over-weening Balliolity we forget God. We pulled down the good to make way for the bad; you, on the contrary, have made the world out of nothing—a more divine procedure."

The Warden, maneuvering uneasily on this slippery ground between jest and earnest, found foothold:

"It is quite true that we have had to make what we can out of very little—and that, you know, is typical of our whole position here."

"Yes; you are practically without endowments?"

The question was so offered as to include the Dean, who said cheerfully:

"Quite right. All done by cheeseparing."

"That being so," he said, seriously, "even to admire seems to be a kind of impertinence. This is a very fine hall —who is the architect?"

The Warden supplied him with a little local history, breaking off to say:

"But probably you are not specially interested in all this question of women's education."

"Is it still a question? It ought not to be. I hope you are not going to ask me whether I approve of women's doing this and that."

"Why not?"

"You should not imply that I have any right either to approve or disapprove."

"I assure you," said the Warden, "that even in Oxford we still encounter a certain number of people who maintain their right to disapprove."

"And I had hoped I was returning to civilization."

The removal of fish plates caused a slight diversion, and the Warden took the opportunity to turn her inquiries upon the situation in Europe. Here the guest was on his own ground. Harriet caught the Dean's eye and smiled. But the more formidable challenge was coming. International politics led to history, and history—in Dr. Baring's mind— to philosophy. The ominous name of Plato suddenly emerged from a tangle of words, and Dr. Baring moved out a philosophical speculation, like a pawn, and planted it temptingly *en prise*.

Many persons had plunged to irretrievable disaster over the Warden's philosophic pawn. There were two ways of taking it: both disastrous. One was to pretend to knowledge; the other, to profess an insincere eagerness for instruction. His lordship smiled gently and refused the gambit:

"That is out of my stars. I have not the philosophic mind."

"And how would you define the philosophic mind, Lord Peter?"

"I wouldn't; definitions are dangerous. But I know that philosophy is a closed book to me, as music is to the tone-deaf."

The Warden looked at him quickly; he presented her with an innocent profile, drooping and contemplative over his plate, like a heron brooding by a pond.

"A very apt illustration," said the Warden; "as it happens, I am tone-deaf myself."

"Are you? I thought you might be," he said, equably.

"That is very interesting. How can you tell?"

"There is something in the quality of the voice." He offered candid grey eyes for examination. "But it's not a very safe conclusion to draw, and, as you may have noticed, I didn't draw it. That is the art of the charlatan—to induce a confession and present it as the result of deduction."

"I see," said Dr. Baring. "You expose your technique very frankly."

"You would have seen through it in any case, so it is better to expose one's self and acquire an unmerited reputation for candor. The great advantage about telling the truth is that nobody ever believes it—that is at the bottom of the *ψευδῆ λέγειν ὡς δεῖ*."

"So there is one philosopher whose books are not closed to you? Next time, I will start by way of Aristotle."

She turned to her left-hand neighbor and released him.

"I am sorry," said the Dean, "we have no strong drink to offer you."

His face was eloquent of mingled apprehension and mischief.

"The toad beneath the harrow knows where every separate tooth-point goes. Do you always prove your guests with hard questions?"

"Till they show themselves to be Solomons. You have passed the test with great credit."

"Hush! there is only one kind of wisdom that has any

social value, and that is the knowledge of one's own limitations."

"Nervous young dons and students have before now been carried out in convulsions through being afraid to say boldly that they did not know."

"Showing themselves," said Miss Pyke across the Dean, "less wise than Socrates, who made the admission fairly frequently."

"For Heaven's sake," said Wimsey, "don't mention Socrates. It might start all over again."

"Not now," said the Dean. "She will ask no questions now except for instruction."

"There is a question on which I am anxious to be instructed," said Miss Pyke, "if you will not take it amiss."

Miss Pyke, of course, was still worried about Dr. Threep's shirt-front, and determined on getting enlightenment. Harriet hoped that Wimsey would recognize her curiosity for what it was: not skittishness, but the embarrassing appetite for exact information which characterizes the scholarly mind.

"That phenomenon," he said, readily, "comes within my own sphere of knowledge. It occurs because the human torso possesses a higher factor of variability than the ready-made shirt. The explosive sound you mention is produced when the shirt-front is slightly too long for the wearer. The stiff edges, being forced slightly apart by the inclination of the body, come back into contact with a sharp click, similar to that emitted by the elytra of certain beetles. It is not to be confused, however, with the ticking of the Death-watch, which is made by tapping with the jaws and is held to be a love-call. The clicking of the shirt-front has no amatory significance, and is, indeed, an embarrassment to the insect. It may be obviated by an increased care in selection or, in extreme cases, by having the garment made to measure."

"Thank you so much," said Miss Pyke. "That is a most satisfactory explanation. At this time of day, it is perhaps not improper to adduce the parallel instance of the old-fashioned corset, which was subject to a similar inconvenience."

"The inconvenience," added Wimsey, "was even greater in the case of plate armor, which had to be very well tailored to allow of movement at all."

At this point, Miss Barton captured Harriet's attention with some remark or other, and she lost track of the conversation on the other side of the table. When she picked up the threads again, Miss Pyke was giving her neighbors some curious details about Ancient Minoan civilization, and the Warden was apparently waiting till she had finished to pounce on Peter again. Turning to her right, Harriet saw that Miss Hillyard was watching the group with a curiously concentrated expression. Harriet asked her to pass the sugar, and she came back to earth with a slight start.

"They seem to be getting on very well over there," said Harriet.

"Miss Pyke likes an audience," said Miss Hillyard, with so much venom that Harriet was quite astonished.

"It's good for a man to have to do the listening sometimes," she suggested.

Miss Hillyard agreed absently. After a slight pause, during which dinner proceeded without incident, she said:

"Your friend tells me he can obtain access for me to some private collections of historical documents in Florence. Do you suppose he means what he says?"

"If he says so, you may be sure he can and will."

"That is a testimonial," said Miss Hillyard. "I am very glad to hear it."

Meanwhile, the Warden had effected her capture, and was talking to Peter in a low tone and with some earnestness. He listened attentively, while he peeled an apple, the narrow coils of the rind sliding slowly over his fingers. She concluded with some question; and he shook his head.

"It is very unlikely. I should say there was no hope of it at all."

Harriet wondered whether the subject of the Poison-Pen had risen at last to the surface; but presently he said:

"Three hundred years ago it mattered comparatively little. But now that you have the age of national self-realization, the age of colonial expansion, the age of the barbarian invasions and the age of the decline and fall, all jammed cheek by jowl in time and space, all armed alike with poison-gas and going through the outward motions of an advanced civilization, principles have become more dangerous than passions. It's getting uncommonly easy to kill people in large numbers, and the first thing a principle does—if it really is a principle—is to kill somebody."

" 'The real tragedy is not the conflict of good with evil but of good with good'; that means a problem with no solution."

"Yes. Afflicting, of course, to the tidy mind. One may either hulloo on the inevitable, and be called a bloodthirsty progressive; or one may try to gain time and be called a bloodthirsty reactionary. But when blood is their argument, all argument is apt to be—merely bloody."

The Warden passed the adjective at its face value.

"I sometimes wonder whether we gain anything by gaining time."

"Well—if one leaves letters unanswered long enough, some of them answer themselves. Nobody can prevent the Fall of Troy, but a dull, careful person may manage to smuggle out the Lares and Penates—even at the risk of having the epithet *pius* tacked to his name."

"The Universities are always being urged to march in the van of progress."

"But epic actions are all fought by the rearguard—at Roncevaux and Thermopylae."

"Very well," said the Warden, laughing, "let us die in our tracks, having accomplished nothing but an epic."

She collected the High Table with her eye, rose, and made a stately exit. Peter effaced himself politely against the paneling while the dons filed past him, arriving at the edge of the dais in time to pick up Miss Shaw's scarf as it slipped from her shoulders. Harriet found herself descending the staircase between Miss Martin and Miss de Vine, who remarked:

"You are a courageous woman."

"Why?" said Harriet lightly. "To bring my friends here and have them put to the question?"

"Nonsense," interrupted the Dean. "We all behaved beautifully. Daniel is still uneaten—in fact, at one point he bit the lion. Was that genuine, by the way?"

"About tone-deafness? Probably just a little more genuine than he made out."

"Will he lay traps all evening for us to walk into?"

Harriet realized for a moment how queer the whole situation was. Once again, she felt Wimsey as a dangerous alien and herself on the side of the women, who, with so strange a generosity, were welcoming the inquisitor among them. She said, however:

"If he does, he will display all the mechanism in the most obliging manner."

"After one is inside. That's very comforting."

"That," said Miss de Vine, brushing aside these surface commentaries, "is a man able to subdue himself to his own ends. I should be sorry for anyone who came up against *his* principles—whatever they are, and if he has any."

She detached herself from the other two, and went on into the Senior Common Room with a somber face.

"Curious," said Harriet. "She is saying about Peter Wimsey exactly what I have always thought about herself."

"Perhaps she recognizes a kindred spirit."

"Or a foe worthy of—I ought not to say that."

Here Peter and his companion caught them up, and the Dean, joining Miss Shaw, went on in with her. Wimsey smiled at Harriet, an odd, interrogative smile.

"What's worrying you?"

"Peter—I feel exactly like Judas."

"Feeling like Judas is part of the job. No job for a gentleman, I'm afraid. Shall we wash our hands like Pilate and be thoroughly respectable?"

She slid her hand under his arm.

"No; we're in for it now. We'll be degraded together."

"That will be nice. Like the lovers in that Strohheim film, we'll go and sit on the sewer." She could feel his bone and muscle, reassuringly human, under the fine broadcloth. She thought: "He and I belong to the same world, and all these others are the aliens." And then: "Damn it all! this is our private fight—why should they have to join in?" But that was absurd.

"What do you want me to do, Peter?"

"Chuck the ball back to me if it runs out of the circle. Not obviously. Just exercise your devastating talent for keeping to the point and speaking the truth."

"That sounds easy."

"It is—for you. That's what I love you for. Didn't you know? Well, we can't stop to argue about it now; they'll think we're conspiring about something."

She released his arm and went into the room ahead of him, feeling suddenly embarrassed and looking, in consequence, defiant. The coffee was already on the table, and the S.C.R. were gathered about it, helping themselves. She saw Miss Barton advance upon Peter, with a courteous offer of refreshment on her lips but the light of determination in her eye. Harriet did not for the moment care what happened to Peter. He had given her a new bone to worry. She provided herself with coffee and a cigarette, and retired with them and the bone into a corner. She had often wondered, in a detached kind of way, what it was that Peter valued in her and had apparently valued from that first day when she had stood in the dock and spoken for her own life. Now that she knew, she thought that a more unattractive pair of qualities could seldom have been put forward as an excuse for devotion.

"But do you really feel comfortable about it, Lord Peter?"

"No—I shouldn't recommend it as a comfortable occupation. But is your or my or anybody's comfort of very great importance?"

Miss Barton probably took that for flippancy; Harriet recognized the ruthless voice that had said, "What does it matter if it hurts . . . ?" Let them fight it out. . . . Unattractive; but if he meant what he said, it explained a great many things. Those were qualities that could be recognized under the most sordid conditions . . . "Detachment . . . if you ever find a person who likes you because of it, that liking is sincere." That was Miss de Vine; and Miss de Vine was sitting not very far away, her eyes, behind their thick glasses, fixed on Peter with a curious, calculating look.

Conversations, carried on in groups, were beginning to falter and fall into silence. People were sitting down. The voices of Miss Allison and Miss Stevens rose into prominence. They were discussing some collegiate question, and they were doing it intently and desperately. They called upon Miss Burrows to give an opinion. Miss Shaw turned to Miss Chilperic and made a remark about the bathing at "Spinsters' Splash." Miss Chilperic replied elaborately—too elaborately; her answer took too long and attracted attention; she hesitated, became confused, and stopped speaking. Miss Lydgate, with a troubled face, was listening to an anecdote that Mrs. Goodwin was telling about her little boy; in the middle of it, Miss Hillyard, who was within earshot, rose pointedly, stabbed out her cigarette on a distant ashtray, and moved slowly, and as though despite herself, to a windowseat close to where Miss Barton was still standing. Harriet could see her angry, smoldering glance fix itself on Peter's bent head and then jerk away across the quad, only to return again. Miss Edwards, close to Harriet and a little in front of her on a low chair, had her hands set squarely and rather mannishly on her knees, and was leaning forward; she had the air of waiting for something. Miss Pyke, on her feet, lighting a cigarette, was apparently looking for an opportunity to engage Peter's attention; she appeared eager and interested, and more at her ease than most of the others. The Dean, curled on a humpty, was frankly listening to what Peter and Miss Barton were saying. They were all listening, really, and at the same time most of them were trying to pretend that he was there as an ordinary guest—that he was not an enemy—not a spy. They were trying to prevent him from becoming openly the center of attention as he was already the center of consciousness.

The Warden, seated in a deep chair near the fireplace, gave nobody any help. One by one, the spurts of talk failed and died, leaving the one tenor floating, like a solo instrument executing a cadenza when the orchestra has fallen silent:

"The execution of the guilty is unpleasant—but not nearly so disturbing as the slaughter of the innocents. If you are out for my blood, won't you allow me to hand you a more serviceable weapon?"

He glanced round and, finding that everybody but Miss Pyke and themselves was sitting down silent, made a brief, interrogative pause, which looked like politeness, but which Harriet mentally classed as "good theater."

Miss Pyke led the way to a large sofa near Miss Hillyard's windowseat and said, as she settled herself in the corner of it:

"Do you mean the murderer's victims?"

"No," said Peter, "I meant my own victims."

He sat down between Miss Pyke and Miss Barton, and went on in a pleasantly conversational tone:

"For example; I happened to find out that a young woman had murdered an old one for her money. It didn't matter much: the old woman was dying in any case, and the girl (though she didn't know that) would have inherited the money in any case. As soon as I started to meddle, the girl set to work again, killed two innocent people to cover her tracks and murderously attacked three others. Finally she killed herself. If I'd left her alone, there might have been only one death instead of four."

"Good gracious!" said Miss Pyke. "But the woman would have been at large."

"Oh, yes. She wasn't a nice woman, and she had a nasty

influence on certain people. But who killed those other two innocents—she or society?"

"They were killed," said Miss Barton, "by her fear of the death penalty. If the unfortunate woman had been medically treated, they and she would still be alive today."

"I told you it was a good weapon. But it isn't as simple as all that. If she hadn't killed those others, we should probably never have caught her, and so far from being medically treated she would be living in prosperity—and incidentally corrupting one or two people's minds, if you think that of any importance."

"You are suggesting, I think," said the Warden, while Miss Barton rebelliously grappled with this problem, "that those innocent victims died for the people; sacrificed to a social principle."

"At any rate, to *your* social principles," said Miss Barton.

"Thank you. I thought you were going to say, to my inquisitiveness."

"I might have done so," said Miss Barton, frankly. "But you lay claim to a principle, so we'll stick to that."

"Who were the other three people attacked?" asked Harriet. (She had no fancy to let Miss Barton get away with it too easily.)

"A lawyer, a colleague of mine and myself. But that doesn't prove that I have any principles. I'm quite capable of getting killed for the fun of the thing. Who isn't?"

"I know," said the Dean. "It's funny that we get so solemn about murders and executions and mind so little about taking risks in motoring and swimming and climbing mountains and so on. I suppose we *do* prefer to die for the fun of the thing."

"The social principle seems to be," suggested Miss Pyke, "that we should die for our own fun and not other people's."

"Of course I admit," said Miss Barton, rather angrily, "that murder must be prevented and murderers kept from doing further harm. But they ought not to be punished and they certainly ought not to be killed."

"I suppose they ought to be kept in hospitals at vast expense, along with other unfit specimens," said Miss Edwards. "Speaking as a biologist, I must say I think public money might be better employed. What with the number of imbeciles and physical wrecks we allow to go about and propagate their species, we shall end by devitalizing whole nations."

"Miss Schuster-Slatt would advocate sterilization," said the Dean.

"They're trying it in Germany, I believe," said Miss Edwards.

"Together," said Miss Hillyard, "with the relegation of woman to her proper place in the home."

"But they execute people there quite a lot," said Wimsey, "so Miss Barton can't take over their organization lock, stock and barrel."

Miss Barton uttered a loud protest against any such suggestion, and returned to her contention that *her* social principles were opposed to violence of every description.

"Bosh!" said Miss Edwards. "You can't carry through any principle without doing violence to somebody. Either directly or indirectly. Every time you disturb the balance of nature you let in violence. And if you leave nature alone you get violence in any case. I quite agree that murderers shouldn't be hanged—it's wasteful and unkind. But I don't agree that they should be comfortably fed and housed while decent people go short. Economically speaking, they should be used for laboratory experiments."

"To assist the further preservation of the unfit?" asked Wimsey, drily.

"To assist in establishing scientific facts," replied Miss Edwards, more drily still.

"Shake hands," said Wimsey. "Now we have found common ground to stand on. Establish the facts, no matter what comes of it."

"On that ground, Lord Peter," said the Warden, "your

inquisitiveness becomes a principle. And a very dangerous one."

"But the fact that A killed B isn't necessarily the whole of the truth," persisted Miss Barton. "A's provocation and state of health are facts, too."

"Nobody surely disputes that," said Miss Pyke. "But one can scarcely ask the investigator to go beyond his job. If we mayn't establish any conclusion for fear somebody should make an injudicious use of it, we are back in the days of Galileo. There would be an end to discovery."

"Well," said the Dean, "I wish we could stop discovering things like poison gas."

"There can be no objection to the making of discoveries," said Miss Hillyard; "but is it always expedient to publish them? In the case of Galileo, the Church—"

"You'll never get any scientist to agree there," broke in Miss Edwards. "To suppress a fact is to publish a falsehood."

For a few minutes Harriet lost the thread of the discussion, which now became general. That it had been deliberately pushed to this point, she could see; but what Peter wanted to make of it, she had no idea. Yet he was obviously interested. His eyes, under their half-closed lids, were alert. He was like a cat waiting at a mousehole. Or was she half-consciously connecting him with his own blazon? "Sable: three mice courant argent; a crescent for difference. The crest, a domestick catt. . . ."

"Of course," said Miss Hillyard, in a hard, sarcastic voice, "if you think private loyalties should come before loyalty to one's job. . . ."

("Couched as to spring, proper.") That was what he had been waiting for, then. One could almost see the silken fur ripple.

"Of course, I don't say that one should be disloyal to one's job for private reasons," said Miss Lydgate. "But surely, if one takes on personal responsibilities, one owes a duty in that direction. If one's job interferes with them, perhaps one should give up the job."

"I quite agree," said Miss Hillyard. "But then, my private responsibilities are few, and possibly I have no right to speak. What is your opinion, Mrs. Goodwin?"

There was a most unpleasant pause.

"If you mean that personally," said the Secretary, getting up and facing the Tutor, "I am so far of your opinion that I have asked Dr. Baring to accept my resignation. Not because of any of the monstrous allegations that have been made about me, but because I realize that under the circumstances I can't do my work as well as I ought. But you are all very much mistaken if you think *I* am at the bottom of the trouble in this college. I'm going now, and you can say what you like about me—but may I say that anybody with a passion for facts will do better to collect them from unprejudiced sources. Miss Barton at least will admit that mental health is a fact like another."

Into the horrified silence that followed, Peter dropped three words like lumps of ice.

"Please don't go."

Mrs. Goodwin stopped short with her hand on the door.

"It would be a great pity," said the Warden, "to take anything personally that is said in a general discussion. I feel sure Miss Hillyard meant nothing of that kind. Naturally, some people have better opportunities than others for seeing both sides of a question. In your own line of work, Lord Peter, such conflicts of loyalty must frequently occur."

"Oh, yes. I once thought I had the agreeable choice between hanging either my brother or my sister. Fortunately, it came to nothing."

"But supposing it had come to something?" demanded Miss Barton, pinning the *argumentum ad hominem* with a kind of relish.

"Oh, well— What does the ideal detective do then, Miss Vane?"

"Professional etiquette," said Harriet, "would suggest an extorted confession, followed by poison for two in the library."

"You see how easy it is, when you stick to the rules,"

said Wimsey. "Miss Vane feels no compunction. She wipes me out with a firm hand, rather than damage my reputation. But the question isn't always so simple. How about the artist of genius who has to choose between letting his family starve and painting pot-boilers to keep them?"

"He's no business to have a wife and family," said Miss Hillyard.

"Poor devil! Then he has the further interesting choice between repressions and immorality. Mrs. Goodwin, I gather, would object to the repressions and some people might object to the immorality."

"That doesn't matter," said Miss Pyke. "You have hypothesized a wife and family. Well—he could stop painting. That, if he really is a genius, would be a loss to the world. But he mustn't paint bad pictures—that would be really immoral."

"Why?" asked Miss Edwards. "What do a few bad pictures matter, more or less?"

"Of course they matter," said Miss Shaw. She knew a good deal about painting. "A bad picture by a good painter is a betrayal of truth—his own truth."

"That's only a relative kind of truth," objected Miss Edwards.

The Dean and Miss Burrows fell headlong upon this remark, and Harriet, seeing the argument in danger of getting out of hand, thought it time to retrieve the ball and send it back. She knew now what was wanted, though not why it was wanted.

"If you can't agree about painters, make it someone else. Make it a scientist."

"I've no objection to scientific pot-boilers," said Miss Edwards. "I mean, a popular book isn't necessarily unscientific."

"So long," said Wimsey, "as it doesn't falsify the facts. But it might be a different kind of thing. To take a concrete instance—somebody wrote a novel called *The Search*—"

"C. P. Snow," said Miss Burrows. "It's funny you should mention that. It was the book that the—"

"I know," said Peter. "That's possibly why it was in my mind."

"I never read the book," said the Warden.

"Oh, I did," said the Dean. "It's about a man who starts out to be a scientist and gets on very well till, just as he's going to be appointed to an important executive post, he finds he's made a careless error in a scientific paper. He didn't check his assistant's results, or something. Somebody finds out, and he doesn't get the job. So he decides he doesn't really care about science after all."

"Obviously not," said Miss Edwards. "He only cared about the post."

"But," said Miss Chilperic, "if it was only a mistake—"

"The point about it," said Wimsey, "is what an elderly scientist says to him. He tells him: 'The only ethical principle which has made science possible is that the truth shall be told all the time. If we do not penalize false statements made in error, we open up the way for false statements by intention. And a false statement of fact, made deliberately, is the most serious crime a scientist can commit.' Words to that effect. I may not be quoting quite correctly."

"Well, that's true, of course. Nothing could possibly excuse deliberate falsification."

"There's no sense in deliberate falsification, anyhow," said the Bursar. "What could anybody gain by it?"

"It has been done," said Miss Hillyard, "frequently. To get the better of an argument. Or out of ambition."

"Ambition to be what?" cried Miss Lydgate. "What satisfaction could one possibly get out of a reputation one knew one didn't deserve? It would be horrible."

Her innocent indignation upset everybody's gravity.

"How about the Forged Decretals . . . Chatterton . . . Ossian . . . Henry Ireland . . . those Nineteenth-Century Pamphlets the other day . . . ?"

"I know," said Miss Lydgate, perplexed. "I know people do it. But *why?* They must be mad."

"In the same novel," said the Dean, "somebody deliberately falsifies a result—later on, I mean—in order to get a job. And the man who made the original mistake finds it out. But he says nothing, because the other man is very badly off and has a wife and family to keep."

"These wives and families!" said Peter.

"Does the author approve?" inquired the Warden.

"Well," said the Dean, "the book ends there, so I suppose he does."

"But does anybody here approve? A false statement is published and the man who could correct it lets it go, out of charitable considerations. Would anybody here do that? There's your test case, Miss Barton, with no personalities attached."

"Of course one couldn't do that," said Miss Barton. "Not for ten wives and fifty children."

"Not for Solomon and all his wives and concubines? I congratulate you, Miss Barton, on striking such a fine, unfeminine note. Will nobody say a word for the women and children?"

("I knew he was going to be mischievous," thought Harriet.)

"You'd like to hear it, wouldn't you?" said Miss Hillyard.

"You've got us in a cleft stick," said the Dean. "If we say it, you can point out that womanliness unfits us for learning; and if we don't, you can point out that learning makes us unwomanly."

"Since I can make myself offensive either way," said Wimsey, "you have nothing to gain by not telling the truth."

"The truth is," said Mrs. Goodwin, "that nobody could possibly defend the indefensible."

"It sounds, anyway, like a manufactured case," said Miss Allison, briskly. "It could very seldom happen; and if it did—"

"Oh, it happens," said Miss De Vine. "It has happened. It happened to me. I don't mind telling you—without names, of course. When I was at Flamborough College, examining for the professorial theses in York University, there was a man who sent in a very interesting paper on a historical subject. It was a most persuasive piece of argument; only I happened to know that the whole contention was quite untrue, because a letter that absolutely contradicted it was actually in existence in a certain very obscure library in a foreign town. I'd come across it when I was reading up something else. That wouldn't have mattered, of course. But the internal evidence showed that the man must have had access to that library. So I had to make an inquiry, and I found that he really had been there and must have seen the letter and deliberately suppressed it."

"But how could you be so sure he had seen the letter?" asked Miss Lydgate anxiously. "He might carelessly have overlooked it. That would be a very different matter."

"He not only had seen it," replied Miss de Vine; "he stole it. We made him admit as much. He had come upon that letter when his thesis was nearly complete, and he had no time to rewrite it. And it was a great blow to him apart from that, because he had grown enamored of his own theory and couldn't bear to give it up."

"That's the mark of an unsound scholar, I'm afraid," said Miss Lydgate in a mournful tone, as one speaks of an incurable cancer.

"But here is the curious thing," went on Miss de Vine. "He was unscrupulous enough to let the false conclusion stand; but he was too good a historian to destroy the letter. He kept it."

"You'd think," said Miss Pyke, "it would be as painful as biting on a sore tooth."

"Perhaps he had some idea of rediscovering it some day," said Miss de Vine, "and setting himself right with his conscience. I don't know, and I don't think he knew very well himself."

"What happened to him?" asked Harriet.

"Well, that was the end of him, of course. He lost the professorship, naturally, and they took away his M.A. degree as well. A pity, because he was brilliant in his own way—and very good-looking, if that has anything to do with it."

"Poor man!" said Miss Lydgate. "He must have needed the post very badly."

"It meant a good deal to him financially. He was married and not well off. I don't know what became of him. That was about six years ago. He dropped out completely. One was sorry about it, but there it was."

"You couldn't possibly have done anything else," said Miss Edwards.

"Of course not. A man as undependable as that is not only useless, but dangerous. He might do anything."

"You'd think it would be a lesson to him," said Miss Hillyard. "It didn't pay, did it? Say he sacrificed his professional honor for the women and children we hear so much about—but in the end it left him worse off."

"But that," said Peter, "was only because he committed the extra sin of being found out."

"It seems to me," began Miss Chilperic, timidly—and then stopped.

"Yes?" said Peter.

"Well," said Miss Chilperic, "oughtn't the women and children to have a point of view? I mean—suppose the wife knew that her husband had done a thing like that for her, what would she feel about it?"

"That's a very important point," said Harriet. "You'd think she'd feel too ghastly for words."

"It depends," said the Dean. "I don't believe nine women out of ten would care a dash."

"That's a monstrous thing to say," cried Miss Hillyard.

"You think a wife might feel sensitive about her husband's honor—even if it was sacrificed on her account?" said Miss Stevens. "Well—I don't know."

"I should think," said Miss Chilperic, stammering a little in her earnestness, "she would feel like a man who—I mean, wouldn't it be like living on somebody's immoral earnings?"

"There," said Peter, "if I may say so, I think you are

exaggerating. The man who does that—if he isn't too far gone to have any feelings at all—is hit by other considerations, some of which have nothing whatever to do with ethics. But it is extremely interesting that you should make the comparison." He looked at Miss Chilperic so intently that she blushed.

"Perhaps that was rather a stupid thing to say."

"No. But if it ever occurs to people to value the honor of the mind equally with the honor of the body, we shall get a social revolution of a quite unparalleled sort—and very different from the kind that is being made at the moment."

Miss Chilperic looked so much alarmed at the idea of fostering a social revolution that only the opportune entry of two Common Room scouts to remove the coffee cups and relieve her of the necessity of replying seemed to have saved her from sinking through the floor.

"Well," said Harriet, "I agree absolutely with Miss Chilperic. If anybody did a dishonorable thing and then said he did it for one's own sake, it would be the last insult. How could one ever feel the same to him again?"

"Indeed," said Miss Pyke, "it must surely vitiate the whole relationship."

"Oh, nonsense!" cried the Dean. "How many women care two hoots about anybody's intellectual integrity? Only over-educated women like us. So long as the man didn't forge a check or rob the till or do something socially degrading, most women would think he was perfectly justified. Ask Mrs. Bones the Butcher's Wife or Miss Tape the Tailor's Daughter how much they would worry about suppressing a fact in a moldy old historical thesis."

"They'd back up their husbands, in any case," said Miss Allison. "My man, right or wrong, they'd say. Even if he *did* rob the till."

"Of course they would," said Miss Hillyard. "That's what the man wants. *He* wouldn't say thank you for a critic on the hearth."

"He must have the womanly woman, you think?" said

Harriet. "What is it, Annie? My coffee cup? Here you are. . . . Somebody who will say, 'The greater the sin the greater the sacrifice—and consequently the greater devotion.' Poor Miss Schuster-Slatt! . . . I suppose it is comforting to be told that one is loved whatever one does."

"Ah, yes," said Peter, in his reediest woodwind voice:

"And these say: 'No more now my knight
Or God's knight any longer'—you,
Being than they so much more white,
So much more pure and good and true,

"Will cling to me for ever—

William Morris had his moments of being a hundred percent manly man."

"Poor Morris!" said the Dean.

"He was young at the time," said Peter, indulgently. "It's odd, when you come to think of it, that the expressions 'manly' and 'womanly' should be almost more offensive than their opposites. One is tempted to believe that there may be something indelicate about sex after all."

"It all comes of this here eddication," pronounced the Dean, as the door shut behind the last of the coffee service. "Here we sit round in a ring, dissociating ourselves from kind Mrs. Bones and that sweet girl, Miss Tape—"

"Not to mention," put in Harriet, "those fine, manly fellows, the masculine Tapes and Boneses—"

"And clacking on in the *most* unwomanly manner about intellectual integrity."

"While I," said Peter, "sit desolate in the midst, like a lodge in a garden of cucumbers."

"You look it," said Harriet, laughing. "The sole relic of humanity in a cold, bitter and indigestible wilderness."

There was a laugh, and a momentary silence. Harriet could feel a nervous tension in the room—little threads of anxiety and expectation strung out, meeting, crossing, quivering. Now, they were all saying to themselves, now something is going to be said about IT. The ground has been surveyed, the coffee has been cleared out of the road, the combatants are stripped for action—now, this amiable gentleman with the well-filed tongue will come out in his true colors as an inquisitor, and it is all going to be very uncomfortable.

Lord Peter took out his handkerchief, polished his monocle carefully, readjusted it, looked rather severely at the Warden, and lifted up his voice in emphatic, pained and querulous complaint about the Corporation dump.

The Warden had gone, expressing courteous thanks to Miss Lydgate for the hospitality of the Senior Common Room, and graciously inviting his lordship to call upon her in her own house at any convenient time during his stay in Oxford. Various dons rose up and drifted away, murmuring that they had essays to look through before they went to bed. The talk had ranged pleasantly over a variety of topics. Peter had let the reins drop from his hands and let it go whither it would, and Harriet, realizing this, had scarcely troubled to follow it. In the end, there remained only herself and Peter, the Dean, Miss Edwards (who seemed to have taken a strong fancy to Peter's conversation), Miss Chilperic, silent and half-hidden in an obscure position and, rather to Harriet's surprise, Miss Hillyard.

The clocks struck eleven. Wimsey roused himself and said he thought he had better be getting along. Everybody rose. The Old Quad was dark, except for the gleam of lighted windows; the sky had clouded, and a rising wind stirred the boughs of the beechtrees.

"Well, goodnight," said Miss Edwards. "I'll see that you get a copy of that paper about blood-groups. I think you'll find it of interest."

"I shall, indeed," said Wimsey. "Thank you very much."

Miss Edwards strode briskly away.

"Goodnight, Lord Peter."

"Goodnight, Miss Chilperic. Let me know when the

social revolution is about to begin and I'll come to die upon the barricades."

"I think you would," said Miss Chilperic, astonishingly, and, in defiance of tradition, gave him her hand.

"Goodnight," said Miss Hillyard, to the world in general, and whisked quickly past them with her head high.

Miss Chilperic flitted off into the darkness like a pale moth, and the Dean said, "Well!" And then, interrogatively, "Well?"

"Pass, and all's well," said Peter, placidly.

"There were one or two moments, weren't there?" said the Dean. "But on the whole—as well as could be expected."

"I enjoyed myself very much," said Peter, with the mischievous note back in his voice.

"I bet you did," said the Dean. "I wouldn't trust you a yard. Not a yard."

"Oh, yes, you would," said he. "Don't worry."

The Dean, too, was gone.

"You left your gown in my room yesterday," said Harriet. "You'd better come and fetch it."

"I brought yours back with me and left it at the Jowett Walk Lodge. Also your dossier. I expect they've been taken up."

"You didn't leave the dossier lying about!"

"What do you take me for? It's wrapped up and sealed."

They crossed the quad slowly.

"There are a lot of questions I want to ask, Peter."

"Oh, yes. And there's one I want to ask you. What is your second name? The one that begins with a D?"

"Deborah, I'm sorry to say. Why?"

"Deborah? Well, I'm damned. All right. I won't call you by it. There's Miss de Vine, I see, still working."

The curtains of the Fellow's window were drawn back this time, and they could see her dark, untidy head, bent over a book.

"She interests me very much," said Peter.

"I like her, you know."

"So do I."

"But I'm afraid those are her kind of hairpins."

"I know they are," said he. He took his hand from his pocket and held it out. They were close under Tudor, and the light from an adjacent window showed a melancholy, spraddle-legged hairpin lying across his palm. "She shed this on the dais after dinner. You saw me pick it up."

"I saw you pick up Miss Shaw's scarf."

"Always the gentleman. May I come up with you, or is that against the regulations!"

"You can come up."

There were a number of students scurrying about the corridors in undress, who looked at Peter with more curiosity than annoyance. In Harriet's room, they found her gown lying on the table, together with the dossier. Peter picked up the book, examined the paper and string and the seals which secured them, each one stamped with the crouching cat and arrogant Wimsey motto.

"If that's been opened, I'll make a meal of hot sealing wax."

He went to the window and looked out into the quad.

"Not a bad observation post—in its way. Thanks. That's all I wanted to look at."

He showed no further curiosity, but took the gown she handed to him and followed her downstairs again.

They were halfway across the quad when he said suddenly:

"Harriet. Do you really prize honesty above every other thing?"

"I think I do. I hope so. Why?"

"If you don't, I am the most blazing fool in Christendom. I am busily engaged in sawing off my own branch. If I am honest, I shall probably lose you altogether. If I am not—"

His voice was curiously rough, as though he were trying to control something; not, she thought, bodily pain or passion, but something more fundamental.

"If you are not," said Harriet, "then *I* shall lose *you*, because you wouldn't be the same person, should you?"

"I don't know. I have a reputation for flippant insincerity. You think I'm honest?"

"I know you are. I couldn't imagine your being anything else."

"And yet at this moment I'm trying to insure myself against the effects of my own honesty. 'I have tried if I could reach that great resolution, to be honest without a thought of heaven or hell.' It looks as though I should get hell either way, though; so I need scarcely bother about the resolution. I believe you mean what you say—and I hope I should do the same thing if I didn't believe a word of it."

"Peter, I haven't an idea what you're talking about."

"All the better. Don't worry. I won't behave like this another time. 'The Duke drained a dipper of brandy-and-water and became again the perfect English gentleman.' Give me your hand."

She gave it to him, and he held it for a moment in a firm clasp, and then drew her arm through his. They moved on into the New Quad, arm in arm, in silence. As they passed the archway at the foot of the Hall stairs, Harriet fancied she heard somebody stir in the darkness and saw the faint glimmer of a watching face; but it was gone before she could draw Peter's attention to it.

Padgett unlocked the gate for them; Wimsey, stepping preoccupied over the threshold, tossed him a heedless goodnight.

"Goodnight, Major Wimsey, sir!"

"Hullo!" Peter brought back the foot that was already in St. Cross Road, and looked closely into the porter's smiling face.

"My God, yes! Stop a minute. Don't tell me. Caudry—1918—I've got it! Padgett's the name. Corporal Padgett."

"Quite right, sir."

"Well, well, well. I'm damned glad to see you. Looking dashed fit, too. How are you keeping?"

"Fine, thank you, sir." Padgett's large and hairy paw

closed warmly over Peter's long fingers. "I says to my wife, when I 'eard you was 'ere, 'I'll lay you anything you like,' I says, 'the Major won't have forgotten.' "

"By jove, no. Fancy finding you here! Last time I saw you, I was being carried away on a stretcher."

"That's right, sir. I 'ad the pleasure of 'elping to dig you out."

"I know you did. I'm glad to see you now, but I was a dashed sight gladder to see you then."

"Yes, sir. Gorblimey, sir—well, there! We thought you was gone that time. I says to Hackett—remember little Hackett, sir?"

"The little red-headed blighter? Yes, of course. What's become of him?"

"Driving a lorry over at Reading, sir, married and three kids. I says to Hackett, 'Lor' lumme!' I says, 'there's old Winderpane gawn'—excuse me, sir—and he says, ''Ell! wot ruddy luck!' So I says, 'Don't stand there grizzlin'—maybe 'e ain't gawn after all.' So we—"

"No," said Wimsey. "I fancy I was more frightened than hurt. Unpleasant sensation, being buried alive."

"Well, sir! W'en we finds yer there at the bottom o' that there old Boche dug-out with a big beam acrost yer, I says to Hackett, 'Well,' I says, ''e's all 'ere, anyhow.' And he says, 'Thank gawd for Jerry!' 'e says—meanin', if it 'adn't been for that there dug-out—"

"Yes," said Wimsey, "I had a bit of luck there. We lost poor Mr. Danbury, though."

"Yes, sir. Bad thing, that was. A nice young gentleman. Ever see anything of Captain Sidgwick nowadays, sir?"

"Oh, yes. I saw him only the other day at the Bellona Club. He's not very fit these days, I'm sorry to say. Got a dose of gas, you know. Lungs groggy."

"Sorry to hear that, sir. Remember how put about 'e was over that there pig—"

"Hush, Padgett. The less said about that pig, the better."

"Yes, sir. Nice bit o' crackling that pig 'ad on 'im. Coo!"

Padgett smacked reminiscent lips. "You 'eard wot 'appened to Sergeant-Major Toop?"

"Toop? No—I've quite lost sight of him. Nothing unpleasant, I hope. Best sergeant-major I ever had."

"Ah! he was a one." Padgett's grin widened. "Well, sir, 'e found 'is match all right. Little bit of a thing—no 'igher than that, but, lummy!"

"Go on, Padgett. You don't say so."

"Yes, sir. When I was workin' in the camel 'ouse at the Zoo—"

"Good God, Padgett!"

"Yes, sir—I see them there and we passed the time o' day. Went round to look 'em up afterwards. Well, there! She give 'im sergeant-major all right. Put 'im through the 'oop proper. You know the old song: Naggin' at a feller as is six foot three—"

"And her only four foot two! Well, well! How are the mighty fallen! By the bye, I'll tell you who I ran into the other day—now, this will surprise you—"

The stream of reminiscence ran remorselessly on, till Wimsey, suddenly reminded of his manners, apologized to Harriet and plunged hastily out, with a promise to return for another chat over old times. Padgett, still beaming, swung the heavy gate to, and locked it.

"Ah!" said Padgett, "he ain't changed much, the major 'asn't. He was a lot younger then, o' course—only just gazetted—but he was regular good officer for all that—and a terror for eye-wash. *And* shavin'—lummy!"

Padgett, supporting himself with one hand against the brickwork of the lodge, appeared lost in the long ago.

" 'Now, men,' 'e'd say, when we was expectin' a bit of a strafe, 'if you gotter face your Maker, fer gawd's sake, face 'Im with a clean chin.' Ah! Winderpane, we called 'im, along of the eyeglass, but meanin' no disrespect. None on us wouldn't 'ear a word agin 'im. Now, there was a chap came to us from another unit—'ulkin' foul-mouthed fellow, wot nobody took to much—'Uggins, that was the name, 'Uggins. Well, this bloke thinks 'e's goin' to be funny, see

—and 'e starts callin' the major Little Percy, and usin' opprobrious epithets—"

Here Padgett paused, to select an epithet fit for a lady's ear, but, failing, repeated:

"Opprobrious epithets, miss. And I says to 'im—mind you, this was afore I got my stripes; I was jest a private then, same as 'Uggins—I says to 'im, 'Now, that's quite enough o' that.' And 'e says to me—Well, anyway, the end of it was, we 'ad a lovely scrap, all round the 'ouses."

"Dear me," said Harriet.

"Yes, miss. We was in rest at the time, and next morning, when the sergeant-major falls us in for parade—coo, lummy! we was a pair o' family portraits. The sergeant-major—Sergeant-Major Toop, that was, 'im wot got married like I was sayin'—'e didn't say nothin'—'e knew. And the adjutant, 'e knew too, and 'e didn't say nothin' neither. And blest if, in the middle of it all, we don't see the Major comin' strollin' out. So the adjutant forms us up into line, and I stands there at attention, 'oping as 'Uggins's face looked worse nor what mine did. 'Mornin',' says the Major; and the adjutant and Sergeant-Major Toop says, 'Morning, sir.' So 'e starts to chat casual-like to the sergeant-major, and I see 'is eye goin' up and down the line. 'Sergeant-major!' says he, all of a sudden. 'Sir!' says the sergeant-major. 'What's that man there been doin' to 'imself?' says 'e, meanin' me. 'Sir?' says the sergeant-major, starin' at me like 'e was surprised to see me. 'Looks as if he'd had a nasty accident,' says the Major. 'And what about that other fellow? Don't like to see that sort of thing. Not smart. Fall 'em out.' So the sergeant-major falls us both out. 'H'm,' says the Major, 'I see. What's this man's name?' 'Padgett, sir,' says the sergeant-major. 'Oh,' says he. 'Well, Padgett, what have you been doing to get yourself into a mess like that?' 'Fell over a bucket, sir,' says I, starin' 'ard over 'is shoulder with the only eye I could see out of. 'Bucket?' says 'e, 'very awkward things, buckets. And this other man—I suppose he trod on the mop, eh, sergeant-major?' 'Major wants to know if you trod on the mop,' says Sergeant-

Major Toop. 'Yessir,' says 'Uggins, talkin' like 'is mouth 'urt 'im. 'Well,' says the Major, 'when you've got this lot dismissed, give these two men a bucket and a mop apiece and put 'em on fatigue. That'll learn 'em to 'andle these dangerous implements.' 'Yessir,' says Sergeant-Major Toop. 'Carry on,' says the Major. So we carries on. 'Uggins says to me arterwards, 'D'you think 'e knew?' 'Knew?' says I, 'course 'e knew. Ain't much 'e don't know.' Arter that, 'Uggins kep' 'is epithets to 'isself."

Harriet expressed due appreciation of this anecdote, which was delivered with a great deal of gusto, and took leave of Padgett. For some reason, this affair of a mop and a bucket seemed to have made Padgett Peter's slave for life. Men were very odd.

There was nobody under the Hall arches as she returned, but as she passed the West end of the Chapel, she thought she saw something dark pass like a shadow into the Fellows' Garden. She followed it. Her eyes were growing accustomed to the dimness of the summer night and she could see the figure walking swiftly up and down, up and down, and hear the rustle of its long skirt upon the grass.

There was only one person in College who had worn a trailing frock that evening, and that was Miss Hillyard. She walked in the Fellows' Garden for an hour and a half.

CHAPTER XVIII

Go tell that witty fellow, my godson, to get home.
It is no season to fool it here!
QUEEN ELIZABETH

"Lor'!" said the Dean.

She gazed with interest from the Senior Common Room window, teacup in hand.

"What's the matter?" inquired Miss Allison.

"*Who* is that incredibly beautiful young man?"

"Flaxman's fiancé, I expect, isn't it?"

"A beautiful young man?" said Miss Pyke. "I should like to see him." She moved to the window.

"Don't be ridiculous," said the Dean. "I know Flaxman's Byron by heart. This is an ash-blond in a House blazer."

"Oh, dear me!" said Miss Pyke. "Apollo Belvedere in spotless flannels. He appears to be unattached. Remarkable."

Harriet put down her cup and rose from the depths of the largest armchair.

"Perhaps he belongs to that bunch playing tennis," hazarded Miss Allison.

"Little Cooke's scrubby friends? My *dear*!"

"Why all the excitement, anyway?" asked Miss Hillyard.

"Beautiful young men are always exciting," said the Dean.

"That," said Harriet, at length getting a glimpse of the wonder-youth over Miss Pyke's shoulder, "is Viscount Saint-George."

"Another of your aristocratic friends?" asked Miss Barton.

"His nephew," replied Harriet; not very coherently.

"Oh!" said Miss Barton. "Well, I don't see why you need all gape at him like a lot of schoolgirls."

She crossed over to the table, cut herself a slice of cake and glanced casually out of the farther window.

Lord Saint-George stood, with a careless air of owning the place, at the corner of the Library Wing, watching a game of tennis being played between two bare-backed students and two young men whose shirts kept on escaping from their belts. Growing tired of this, he sauntered past the windows towards Queen Elizabeth, his eye roving over a group of Shrewsburians a-sprawl under the beeches, like that of a young Sultan inspecting a rather unpromising consignment of Circassian slaves.

"Supercilious little beast!" thought Harriet; and wondered if he was looking for her. If he was, he could wait, or ask properly at the Lodge.

"Oho!" said the Dean. "So *that's* how the milk got into the coconut!"

From the door of the Library Wing there issued slowly Miss de Vine, and behind her, grave and deferential, Lord Peter Wimsey. They skirted the tennis-court in earnest conversation. Lord Saint-George, viewing them from afar, advanced to meet them. They joined forces on the path. They stood for a little time talking. They moved away towards the Lodge.

"Dear me!" said the Dean. "Abduction of Helen de Vine by Paris and Hector."

"No, no," said Miss Pyke. "Paris was the brother of Hector, not his nephew. I do not think he had any uncles."

"Talking of uncles," said the Dean, "is it true, Miss Hillyard, that Richard III—I thought she was here."

"She *was* here," said Harriet.

"Helen is being returned to us," said the Dean. "The siege of Troy is postponed."

The trio were returning again up the path. Half-way

along Miss de Vine took leave of the two men and returned towards her own room.

At that moment, the watchers in the S.C.R. were petrified to behold a portent. Miss Hillyard emerged from the foot of the Hall stair, bore down upon the uncle and nephew, addressed them, cut Lord Peter neatly off from his convoy and towed him firmly away towards the New Quad.

"Glory *alleluia!*" said the Dean. "Hadn't you better go out and rescue your young friend? He's been deserted again."

"You could offer him a cup of tea," suggested Miss Pyke. "It would be an agreeable diversion for us."

"I'm surprised at you, Miss Pyke," said Miss Barton. "No man is safe from women like you."

"Now, where have I heard that sentiment before?" said the Dean.

"In one of the Poison-letters," said Harriet.

"If you're suggesting—" began Miss Barton.

"I'm only suggesting," said the Dean, "that it's a bit of a cliché."

"I meant it for a joke," retorted Miss Barton, angrily. "Some people have no sense of humor."

She went out and slammed the door. Lord Saint-George had wandered back and was sitting in the loggia leading up to the Library. He rose politely as Miss Barton stalked past him on the way to her room, and made some remark, to which the Fellow replied briefly, but with a smile.

"Insinuating men, these Wimseys," said the Dean. "Vamping the S.C.R. right and left."

Harriet laughed, but in Saint-George's quick, appraising glance at Miss Barton she had again seen his uncle look for a moment out of his eyes. These family resemblances were unnerving. She curled herself into the window seat and watched for nearly ten minutes. The viscount sat still, smoking a cigarette, and looking entirely at his ease. Miss Lydgate, Miss Burrows and Miss Shaw came in and began to pour out tea. The tennis party finished the set and moved away. Then, from the left, came a quick, light step along the gravel walk.

"Hullo!" said Harriet to the owner of the step.

"Hullo!" said Peter. "Fancy seeing you here!" He grinned. "Come and talk to Gerald. He's in the loggia."

"I see him quite plainly," said Harriet. "His profile has been much admired."

"As a good adopted aunt, why didn't you go and be kind to the poor lad?"

"I never was one to interfere. I keep myself *to* myself."

"Well, come now."

Harriet got down from the window seat and joined Wimsey outside.

"I brought him here," said Peter, "to see if he could make any identifications. But he doesn't seem able to."

Lord Saint-George greeted Harriet enthusiastically.

"There was another female went past me," he said, turning to Peter. "Grey hair badly bobbed. Earnest manner. Dressed in sack cloth. Institutional touch about her. I got speech of her."

"Miss Barton," said Harriet.

"Right sort of eyes; wrong sort of voice. I don't think it's her. It might be the one that collared you, Uncle. She had a kind of a lean and hungry look."

"H'm!" said Peter. "How about the first one?"

"I'd like to see her without her glasses."

"If you mean Miss de Vine," said Harriet, "I doubt whether she could see very far without them."

"That's a point," said Peter, thoughtfully.

"I'm sorry to be so vague and all that," said Lord Saint-George. "But it's not easy to identify a hoarse whisper and a pair of eyes seen once by moonlight."

"No," said Peter, "it needs a good deal of practice."

"Practice be blowed," retorted his nephew. "I'm not going to make a practice of it."

"It's not a bad sport," said Peter. "You might take it up till you can start games again."

"How's the shoulder getting on?" inquired Harriet.

"Oh, not too bad, thanks. The massage bloke is working wonders with it. I can lift the old arm shoulder high now. It's quite serviceable—for some things."

By way of demonstration he threw the damaged arm round Harriet's shoulders, and kissed her rapidly and expertly before she could dodge him.

"Children, children!" cried his uncle, plaintively, "remember where you are."

"It's all right for *me*," said Lord Saint-George. "*I'm* an adopted nephew. Isn't that right, Aunt Harriet?"

"Not bang underneath the windows of the S.C.R.," said Harriet.

"Come round the corner, then," said the viscount, impenitently, "and I'll do it again. As Uncle Peter says, these things need a good deal of practice."

He was impudently set upon tormenting his uncle, and Harriet felt extremely angry with him. However, to show annoyance was to play into his hands. She smiled upon him pityingly and uttered the Brasenose porter's classic rebuke:

"It's no good you making a noise, gentlemen. The Dean ain't a-coming down tonight."

This actually silenced him for the moment. She turned to Peter, who said:

"Have you any commissions in Town?"

"Why, are you going back?"

"I'm running up tonight and on to York in the morning. I expect to get back on Thursday."

"York?"

"Yes; I want to see a man there—about a dog, and all that."

"Oh, I see. Well—if it wouldn't be out of your way to call at my flat, you might take up a few chapters of manuscript to my secretary. I'd rather trust you than the post. Could you manage it?"

"With very great pleasure," said Wimsey, formally.

She ran up to her room to get the papers, and from the window observed that the Wimsey family was having the matter out with itself. When she came down with the parcel, she found the nephew waiting at the door of Tudor, rather red in the face.

"Please, I am to apologize."

"I should think so," said Harriet, severely. "I can't be disgraced like this in my own quad. Frankly, I can't afford it."

"I'm most frightfully sorry," said Lord Saint-George. "It was rotten of me. Honestly, I wasn't thinking of anything except getting Uncle Peter's goat. And if it's any satisfaction to you," he added, ruefully, "I got it."

"Well, be decent to him; he's very decent to you."

"I will be good," said Peter's nephew, taking the parcel from her, and they proceeded amicably together till Peter rejoined them at the Lodge.

"Damn that boy!" said Wimsey, when he had sent Saint-George ahead to start up the car.

"Oh, Peter, don't worry about every little thing so dreadfully. What does it matter? He only wanted to tease you."

"It's a pity he can't find some other way to do it. I seem to be a perfect millstone tied round your neck, and the sooner I clear out the better."

"Oh, for goodness' sake!" said Harriet, irritated. "If you're going to be morbid about it, it certainly would be better for *you* if you *did* clear out. I've told you so before."

Lord Saint-George, finding his elders dilatory, blew a cheerful "hi-tiddley-hi-ti, pom, pom" on the horn.

"Damn and blast!" said Peter. He took gate and path at a bound, pushed his nephew angrily out of the driving seat, jerked the door of the Daimler to noisily and shot off up the road with a bellowing roar. Harriet, finding herself unexpectedly possessed of a magnificent fit of bad temper, went back, determined to extract the last ounce of enjoyment out of it; an exercise in which she was greatly helped by the discovery that the little episode on the loggia had greatly intrigued the Senior Common Room, and by learning from Miss Allison, after Hall, that Miss Hillyard, when she heard of it, had made some very unpleasant observations, which it was only right that Miss Vane should know about.

Oh, God! thought Harriet, alone in her room, what have I done, more than thousands of other people, except have the rotten luck to be tried for my life and have the whole miserable business dragged out into daylight? . . . Anybody would think I'd been punished enough. . . . But nobody can forget it for a moment. . . . I can't forget it. . . . Peter can't forget it. . . . If Peter wasn't a fool he'd chuck it. . . . He must see how hopeless it all is. . . . Does he think I like to see him suffering vicarious agonies? . . . Does he really suppose I could ever marry him for the pleasure of seeing him suffer agonies? . . . Can't he see that the only thing for me to do is to keep out of it all? . . . What the devil possessed me to bring him to Oxford? . . . Yes—and I thought it would be so nice to retire to Oxford . . . to have "unpleasant observations" made about me by Miss Hillyard, who's half potty, if you ask me. . . . Somebody's potty, anyhow . . . that seems to be what happens to one if one keeps out of the way of love and marriage and all the rest of the muddle. . . . Well if Peter fancies I'm going to "accept the protection of his name" and be grateful, he's damn well mistaken. . . . A nice, miserable business that'd be for him. . . . It's a nice, miserable business for him, too, if he really wants me —if he does—and can't have what he wants because I had the rotten luck to be tried for a murder I didn't do. . . . It looks as if he was going to get hell either way. . . . Well, let him get hell, it's his lookout. . . . It's a pity he saved me from being hanged—he probably wishes by now he'd left me alone. . . . I suppose any decently grateful person would give him what he wants. . . . But it wouldn't be much gratitude to make him miserable. . . . We should both be perfectly miserable, because neither of us could ever forget. . . . I very nearly did forget the other day on the river. . . . And I had forgotten this afternoon, only he remembered it first. . . . Damn that impudent little beast! how horribly cruel the young can be to the middle-aged! . . . I wasn't frightfully kind myself. . . . And I did know what I was doing. . . . It's a good thing Peter's gone . . . but I wish he hadn't gone and left me in this ghastly place where people go off their heads and write horrible letters. . . . "When I am from him I am dead till I be with him." . . . No, it won't do to feel like that. . . . I won't get mixed up with that kind of thing again. . . . I'll stay out of it. . . . I'll stay here . . . where people go queer in their heads. . . . Oh, God, what have I done, that I should be such a misery to myself and other people? Nothing more than thousands of women . . .

Round and round, like a squirrel in a cage, till at last Harriet had to say firmly to herself: This won't do, or I shall go potty myself. I'd better keep my mind on the job. What's taken Peter to York? Miss de Vine? If I hadn't lost my temper I might have found out, instead of wasting time in quarreling. I wonder if he's made any notes on the dossier.

She took up the looseleaf book, which was still wrapped in its paper and string and sealed all over with the Wimsey crest. "As my Whimsy takes me"—Peter's whimsies had taken him into a certain amount of trouble. She broke the seals impatiently; but the result was disappointing. He had marked nothing—presumably he had copied out anything he wanted. She turned the pages, trying to piece some sort of solution together, but too tired to think coherently. And then—yes; here was his writing, sure enough, but not on a page of the dossier. This was the unfinished sonnet—and of all the idiotic things to do, to leave half-finished sonnets mixed up with one's detective work for other people to see! A schoolgirl trick, enough to make anybody blush. Particularly since, from what she remembered of the sonnet, its sentiments had become remarkably inappropriate to the state of her feelings.

But here it was: and in the interval it had taken to itself a sestet and stood, looking a little unbalanced, with her own sprawling hand above and Peter's deceptively neat script below, like a large top on a small spindle.

Here then at home, by no more storms distrest,
Folding laborious hands we sit, wings furled;
Here in close perfume lies the rose-leaf curled,
Here the sun stands and knows not east nor west,
Here no tide runs; we have come, last and best,
From the wide zone in dizzying circles hurled
To that still center where the spinning world
Sleeps on its axis, to the heart of rest.

Lay on thy whips, O Love, that we upright,
Poised on the perilous point, in no lax bed
May sleep, as tension at the verberant core
Of music sleeps; for, if thou spare to smite,
Staggering, we stoop, stooping, fall dumb and dead,
And, dying so, sleep our sweet sleep no more.

Having achieved this, the poet appeared to have lost countenance; for he had added the comment:

"A very conceited, metaphysical conclusion!"

So. So there was the turn she had vainly sought for the sestet! Her beautiful, big, peaceful humming-top turned to a whip-top, and sleeping, as it were, upon compulsion. (And, damn him! how *dared* he pick up her word "sleep" and use it four times in as many lines, and each time in a different foot, as though juggling with the accent-shift were child's play? And drag out the last halfline with those great, heavy, drugged, drowsy monosyllables, contradicting the sense so as to deny their own contradiction? It was not one of the world's great sestets, but it was considerably better than her own octave: which was monstrous of it.)

But if she wanted an answer to her questions about Peter, there it was, quite appallingly plain. He did not want to forget, or to be quiet, or to be spared things, or to stay put. All he wanted was some kind of central stability, and he was apparently ready to take anything that came along, so long as it stimulated him to keep that precarious balance. And of course, if he really felt like that, everything he had ever said or done, as far as she was concerned, was perfectly consistent. "Mine is only a balance of opposing forces." . . . "What does it matter if it hurts like hell, so long as it makes a good book?" . . . "What is the use of making mistakes if you don't make use of them?" . . . "Feeling like Judas is part of the job." . . . "The first thing a principle does is to kill somebody." . . . If that was his attitude, it was clearly ridiculous to urge him, in kindly tones, to stand aside for fear he might get a rap over the shins.

He had tried standing aside. "I have been running away from myself for twenty years, and it doesn't work." He no longer believed that the Ethiopian could change his skin to rhinoceros hide. Even in the five years or so that she had known him, Harriet had seen him strip off his protections, layer by layer, till there was uncommonly little left but the naked truth.

That, then, was what he wanted her for. For some reason, obscure to herself and probably also to him, she had the power to force him outside his defenses. Perhaps, seeing her struggling in a trap of circumstance, he had walked out deliberately to her assistance. Or perhaps the sight of her struggles had warned him what might happen to him, if he remained in a trap of his own making.

Yet with all this, he seemed willing to let her run back behind the barriers of the mind, provided—yes, he was consistent after all—provided she would make her own way of escape through her work. He was, in fact, offering her the choice between himself and Wilfrid. He did recognize that she had an outlet which he had not.

And that, she supposed, was why he was so morbidly sensitive about his own part in the comedy. His own needs were (as he saw the matter) getting between her and her legitimate way of escape. They involved her in difficulties which he could not share, because she had consistently refused him the right to share them. He had nothing of his nephew's cheerful readiness to take and have. Careless, selfish little beast, thought Harriet (meaning the viscount), can't he leave his uncle alone?

. . . It was just conceivable, by the way, that Peter was quite plainly and simply and humanly jealous of his nephew—not, of course, of his relations with Harriet (which would be disgusting and ridiculous), but of the careless young egotism which made those relations possible.

And, after all, Peter had been right. It was difficult to account for Lord Saint-George's impertinence without allowing people to assume that she was on terms with Peter which would explain that kind of thing. It had undoubtedly made an awkwardness. It was easy to say, "Oh, yes. I knew him slightly and went to see him when he was laid up after a motor accident." She did not really very much mind if Miss Hillyard supposed that with a person of her dubious reputation all and any liberties might be taken. But she did mind the corollary that might be drawn about Peter. That after five years' patient friendship he should have acquired only the right to look on while his nephew romped in public went near to making him look a fool. But anything else would not be true. She had placed him in exactly that imbecile position, and she admitted that that was not very pretty conduct.

She went to bed thinking more about another person than about herself. This goes to prove that even minor poetry may have its practical uses.

On the following night, a strange and sinister thing happened.

Harriet had gone, by appointment, to dine with her Somerville friend, and to meet a distinguished writer on the mid-Victorian period, from whom she expected to gain some useful information about Lefanu. She was sitting in the friend's room, where about half a dozen people were gathered to do honor to the distinguished writer, when the telephone rang.

"Oh, Miss Vane," said her hostess. "Somebody wants you from Shrewsbury."

Harriet excused herself to the distinguished guest, and went out into the small lobby in which the telephone was placed. A voice which she could not quite recognize answered her "Hullo!"

"Is that Miss Vane?"

"Yes—who's that speaking?"

"This is Shrewsbury College. Could you please come round quickly. There's been another disturbance."

"Good heavens! What's happened? Who is speaking, please?"

"I'm speaking for the Warden. Could you please—?"

"Is that Miss Parsons?"

"No, miss. This is Dr. Baring's maid."

"But what has happened?"

"I don't know, miss. The Warden said I was to ask you to come at once."

"Very well. I'll be there in about ten or fifteen minutes. I haven't got the car. I'll be there about eleven."

"Very good, miss. Thank you."

The connection was severed. Harriet hurriedly got hold of her friend, explained that she had been called away suddenly, said her good-byes and hurried out.

She had crossed the Garden Quad and was just passing between the Old Hall and the Maitland Buildings, when she was visited with an absurd recollection. She remembered Peter's saying to her one day:

"The heroines of thrillers deserve all they get. When a mysterious voice rings them up and says it is Scotland Yard, they never think of ringing back to verify the call. Hence the prevalence of kidnapping."

She knew where Somerville kept its public call box; presumably she could get a call from there. She went in; tried it; found that it was through to the Exchange; dialed the Shrewsbury number, and on getting it asked to be put through to the Warden's Lodgings.

A voice answered her; not the same person's that had rung her up before.

"Is that Dr. Baring's maid?"

"Yes, madam. Who is speaking, please?"

("Madam"—the other voice had said "miss." Harriet knew now why she had felt vaguely uneasy about the call. She had subconsciously remembered that the Warden's maid said "Madam.")

"This is Miss Harriet Vane, speaking from Somerville. Was it you who rang me up just now?"

"No, madam."

"Somebody rang me up, speaking for the Warden. Was it Cook, or anybody else in the house?"

"I don't think anybody has telephoned from here, madam."

(Some mistake. Perhaps the Warden had sent her message from somewhere in College and she had misunderstood the speaker or the speaker her.)

"Could I speak to the Warden?"

"The Warden isn't in College, madam. She went out to the theater with Miss Martin. I'm expecting them back any minute."

"Oh, thank you. Never mind. There must have been some mistake. Would you please put me back to the Lodge?"

When she heard Padgett's voice again she asked for Miss Edwards, and while the connection was being made, she thought fast.

It was beginning to look very much like a bogus call. But why, in Heaven's name? What would have happened if she had gone back to Shrewsbury straight away? Since she had not the car with her, she would have gone in by the private gate, past the thick bushes by the Fellows' Garden—the Fellows' Garden, where people walked by night—

"Miss Edwards isn't in her room, Miss Vane."

"Oh! The scouts are all in bed, I suppose."

"Yes, miss. Shall I ask Mrs. Padgett to see if she can find her?"

"No—see if you can get Miss Lydgate."

Another pause. Was Miss Lydgate also out of her room? Was every reliable don in College out, or out of her room? Yes—Miss Lydgate was out, too; and then it occurred to Harriet that, of course, they were dutifully patrolling the College before turning in to bed. However, there was Padgett. She explained matters as well as she could to him.

"Very good, miss," said Padgett, comfortingly. "Yes, miss —I can leave Mrs. Padgett on the Lodge. I'll get down to the private gate and have a look round. Don't you worry, miss. If there's anybody a-laying in wait for you, miss, I'm sorry for 'em, that's all. No, miss, there ain't been no disturbance tonight as I knows on; but if I catches anybody a-laying in wait, miss, then the disturbance will proceed according to schedule, miss, trust me."

"Yes, Padgett; but don't make a row about it. Slip down quietly and see if there's anybody hanging round—but don't let them see you. If anybody attacks me when I come in, you can come to the rescue; but if not, keep out of sight."

"Very good, miss."

Harriet hung up again and stepped out of the call box. A center light burned dimly in the entrance hall. She looked at the clock. Seven minutes to eleven. She would be late. However, the assailant, if there was one, would wait for her. She knew where the trap would be—must be. Nobody would start a riot just outside the Infirmary or the Warden's Lodgings, where people might overhear and come out. Nor would anyone hide under or behind the walls on that side of the path. The only reasonable lurking place was the bushes in the Fellows' Garden, near the gate, on the right side of the path as you went up.

One would be prepared, and that was an advantage; and Padgett would be somewhere at hand; but there would be a nasty moment when one had to turn one's back and lock the private gate from the inside. Harriet thought of the bread knife in the dummy, and shuddered.

If she bungled it and got killed—melodramatic, but possible, when people weren't quite sane—Peter would have something to say about it. Perhaps it would be only decent to apologize beforehand, in case. She found somebody's notebook astray on a window seat, borrowed a sheet of it, scribbled half a dozen words with the pencil from her bag, folded the note, addressed it and put it away with the pencil. If anything happened, it would be found.

The Somerville porter let her out into the Woodstock Road. She took the quickest way: by St. Giles' Church, Blackhall Road, Museum Road, South Parks Road, Mansfield Road, walking briskly, almost running. When she turned into Jowett Walk, she slowed down. She wanted her breath and her wits.

She turned the corner into St. Cross Road, reached the gate and took out her key. Her heart was thumping.

And then, the whole melodrama dissipated itself into polite comedy. A car drew up behind her; the Dean deposited the Warden and drove on round to the tradesmen's entrance to garage her Austin, and Dr. Baring said pleasantly:

"Ah! it's you, Miss Vane? Now I shan't have to look for my key. Did you have an interesting evening? The Dean and I have been indulging in a little dissipation. We suddenly made up our minds after dinner . . ."

She walked on up the path with Harriet, chatting with great amiability about the play she had seen. Harriet left her at her own gate, refusing an invitation to come in and have coffee and sandwiches. Had she, or had she not, heard something stir behind the bushes? At any rate, the opportunity was by now lost. She had offered herself as the cheese, but, owing to the slight delay in setting the trap, the Warden had innocently sprung it.

Harriet stepped into the Fellows' Garden, switched on her torch and looked round. The garden was empty. She suddenly felt a complete fool. Yet, when all was said and done, there must have been some reason for that telephone call.

She made her way towards the St. Cross Lodge. In the New Quad she met Padgett.

"Ah!" said Padgett, cautiously. "She was there right enough, miss." His right hand moved at his side, and Harriet fancied it held something suspiciously like a cosh. "Sittin' on the bench be'ind them laurels near the gate. I crep' along careful, like it was a night reconnaissance, miss, and 'id be'ind them center shrubs. She didn't tumble to me, miss. But when you an' Dr. Baring come through the gate a-talking, she was up and orf like a shot."

"Who was it, Padgett?"

"Well, miss, not to put too fine a point upon it, miss, it was Miss 'Illyard. She come out at the top end of the Garden, miss, and away to her own rooms. I follered 'er and see 'er go up. Going very quick, she was. I stepped out o' the gate, and I see the light go up in her window."

"Oh!" said Harriet. "Look here, Padgett. I don't want anything said about this. I know Miss Hillyard does sometimes take a stroll in the Fellows' Garden at night. Perhaps the person who sent the telephone call saw her there and went away again."

"Yes, miss. It's a funny thing about that there telephone call. It didn't come through the Lodge, miss."

"Perhaps one of the other instruments was through to the Exchange."

"No, they wasn't, miss. I 'ad a look to see. Afore I goes to bed at 11 o'clock, I puts the Warden, the Dean, and the Infirmary and the public box through, miss, for the night. But they wasn't through at 10:40, miss, that I'll swear."

"Then the call must have come from outside."

"Yes, miss. Miss 'Illyard come in at 10:50, miss, jest afore you rang up."

"Did she? Are you sure?"

"I remember quite well, miss, because of Annie passing a remark about her. There's no love lost between her and

Annie," added Padgett, with a chuckle. "Faults o' both sides, that's what I say, miss, and a 'asty temper—"

"What was Annie doing in the Lodge at that hour?"

"Jest come in from her half-day out, miss. She set in the Lodge a bit with Mrs. Padgett."

"Did she? You didn't say anything about this business to her, did you, Padgett? She doesn't like Miss Hillyard, and if you ask me, I think she's a mischief maker."

"I didn't say one word, miss, not even to Mrs. Padgett, and nobody could 'ave 'eard me on the 'phone, because, after I couldn't find Miss Lydgate and Miss Edwards and you begins to tell me, I shuts the door between me an' the settin' room. Then I jest puts me 'ead in afterwards and says to Mrs. Padgett, 'Look after the gate, would you?' I says, 'I jest got to step over and give Mullins a message.' So this here remains wot I might call confidential between you an' me, miss."

"Well, see that it stays confidential, Padgett. I may have been imagining something quite absurd. The 'phone call was certainly a hoax, but there's no proof that anybody meant mischief. Did anybody else come in between 10:40 and 11?"

"Mrs. Padgett will know, miss. I'll send you up a list of the names. Or if you like to step into the Lodge now—"

"Better not. No—give me the list in the morning."

Harriet went away and found Miss Edwards, of whose discretion and common sense she had a high opinion, and told her the story of the 'phone call.

"You see," said Harriet, "if there *had* been any disturbance, the call might have been intended to prove an alibi, though I don't quite see how. Otherwise, why try to get me back at eleven? I mean, if the disturbance was due to start then, and I was brought there as a witness, the person might have wangled something so as to appear to be elsewhere at the time. But why was it necessary to have me as a witness?"

"Yes—and why say the disturbance had already happened, when it hadn't? And why wouldn't you do as a witness when you had the Warden with you?"

"Of course," said Harriet, "the idea might have been to make a disturbance and bring me on to the scene in time to be suspected of having done it myself."

"That would be silly; everybody knows *you* can't be the Poltergeist."

"Well, then, we come back to my first idea. I was to be attacked. But why couldn't I be attacked at midnight or any other time? Why bring me back at eleven?"

"It couldn't have been something timed to go off at eleven, while the alibi was being established?"

"Nobody could know to a moment the exact time I should take coming from Somerville to Shrewsbury. Unless you are thinking of a bomb or something that would go off when the gate was opened. But that would work equally well at any time."

"But if the alibi was fixed for eleven—"

"Then why didn't the bomb go off? As a matter of fact, I simply can't believe in a bomb at all."

"Nor can I—not really," said Miss Edwards. "We're just being theoretical. I suppose Padgett saw nothing suspicious?"

"Only Miss Hillyard," replied Harriet, lightly, "sitting in the Fellows' Garden."

"Oh!"

"She does go there sometimes at night; I've seen her. Perhaps she frightened away—whatever it was."

"Perhaps," said Miss Edwards. "By the way, your noble friend seems to have overcome her prejudices in a remarkable manner. I don't mean the one who saluted you in the quad—the one who came to dinner."

"Are you trying to make a mystery out of yesterday afternoon?" asked Harriet, smiling. "I think it was only a matter of introductions to some man in Italy who owns a library."

"So she informed us," said Miss Edwards. Harriet realized that, when her own back was turned, a good deal of chaff must have been flying about the History Tutor's ears. "Well," Miss Edwards went on, "I promised him a paper on blood groups, but he hasn't started to badger me for it yet. He's an interesting man, isn't he?"

"To the biologist?"

Miss Edwards laughed. "Well, yes—as a specimen of the pedigree animal. Shockingly overbred, but full of nervous intelligence. But I didn't mean that."

"To the woman, then?"

Miss Edwards turned a candid eye on Harriet.

"To many women, I should imagine."

Harriet met the eye with a level gaze.

"I have no information on that point."

"Ah!" said Miss Edwards. "In your novels, you deal more in material facts than in psychology, don't you?"

Harriet readily admitted that this was so.

"Well, never mind," said Miss Edwards; and said good-night rather brusquely.

Harriet asked herself what all this was about. Oddly enough, it had never yet occurred to her to wonder what other women made of Peter, or he of them. This must argue either very great confidence or very great indifference on her own part; for, when one came to think of it, eligibility was his middle name.

On reaching her room, she took the scribbled note from her bag and destroyed it without rereading it. Even the thought of it made her blush. Heroics that don't come off are the very essence of burlesque.

Thursday was chiefly remarkable for a violent, prolonged and wholly inexplicable row between Miss Hillyard and Miss Chilperic, in the Fellows' Garden after Hall. How it started or what it was about, nobody could afterwards remember. Somebody had disarranged a pile of books and papers on one of the Library tables, with the result that a History Schools candidate had arrived for a coaching with a tale of a set of notes mislaid or missing. Miss Hillyard, whose temper had been exceedingly short all day, was moved to take the matter personally and, after glowering all through dinner, burst out—as soon as the Warden had gone—into a storm of indignation against the world in general.

"Why *my* pupils should always be the ones to suffer from other people's carelessness, I don't know," said Miss Hillyard.

Miss Burrows said she didn't see that they suffered more than anybody else. Miss Hillyard angrily adduced instances extending over the past three terms of History students whose work had been interfered with by what looked like deliberate persecution.

"Considering," she went on, "that the History School is the largest in the College and certainly not the least important—"

Miss Chilperic pointed out, quite correctly, that in that particular year there happened to be more candidates for the English School than any other.

"Of course you would say that," said Miss Hillyard. "There may be a couple more this year—I dare say there may—though why we should need an extra English tutor to cope with them, when I have to grapple single-handed—"

It was at that point that the origin of the quarrel became lost in a fog of personalities, in the course of which Miss Chilperic was accused of insolence, arrogance, inattention to her work, general incompetence and a desire to attract notice to herself. The extreme wildness of these charges left poor Miss Chilperic quite bewildered. Indeed, nobody seemed to be able to make anything of it, except, perhaps, Miss Edwards, who sat with a grim smile knitting herself a silk jumper. At length the attack extended itself from Miss Chilperic to Miss Chilperic's fiancé, whose scholarship was submitted to scathing criticism.

Miss Chilperic rose up, trembling.

"I think, Miss Hillyard," she said, "you must be beside yourself. I do not mind what you say about me, but I cannot sit here while you insult Jacob Peppercorn." She stumbled a little over the syllables of this unfortunate name, and Miss Hillyard laughed unkindly. "Mr. Peppercorn is a very fine scholar," pursued Miss Chilperic, with rising anger as of an exasperated lamb, "and I insist that—"

"I'm glad to hear you say so," said Miss Hillyard. "If I were you, I should make do with him."

"I don't know what you mean," cried Miss Chilperic.

"Perhaps Miss Vane could tell you," retorted Miss Hillyard, and walked away without another word.

"Good gracious!" cried Miss Chilperic, turning to Harriet. "Whatever is she talking about?"

"I haven't the least idea," said Harriet.

"I don't know, but I can guess," said Miss Edwards. "If people will bring dynamite into a powder factory, they must expect explosions." While Harriet was rooting about in the back of her mind for some association that these words called up, Miss Edwards went on:

"If somebody doesn't get to the bottom of these disturbances within the next few days, there'll be murder done. If we're like this now, what's going to happen to us at the end of term? You ought to have had the police in from the start, and if I'd been here, I'd have said so. I'd like to deal with a good, stupid sergeant of police for a change."

Then she, too, got up and stalked away, leaving the rest of the dons to stare at one another.

CHAPTER XIX

O well-knit Samson! strong-jointed Samson! I do excel thee in my rapier, as much as thou didst excel me in carrying gates. I am in love, too.
WILLIAM SHAKESPEARE

Harriet had been only too right about Wilfrid. She had spent portions of four days in altering and humanizing Wilfrid, and today, after a distressful morning with him, had reached the dismal conclusion that she would have to rewrite the whole thing from the beginning. Wilfrid's tormented humanity stood out now against the competent vacuity of the other characters like a wound. Moreover, with the reduction of Wilfrid's motives to what was psychologically credible, a large lump of the plot had fallen out, leaving a gap through which one could catch glimpses of new and exciting jungles of intrigue. She stood aimlessly staring into the window of the antique shop. Wilfrid was becoming like one of those coveted ivory chessmen. You probed into his interior and discovered an intricate and delicate carved sphere of sensibilities, and, as you turned it in your fingers, you found another inside that, and within that, another again.

Behind the table where the chessmen stood was a Jacobean dresser in black oak, and, as she stood at gaze, a set of features limned themselves pallidly against the dark background, like Pepper's ghost.

"What is it?" asked Peter over her shoulder; "Toby jugs or pewter pots or the dubious chest with Brummagem handles?"

"The chessmen," said Harriet. "I have fallen a victim to them. I don't know why. I have no possible use for them. It's just one of those bewitchments."

" 'The reason no man knows, let it suffice What we behold is censured by our eyes.' To be possessed is an admirable reason for possessing."

"What would they want for them, I wonder?"

"If they're complete and genuine, anything from forty to eighty pounds."

"Too much. When did you get back?"

"Just before lunch. I was on my way to see you. Were you going anywhere in particular?"

"No—just wandering. Have you found out anything useful?"

"I have been scouring England for a man called Arthur Robinson. Does the name mean anything to you?"

"Nothing whatever."

"Nor to me. I approached it with a refreshing absence of prejudice. Have there been any developments in College?"

"Well, yes. Something rather queer happened the other night. Only I don't quite understand it."

"Will you come for a run and tell me about it? I've got the car, and it's a fine afternoon."

Harriet looked round, and saw the Daimler parked by the curb.

"I'd love to."

"We'll dawdle along the lanes and have tea somewhere," he added, conventionally, as he handed her in.

"How original of you, Peter!"

"Isn't it?" They moved decorously down the crowded High Street. "There's something hypnotic about the word tea. I am asking you to enjoy the beauties of the English countryside, to tell me your adventures and hear mine, to plan a campaign involving the comfort and reputation of two hundred people, to honor me with your sole presence and bestow upon me the illusion of Paradise—and I speak as though the preeminent object of all desire were a pot of boiled water and a plateful of synthetic pastries in Ye Olde Worlde Tudor Tea-Shoppe."

"If we dawdle till after opening time," said Harriet, practically, "we can get bread-and-cheese and beer in the village pub."

"Now you have said something.

The crystal springs, whose taste illuminates
Refinèd eyes with an eternal sight,
Like trièd silver, run through Paradise
To entertain divine Zenocrate."

Harriet could find no adequate reply to this, but sat watching his hands as they lay lightly on the driving wheel. The car passed on through Long Marston out to Marston and Elsfield. Presently he turned it into a side road and thence into a lane and there drew up.

"There comes a moment when one must cease voyaging through strange seas of thought alone. Will you speak first, or shall I?"

"Who is Arthur Robinson?"

"Arthur Robinson is the gentleman who behaved so strangely in the matter of a thesis. He was an M.A. of York University, held various tutorships from time to time in various seats of learning, applied for the Chair of Modern History at York, and there came up against the formidable memory and detective ability of your Miss de Vine, who was then Head of Flamborough College and on the examining body. He was a fair, handsome man, aged about thirty-five at the time, very agreeable and popular, though hampered a little in his social career by having in a weak moment married his landlady's daughter. After the unfortunate episode of the thesis, he disappeared from academic circles, and was no more heard of. At the time of his disappearance he had one female child of two years of age and another expected. I managed to hunt up a former friend of his, who said that he had heard nothing of Robinson since the disaster, but fancied that he had gone abroad and changed his name. He referred me to a man called Simpson, living in Nottingham. I pursued Simpson, and found that he had, in the most inconvenient way, died last year. I returned to London and dispatched sundry members of Miss Climpson's Bureau in search of other friends and colleagues of Mr. Arthur Robinson, and also to Somerset House to hunt through the Marriage and Birth Registers. That is all I have to show for two days of intensive activity —except that I honorably delivered your manuscript to your secretary."

"Thank you very much. Arthur Robinson. Do you think he can possibly have anything to do with it?"

"Well, it's rather a far cry. But it's a fact that until Miss de Vine came here there were no disturbances, and the only thing she has ever mentioned that might suggest a personal enmity is the story of Arthur Robinson. It seemed just worth while following up."

"Yes, I see. . . . I hope you're not going to suggest that Miss Hillyard is Arthur Robinson in disguise, because I've known her for ten years."

"Why Miss Hillyard? What's she been doing?"

"Nothing susceptible of proof."

"Tell me."

Harriet told him the story of the telephone call, to which he listened with a grave face.

"Was I making a mountain out of a mole hill?"

"I think not. I think our friend has realized that you are a danger and is minded to tackle you first. Unless it is a quite separate feud—which is just possible. On the whole it's as well that you thought of ringing back."

"You may take the credit for that. I hadn't forgotten your scathing remarks about the thriller-heroine and the bogus message from Scotland Yard."

"Hadn't you? . . . Harriet, will you let me show you how to meet an attack if it ever does come?"

"Meet a—? Yes, I should like to know. Though I'm fairly strong, you know. I think I could cope with most things, except a stab in the back. That was what I rather expected."

"I doubt if it will be that," said he, coolly. "It makes a mess and leaves a messy weapon to be disposed of. Strangling is cleaner and quicker and makes no noise to speak of."

"Yeough!"

"You have a nice throat for it," pursued his lordship, thoughtfully. "It has a kind of arum-lily quality that is in itself a temptation to violence. I do not want to be run in by the local bobby for assault; but if you will kindly step aside with me into this convenient field, it will give me great pleasure to strangle you scientifically in several positions."

"You're a gruesome companion for a day's outing."

"I'm quite serious." He had got out of the car and was holding the door open for her. "Come, Harriet. I am very civilly pretending that I don't care what dangers you run. You don't want me to howl at your feet, do you?"

"You're going to make me feel ignorant and helpless," said Harriet, following him nevertheless to the nearest gate. "I don't like it."

"This field will do charmingly. It is not laid down for hay, it is reasonably free from thistles and cow pats, and there is a high hedge to screen us from the road."

"And it is soft to fall on and has a pond to throw the corpse into if you get carried away by your enthusiasm. Very well. I have said my prayers."

"Then kindly imagine me to be an unpleasant-faced thug with designs on your purse, your virtue and your life."

The next few minutes were rather breathless.

"Don't thrash about," said Peter, mildly. "You'll only exhaust yourself. Use *my* weight to upset me with. I'm putting it entirely at your disposal, and I can't throw it about in two directions at once. If you let my vaulting ambition overleap itself, I shall fall on the other side with the beautiful precision of Newton's apple."

"I don't get that."

"Try throttling me for a change, and I'll show you."

"Did I say this field was soft?" said Harriet, when her feet had been ignominiously hooked from under her. She rubbed herself resentfully. "Just let me do it to you, that's all."

And this time, whether by skill or favor, she did contrive to bring him off his balance, so that he only saved himself from sprawling by a complicated twist suggestive of an eel on a hook.

"We'd better stop now," said Peter, when he had instructed her in the removal of the thug who leaps from in front, the thug who dives in from behind, and the more sophisticated thug who starts operations with a silk scarf. "You'll feel tomorrow as if you'd been playing football."

"I think I shall have a sore throat."

"I'm sorry. Did I let my animal nature get the better of me? That's the worst of these rough sports."

"It would be a good bit rougher if it was done in earnest. I shouldn't care to meet *you* in a narrow lane on a dark night, and I only hope the Poison-Pen hasn't been making a study of the subject. Peter, you don't seriously think—"

"I avoid serious thought like the plague. But I assure you I haven't been knocking you about for the fun of it."

"I believe you. No gentleman could throttle a lady more impersonally."

"Thank you for the testimonial. Cigarette?"

Harriet took the cigarette, which she felt she had deserved, and sat with her hands about her knees, mentally turning the incidents of the last hour into a scene in a book (as is the novelist's unpleasant habit) and thinking how, with a little vulgarity on both sides, it could be worked up into a nice piece of exhibitionism for the male and provocation for the female concerned. With a little manipulation it might come in for the chapter where the wart Everard was due to seduce the glamorous but neglected wife, Sheila. He could lock her to him, knee to knee and breast to breast in an unbreakable grip and smile challengingly into her flushed face; and Sheila could go all limp—at which point Everard could either rain fierce kisses on her mouth, or say, "My God! don't tempt me!" which would come to exactly the same thing in the end. "It would suit them very well," thought Harriet, "the cheap skates!" and passed an exploring finger under the angle of her jaw, where the pressure of a relentless thumb had left its memory.

"Cheer up," said Peter. "It'll wear off."

"Do you propose to give Miss de Vine lessons in self defense?"

"I'm rather bothered about her. She's got a groggy heart, hasn't she?"

"She's supposed to have. She wouldn't climb Magdalen Tower."

"And presumably she wouldn't rush round College and steal fuses or climb in and out of windows. In which case the hairpins would be a plant. Which brings us back to the Robinson theory. But it's easy to pretend your heart is worse than it is. Ever seen her have a heart attack?"

"Now you mention it, I have not."

"You see," said Peter, "she put me on to Robinson. I gave her the opportunity to tell a story, and she told it. Next day, I went to see her and asked for the name. She made a good show of reluctance, but she gave it. It's easy to throw suspicion on people who owe you a grudge, and that without telling any lies. If I wanted you to believe that somebody was having a smack at me, I could give you a list of enemies as long as my arm."

"I suppose so. Do they ever try to do you in?"

"Not very often. Occasionally they send silly things by post. Shaving cream full of nasty bugs and so on. And there was a gentleman with a pill calculated to cure lassitude and debility. I had a long correspondence with him, all in plain envelopes. The beauty of his system was that he made you pay for the pill, which still seems to me a very fine touch. In fact, he took me in completely; he only made the one trifling miscalculation of supposing that I wanted the pill—and I can't really blame him for that, because the list of symptoms I produced for him would have led anybody to suppose I needed the whole pharmacopoeia. However, he sent me a week's supply—seven pills—at shocking expense; so I virtuously toddled round with them to my friend at the Home Office who deals with charlatans and immoral advertisements and so on, and he was inquisitive enough to analyze them. 'H'm,' said he, 'six of 'em would neither make nor mar you; but the other would cure lassitude all right.' So I naturally asked what was in it. 'Strychnine,' said he. 'Full lethal dose. If you want to go rolling round the room like a hoop with your head touching your heels, I'll guarantee the result.' So we went out to look for the gentleman."

"Did you find him?"

"Oh, yes. Dear old friend of mine. Had him in the dock before on a cocaine charge. We put him in jug—and I'm dashed if, when he came out, he didn't try to blackmail me on the strength of the pill correspondence. I never met a scoundrel I liked better. . . . Would you care for a little more healthy exercise, or shall we take the road again?"

It was when they were passing through a small town that Peter caught sight of a leather-and-harness shop, and pulled up suddenly.

"I know what you want," he said. "You want a dog collar. I'm going to get you one. The kind with brass knobs."

"A dog collar? Whatever for? As a badge of ownership?"

"God forbid. To guard against the bites of sharks. Excellent also against thugs and throat slitters."

"My dear man!"

"Honestly. It's too stiff to squeeze and it'll turn the edge of a blade—and even if anybody hangs you by it, it won't choke you as a rope would."

"I can't go about in a dog collar."

"Well, not in the daytime. But it would give confidence when patrolling at night. And you could sleep in it with a little practice. You needn't bother to come in—I've had my hands round your neck often enough to guess the size."

He vanished into the shop and was seen through the window conferring with the proprietor. Presently he came out with a parcel and took the wheel again.

"The man was very much interested," he observed, "in my bull terrior bitch. Extremely plucky animal, but reckless and obstinate fighter. Personally, he said, he preferred greyhounds. He told me where I could get my name and address put on the collar, but I said that could wait. Now we're out of the town, you can try it on."

He drew in to the side of the road for this purpose, and assisted her (with, Harriet fancied, a touch of self satisfaction), to buckle the heavy strap. It was a massive kind of necklace and quite surprisingly uncomfortable. Harriet fished in her bag for a hand mirror and surveyed the effect.

"Rather becoming, don't you think?" said Peter. "I don't see why it shouldn't set a new fashion."

"I do," said Harriet. "Do you mind taking it off again."

"Will you wear it?"

"Suppose somebody grabs at it from behind."

"Let go and fall back on them—heavily. You'll fall soft, and with luck they'll crack their skull open."

"Bloodthirsty monster. Very well. I'll do anything you like if you'll take it off now."

"That's a promise," said he, and released her. "That collar," he added, wrapping it up again and laying it on her knee, "deserves to be put in a glass case."

"Why?"

"It's the only thing you've ever let me give you."

"Except my life—except my life—except my life."

"Damn!" said Peter, and stared out angrily over the windscreen. "It must have been a pretty bitter gift, if you can't let either of us forget it."

"I'm sorry, Peter. That was ungenerous and beastly of me. You *shall* give me something if you want to."

"May I? What shall I give you? Roc's eggs are cheap today."

For a moment her mind was a blank. Whatever she asked him for, it must be something adequate. The trivial, the commonplace or the merely expensive would all be equally insulting. And he would know in a moment if she was inventing a want to please him. . . .

"Peter—give me the ivory chessmen."

He looked so delighted that she felt sure he had expected to be snubbed with a request for something costing seven-and-sixpence.

"My dear—of course! Would you like them now?"

"This instant! Some miserable undergraduate may be snapping them up. Every day I go out I expect to find them gone. Be quick."

"All right. I'll engage not to drop below seventy, except in the thirty mile limit."

"Oh, God!" said Harriet, as the car started. Fast driving terrified her, as he very well knew. After five breathtaking miles, he shot a glance sideways at her, to see how she was standing it, and slacked his foot from the accelerator.

"That was my triumph song. Was it a bad four minutes?"

"I asked for it," said Harriet, with set teeth. "Go on."

"I'm damned if I will. We will go at a reasonable pace and risk the undergraduate, damn his bones!"

The ivory chessmen were, however, still in the window when they arrived. Peter subjected them to a hard and monocled stare, and said:

"They *look* all right."

"They're lovely. Admit that when I do do a thing, I do it handsomely. I've asked you now for thirty-two presents at once."

"It sounds like *Through the Looking Glass*. Are you coming in, or will you leave me to fight it out by myself?"

"Of course I'm coming in. Why?—Oh! Am I looking too keen?"

"Much too keen."

"Well, I don't care. I'm coming in."

The shop was dark, and crowded with a strange assortment of first class stuff, junk, and traps for the unwary. The proprietor, however, had all his wits about him and, recognizing after a preliminary skirmish of superlatives that he had to do with an obstinate, experienced and well-informed customer, settled down with something like enthusiasm to a prolonged siege of the position. It had not previously occurred to Harriet that anybody could spend an hour and forty minutes in buying a set of chessmen. Every separate carved ball in every one of thirty-two pieces had to be separately and minutely examined with fingertips and the naked eye and a watchmaker's lens for signs of damage, repair, substitution or faulty workmanship; and only after a sharp catechism directed to the "provenance" of the set, and a long discussion about trade conditions in China, the state of the antique market generally and the effect of the American slump on prices, was any figure mentioned at all; and when it was mentioned, it was instantly challenged, and a further discussion followed, during which all the pieces were scrutinized again. This ended at length in Peter's agreeing to purchase the set at the price named (which was considerably above his minimum, though within his maximum estimate) provided the board was included. The unusual size of the pieces made it necessary that they should have their own board; and the dealer rather reluctantly agreed, after having it firmly pointed out to him that the board was sixteenth-century Spanish—clean out of the period—and that it was therefore almost a condescension on the purchaser's part to accept it as a gift.

The combat being now brought to an honorable conclusion, the dealer beamed pleasantly and asked where the parcel should be sent.

"We'll take it with us," said Peter, firmly. "If you'd rather have notes than a check—"

The dealer protested that the check would be quite all right but that the parcel would be a large one and take some time to make up, since the pieces ought all to be wrapped separately.

"We're in no hurry," said Peter. "We'll take it with us"; thus conforming to the first rule of good nursery behavior, that presents must always be taken and never delivered by the shop.

The dealer vanished upstairs to look for a suitable box, and Peter turned apologetically to Harriet.

"Sorry to be so long about it. You've chosen better than you knew. I'm no expert, but I'm very much mistaken if that isn't a very fine and ancient set, and worth a good bit more than he wants for it. That's why I haggled so much. When a thing looks like a bargain, there's usually a snag about it somewhere. If one of those dashed pawns wasn't the original, it would make the whole lot worthless."

"I suppose so." A disquieting thought struck Harriet. "If the set hadn't been perfect, should you have bought it?"

"Not at any price."

"Not if I still wanted it?"

"No. That's the snag about *me*. Besides, you wouldn't want it. You have the scholarly mind and you'd always feel uncomfortable knowing it was wrong, even if nobody else knew."

"That's true. Whenever anybody admired it I should feel obliged to say, 'Yes, but one of the pawns is modern'—and that would get so tedious. Well, I'm glad they're all right, because I love them with a perfectly idiotic passion. They have been haunting my slumbers for weeks. And even now I haven't said thank you."

"Yes, you have—and anyway, the pleasure is all mine. . . . I wonder whether that spinet's in order."

He threaded his way through the dark backward and abysm of the antique shop, clearing away a spinning wheel, a Georgian wine cooler, a brass lamp and a small forest of Burmese idols that stood between him and the instrument. "Variations on a musical box," he said, as he ran his fingers over the keys, and, disentangling a coffin stool from his surroundings, sat down and played, first a minuet from a Bach suite and then a gigue, before striking into the air of *Greensleeves*.

"*Alas! my love, you do me wrong*
To cast me off discourteously,

And I have loved you so long,
Delighting in your company."

He shall see that I don't mind that, thought Harriet, and raised her voice cheerfully in the refrain:

"For O Greensleeves was all my joy,
And O Greensleeves was my delight—"

He stopped playing instantly.

"Wrong key for you. God meant you for a contralto." He transposed the air into E minor, in a tinkling cascade of modulations. "You never told me you could sing. . . . No, I can hear you're not trained . . . chorus singer? Bach Choir? . . . of course—I might have guessed it. . . . 'And O Greensleeves was my heart of gold And who but my Lady Greensleeves' . . . Do you know any of Morley's *Canzonets for Two Voices?* . . . Come on, then, 'When lo! by Break of Morning' . . . Whichever part you like—they're exactly the same. . . . 'My love herself adorning.' . . . G natural, my dear, G natural. . . ."

The dealer, descending with his arms full of packing materials, paid no attention to them. He was well accustomed to the eccentricities of customers; and, moreover, probably cherished hopes of selling them the spinet.

"This kind of thing," said Peter, as tenor and alto twined themselves in a last companionable cadence, "is the body and bones of music. Anybody can have the harmony, if they will leave us the counterpoint. What next? . . . 'Go to Bed, sweet Muse'? Come, come! Is it true? is it kind? is it necessary? . . . 'Love is a fancy, love is a frenzy.' . . . Very well, I owe you one for that," and with a mischievous eye he played the opening bars of "Sweet Cupid, Ripen Her Desire."

"No," said Harriet, reddening.

"No. Not in the best of taste. Try again."

He hesitated; ran from one tune to another; then settled down to that best known of all Elizabethan love songs.

"Fain would I change that note
To which fond love hath charmed me. . . ."

Harriet, with her elbows on the lid of the spinet and her chin propped on her hands, let him sing alone. Two young gentlemen, who had strayed in and were talking rather loudly in the front part of the shop, abandoned a half-hearted quest for brass candlesticks and came stumbling through the gloom to see who was making the noise.

"True house of joy and bliss
Where sweetest pleasure is
I do adore thee;
I see thee what thou art,
I love thee in my heart
And fall before thee."

Tobias Hume's excellent air rises to a high pitched and triumphant challenge in the penultimate line, before tumbling with a clatter to the key note. Too late, Harriet signed to the singer to moderate his voice.

"Here, you!" said the larger of the two young gentlemen, belligerently. "You're making a filthy row. Shut up!"

Peter swung round on the stool.

"Sir?" He polished his monocle with exaggerated care, adjusted it and let his eye travel up the immense tweedy form lowering over him. "I beg your pardon. Was that obligin' observation addressed to me?"

Harriet started to speak, but the young man turned to her.

"Who," he demanded loudly, "is this effeminate bounder?"

"I have been accused of many things," said Wimsey, interested; "but the charge of effeminacy is new to me. Do you mind explaining yourself?"

"I don't like your song," said the young man, rocking slightly on his feet, "and I don't like your voice, and I don't like your tom-fool eyeglass."

"Steady on, Reggie," said his friend.

"You're annoying this lady," persisted the young man. "You're making her conspicuous. Get out!"

"Good God!" said Wimsey, turning to Harriet. "Is this by any chance Mr. Jones of Jesus?"

"Who are you calling a bloody Welshman?" snarled the young man, much exasperated. "My name's Pomfret."

"Mine's Wimsey," said Peter. "Quite as ancient though less euphonious. Come on, son, don't be an ass. You mustn't behave like this to senior members and before ladies."

"Senior member be damned!" cried Mr. Pomfret, to whom this unfortunate phrase conveyed only too much. "Do you think I'm going to be sneered at by you? Stand up, blast you! why can't you stand up for yourself?"

"First," replied Peter, mildly, "because I'm twenty years older than you are. Secondly, because you're six inches taller than I am. And thirdly, because I don't want to hurt you."

"Then," said Mr. Pomfret, "take that, you sitting rabbit!"

He launched an impetuous blow at Peter's head, and found himself held by the wrist in an iron grip.

"If you don't keep quiet," said his lordship, "you'll break something. Here, you, sir. Take your effervescent friend home, can't you? How the devil does he come to be drunk at this time of the day?"

The friend offered a confused explanation about a lunch party and subsequent cocktail binge. Peter shook his head.

"One damn gin after another," he said, sadly. "Now, sir. You had better apologize to the lady and beetle off."

Mr. Pomfret, much subdued and tending to become lachrymose, muttered that he was sorry to have made a row. "But why did you make fun of me with that?" he asked Harriet, reproachfully.

"I didn't, Mr. Pomfret. You're quite mistaken."

"Damn your senior members!" said Mr. Pomfret.

"Now, don't begin all over again," urged Peter, kindly.

He got up, his eyes about on a level with Mr. Pomfret's chin. "If you want to continue the discussion, you'll find me at the Mitre in the morning. This way out."

"Come on, Reggie," said the friend.

The dealer, who had returned to his packing after assuring himself that it would not be necessary to send for the police or the proctors, leapt helpfully to open the door, and said "*Good* afternoon, gentlemen," as though nothing out of the way had happened.

"I'm damned if I'll be sneered at," said Mr. Pomfret, endeavoring to stage a comeback on the doorstep.

"Of course not, old boy," said his friend. "Nobody's sneering at you. *Come* on! You've had quite enough fun for one afternoon."

The door shut them out.

"Well, well!" said Peter.

"Young gentlemen will be lively," said the dealer. "I'm afraid it's a bit bulky, sir. I've put the board up separate."

"Stick 'em in the car," said Peter. "They'll be all right."

This was done; and the dealer, glad enough to get his shop cleared, began to put up his shutters, as it was now long past closing time.

"I apologize for my young friend," said Harriet.

"He seems to have taken it hard. What on earth was there so infuriating about my being a senior?"

"Oh, poor lamb! He thought I'd been telling you about him and me and the proctor. I suppose I *had* better tell you now."

Peter listened and laughed a little ruefully.

"I'm sorry," he said. "That kind of thing hurts like hell when you're his age. I'd better send him a note and set that right. I say!"

"What?"

"We never had that beer. Come round and have one with me at the Mitre, and we'll concoct a salve for wounded feelings."

With two half pint tankards on the table before them, Peter produced his epistle.

The Mitre Hotel,
Oxford

To Reginald Pomfret, Esq.

Sir,

I am given to understand by Miss Vane that in the course of our conversation this afternoon I unhappily made use of an expression which might have been misconstrued as a reference to your private affairs. Permit me to assure you that the words were uttered in complete ignorance, and that nothing could have been farther from my intentions than to make any such offensive allusion. While deprecating very strongly the behavior you thought fit to use, I desire to express my sincere regret for any pain I may have inadvertently caused you, and beg to remain,

Your obedient servant,
Peter Death Bredon Wimsey

"Is that pompous enough?"

"Beautiful," said Harriet. "Scarcely a word under three syllables and all the names you've got. What your nephew calls 'Uncle Peter at his stuffiest.' All it wants is the crest and sealing wax. Why not write the child a nice, friendly note?"

"He doesn't want friendliness," said his lordship, grinning. "He wants satisfaction." He rang the bell and sent the waiter for Bunter and the sealing wax. "You're right about the beneficial effects of a red seal—he'll think it's a challenge. Bunter, bring me my seal ring. Come to think of it, that's an idea. Shall I offer him the choice of swords or pistols on Port Meadow at daybreak?"

"I think it's time you grew up," said Harriet.

"Is it?" said Peter, addressing the envelope. "I've never challenged anybody. It would be fun. I've been challenged three times and fought twice; the third time the police butted in. I'm afraid that was because my opponent didn't fancy my choice of weapon. . . . Thanks, Bunter. . . .

A bullet, you see, may go anywhere, but steel's almost bound to go somewhere."

"Peter," said Harriet, looking gravely at him, "I believe you're showing off."

"I believe I am," said he, setting the heavy ring accurately down upon the wax. "Every cock will crow upon his own dung-hill." His grin was half petulant, half deprecating. "I hate being loomed over by gigantic undergraduates and made to feel my age."

CHAPTER XX

For, to speak in a word, envy is naught else but tristitia de bonis alienis, *sorrow for other men's good, be it present, past, or to come: and* gaudium de adversis, *and joy at their harms. . . . 'Tis a common disease, and almost natural to us, as* Tacitus *holds, to envy another man's prosperity.*

ROBERT BURTON

It is said that love and a cough cannot be hid. Nor is it easy to hide two-and-thirty outsize ivory chessmen; unless one is so inhuman as to leave them swaddled in their mummy-clothes of wadding and entombed within the six sides of a wooden sarcophagus. What is the use of acquiring one's heart's desire if one cannot handle and gloat over it, show it to one's friends and gather an anthology of envy and admiration? Whatever awkward deductions might be drawn about the giver —and, after all, was that anybody's business?—Harriet knew that she must needs display the gift or burst in solitary ecstasy.

Accordingly, she put a bold face on it, marched her forces openly into the Senior Common Room after Hall, and deployed them upon the table, with the eager assistance of the dons.

"But where are you going to keep them?" asked the Dean, when everybody had sufficiently exclaimed over the fineness of the carving, and had taken her turn at twisting and examining the nests of concentric globes. "You can't just leave them in the box. Look at those fragile little spears and things and the royal head-dresses. They ought to be put in a glass case."

"I know," said Harriet. "It's just like me to want something completely impracticable. I shall have to wrap them all up again."

"Only then," said Miss Chilperic, "you won't be able to look at them. I know, if they were mine, I shouldn't be able to take my eyes off them for a moment."

"You can have a glass case if you like," said Miss Edwards. "Out of the Science Lecture-Room."

"The very thing," said Miss Lydgate. "But how about the terms of the bequest? I mean, the glass cases—"

"Oh, blow the bequest!" cried the Dean. "Surely one can *borrow* a thing for a week or two. We can lump some of those hideous geological specimens together and have one of the small cases taken up to your room."

"By all means," said Miss Edwards. "I'll see to it."

"Thank you," said Harriet; "that will be lovely."

"Aren't you simply aching to play with the new toy?" asked Miss Allison. "Does Lord Peter play chess?"

"I don't know," said Harriet. "I'm not much of a player. I just fell in love with the pieces."

"Well," said Miss de Vine, kindly, "let us have a game. They are so beautiful, it would be a pity not to use them."

"But I expect you could play my head off."

"Oh, do play with them!" cried Miss Shaw, sentimentally. "Think how they must be longing for a little life and movement after sitting all that time in a shop-window."

"I will give you a pawn," suggested Miss de Vine.

Even with this advantage, Harriet suffered three humiliating defeats in quick succession: first, because she was but a poor player; secondly, because she found it difficult to remember which piece was which; thirdly, because the anguish of parting at one fell swoop with a fully-armed warrior, a prancing steed and a complete nest of ivory balls was such that she could scarcely bear to place so much as a pawn in jeopardy. Miss de Vine, viewing with perfect equanimity the disappearance even of a robed counselor with long moustaches or an elephant carrying a castleful of combatants, soon had Harriet's king penned helplessly among his own defenders. Nor was the game made any easier for the weaker party by being played under the derisive eye of Miss Hillyard, who, pronouncing chess to be the world's most wearisome amusement, yet would not go away and get on with her work, but sat staring at the board as though fascinated and (what was worse) fiddling with the captured pieces and putting Harriet into an agony for fear she would drop one.

Moreover, when the games were finished, and Miss Edwards had announced that a glass case had been dusted and taken up to Harriet's room by a scout, Miss Hillyard insisted on helping to carry the pieces over, grasping for the purpose the white king and queen, whose headgear bore delicate waving ornaments like antennae, extremely liable to damage. Even when the Dean had discovered that the pieces could be more safely transported standing upright in their box, Miss Hillyard attached herself to the party that escorted them across the quad, and was officious in helping to set the glass case in a convenient position opposite the bed, "so that," as she observed, "you can see them if you wake up in the night."

The following day happened to be the Dean's birthday. Harriet, going shortly after breakfast to purchase a tribute of roses in the Market, and coming out into the High Street with the intention of making an appointment at the hairdresser's, was rewarded by the rather unexpected sight of two male backs, issuing from the Mitre and proceeding, apparently in perfect amity, in an easterly direction. The shorter and slighter of the two she could have singled out from a million backs anywhere; nor was it easy to mistake the towering bulk and breadth of Mr. Reginald Pomfret. Both parties were smoking pipes, and she concluded from this that the object of their excursion could scarcely be swords or pistols on Port Meadow. They were strolling in a leisurely after-breakfast manner, and she took care not to catch them up. She hoped that what Lord Saint-George called the "famous family charm" was being exerted to good purpose; she was too old to enjoy the sensation of being squabbled over—it made all three of them ridiculous. Ten years ago, she might have felt flattered; but it seemed that the lust to power was a thing one grew out of. What one wanted, she thought, standing amid the stuffy perfumes of the hair-dresser's establishment, was peace, and freedom from the pressure of angry and agitated personalities. She booked an appointment for the afternoon and resumed her way. As she passed Queen's, Peter came down the steps alone.

"Hullo!" said he. "Why the floral emblems?"

Harriet explained.

"Good egg!" said his lordship. "I like your Dean." He relieved her of the roses. "Let me also be there with a gift.

"*Make her a goodly chapilet of azur'd Colombine,*
And wreathe about her coronet with sweetest Eglantine,
With roses damask, white, and red, and fairest flower delice,
With Cowslips of Jerusalem, and cloves of Paradice.

Though what Cowslips of Jerusalem may be I do not know, and they are probably not in season."

Harriet turned back with him marketwards.

"Your young friend came to see me," pursued Peter.

"So I observed. Did you 'fix a vacant stare and slay him with your noble birth'?"

"And he my own kin in the sixteenth degree on the father's mother's side? No; he's a nice lad, and the way to his heart is through the playing-fields of Eton. He told me all his griefs and I sympathized very kindly, mentioning that there were better ways of killing care than drowning it in a butt of malmsey. But, O God, turn back the universe and give me yesterday! He was beautifully sozzled last night, and had one breakfast before he came out and another with me at the Mitre. I do not envy the heart of youth, but only its head and stomach."

"Have you heard anything fresh about Arthur Robinson?"

"Only that he married a young woman called Charlotte Ann Clarke, and had by her a daughter, Beatrice Maud. That was easy, because we know where he was living eight years ago, and could consult the local registers. But they're still hunting the registers to find either his death—supposing him to be dead, which is rather less likely than otherwise—or the birth of the second child, which—if it ever occurred—might tell us where he went to after the trouble at York. Unfortunately, Robinsons are as plentiful as blackberries, and Arthur Robinsons not uncommon. And if he really did change his name, there may not be any Robinson entries at all. Another of my searchers has gone to his old lodgings—where, you may remember, he very imprudently married the landlady's daughter; but the Clarkes have moved, and it's going to be a bit of a job finding them. Another line is to inquire among the scholastic agencies and the small and inferior private schools, because it seems probable—You're not attending."

"Yes, I am," said Harriet, vaguely. "He had a wife called Charlotte and you're looking for him in a private school." A rich, damp fragrance gushed out upon them as they turned into the Market, and she was overcome by a sense of extravagant well-being. "I love this smell—it's like the cactus-house in the Botanical Gardens."

Her companion opened his mouth to speak, looked at her, and then, as one that will not interfere with fortune, let the name of Robinson die upon his lips.

"*Mandragorae dederunt odorem.*"

"What do you say, Peter?"

"Nothing. The words of Mercury are harsh after the songs of Apollo." He laid his hand gently upon her arm. "Let us interview the merchant with the sops-in-wine."

And when both roses and carnations had been dispatched—this time by a messenger—to their destination, it seemed natural, since the Botanical Gardens had been mentioned, to go there. For a garden, as Bacon observes, is the purest of human pleasures and the greatest refreshment to the spirit of man; and even idle and ignorant people who cannot distinguish *Leptosiphon hybridus* from *Kaulfussia amelloides* and would rather languish away in a wilderness than break their backs with dibbling and weeding may get a good deal of pleasant conversation out of it, especially if they know the old-fashioned names of the commoner sorts of flowers and are both tolerably well acquainted with the minor Elizabethan lyrists.

It was only when they had made the round of the Gardens and were sitting idly on the bank of the river that Peter, wrenching his attention back to the sordid present, remarked suddenly:

"I think I shall have to pay a visit to a friend of yours. Do you know how Jukes came to be caught with the stuff on him?"

"I've no idea."

"The police got an anonymous letter."

"Not—?"

"Yes. One of them there. By the way, did you ever try and find out what was to have been the last word of that message to you? The one we found in the Science Lecture-Room?"

"No—she couldn't have finished it, anyhow. There wasn't a single vowel left in the box. Not even a B and a dash!"

"That was an oversight. I thought so. Well, Harriet, it's easy to put a name to the person we want, isn't it? But proof's a different matter. We've tied the thing up so tight. That lecture-room episode was meant to be the last of the nocturnal prowls, and it probably will be. And the best bit of evidence will be at the bottom of the river by this time. It's too late to seal the doors and set a watch."

"On whom?"

"Surely you know by this time? You *must* know, Harriet, if you're giving your mind to the thing at all. Opportunity, means, motive—doesn't it stand out a mile? For God's sake, put your prejudices aside and think it out. What's happened to you that you can't put two and two together?"

"I don't know."

"Well," said he drily, "if you really don't know, it's not for me to tell you. But if you will turn your attention for one moment to the matter in hand and go through your own dossier of the case carefully—"

"Undeterred by any casual sonnets I may find by the way?"

"Undeterred by any personal consideration whatever," he burst out, almost angrily. "No; you're quite right. That was a stupidity. My talent for standing in my own light amounts to genius, doesn't it? But when you have come to a conclusion about all this, will you remember that it was *I* who asked *you* to take a dispassionate view and *I* who told *you* that of all devils let loose in the world there was no devil like devoted love. . . . I don't mean passion. Passion's a good, stupid horse that will pull the plough six days a week if you give him the run of his heels on Sundays. But love's a nervous, awkward, over-mastering brute; if you can't rein him, it's best to have no truck with him."

"That sounds very topsy-turvy," said Harriet, mildly. But his unwonted excitement had already flickered out.

"I'm only walking on my head, after the manner of clowns. If we went along to Shrewsbury now, do you think the Warden would see me?"

Later in the day, Dr. Baring sent for Harriet.

"Lord Peter Wimsey has been to see me," she said, "with a rather curious proposition which, after a little consideration, I refused. He told me that he was almost certain in his own mind of the identity of the—the offender, but that he was not in a position at the moment to offer a complete proof. He also said that the person had, he thought, taken the alarm, and would be doubly careful from now on to escape detection. The alarm might, in fact, be sufficient to prevent further outbreaks until the end of the term at any rate; but as soon as our vigilance was relaxed, the trouble would probably break out again in a more violent form. I said that that would be very unsatisfactory, and he agreed. He asked whether he should name the person to me, in order that a careful watch might be kept upon her movements. I said I saw two objections to that: first, that the person might discover that she was being spied upon and merely increase her caution, and secondly, that if he happened to be mistaken as to the offender's identity, the person spied upon would be subjected to the most intolerable suspicions. Supposing, I said, the persecutions merely ceased, and we were left suspecting this person—who might be quite innocent—without proof either way. He replied that those were precisely the objections that had occurred to him. Do you know the name of the person to whom he alludes, Miss Vane?"

"No," said Harriet, who had been exercising her wits in the interval. "I am beginning to have an idea; but I can't make it fit. In fact, I simply can't believe it."

"Very well. Lord Peter then made a very remarkable proposition. He asked whether I would allow him to interrogate this person privately, in the hope of surprising her into some admission. He said that if this bluff, as he called it, came off, the culprit could then make her confession to me and be suffered to depart quietly, or be dealt with medically, as we might decide was advisable. If, however, it did not come off and the person denied everything, we might be placed in a very disagreeable position. I replied that I quite saw that, and could not possibly consent to have such methods used upon anybody in this College. To which he replied that that was exactly what he had expected me to say.

"I then asked him what evidence, if any, he had against this person. He said that all his evidence was circumstantial; that he hoped to have more of it in the course of the next few days, but that in default of a fresh outbreak and the capture of the culprit red-handed, he doubted whether any direct evidence could be produced at this stage. I inquired whether there was any reason why we should not at least wait for the production of the additional evidence."

Dr. Baring paused and looked keenly at Harriet.

"He replied that there was only one reason, and that was that the culprit, instead of becoming more cautious, might throw caution to the winds and proceed to direct violence. 'In which case,' he said, 'we should very likely catch her, but only at the cost of somebody's death or serious injury.' I asked what persons were threatened with death or injury. He said the most probable victims were—yourself, Miss de Vine and another person whom he could not name, but whose existence, he said, he deduced. He also surprised me by saying that an abortive attack had already been made upon you. Is that true?"

"I shouldn't have put it as strongly as that," said Harriet. She briefly outlined the story of the telephone call. At the name of Miss Hillyard, the Warden looked up:

"Do I understand that you entertain a definite suspicion of Miss Hillyard?"

"If I did," said Harriet, cautiously, "I shouldn't be the only person to do so. But I'm bound to say that she doesn't seem to fit in at all with the line of Lord Peter's inquiries, so far as I am acquainted with them."

"I am glad to hear you say that," replied Dr. Baring. "Representations have been made to me which—in default of evidence—I have been very unwilling to listen to."

So Dr. Baring had kept abreast of the feeling in the S.C.R. Miss Allison and Mrs. Goodwin had probably been talking. Well!

"In the end," pursued the Warden, "I informed Lord Peter that I thought it would be better to wait for the further evidence. But that decision must, of course, be subject to the willingness of yourself and Miss de Vine to face the risks involved. The willingness of the unknown third party cannot, naturally, be ascertained."

"I don't in the least mind what risks *I* take," said Harriet. "But Miss de Vine ought to be warned, I suppose."

"That is what I said. Lord Peter agreed."

So, thought Harriet, something has decided him to acquit Miss de Vine. I'm glad. Unless this is a Machiavellian ruse to throw her off her guard.

"Have you said anything to Miss de Vine, Warden?"

"Miss de Vine is in Town, and will not return till tomorrow evening. I propose to speak to her then."

So there was nothing to do but to wait. And in the meantime, Harriet became aware of a curious change in the atmosphere of the Senior Common Room. It was as though they had lost sight of their mutual distrust and their general apprehensions and had drawn together like spectators at the ring-side to watch another kind of conflict, in which she was one of the principals. The curious tension thus produced was scarcely relieved by the Dean's announcement to a few select spirits that in *her* opinion, Flaxman's young man had given her the chuck and serve her right; to which Miss Flaxman's tutor sourly replied that she wished people wouldn't have these upheavals in the Summer Term, but that, fortunately, Miss Flaxman didn't take her final Schools till next year. This prompted Harriet to ask Miss Shaw how Miss Newland was getting on. It appeared that Miss Newland was doing well, having completely got over the shock of her immersion in the Cherwell, so that her chances for a First looked pretty good.

"Splendid!" said Harriet. "I've ear-marked my winnings already. By the way, Miss Hillyard, how is our young friend Cattermole?"

It seemed to her that the room waited breathlessly for the answer. Miss Hillyard replied, rather shortly, that Miss Cattermole seemed to have recovered such form as she had ever possessed, thanks, as she understood from the young woman herself, to Miss Vane's good advice. She added that it was very kind of Harriet, amid her many preoccupations, to interest herself in the History students. Harriet made some vague reply and the room, as it seemed to her, breathed again.

Later in the day, Harriet took an outrigger on the river with the Dean, and, rather to her surprise, observed Miss Cattermole and Mr. Pomfret sharing a punt. She had received the "penitent letter" from Mr. Pomfret, and waved a cheerful hand as the boats passed, in token of peace restored. If she had known that Mr. Pomfret and Miss Cattermole had found a bond of sympathy in devotion to herself, she might have speculated on what may happen to rejected lovers who confide their troubles to willing ears; but this did not occur to her, because she was wondering what, exactly, had happened that morning at the Mitre; and her thoughts had strayed away into the Botanical Gardens before the Dean pointed out, rather sharply, that she was setting a very irregular and leisurely stroke.

It was Miss Shaw who innocently precipitated a flare-up.

"That's a very handsome scarf," she said to Miss Hillyard. The dons were assembling, as usual, for Hall, outside the S.C.R.; but the evening was dull and chilly and a thick silk scarf was a grateful addition to evening dress.

"Yes," said Miss Hillyard. "Unfortunately it isn't mine. Some careless person left it in the Fellows' Garden last night and I rescued it. I brought it along to be identified—but I'm ready to admit that I can do with it this evening."

"I don't know whose it can be," said Miss Lydgate. She fingered it admiringly. "It looks more like a man's scarf," she added.

Harriet, who had not been paying much attention, turned round, conscience-stricken.

"Good lord!" she said, "that's mine. At least, it's Peter's. I couldn't think where I'd left it."

It was, in fact, the very scarf that had been used for a strangling demonstration on the Friday, and been brought back to Shrewsbury by accident together with the chessmen and the dog collar. Miss Hillyard turned brick-red and snatched it off as though it were choking her.

"I *beg* your pardon, Miss Vane," she said, holding it out.

"It's all right. I don't want it now. But I'm glad to know where it is. I'd have got into trouble if I'd lost it."

"Will you kindly take your property," said Miss Hillyard.

Harriet, who was already wearing a scarf of her own, said:

"Thank you. But are you sure you won't—"

"I will *not*," said Miss Hillyard, dropping the scarf angrily on the steps.

"Dear me!" said the Dean, picking it up. "Nobody seems to want this nice scarf. I shall borrow it. I call it a nasty, chilly evening, and I don't know why we can't all go inside."

She twisted the scarf comfortably round her neck and, the Warden mercifully arriving at that moment, they went in to dinner.

At a quarter to ten, Harriet, after an hour or so spent with Miss Lydgate on her proofs—now actually nearing the stage when they might really be sent to the printer—crossed the Old Quad to Tudor Building. On the steps, just coming out, she met Miss Hillyard.

"Were you looking for me?" asked Harriet, a little aggressively.

"No," said Miss Hillyard, "I wasn't. Certainly not." She spoke hurriedly, and Harriet fancied that there was something in her eyes both furtive and malicious; but the evening was dark for the middle of May, and she could not be sure.

"Oh!" said Harriet. "I thought you might be."

"Well, I wasn't," said Miss Hillyard again. And as Harriet passed her she turned back and said, almost as though the words were forced out of her:

"Going to work—under the inspiration of your beautiful chessmen?"

"More or less," said Harriet, laughing.

"I hope you will have a pleasant evening," said Miss Hillyard.

Harriet went on upstairs and opened the door of her room.

The glass case had been shattered, and the floor was strewn with broken glass and with smashed and trampled fragments of red and white ivory.

For about five minutes, Harriet was the prey of that kind of speechless rage which is beyond expression or control. If she had thought of it, she was at that moment in a mood to sympathize with the Poltergeist and all her works. If she could have beaten or strangled anybody, she would have done it and felt the better for it. Happily, after the first devastating fury, she found the relief of bad language. When she found she could keep her voice steady, she locked her bedroom door behind her and went down to the telephone.

Even so, she was at first so incoherent that Peter could hardly understand what she said. When he did understand, he was maddeningly cool about it, merely asking whether she had touched anything or told anybody. When assured that she had not, he replied cheerfully that he would be along in a few minutes.

Harriet went out and raged distractedly about the New Quad till she heard him ring—for the gates were just shut—and only a last lingering vestige of self-restraint prevented her from rushing at him and pouring out her indignation in the presence of Padgett. But she waited for him in the middle of the quad.

"Peter—oh, Peter!"

"Well," said he, "this is rather encouraging. I was afraid we might have choked off these demonstrations for good and all."

"But my chessmen! I could kill her for that."

"My dear, it's sickening that it should be your chessmen. But don't let's lose all sense of proportion. It might have been you."

"I wish it had been. I could have hit back."

"Termagant. Let's go and look at the damage."

"It's horrible, Peter. It's like a massacre. It's—it's rather frightening, somehow—they've been hit so hard."

When he saw the room, Wimsey looked grave enough.

"Yes," he said, kneeling amid the wreckage. "Blind, bestial malignity. Not only broken but ground to powder. There's been a heel at work here, as well as the poker; you can see the marks on the carpet. She hates you, Harriet. I didn't realize that. I thought she was only afraid of you. . . . Is there yet any that is left of the house of Saul? . . . Look! one poor warrior hiding behind the coal-scuttle—remnant of a mighty army."

He held up the solitary red pawn, smiling; and then scrambled hurriedly to his feet.

"My dear girl, don't cry about it. What the hell does it matter?"

"I loved them," said Harriet, "and you gave them to me."

He shook his head.

"It's a pity it's that way round. 'You gave them to me, and I loved them' is all right, but 'I loved them and you gave them to me' is irreparable. Fifty thousand rocs' eggs won't supply their place. 'The Virgin's gone and I am gone; she's gone, she's gone and what shall I do?' But you needn't weep over the chest of drawers while I have a shoulder at your disposal, need you?"

"I'm sorry. I'm being a perfect idiot."

"I told you love was the devil and all. Two-and-thirty chessmen, baked in a pie. 'And all the powerful kings and all the beautiful queens of this world were but as a bed of flowers' . . ."

"I might have had the decency to take care of them."

"That's foolish," said he, with his mouth muffled in her hair. "Don't talk so soft, or I shall get foolish too. Listen. When did all this happen?"

"Between Hall and a quarter to ten."

"Was anybody absent from Hall? Because this must have made a bit of a noise. After Hall, there'd be students about, who might hear the glass smash or notice if anybody unusual was wandering about."

"There might be students here all through Hall—they often have eggs in their rooms. And—good God!—there was somebody unusual—She said something about the chessmen, too. And she was queer about them last night."

"Who was that?"

"Miss Hillyard."

"Again!"

While Harriet told her story he fidgeted restlessly about the room, avoiding the broken glass and ivory on the floor with the automatic precision of a cat, and stood at length in the window with his back to her. She had drawn the curtains together when she had brought him up, and his gaze at them seemed purely preoccupied.

"Hell!" he said, presently. "That's a devil of a complication." He still had the red pawn in his hand, and he now came back, and set it with great precision in the center of the mantelpiece. "Yes. Well, I suppose you'll have to find out—"

Somebody knocked at the door, and Harriet went to open it.

"Excuse me, madam, but Padgett sent over to the Senior Common Room to see if Lord Peter Wimsey was there, and seeing he thought you might know—"

"He's here, Annie. It's for you, Peter."

"Yes?" said Peter, coming to the door.

"If you please, sir, they've rung up from the Mitre to say there's a message come from the Foreign Office and would you kindly ring up at once."

"What? Oh, Lord, that *would* happen! Very well, thank you, Annie. Oh, one moment. Was it you who saw the—er—the person who was playing tricks in the Lecture-Room?"

"Yes, sir. Not to know her again, sir."

"No; but you did see her, and she may not know you couldn't recognize her. I think if I were you I'd be rather careful how you go about the College after dark. I don't want to frighten you, but you see what's happened to Miss Vane's chessmen?"

"Yes, I see, sir. What a pity, isn't it?"

"It would be more than a pity if anything unpleasant happened to you personally. Now, don't get the wind up—but if I were you, I'd take somebody with me when I went out after sunset. And I should give the same advice to the scout who was with you."

"To Carrie? Very well, I'll tell her."

"It's only a precaution, you know. Good-night, Annie."

"Good-night, sir. Thank you."

"I shall have to make quite an issue of dog-collars," said Peter. "You never know whether to warn people or not. Some of them get hysterics, but she looks fairly level-headed. Look here, my dear, this is all very tiresome. If it's another summons to Rome, I shall have to go. (I should lock that door.) Needs must when duty calls, and all that. If it *is* Rome, I'll tell Bunter to bring round all the notes I've got at the Mitre and instruct Miss Climpson's sleuths to report direct to you. In any case, I'll ring you up this evening as soon as I know what it's all about. If it isn't Rome, I'll come round again in the morning. And in the meantime, don't let anybody into your room. I think I'd lock it up and sleep elsewhere tonight."

"I thought you didn't expect any more night disturbances."

"I don't; but I don't want people walking over that floor." He stopped on the staircase to examine the soles of his shoes. "I haven't carried away any bits. Do you think you have?"

Harriet stood first on one leg and then another.

"Not this time. And the first time I didn't walk into the mess at all. I stood in the doorway and swore."

"Good girl. The paths in the quad are a bit damp, you know, and something might have stuck. As a matter of fact, it's raining a little now. You'll get wet."

"It doesn't matter. Oh, Peter! I've got that white scarf of yours."

"Keep it till I come again—which will be tomorrow, with luck, and otherwise, God knows when. Damn it! I knew there was trouble coming." He stood still under the beech-trees. "Harriet, don't choose the moment my back's turned to get yourself wiped out or anything—not if you can help it; I mean, you're not very good at looking after valuables."

"I might have the decency to take care? All right, Peter. I'll do my best this time. Word of honor."

She gave him her hand and he kissed it. Once again Harriet thought she saw somebody move in the darkness, as on the last occasion they had walked through the shadowy quads. But she dared not delay him and so again said nothing. Padgett let him out through the gate and Harriet, turning away, found herself face to face with Miss Hillyard.

"Miss Vane, I should like to speak to you."

"Certainly," said Harriet. "I should rather like to speak to *you*."

Miss Hillyard, without another word, led the way to her own rooms. Harriet followed her up the stairs and into the sitting-room. The tutor's face was very white as she shut the door after them and said, without asking Harriet to sit down:

"Miss Vane. What are the relations between that man and you?"

"What do you mean by that?"

"You know perfectly well what I mean. If nobody else will speak to you about your behavior, I must. You bring the man here, knowing perfectly well what his reputation is—"

"I know what his reputation as a detective is."

"I mean his moral reputation. You know as well as I do that he is notorious all over Europe. He keeps women by the score—"

"All at once or in succession?"

"It's no use being impertinent. I suppose that to a person with your past history, that kind of thing is merely amusing. But you must try to conduct yourself with a little more decency. The way you look at him is a disgrace. You pretend to be the merest acquaintance of his and call him by his title in public and his Christian name in private. You take him up to your room at night—"

"Really, Miss Hillyard, I can't allow—"

"I've seen you. Twice. He was there tonight. You let him kiss your hands and make love to you—"

"So that was you, spying about under the beeches."

"How dare you use such a word?"

"How dare you say such a thing?"

"It's no affair of mine how you behave in Bloomsbury. But if you bring your lovers here—"

"You know very well that he is not my lover. And you know very well why he came to my room tonight."

"I can guess."

"And *I* know very well why *you* came there."

"I came there? I don't know what you mean."

"You do. And you know that he came to see the damage you did in my room."

"I never went into your room."

"You didn't go into my room and smash up my chessmen?"

Miss Hillyard's dark eyes flickered.

"Certainly I did not. I told you I hadn't been anywhere near your room tonight."

"Then," said Harriet, "you told a lie."

She was too angry to be frightened, though it did cross her mind that if the furious white-faced woman attacked her, it might be difficult to summon assistance on this isolated staircase, and she thought of the dog-collar.

"I know it's a lie," said Harriet, "because there's a piece of broken ivory on the carpet under your writing-table and another stuck on the sole of your right shoe. I saw it, coming upstairs."

She was prepared for anything after that, but to her surprise, Miss Hillyard staggered a little, sat down suddenly, and said, "Oh, my God!"

"If you had nothing to do with smashing those chessmen," went on Harriet, "or with the other pranks that have been played in this College, you'd better explain those pieces of ivory."

(Am I a fool, she thought, showing my hand like this? But if I didn't, what would become of the evidence?)

Miss Hillyard, in a bewildered way, pulled off her slipper and looked at the sliver of white that clung to the heel, embedded in a little patch of damp gravel.

"Give it to me," said Harriet, and took slipper and all.

She had expected an outburst of denial, but Miss Hillyard said, faintly:

"That's evidence . . . . incontrovertible. . . ."

Harriet thanked Heaven, with grim amusement, for the scholarly habit; at least, one did not have to argue about what was or was not evidence.

"I did go into your room. I went there to say to you what I said just now. But you weren't there. And when I saw the mess on the mess on the floor I thought—I was afraid you'd think—"

"I did think."

"What did he think?"

"Lord Peter? I don't know what he thought. But he'll probably think something now."

"You've no evidence that I did it," said Miss Hillyard, with sudden spirit. "Only that I was in the room. It was done when I got there. I saw it, I went to look at it. You can tell your lover that I saw it and was glad to see it. But he'll tell you that's no proof that I did it."

"Look here, Miss Hillyard," said Harriet, divided between anger, suspicion and a dreadful kind of pity, "you must understand, once and for all, that he is not my lover. Do you really imagine that if he were, we should—" here her sense of the ludicrous overcame her and made it difficult to control her voice—"we should come and misbehave ourselves in the greatest possible discomfort at Shrewsbury? Even if I had no respect for the College—where would be the point of it? With all the world and all the time there is at our disposal, why on earth should we come and play the fool down here? It would be silly. And if you really were down there in the quad just now, you must know that people who are lovers don't treat each other like that. At least," she added rather unkindly, "if you knew anything about it at all, you'd know that. We're very old friends, and I owe him a great deal—"

"Don't talk nonsense," said the tutor roughly. "You know you're in love with the man."

"By God!" said Harriet, suddenly enlightened, "if I'm not, I know who is."

"You've no right to say that!"

"It's true, all the same," said Harriet. "Oh, damn! I suppose it's no good my saying I'm frightfully sorry." (Dynamite in a powder factory? Yes, indeed, Miss Edwards, you saw it before anybody else. Biologically interesting!) "This kind of thing is the devil and all." ("That's the devil of a complication," Peter had said. He'd seen it, of course. Must have. Too much experience not to. Probably happened scores of times—scores of women—all over Europe. Oh, dear! Oh, dear! And was that a random accusation, or had Miss Hillyard been delving into the past and digging up Viennese singers?)

"For Heaven's sake," said Miss Hillyard, "go away!"

"I think I'd better," said Harriet.

She did not know how to deal with the situation at all. She could no longer feel outraged or angry. She was not alarmed. She was not jealous. She was only sorry, and quite incapable of expressing any sympathy which would not be an insult. She realized that she was still clutching Miss Hillyard's slipper. Had she better give it back? It was evidence—of something. But of what? The whole business of the Poltergeist seemed to have retreated over the horizon, leaving behind it the tormented shell of a woman staring blindly into vacancy under the cruel harshness of the electric light. Harriet picked up the other fragment of ivory from under the writing-table—the little spearhead from a red pawn.

Well, whatever one's personal feelings, evidence was evidence. Peter—she remembered that Peter had said he would ring up from the Mitre. She went downstairs with the slipper in her hand, and in the New Quad ran into Mrs. Padgett, who was just coming to look for her.

The call was switched through to the box in Queen Elizabeth.

"It's not so bad after all," said Peter's voice. "It's only the Grand Panjandrum wanting a conference at his private house. Sort of Pleasant Sunday Afternoon in Wild Warwickshire. It may mean London or Rome after that, but we'll hope not. At any rate, it'll do if I'm there by half-past eleven, so I'll pop round and see you about nine."

"Please do. Something's happened. Not alarming, but upsetting. I can't tell you on the 'phone."

He again promised to come, and said good-night. Harriet, after locking the slipper and the piece of ivory carefully away, went to the Bursar, and was accommodated with a bed in the Infirmary.

CHAPTER XXI

Thus she there wayted untill eventyde,
Yet living creature none she saw appeare.
And now sad shadows gan the world to hyde
From mortall vew, and wrap in darkenes dreare;
Yet nould she d'off her weary armes, for feare
Of secret daunger, ne let sleepe oppresse
Her heavy eyes with nature's burdein deare,
But drew her self aside in sickernesse,
And her well-pointed wepons did about her dresse.

EDMUND SPENSER

Harriet left word at the Lodge that she would wait for Lord Peter Wimsey in the Fellows' Garden. She had breakfasted early, thus avoiding Miss Hillyard, who passed through the New Quad like an angry shadow while she was talking to Padgett.

She had first met Peter at a moment when every physical feeling had been battered out of her by the brutality of circumstance; by this accident she had been aware of him from the beginning as a mind and spirit localized in a body. Never—not even in those later dizzying moments on the river—had she considered him primarily as a male animal, or calculated the promise implicit in the veiled eyes, the long, flexible mouth, the curiously vital hands. Nor, since of her he had always asked and never demanded, had she felt in him any domination but that of intellect. But now, as he advanced towards her along the flower-bordered path, she saw him with new eyes—the eyes of women who had seen him before they knew him—saw him, as they saw him, dynamically. Miss Hillyard, Miss Edwards, Miss de Vine, the Dean even, each in her own way had recognized the same thing: six centuries of possessiveness, fastened under the yoke of urbanity. She herself, seeing it impudent and uncontrolled in the nephew, had known it instantly for what it was; it astonished her that in the older man she should have been blind to it so long and should still retain so strong a defense against it. And she wondered whether it was only accident that had sealed her eyes till it was too late for realization to bring disaster.

She sat still where she was till he stood looking down at her.

"Well?" he said, lightly, "how doth my lady? What, sweeting, all amort? . . . Yes, something has happened; I see it has. What is it, domina?"

Though the tone was half-jesting, nothing could have reassured her like that grave, academic title. She said, as though she were reciting a lesson:

"When you left last night, Miss Hillyard met me in the New Quad. She asked me to come up to her room because she wanted to speak to me. On the way up, I saw there was a little piece of white ivory stuck on the heel of her slipper. She—made some rather unpleasant accusations; she had misunderstood the position—"

"That can and shall be put right. Did you say anything about the slipper?"

"I'm afraid I did. There was another bit of ivory on the floor. I accused her of having gone into my room, and she denied it till I showed her the evidence. Then she admitted it; but she said the damage was already done when she got there."

"Did you believe her?"

"I might have done . . . if . . . if she hadn't shown me a motive."

"I see. All right. You needn't tell me."

She looked up for the first time into a face as bleak as winter, and faltered:

"I brought the slipper away with me. I wish I hadn't."

"Are you going to be afraid of the facts?" he said. "And you a scholar?"

"I don't think I did it in malice. I hope not. But I was bitterly unkind to her."

"Happily," said he, "a fact is a fact, and your state of mind won't alter it by a hair's breadth. Let's go now and have the truth at all hazards."

She led him up to her room, where the morning sun cast a long rectangle of brilliance across the ruin on the floor. From the chest near the door she took out the slipper and handed it to him. He lay down flat, squinting sideways along the carpet in the place where neither he nor she had trodden the night before. His hand went to his pocket, and he smiled up sideways into her troubled face.

"If all the pens that ever poets held had had the feeling of their masters' thoughts, they could not write as much solid fact as you can hold in a pair of callipers." He measured the heel of the slipper in both directions, and then turned his attention to the pile of the carpet. "She stood here, heels together, looking." The callipers twinkled over the sunlit rectangle. "And here is the heel that stamped and trampled and ground beauty to dust. One was a French heel and one was a Cuban heel—isn't that what the footwear specialists call them?" He sat up and tapped the sole of the slipper lightly with the callipers. "Who goes there? France—Pass, France, and all's well."

"Oh, I'm glad," said Harriet, fervently. "I'm glad."

"Yes. Meanness isn't one of your accomplishments, is it?" He turned his eyes to the carpet again, this time to a place near the edge.

"Look! now that the sun's out you can see it. Here's where Cuban Heel wiped her soles before she left. There are very few flies on Cuban Heel. Well, that saves us a back-breaking search all over the College for the dust of kings and queens." He picked the sliver of ivory from the French heel, put the slipper in his pocket and stood up. "This had better go back to its owner, furnished with a certificate of innocence."

"Give it to me. I must take it."

"No, you will not. If anybody has to face unpleasantness, it shan't be you this time."

"But, Peter—you won't—"

"No," he said, "I won't. Trust me for that."

Harriet was left staring at the broken chessman. Presently she went out into the corridor, found a dustpan and brush in a scout's pantry and returned with them to sweep up the debris. As she was replacing the brush and pan in the pantry, she ran into one of the students from the annex.

"By the way, Miss Swift," said Harriet, "you didn't happen to hear any noise in my room like glass being smashed last night, did you? Some time during or after Hall?"

"No, I didn't, Miss Vane. I was in my own room all evening. But wait a moment. Miss Ward came along about half-past nine to do some Morphology with me and"—the girl's mouth dimpled into laughter—"she asked if you were a secret toffee-eater, because it sounded as though you were smashing up toffee with the poker. Has the College Ghost been visiting you?"

"I'm afraid so," said Harriet. "Thank you; that's very helpful. I must see Miss Ward."

Miss Ward, however, could help no farther than by fixing the time a little more definitely as "certainly not later than half-past nine."

Harriet thanked her, and went out. Her very bones seemed to ache with restlessness—or perhaps it was with having slept badly in an unfamiliar bed and with a disturbed mind. The sun had scattered diamonds among the wet grass of the quadrangle, and the breeze was shaking the rain in a heavy spatter of drops from the beeches. Students came and went. Somebody had left a scarlet cushion out all night in the rain; it was sodden and mournful-looking; its owner came and picked it up, with an air between laughter and disgust; she threw it on a bench to dry in the sunshine.

To do nothing was intolerable. To be spoken to by any member of the Senior Common Room would be still more intolerable. She was penned in the Old Quad, for she was sensitive to the mere neighborhood of the New Quad as a person that has been vaccinated is sensitive to everything that lies on the sore side of his body. Without particular aim or intention, she skirted the tennis-court and turned in at the Library entrance. She had intended to go upstairs but, seeing the door of Miss de Vine's set stand open, she altered her mind; she could borrow a book from there. The little lobby was empty, but in the sitting-room a scout was giving the writing-table a Sunday morning flick with the duster. Harriet remembered that Miss de Vine was in town, and that she was to be warned when she returned.

"What time does Miss de Vine get back tonight? Do you know, Nellie?"

"I think she gets in by the 9:39, miss."

Harriet nodded, took a book from the shelves at random, and went to sit on the steps of the loggia, where there was a deck chair. The morning, she told herself, was getting on. If Peter had to get to his destination by 11:30, it was time he went. She vividly remembered waiting in a nursing-home while a friend underwent an operation; there had been a smell of ether, and, in the waiting-room, a large black Wedgwood jar, filled with delphiniums.

She read a page without knowing what was in it, and looked up at an approaching footstep into the face of Miss Hillyard.

"Lord Peter," said Miss Hillyard, without preface, "asked me to give you this address. He was obliged to leave quickly to keep his appointment."

Harriet took the paper and said, "Thank you."

Miss Hillyard went on resolutely: "When I spoke to you last night I was under a misapprehension. I had not fully realized the difficulty of your position. I am afraid I have unwittingly made it harder for you, and I apologize."

"That's all right," said Harriet, taking refuge in formula. "I am sorry too. I was rather upset last night and said a great deal more than I should. This wretched business has made everything so uncomfortable."

"Indeed it has," said Miss Hillyard, in a more natural voice. "We are all feeling rather overwrought. I wish we could get at the truth of it. I understand that you now accept my account of my movements last night."

"Absolutely. It was inexcusable of me not to have verified my data."

"Appearances can be very misleading," said Miss Hillyard.

There was a pause.

"Well," said Harriet at last, "I hope we may forget all this." She knew as she spoke that one thing at least had been said which could never be forgotten: she would have given a great deal to recall it.

"I shall do my best," replied Miss Hillyard. "Perhaps I am too much inclined to judge harshly of matters outside my experience."

"It is very kind of you to say that," said Harriet. "Please believe that I don't take a very self-satisfied view of myself either."

"Very likely not. I have noticed that the people who get opportunities always seem to choose the wrong ones. But it's no affair of mine. Good morning."

She went as abruptly as she had come. Harriet glanced at the book on her knee and discovered that she was reading *The Anatomy of Melancholy*.

"*Fleat Heraclitus an rideat Democritus?* in attempting to speak of these Symptoms, shall I laugh with *Democritus* or weep with *Heraclitus?* they are so ridiculous and absurd on the one side, so lamentable and tragical on the other."

Harriet got the car out in the afternoon and took Miss Lydgate and the Dean for a picnic in the neighborhood of Hinksey. When she got back, in time for supper, she found an urgent message at the Lodge, asking her to ring up Lord Saint-George at the House as soon as she got back. His voice, when he answered the call, sounded agitated.

"Oh, look here! I can't get hold of Uncle Peter—he's

vanished again, curse him! I say, I saw your ghost this afternoon, and I do think you ought to be careful."

"Where did you see her? When?"

"About half-past two—walking over Magdalen Bridge in broad daylight. I'd been lunching with some chaps out Iffley way, and we were just pulling over to put one of 'em down at Magdalen, when I spotted her. She was walking along, muttering to herself, and looking awfully queer. Sort of clutching with her hands and rolling her eyes about. She spotted me, too. Couldn't mistake her. A friend of mine was driving and I tried to catch his attention, but he was pulling round behind a bus and I couldn't make him understand. Anyhow, when we stopped at Magdalen gate, I hopped out and ran back, but I couldn't find her anywhere. Seemed to have faded out. I bet she knew I was on to her and made tracks. I was scared. Thought she looked up to anything. So I rang up your place and found you were out and then I rang up the Mitre and that wasn't any good either, so I've been sitting here all evening in a devil of a stew. First I thought I'd leave a note, and then I thought I'd better tell you myself. Rather devoted of me, don't you think? I cut a supper-party so as not to miss you."

"That was frightfully kind of you," said Harriet. "What was the ghost dressed in?"

"Oh—one of those sort of dark-blue frocks with spriggy bits on it and a hat with a brim. Sort of thing most of your dons wear in the afternoon. Neat, not gaudy. Not smart. Just ordinary. It was the eyes I recognized. Made me feel all gooseflesh. Honest. That woman's not safe, I'll swear she isn't."

"It's very good of you to warn me," said Harriet again. "I'll try and find out who it could have been. And I'll take precautions."

"Please do," said Lord Saint-George. "I mean, Uncle Peter's getting the wind up horribly. Gone clean off his oats. Of course I know he's a fidgety old ass and I've been doing my best to soothe the troubled beast and all that, but I'm beginning to think he's got some excuse. For goodness' sake, Aunt Harriet, do something about it. I can't afford to have a valuable uncle destroyed under my eyes. He's getting like the Lord of Burleigh, you know—walking up and pacing down and so on—and the responsibility is very wearing."

"I'll tell you what," said Harriet. "You'd better come and dine in College tomorrow and see if you can spot the lady. It's no good this evening, because so many people don't turn up to Sunday supper."

"Right-ho!" said the viscount. "That's a dashed good idea. I'd get a dashed good birthday-present out of Uncle Peter if I solved his problem for him. So long and take care of yourself."

"I ought to have thought of that before," said Harriet, retailing this piece of news to the Dean; "but I never imagined he'd recognize the woman like that after only seeing her once."

The Dean, to whom the whole story of Lord Saint-George's ghostly encounter had come as a novelty, was inclined to be skeptical. "Personally, I wouldn't undertake to identify anybody after one glimpse in the dark—and I certainly wouldn't trust a young harum-scarum like that. The only person here I know of with a navy sprigged foulard is Miss Lydgate, and I absolutely refuse to believe *that!* But ask the young man to dinner by all means. I'm all for excitement, and he's even more ornamental than the other one."

It was borne in upon Harriet that things were coming to a crisis. "Take precautions." A nice fool she would look, going about with a dog-collar round her neck. Nor would it be any defense against pokers and such things. . . . The wind must be in the south-west, for the heavy boom of Tom tolling his hundred-and-one came clearly to her ears as she crossed the Old Quad.

"Not later than half-past nine," Miss Ward had said. If the peril had ceased to walk by night, it was still abroad of an evening.

She went upstairs and locked the door of her room before opening a drawer and taking out the heavy strap of brass and leather. There was something about the description of that woman walking wild-eyed over Magdalen Bridge and "clutching with her hands" that was very unpleasant to think of. She could feel Peter's grip on her throat now like a band of iron, and could hear him saying serenely, like a textbook:

"*That* is the dangerous spot. Compression of the big blood vessels *there* will cause almost instant unconsciousness. And then, you see, you're done for."

And at the momentary pressure of his thumbs the fire had swum in her eyes.

She turned with a start as something rattled the door handle. Probably the passage-window was open and the wind blowing in. She was getting ridiculously nervous.

The buckle was stiff to her fingers. (Is thy servant a dog that she should do this thing?) When she saw herself in the glass, she laughed. "An arum-lily quality that is in itself an invitation to violence." Her own face, in the drowned evening light, surprised her—softened and startled and drained of color, with eyes that looked unnaturally large under the heavy black brows, and lips a little parted. It was like the head of someone who had been guillotined; the dark band cut it off from the body like the stroke of the headsman's steel.

She wondered whether her lover had seen it like that, through that hot unhappy year when she had tried to believe that there was happiness in surrender. Poor Philip—tormented by his own vanities, never loving her till he had killed her feeling for him, and yet perilously clutching her as he went down into the slough of death. It was not to Philip she had submitted, so much as to a theory of living. The young were always theoretical; only the middle-aged could realize the deadliness of principles. To subdue one's self to one's own ends might be dangerous, but to subdue one's self to other people's ends was dust and ashes. Yet there were those, still more unhappy, who envied even the ashy saltness of those dead sea apples.

Could there ever be any alliance between the intellect and the flesh? It was this business of asking questions and analyzing everything that sterilized and stultified all one's passions. Experience perhaps had a formula to get over this difficulty: one kept the bitter, tormenting brain on one side of the wall and the languorous sweet body on the other, and never let them meet. So that if you were made that way, you could argue about loyalties in an Oxford common-room and refresh yourself elsewhere with—say—Viennese singers, presenting an unruffled surface on both sides of yourself. Easy for a man, and possible even for a woman, if one avoided foolish accidents like being tried for murder. But to seek to force incompatibles into a compromise was madness; one should neither do it nor be a party to it. If Peter wanted to make the experiment, he must do it without Harriet's connivance. Six centuries of possessive blood would not be dictated to by a bare forty-five years of over-sensitized intellect. Let the male animal take the female and be content; the busy brain could very well be "left talking" like the hero of *Man and Superman*. In a long monologue, of course; for the female animal could only listen without contributing. Otherwise one would get the sort of couple one had in *Private Lives*, who rolled on the floor and hammered one another when they weren't making love, because they (obviously) had no conversational resources. A vista of crashing boredom, either way.

The door rattled again, as a reminder that even a little boredom might be welcome by way of change from alarms. On the mantelpiece, a solitary red pawn mocked all security. . . . How quietly Annie had taken Peter's warning. Did she take it seriously? Was she looking after herself? She had been her usual refined and self-contained self when she brought in the Common-room coffee that night—perhaps a little brighter looking than usual. Of course, she had had her afternoon off with Beatie and Carola. . . . Curious, thought Harriet, this desire to possess children and dictate their tastes, as though they were escaping fragments of one's self, and not separate individuals. Even if the taste ran to motor-bikes. . . . Annie was all right. How about Miss de Vine, traveling down from Town in happy ignorance?—With a start, Harriet saw that it was nearly a quarter to ten. The train must be in. Had the Warden remembered about warning Miss de Vine? She ought not to be left to sleep in the ground-floor room without being fore-armed. But the Warden never forgot anything.

Nevertheless, Harriet was uneasy. From her window she could not see whether any lights were on in the Library Wing. She unlocked the door and stepped out (yes—the passage-window was open; nobody but the wind had rattled the handle). A few dim figures were still moving at the far end of the quad as she passed along beside the tennis-court. In the Library Wing, all the ground-floor windows were dark except for the dim glow of the passage-light. Miss Barton, at any rate, was not in her room; nor was Miss de Vine back yet. Or—yes, she must be; for the window-curtains were drawn in her sitting-room, though no light shone as yet behind them.

Harriet went into the building. The door of Miss Burrows's set stood open, and the lobby was dark. Miss de Vine's door was shut. She knocked, but there was no answer—and it suddenly struck her as odd that the curtains should be drawn and no light on. She opened the door and pressed down the wall-switch in the lobby. Nothing happened. With a growing sense of disquiet, she went on to the sitting-room door and opened that. And then, as her fingers went out to the switch, the fierce clutch took her by the throat.

She had two advantages: she was partly prepared, and the assailant had not expected the dog-collar. She felt and heard the quick gasp in her face as the strong, cruel fingers fumbled on the stiff leather. As they shifted their hold, she had time to remember what she had been taught—to catch and jerk the wrists apart. But as her feet felt for the other's feet, her high heels slipped on the parquet—and she was falling—they were falling together and she was undermost; they seemed to take years to fall; and all the time a stream of hoarse, filthy abuse was running into her ears. Then the world went black in fire and thunder.

Faces—swimming confusedly through crackling waves of pain—swelling and diminishing anxiously—then resolving themselves into one—Miss Hillyard's face, enormous and close to her own. Then a voice, agonizingly loud, blaring unintelligibly like a fog-horn. Then, suddenly and quite clearly, like the lighted stage of a theater, the room, with Miss de Vine, white as marble, on the couch and the Warden bending over her, and in between, on the floor, a white bowl filled with scarlet and the Dean kneeling beside it. Then the fog-horn boomed again, and she heard her own voice, incredibly far-off and thin: "Tell Peter—" Then nothing.

Somebody had a headache—a quite unbearably awful headache. The white bright room in the Infirmary would have been very pleasant, if it hadn't been for the oppressive neighborhood of the person with the headache, who was, moreover, groaning very disagreeably. It was an effort to pull one's self together and find out what the tiresome person wanted. With an effort like that of a hippopotamus climbing out of a swamp, Harriet pulled herself together and discovered that the headache and the groans were her own, and that the Infirmarian had realized what she was about and was coming to lend a hand.

"What in the world—?" said Harriet.

"Ah!" said the Infirmarian, "that's better. No—don't try to sit up. You've had a nasty knock on the head, and the quieter you keep the better."

"Oh, I see," said Harriet. "I've got a beast of a headache." A little thought located the worst part of the headache somewhere behind the right ear. She put up an exploratory hand and encountered a bandage. "What happened?"

"That's what we'd all like to know," said the Infirmarian.

"Well, I can't remember a thing," said Harriet.

"It doesn't matter. Drink this."

Like a book, thought Harriet. They always said, "Drink this." The room wasn't really so bright after all; the Venetian shutters were closed. It was her own eyes that were extraordinarily sensitive to light. Better shut them.

"Drink this" must have had something helpfully potent about it, because when she woke up again, the headache was better and she felt ravenously hungry. Also, she was beginning to remember things—the dog-collar and the lights that wouldn't go on—and the hands that had come clutching out of the darkness. There, memory obstinately stopped short. How the headache had come into existence she had no idea. Then she saw again the picture of Miss de Vine stretched on the couch. She asked after her.

"She's in the next room," said the Infirmarian. "She's had rather a nasty heart-attack, but she's better now. She would try to do too much, and of course, finding you like that was a shock to her."

It was not till the evening, when the Dean came in and found the patient fretting herself into a fever of curiosity, that Harriet got a complete story of the night's adventures.

"Now, if you'll keep quiet," said the Dean, "I'll tell you. If not, not. And your beautiful young man has sent you a young gardenful of flowers and will call again in the morning. Well, now! Poor Miss de Vine got here about 10 o'clock—her train was a bit late—and Mullins met her with a message to go and see the Warden *at* once. However, she thought she'd better take her hat off first, so she went along to her rooms—all in a hurry, so as not to keep Dr. Baring waiting. Well, of course, the first thing was that the lights wouldn't go on; and then to her horror she heard *you*, my dear, snorting on the floor in the dark. So then she tried the table lamp and that worked—and there you were, a nasty bluggy sight for a respectable female don to find in her sitting-room. You've got two beautiful stitches in you, by the way; it was the corner of the bookcase did that. . . . So Miss de Vine rushed out calling for help, but there wasn't a soul in the building, and then, my dear, she ran like fury over to Burleigh and some students tore out to see what was happening and then somebody fetched the Warden and somebody else fetched the Infirmarian and somebody else fetched Miss Stevens and Miss Hillyard and me who were having a quiet cup of tea in my room, and we rang up the doctor, and Miss de Vine's groggy heart went back on her, what with shock and running about, and she went all blue on us—we had a lovely time."

"You must have. One other gaudy night! I suppose you haven't found who did it?"

"For quite a long time we hadn't a moment to think about that part of it. And then, just as we were settling down, all the fuss started again about Annie."

"Annie? What's happened to her?"

"Oh, didn't you know? We found her in the coal-hole, my dear, in such a state, what with coal-dust and hammering her fists on the door; and I wonder she wasn't clean off her head, poor thing, locked up there all that time. And if it hadn't been for Lord Peter we mightn't even have begun to look for her till next morning, what with everything being in such an uproar."

"Yes—he warned her she might be attacked. . . . How did he—? Did you get him on the 'phone, or what?"

"Oh, yes. Well, after we'd got you and Miss de Vine to bed and had made up our minds you wouldn't either of you peg out yet awhile, somebody brightly remembered that the first thing you said when we picked you up was 'Tell Peter.' So we rang up the Mitre and he wasn't there; and then Miss Hillyard said she knew where he was and 'phoned through. That was after midnight. Fortunately, he hadn't gone to bed. He said he'd come over at once, and then he asked what had happened to Annie Wilson. Miss Hillyard thought the shock had affected his wits, I think. However, he insisted that she ought to be kept an eye on, so we all started to look for her. Well, you know what a job it is tracking anybody down in this place, and we hunted and hunted and nobody had seen anything of her. And then, just before two, Lord Peter arrived, looking like death, and said we were to turn the place upsidedown if we didn't want a corpse on our hands. Nice and reassuring *that* was!"

"I wish I hadn't missed it all," said Harriet. "He must have thought I was an awful ass to let myself be knocked out like that."

"He didn't say so," said the Dean, drily. "He came in to see you, but of course you were well under the weather. And of course he explained about the dog-collar, which had puzzled us all dreadfully."

"Yes. She went for my throat. I do remember that. I suppose she really meant to get Miss de Vine."

"Obviously. And with her weak heart—and no dog-collar—she wouldn't have had much chance, or so the doctor said. It was very lucky for her you happened to go in there. Or did you know?"

"I think," said Harriet, her memory still rather confused, "I went to tell her about Peter's warning and—oh, yes! there was something funny about the window-curtains. And the lights were all off."

"The bulbs had been taken out. Well, anyway, somewhere about four o'clock, Padgett found Annie. She was locked up in the coal-cellar under the Hall Building, at the far end of the boiler-house. The key'd been taken away and Padgett had to break in the door. She was pounding and shouting—but of course, if we hadn't been searching for her she might have yelled till Doomsday, especially as the radiators are off, and we're not using the furnace. She was in what they call a state of collapse and couldn't give us a coherent story for ever so long. But there's nothing really the matter with her except shock and bruises where she was flung down on the coal-heap. And of course her hands and arms were pretty well skinned with battering on the door and trying to climb out of the ventilator."

"What did she say happened?"

"Why, she was putting away the deck-chairs in the loggia about half-past nine, when somebody seized her round the neck from behind and frog's-marched her off to the cellar. She said it was a woman, and very strong—"

"She was," said Harriet. "I can bear witness to that. Grip like steel. And a most unfeminine vocabulary."

"Annie says she never saw who it was, but she thought that the arm that was round her face had a dark sleeve on. Annie's own impression was that it was Miss Hillyard; but she was with the Bursar and me. But a good many of our strongest specimens haven't got alibis—particularly Miss Pyke, who says she was in her room, and Miss Barton, who claims to have been in the Fiction Library, looking for a 'nice book to read.' And Mrs. Goodwin, and Miss Burrows aren't very well accounted for, either. According to their own story, they were each seized at the same moment with an unaccountable desire to wander. Miss Burrows went to commune with Nature in the Fellows' Garden and Mrs. Goodwin to commune with a higher Authority in the Chapel. We are looking rather askance at one another today."

"I wish to goodness," said Harriet, "I'd been a trifle more efficient." She pondered a moment. "I wonder why she didn't stay to finish me off."

"Lord Peter wondered that, too. He said he thought she must either have thought you were dead, or been alarmed by the blood and finding she'd got the wrong person. When you went limp, she'd probably feel about and she'd know you were not Miss de Vine—short hair and no spectacles, you see—and she'd hurry off to get rid of any bloodstains before somebody came along. At least, that was his theory. He looked pretty queer about it."

"Is he here now?"

"No; he had to go back. . . . Something about getting an early 'plane from Croydon. He rang up and made a great to-do, but apparently it was all settled and he had to go. If any of his prayers are heard, I shouldn't think anybody in the Government would have a whole place in his body this morning. So I comforted him with hot coffee and he went off, leaving orders that neither you nor Miss de Vine nor

Annie was to be left alone for a single moment. And he's rung up once from London and three times from Paris."

"Poor old Peter!" said Harriet. "He never seems to get a night's rest."

"Meanwhile, the Warden is valiantly issuing an unconvincing statement to the effect that somebody played a foolish practical joke on Annie, that you accidentally slipped and cut your head and that Miss de Vine was upset by the sight of blood. And the College gates are shut to all comers, for fear they should be reporters in disguise. But you can't keep the scouts quiet—goodness knows what reports are going out by the tradesmen's entrance. However, the great thing is that nobody's killed. And now I must be off, or the Infirmarian will have my blood and there really *will* be an inquest."

The next day brought Lord Saint-George. "My turn to visit the sick," he said. "You're a nice, restful aunt for a fellow to adopt, I don't think. Do you realize that you've done me out of a dinner?"

"Yes," said Harriet. "It's a pity—Perhaps I'd better tell the Dean. You might be able to identify—"

"Now don't you start laying plots," said he, "or your temperature will go up. You leave it to Uncle. He says he'll be back tomorrow, by the way, and the evidence is rolling in nicely and you're to keep quiet and not worry. Honor bright. Had him on the 'phone this morning. He's all of a doodah. Says anybody could have done his business in Paris, only they've got it into their heads he's the only person who can get on the right side of some tedious old mule or other who has to be placated or conciliated or something. As far as I can make out, some obscure journalist has been assassinated and somebody's trying to make an international incident of it. Hence the pyramids. I told you Uncle Peter had a strong sense of public duty; now you see it in action."

"Well, he's quite right."

"What an unnatural woman you are! He ought to be

here, weeping into the sheets and letting the international situation blow itself to blazes." Lord Saint-George chuckled. "I wish I'd been on the road with him on Monday morning. He collected five summonses in the round trip between Warwickshire and Oxford and London. My mother will be delighted. How's your head?"

"Doing fine. It was more the cut than the bump, I think."

"Scalp-wounds do bleed, don't they? Completely pig-like. Still, it's as well you're not a 'corpse in the case with a sad, swelled face.' You'll be all right when they get the stitches out. Only a bit convict-like that side of the head. You'll have to be cropped all round to even matters up and Uncle Peter can wear your discarded tresses next his heart."

"Come, come," said Harriet. "He doesn't date back to the seventies."

"He's aging rapidly. I should think he'd nearly got to the sixties by now. With beautiful, golden side whiskers. I really think you ought to rescue him before his bones start to creak and the spiders spin webs over his eyes."

"You and your uncle," said Harriet, "should be set to turn phrases for a living."

CHAPTER XXII

O no, there is no end: the end is death and madness! As I am never better than when I am mad: then methinks I am a brave fellow; then I do wonders: but reason abuseth me, and there's the torment, there's the hell. At the last, sir, bring me to one of the murderers: were he as strong as Hector, thus would I tear and drag him up and down.

BEN JONSON

Thursday. A heavy, gloomy and depressing Thursday, pouring down uninteresting rain from a sky like a grey boxlid. The Warden had called a meeting of the Senior Common Room for half-past two—an unconsoling hour. All three invalids were up and about again. Harriet had exchanged her bandages for some very unbecoming and unromantic strappings, and had not exactly a headache, but the sensation that a headache might begin at any moment. Miss de Vine looked like a ghost. Annie, though she had suffered less than the others physically, seemed to be still haunted by nervous terrors, and crept unhappily about her duties with the other Common Room maid always closely in attendance.

It was understood that Lord Peter Wimsey would attend the S.C.R. meeting in order to lay certain information before the staff. Harriet had received from him a brief and characteristic note, which said:

"Congratulations on not being dead yet. I have taken your collar away to have my name put on."

She had already missed the collar. And she had had,

from Miss Hillyard, a strangely vivid little picture of Peter, standing at her bedside between night and dawn, quite silent, and twisting the thick strap over and over in his hands.

All morning she had expected to see him; but he arrived only at the last moment, so that their meeting took place in the Common Room, under the eyes of all the dons. He had driven straight from Town without changing his suit, and above the dark cloth his head had the bleached look of a faint water-color. He paid his respects politely to the Warden and the Senior dons before coming over and taking her hand.

"Well, and how are you?"

"Not too bad, considering."

"That's good."

He smiled and went to sit by the Warden. Harriet, at the opposite side of the table, slipped into a place beside the Dean. Everything that was alive in him lay in the palm of her hand, like a ripe apple. Dr. Baring was asking him to begin, and he was doing so, in the flat voice of a secretary reading the minutes of a company meeting. He had a sheaf of papers before him, including (Harriet noticed) her dossier, which he must have taken away on the Monday morning. But he went on without referring to so much as a note, addressing himself to a bowl filled with marigolds that stood on the table before him.

"I need not take up your time by going over all the details of this rather confusing case. I will first set out the salient points as they presented themselves to me when I came to Oxford last Sunday week, so as to show you the basis upon which I founded my working theory. I will then formulate that theory, and adduce the supporting evidence which I hope and think you will consider conclusive. I may say that practically all the data necessary to the formation of the theory are contained in the very valuable digest of the events prepared for me by Miss Vane and handed to me on my arrival. The rest of the proof was merely what the police call routine work."

(This, thought Harriet, is suiting your style to your company with a vengeance. She looked round. The Common Room had the hushed air of a congregation settling down to a sermon, but she could feel the nervous tension everywhere. They did not know what they might be going to hear.)

"The first point to strike an outsider," went on Peter, "is the fact that these demonstrations began at the Gaudy. I may say that that was the first bad mistake the perpetrator made. By the way, it will save time and trouble if I refer to the perpetrator in the time-honored way as X. If X had waited till term began, we should have had a much wider field for suspicion. I therefore asked myself what it was that so greatly excited X at the Gaudy that she could not wait for a more suitable time to begin.

"It seemed unlikely that any of the Old Students present could have roused X's animosity, because the demonstrations continued in the following term. But they did not continue during the Long Vacation. So my attention was immediately directed to any person who entered the College for the first time at Gaudy and was in residence the following term. Only one person answered these requirements, and that was Miss de Vine."

The first stir went round the table, like the wind running over a cornfield.

"The first two communications came into the hands of Miss Vane. One of them, which amounted to an accusation of murder, was slipped into the sleeve of her gown and might, by a misleading coincidence, have been held to apply to her. But Miss Martin may remember that she placed Miss Vane's gown in the Senior Common Room side by side with that of Miss de Vine. I believe that X, misreading 'H. D. Vane' as 'H. de Vine' put the note in the wrong gown. This belief is, of course, not susceptible of proof; but the possibility is suggestive. The error, if it was one, distracted attention at the start from the central object of the campaign."

Nothing altered in the level voice as he lifted the old

infamy into view only to cast it in the next breath into oblivion, but the hand that had held hers tightened for a moment and relaxed. She found herself watching the hand as it moved now among the sheaf of papers.

"The second communication, picked up accidentally by Miss Vane in the quad, was destroyed like the other; but from the description I gather that it was a drawing similar to this." He slipped out a paper from under the clip and passed it to the Warden. "It represents a punishment inflicted by a naked, female figure upon another, which is clothed in academical dress and epicene. This appears to be the symbolical key to the situation. In the Michaelmas Term, other drawings of a similar kind appear, together with the motif of the hanging of some academical character—a motif which is repeated in the incident of the dummy found later on suspended in the Chapel. There were also communications of a vaguely obscene and threatening sort which need not be particularly considered. The most interesting and important one, perhaps, is the message addressed to (I think) Miss Hillyard. 'No man is safe from women like you'; and the other, sent to Miss Flaxman, demanding that she should leave another student's fiancé alone. These suggested that the basis of X's grievance was sexual jealousy of the ordinary kind—a suggestion which, again, I believe to be entirely erroneous and to have obscured the issue in a quite fantastic manner.

"We next come (passing over the episode of the bonfire of gowns in the quad) to the more serious matter of Miss Lydgate's manuscript. I do not think it is a coincidence that the portions most heavily disfigured and obliterated were those in which Miss Lydgate attacked the conclusions of other scholars, and those scholars, men. If I am right, we see that X is a person capable of reading, and to some extent understanding, a work of scholarship. Together with this outrage we may take the mutilation of the novel called *The Search* at the exact point where the author upholds, or appears for the moment to uphold, the doctrine that loyalty to the abstract truth must over-ride all personal considerations; and also the burning of Miss Barton's book in which she attacks the Nazi doctrine that woman's place in the State should be confined to the 'womanly' occupations of *Kinder, Kirche, Küche*.

"In addition to these personal attacks upon individuals, we get the affair of the bonfire and the sporadic outbursts of obscenity upon the walls. When we come to the disfigurement of the Library, we get the generalized attack in a more spectacular form. The object of the campaign begins to show itself more clearly. The grievance felt by X, starting from a single person, has extended itself to the entire College, and the intention is to provoke a public scandal, which may bring the whole body into disrepute."

Here for the first time the speaker lifted his gaze from the bowl of marigolds, let it travel slowly round the table, and brought it to rest upon the Warden's intent face.

"Will you let me say, here and now, that the one thing which frustrated the whole attack from first to last was the remarkable solidarity and public spirit displayed by your college as a body. I think that was the last obstacle that X expected to encounter in a community of women. Nothing but the very great loyalty of the Senior Common Room to the College and the respect of the students for the Senior Common Room stood between you and a most unpleasant publicity. It is the merest presumption in me to tell you what you already know far better than I do; but I say it, not only for my own satisfaction, but because this particular kind of loyalty forms at once the psychological excuse for the attack and the only possible defense against it."

"Thank you," said the Warden. "I feel sure that everybody here will know how to appreciate that."

"We come next," resumed Wimsey, his eyes once more on the marigolds, "to the incident of the dummy in the Chapel. This merely repeats the theme of the early drawings, but with a greater eye to dramatic effect. Its evidential importance lies in the 'Harpy' quotation pinned to the dummy; the mysterious appearance of a black figured frock which nobody could identify; the subsequent conviction of the ex-porter Jukes for theft; and the finding of the mutilated newspaper in Miss de Vine's room, which closed that sequence of events. I will take up those points later.

"It was about this time that Miss Vane made the acquaintance of my nephew Saint-George, and he mentioned to her that, under circumstances into which we need not, perhaps, inquire, he had met a mysterious woman one night in your Fellows' Garden, and that she had told him two things. One: that Shrewsbury College was a place where they murdered beautiful boys like him and ate their hearts out; secondly: that 'the other had fair hair, too.'"

This piece of information was new to most of the Senior Common Room, and caused a mild sensation.

"Here we have the 'murder-motif' emphasized, with a little detail about the victim. He is a man, fair, handsome and comparatively young. My nephew then said he would not undertake to recognize the woman again; but on a subsequent occasion he saw and did recognize her."

Once again the tremor passed round the table.

"The next important disturbance was the affair of the missing fuses."

Here the Dean could contain herself no longer and burst out:

"What a lovely title for a thriller!"

The veiled eyes lifted instantly, and the laughter-lines gathered at the corners.

"Perfect. And that was all it was. X retired, having accomplished nothing but a thriller with good publicity value."

"And it was after *that*," said Miss de Vine, "that the newspaper was found in my room."

"Yes," said Wimsey; "mine was a rational, not a chronological, grouping. . . . That brings us to the end of the Hilary Term. The Vacation passed without incident. In the Summer Term, we are faced with the cumulative effect of long and insidious persecution upon a scholar of sensitive temperament. That was the most dangerous phase of X's activities. We know that other students besides Miss Newland had received letters wishing them bad luck in their Schools; happily, Miss Layton and the rest were of tougher fiber. But I should like particularly to draw your attention to the fact that, with a few unimportant exceptions, the animus was all directed against dons and scholars."

Here the Bursar, who had been manifesting irritation for some time, broke in:

"I cannot imagine why they are making all that noise underneath this building. Do you mind, Warden, if I send out and stop it?"

"I am sorry," said Wimsey. "I am afraid I am responsible for that. I suggested to Padgett that a search in the coal cellar might be profitable."

"Then," pronounced the Warden, "I fear we must put up with it, Bursar." She inclined her head towards Wimsey, who went on:

"That is a brief summary of the events as presented to me by Miss Vane, when, with your consent, Warden, she laid the case before me. I rather gathered"—here the right hand became restless and began to beat out a silent tattoo upon the tabletop—"that she and some others among you were inclined to look upon the outrages as the outcome of repressions sometimes accompanying the celibate life and issuing in an obscene and unreasoning malice directed partly against the conditions of that life and partly against persons who enjoyed or had enjoyed or might be supposed to enjoy a wider experience. There is no doubt that malice of that kind exists. But the history of the case seemed to me to offer a psychological picture of an entirely different kind. One member of this Common Room has been married, and another is engaged to be married; and neither of these, who ought to have been the first victims, were (so far as I know) persecuted at all. The dominance of the naked female figure in the early drawing is also highly significant. So is the destruction of Miss Barton's book. Also, the bias displayed by X seemed to be strongly antischolastic, and to have a more or less rational motive, based on some injury amounting in X's mind to murder, inflicted upon a male person by a female scholar. The grievance seemed, to my mind, to be felt principally against Miss de Vine, and to be extended, from her, to the whole College and possibly to educated women in general. I therefore felt we should look for a woman either married or with sexual experience, of limited education but some acquaintance with scholars and scholarship, whose past was in some way linked with that of Miss de Vine, and (though this was an assumption) who had probably come into residence later than last December."

Harriet twisted her glance away from Peter's hand, which had ceased its soft drumming and now lay flat on the table, to estimate the effect of this on his hearers. Miss de Vine was frowning as though her mind, running back over the years, were dispassionately considering her claim to have done murder; Miss Chilperic's face wore a troubled blush, and Mrs. Goodwin's an air of protest; in Miss Hillyard's eyes was an extraordinary mixture of triumph and embarrassment; Miss Barton was nodding quiet assent, Miss Allison smiling, Miss Shaw faintly affronted; Miss Edwards was looking at Peter with eyes that said frankly, "You are the sort of person I can deal with." The Warden's grave countenance was expressionless. The Dean's profile gave no clue to her feelings, but she uttered a little, quick sigh that sounded like relief.

"I will now come," said Peter, "to the material clues. First, the printed messages. It seemed to me extremely unlikely that these could have been produced, in such quantity, within the College walls, without leaving some trace of their origin. I was inclined to look for an outside source. Similarly with the figured dress found on the dummy; it seemed very strange that nobody should ever have set eyes on it before, though it was several seasons old. Thirdly, there was the odd circumstance that the letters which came by post were always received either on a Monday or a Thursday, as though Sunday and Wednesday were the only days on which letters could conveniently be posted from a distant post-office or box. These three considerations might have suggested someone living at a distance, who visited Oxford only twice a week. But the nightly disturbances made it plain that the person actually lived within the walls, with fixed days for going outside them and a place somewhere outside, where clothes could be kept and letters prepared. The person who would fulfill these conditions best would be one of the scouts."

Miss Stevens and Miss Barton both stirred.

"The majority of the scouts, however, seemed to be ruled out. Those who were not confined within the Scouts' Wing at night were trusted women of long service here—most unlikely to fulfill any of the other conditions. Most of those in the Scouts' Wing slept two in a room, and therefore (unless two of them were in collusion) could not possibly escape into the College night after night without being suspected. This left only those who had separate bedrooms: Carrie, the head Scout; Annie, the scout attached first to Miss Lydgate's staircase and subsequently to the Senior Common Room, and a third scout, Ethel, an elderly and highly reputable woman. Of these three, Annie corresponded most closely to the psychological picture of X; for she had been married and had the afternoon of Sunday and the afternoon and evening of Wednesday free; she also had her children domiciled in the town and therefore a place where she could keep clothes and prepare letters."

"But—" began the Bursar, indignantly.

"This is only the case as I saw it last Sunday week," said Wimsey. "Certain powerful objections at once presented themselves. The Scouts' Wing was shut off by locked doors and gates. But it was made clear at the time of the Library episode that the buttery hatch was occasionally left open for the convenience of students wishing to obtain supplies late at night. Miss Hudson had, in fact, expected to find it open that very night. When Miss Vane tried it, it was, in fact, locked. But that was *after* X had left the Library, and you will remember that X was shown to have been trapped in the Hall Building by Miss Vane and Miss Hudson at one end and Miss Barton at the other. The assumption made at the time was that she had been hiding in the Hall.

"After that episode, greater care was taken to see that the buttery hatch was kept locked, and I learn that the key, which was previously left on the inner side of the hatch, was removed and placed on Carrie's key-ring. But a key can very readily be cut in a single day. Actually, it was a week before the next nocturnal episode occurred, which carries us over the following Wednesday, when a key abstracted from Carrie's bunch might readily have been copied and returned. (I know for a fact that such a key was cut on that Wednesday by an ironmonger in the lower part of the town, though I have not been able to identify the purchaser. But that is merely a routine detail.) There was one consideration which inclined Miss Vane to exonerate all the scouts, and that was, that no woman in that position would be likely to express her resentment in the Latin quotation from the *Aeneid* found attached to the dummy.

"This objection had some weight with me, but not a great deal. It was the only message that was not in English, and it was one to which any school child might easily have access. On the other hand, the fact that it was unique among the other scripts made me sure that it had some particular significance. I mean, it wasn't that X's feelings habitually expressed themselves in Latin hexameters. There must be something special about that passage besides its general applicability to unnatural females who snatch the meat from men's mouths. *Nec saevior ulla pestis.*"

"When I first heard of that," broke in Miss Hillyard, "I felt sure that a man was behind all this."

"That was probably a sound instinct," said Wimsey. "I feel sure that a man did write that. . . . Well, I need not take up time with pointing out how easy it was for anybody to wander about the College at night and play tricks on people. In a community of two hundred people, some of whom scarcely know one another by sight, it is harder to find a person than to lose her. But the intrusion of Jukes upon the situation at that moment was rather awkward for

X. Miss Vane showed, and announced, a disposition to inquire rather too closely into Jukes's home-life. As a result somebody who knew a good deal about Jukes's little habits laid an information and Jukes was removed to goal. Mrs. Jukes took refuge with her relations and Annie's children were sent away to Headington. And in order that we should feel quite sure that the Jukes household had nothing to do with the matter, a mutilated newspaper appeared shortly afterwards in Miss de Vine's room."

Harriet looked up.

"I did work that out—eventually. But what happened last week seemed to make it quite impossible."

"I don't think," said Peter, "you approached the problem—forgive me for saying so—with an unprejudiced mind and undivided attention. Something got between you and the facts."

"Miss Vane has been helping me so generously with my books," murmured Miss Lydgate, contritely; "and she has had her own work to do as well. We really ought not to have asked her to spare any time for our problems."

"I had plenty of time," said Harriet. "I was only stupid."

"At any rate," said Wimsey, "Miss Vane did enough to make X feel she was dangerous. At the beginning of this term, we find X becoming more desperate and more deadly in intention. With the lighter evenings, it becomes more difficult to play tricks at night. There is the psychological attempt on Miss Newland's life and reason and, when that fails, an effort is made to create a stink in the University by sending letters to the Vice-Chancellor. However, the University proved to be as solid as the College; having let the women in, it was not prepared to let them down. This was no doubt exasperating to the feelings of X. Dr. Threep acted as intermediary between the Vice-Chancellor and yourselves, and the matter was presumably dealt with."

"I informed the Vice-Chancellor," said the Warden, "that steps were being taken."

"Quite so; and you complimented me by asking me to take those steps. I had very little doubt from the start as to the identity of X; but suspicion is not proof, and I was anxious not to cast any suspicion that could not be justified. My first task was obviously to find out whether Miss de Vine had actually ever murdered or injured anybody. In the course of a very interesting after-dinner conversation in this room, she informed me that, six years ago, she had been instrumental in depriving a man of his reputation and livelihood—and we decided, if you remember, that this was an action which any manly man or womanly woman might be disposed to resent."

"Do you mean to say," cried the Dean, "that all that discussion was intended merely to bring out that story?"

"I offered an opportunity for the story's appearance, certainly; but if it hadn't come out then, I should have asked for it. Incidentally, I established for a certainty, what I was sure of in my own mind from the start, that there was not a woman in this Common Room, married or single, who would be ready to place personal loyalties above professional honor. That was a point which it seemed necessary to make clear—not so much to me, as to yourselves."

The Warden looked from Miss Hillyard to Mrs. Goodwin and back at Peter.

"Yes," she said, "I think it was wise to establish that."

"The next day," said Peter, "I asked Miss de Vine for the name of the man in question, whom we already knew to be handsome and married. The name was Arthur Robinson; and with this information I set out to find what had become of him. My working theory was that X was either the wife or some relation of Robinson: that she had come here when Miss de Vine's appointment was announced, with the intention of revenging his misfortunes upon Miss de Vine, the College and academic women in general; and that in all probability X was a person who stood in some close relation to the Jukes family. This theory was strengthened by the discovery that information was laid against Jukes by an anonymous letter similar to those circulated here.

"Now, the first thing that happened after my arrival was

the appearance of X in the Science Lecture Room. The idea that X was courting discovery by preparing letters in that public and dangerous manner was patently absurd. The whole thing was a clear fake, intended to mislead, and probably to establish an alibi. The communications had been prepared elsewhere and deliberately planted—in fact, there were not enough letters left in the box to finish the message that had been begun to Miss Vane. The room chosen was in full view of the Scouts' Wing, and the big ceiling light was conspicuously turned on, though there was a reading-lamp in the room, in good working order; it was Annie who drew Carrie's attention to the light in the window; Annie was the only person who claimed to have actually seen X; and while the alibi was established for both scouts, Annie was the one who most closely corresponded to the conditions required to X."

"But Carrie heard X in the room," said the Dean.

"Oh, yes," said Wimsey, smiling. "And Carrie was sent to fetch you while Annie removed the strings that had switched out the light and overturned the blackboard from the other side of the door. I pointed out to you, you know, that the top of the door had been thoroughly dusted, so that the mark of the string shouldn't show."

"But the marks on the dark-room window-sill—" said the Dean.

"Quite genuine. She got out there the first time, leaving the doors locked on the inside and strewing a few of Miss de Vine's hairpins about to produce conviction. Then she let herself into the Scouts' Wing through the Buttery, called up Carrie and brought her along to see the fun. . . . I think, by the way, that some one of the scouts must have had her suspicions. Perhaps she had found Annie's bedroom door mysteriously locked on various occasions, or had met her in the passage at inconvenient times. Anyhow, the time had obviously arrived for establishing an alibi. I hazarded the suggestion that nocturnal ramblings would cease from that time on; and so they did. And I don't suppose we shall ever find that extra key to the Buttery."

"All very well," said Miss Edwards. "But you still have no proof."

"No. I went away to get it. In the meantime, X—if you don't like my identification—decided that Miss Vane was dangerous, and laid a trap to catch her. This didn't come off, because Miss Vane very sensibly telephoned back to College to confirm the mysterious message she had received at Somerville. The message was sent from an outside call-box on the Wednesday night at 10:40. Just before eleven, Annie came in from her day off and heard Padgett speak to Miss Vane on the 'phone. She didn't hear the conversation, but she probably heard the name.

"Although the attempt had not come off, I felt sure that another would be made, either on Miss Vane, Miss de Vine or the suspicious scout—or on all three. I issued a warning to that effect. The next thing that happened was that Miss Vane's chessmen were destroyed. That was rather unexpected. It looked less like alarm than personal hatred. Up till that time, Miss Vane had been treated with almost as much tenderness as though she had been a womanly woman. Can you think of anything that can have given X that impression, Miss Vane?"

"I don't know," said Harriet, confused. "I asked kindly after the children and spoke to Beatie—good heavens, yes, Beatie!—when I met them. And I remember once agreeing politely with Annie that marriage might be a good thing if one could find the right person."

"That was politic if unprincipled. And how about the attentive Mr. Jones of Jesus? If you will bring young men into the College at night and hide them in the Chapel—"

"Good gracious!" exclaimed Miss Pyke.

"—you must be expected to be thought a womanly woman. However; that is of no great importance. I fear the illusion was destroyed when you publicly informed me that personal attachments must come second to public duties."

"But," said Miss Edwards, impatiently, "what happened to Arthur Robinson?"

"He was married to a woman called Charlotte Ann

Clarke, who had been his landlady's daughter. His first child, born eight years ago, was called Beatrice. After the trouble at York, he changed his name to Wilson and took a post as junior master in a small preparatory school, where they didn't mind taking a man who had been deprived of his M.A., so long as he was cheap. His second daughter, born shortly afterwards, was named Carola. I'm afraid the Wilsons didn't find life too easy. He lost his first job—drink was the reason, I'm afraid—took another—got into trouble again and three years ago blew his brains out. There were photographs in the local paper. Here they are, you see. A fair, handsome man of about thirty-eight—irresolute, attractive, something of my nephew's type. And here is the photograph of the widow."

"You are right," said the Warden. "That is Annie Wilson."

"Yes. If you read the report of the inquest, you will see that he left a letter, saying that he had been hounded to death—rather a rambling letter, containing a Latin quotation, which the coroner obligingly translated."

"Good gracious!" said Miss Pyke. "*Tristius haud illis monstrum—?*"

"*Ita*. A man wrote that after all, you see; so Miss Hillyard was so far right. Annie Wilson, being obliged to do something to support her children and herself, went into service."

"I had very good references with her," said the Bursar.

"No doubt; why not? She must somehow have kept track of Miss de Vine's movements; and when the appointment was announced last Christmas, she applied for a job here. She probably knew that, as an unfortunate widow with two small children, she would receive kindly consideration—"

"What did I tell you?" cried Miss Hillyard. "I always said that this ridiculous sentimentality about married women would be the ruin of all discipline in this College. Their minds are not, and cannot be, on their work."

"Oh, dear!" said Miss Lydgate. "Poor soul! brooding

over that grievance in this really unbalanced way! If only we had known, we could surely have done something to make her see the thing in a more rational light. Did it never occur to you, Miss de Vine, to inquire what happened to this unhappy man Robinson?"

"I am afraid it did not."

"Why should you?" demanded Miss Hillyard.

The noise in the coal-cellar had ceased within the last few minutes. As though the silence had roused a train of association in her mind, Miss Chilperic turned to Peter and said, hesitatingly:

"If poor Annie really did all these dreadful things, how did she get shut up in the coal-hole?"

"Ah!" said Peter. "That coal-hole very nearly shook my faith in my theory; especially as I didn't get the report from my research-staff till yesterday. But when you come to think of it, what else could she do? She laid a plot to attack Miss de Vine on her return from Town—the scouts probably knew which train she was coming by."

"Nellie knew," said Harriet.

"Then she could have told Annie. By an extraordinary piece of good fortune, the attack was delivered—not against Miss de Vine, who would have been taken unawares and whose heart is not strong, but against a younger and stronger woman, who was, up to the certain point, prepared to meet it. Even so, it was serious enough, and might easily have proved fatal. I find it difficult to forgive myself for not having spoken earlier—with or without proof—and put the suspect under observation."

"Oh, nonsense!" said Harriet, quickly. "If you had, she might have chucked the whole thing for the rest of the term, and we should still not know anything definite. I wasn't much hurt."

"No. But it might not have been you. I knew you were ready to take the risk; but I had no right to expose Miss de Vine."

"It seems to me," said Miss de Vine, "that the risk was rightly and properly mine."

"The worst responsibility rests on me," said the Warden. "I should have telephoned the warning to you before you left Town."

"Whosever fault it was," said Peter, "it was Miss Vane who was attacked. Instead of a nice, quiet throttling, there was a nasty fall and a lot of blood, some of which, no doubt, got on to the assailant's hands and dress. She was in an awkward position. She had got the wrong person, she was bloodstained and disheveled, and Miss de Vine or somebody else might arrive at any moment. Even if she ran quickly back to her own room, she might be seen—her uniform was stained—and when the body was found (alive or dead) she would be a marked woman. Her only possible chance was to stage an attack on herself. She went out through the back of the Loggia, threw herself into the coal-cellar, locked the door on herself and proceeded to cover up Miss Vane's bloodstains with her own. By the way, Miss Vane, if you remembered anything of your lesson, you must have marked her wrists for her."

"I'll swear I did," said Harriet.

"But any amount of bruising may be caused by trying to scramble through a ventilator. Well. The evidence, you see, is still circumstantial—even though my nephew is prepared to identify the woman he saw crossing Magdalen Bridge on Wednesday with the woman he met in the garden. One can catch a Headington bus from the other side of Magdalen Bridge. Meanwhile, you heard this fellow in the cellarage? If I am not mistaken, somebody is arriving with something like direct proof."

A heavy step in the passage was followed by a knock on the door; and Padgett followed the knock almost before he was told to come in. His clothes bore traces of coal-dust, though some hasty washing had evidently been done to his hands and face.

"Excuse me, madam Warden, miss," said Padgett. "Here you are, Major. Right down at the bottom of the 'eap. 'Ad to shift the whole lot, I had."

He laid a large key on the table.

"Have you tried it in the cellar-door?"

"Yes, sir. But there wasn't no need. 'Ere's my label on it. 'Coal-cellar'—see?"

"Easy to lock yourself in and hide the key. Thank you, Padgett."

"One moment, Padgett," said the Warden. "I want to see Annie Wilson. Will you please find her and bring her here."

"Better not," said Wimsey, in a low tone.

"I certainly shall," said the Warden, sharply. "You have made a public accusation against this unfortunate woman, and it is only right that she should be given an opportunity to answer it. Bring her here at once, Padgett."

Peter's hands made a last eloquent gesture of resignation as Padgett went out.

"I think it is *very* necessary," said the Bursar, "that this matter should be cleared up completely and at once."

"Do you really think it wise, Warden?" asked the Dean.

"Nobody shall be accused in this College," said the Warden, "without a hearing. Your arguments, Lord Peter, appear to be most convincing; but the evidence may bear some other interpretation. Annie Wilson is, no doubt, Charlotte Ann Robinson; but it does not follow that she is the author of the disturbances. I admit that appearances are against her, but there may be falsification or coincidence. The key, for example, may have been put into the coal-cellar at any time within the last three days."

"I have been down to see Jukes," began Peter; when the entrance of Annie interrupted him. Neat and subdued as usual, she approached the Warden:

"Padgett said you wished to see me, madam." Then her eye fell on the newspaper spread out upon the table, and she drew in her breath with a long, sharp hiss, while her eyes went round the room like the eyes of a hunted animal.

"Mrs. Robinson," said Peter, quickly and quietly. "We can quite understand how you came to feel a grievance—perhaps a justifiable grievance—against the persons responsible for the sad death of your husband. But how could you bring yourself to let your children help you to prepare those horrible messages? Didn't you realize that if anything had happened they might have been called upon to bear witness in court?"

"No, they wouldn't," she said quickly. "They knew nothing about it. They only helped to cut out the letters. Do you think I'd let them suffer? . . . My God! You can't do that. . . . I say you can't do it. . . . You beasts, I'd kill myself first."

"Annie," said Dr. Baring, "are we to understand that you admit being responsible for all these abominable disturbances? I sent for you in order that you might clear yourself of certain suspicions which—"

"Clear myself! I wouldn't trouble to clear myself. You smug hypocrites—I'd like to see you bring me into court. I'd laugh in your faces. How would you look, sitting there while I told the judge how that woman there killed my husband?"

"I am exceedingly disturbed," said Miss de Vine, "to hear about all this. I knew nothing of it till just now. But indeed I had no choice in the matter. I could not foresee the consequences—and even if I had—"

"You wouldn't have cared. You killed him and you didn't care. I say you murdered him. What had he done to you? What harm had he done to anybody? He only wanted to live and be happy. You took the bread out of his mouth and flung his children and me out to starve. What did it matter to you? You had no children. You hadn't a man to care about. I know all about you. You had a man once and you threw him over because it was too much bother to look after him. But couldn't you leave my man alone? He told a lie about somebody else who was dead and dust hundreds of years ago. Nobody was the worse for that. Was a dirty bit of paper more important than all our lives and happiness? You broke him and killed him—all for nothing. Do you think that's a woman's job?"

"Most unhappily," said Miss de Vine, "it was my job."

"What business had you with a job like that? A

woman's job is to look after a husband and children. I wish I had killed you. I wish I could kill you all. I wish I could burn down this place and all the places like it—where you teach women to take men's jobs and rob them first and kill them afterwards."

She turned to the Warden.

"Don't you know what you're doing? I've heard you sit round sniveling about unemployment—but it's you, it's women like you who take the work away from the men and break their hearts and lives. No wonder you can't get men for yourselves and hate the women who can. God keep the men out of your hands, that's what I say. You'd destroy your own husbands, if you had any, for an old book or bit of writing. . . . I loved my husband and you broke his heart. If he'd been a thief or a murderer, I'd have loved him and stuck to him. He didn't mean to steal that old bit of paper—he only put it away. It made no difference to anybody. It wouldn't have helped a single man or woman or child in the world—it wouldn't have kept a cat alive; but you killed him for it."

Peter had got up and stood behind Miss de Vine, with his hand over her wrist. She shook her head. Immovable, implacable, thought Harriet; this won't make her pulse miss a single beat. The rest of the Common Room looked merely stunned.

"Oh, no!" said Annie, echoing Harriet's thoughts. "*She* feels nothing. None of them feel anything. You brazen devils—you all stand together. You're only frightened for your skins and your miserable reputations. I scared you all, didn't I? God! how I laughed to see you all look at one another! You didn't even trust each other. You can't agree about anything except hating decent women and their men. I wish I'd torn the throats out of the lot of you. It would have been too good for you, though. I wanted to see you thrown out to starve, like us. I wanted to see you all dragged into the gutter. I wanted to see you—you—sneered at and trampled on and degraded and despised as we were. It would do you good to learn to scrub floors for a living as I've done, and use your hands for something, and say 'madam' to a lot of scum. . . . But I made you shake in your shoes, anyhow. You couldn't even find out who was doing it—that's all your wonderful brains come to. There's nothing in your books about life and marriage and children, is there? Nothing about desperate people—or love—or hate or anything human. You're ignorant and stupid and helpless. You're a lot of fools. You can't do anything for yourselves. Even you, you silly old hags—you had to get a man to do your work for you.

"*You* brought him here." She leaned over Harriet with her fierce eyes, as though she would have fallen on her and torn her to pieces. "And you're the dirtiest hypocrite of the lot. I know who you are. You had a lover once, and he died. You chucked him out because you were too proud to marry him. You were his mistress and you sucked him dry, and you didn't value him enough to let him make an honest woman of you. He died because you weren't there to look after him. I suppose you'd say you loved him. You don't know what love means. It means sticking to your man through thick and thin and putting up with everything. But you take men and use them and throw them away when you've finished with them. They come after you like wasps round a jam-jar, and then they fall in and die. What are you going to do with that one there? You send for him when you need him to do your dirty work, and when you've finished with him you'll get rid of him. You don't want to cook his meals and mend his clothes and bear his children like a decent woman. You'll use him, like any other tool, to break me. You'd like to see me in prison and my children in a home, because you haven't the guts to do your proper job in the world. The whole bunch of you together haven't flesh and blood enough to make you fit for a man. As for *you*—"

Peter had come back to his place and was sitting with his head in his hands. She went over and shook him furiously by the shoulder, and as he looked up, spat in his face. "You! you dirty traitor! You rotten little white-faced rat!

It's men like you that make women like this. You don't know how to do anything but talk. What do you know about life, with your title and your money and your clothes and motor-cars? You've never done a hand's turn of honest work. You can buy all the women you want. Wives and mothers may rot and die for all you care, while you chatter about duty and honor. Nobody would sacrifice anything for you—why should they? That woman's making a fool of you and you can't see it. If she marries you for your money she'll make a worse fool of you, and you'll deserve it. You're fit for nothing but to keep your hands white and father other men's children. . . . What are you going to do now, all of you? Run away and squeal to the magistrate because I made fools of you all? You daren't. You're afraid to come out into the light. You're afraid for your precious college and your precious selves. *I'm* not afraid. I did nothing but stand up for my own flesh and blood. Damn you! I can laugh at you all! You daren't touch me. You're afraid of me. I had a husband and I loved him—and you were jealous of me and you killed him. Oh, God! You killed him among you, and we never had a happy moment again."

She suddenly burst out crying—half dreadful and half grotesque, with her cap crooked and her hands twisting her apron into a knot.

"For Heaven's sake," muttered the Dean, desperately, "can't this be stopped?"

Here Miss Barton got up.

"Come, Annie," she said, briskly. "We are all very sorry for you, but you mustn't behave in this foolish and hysterical way. What would the children think if they saw you now? You had better come and lie down quietly and take some aspirin. Bursar! will you please help me out with her?"

Miss Stevens, galvanized, got up and took Annie's other arm, and all three went out together. The Warden turned to Peter, who stood mechanically wiping his face with his hand kerchief and looking at nobody.

"I apologize for allowing this scene to take place. I ought to have known better. You were perfectly right."

"Of course he was right!" cried Harriet. Her head was throbbing like an engine. "He's always right. He said it was dangerous to care for anybody. He said love was a brute and a devil. You're honest, Peter, aren't you? Damned honest—Oh, God! let me get out of here. I'm going to be sick."

She stumbled blindly against him as he held the door open for her, and he had to steer her with a firm hand to the cloakroom door. When he came back, the Warden had risen, and the dons with her. They looked stupefied with the shock of seeing so many feelings stripped naked in public.

"Of course, Miss de Vine," the Warden was saying, "no sane person could possibly think of blaming you."

"Thank you, Warden," said Miss de Vine. "Nobody, perhaps, but myself."

"Lord Peter," said the Warden, "a little later on, when we are all feeling more ourselves, I think we should all like to say—"

"Please don't," said he. "It doesn't matter at all."

The Warden went out, and the rest followed her like mutes at a funeral, leaving only Miss de Vine, sitting solitary beneath the window. Peter shut the door after them and came up to her. He was still passing his handkerchief across his mouth. Becoming aware of this, he tossed the linen into the wastepaper basket.

"I do blame myself," said Miss de Vine, less to him than to herself. "Most bitterly. Not for my original action, which was unavoidable, but for the sequel. Nothing you can say to me could make me feel more responsible than I do already."

"I can have nothing to say," said he. "Like you and every member of this Common Room, I admit the principle and the consequences must follow."

"That won't do," said the Fellow, bluntly. "One ought to take some thought for other people. Miss Lydgate would have done what I did in the first place; but she would have made it her business to see what became of that unhappy man and his wife."

"Miss Lydgate is a very great and a very rare person. But she could not prevent other people from suffering for her principles. That seems to be what principles are for, somehow. . . . I don't claim, you know," he added, with something of his familiar diffidence, "to be a Christian or anything of that kind. But there's one thing in the Bible that seems to me to be a mere statement of brutal fact—I mean, about bringing not peace but a sword."

Miss de Vine looked up at him curiously.

"How much are *you* going to suffer for this?"

"God knows," he said. "That's my lookout. Perhaps not at all. In any case, you know, I'm with you—every time."

When Harriet emerged from the cloak-room, she found Miss de Vine alone.

"Thank Heaven, they've gone," said Harriet. "I'm afraid I made an exhibition of myself. It was rather—shattering, wasn't it? What's happened to Peter?"

"He's gone," said Miss de Vine.

She hesitated, and then said:

"Miss Vane—I've no wish to pry impertinently into your affairs. Stop me if I am saying too much. But we have talked a good deal about facing the facts. Isn't it time you faced the facts about that man?"

"I have been facing one fact for some time," said Harriet, staring out with unseeing eyes into the quad, "and that is, that if I once gave way to Peter, I should go up like straw."

"That," said Miss de Vine, drily, "is moderately obvious. How often has he used that weapon against you?"

"Never," said Harriet, remembering the moments when he might have used it. "Never."

"Then what are you afraid of? Yourself?"

"Isn't this afternoon warning enough?"

"Perhaps. You have had the luck to come up against a very unselfish and a very honest man. He has done what you asked him without caring what it cost him and without shirking the issue. He hasn't tried to disguise the facts or bias your judgment. You admit that, at any rate."

"I suppose he realized how I should feel about it?"

"Realized it?" said Miss de Vine, with a touch of irritation. "My dear girl, give him the credit for the brains he's got. They are very good ones. He is painfully sensitive and far more intelligent than is good for him. But I really don't think you can go on like this. You won't break his patience or his control or his spirit; but you may break his health. He looks like a person pushed to the last verge of endurance."

"He's been rushing about and working very hard," said Harriet, defensively. "I shouldn't be at all a comfortable person for him to live with. I've got a devilish temper."

"Well, that's his risk, if he likes to take it. He doesn't seem to lack courage."

"I should only make his life a misery."

"Very well. If you are determined that you're not fit to black his boots, tell him so and send him away."

"I've been trying to send Peter away for five years. It doesn't have that effect on him."

"If you had really tried, you could have sent him away in five minutes. . . . Forgive me. I don't suppose you've had a very easy time with yourself. But it can't have been easy for him, either—looking on at it, and quite powerless to interfere."

"Yes. I almost wish he had interfered, instead of being so horribly intelligent. It would be quite a relief to be ridden over rough-shod for a change."

"He will never do that. That's *his* weakness. He'll never make up your mind for you. You'll have to make your own decisions. You needn't be afraid of losing your independence; he will always force it back on you. If you ever find any kind of repose with him, it can only be the repose of very delicate balance."

"That's what he says himself. If you were me, should you like to marry a man like that?"

"Frankly," said Miss de Vine, "I should not. I would not do it for any consideration. A marriage of two independent and equally irritable intelligences seems to me reckless to the point of insanity. You can hurt one another so dreadfully."

"I know. And I don't think I can stand being hurt any more."

"Then," said Miss de Vine, "I suggest that you stop hurting other people. Face the facts and state a conclusion. Bring a scholar's mind to the problem and have done with it."

"I believe you're quite right," said Harriet. "I will. And that reminds me. Miss Lydgate's *History of Prosody* was marked PRESS with her own hand this morning. I fled with it and seized on a student to take it down to the printers. I'm almost positive I heard a faint voice crying from the window about a footnote on page 97—but I pretended not to hear."

"Well," said Miss de Vine, laughing, "thank goodness, *that* piece of scholarship has achieved a result at last!"

CHAPTER XXIII

The last refuge and surest remedy, to be put in practice in the utmost place, when no other means will take effect, is, to let them go together and enjoy one another; potissima cura est ut heros amasia sua potiatur, *saith* Guianerius. . . . Aesculapius *himself, to this malady, cannot invent a better remedy,* quam ut amanti cedat amatum *. . . than that a Lover have his desire.*

ROBERT BURTON

There was no word from Peter in the morning. The Warden issued a brief and discreet announcement to the College that the offender had been traced and the trouble ended. The Senior Common Room, recovering a little from its shock, went quietly about the business of the term. They were all normal again. They had never been anything else. Now that the distorting-glass of suspicion was removed, they were kindly, intelligent human beings—not seeing, perhaps, very much farther beyond their own interests than the ordinary man beyond his job or the ordinary woman beyond her own household—but as understandable and pleasant as daily bread.

Harriet, having got Miss Lydgate's proofs off her mind, and feeling that she could not brace herself to deal with Wilfrid, took her notes on Lefanu, and went down to put in a little solid work at the Camera.

Shortly before noon, a hand touched her shoulder.

"They told me you were here," said Peter. "Can you spare a moment? We can go up on to the roof."

Harriet put down her pen and followed him across the circular chamber with its desks full of silent readers.

"I understand," he said, pushing open the swing-door that leads to the winding staircase, "that the problem is being medically dealt with."

"Oh, yes. When the academic mind has really grasped a hypothesis—which may take a little time—it copes with great thoroughness and efficiency. Nothing will be overlooked."

They climbed in silence, and came out at length through the little turret upon the gallery of the Camera. The previous day's rain had passed and left the sun shining upon a shining city. Stepping cautiously over the slatted flooring towards the south-east segment of the circle, they were a little surprised to come upon Miss Cattermole and Mr. Pomfret, who were seated side by side upon a stone projection and rose as they approached, in a flutter, like daws disturbed from a belfry.

"Don't move," said Wimsey, graciously. "Plenty of room for all of us."

"It's quite all right, sir," said Mr. Pomfret. "We were just going. Really. I've got a lecture at twelve."

"Dear me!" said Harriet, watching them disappear into the turret. But Peter had already lost interest in Mr. Pomfret and his affairs. He was leaning with his elbows on the parapet, looking down into Cat Street. Harriet joined him.

There, eastward, within a stone's throw, stood the twin towers of All Souls, fantastic, unreal as a house of cards, clear-cut in the sunshine, the drenched oval in the quad beneath brilliant as an emerald in the bezel of a ring. Behind them, black and grey, New College frowning like a fortress, with dark wings wheeling about her belfry louvres; and Queen's with her dome of green copper; and, as the eye turned southward, Magdalen, yellow and slender, the tall lily of towers; the Schools and the battlemented front of University; Merton, square-pinnacled, half-hidden behind the shadowed North side and mounting spire of St. Mary's. Westward again, Christ Church, vast between Cathedral spire and Tom Tower; Brasenose close at hand; St. Aldate's and Carfax beyond; spire and tower and quadrangle, all Oxford springing underfoot in living leaf and enduring stone, ringed far off by her bulwark of blue hills.

Towery City, and branchy between towers,
Cuckoo-echoing, bell-swarmed, lark-charmed,
rook-racked, river-rounded,
The dapple-eared lily below.

"Harriet," said Peter; "I want to ask your forgiveness for these last five years."

"I think," said Harriet, "it ought to be the other way round."

"I think not. When I remember how we first met—"

"Peter, don't think about that ghastly time. I was sick of myself, body and soul. I didn't know what I was doing."

"And I chose that time, when I should have thought only of you, to thrust myself upon you, to make demands of you, like a damned arrogant fool—as though I had only to ask and have. Harriet, I ask you to believe that, whatever it looked like, my blundering was nothing worse than vanity and a blind, childish impatience to get my own way."

She shook her head, finding no words.

"I had found you," he went on, a little more quietly, "beyond all hope or expectation, at a time when I thought no woman could ever mean anything to me beyond a little easy sale and exchange of pleasure. And I was so terrified of losing you before I could grasp you that I babbled out all my greed and fear as though, God help me, you had nothing to think of but me and my windy self-importance. As though it mattered. As though the very word of love had not been the most crashing insolence a man could offer you."

"No, Peter. Never that."

"My dear—you showed me what you thought of me when you said you would live with me but not marry me."

"Don't. I am ashamed of that."

"Not so bitterly ashamed as I have been. If you knew how I have tried to forget it. I told myself that you were only afraid of the social consequences of marriage. I comforted myself with pretending that it showed you liked me a little. I bolstered up my conceit for months, before I would admit the humiliating truth that I ought to have known from the beginning—that you were so sick of my pestering that you would have thrown yourself to me as one throws a bone to a dog, to stop the brute from yelping."

"Peter, that isn't true. It was myself I was sick of. How could I give you base coin for a marriage-portion?"

"At least I had the decency to know that I couldn't take it in settlement of a debt. But I have never dared to tell you what that rebuke meant to me, when at last I saw it for what it was. . . . Harriet; I have nothing much in the way of religion, or even morality, but I do recognize a code of behavior of sorts. I do know that the worst sin—perhaps the only sin—passion can commit, is to be joyless. It must lie down with laughter or make its bed in hell—there is no middle way. . . . Don't misunderstand me. I have bought it, often—but never by forced sale or at 'stupendous sacrifice.' . . . Don't, for God's sake, ever think you owe me anything. If I can't have the real thing, I can make do with the imitation. But I will not have surrenders or crucifixions. . . . If you have come to feel any kindness for me at all, tell me that you would never make me that offer again."

"Not for anything in the world. Not now or at any time since. It isn't only that I have found a value for myself. But when I made you the offer, it meant nothing to me—now it would mean something."

"If you have found your own value," he said, "that is immeasurably the greatest thing. . . . It has taken me a long time to learn my lesson, Harriet. I have had to pull down, brick by brick, the barriers I had built up by my own selfishness and folly. If, in all these years, I have managed to get back to the point at which I ought to have started, will you tell me so and give me leave to begin again? Once or twice in the last few days I have fancied that you might feel as though this unhappy interval might be wiped out and forgotten."

"No; not that. But as though I could be glad to remember it."

"Thank you. That is far more than I expected or deserved."

"Peter—it's not fair to let you talk like this. It's I who ought to apologize. If I owe you nothing else, I owe you my self respect. And I owe you my life—"

"Ah!" said he, smiling. "But I have given you that back by letting you risk it. That was the last kick that sent my vanity out of doors."

"Peter, I did manage to appreciate that. Mayn't I be grateful for that?"

"I don't want gratitude—"

"But won't you take it, now that I want to give it you?"

"If you feel like that about it, then I have no right to refuse. Let that clear all scores, Harriet. You have given me already far more than you know. You are free now and for ever, so far as I am concerned. You saw yesterday what personal claims might lead to—though I didn't intend you to see it in quite that brutal way. But if circumstances made me a little more honest than I meant to be, still, I did mean to be honest up to a point."

"Yes," said Harriet, thoughtfully. "I can't see you burking a fact to support a thesis."

"What would be the good? What could I ever have gained by letting you imagine a lie? I set out in a lordly manner to offer you heaven and earth. I find that all I have to give you is Oxford—which was yours already. Look! Go round about her and tell the towers thereof. It has been my humble privilege to clean and polish your property and present her for your inspection upon a silver salver. Enter into your heritage and do not, as is said in another connection, be afraid with any amazement."

"Peter dear," said Harriet. She turned her back upon the

shining city, leaning back against the balustrade, and looking at him. "Oh, *damn!*"

"Don't worry," said Peter. "It's quite all right. By the way, it looks as though it was Rome again for me next week. But I shan't leave Oxford till Monday. On Sunday there's a Balliol Concert. Will you come to it? We'll have one other gaudy night, and comfort our souls with the Bach Concerto for two violins. If you will bear with me so far. After that, I shall be clearing off and leaving you to—"

"To Wilfrid and Co.," said Harriet, in a kind of exasperation.

"Wilfrid?" said Peter, momentarily at a loss, with his mind scampering after rabbits.

"Yes, I'm re-writing Wilfrid."

"Good God, yes. The chap with the morbid scruples. How's he getting on?"

"He's better, I think. Almost human. I shall have to dedicate the book to you, I think. 'To Peter, who made Wilfrid what he is'—that sort of thing. . . . Don't laugh like that. I'm really *working* at Wilfrid."

For some reason, that anxious assurance shook him as nothing else had done.

"My dear—if anything I have said . . . If you have let me come as far as your work and your life . . . Here! I think I'd better remove myself before I do anything foolish. . . . I shall be honored to go down to posterity in the turn-up of Wilfrid's trouser. . . . You will come on Sunday? I am dining with the Master, but I will meet you at the foot of the stairs. . . . Till then."

He slipped away along the gallery and was gone. Harriet was left to survey the kingdom of the mind, glittering from Merton to Bodley, from Carfax to Magdalen Tower. But her eyes were on one slight figure that crossed the cobbled Square, walking lightly under the shadow of St. Mary's into the High. All the kingdoms of the world and the glory of them.

• • • • •

Masters, undergraduates, visitors; they sat huddled closely together on the backless oak benches, their elbows on the long tables, their eyes shaded with their fingers, or turned intelligently towards the platform where two famous violinists twisted together the fine, strong strands of the Concerto in D Minor. The Hall was very full; Harriet's gowned shoulder touched her companion's, and the crescent of his long sleeve lay over her knee. He was wrapt in the motionless austerity with which all genuine musicians listen to genuine music. Harriet was musician enough to respect this aloofness; she knew well enough that the ecstatic rapture on the face of the man opposite meant only that he was hoping to be thought musical, and that the elderly lady over the way, waving her fingers to the beat, was a musical moron. She knew enough, herself, to read the sounds a little with her brains, laboriously unwinding the twined chains of melody link by link. Peter, she felt sure, could hear the whole intricate pattern, every part separately and simultaneously, each independent and equal, separate but inseparable, moving over and under and through, ravishing heart and mind together.

She waited till the last movement had ended and the packed hall was relaxing its attention in applause.

"Peter—what did you mean when you said that anybody could have the harmony if they would leave us the counterpoint?"

"Why," said he, shaking his head, "that I like my music polyphonic. If you think I meant anything else, you know what I meant."

"Polyphonic music takes a lot of playing. You've got to be more than a fiddler. It needs a musician."

"In this case, two fiddlers—both musicians."

"I'm not much of a musician, Peter."

"As they used to say in my youth: 'All girls should learn a little music—enough to play a simple accompaniment.' I admit that Bach isn't a matter of an autocratic virtuoso and a meek accompanist. But do you want to be either? Here's a gentleman coming to sing a group of ballads. Pray silence for the soloist. But let him be soon over, that we may hear the great striding fugue again."

The final Chorale was sung, and the audience made their way out. Harriet's way lay through the Broad Street gate; Peter followed her through the quad.

"It's a beautiful night—far too good to waste. Don't go back yet. Come down to Magdalen Bridge and send your love to London River."

They turned along the Broad in silence, the light wind fluttering their gowns as they walked.

"There's something about this place," said Peter presently, "that alters all one's values." He paused, and added a little abruptly: "I have said a good deal to you one way and another, lately; but you may have noticed that since we came to Oxford I have not asked you to marry me."

"Yes," said Harriet, her eyes fixed upon the severe and delicate silhouette of the Bodleian roof, just emerging between the Sheldonian and the Clarendon Building. "I had noticed it."

"I have been afraid," he said, simply; "because I knew that from anything you said to me here, there could be no going back. . . . But I will ask you now, and if you say No, I promise you that this time I will accept your answer. Harriet; you know that I love you: will you marry me?"

The traffic lights winked at the Holywell Corner: Yes; No; Wait. Cat Street was crossed and the shadows of New College walls had swallowed them up before she spoke:

"Tell me one thing, Peter. Will it make you desperately unhappy if I say No?"

"Desperately? . . . My dear, I will not insult either you or myself with a word like that. I can only tell you that if you will marry me it will give me very great happiness."

They passed beneath the arch of the bridge and out into the pale light once more.

"Peter!"

She stood still; and he stopped perforce and turned towards her. She laid both hands upon the fronts of his gown, looking into his face while she searched for the word that should carry her over the last difficult breach.

It was he who found it for her. With a gesture of submission he bared his head and stood gravely, the square cap dangling in his hand.

"*Placetne, magistra?*"

"*Placet.*"

The Proctor, stumping grimly past with averted eyes, reflected that Oxford was losing all sense of dignity. But what could he do? If Senior Members of the University chose to stand—in their gowns, too!—closely and passionately embracing in New College Lane right under the Warden's windows, he was powerless to prevent it. He primly settled his white bands and went upon his walk unheeded; and no hand plucked his velvet sleeve.

BUSMAN'S HONEYMOON

To Muriel St. Clare Byrne, Helen Simpson and Marjorie Barber

Dear Muriel, Helen and Bar,

With what extreme of womanly patience you listened to the tale of *Busman's Honeymoon* while it was being written, the Lord He knoweth. I do not like to think how many times I tired the sun with talking—and if at any time they had told me you were dead, I should easily have believed that I had talked you into your graves. But you have strangely survived to receive these thanks.

You, Muriel, were in some sort a predestined victim, since you wrote with me the play to which this novel is but the limbs and outward flourishes; my debt and your long-suffering are all the greater. You, Helen and Bar, were wantonly sacrificed on the altar of that friendship of which the female sex is said to be incapable; let the lie stick i' the wall!

To all three I humbly bring, I dedicate with tears, this sentimental comedy.

It has been said, by myself and others, that a love-interest is only an intrusion upon a detective story. But to the characters involved, the detective-interest might well seem an irritating intrusion upon their love-story. This book deals with such a situation. It also provides some sort of answer to many kindly inquiries as to how Lord Peter and his Harriet solved their matrimonial problem. If there is but a ha'porth of detection to an intolerable deal of saccharine, let the occasion be the excuse.

Yours in all gratitude,
Dorothy L. Sayers

That will ask some tears in the true performing of it; if I do it, let the audience look to their eyes; I will move storms, I will condole in some measure. . . . I could play Ercles rarely, or a part to tear a cat in, to make all split . . . a lover is more condoling.

—SHAKESPEARE,
A Midsummer Night's Dream

Contents

PROTHALAMION

MARRIAGES

WIMSEY-VANE. On the 8th October, at St. Cross Church, Oxford, Peter Death Bredon Wimsey, second son of the late Gerald Mortimer Bredon Wimsey, 15th Duke of Denver, to Harriet Deborah Vane, only daughter of the late Henry Vane, M.D. of Great Pagford, Herts.

MIRABELLE, COUNTESS OF SEVERN AND THAMES, TO HONORIA LUCASTA, DOWAGER DUCHESS OF DENVER

MY DEAR HONORIA,

So Peter is really married: I have ordered willow-wreaths for half my acquaintance. I understand that it is a deciduous tree; if nothing is available but the bare rods, I shall distribute them all the same, for the better beating of breasts.

Honestly, as one frank old woman to the other, how do you feel about it? A cynic should have cause to be grateful, since to see your amorous sweet devil of a son wedded to an Oxford-Bloomsbury bluestocking should add considerably to the gaiety of the season. I am not too blind to see through Peter, with all his affectations, and if I had been half a century younger I would have married him myself, for the fun of it. But is this girl flesh and blood? You say she is passionately devoted to him, and I know, of course, that she once had a half-baked affair with a poet—but, Heaven deliver us, what's a poet? Something that can't go to bed without making a song about it. Peter wants more than a devoted admirer to hold his hand and recite verses to him; and he has a foolish, pleasant trick of keeping to one woman at a time, which he may find inconvenient in a permanent relationship. Not that many marriages can be called permanent these days, but I can't see Peter exhibiting himself in the Divorce Courts for his own amusement, though, no doubt, if asked to oblige, he would carry it through with an air. (Which reminds me that my idiot great-nephew, Hughie, has bungled matters as usual. Having undertaken to do the thing like a gentleman, he sneaked off to Brighton with a hired nobody, and the Judge wouldn't believe either the hotel bills or the chambermaid—knowing them all too well by sight. So it means starting all over again from the beginning.)

Well, my dear, we shall see what we shall see, and you may be sure I shall do my best for Peter's wife, if only to spite Helen, who will doubtless make everything as unpleasant as possible for her new sister-in-law. Naturally, I pay no attention to her snobbish nonsense about misalliances, which is ridiculous and out-of-date. Compared with the riff-raff we are getting in now from the films and the night-clubs, a country doctor's daughter, even with a poet in her past, is a miracle of respectability. If the young woman has brains and bowels, she will suit well enough. Do you suppose they intend to have any children? Helen will be furious if they do, as she has always counted on Peter's money going to Saint-George. Denver, if I know anything about him, will be more concerned to secure the succession in case Saint-George breaks his neck in that car of his. Whatever they do, somebody will be indignant, so I imagine they will please themselves.

I was sorry I could not come to the reception—you seem to have diddled the Press very neatly—but my asthma has been very bad lately. Still, I must be thankful to have retained my faculties and my sense of humour so long. Tell Peter to bring his Harriet to see me as soon as they return from this mysterious honeymoon of theirs, and believe me, dear Honoria, always (in spite of my venomous old tongue) most affectionately yours,

MIRABELLE SEVERN AND THAMES

Mrs. Chipperly James To Hon. Mrs. Trumpe-Harte

. . . Well, dear, prepare for a shock! Peter Wimsey is married—yes, actually *married*—to that extraordinary young woman who lived with a Bolshevist or a musician or something, and murdered him, or something—I forget exactly, it was all ages ago, and such odd things happen every day, don't they? It seems a sad waste, with all that money—but it does rather go to show, doesn't it, that there is something not quite right about the Wimseys—the third cousin, you know, the one that lives shut up in a little villa at Monte, is *more* than eccentric—and in any case Peter must be forty-five if he's a day. You know, dear, I always thought you were a little unwise to try to get him for Monica, though of course I didn't like to say so when you were working so hard to bring it off. . . .

Mrs. Dalilah Snype to Miss Amaranth Sylvester-Quicke

. . . Of course, *the* sensation is the Wimsey-Vane marriage. It must be a sort of sociological experiment, I should think, because, as *you* know, darling, he is the *world's* chilliest prig and I'm *definitely* sorry for the girl, in spite of the money and the title and everything, because *nothing* would make up for being tied to a chattering icicle in an eyeglass, my dear, *too* weary-making. Not that it's likely to last. . . .

Helen, Duchess of Denver, to Lady Grummidge

MY DEAR MARJORIE,

Thank you for your kind inquiries. Tuesday was indeed a most exhausting day, though I am feeling rather more rested this evening. But it has been a very trying time for all of us. Peter, of course, was just as tiresome as he could be, and that is saying a good deal. First of all, he insisted on being married in church, though, considering everything, I should have thought the Registrar's Office would have been more appropriate. However, we resigned ourselves to St. George's, Hanover Square, and I was prepared to do everything in my power to see that the thing was done properly, if it had to be done at all. But my mother-in-law took it all out of my hands, though I am sure we were distinctly given to understand that the wedding would take place on the day *I* had suggested, that is, next Wednesday. But this, as you will see, was just one of Peter's monkey tricks. I feel the slight *very much*, particularly as we had gone out of our way to be civil to the girl, and had asked her to dinner.

Well! Last Monday evening, when we were down at Denver, we got a wire from Peter, which coolly said, "If you really want to see me married, try St. Cross Church, Oxford, tomorrow at two." I was furious—all that distance and my frock not ready, and to make things worse, Gerald, who had asked sixteen people down for the shooting, laughed like an idiot, and said, "Good for Peter!" He insisted on our both going, just like that, leaving all our guests to look after themselves. I strongly suspect Gerald of having known all about it beforehand, though he swears he didn't. Anyway, Jerry knew all right, and that's why he stayed in London. I am always telling Jerry that his uncle means more to him than his own parents; and I needn't tell *you* that I consider Peter's influence most pernicious for a boy of his age. Gerald, manlike, said Peter had a right to get married when and where he liked; he never considers the embarrassment and discomfort these eccentricities cause to other people.

We went to Oxford and found the place—an obscure little church in a side-street, very gloomy and damp-looking. It turned out that the bride (who, *mercifully*, has no living relations) was being married from a Women's College, of all places. I was relieved to see Peter in proper morning dress; I really had begun to think he meant to get married in a cap and gown. Jerry was there as best man, and my mother-in-law arrived in great state, beaming away as though they had all done something clever. And they had raked out old Uncle Paul Delagardie, creaking with arthritis, poor old creature, with a gardenia in his buttonhole and trying to look sprightly, which at his age is disgusting. There were all kinds of queer people in the church—practically none of our own friends, but that ridiculous old Climpson woman, and some hangers-on that Peter had picked up in the course of his "cases," and several policemen. Charles and Mary appeared at the last moment, and Charles pointed out to me a man in a Salvation Army uniform, who he *said* was a retired burglar; but I can scarcely believe this, even of Peter.

The bride came attended by the most incredible assortment of bridesmaids—all female dons!—and an odd, dark woman to give her away, who was supposed to be the Head of the College. I am thankful to say, considering her past history, that Harriet (as I suppose I must now call her) had enough sense of propriety not to get herself up in white satin and orange-blossom; but I could not help thinking that a plain costume would have been more suitable than cloth of gold. I can see that I shall have to speak to her presently about her clothes, but I am afraid she will be difficult. I have never seen anybody look so indecently triumphant—I suppose, in a way, she had a right to; one must admit that she has played her cards very cleverly. Peter was as white as a sheet; I thought he was going to be sick. Probably he was realizing what he had let himself in for. Nobody can say that I did not do my best to open his eyes. They were married in the old, coarse Prayer-book form, and the bride said "Obey"—I take this to be their idea of humor, for she looks as obstinate as a mule.

There was a great deal of promiscuous kissing in the vestry, and then all the oddities were bundled into cars (at Peter's expense, no doubt) and we started back to

Town, closely pursued by the local newspaper men. We went to my mother-in-law's little house—*all* of us, including the policemen and the ex-burglar—and after a wedding-breakfast (which I must admit was very good) Uncle Delagardie made a speech, garnished with flowers of French eloquence. There were a lot of presents, some of them very absurd; the ex-burglar's was a thick book of ranting and vulgar hymns! Presently the bride and bridegroom vanished, and we waited a long time for them, till my mother-in-law came down, all smiles, to announce that they had been gone half an hour, leaving no address. At this moment, I have no idea *where* they are, nor has anybody.

The whole business has left us in a most painful and ridiculous position. I consider it a disgraceful ending to a most disastrous affair, and it is no consolation to think that I shall have to produce this appalling young woman as my sister-in-law. Mary's policeman was bad enough, but he is, at any rate, quiet and well behaved; whereas, with Peter's wife, we may look for notoriety, if not for open scandal, from one day to another. However, we must put as good a face on it as we can; I wouldn't say as much as I *have* said to anybody but you.

With all gratitude for your sympathy,

Yours affectionately,

HELEN DENVER

MR. MERVYN BUNTER TO MRS. BUNTER, SENR.

DEAR MOTHER,

I write from an "unknown destination" in the country, hoping this finds you as it leaves me. Owing to a trifling domestic catastrophe, I have only a candle to see by, so trust you will excuse my bad writing.

Well, Mother, we were happily married this morning and a very pretty wedding it was. I only wish you could have been present at his lordship's kind invitation, but as I said to him, at eighty-seven some physical infirmities are only to be expected. I hope your leg is better.

As I told you in my last, we were all set to escape Her Grace's interfering ways, and so we did, everything going off like clockwork. Her new ladyship, Miss Vane that was, went down to Oxford the day before, and his lordship with Lord Saint-George and myself followed in the evening, staying at the Mitre. His lordship spoke very kindly to me indeed, alluding to my twenty years' service, and trusting that I should find myself comfortable in the new household. I told him I hoped I knew when I was well suited, and should endeavor to give satisfaction. I am afraid I said more than was my place, for his lordship was sincerely affected and told me not to be a bloody fool. I took the liberty to prescribe a dose of bromide and got him to sleep at last, when I could persuade his young lordship to leave him alone. Considerate is not the term I would employ of Lord Saint-George, but some of his teasing must be put down to the champagne.

His lordship appeared calm and resolute in the morning, which was a great relief to my mind, there being a good deal to do. A number of humble friends arriving by special transport, it was my task to see that they were made comfortable and not permitted to lose themselves.

Well, dear Mother, we partook of a light and early lunch, and then I had to get their lordships dressed and down to the church. My own gentleman was as quiet as a lamb and gave no trouble, not even his usual joking, but Lord Saint-George was in tearing high spirits and I had my hands full with him. He pretended five times that he had lost the ring, and just as we were setting out he mislaid it in earnest; but his lordship, with his customary detective ability, discovered it for him and took charge of it personally. In spite of this misadventure, I had them at the chancel steps dead on time, and I will say they both did me credit. I do not know where you would beat his young lordship for handsome looks, though to my mind there is no comparison which is the finer gentleman.

The lady did not keep us waiting, I am thankful to say, and very well she looked, all in gold, with a beautiful bouquet of chrysanthemums. She is not pretty, but what you would call striking-looking, and I am sure she had no eyes for anyone but his lordship. She was attended by four ladies from the College, not dressed as bridesmaids, but all neat and ladylike in appearance. His lordship was very serious all through the ceremony.

Then we all went back to a reception at Her Grace the Dowager's Town house. I was very much pleased with her new ladyship's behavior towards the guests, which was frank and friendly to all stations, but, of course, his lordship would not choose any but a lady in all respects. I do not anticipate any trouble with her.

After the reception, we got the bride and bridegroom quietly away by the back door, having incarcerated all the newspaper reporters in the little drawing-room. And now, dear Mother, I must tell you . . .

MISS LETITIA MARTIN, DEAN OF SHREWSBURY COLLEGE, OXFORD, TO MISS JOAN EDWARDS, LECTURER AND TUTOR IN SCIENCE IN THE SAME FOUNDATION

DEAR TEDDY,

Well! we have had our wedding—quite a red-letter day in College history! Miss Lydgate, Miss de Vine, little Chilperic and yours truly were bridesmaids, with the Warden to give the bride away. No, my dear, we did *not* array ourselves in fancy costumes. Personally, I thought we should have looked more symmetrical in academic dress, but the bride said she thought "poor Peter" would be *quite* sufficiently harrowed by headlines as it was. So we just turned up in our Sunday best, and I wore my new furs. It took all our united efforts to *put* Miss de Vine's hair up and *keep* it put.

The Denver family were all there; the Dowager is a

darling, like a small eighteenth-century marquise, but the Duchess looked a tartar, *very* cross, and as stiff as a poker. It was great fun seeing her try to patronize the Warden—needless to say, she got no change out of *her!* However, the Warden had her turn to be disconcerted in the vestry. She was advancing upon the bridegroom with outstretched hand and a speech of congratulation, when he firmly took and kissed her, and *what* the speech was to have been we shall now never know! He then proceeded to kiss us all round (brave man!) and Miss Lydgate was so overcome by her feelings that she returned the salute good and hearty. After that, the best man—(the good-looking Saint-George boy)—started in, so there was quite an orgy of embraces, and we had to put Miss de Vine's hair up again. The bridegroom gave each bridesmaid a lovely crystal decanter and set of cut glasses (for sherry-parties, bless his frivolous heart!) and the Warden got a check for £250 for the Latymer Scholarship, which I call handsome.

However, in my excitement I am forgetting all about the bride. I had never imagined that Harriet Vane could look so impressive. I'm always apt to think of her, still, as a gawky and dishevelled First-Year, all bones, with a discontented expression. Yesterday she looked like a Renaissance portrait stepped out of its frame. I put it down first of all to the effect of gold lamé, but on consideration, I think it was probably due to "lerve." There was something rather splendid about the way those two claimed one another, as though nothing and nobody else mattered or even existed; he was the only bridegroom I have ever seen who looked as though he knew exactly what he was doing and meant to do it.

On the way up to Town—oh! by the way, Lord Peter put his foot *resolutely* down on Mendelssohn and *Lohengrin*, and we were played out with Bach—the Duke was mercifully taken away from his cross Duchess and handed over to me to entertain. He is handsome and stupid in a county-family kind of way, and looks rather like Henry VIII, de-bloated and de-bearded and brought up to date. He asked me, a little anxiously, whether I thought "the girl" was really keen on his brother, and when I said I was sure of it, confided to me that he had never been able to make Peter out, and had never expected him to settle down, and hoped it would turn out all right, what? Somewhere in the dim recesses of his mind, I think he has a lurking suspicion that Brother Peter may have that little extra something he hasn't got himself, and that it might even be a good thing to have, if one didn't have to consider the County.

The reception at the Dowager's was great fun—and for once, at a wedding, one got enough to eat!—and drink! The people who came off badly were the unhappy reporters, who by this time had got wind of something, and turned up in battalions. They were firmly collared at the doors by two gigantic footmen, and penned up in a room, with the promise that "his lordship would see them in a few moments." Eventually "his lordship" did go to them—not Lord Peter, but Lord Wellwater, the F.O. man, who delivered to them at great length a highly important statement about Abyssinia, to which they didn't dare not listen. By the time he had finished, *our* lord and lady had sneaked out by the back door, and all that was left them was a roomful of wedding-presents and the remains of the cake. However, the Dowager saw them and was quite nice to them, so they tooled off, fairly happy, but without any photographs or any information about the honeymoon. As a matter of fact, I don't believe anybody, except the Dowager, knows where the bride and bridegroom really have gone to.

Well—that was that; and I do hope they'll be most frightfully happy. Miss de Vine thinks there is too much intelligence on both sides—but I tell her not to be such a confirmed pessimist. I know heaps of couples who are both as stupid as owls and not happy at all—so it doesn't really follow, one way or the other, does it?

Yours ever,
LETITIA MARTIN

EXTRACTS FROM THE DIARY OF HONORIA LUCASTA, DOWAGER DUCHESS OF DENVER

20 MAY.

Peter rang up this morning, terribly excited, poor darling, to say that he and Harriet were really and truly engaged, and that the ridiculous Foreign Office had ordered him straight off to Rome again after breakfast—so like them—you'd think they did it on purpose. What with exasperation and happiness, he sounded perfectly distracted. Desperately anxious I should get hold of H. and make her understand she was welcome—poor child, it is hard for her, left here to face us all, when she can scarcely feel sure of herself or anything yet. Have written to her at Oxford, telling her as well as I could how very, very glad I was she was making Peter so happy, and asking when she would be in Town, so that I could go and see her. Dear Peter! Hope and pray she really loves him in the way he needs; shall know in a minute when I see her.

21 MAY.

Was reading *The Stars Look Down* (Mem. very depressing, and not what I expected from the title—think I must have had a Christmas carol in mind, but remember now it has something to do with the Holy Sepulchre—must ask Peter and make sure) after tea, when Franklin announced "Miss Vane." Was so surprised and delighted, I jumped up quite forgetting poor Ahasuerus, who was asleep on my knee, and was dreadfully affronted. I said, "My dear, how sweet of you to come"—she looked so different I shouldn't have known her—but of course it was 5½ years ago, and nobody can look her best in the dock at that dreary Old Bailey. She walked straight up to me, rather as if she was facing a firing-squad, and said abruptly, in that queer deep voice of hers, "Your letter was so kind—I didn't quite know how to answer it, so I thought I'd better come. Do you honestly not mind too much, about Peter and me? Because I love him quite dreadfully, and there's just nothing to be done about it." So I said, "Oh, do please go on loving him, because he wants it so much, and he really is the dearest of all my children, only it doesn't do for parents to say so—but *now* I *can* say it to *you*, and I'm so glad about it." So I kissed her, and Ahasuerus was so furious that he ran *all* his claws *hard* into her legs and I apologized and smacked him and we sat down on the sofa, and she said, "Do you know, I've been saying to myself all the way up from Oxford, 'If only I can face her and it really is all right, I shall have somebody I can talk to about Peter.' That's the one thing that kept me from turning back half-way." Poor child, that really was all she wanted—she was quite in a daze, because apparently it all happened quite late on Sunday evening, and they sat up half the night, kissing one another madly in a punt, poor things, and then he had to go, making no arrangements for anything, and if it hadn't been for his signet-ring that he put on her hand all in a hurry at the last moment it might have been all a dream. And after holding out against him all these years, she'd given way all of a piece, like falling down a well, and didn't seem to know what to do with herself. Said she couldn't remember ever having been absolutely and shatteringly happy since she was a small child, and it made her feel quite hollow inside. On inquiry, I found she must be *literally* hollow inside, because as far as I could make out she hadn't eaten or slept to speak of since Sunday. Sent Franklin for sherry and biscuits, and made her—H., I mean—stay to dinner. Talked Peter till I could almost *hear* him saying, "Mother dear, you are having an orgy" (or is it orgie?). . . . H. caught sight of that David Bellezzi photograph of Peter which he dislikes so much, and I asked what she thought of it. She said, "Well, it's a nice English gentleman, but it isn't either the lunatic, the lover or the poet, is it?" Agree with her. (Can't think why I keep the thing about, except to please David.) Brought out family album. *Thankful* to say she didn't go all broody and possessive over Peter kicking baby legs on a rug—can't stand maternal young women, though P. really a very comic infant with his hair in a tuft, but he controls it very well now, so why rake up the past? She instantly seized on the ones Peter calls "Little Mischief" and "The Lost Chord" and said, "Somebody who understood him took those—was it Bunter?"—which looked like second sight. Then she confessed she felt horribly guilty about Bunter and hoped his feelings weren't going to be hurt, because if he gave notice it would break Peter's heart. Told her quite frankly it would depend entirely on her, and I felt sure Bunter would never go unless he was pushed out. H. said, "But you don't think I'd do that. That's just it. I don't want Peter to lose *anything*." She looked quite distressed, and we both wept a little, till it suddenly struck us as funny that we should both be crying over Bunter, who would have been shocked out of his wits if he'd known it. So we cheered up and I gave her the photographs and asked what plans they had, if they had got so far. She said P. didn't know when he'd be back, but she thought she'd better finish her present book quickly, so as to be ready when the time came and have enough money for clothes. Asked if I could tell her the right tailor—shows sense, and would pay for really *inspired* dressing, but must be careful what I advise, as find I have *no* idea what people make by writing books. Ignorant and stupid of me—so important not to hurt her pride. . . . Altogether most reassuring evening. Telephoned long enthusiastic wire to Peter before bed. Hope Rome is not too stuffy and hot, as heat does not suit him.

24 MAY.

Harriet to tea. Helen came in—very rude and tiresome when I introduced Harriet. Said, "Oh, really! and where *is* Peter? Run off abroad again? How absurd and unaccountable he is!" Went on to talk Town and Country solidly, saying every so often, "Do you know the so-and-so's, Miss Vane? No? They're *very* old friends of Peter's." "Do you hunt, Miss Vane? No? What a pity! I do hope Peter doesn't mean to give it up. It does him good to get out." Harriet very sensibly said "No" and "Certainly" to everything, without any explanations or apologies, which are always so dangerous (dear Disraeli!). I asked Harriet how the book was getting on and if Peter's suggestions had helped. Helen said, "Oh, yes, you write, don't you?" as if she'd never heard of her, and asked what the title was, so that she could get it from the library. Harriet said, quite gravely, "That is very kind of you, but do let me send you one—I am allowed six free copies, you know." First sign of temper, but I don't blame her. Apologized for Helen after she'd gone, and said I was glad my *second* son was marrying for love. Fear my vocabulary remains hopelessly old-fashioned in spite of carefully chosen reading. (Must remember to ask Franklin what I have done with *The Stars Look Down*.)

1 JUNE.

Letter from Peter, about taking the Belchesters' house in Audley Square from Michaelmas and furnishing it. H., thank Heaven, ready to prefer eighteenth-century elegance to chromium tubes. H. alarmed by size of house, but relieved she is not called upon to "make a home" for Peter. I explained it was his business to make the home and take his bride to it—privilege now apparently confined to aristocracy and clergymen, who can't choose their vicarages, poor dears, usually much too big for them. H. pointed out that Royal brides always seemed to be expected to run about choosing cretonnes, but I said this was duty they owed to penny papers which like domestic women—Peter's wife fortunately without duties. Must see about housekeeper for them—someone capable—Peter insistent wife's work must not be interrupted by uproars in servants' hall.

5 JUNE.

Sudden outburst of family feeling in most tiresome form. Gerald first—worried of course by Helen—to ask if girl is presentable and has she got modern ideas, meaning children of course, that is to say not wanting children. Told Gerald to mind his own business, which is Saint-George. Next Mary, to say Small Peter sickening for chicken-pox and will this girl really look after Peter? Told her, Peter perfectly capable of looking after himself, and probably not wanting wife with head stuffed with chicken-pox and best way to boil fish. Found beautiful Chippendale mirror and set tapestry chairs at Harrison's.

25 JUNE.

Love's dream troubled by solemn interview with Murbles about Settlements—appalling long document providing for every conceivable and inconceivable situation and opening up ramifications into everybody's death and remarriage, "covered," as Murbles observes, "by THE WILL" (in capitals). Had not realized Peter was doing so well out of the London property. H. more and more uncomfortable at every clause. Rescued her in depressed state and took her to tea at Rumpelmeyer's. She finally told me, "Ever since I left College, I've never spent a penny I hadn't earned." Said to her, "Well, my dear, tell Peter what you feel, but do remember he's just as vain and foolish as most men and not a chameleon to smell any sweeter for being trodden on." On consideration, think I meant "camomile" (Shakespeare? Must ask Peter.) Considered writing to P. about this, but better not—young people must fight their own battles.

10 AUGUST.

Returned from country yesterday to find question of Settlements settled. H. showed me three pages of intelligent sympathy from P., beginning, "Of course I had foreseen the difficulty," and ending, "Either your pride or mine will have to be sacrificed—I can only appeal to your generosity to let it be yours." H. said, "Peter can always see the difficulty—that's what's so disarming." Agree heartily—can't stand people who "can't see what the fuss is about." H. now meekly prepared to accept suitable income, but has solaced pride by ordering two dozen silk shirts in Burlington Arcade, and paying cash for them. Evinces dogged determination to do thing properly while she is about it—has grasped that if Helen can pick holes, Peter will suffer for it, and resolutely applies intelligence to task. Something apparently to be said for education—teaches grasp of facts. H. grappling with fact of P.'s position—interesting to watch. Long letter from Peter, very dubious about League of Nations, and sending detailed instructions about library shelving and a William-and-Mary bedstead, also irritable about being left in Rome, "like a plumber, to stop diplomatic leaks." English very unpopular in Italy, but P. had soothing discussion with the Pope about a historical manuscript—must have made a pleasant change for both of them.

16 AUGUST.

Harriet, who has been down to the country to look at a water-mill (something to do with her new book), said she had motored back through Herts, and paid a visit to her old home at Great Pagford. Talked about her people—quiet country doctor and wife. Father made quite good income, but never thought of saving anything (thought he'd live forever, I suppose)—very anxious, however, H. should have good education—just as well, as things turned out. H. said her own childish ambition had been to make enough money to buy quaint old farmhouse called Talboys in next village. Had seen it again on her trip—Elizabethan, very pretty. Said how differently things turned out from what one expected. I said it sounded just the sort of place she and P. would want for weekend cottage. H. rather taken aback—said, Yes, she supposed so. Left it at that.

19 AUGUST.

Found the exact right hangings for the bedstead. Helen says all that kind of thing highly insanitary. Says Gerald has had bad reports of the partridges and thinks country going to the dogs.

20 AUGUST.

H. has written to Peter about buying Talboys. Explained she thought Peter "liked giving people things." So he does, poor boy! Facts now apparently faced once for all—looks as though he was going to get five-and-a-half years' arrears of patience repaid in a lump. Said mildly I thought nothing would give P. greater pleasure. When she had gone, danced quiet jig in drawing-room, to surprise of Franklin (silly woman—she ought to know me by this time).

21 AUGUST.

Harriet's book finished and sent to publisher. This unfortunately leaves her mind free to worry about Abyssinia, so tiresome. Convinced civilization will perish and Peter never be seen again. Like cat on hot bricks saying she wasted five years of P.'s life and can't forgive herself and it's no good saying he's over age because he has M.I. written all over his conscience and if he was seventy he might still be gassed or bombed in an air-raid. Earnestly hope we shall *not* have another war with meat-coupons and no sugar and people being killed—ridiculous and unnecessary. Wonder whether Mussolini's mother spanked him too much or too little—you never know, these psychological days. Can distinctly remember spanking Peter, but it doesn't seem to have warped him much, so psychologists very likely all wrong.

24 AUGUST.

Peter has instructed agent to negotiate for Talboys with present owner—man called Noakes. His letter to me very discreet—but he *is* delighted. Situation in Rome apparently clearing, so far as his own job is concerned. H. still uneasy about prospects of war.

30 AUGUST.

Harriet completely exalted by letter from Peter saying, "Even if it is the twilight of the world, before night falls I will sleep in your arms." . . . (How well I recognize the old, magniloquent Peter of twenty years back) . . . and adding that his plumbing is done and he has asked for his papers, which is more to the point.

4 SEPTEMBER.

They have made a good job of the chandeliers for the hall and great saloon. Gerald says they can have the tapestries from the Blue Room—they will look well on the upper landing, I think—have sent them to be overhauled and cleaned, which they badly need. (Peter would say, so do my pronouns, but I know quite well what I mean.) Ahasuerus sick in Franklin's bedroom—funny how fond he is of her, seeing she doesn't really like cats.

7 SEPTEMBER.

Peter wires he will be back next week. Harriet insisted on taking me out to dinner and standing me champagne. Said, hilariously, her last opportunity, as Peter doesn't care for champagne. Condoled with her on loss of freedom in brief and witty speech (brief for me, anyway). Should like to see Helen taking me out to dinner and listening to a speech.

14 SEPTEMBER.

Peter came back. He dined somewhere with Harriet and then came round to see me—alone, so nice of them, because of course I had said, bring her too. He looks thin and tired, but I think that must be Mussolini or the weather or something, because he obviously has no doubts about anything (except the League, naturally)—and it struck me so much that he sat absolutely quiet for nearly two hours without fidgeting or saying very much, so unusual, because as a rule peas on a hot shovel are nothing to it. Very sweet about what I had done as regards the house. Will leave it to me to engage staff, as Harriet not experienced. They will need about eight servants, besides Bunter and the housekeeper—so I shall have a nice busy time.

15 SEPTEMBER.

Harriet came round this morning to show me her ring—big solitaire ruby—old Abrahams had it cut and set specially to instructions. Poor H. laughed at herself, because when Peter gave it to her yesterday she was looking at *him* and ten minutes afterwards, when challenged, couldn't even tell him the color of the stone. Said she was afraid she never would learn to behave like other people, but Peter had only said it was the first time his features had ever been prized above rubies. Peter joined us at lunch—also Helen, who demanded to see the ruby and said, sharply, "Good Heavens! I hope it's insured." To do her justice, I can't see that she could have found anything nastier to say if she'd thought it out with both hands for a fortnight. She then went on to say she supposed they intended to get married quietly before the Registrar, but Peter said, No, he would as soon be married in a railway-station waiting-room, and that if Helen had developed religious scruples she need not lend her countenance to the proceedings. So Helen said, "Oh, I see—St. George's Hanover Square, I suppose"—and went on to arrange everything for them, including the date, the parson, the guests and the music. When she got to "The voice that Breathed o'er Eden," Peter said, "Oh, for God's sake, cut out the League of Nations!" and he and Harriet began to invent rude rhymes, which left Helen rather out of it, as she never was good at drawing-room games.

16 SEPTEMBER.

Helen obligingly presented us with a copy of the new form of marriage service, with all the vulgar bits left out—which was asking for trouble. Peter very funny about it—said he knew all about the "procreation of children," in theory though not in practice, but that the "increase of mankind" by any other method sounded too advanced for him, and that, if he ever did indulge in such dangerous amusements, he would, with his wife's permission, stick to the old-fashioned procedure. He also said that, as for the "gift of continence," he wouldn't have it as a gift, and had no objection to admitting as much. At this point, Helen got up and left the house, leaving P. and Harriet to wrangle over the word "obey." P. said he would consider it a breach of manners to give orders to his wife, but H. said, Oh, no—he'd give orders fast enough if the place was on fire or a tree falling down and he wanted her to stand clear. P. said, in that case they ought both to say "obey," but it would be too much jam for the reporters. Left them to fight it out. When I came back, found Peter had consented to be obeyed on condition he might "endow" and not "share" his worldly goods. Shocking victory of sentiment over principle.

18 SEPTEMBER.

Must really say "*Damn!*" Disgusting newspapers have raked up all that old story about Harriet and Philip Boyes. Peter *furious*. Harriet says, "Only to be expected." Was horribly afraid she might offer to release P. from engagement, but she controlled herself nobly—expect she realizes it would nearly kill him to go through that again. Think it is probably fault of that Sylvester-Quicke woman who tried so hard to get hold of Peter—have always suspected her of writing gossip-column for Sunday papers. Helen (coming down strong, but heavy-footed, on family side) determined that best plan is to have colossal Society wedding and face it out. Has decided, for reasons best known to herself, 16th October most suitable date. Kindly undertaken choice of bridesmaids—our own friends, as H.'s friends "obviously impossible"—and offered loan of house for reception—also ten villas belonging to impoverished nobility for honeymoon. Peter, losing patience, said, "Who's getting married, Helen? You or we?" Gerald tried to take Head of Family line—well snubbed all round. Helen again gave her views, and ended by saying, "Then I take it the 16th is settled." Peter said, "Take what you like." Helen said she would take her departure till he chose to realize she was only doing her *best* for them—and Gerald looked so imploring that Peter apologized for incivility.

20 SEPTEMBER.

Agent reports price for Talboys settled. Many alterations and repairs needed, but fabric sound. Agreement to purchase with immediate possession—present owner to be left there till after honeymoon, when Peter will go down and see what they want done and send the workmen in.

25 SEPTEMBER.

Situation, what with Helen and newspapers, becoming impossible. Peter upset at idea of St. George's and general hullaballoo. Harriet suffering from return of inferiority complex which she tries hard not to show. Have held up all invitations.

27 SEPTEMBER.

Peter came to me and said that if this went on they would both be driven mad. He and H. have decided to do the whole thing quietly, without telling anybody except their own personal friends. Small wedding at Oxford, reception *here,* honeymoon in some peaceful spot in the country. I have readily agreed to help them.

30 SEPTEMBER.

They have fixed up with Noakes to have honeymoon at Talboys, nobody to know anything about it. Apparently N. can clear out at short notice and lend all furniture, &c. I asked, "What about DRAINS?" Peter said, Damn drains—no drains (to speak of) at the Hall when he was a boy (well I remember it!). Wedding (Archbp's licence) on the 8th October and let Helen think what she likes till last moment—also newspapers. Harriet very much relieved. Peter adds, anyway, honeymoon in hotels disgusting—own roof (especially if Elizabethan) much more suited to English gentleman. Fierce bustle about wedding-dress—Worth's—period gown in stiff gold brocade, long sleeves, square neck, off-the-face head-dress, no jewels except my long ear-rings that belonged to great-aunt Delagardie. (*N.B.*—Publisher must have come well up to scratch on new book.) H. to be married from her College (rather nice, I think)—tremendous wirings and swearings to secrecy. Bunter to go ahead and see that all is in order at Talboys.

2 OCTOBER.

We have had to cancel Bunter. He is being dogged by pressmen. Found one forcing his way into Peter's flat via service lift. B. narrowly escaped summons for assault. P. said, better take Talboys (including drains) on trust. Payment completed, and Noakes says he will have everything ready—quite accustomed to letting house for summer holidays, so it should be all right—Helen agitated because no invitations yet sent out for 16th. Told her I believed 16th not yet officially settled (!) Helen asked, Why the delay? Had Peter got cold feet, or was that girl playing him up again? . . . I suggested, wedding their own affair, both being well over age. . . . They are taking no servants but Bunter, who is a host in himself, and can do all they want, with local help. I fancy Harriet rather shrinks from starting off at once with a strange staff, and Peter wants to spare her. And Town maids are always a perfect nuisance in the country. If Harriet can once establish herself with Bunter, she will have no further trouble with domestics!

4 OCTOBER.

Went round to Peter's flat to advise about settings for some stones he picked up in Italy. While there, registered post brought large, flat envelope—Harriet's writing. Wondered what it was she wanted to send and not bring! (Inquisitive me!) Watched Peter open it, while pretending to examine zircon (such a lovely color!). He flushed up in that absurd way he has when anybody says anything rather personal to him, and stood staring at the thing till I got quite wound up, and said, "What is it?" He said, in an odd sort of voice, "The bride's gift to the bridegroom." It had been worrying me for some time how she'd grapple with that, because there isn't an awful lot, *really*, one can give a very well-off man, unless one is frightfully well off oneself, and the wrong thing is worse than nothing, but all the same, nobody really wants to be kindly told that they can't bring a better gift than their sweet selves—very pretty but so patronizing and Lord of Burleigh—and after all, we all have human instincts, and giving people things is one of them. So I dashed up to look, and it was a letter written on a single sheet in a very beautiful seventeenth-century hand. Peter said, "The funny thing is that the catalogue was sent to me in Rome, and I wired for this, and was ridiculously angry to learn it had been sold." I said, "But you don't collect manuscripts." And he said, "No, but I wanted this for Harriet." And he turned it over, and I could read the signature, "John Donne," and that explained a lot, because of course Peter has always been queer about Donne. It seems it's a very beautiful letter from D. to a parishioner—Lady Somebody—about Divine and human love. I was trying to read it, only I never can make out that old-fashioned kind of writing (wonder what Helen will make of it—no doubt she'll think a gold cigarette-lighter would have been much more suitable)—when I found Peter had got on the phone, and was saying, "Listen, dear heart," in a voice I'd never heard him use in his life. So I shot out of the room, and ran slap into Bunter, just coming in from the hall-door. Afraid Peter is getting out of hand, because when he came out after telephoning, Bunter reported that he had "booked the best room at the Lord Warden, my lord, for the night of the 16th, and reserved cabin and train accommodation for Mentone as instructed." P. asked, were the hell-hounds on the trail? B. said, Yes—leading hell-hound had approached him as expected with pump working full blast. Had asked, Why Lord

Warden and not night boat or aeroplane? B. had replied, Lady a martyr to sea-and-air-sickness. Hound appeared satisfied and tipped B. 10*s.*, which B. says he will take liberty of forwarding to Prisoners' Aid Society. I said, "Really, Peter!" but he said, Why shouldn't he arrange continental trip for deserving couple? and posted off reservations to Miss Climpson, for benefit of tubercular accountant and wife in reduced circumstances. (Query: How does one reduce a circumstance?)

5 OCTOBER.

Worth has made magnificent effort and delivered dress. Few select friends invited to see trousseau—including Miss Climpson, miraculously reduced to *speechlessness* by Peter's gift of mink cloak—950 guineas admittedly perhaps a trifle extravagant, but his *sole* contribution, and he looked as scared and guilty when he presented it as he did when he was a small boy and his father caught him with his pocket full of rabbits after a night out with that rascally old poacher Merryweather he took such a fancy to—and *how* that man's cottage did *smell!* But it *is* a lovely cloak, and H. hadn't the heart to say more than, "Oh, Mr. Rochester!"—in fun, and meaning Jane Eyre, who I always think behaved so ungraciously to that poor man—so gloomy to have your bride, however bigamous, insisting on grey alpaca or merino or whatever it was, and damping to a lover's feelings. . . . Hell-hound's paragraph in *Morning Star*—discreetly anonymous but quite unmistakable. Helen rang up to know if it was true. I replied, with exactness, that it must be all invention! In evening, took Peter and Harriet to Cheyne Walk to dine with Paul—who insists on coming to wedding, arthritis or no arthritis. Noticed unusual constraint between P. and H., who had been all right when I saw them off to dinner and theater last night. Paul gave one look at them, and started off to chatter about his eternal *cloisonné* and the superiority of naturally matured French wines over port. Uncomfortable evening, with everybody unlike themselves. At last, Paul sent P. and H. off by themselves in a taxi, saying he wanted to talk business with me—obvious excuse. I asked, did he think anything was wrong? Paul said, "*Au contraire, ma soeur, c'est nous qui sommes de trop. Il arrive toujours le moment où l'on apprend à distinguer entre embrasser et baiser*"—adding with one of his grins, "I was wondering how long Peter would last before he let the bars down—he's his father all over again, with a touch of myself, Honoria, with a touch of myself!" Couldn't waste time and breath being annoyed with Paul—who has always been the complete polygamist—and so was Peter's father, of course, dearly as I loved him—so I said, "Yes, but, Paul, do you think Harriet—?" Paul said, "Bah! the wine she drinks is made of grapes. *Il y a des femmes qui ont le génie*—" I really could *not* stand Paul on *le génie de l'amour*, because he goes on and *on*, getting more and more conscientiously French every moment, with illustrative anecdotes from his own career, and anyway, he's only as much French as I am—exactly one-eighth—so I told him hastily I was sure his diagonal was the right one (wonder whether I meant "angle" or "diagnosis"), and I expect it is—have never known Paul mistaken about the progress of a love-affair. Realize that this explains why he and Harriet have always got on so well together, though one would never have expected it, considering her reserve and his usual taste in women. Suggested to Paul it was time he went to bed; so he said rather dismally, "Yes, Honoria—I'm getting very old and my bones ache. My sins are deserting me, and if I could only have my time over again I'd take care to commit more of them. Confound Peter! *Il ne sait pas vivre. Mais je voudrais bien être dans ses draps.*" "You'll be in your own winding-sheet soon," I said, very crossly; "no wonder Peter calls you Uncle Pandarus, you evil old wretch." Paul said, "Well, you can't deny I had him taught his job, and he's no disgrace to either of us." There was no answer to that, so I came away. . . . Tried *The Stars Look Down* again, and found it full of most unpleasant people. . . . The fact is, one never really *visual-*

izes one's own son. . . . But I needn't have been so cross with Paul.

7 OCTOBER.

Harriet came to see me before starting for Oxford—very nice to me. I think she will give Peter *all* he wants—yes, I really do. If anybody can. . . . Felt depressed, all the same, for nearly half an hour. . . . Later on, while coping with preparations for wedding-breakfast—all made more difficult by need for secrecy—interrupted by Peter on phone, gone suddenly all fractious because it had rained in the night and roads would be slippery, and convinced Harriet would have a skid and be killed on way to Oxford. Begged him not to behave like a half-wit and said, if he wanted healthy occupation he could come and help Franklin wash all the ornaments out of drawing-room cabinets. He didn't come—but Jerry did, in high spirits at idea of being best man, and broke a Dresden shepherdess.

LATER.

Peter and Jerry got (thank goodness!) safely out of the way to Oxford. Preparations completed and all wished-for guests summoned and transport arranged for the impecunious. . . . In evening, furious trunk-call from Helen at Denver, having had wire from Peter and demanding what we meant by inconsiderate behavior. Took great pleasure in telling her (at considerable length and her expense) nothing to thank but her own tactlessness.

8 OCTOBER.

Peter's wedding-day. Too exhausted to do more than put down that it all went off very well. H. looked genuinely lovely, like a ship coming into harbor with everything shining and flags flying at wherever modern ships do fly flags—Peter terribly white, poor darling, like the day he had his first watch, and could hardly bear himself for fear it would come to pieces in his hands or turn out not to be real, or something—but he pulled himself together to be specially nice to all the guests (believe if he were in Inquisition he would exert social talents to entertain executioners). . . . Got back to Town at 5:30 (Peter's face a study when he realized he had to go 60 miles over crowded roads in a closed car with somebody else driving!—but one really couldn't let him drive H. back in the open Daimler, all in wedding-garments and a top-hat!) . . . Got them smuggled out of the house at a quarter to 7—Bunter was waiting for them with the car on the far side of the Park. . . .

11 P.M.

Hope all is really well with them—must stop now and try to get some sleep or shall be a rag in the morning. Find *The Stars Look Down* not quite soothing enough for a bed-book —will fall back on *Through the Looking-Glass*.

CHAPTER I

NEW-WEDDED LORD

I agree with Dryden, that "Marriage is a noble daring."

—SAMUEL JOHNSON, *TABLE TALK*

Mr. Mervyn Bunter, patiently seated in the Daimler on the far side of Regent's Park, reflected that time was getting on. Packed in eiderdowns in the back of the car was a case containing two and a half dozen of vintage port, and he was anxious about it. Great speed would render the wine undrinkable for a fortnight; excessive speed would render it undrinkable for six months. He was anxious about the arrangements—or the lack of them—at Talboys. He hoped everything would be found in good order when they arrived—otherwise, his lady and gentleman might get nothing to eat till goodness knew when. True, he had brought ample supplies from Fortnum's, but suppose there were no knives or forks or plates available. He wished he could have gone ahead, as originally instructed, to see to things. Not but what his lordship was always ready to put up with what couldn't be helped; but it was unsuitable that his lordship should be called on to put up with anything—besides, the lady was still, to some extent, an unknown factor. What his lordship had had to put up with from *her* during the past five or six years, only his lordship knew, but Mr. Bunter could guess. True, the lady seemed now to be in a very satisfactory way of amendment; but it was yet to be ascertained what her conduct would be under the strain of trivial inconvenience. Mr. Bunter was professionally accustomed to judge human beings by their behavior, not in great crises, but in the minor adjustments of daily life. He had seen one lady threatened with dismissal from his lordship's service (including all emoluments and the enjoyment of an *appartement meublé*, Ave. Kléber) for having, in his presence, unreasonably lost her temper with a lady's maid: but wives were not subject to peremptory dismissal. Mr. Bunter was anxious, also, about how things were going at the Dowager's; he did not really believe that anything could be suitably organized or carried out without his assistance.

He was unspeakably relieved to see the taxi arrive and to assure himself that there was no newspaper man perched on the spare wheel, or lurking in a following vehicle.

"Here we are, Bunter. All serene? Good man. I'll drive. Sure you won't be cold, Harriet?"

Mr. Bunter tucked a rug about the bride's knees.

"Your lordship will bear in mind that we are conveying the port?"

"I will go as gingerly as if it were a baby in arms. What's the matter with the rug?"

"A few grains of cereal, my lord. I have taken the liberty of removing approximately a pound and three-quarters from among the hand-luggage, together with a quantity of assorted footgear."

"That must have been Lord Saint-George," said Harriet.

"Presumably so, my lady."

"My *lady*"—she had never really thought it possible that Bunter would accept the situation. Everybody else, perhaps, but not Bunter. Yet apparently he did. And that being so, the incredible must have happened. She must be actually married to Peter Wimsey. She sat looking at Peter, as the car twisted smoothly in and out of the traffic. The high, beaked profile, and the long hands laid on the wheel had been familiar to her for a long time now; but they were suddenly the face and hands of a stranger. (Peter's hands, holding the keys of hell and heaven . . . that was the novelist's habit, of thinking of everything in terms of literary allusions.)

"Peter!"

"My dear?"

"I was just wondering whether I should recognize your voice—your face seems to have got rather remote, somehow."

She saw the corner of his long mouth twitch.

"Not quite the same person?"

"No."

"Don't worry," he said, imperturbably, "it'll be all right on the night."

Too much experience to be surprised, and too much honesty to pretend not to understand. She remembered what had happened four days earlier. He had brought her home after the theater, and they were standing before the fire, when she had said something—quite casually, laughing at him. He had turned and said, suddenly and huskily:

"*Tu m'enivres!*"

Language and voice together had been like a lightning-flash, showing up past and future in a single crack of fire that hurt your eyes and was followed by a darkness like thick, black velvet. . . . When his lips had reluctantly freed themselves, he had said:

"I'm sorry. I didn't mean to wake the whole zoo. But I'm glad, my God! to know it's there—and no shabby tigers either."

"Did you think mine would be a shabby tiger?"

"I thought it might, perhaps, be a little daunted."

"Well, it isn't. It seems to be an entirely new tiger. I never had one before—only kindness to animals."

"My *lady gave me a tiger,*
A *sleek and splendid tiger,*
A *striped and* shining *tiger,*
All under the leaves of life."

Nobody else, thought Harriet, had apparently suspected the tiger—except of course, old Paul Delagardie, whose ironic eyes saw everything.

Peter's final comment had been:

"I have now completely given myself away. No English vocabulary. No other Englishwoman. And that is the most I can say for myself."

Gradually, they were shaking off the clustering lights of London. The car gathered speed. Peter looked back over his shoulder.

"Not waking the baby, are we, Bunter?"

"The vibration is at present negligible, my lord."

That led memory farther back.

"This question of children, Harriet. Do you feel strongly about it?"

"Well, I'm not quite sure. I'm not marrying you for the sake of having them, if that's what you mean."

"Thank Heaven! He does not wish to regard himself, nor yet to be regarded, in that agricultural light. . . . You don't particularly care about children?"

"Not children, in the lump. But I think it's just possible that I might some day come to want—"

"Your own?"

"No—yours."

"Oh!" he had said, unexpectedly disconcerted. "I see. That's rather—Have you ever considered what kind of a father I should make?"

"I know quite well. Casual, apologetic, reluctant and adorable."

"If I was reluctant, Harriet, it would only be because I have a profound distrust of myself. Our family's been going a pretty long time. There's Saint-George, who has no character, and his sister, with no vitality—to say nothing of the next heir after Saint-George and myself, who is a third cousin and completely gaga. And if you think about my own compound of what Uncle Paul calls nerves and nose—"

"I am reminded of what Clare Clairemont said to Byron: 'I shall always remember the gentleness of your manners and the wild originality of your countenance.' "

"No, Harriet—I mean that."

"Your brother married his own cousin. Your sister married a commoner and *her* children are all right. You wouldn't be doing it all yourself, you know—*I'm* common enough. What's wrong with *me?*"

"Nothing, Harriet. That's true. By God, that's true. The fact is, I'm a coward about responsibility and always have been. My dear—if you want it and are ready to take the risk—"

"I don't believe it's such a risk as all that."

"Very well. I leave it to you. If you will and when you will. When I asked you, I rather expected you to say, No."

"But you had a horrible fear I might say, 'Yes, of course'!"

"Well, perhaps. I didn't expect what you did say. It's embarrassing to be taken seriously—as a person."

"But, Peter, putting aside my own feelings and your morbid visions of twin gorgons or nine-headed hydras or whatever it is you look forward to—would *you* like children?"

She had been amused by the conflict in his self-conscious face.

"Egotistical idiot that I am," he had said finally, "yes. Yes. I should. Heaven knows why. Why does one? To prove one can do it? For the fun of boasting about 'my boy at Eton'? or because—?"

"Peter! When Mr. Murbles drew up that monstrous great long will for you, after we were engaged—"

"Oh, Harriet!"

"How did you leave your property? I mean, the real estate?"

"All right," he said with a groan, "the murder's out. Entailed.—I admit it. But Murbles expects that every man

—damn it, don't laugh like that, I couldn't argue the point with Murbles—and *every* contingency was provided for."

A town, with a wide stone bridge, and lights reflected in the river—taking memory no further back than that morning. The Dowager's closed car, with the Dowager discreetly seated beside the chauffeur; herself in cloth of gold and a soft fur cloak, and Peter, absurdly upright in morning dress, with a gardenia in his lapel, balancing a silk hat on his knee.

"Well, Harriet, we've passed the Rubicon. Any qualms?"

"No more than when we went up the Cherwell that night and moored on the far bank, and you asked the same question."

"Thank God! Stick to it, sweetheart. Only one more river."

"And that's the river of Jordan."

"If I kiss you now I shall lose my head and something irreparable will happen to this accursed hat. Let us be very strange and well bred—as if we were not married at all."

One more river.

"Are we getting anywhere near?"

"Yes—this is Great Pagford, where we used to live. Look! that's our old house with the three steps up to the door—there's a doctor there still, you can see the surgery lamp. . . . After two miles you take the right hand turn for Pagford Parva, and then it's another three miles to Paggleham, and sharp left by a big barn and straight on up the lane."

When she was quite small, Dr. Vane had had a dog-cart—just like doctors in old-fashioned books. She had gone along this road, ever so many times, sitting beside him, sometimes allowed to pretend to hold the reins. Later on, it had been a car—a small and noisy one, very unlike this smooth, long-bonneted monster. The doctor had had to start on his rounds in good time, so as to leave a margin for break-downs. The second car had been more reliable—a pre-war Ford. She had learned to drive that one. If her father had lived, he would be getting on for seventy—his strange new son-in-law would have been calling him "sir." An odd way, this, to be coming home, and not home. This was Paggleham, where the old woman lived who had such terrible rheumatism in her hands—old Mrs., Mrs., Mrs. Warner, that was it—*she* must have gone long ago.

"That's the barn, Peter."

"Right you are. Is that the house?"

The house where the Batesons had lived—a dear old couple, a pleasantly tottering, Darby and Joan pair, always ready to welcome little Miss Vane and give her strawberries and seedy-cake. Yes—the house—a huddle of black gables, with two piled chimney-stacks, blotting out the stars. One would open the door and step straight in, through the sanded entry into the big kitchen with its wooden settles and its great oak rafters, hung with home-cured hams. Only, Darby and Joan were dead by now, and Noakes (she vaguely remembered him—a hard-faced, grasping man who hired out bicycles) would be waiting to receive them. But —there was no light in any of the windows at Talboys.

"We're a bit late," said Harriet, nervously; "he may have given us up."

"Then we shall firmly hand ourselves back to him," said Peter, cheerfully. "People like you and me are not so easily got rid of. I told him, any time after eight o'clock. This looks like the gate."

Bunter climbed out and approached the gate in eloquent silence. He had known it; he had felt it in his bones; the arrangements had fallen through. At whatever cost, even if he had had to strangle pressmen with his bare hands, he ought to have come ahead to see to things. In the glare of the headlights a patch of white paper showed clearly on the top bar of the gate; he looked suspiciously at it, removed, with careful fingers, the tintack that secured it to the wood and brought it, still without a word, to his master.

"NO BREAD AND MILK" (it said) "TILL FURTHER NOTISE."

"H'm!" said Peter. "The occupier, I gather, has already taken his departure. This has been up for several days, by the look of it."

"He's got to be there to let us in," said Harriet.

"He's probably deputed somebody else. He didn't write this himself—he can spell 'notice' in his letter to us. The 'somebody' is a little lacking in thought not to realize that *we* might want bread and milk. However, we can remedy the matter."

He reversed the paper, wrote in pencil on the back "BREAD AND MILK, PLEASE," and restored it to Bunter, who tin-tacked it back and gloomily opened the gate. The car moved slowly past him, up a short and muddy approach, on either side of which were flower-beds, carefully tended and filled with chrysanthemums and dahlias, while behind them rose the dark outlines of some sheltering bushes.

"A load of gravel would have done them no harm," observed Bunter to himself, as he picked a disdainful way through the mud. When he reached the door—massive and uncompromising, within an oaken porch having seats on either side—his lordship was already performing a brisk fantasia upon the horn. There was no reply; nothing stirred in the house; no candle darted its beams; no casement was thrown open; no shrill voice demanded to know their business; only, in the near distance, a dog barked irritably.

Mr. Bunter, gloomily self-restrained, grasped the heavy knocker and let its summons thunder through the night. The dog barked again. He tried the handle, but the door was fast.

"Oh, dear!" said Harriet.

This, she felt, was her fault. Her idea in the first place. Her house. Her honeymoon. Her—and this was the incalculable factor in the thing—her husband. (A repressive word, that, when you came to think of it, compounded of a grumble and a thump.) The man in possession. The man with rights—including the right not to be made a fool of by his belongings. The dashboard light was switched off, and she could not see his face; but she felt his body turn and his left arm move along the back of the seat as he leaned to call across her:

"Try the back!"—and something in his assured tone reminded her that he had been brought up in the country and knew well enough that farm houses were more readily assailable in the rear. "If you can't find anybody there, make for the place where the dog is."

He tootled on the horn again, the dog responded with a volley of yelps, and the shadowy bulk that was Bunter moved round the side of the building.

"That," continued Peter, with satisfaction, and throwing his hat into the back of the car, "will keep him busy for quite a bit. We shall now give one another that attention which, for the last thirty-six hours, has been squandered on trivialities. . . . *Da mihi basia mille, deinde centum*. . . . Do you realize, woman, that I've done it? . . . that I've got you? . . . that you can't get rid of me now, short of death or divorce? . . . *Et tot millia millies quot sunt sidera cœlo*. . . . Forget Bunter. I don't care a rap whether he goes for the dog or the dog goes for him."

"Poor Bunter!"

"Yes, poor devil! No wedding bells for Bunter. . . . Not fair, is it? All the kicks for him and all the kisses for me. . . . Stick to it, old son! Wake Duncan with thy knocking. But there's no hurry for the next few minutes."

The fusillade of knocks had begun again, and the dog was growing hysterical.

"Somebody must come sometime," said Harriet, still with a sense of guilt that no embraces could stifle, "because, if not—"

"If not . . . Last night you slept in a goosefeather bed, and all that. But the goosefeather bed and the new-wedded lord are inseparable only in ballads. Would you rather wed with the feathers or bed with the goose—I mean the gander? Or would you make shift with the lord in the cold open field?"

"He wouldn't be stranded in a cold open field if I hadn't been so idiotic about St. George's, Hanover Square."

"No—and if I hadn't refused Helen's ten villas on the Riviera! . . . Hurray! somebody's throttled the hound—that's a step in the right direction. . . . Cheer up! the night is yet young, and we may even find a goosefeather bed in the village pub—or in the last resort sleep under a haystack. I believe, if I'd had nothing but a haystack to offer you, you'd have married me years ago."

"I shouldn't be surprised."

"Damnation! Think what I've missed."

"Me too. At this moment I could have been tramping at your heels with five babies and a black eye, and saying to a sympathetic bobby, 'You leave 'im be—'e's my man, ain't 'e?—'E've a right to knock me abaht.' "

"You seem," said her husband, reprovingly, "to regret the black eye more than the five babies."

"Naturally. You'll never give me the black eye."

"Nothing so easily healed, I'm afraid. Harriet—I wonder what sort of shot I'm going to make at being decent to you."

"My dear Peter—"

"Yes, I know. But I've never—now I come to think of it—inflicted myself on anyone for very long together. Except Bunter, of course. Have you consulted Bunter? Do you think he would give me a good character?"

"It sounds to me," said Harriet, "as though Bunter had picked up a girl friend."

The footsteps of two people were, in fact, approaching from behind the house. Somebody was expostulating with Bunter in high-pitched tones:

"I'll believe it w'en I sees it, and not before. Mr. Noakes is at Broxford, I tell you, and has been ever since last Wednesday night as ever is, and he ain't never said nothing to me nor nobody, not about sellin' no 'ouse nor about no lords nor ladies neither."

The speaker, now emerging into the blaze of the headlights, was a hard-faced angular lady of uncertain age, dressed in a mackintosh, a knitted shawl, and a man's cap secured rakishly to her head with knobbed and shiny hatpins. Neither the size of the car, the polish of its chromium plating nor the brilliance of its lamps appeared to impress her, for advancing with a snort to Harriet's side she said, belligerently:

"Now then, 'oo are you and wot d'you want, kicking up all this noise? Let's 'ave a look at yer!"

"By all means," said Peter. He switched on the dashboard light. His yellow hair and his eye-glass seemed to produce an unfortunate impression.

"H'mph!" said the lady, "film actors, by the look of yer. And—" (with a withering glance at Harriet's furs) "no better than you should be, I'll be bound."

"We are very sorry to have disturbed you," began Peter, "Mrs.—er—"

"Ruddle is my name," said the lady of the cap. "Mrs. Ruddle, and a respectable married woman with a grown son of her own. He's a-coming over from the cottage now with his gun, as soon as he's put his trousis on, which he had just took 'em off to go to bed in good time, 'aving to be up early to 'is work. Now then! Mr. Noakes is over at Broxford, same as I was sayin' to this other chap of yours, and you can't get nothing out of me, for it ain't no business of mine, except that I obliges 'im in the cleaning way."

"Ruddle?" said Harriet. "Didn't he work at one time for Mr. Vickey at Five Elms?"

"Yes, 'e did," said Mrs. Ruddle quickly, "but that's fifteen years agone. I lost Ruddle last Michaelmas five year, and a good 'usband 'e was, when he was himself, that is. 'Ow do you come to know Ruddle?"

"I'm Dr. Vane's daughter, that used to live at Great Pagford. Don't you remember him? I know your name, and I think I remember your face. But you didn't live here then. The Batesons had the farm, and there was a woman called Sweeting at the cottage who kept pigs and had a niece who wasn't quite right in the head."

"Lor' now!" cried Mrs. Ruddle. "To think 'o that! Dr. Vane's daughter, is you, miss? Now I come to look at you, you *'ave* got a look of 'er. But it's gettin' on for seventeen years since you and the doctor left Pagford. I did 'ere as 'e'd passed away, and sorry I was—'e was a wonderful clever doctor, was your dad, miss—I 'ad 'im for my Bert, and I'm sure it's a mercy I did, 'im comin' into the world wrong end up as you might say, which is a sad trial for a woman. And how *are* you, miss, after all this time? We *did* 'ear as you'd been in trouble with the perlice, but as I said to Bert, you can't believe the stuff they puts into them papers."

"It was quite true, Mrs. Ruddle—but they'd got hold of the wrong person."

"Just like 'em!" said Mrs. Ruddle. "There's that Joe Sellon. Tried to make out as my Bert 'ad been stealin' Aggie Twitterton's 'ens. ''Ens,' I said. 'You'll be making out next as 'e took that there pocket-book of Mr. Noakes's, wot 'e made all the fuss about. You look for your 'ens in George Withers's back kitchen,' I says, and sure enough, there they was. 'Call yourself a perliceman,' I says, 'I'd make a better perliceman than you any day, Joe Sellon.' That's what I ses to 'im. I'd never believe nothing none of them perlicemen said, not if I was to be paid for it, so don't you think it, miss. I'm sure I'm very pleased to see you, miss, looking so well, but if you and the gentleman was wanting Mr. Noakes—"

"We did want him, but I expect you can help us. This is my husband and we've bought Talboys and we arranged with Mr. Noakes to come here for our honeymoon."

"You don't say!" ejaculated Mrs. Ruddle. "I'm sure I congratulate you, miss—mum, and sir." She wiped a bony hand on the mackintosh and extended it to bride and groom in turn. " 'Oneymoon—well, there!—it won't take me a minnit to put on the clean sheets, which is all laying aired and ready at the cottage, so if you'll let me 'ave the keys—"

"But," said Peter, "that's just the trouble. We haven't got the keys. Mr. Noakes said he'd make all the preparations and be here to let us in."

"Ho!" said Mrs. Ruddle. "Well, 'e never told me nothing about it. Off to Broxford 'e was, by the ten o'clock bus Wednesday night, and never said nothing to nobody, not to mention leave me my week's money."

"But," said Harriet, "if you do his cleaning, haven't you got a key to the house?"

"No, I have *not*," replied Mrs. Ruddle. "You don't ketch *'im* givin' me no keys. Afraid I'll pinch sommink, I suppose. Not that *'e* leaves much as 'ud be worth pinchin'. But there you are, that's 'im all over. *And* burglar-proof bolts on all the winders. Many's the time I've said to Bert, supposin' the 'ouse was to go on fire with 'im away an' no keys nearer than Pagford."

"Pagford?" said Peter. "I thought you said he was at Broxford."

"So 'e is—sleeps over the wireless business. But you'd 'ave a job ter get him, I reckon, 'im bein' a bit deaf and the bell ringin' inter the shop. Your best way'll be ter run over ter Pagford an' git Aggie Twitterton."

"The lady who keeps hens?"

"That's 'er. You mind the little cottage down by the river, miss—mum, I should say—where old Blunt useter live? Well, that's it, an' she's got a key to the 'ouse—comes over ter see ter things w'en 'e's away, though, come ter think of it, I ain't seen 'er this last week. Maybe she's poorly, because, come to think of it, if 'e knowed you was coming it's Aggie Twitterton, 'e'd a-told about it."

"I expect that's it," said Harriet. "Perhaps she meant to let you know, and got ill and couldn't see to it. We'll go over. Thank you very much. Do you think she could let us have a loaf of bread and some butter?"

"Bless you, miss—mum—I can do that. I got a nice loafer bread, 'ardly touched, and 'arf a pound er butter at 'ome this minnit. And," said Mrs. Ruddle, not for an instant losing her grasp upon essentials, "the clean sheets, like I was sayin'. I'll run and fetch them up directly, and it won't take no time to get straight w'en you and your good gentleman comes back with the keys. Excuse me, mum, wot might your married name be?"

"Lady Peter Wimsey," said Harriet, feeling not at all sure that it was her name.

"I never!" said Mrs. Ruddle. "That's wot 'e said"—she jerked her head at Bunter—"but I didn't pay no 'eed to 'im. Begging your pardon, mum, but there's some of these commercial fellers 'ud say anythink, wouldn't they, sir?"

"Oh, we all have to pay heed to Bunter," said Wimsey. "He's the only really reliable person in the party. Now, Mrs. Ruddle, we'll run over and get the keys from Miss Twitterton and be back in twenty minutes. Bunter, you'd better stay here and give Mrs. Ruddle a hand with the things. Is there room to turn?"

"Very good, my lord. No, my lord. I fancy there is *not* room to turn. I will open the gate for your lordship. Allow me, my lord. Your lordship's hat."

"Give it to me," said Harriet, Peter's hands being occupied with the ignition switch and the self-starter.

"Yes, my lady. Thank you, my lady."

"After which," said Peter, when they had reversed through the gate and were once again headed for Great Pagford, "Bunter will proceed to make it quite plain to Mrs. Ruddle—in case she hasn't grasped the idea—that Lord and Lady Peter Wimsey are my lord and lady. Poor old Bunter! Never have his feelings been so harrowed. Film-actors, by the look of you! No better than you should be! These commercial fellers will say anythink!"

"Oh, Peter! I wish I could have married Bunter. I do love him so."

"Bride's Wedding-Night Confession; Titled Clubman Slays Valet and Self. I'm glad you take to Bunter—I owe him a lot. . . . Do you know anything about this Twitterton woman we're going to see?"

"No—but I've an idea there was an elderly laborer of that name in Pagford Parva who used to beat his wife or something. They weren't Dad's patients. It's funny, even if she's ill, that she shouldn't have sent Mrs. Ruddle a message."

"Dashed funny. I've got my own ideas about Mr. Noakes. Simcox—"

"Simcox? Oh, the agent, yes?"

"He was surprised to find the place going so cheap. It's true it was only the house and a couple of fields—Noakes seems to have sold part of the property. I paid Noakes last Monday, and the check was cleared in London on Thursday, I shouldn't wonder if another bit of clearing was done at the same time."

"What?"

"Friend Noakes. It doesn't affect our purchase of the house—the title is all right and there's no mortgage, I made sure of that. The fact that there was no mortgage cuts both ways. If he was in difficulties, you'd expect a mortgage; but if he was in great difficulties, he might have kept the property free for a quick sale. He kept a bicycle shop in your day. Was he ever in difficulties with that?"

"I don't know. I think he sold it and the man who bought it said he'd been cheated. Noakes was supposed to be pretty sharp over a bargain."

"Yes. He got Talboys dirt cheap, I fancy from what Simcox said. Got some kind of squeeze on the old people and put the brokers in. I've an idea he was fond of buying and selling things as a speculation."

"He used to be spoken of as a warm man. Always up to something."

"All sorts of little enterprises, h'm? Picking things up cheap on the chance of patching 'em up for resale at a profit—that sort?"

"Rather that sort."

"Um. Sometimes it works, sometimes not. There's a London tenant of mine who started twenty years ago with a few second-hand oddments in a cellar. I've just built him a very handsome block of flats with sunshine balconies and vitaglass and things. He'll do very well with them. But then he's a Jew, and knows exactly what he's doing. I shall get my money back and so will he. He's got the knack of making money turn over. We'll have him to dinner one day and he'll tell you how he did it. He started in the War, with the double handicap of a slight deformity and a German name, but before he dies he'll be a damn sight richer than I am."

Harriet asked a question or two, which her husband answered, but in so abstract a tone that she realized he was giving only about a quarter of his mind to the virtuous Jew of London and none of it to herself. He was probably mulling over the mysterious behavior of Mr. Noakes. She was quite accustomed to his sudden withdrawals into the recesses of his own mind, and did not resent them. She had known him stop short in the middle of a proposal of marriage to her because some chance sight or sound had offered him a new piece to fit into a criminal jig-saw. His meditations did not last long, for within five minutes they were running into Great Pagford, and he was obliged to rouse himself to ask his companion the way to Miss Twitterton's cottage.

CHAPTER II

GOOSEFEATHER BED

But for the Bride-bed, what were fit,
That hath not been talk'd of yet.
—DRAYTON, *EIGHTH NIMPHALL*

The cottage, which had three yellow brick sides and a red-brick front, like the uglier kind of doll's house, stood rather isolated from the town, so that it was perhaps not unreasonable in Miss Twitterton to interrogate her visitors, in sharp and agitated tones from an upper window, as to their intentions and *bona fides*, before cautiously opening the door to them. She revealed herself as a small, fair and flustered spinster in her forties, wrapped in a pink flannel dressing-gown, and having in one hand a candle and in the other a large dinner-bell. She could not understand *what* it was all about. Uncle William had said *nothing* to her. She did not even know he was away. He *never* went away without letting her know. He would *never* have sold the house without telling her. She kept the door on the chain while repeating these asseverations, holding the dinner-bell ready to ring in case the odd-looking person in the eye-glass should become violent and oblige her to summon assistance. Eventually, Peter produced Mr. Noakes's last letter from his pocketbook (where he had thoughtfully placed it before starting, in case of any difference of opinion about the arrangements) and passed it in through the partly-opened door. Miss Twitterton took it gingerly, as though it were a bomb, shut the door promptly in Peter's face, and retired with the candle into the front room to examine the document at her leisure. Apparently the perusal was satisfactory, and at the end of it she returned, opened the door wide and begged her visitors to enter.

"I beg your pardon," said Miss Twitterton, leading the way into a sitting-room furnished with a suite in green velvet and walnut veneer, and a surprising variety of knick-knacks, "for receiving you like this—do please sit down, Lady Peter—I do hope you will both forgive my attire—dear me!—but my house is a little lonely and it's only a *short* time ago since my *henroost* was robbed—and really, the whole thing is so *inexplicable*, I scarcely know what to think—it really is *most* upsetting—so *peculiar* of uncle—and what you must be thinking of both of us I cannot *imagine*."

"Only that it's a great shame to knock you up at this time of night," said Peter.

"It's only a quarter to ten," replied Miss Twitterton, with a deprecating glance at a little china clock in the shape of a pansy, "nothing, of *course*, to you—but you know we keep *early* hours in the country. I have to be up at *five* to feed my birds, so I'm rather an *early bird* myself—except on choir-practice nights, you know—Wednesday, such an awkward day for me with Thursday market-day, but then it's more convenient for the dear Vicar. But, of *course*, if I'd had the *smallest* idea that Uncle William would *do* such an *extraordinary* thing, I'd have come over and been there to let you in. If you could wait five—or perhaps *ten*—minutes while I made a more suitable toilet, I could come now—as I see you have your beautiful *car*, perhaps—"

"Please don't bother, Miss Twitterton," said Harriet, a little alarmed at the prospect. "We have plenty of supplies with us and Mrs. Ruddle and our man can look after us quite well for tonight. If you could just let us have the keys—"

"The keys—yes, of course. So *dreadful* for you not being

able to get in and really such a cold night for the time of year—what Uncle William can have been *thinking* of—and did he say—dear me! his letter upset me so I hardly knew what I was reading—your honeymoon, didn't you say?—how terrible for you—and I do hope at any rate you've had supper? No *supper?*—I simply can't *understand* how Uncle could—but you *will* take a little bit of cake and a glass of my homemade wine?"

"Oh, really, we mustn't trouble you—" began Harriet, but Miss Twitterton was already hunting in a cupboard. Behind her back, Peter put his hands to his face in a mute gesture of horrified resignation.

"There!" said Miss Twitterton, triumphantly, "I'm sure you will feel better for a little refreshment. My parsnip wine is really *extra* good this year. Dr. Jellyfield always takes a glass when he comes—which isn't very often, I'm pleased to say, because my health is always *remarkably* good."

"That will not prevent me from drinking to it," said Peter, disposing of the parsnip wine with a celerity which might have been due to eagerness but, to Harriet, rather suggested a reluctance to let the draught linger on the palate. "May I pour out a glass for yourself?"

"How kind of you!" cried Miss Twitterton. "Well—it's *rather* late at night—but I really *ought* to drink to your wedded happiness, oughtn't I?—*Not* too much, Lord Peter, please. The dear Vicar always says my parsnip wine is not *nearly* so innocent as it looks—dear me!—But *you* will take just a little more, won't you? A gentleman always has a stronger head than a lady."

"Thanks so much," said Peter, meekly, "but you must remember I've got to drive my wife back to Paggleham."

"*One* more I'm *sure* won't do any harm—Well, just *half* a glass, then—there! Now of course, you want the keys. I'll run upstairs for them at once—I know I mustn't keep you—I won't be a *minute*, Lady Peter, so *please* have another slice of cake—it's home-made—I do all my own baking, and Uncle's too—whatever can have come over him I can't *think!*"

Miss Twitterton ran out, leaving the pair to gaze at one another in the light of the candle.

"Peter, my poor, long-suffering, heroic lamb—pour it into the aspidistra."

Wimsey lifted his eyebrows at the plant.

"It looks rather unwell already, Harriet. I think my constitution is the better of the two. Here goes. But you might kiss me to take the taste away. . . . Our hostess has a certain refinement (I think that's the word) about her which I had not expected. She got your title right first shot, which is unusual. Her life has had some smatch of honor in it. Who was her father?"

"I think he was a cowman."

"Then he married above his station. His wife, presumably, was a Miss Noakes."

"It comes back to me that she was a village schoolmistress over at some place near Broxford."

"That explains it. . . . Miss Twitterton is coming down. At this point we rise up, buckle the belt of the old leather coat, grab the gent's soft hat and make the motions of imminent departure."

"The keys," said Miss Twitterton, arriving breathless with a second candle. "The big one is the *back* door, but you'll find that *bolted*. The *little* one is the *front* door—it's a *patent, burglar-proof* lock—you may find it a little *difficult* if you don't know the way it works. Perhaps, after all, I ought to come over and show you—"

"Not a bit of it, Miss Twitterton. I know these locks quite well. Really. Thank you ever so much. Good night. And many apologies."

"I must apologize for Uncle. I really *cannot* understand his treating you in this *cavalier* way. I *do* hope you'll find everything all right. Mrs. Ruddle is *not* very intelligent."

Harriet assured Miss Twitterton that Bunter would see to everything, and they succeeded at length in extricating themselves. Their return to Talboys was remarkable only for Peter's observing that unforgettable was the epithet for Miss Twitterton's parsnip wine and that if one was going to be sick on one's wedding night one might just as well have done it between Southampton and Le Havre.

Bunter and Mrs. Ruddle had by now been joined by the dilatory Bert (with his "trousis" but without his gun); yet even thus supported, Mrs. Ruddle had a chastened appearance. The door being opened, and Bunter having produced an electric torch, the party stepped into a wide stone passage strongly permeated by an odor of dry-rot and beer. On the right, a door led into a vast, low-ceilinged, stone-paved kitchen, its rafters black with time, its enormous, old-fashioned range clean and garnished under the engulfing chimney-breast. On the whitewashed hearth stood a small oil cooking-stove and before it an arm-chair whose seat sagged with age and use. The deal table held the remains of two boiled eggs, the heel of a stale loaf and a piece of cheese, together with a cup which had contained cocoa, and a half-burnt candle in a bedroom candlestick.

"There!" exclaimed Mrs. Ruddle. "If Mr. Noakes 'ad a-let me know, I'd a-cleaned all them things away. That'll be 'is supper wot 'e 'ad afore 'e caught the ten o'clock. But me not knowing and 'avin' no key, you see, I couldn't. But it won't take me a minnit, m'lady, now we *are* here. Mr. Noakes took all 'is meals in 'ere, but you'll find it comfortabler in the settin'-room m'lady, if you'll come this way—it's a much brighter room, like, and furnished beautiful, as you'll see, m'lord." Here Mrs. Ruddle dropped something like a curtsy.

The sitting-room was, indeed, "brighter" than the kitchen. Two ancient oak-settles, flanking the chimney-piece at right angles, and an old-fashioned American eight-day clock on the inner wall, were all that remained of the old farm-house furniture that Harriet remembered. The flame of the kitchen candle, which Mrs. Ruddle had lit, danced flickeringly over a suite of Edwardian chairs with crimson upholstery, a top-heavy sideboard, a round mahogany table with wax fruit on it, a bamboo what-not with mirrors and little shelves sprouting from it in all directions, a row of aspidistras in pots in the window-ledge, with strange hanging plants above them in wire baskets, a large radio cabinet, over which hung an unnaturally distorted cactus in a brass Benares bowl, mirrors with roses painted on the glass, a chesterfield sofa upholstered in electric blue plush, two carpets of violently colored and mutually intolerant patterns juxtaposed to hide the black oak floorboards—a collection of objects, in fact, suggesting that Mr. Noakes had furnished his house out of auction-sale bargains that he had not been able to re-sell, together with a few remnants of genuine old stuff and a little borrowing from the stock-in-trade of the wireless business. They were allowed every opportunity to inspect this collection of bric-à-brac, for Mrs. Ruddle made the round of the room, candle in hand, to point out all its beauties.

"Fine!" said Peter, cutting short Mrs. Ruddle's panegyric on the radio cabinet ("which you can hear it lovely right over at the cottage if the wind sets that way"). "Now, what we want at the moment, Mrs. Ruddle, is fire and food. If you'll get us some more candles and let your Bert help Bunter to bring in the provisions out of the back of the car, then we can get the fires lit—"

"Fires?" said Mrs. Ruddle in doubtful accents. "Well, there, sir—m'lord I should say—I ain't sure as there's a mite of coal in the place. Mr. Noakes, 'e ain't 'ad no fires this long time. Said these 'ere great chimbleys ate up too much of the 'eat. Oil-stoves, that's wot Mr. Noakes 'ad, for cookin' an' for settin' over of an evenin'. I don't rackollect w'en there was fires 'ere last—except that young couple we 'ad 'ere August four year, w'en we had sich a cold summer —and they couldn't get the chimbley to go. Thought there must be a bird's nest in it or somethink, but Mr. Noakes said 'e wasn't goin' to spend good money 'aving they chimbleys cleared. Coal, now. There ain't none in the oil-shed, that I do know—without there might be a bit in the wash'us—but it'll have been there a long time," she concluded dubiously, as though its qualities might have been lost by keeping.

"I might fetch up a bucket or so of coal from the cottage, mum," suggested Bert.

"So you might, Bert," agreed his mother. "My Bert's got a wonderful 'ead. So you might. And a bit o' kindlin' with it. You can cut across the back way—and, 'ere, Bert—jest shet that cellar door as you goes by—sech a perishin' draught as it do send up. And, Bert, I declare if I ain't forgot the sugar—you'll find a packet in the cupboard you could put in your pocket. There'll be tea in the kitchen, but Mr. Noakes never took no sugar, only the gran, and that ain't right for 'er ladyship."

By this time, the resourceful Bunter had ransacked the kitchen for candles, which he was putting in a couple of tall brass candlesticks (part of Mr. Noakes's more acceptable possessions) which stood on the sideboard; carefully scraping the guttered wax from the sockets with a penknife with the air of one to whom neatness and order came first, even in a crisis.

"And if your ladyship will come this way," said Mrs. Ruddle, darting to a door in the panelling, "I'll show you the bedrooms. Beautiful rooms they is, but only the one of 'em in use, of course, except for summer visitors. Mind the stair, m'lady, but there—I'm forgettin' you knows the 'ouse. I'll jest pop the bed again the fire, w'en we gets it lit, though damp it cannot be, 'avin' been in use till last Wednesday, and the sheets is aired beautiful, though linen, which, if folks don't suffer from the rheumatics, most ladies and gentlemen is partial to. I 'opes as you don't mind them old four-posters, miss—mum—m'lady. Mr. Noakes did want to sell them, but the gentleman as come down to look at them said as 'ow they wasn't wot 'e called original owing to being mended on account of the worm and wouldn't give Mr. Noakes the price 'e put on 'em. Nasty old things I calls 'em—w'en Ruddle and me was to be wedded I says to 'im, 'Brass knobs,' I ses, 'or nothing'—and, bein' wishful to please, brass knobs it was, beautiful."

"How lovely," said Harriet, as they passed through a deserted bedroom, with the four-poster stripped naked and the rugs rolled together and emitting a powerful odor of mothballs.

"That it is, m'lady," said Mrs. Ruddle. "Not but what some o' the visitors likes these old-fashioned things—quaint, they calls 'em—and the curtains you will find in good order if wanted, Miss Twitterton and me doin' of 'em up careful at the end of the summer, and I do assure you, m'lady, if you and your good gentleman—your good lord, m'lady—was a-wantin' a bit of 'elp in the 'ouse you will find Bert an' me allus ready to oblige, as I was a-sayin' only jest now to Mr. Bunter. Yes, m'lady, thank you. Now, this" —Mrs. Ruddle opened the farther door—"is Mr. Noakes's own room, as you may see, and all ready to okkerpy, barrin' 'is odds-and-ends, which it won't take me a minnit to put aside."

"He seems to have left all his things behind him," said Harriet, looking at an old-fashioned nightshirt laid ready for use on the bed and at the shaving tackle and sponge on the washstand.

"Oh, yes, m'lady. Kept a spare set of everythink over at Broxford, 'e did, so 'e 'adn't to do nothing but step into the 'bus. More often at Broxford than not 'e was, lookin' after the business. But I'll 'ave everythink straight in no time—only jest to change the sheets and run a duster over. Maybe you'd like me to bile yer a kittle of water on the Beetrice, m'lady—*and,*" Mrs. Ruddle's tone suggested that this consideration had often influenced the wavering decision of prospective summer visitors—"*down* this 'ere little stair—mind yer 'ead, mum—everythink is modern, put in by Mr. Noakes w'en 'e took to lettin' for the summer."

"A bathroom?" asked Harriet hopefully.

"Well, no, m'lady, not a *bath*room," replied Mrs. Ruddle, as though that were too much to expect, "but everythink else is quite modern as you'll find—only requirin' to be pumped up night and morning in the scullery."

"Oh, I see," said Harriet, "how nice." She peered from the lattice. "I wonder if they've brought in the suitcases."

"I'll run and see this minnit," said Mrs. Ruddle, gathering all Mr. Noakes's toilet apparatus dexterously into her apron as she passed the dressing-table and whisking his nightgear in after it; "and I'll 'ave it all up before you can look round."

It was Bunter, however, who brought the luggage. He looked, Harriet thought, a little worn, and she smiled deprecatingly at him.

"Thank you, Bunter. I'm afraid this is making a lot of work for you. Is his lordship—?"

"His lordship is with the young man they call Bert, clearing out the woodshed to put the car away, my lady." He looked at her and his heart was melted. "He is singing songs in the French language, which I have observed to be a token of high spirits with his lordship. It has occurred to me, my lady, that if you and his lordship would kindly overlook any temporary deficiencies in the arrangements, the room adjacent to this might be suitably utilized as a dressing-room for his lordship's use, so as to leave more accommodation here for your ladyship. Allow me."

He opened the wardrobe door, inspected Mr. Noakes's garments hanging within, shook his head over them, removed them from the hooks and carried them away over his arm. In five minutes, he had cleared the chest of drawers of all its contents and, in five minutes more, had relined all the drawers with sheets of the *Morning Post,* which he produced from his coat-pocket. From the other pocket he drew out two new candles, which he set in the two empty sticks that flanked the mirror. He took away Mr. Noakes's chunk of yellow soap, his towels and the ewer, and presently returned with fresh towels and water, a virgin tablet of soap wrapped in cellophane, a small kettle and a spirit-lamp, observing, as he applied a match to the spirit, that Mrs. Ruddle had placed a ten-pint kettle on the oil-stove, which, in his opinion, would take half an hour to boil, and would there be anything further at the moment, as he rather thought they were having a little difficulty with the sitting-room fire, and he would like to get his lordship's suitcase unpacked before going down to give an eye to it.

Under the circumstances, Harriet made no attempt to change her dress. The room, though spacious and beautiful in its half-timbered style, was cold. She wondered whether, all things considered, Peter would not have been happier in the Hotel Gigantic somewhere-or-other on the Continent. She hoped that, after his struggles with the woodshed, he would find a good, roaring fire to greet him and be able to eat his belated meal in comfort.

Peter Wimsey rather hoped so, too. It took a long time to clear the woodshed, which contained not very much wood, but an infinite quantity of things like dilapidated mangles and wheelbarrows, together with the remains of an old pony-trap, several disused grates and a galvanized iron boiler with a hole in it. But he had his doubts about the weather, and was indisposed to allow Mrs. Merdle (the ninth Daimler of that name) to stand out all night. When he thought of his lady's expressed preference for haystacks, he sang songs in the French language; but from time to time he stopped singing and wondered whether, after all, she might not have been happier at the Hotel Gigantic, somewhere-or-other on the Continent.

The church clock down in the village was chiming the three-quarters before eleven when he finally coaxed Mrs. Merdle into her new quarters and re-entered the house, brushing the cobwebs from his hands. As he passed the threshold a thick cloud of smoke caught him by the throat and choked him. Pressing on, nevertheless, he arrived at the door of the kitchen, where a first hasty glance convinced him that the house was on fire. Recoiling into the sitting-room, he found himself enveloped in a kind of London fog, through which he dimly decried dark forms struggling about the hearth like genies of the mist. He said "Hallo!" and was instantly seized by a fit of coughing. Out of the thick rolls of smoke came a figure that he vaguely remembered promising to love and cherish at some earlier period in the day. Her eyes were streaming and her progress blind. He extended an arm, and they coughed convulsively together.

"Oh, Peter!" said Harriet, "I think all the chimneys are bewitched."

The windows in the sitting-room had been opened and the draught brought fresh smoke billowing out into the passage. With it came Bunter, staggering but still in possession of his faculties, and flung wide both the front door and the back. Harriet reeled out into the sweet cold air of the porch and sat down on a seat to recover herself. When she could see and breathe again, she made her way back to the sitting-room, only to meet Peter coming out of the kitchen in his shirt-sleeves.

"It's no go," said his lordship. "No can do. Those chimneys are blocked. I've been inside both of them and you can't see a single star and there's about fifteen bushels of soot in the kitchen chimney-ledges, because I felt it." (As indeed his right arm bore witness.) "I shouldn't think they'd been swept for twenty years."

"They ain't been swep' in *my* memory," said Mrs. Ruddle, "and I've lived in that cottage eleven year come next Christmas quarter-day."

"Then it's time they were," said Peter, briskly. "Send for the sweep tomorrow, Bunter. Heat up some of the turtle soup on the oil-stove and give us the foie gras, the quails in aspic and a bottle of hock in the kitchen."

"Certainly, my lord."

"And I want a wash. Did I see a kettle in the kitchen?"

"Yes, m'lord," quavered Mrs. Ruddle, "oh, yes—a beautiful kittle as 'ot at 'ot. And if I was jest to put the bed down before the Beetrice in the settin'-room and git the clean sheets on—"

Peter fled with the kettle into the scullery, whither his bride pursued him.

"Peter, I'm past apologizing for my ideal home."

"Apologize if you dare—and embrace me at your peril. I am as black as Belloc's scorpion. He is a most unpleasant brute to find in bed at night."

"Among the clean sheets. And, Peter—oh, Peter! the ballad was right. It *is* a goosefeather bed!"

CHAPTER III

JORDAN RIVER

The feast with gluttonous delays
Is eaten . . .
. . . night is come; and yet we see
Formalities retarding thee. . . .
A bride, before a "Good-night!" could be said,
Should vanish from her clothes into her bed,
As souls from bodies steal, and are not spied.
But now she's laid; what though she be?
Yet there are more delays, for where is he?
He comes and passeth through sphere after sphere;
First her sheets, then her arms, then anywhere.
Let not this day, then, but this night be thine;
Thy day was but the eve to this, O Valentine.

—JOHN DONNE, *AN EPITHALAMION ON THE LADY ELIZABETH AND COUNT PALATINE*

Peter, dispensing soup and pâté and quails from a curious harlequin assortment of Mr. Noakes's crockery, had said to Bunter:

"We'll do our own waiting. For God's sake get yourself some grub and make Mrs. Ruddle fix you up something to sleep on. My egotism has reached an acute stage tonight, but there's no need for you to pander to it."

Bunter smiled gently and vanished, with the assurance that he should "do very well, my lord, thank you."

He returned, however, about the quail stage, to announce that the chimney in her ladyship's room was clear, owing (he suggested) to the circumstance that nothing had been burned in it since the days of Queen Elizabeth. He had consequently succeeded in kindling upon the hearthstone a small fire of wood which, though restricted in size and scope by the absence of dogs, would, he trusted, somewhat mitigate the inclemency of the atmosphere.

"Bunter," said Harriet, "you are marvelous."

"Bunter," said Wimsey, "you are becoming thoroughly demoralized. I told you to look after *yourself*. This is the first time you have ever refused to take my orders. I hope you will not make it a precedent."

"No, my lord. I have dismissed Mrs. Ruddle, after enlisting her services for tomorrow, subject to her ladyship's approval. Her manner is unpolished, but I have observed that her brass is not and that she has hitherto maintained the house in a state of commendable cleanliness. Unless your ladyship desires to make other arrangements—"

"Let's keep her on if we can," said Harriet, a little confused at being deferred to (since Bunter, after all, was likely to suffer most from Mrs. Ruddle's peculiarities). "She's always worked here and she knows where everything is, and she seems to be doing her best."

She glanced doubtfully at Peter, who said:

"The worst I know of her is that she doesn't like my face, but that will hurt her more than it will me. I mean, you know, she's the one that's got to look at it. Let her carry on. . . . In the meantime, there is this matter of Bunter's insubordination, from which I refuse to be diverted by Mrs. Ruddle or any other red herring."

"My lord?"

"If, Bunter, you do not immediately sit down here and have your supper, I will have you drummed out of the Regiment. My God!" said Peter, putting a formidable wedge of foie gras on a cracked plate and handing it to his man, "do you realize what will happen to us if you die of neglect and starvation? There appear to be only two tumblers, so your punishment shall be to take your wine in a teacup and make a speech afterwards. There was a little supper below-stairs at my mother's on Sunday night, I fancy. The speech you made then will serve the purpose, Bunter, with suitable modifications to fit it for our chaste ears."

"May I respectfully inquire," asked Bunter, drawing up an obedient chair, "how your lordship comes to know about that?"

"You know my methods, Bunter. As a matter of fact, James blew—if I may call it so—the gaff."

"Ah, James!" said Bunter, in a tone that boded James no good. He brooded a little over his supper, but, when called upon, rose without overmuch hesitation, teacup in hand.

"My orders are," said Mr. Bunter, "to propose the health of the happy couple shortly to—the happy couple now before us. To obey orders in this family has been my privilege for the last twenty years—a privilege which has been an unqualified pleasure, except perhaps when connected with the photography of deceased persons in an imperfect state of preservation."

He paused, and seemed to expect something.

"Did the kitchen-maid shriek at that point?" asked Harriet.

"No, my lady—the housemaid; the kitchen-maid having been sent out for giggling when Miss Franklin was speaking."

"It's a pity we let Mrs. Ruddle go," said Peter. "In her absence we will deem the shriek to have been duly uttered. Proceed!"

"Thank you, my lord. . . . I should, perhaps," resumed Mr. Bunter, "apologize for alarming the ladies with so unpleasant an allusion, but that her ladyship's pen has so adorned the subject as to render the body of a murdered millionaire as agreeable to the contemplative mind as is that of a ripe burgundy to the discriminating palate. (*Hear, hear!*) His lordship is well known as a connoisseur, both of a fine body (*Keep it clean, Bunter!*)—in every sense of the word (*Laughter*)—and of a fine spirit (*Cheers*)—also in every sense of the word (*Renewed laughter and applause*). May I express the hope that the present union may happily exemplify that which we find in a first-class port—strength of body fortified by a first-class spirit and mellowing through many years to a noble maturity. My lord and my lady—your very good health!" (*Prolonged applause, during which the orator drained his cup and sat down.*)

"Upon my word," said Peter, "I have seldom heard an after-dinner speech more remarkable for brevity and—all things considered—propriety."

"You'll have to reply to it, Peter."

"I am no orator as Bunter is, but I'll try. . . . Am I mistaken, by the way, in imagining that that oil-stove is stinking to heaven?"

"It's smoking, at any rate," said Harriet, "like nothing on earth."

Bunter, whose back was towards it, got up in alarm.

"I fear, my lord," he observed, after some minutes of silent struggle, "that some catastrophe has occurred to the burner."

"Let's have a look," said Peter.

The ensuing struggle was neither silent nor successful.

"Turn the blasted thing out and take it away," said Peter at length. He came back to the table, his appearance in no way improved by several long smears from the oily smuts which were now falling in every part of the room. "Under the present conditions, I can only say, Bunter, in reply to your good wishes for our welfare, that my wife and I thank you sincerely and shall hope that they may be fulfilled in every particular. For myself, I should like to add that any man is rich in friends who has a good wife and a good servant, and I hope I may be dead, as I shall certainly be damned, before I give either of you cause to leave me (as they say) for another. Bunter, your health—and may heaven send her ladyship and you fortitude to endure me, so long as we all shall live. I may as well warn you that I for one am firmly resolved to live as long as I possibly can."

"To which," said Mr. Bunter, "always excepting the fortitude as being unnecessary, I should wish—if the expression may be permitted—to observe, Amen."

Here everybody shook hands, and there was a pause, broken by Mr. Bunter's saying with slightly self-conscious haste, that he thought he had better attend to the bedroom fire.

"And in the meantime," said Peter, "we can have a final cigarette over the Beatrice in the sitting-room. I suppose, by the way, Beatrice is capable of heating us a little washing water."

"No doubt of it, my lord," said Mr. Bunter, "always supposing that one could find a new wick for it. The present wick appears, I regret to say, inadequate."

"Oh!" said Peter, a little blankly.

And indeed, when they reached the sitting-room, Beatrice was seen to be at her last expiring blue glimmer.

"You must see what you can do with the bedroom fire," was Harriet's suggestion.

"Very good, my lady."

"At any rate," said Peter, lighting the cigarettes, "the matches still seem to strike on the box; all the laws of Nature have not been suspended for our confusion. We will muffle ourselves in overcoats and proceed to keep each other warm in the accepted manner of benighted travelers in a snowbound country. 'If I were on Greenland's coast,' and all that. Not that I see any prospect of a six-months' night; I wish I did; it is already past midnight."

Bunter vanished upstairs, kettle in hand.

"If," said her ladyship a few minutes later, "you would remove that contraption from your eye, I could clean the bridge of your nose. Are you sorry we didn't go to Paris or Mentone after all?"

"No, definitely not. There is a solid reality about this. It's convincing, somehow."

"It's beginning to convince me, Peter. Such a series of domestic accidents could only happen to married people. There's none of that artificial honeymoon glitter that prevents people from discovering each other's real characters. You stand the test of tribulation remarkably well. It's very encouraging."

"Thank you—but I really don't know that there's a great deal to complain of. I've got you, that's the chief thing, and food and fire of sorts, and a roof over my head. What more could any man want?—Besides, I should hate to have missed Bunter's speech and Mrs. Ruddle's conversation—and even Miss Twitterton's parsnip wine adds a distinct flavor to life. I might, perhaps, have preferred rather more hot water and less oil about my person. Not that there is anything essentially effeminate about paraffin—but I disapprove on principle of perfumes for men."

"It's a nice, clean smell," said his wife, soothingly, "much more original than all the powders of the merchant. And I expect Bunter will manage to get it off you."

"I hope so," said Peter. He remembered that it had once been said of "*ce blond cadet de famille ducale anglaise*"—said, too, by a lady who had every opportunity of judging—that "*il tenait son lit en Grand Monarque et s'y démenait en Grand Turc.*" The Fates, it seemed, had determined to strip him of every vanity save one. Let them. He could fight this battle naked. He laughed suddenly.

"*Enfin, du courage! Embrasse-moi, chérie. Je trouverai quand même le moyen de te faire plaisir. Hein? tu veux? dis donc!*"

"*Je veux bien.*"

"Dearest!"

"Oh, Peter!"

"I'm sorry—did I hurt you?"

"No. Yes. Kiss me again."

It was at some point during the next five minutes that Peter was heard to murmur, 'Not faint Canaries but ambrosial"; and it is symptomatic of Harriet's state of mind that at the time she vaguely connected the faint canaries with the shabby tigers—only tracing the quotation to its source some ten days later.

• • • • •

Bunter came downstairs. In one hand he held a small and steaming jug, and in the other a case of razors and a spongebag. A bath towel and a pair of pajamas hung from his arm, together with a silk dressing-gown.

"The fire in the bedroom is drawing satisfactorily. I have contrived to heat a small quantity of water for your ladyship's use."

His master looked apprehensive.

"But what to me, my love, but what to me?"

Bunter made no verbal reply, but his glance in the direction of the kitchen was eloquent. Peter looked thoughtfully at his own fingernails and shuddered.

"Lady," said he, "get you to bed and leave me to my destiny."

The wood upon the hearth was flaring cheerfully, and the water, what there was of it, was boiling. The two brass candlesticks bore their flaming ministers bravely, one on either side of the mirror. The big four-poster, with its patchwork quilt of faded blues and scarlets and its chintz hangings dimmed by age and laundering, had, against the pale, plastered walls, a dignified air as though of exiled royalty. Harriet, warm and powdered and free at last from the smell of soot, paused with the hairbrush in her hand to wonder what was happening to Peter. She slipped across the chill dark of the dressing-room, opened the farther door, and listened. From somewhere far below came an ominous clank of iron, followed by a loud yelp and a burst of half-suffocated laughter.

"Poor darling!" said Harriet. . . .

She put out the bedroom candles. The sheets, worn thin by age, were of fine linen, and somewhere in the room there was a scent of lavender. . . . Jordan river. . . . A branch broke and fell upon the hearth in a shower of sparks, and the tall shadows danced across the ceiling.

The door-latch clicked, and her husband sidled apologetically through. His air of chastened triumph made her chuckle, though her blood was thumping erratically and something seemed to have happened to her breath. He dropped to his knees beside her.

"Sweetheart," he said, his voice shaken between passion and laughter, "take your bridegroom. Quite clean and not the least paraffiny, but dreadfully damp and cold. Scrubbed like a puppy under the scullery pump!"

"Dear Peter!"

("*. . . en Grand monarque. . . .*")

"I think," he went on, rapidly and almost indistinguishably, "I *think* Bunter was enjoying himself. I have set him to clean the blackbeetles out of the copper. What does it matter? What does anything matter? We are here. Laugh, lover, laugh. This is the end of the journey and the beginning of all delight."

Mr. Mervyn Bunter, having chased away the beetles, filled the copper and laid the fire ready for lighting, wrapped himself up in two great-coats and a rug and disposed himself comfortably in a couple of armchairs. But he did not sleep at once. Though not precisely anxious, he was filled with a kindly concern. He had (with what exertions!) brought his favorite up to the tape and must leave him now to make the running, but no respect for the proprieties could prevent his sympathetic imagination from following the cherished creature every step of the way. With a slight sigh he drew the candle towards him, took out a fountain pen and a writing pad, and began a letter to his mother. The performance of this filial duty might, he thought, serve to calm his mind.

"DEAR MOTHER,—I write from an 'unknown destination—' "

"What was that you called me?"

"Oh, Peter—how absurd! I wasn't thinking."

"*What* did you call me?"

"My lord!"

"The last two words in the language I ever expected to get a kick out of. One never values a thing till one's earned it, does one? Listen, heart's lady—before I've done I mean to be king and emperor."

It is no part of the historian's duty to indulge in what a critic has called "interesting revelations of the marriage-bed." It is enough that the dutiful Mervyn Bunter at length set aside his writing materials, blew out the candle and composed his limbs to rest; and that, of the sleepers beneath that ancient roof, he that had the hardest and coldest couch enjoyed the quietest slumbers.

CHAPTER IV

HOUSEHOLD GODS

Sir, he made a chimney in my father's house, and the bricks are alive to this day to testify it.
—WILLIAM SHAKESPEARE, *II HENRY VI: IV.2*

Lady Peter Wimsey propped herself cautiously on one elbow and contemplated her sleeping lord. With the mocking eyes hidden and the confident mouth relaxed, his big, bony nose and tumbled hair gave him a gawky, fledging look, like a schoolboy. And the hair itself was almost as light as tow—it was ridiculous that anything male should be as fair as that. No doubt when it was damped and sleeked down for the day his head would go back to its normal barley-corn color. Last night, after Bunter's ruthless pumping, it had affected her much as the murdered Lorenzo's glove affected Isabella, and she had had to rub it dry with a towel before cradling it where, in the country phrase, it "belonged to be."

Bunter? She spared him a stray thought from a mind drugged with sleep and the pleasure that comes with sleep. Bunter was up and about; she could faintly hear doors opening and shutting and furniture being moved down below. What an amazing muddle it had all been! But he would miraculously put everything right—wonderful Bunter—and leave one free to live and not bother one's head. One vaguely hoped Bunter had not spent the whole night chasing blackbeetles, but for the moment what was left of one's mind was concentrated on Peter—being anxious not to wake him, rather hoping he would soon wake up of his own accord and wondering what he would say when he did. If his first words were French one would at least feel certain that he retained an agreeable impression of the night's proceedings; on the whole, however, English would be preferable, as showing that he remembered quite distinctly who one was.

As though this disturbing thought had broken his sleep, he stirred at that moment, and, without opening his eyes felt for her with his hand and pulled her down against him. And his first word was neither French nor English, but a long interrogative, "M'mmm?"

"M'm!" said Harriet, abandoning herself. *"Mais quel tact, mon dieu! Sais-tu enfin qui je suis?"*

"Yes, my Shulamite, I do, so you needn't lay traps for my tongue. In the course of a misspent life I have learned that it is a gentleman's first duty to remember in the morning who it was he took to bed with him. You are Harriet, and you are black but comely. Incidentally, you are my wife, and if you have forgotten it you will have to learn it all over again."

"Ah!" said the baker. "I *thought* there was visitors here. You don't catch old Noakes or Martha Ruddle putting 'please' into an order for bread. How many loaves would you be wanting? I calls every day. Rightyho! a cottage and a sandwich. And a small brown? Okay, chief. Here they are."

"If," said Bunter, retreating into the passage, "you would kindly step in and set them on the kitchen table, I should be obliged, my hands being covered with paraffin."

"Okay," said the baker, obliging him. "Trouble with the stove?"

"A trifle," admitted Bunter. "I have been compelled to dismantle and reassemble the burners, but I am in hopes that it will now function adequately. We should, however, be more comfortable if we could induce the fires to draw. We have sent a message by the milkman to a person called

Puffett who, as I understand, is willing to oblige in the chimney-sweeping way."

"That's okay," agreed the baker. "He's a builder by rights, is Tom Puffett, but he ain't above obliging with a chimbley. You stopping here long? A month? Then maybe you'd like me to book the bread. Where's old Noakes?"

"Over at Broxford as I understand," said Mr. Bunter, "and we should like to know what he means by it. No preparations made for us and the chimneys out of order, after distinct instructions in writing and promises of compliance which have *not* been adhered to."

"Ah!" said the baker. "It's easy to promise, ain't it?" He winked. "Promises cost nothing, but chimbleys is eighteenpence apiece and the soot thrown in. Well, I must scram. Anything I can do for you in a neighborly way in the village?"

"Since you are so good," replied Mr. Bunter, "the dispatch of the grocer's assistant with streaky rashers and eggs would enable us to augment the deficiencies of the breakfast menu."

"Say, boy," said the baker, "that's okay by me. I'll tell Willis to send his Jimmy along."

"Which," observed Mrs. Ruddle, suddenly appearing from the sitting-room in a blue-checked apron and with her sleeves rolled up, "there's no call to let George Willis think 'e's to 'ave all me lord's custom, seein' the 'Ome and Colonial is a 'apenny cheaper per pound not to say better and leaner and I can ketch 'im w'en he goes by as easy as easy."

"You'll 'ave to do with Willis today," retorted the baker, "unless you wants your breakfast at dinner-time, seein' the 'Ome and Colonial don't get here till past eleven or nearer twelve more like. Nothing more today? Okay. 'Mornin', Martha. So long, chief."

The baker hastened down the path, calling to his horse, and leaving Bunter to deduce that somewhere at no great distance the neighborhood boasted a picture-palace.

• • • • •

"Peter!"

"Heart's desire?"

"Somebody's frying bacon."

"Nonsense. People don't fry bacon at dawn."

"That was eight by the church clock and the sun's simply blazing in."

"Busy old fool, unruly sun—but you're right about the bacon. The smell's coming up quite distinctly. Through the window, I think. This calls for investigation. . . . I say, it's a gorgeous morning. . . . Are you hungry?"

"Ravenous."

"Unromantic but reassuring. As a matter of fact, I could do with a large breakfast myself. After all, I work hard for my living. I'll give Bunter a hail."

"For God's sake put some clothes on—if Mrs. Ruddle sees you hanging out of the window like that she'll have a thousand fits."

"It'd be a treat for her. Nothing so desirable as novelty. I expect old man Ruddle went to bed in his boots. Bunter! Bunter! . . . Damn it, here *is* the Ruddle woman. Stop laughing and chuck me my dressing-gown. . . . Er—good-morning, Mrs. Ruddle. Tell Bunter we're ready for breakfast, would you?"

"Right you are, me lord," replied Mrs. Ruddle (for after all, he *was* a lord). But she expressed herself later in the day to her friend, Mrs. Hodges.

"Mother-naked, Mrs. 'Odges, if you'll believe *me*. I declare I was that ashamed I didden know w'ere to look. And no more 'air on 'is chest than wot I 'as meself."

"That's gentry," said Mrs. Hodges, referring to the first part of the indictment. "You've only to look at the pictures of them there sunbathers as they call them on the Ly-doh. Now, my Susan's first were a wunnerful 'airy man, jest like a kerridgerug if you take my meaning. But," she added cryptically, "it don't foller, for they never 'ad no family, not till 'e died and she married young Tyler over at Pigott's."

• • • • •

When Mr. Bunter tapped discreetly at the door and entered with a wooden bucket full of kindling, her ladyship had vanished and his lordship was sitting on the window-ledge smoking a cigarette.

"Good morning, Bunter. Fine morning."

"Beautiful autumn weather, my lord, very seasonable. I trust your lordship found everything satisfactory."

"H'm. Bunter, do you know the meaning of the expression *arrière-pensée?*"

"No, my lord."

"I'm glad to hear it. Have you remembered to pump up the cistern?"

"Yes, my lord. I have put the oil-stove in order and summoned the sweep. Breakfast will be ready in a few minutes, my lord, if you will kindly excuse tea for this morning, the local grocer not being acquainted with coffee except in bottles. While you are breakfasting, I will endeavor to kindle a fire in the dressing-room, which I would not attempt last night, on account of the time being short and there being a board in the chimney—no doubt to exclude draughts and pigeons. I fancy, however, it is readily removable."

"All right. Is there any hot water?"

"Yes, my lord—though I would point out there is a slight leak in the copper which creates difficulty as tending to extinguish the fire. I would suggest bringing up the baths in about forty minutes' time, my lord."

"Baths? Thank God! Yes—that'll do splendidly. No word from Mr. Noakes, I suppose?"

"No, my lord."

"We'll see to him presently. I see you've found the firedogs."

"In the coalhouse, my lord. Will you wear the Lovats or the grey suit?"

"Neither—find me an open shirt and a pair of flannel bags and—did you put in my old blazer?"

"Certainly, my lord."

"Then buzz off and get breakfast before I get like the

Duke of Wellington, nearly reduced to a skellington. . . . I say, Bunter."

"My lord?"

"I'm damned sorry you're having all this trouble."

"Don't mention it, my lord. So long as your lordship is satisfied—"

"Yes. All right, Bunter. Thanks."

He dropped his hand lightly on the servant's shoulder in what might have been a gesture of affection or dismissal as you chose to take it, and stood looking thoughtfully into the fireplace till his wife rejoined him.

"I've been exploring—I'd never been in that part of the house. After you go down five steps to the modern bit you turn a corner and go up six steps and bump your head and there's another passage and a little ramification and two more bedrooms and a triangular cubby-hole and a ladder that goes up to the attics. And the cistern lives in a cupboard to itself—you open the door and fall down two steps *and* bump your head, and bring up with your chin on the ball-cock."

"My God! You haven't put the ball-cock out of order? Do you realize, woman, that country life is entirely conditioned by the ball-cock in the cistern and the kitchen boiler?"

"I do—but I didn't think you would."

"Don't I? If you'd spent your childhood in a house with a hundred and fifty bedrooms and perpetual houseparties, where every drop had to be pumped up by hand and the hot water carried because there were only two bathrooms and all the rest hip-baths, and had the boiler burst when you were entertaining the Prince of Wales, what you didn't know about insanitary plumbing wouldn't be worth knowing."

"Peter, I believe you're a fraud. You may play at being a great detective and a scholar and a cosmopolitan man-about-town, but at bottom you're nothing but an English country gentleman, with his soul in the stables and his mind on the parish pump."

"God help all married men! You would pluck out the heart of my mystery. No—but my father was one of the old school and thought that all these new-fangled luxuries made you soft and merely spoiled the servants. . . . Come in! . . . Ah! I have never regretted Paradise Lost since I discovered that it contained no eggs-and-bacon."

"The trouble with these here chimneys," observed Mr. Puffett oracularly, "is that they wants sweeping."

He was an exceedingly stout man, rendered still stouter by his costume. This had reached what, in recent medical jargon, is known as "a high degree of onionisation," consisting as it did of a greenish-black coat and trousers and a series of variegated pullovers one on top of the other, which peeped out at the throat in a graduated scale of *décolleté*.

"There ain't no sweeter chimneys in the county," pursued Mr. Puffett, removing his coat and displaying the outermost sweater in a glory of red and yellow horizontal stripes, "if they was given half a chance, as who should know better than me what's been up them time and again as a young lad me ole Dad bein' in the chimney-sweeping line."

"Indeed?" said Mr. Bunter.

"The law wouldn't let me do it now," said Mr. Puffett, shaking his head, which was crowned with a bowler hat. "Not as me figure would allow of it at my time of life. But I knows these here chimneys from 'earth to pot as I may say, and a sweeter-drawing pair of chimneys you couldn't wish for. Not when properly swep'. But no chimney can be sweet if not swep', no more than a room can, as I'm sure you'll agree with me, Mr. Bunter."

"Quite so," said Mr. Bunter. "Would you be good enough to proceed to sweep them?"

"To oblige *you*, Mr. Bunter, and to oblige the lady and gentleman, I shall be 'appy to sweep them. I'm a builder by trade, but always 'appy to oblige with a chimney when called upon. I 'ave, as you might say, a soft spot for chimneys, 'avin' been brought up in 'em, like, and though I says it, Mr. Bunter, there ain't no one 'andles a chimney kinder nor wot I does. It's knowing 'em, you see, wot does it—knowing w'ere they wants easin' and 'umourin' and w'ere they wants the power be'ind the rods."

So saying, Mr. Puffett turned up his various sleeves, flexed his biceps once or twice, picked up his rods and brushes, which he had laid down in the passage, and asked where he should begin.

"The sitting-room will be required first," said Mr. Bunter. "In the kitchen I can, for the immediate moment, manage with the oil-stove. This way, Mr. Puffett, if you please."

Mrs. Ruddle, who, as far as the Wimseys were concerned, was a new broom, had made a clean and determined sweep of the sitting-room, draping all the uglier pieces of furniture with particular care in dust-sheets, covering the noisy rugs with newspaper, decorating with handsome dunce's caps two exceptionally rampageous bronze cavaliers which flanked the fireplace on pedestals and were too heavy to move, and tying up in a duster the withered pampas-grass in the painted drainpipe near the door, for, as she observed, "them things do 'old the dust so."

"Ah!" said Mr. Puffett. He removed his top sweater to display a blue one, spread out his apparatus on the space between the shrouded settles and plunged beneath the sacking that enveloped the chimney-breast. He emerged again, beaming with satisfaction. "What did I tell you? Full o' sut this chimney is. Ain't bin swep' for a mort o' years I reckon."

"We reckon so too," said Mr. Bunter. "We should like to have a word with Mr. Noakes on the subject of these chimneys."

"Ah!" said Mr. Puffett. He thrust his brush up the chimney and screwed a rod to its hinder end. "If I was to give you a pound note, Mr. Bunter"—the rod jerked upwards and he added another joint—"a pound note for every penny"—he added another joint—"every penny Mr.

Noakes has paid me"—he added another joint—"or any other practical sweep for that matter"—he added another joint—"in the last ten years or maybe more"—he added another joint—"for sweeping of these here chimneys"—he added another joint—"I give you my word, Mr. Bunter"—he added another joint and swivelled round on his haunches to deliver his peroration with more emphasis—"you wouldn't be one 'apenny better off then you are now."

"I believe you," said Mr. Bunter. "And the sooner that chimney is clear, the better we shall be pleased."

He retired into the scullery, where Mrs. Ruddle, armed with a hand-bowl, was scooping boiling water from the copper into a large bath-can.

"You had better leave it to me, Mrs. Ruddle, to negotiate the baths round the turn of the stairs. You may follow me with the cans, *if* you please."

Returning thus processionally through the sitting-room he was relieved to see only Mr. Puffett's ample base emerging from under the chimney-breast and to hear him utter loud groans and cries of self-encouragement which boomed hollow in the funnel of the brickwork. It is always pleasant to see a fellow-creature toiling still harder than one's self.

In nothing has the whirligig of time so redressed the balance between the sexes as in this business of getting up in the morning. Woman, when not an adept of the Higher Beauty Culture, has now little to do beyond washing, stepping into a garment or so, and walking downstairs. Man, still slave to the button and the razor, clings to the ancient ceremonial of potter and gets himself up by installments. Harriet was knotting her tie before the sound of splashing was heard in the next room. She accordingly classed her new possession as a confirmed potterer and made her way down by what Peter, with more exactness than delicacy, had already named the Privy Stair. This led into a narrow passage, containing the modern convenience before-mentioned, a boot-hole and a cupboard with brooms in it, and debouched at length into the scullery and so to the back door.

The garden, at any rate, had been well looked after. There were cabbages at the back, and celery trenches, also an asparagus bed well strawed up and a number of scientifically pruned apple trees. There was also a small cold-house sheltering a hardy vine with half a dozen bunches of black grapes on it and a number of half-hardy plants in pots. In front of the house, a good show of dahlias and chrysanthemums and a bed of scarlet salvias lent color to the sunshine. Mr. Noakes apparently had some little taste for gardening, or at any rate a good gardener; and this was the pleasantest thing yet known of Mr. Noakes, thought Harriet. She explored the potting-shed, where the tools were in good order, and found a pair of scissors, armed with which she made an assault upon the long trail of vine-leaves and the rigid bronze sheaves of the chrysanthemums. She grinned a little to find herself thus supplying the statutory "feminine touch" to the household and, looking up, was rewarded with the sight of her husband. He was curled on the sill of the open window, in a dressing-gown, with *The Times* on his knee and a cigarette between his lips, and was trimming his nails in a thoughtful leisurely way, as though he had world and time enough at his disposal. At the other side of the casement, come from goodness knew where, was a large ginger cat, engaged in thoroughly licking one forepaw, before applying it to the back of its ear. The two sleek animals, delicately self-absorbed, sat on in a mandarin-like calm till the human one, with the restlessness of inferiority, lifted his eyes from his task, caught sight of Harriet and said "Hey!"—whereupon the cat rose up, affronted, and leapt out of sight.

"That," said Peter, who had sometimes an uncanny way of echoing one's own thoughts, "is a very dainty, ladylike occupation."

"Isn't it?" said Harriet. She stood on one leg to inspect the pound or two of garden mold adhering to her stout brogue shoe. "A garden is a lovesome thing. God wot."

"Her feet beneath her petticoat like little mice stole in and out," agreed his lordship gravely. "Can you tell me, rosyfingered Aurora, whether the unfortunate person in the room below me is being slowly murdered or only having a fit?"

"I was beginning to wonder myself," said Harriet; for strange, strangled cries were proceeding from the sitting-room. "Perhaps I had better go and find out."

"Must you go? You improve the scenery so much. I like a landscape with figures. . . . Dear me! what a shocking sound—like Nell Cook under the paving-stone! It seemed to come right up into the room beside me. I am becoming a nervous wreck."

"You don't look it. You look abominably placid and pleased with life."

"Well, so I am. But one should not be selfish in one's happiness. I feel convinced that somewhere about the house there is a fellow-creature in trouble."

At this point Bunter emerged from the front door, walked backwards across the strip of turf, with eyes cast upwards as though seeking a heavenly revelation, and solemnly shook his head, like Lord Burleigh in *The Critic*.

"Ain't we there yet?" cried the voice of Mrs. Ruddle from the window.

"No," said Bunter, returning, "we appear to be making no progress at all."

"It seems," said Peter, "that we are expecting a happy event. *Parturiunt montes*. At any rate, the creation seems to be groaning and travailing together a good deal."

Harriet got off the flower-bed and scraped the earth from her shoes with a garden label.

"I shall cease to decorate the landscape and go and form part of a domestic interior."

Peter uncoiled himself from the windowsill, took off his dressing-gown and pulled away his blazer from under the ginger cat.

. . . . . .

"All that's the matter with this chimney, Mr. Bunter," pronounced Mr. Puffett, "is, sut." Having thus, as it were, come out by the same road as he had gone in, he began to withdraw his brush from the chimney, unscrewing it with extreme deliberation, rod by rod.

"So," said Mr. Bunter, with an inflection of sarcasm quite lost on Mr. Puffett, "so we had inferred."

"That's it," pursued Mr. Puffett, "corroded sut. No chimney can draw when the pot's full of corroded sut like this 'ere chimney-pot is. You can't ask it. It ain't reasonable."

"I don't ask it," retorted Mr. Bunter. "I asked you to get it clear, that's all."

"Well now, Mr. Bunter," said Mr. Puffett with an air of injury, "I put it to you to just take a look at this 'ere sut." He extended a grimy hand filled with what looked like clinkers. " 'Ard as a crock, that sut is, corroded 'ard. That's wot your chimney-pot's full of, and you can't get a brush through it, not with all the power you puts be'ind it. Near forty feet of rod I've got up that chimney, Mr. Bunter, trying to get through the pot, and it ain't fair on a man nor his rods." He pulled down another section of his apparatus and straightened it out with loving care.

"Some means will have to be devised to penetrate the obstruction," said Mr. Bunter, his eyes on the window, "and without delay. Her ladyship is coming in from the garden. You can take out the breakfast tray, Mrs. Ruddle."

"Ah!" said Mrs. Ruddle, peeping under the dish-covers before lifting the tray from the radio cabinet where Bunter had set it down, "they're taking their vittles well—that's a good sign in a young couple. I remember when me and Ruddle was wed—"

"And the lamps all need new wicks," added Bunter austerely, "and the burners cleaned before you fill them."

"Mr. Noakes ain't used no lamps this long time," said Mrs. Ruddle with a sniff. "Says 'e can see well enough by candlelight. Comes cheaper, I suppose." She flounced out with the tray and, encountering Harriet in the doorway, dropped a curtsy that sent the dish-covers sliding.

"Oh, you've got the sweep, Bunter—that's splendid! We thought we heard something going on."

"Yes, my lady. Mr. Puffett has been good enough to oblige. But I understand that he has encountered some impenetrable obstacle in the upper portion of the chimney."

"How kind of you to come, Mr. Puffett. We had a dreadful time last night."

Judging from the sweep's eye that propitiation was advisable, Harriet extended her hand. Mr. Puffett looked at it, looked at his own, pulled up his sweaters to get at his trousers pocket, extracted a newly laundered red-cotton handkerchief, shook it slowly from its fold, draped it across his palm and so grasped Harriet's fingers, rather in the manner of a royal proxy bedding his master's bride with the sheet between them.

"Well, me lady," said Mr. Puffett, "I'm allus willin' to oblige. Not but what you'll allow as a chimney wot's choked like this chimney is ain't fair to a man nor yet to 'is rods. But I will make bold to say that if any man can get the corroded sut out of this 'ere chimney-pot, I'm the man to do it. It's experience, you see, that's wot it is, and the power I puts be'ind it."

"I'm sure it is," said Harriet.

"As I understand the matter, my lady," put in Bunter, "it is the actual pot that's choked—no structural defect in the stack."

"That's right," said Mr. Puffett, mollified by finding himself appreciated, "the pot's where your trouble is." He stripped off another sweater to reveal himself in emerald green. "I'm a-goin' to try it with the rods alone, without the brush. Maybe, with my power be'ind it, we'll be able to get the rod through the sut. If not, then we'll 'ave to get the ladders."

"Ladders?"

"Access by the roof, my lady," explained Bunter.

"What fun!" said Harriet. "I'm sure Mr. Puffett will manage it somehow. Can you find me a vase or something for these flowers, Bunter?"

"Very good, my lady."

(Nothing, thought Mr. Bunter, not even an Oxford education, would prevent a woman's mind from straying away after inessentials; but he was pleased to note that the temper was, so far, admirably controlled. A vase of water was a small price to pay for harmony.)

"Peter!" cried Harriet up the staircase. (Bunter, had he remained to witness it, might after all have conceded her an instinct for essentials.) "Peter darling! the sweep's here!"

"Oh, frabjous day! I am coming, my own, my sweep." He pattered down briskly. "What a genius you have for saying the right thing! All my life I have waited to hear those exquisite words, *Peter darling, the sweep's come*. We are married, by God! We are married. I thought so once, but now I know it."

"Some people take a lot of convincing."

"One is afraid to believe in good fortune. The sweep! I crushed down my rising hopes. I said, No—it is a thunderstorm, a small earthquake, or at most a destitute cow dying by inches in the chimney. I dared not court disappointment. It is so long since I was taken into anybody's confidence about a sweep. As a rule, Bunter smuggles him in when I am out of the house, for fear my lordship should be inconvenienced. Only a wife would treat me with the disrespect I deserve and summon me to look upon the—good Lord!"

He turned as he spoke to look upon Mr. Puffett, only the soles of whose boots were visible. At this moment a bellow so loud and prolonged issued from the fireplace that Peter turned quite pale.

"He hasn't got stuck, has he?"

"No—it's the power he's putting behind it. There's corroded soot in the pot or something, which makes it very hard work. . . . Peter, I do wish you could have seen the place before Noakes filled it up with bronze horsemen and bamboo whatnots and aspidistras."

"Hush! never blaspheme the aspidistra. It's very unlucky. Something frightful will come down that chimney and *get* you—boo! . . . Oh, my God! look at that bristling horror over the wireless set!"

"Some people would pay pounds for a fine cactus like that."

"They must have very little imagination. It's not a plant—it's a morbid growth—something lingering happening to your kidneys. Besides, it makes me wonder whether I've shaved. Have I?"

"M'm—yes—like satin—no, that'll do! I suppose, if we shot the beastly thing out, it'd die to spite us. They're delicate, though you mightn't think it, and Mr. Noakes would demand its weight in gold. How long did we hire this grisly furniture for?"

"A month, but we might get rid of it sooner. It's a damn shame spoiling this noble old place with that muck."

"Do you like the house, Peter?"

"It's beautiful. It's like a lovely body inhabited by an evil spirit. And I don't mean only the furniture. I've taken a dislike to our landlord, or tenant, or whatever he is. I've a fancy he's up to no good and that the house will be glad to be rid of him."

"I believe it hates him. I'm sure he's starved and insulted and ill-treated it. Why, even the chimneys—"

"Yes, of course, the chimneys. Do you think I could bring myself to the notice of our household god, our little Lar? . . . Er—excuse me one moment, Mr.—er—"

"Puffett is the name."

"Mr. Puffett—hey, Puffett! Just a second, would you?"

"Now then!" expostulated Mr. Puffett, swivelling round on his knees. "Who're you a-poking of in the back with a man's own rods? It ain't fair to a man *nor* his rods."

"I beg your pardon," said Peter. "I did shout but failed to attract your attention."

"No offense," said Mr. Puffett, evidently conceding

something to the honeymoon spirit. "You'll be his lordship, I take it. Hope I sees you well."

"Thank you, we are in the pink. But this chimney seems to be a little unwell. Shortness of wind or something."

"There ain't no call to abuse the chimney," said Mr. Puffett. "The fault's in the pot, like I was saying to your lady. The pot, you see, ain't reconcilable to the size of the chimney, and it's corroded that 'ard with sut as you couldn't 'ardly get a bristle through, let alone a brush. It don't matter 'ow wide you builds the chimney, all the smoke's got to go through the pot in the end, and that—if you foller my meaning—is where the fault is, see?"

"I follow you. Even a Tudor chimney winds somewhere safe to pot."

"Ah!" said Mr. Puffett, "that's just it. If we 'ad the Tooder pot, now, we'd be all right. A Tooder pot is a pot as any practical chimney-sweep might 'andle with pleasure and do justice to 'isself *and* 'is rods. But Mr. Noakes, now 'e tuk down some of the Tooder pots and sold 'em to make sundials."

"Sold them for sundials?"

"That's right, me lady. Catch penny, I calls it. That's 'im all over. And these 'ere fiddlin' modern pots wot 'e's put on ain't no good for a chimney the 'ighth and width of this chimney wot you've got 'ere. It stands to reason they'll corrode up with sut in a month. Once that there pot's clear, the rest is easy. There's loose sut in the bends, of course—but that don't 'urt—not without it was to ketch fire, which is why it didn't oughter be there and I'll 'ave it out in no time once we're done with the pot—but while the sut's corroded 'ard in the pot, you won't get no fire to go in this chimney, me lord, and that's the long and the short of it."

"You make it admirably clear," said Peter. "I see you are an expert. Please go on demonstrating. Don't mind me—I'm admiring the tools of your trade. What is this affair like a Brobdingnagian corkscrew? There's a thing to give a man a thirst—what?"

"Thank-you, me lord," replied Mr. Puffett, evidently taking this for an invitation. "Work first and pleasure afterwards. W'en the job's done, I won't say no."

He beamed kindly at them, peeled off his green uppermost layer and, arrayed now in a Fair-Isle jumper of complicated pattern, addressed himself once more to the chimney.

CHAPTER V

FURY OF GUNS

So Henny-penny, Cocky-locky, Ducky-daddles, Goosey-poosey, Turkey-lurkey, and Foxy-woxy all went to tell the king the sky was a-falling.

—JOSEPH JACOBS, ENGLISH FAIRY TALES

"I do *hope* I'm not disturbing you," exclaimed Miss Twitterton anxiously. "I felt I *must* run over and see how you were getting on. I really couldn't sleep for thinking of you—so strange of Uncle to behave like that—so dreadfully inconsiderate!"

"Oh, please!" said Harriet." It was so nice of you to come, won't you sit down? . . . Oh, *Bunter!* Is that the best you can find?"

"Why!" cried Miss Twitterton, "you've got the Bonzo vase! Uncle won it in a raffle. So *amusing*, isn't it, holding the flowers in his mouth like that, and his little pink waistcoat?—Aren't the chrysanthemums lovely? Frank Crutchley looks after them, he's *such* a good gardener. . . . Oh, thank you, thank you so much—I really mustn't inflict myself on you for more than a moment. But I couldn't help being anxious. I do *hope* you passed a comfortable night."

"Thank you," said Peter, gravely. "Parts of it were excellent."

"I always think the *bed* is the important thing—" began Miss Twitterton. Mr. Puffett, scandalized and seeing Peter beginning to lose control of his mouth, diverted her attention by digging her gently in the ribs with his elbow.

"Oh!" ejaculated Miss Twitterton. The state of the room and Mr. Puffett's presence forced themselves together upon her mind. "Oh, dear, what *is* the matter? *Don't* say the chimney has been smoking again? It always *was* a tiresome chimney."

"Now, see here," said Mr. Puffett, who seemed to feel to the chimney much as a tigress might feel to her offspring, "that's a good chimney, that is. I couldn't build a better chimney meself, allowin' for them upstairs flues and the 'ighth and pitch of the gable. But when a chimney ain't never been swep' through, on account of persons' cheeseparin' 'abits, then it ain't fair on the chimney, nor yet it ain't fair on the sweep. And you knows it."

"Oh, dear, oh, dear!" cried Miss Twitterton, collapsing upon a chair and immediately bouncing up again. "What you must be thinking of us all. Where *can* Uncle be? I'm sure if I'd known—Oh! there's Frank Crutchley! I'm so glad. Uncle may have said something to him. He comes every Wednesday to do the garden, you know. A most *superior* young man. Shall I call him in? I'm sure he could help us. I always send for Frank when anything goes wrong. He's so clever at finding a way out of a difficulty."

Miss Twitterton had run to the window without waiting for Harriet's, "Yes, do have him in," and now cried in agitated tones:

"Frank! Frank! Whatever can have happened? We can't find Uncle!"

"Can't find him?"

"No—he isn't here, and he's sold the house to this lady and gentleman, and we don't know *where* he is and the chimney's smoking and everything upside down; what *can* have become of him?"

Frank Crutchley, peering in at the window and scratching his head, looked bewildered, as well he might.

"Never said nothing to me, Miss Twitterton. He'll be over at the shop, most like."

"Was he here when you came last Wednesday?"

"Yes," said the gardener, "he was here then all right."

He paused, and a thought seemed to strike him. "He did ought to be here today. Can't find him, did you say? What's gone of him?"

"That's just what we don't know. Going off like that without telling anyone! What did he say to you?"

"I thought I'd find him here—leastways—"

"You'd better come in, Crutchley," said Peter.

"Right, sir!" said Crutchley, with some appearance of relief at having a man to deal with. He withdrew in the direction of the back door, where, to judge by the sounds, he was received by Mrs. Ruddle with a volume of explanatory narrative.

"Frank would run over to Broxford, I'm sure," said Miss Twitterton, "and find out what's happened to Uncle. He might be ill—though you'd think he'd have sent for me, wouldn't you? Frank could get a car from the garage—he drives for Mr. Hancock at Pagford you know, and I tried to get him this morning before I came, but he was out with a taxi. He's very clever with cars, and such a good gardener. I'm sure you won't mind my mentioning it, but if you've bought the house and want someone to do the garden—"

"He's kept it awfully well," said Harriet. "I thought it looked lovely."

"I'm so glad you think so. He works so hard, and he's so anxious to get on—"

"Come in, Crutchley," said Peter.

The gardener, hesitating now at the door of the room with his face to the light, showed himself as an alert, well-set-up young man of about thirty, neatly dressed in a suit of working clothes and carrying his cap respectfully in his hand. His crisp dark hair, blue eyes and strong white teeth produced a favorable impression, though at the moment he looked slightly put out. From his glance at Miss Twitterton, Harriet gathered that he had overheard her panegyric of him and disapproved of it.

"This," went on Peter, "comes a little unexpected, what?"

"Well, yes, sir." The gardener smiled, and sent his quick glance roving over Mr. Puffett. "I see it's the chimney."

"It ain't the *chimney*," began the sweep indignantly; when Miss Twitterton broke in:

"But, Frank, don't you understand? Uncle's sold the house and gone away without telling anybody. I can't make it out, it's not *like* him. Nothing done and nothing ready and nobody here last night to let anybody in, and Mrs. Ruddle knew *nothing* except that he'd gone to Broxford—"

"Well, have you sent over there to look for him?" inquired the young man in a vain endeavor to stem the tide.

"No, not yet—unless Lord Peter—did you?—or no, there wouldn't be time, would there?—no keys, even, and I really was ashamed you should have had to come last night like that, but of course I never *dreamt*—and you could so easily have run over this morning, Frank—or I could go myself on my bicycle—but Mr. Hancock told me you were out with a taxi, so I thought I'd better just call and see."

Frank Crutchley's eyes wandered over the room as though seeking counsel from the dust-sheets, the aspidistras, the chimney, the bronze horsemen, Mr. Puffett's bowler, the cactus and the radio cabinet, before at length coming to rest on Peter's in mute appeal.

"Let's start from the right end," suggested Wimsey. "Mr. Noakes was here last Wednesday and went off the same night to catch the ten o'clock bus to Broxford. That was nothing unusual, I gather. But he expected to be back to deal with the matter of our arrival, and you, in fact, expected to find him here today."

"That's right, sir."

Miss Twitterton gave a little jump and her mouth shaped itself into an anxious O.

"Is he usually here when you come on Wednesdays?"

"Well, that depends, sir. Not always."

"Frank!" cried Miss Twitterton, outraged, "it's Lord Peter Wimsey. You ought to say 'my lord.'"

"Never mind that now," said Peter, kindly, but irritated by this interference with his witness. Crutchley looked at

Miss Twitterton with the expression of a small boy who has been publicly exhorted to wash behind the ears, and said:

"Some days he's here, some not. If he ain't" (Miss Twitterton frowned), "I gets the key from her" (he jerked his head at Miss Twitterton) "to come in and wind the clock and see to the pot-plants. But I did reckon to see him this morning, because I had particular business with him. That's why I come up to the house first—came, if you like" (he added, crossly, in response to Miss Twitterton's anxious prompting), "it's all one, I dessay, to my lord."

"To his lordship," said Miss Twitterton, faintly.

"Did he actually tell you he'd be here?"

"Yes—my lord. Leastways he said as he'd let me have back some money I'd put into that business of his. Promised it back today."

"Oh, Frank! You've been worrying Uncle *again*. I've *told* you you're just being *silly* about your money. I *know* it's quite safe with Uncle."

Peter's glance crossed Harriet's over Miss Twitterton's head.

"He said he'd let you have it this morning. May I ask whether it was any considerable sum?"

"Matter o' forty pounds," said the gardener, "as he got me to put into his wireless business. Mayn't seem a lot to you," he went on a little uncertainly, as though trying to assess the financial relationship between Peter's title, his ancient and shabby blazer, his manservant and his wife's non-committal tweeds, "but I've got a better use for it, and so I told him. I asked for it last week and he palavered as usual, sayin' he didn't keep sums like that in the house—puttin' me off—"

"But, Frank, of course he didn't. He might have been robbed. He did lose ten pounds once, in a pocketbook—"

"But I stuck to it," pursued Crutchley, unheeding, "sayin' I must have it, and at last he said he'd let me have it today, as he'd got some money coming in—"

"He said that?"

"Yes, sir—my lord—and I says to him, I hope you do, I says, and if you don't, I'll have the law on you."

"Oh, Frank, you shouldn't have said that!"

"Well, I did say it. Can't you let me tell his lordship what he wants to know?"

Harriet's glance had caught Peter's again, and he had nodded. The money for the house. But if he had told Crutchley as much as that—"

"Did he say where this money of his was coming from?"

"Not him. He's not the sort to tell more than he has to. Matter of fact, I never thought he was expecting no money in particular. Making excuses, he was. Never pays out money till the last moment, and not then if he can 'elp it. Might lose 'arf a day's interest, don't you see," added Crutchley with a sudden half-reluctant grin.

"Sound principle, so far as it goes," said Wimsey.

"That's right; that's the way he's made his bit. He's a warm man, is Mr. Noakes. Still, all the same for that, I told him I wanted the forty pound for my new garridge—"

"Yes, the garahge," put in Miss Twitterton, with a corrective little frown and shake of the head. "Frank's been saving up a long time to start his own garahge."

"So," repeated Crutchley with emphasis, " 'wantin' the money for the garridge,' I said, 'I'll see my money Wednesday,' I said, 'or I'll 'ave the law on you.' That's what I said. And I went out sharp and I ain't seen him since."

"I see. Well—" Peter glanced from Crutchley to Miss Twitterton and back again. "We'll run over to Broxford presently and hunt the gentleman up, and then we can get it straight. In the meantime, we shall want the garden kept in order, so perhaps you'd better carry on as usual."

"Very good, my lord. Shall I come Wednesdays same as before? Five shillings, Mr. Noakes give me by the day."

"I'll give you the same. Do you know anything about running an electric light plant, by the way?"

"Yes, my lord; there's one at the garridge where I work."

"Because," said Peter, with a smile at his wife, "though

candles and oil-stoves have their romantic moments and all that, I think we shall really have to electrify Talboys."

"You'll electrify Paggleham if you do, my lord," said Crutchley, with sudden geniality. "I'm sure I'd be very willing—"

"Frank," said Miss Twitterton brightly, "knows *everything* about machinery!"

The unfortunate Crutchley, on the verge of an explosion, caught Peter's eye and smiled in some embarrassment.

"All right," said his lordship. "We'll talk it over presently. Meanwhile, carry on with whatever it is you do on Wednesdays." Whereupon the gardener thankfully made his escape, leaving Harriet to reflect that school-marming seemed to have got into Miss Twitterton's blood and that nothing was so exasperating to the male sex in general as an attitude of mingled reproof and showmanship.

The click of the distant gate and a footfall on the path broke in on the slightly blank pause which followed Crutchley's exit.

"Perhaps," cried Miss Twitterton, "that's Uncle coming now."

"I hope to God," said Peter, "it's not one of those infernal reporters."

"It's not," said Harriet, running to the window. "It's the vicar—he's coming to call."

"Oh, the dear vicar! perhaps he may know something."

"Ah!" said Mr. Puffett.

"This is magnificent," said Peter. "I collect vicars." He joined Harriet at her observation-post. "This is a very well-grown specimen, six foot four or thereabouts, short-sighted, a great gardener, musical, smokes a pipe—"

"Good gracious!" cried Miss Twitterton, "do you know Mr. Goodacre?"

"—untidy, with a wife who does her best on a small stipend; a product of one of our older seats of learning—1890 vintage—Oxford, at a guess, but not, I fancy, Keble, though as high in his views as the parish allows him to be."

"He'll hear you," said Harriet, as the reverend gentleman withdrew his nose from the middle of a clump of dahlias and cast a vague glance through his eyeglasses towards the sitting-room window. "To the best of my knowledge and belief, you're right. But why the strictly limited High Church views?"

"The Roman vest and the emblem upon the watch-chain point the upward way. You know my methods, Watson. But a bundle of settings for the Te Deum under the arm suggest sung Matins in the Established way; besides, though we heard the church clock strike eight, there was no bell for a daily Celebration."

"However you think of these things, Peter!"

"I'm sorry," said her husband, flushing faintly. "I can't help taking notice, whatever I'm doing."

"Worse and worse," replied his lady. "Mrs. Shandy herself would be shocked." While Miss Twitterton, completely bewildered, made haste to explain:

"It's choir practice tonight, of *course*. Wednesdays, you know. Always Wednesdays. He'll be taking them up to the church."

"Of course, as you say," agreed Peter with relish. "Wednesday always *is* choir practice. *Quod semper, quod ubique, quod ab omnibus*. Nothing ever changes in the English countryside. Harriet, your honeymoon house is a great success. I am feeling twenty years younger."

He retired hastily from the window as the vicar approached, and declaimed with considerable emotion:

"Give me just a country cottage, where the soot of
ages falls,
And, to crown a perfect morning, look! an English
vicar calls!

I, too, Miss Twitterton, though you might not think it, have bawled Maunder and Garrett down the neck of the blacksmith's daughter singing in the village choir, and have proclaimed the company of the spearmen to be scattered abroad among the beasts of the people, with a little fancy pointing of my own."

"Ah!" said Mr. Puffett, "that's an orkerd one, is the beasts of the people."

As though the word "soot" had struck a chord in his mind, he moved tentatively in the direction of the fireplace. The vicar vanished within the porch.

"My dear," said Harriet, "Miss Twitterton will think we are both quite mad; and Mr. Puffett knows it already."

"Oh, no, me lady," said Mr. Puffett. "Not mad. Only 'appy. I knows the feeling."

"As man to man, Puffett," said the bridegroom, "I thank you for those kind and sympathetic words. Where, by the way, did *you* go for your honeymoon?"

" 'Erne Bay, me lord," replied Mr. Puffett.

"Good God, yes! Where George Joseph Smith murdered his first Bride-in-the-Bath. We never thought of that! Harriet—"

"Monster," said Harriet, "do your worst! There are only hip-baths here."

"There!" cried Miss Twitterton, catching at the only word in this conversation that appeared to make sense, "I was *always* saying to Uncle that he really *ought* to put in a bathroom."

Before Peter could give further proofs of insanity, Bunter mercifully announced:

"The Reverend Simon Goodacre."

The vicar, thin, elderly, clean-shaven, his tobacco-pouch bulging from the distended pocket of his suit of "clerical grey" and the left knee of his trousers displaying a large three-cornered tear carefully darned, advanced upon them with that air of mild self-assurance which a consciousness of spiritual dignity bestows upon a naturally modest disposition. His peering glance singled out Miss Twitterton from the group presented to his notice, and he greeted her with a cordial shake of the hand, at the same time acknowledging Mr. Puffett's presence with a nod and a cheerful, " 'Morning, Tom!"

"Good morning, Mr. Goodacre," replied Miss Twitterton in a mournful chirp. "Dear, dear! Did they tell you—?"

"Yes, indeed," said the vicar. "Well, this *is* a surprise!" He adjusted his glasses, beamed vaguely about him, and addressed himself to Peter. "I fear I am intruding. I understand that Mr. Noakes—er—"

"Good morning, sir," said Peter, feeling it better to introduce himself than to wait for Miss Twitterton. "Delighted to see you. My name's Wimsey. My wife."

"I'm afraid we're all at sixes and sevens," said Harriet. Mr. Goodacre, she thought, had not changed much in the last seventeen years. He was a little greyer, a little thinner, a little baggier about the knees and shoulders, but in essentials the same Mr. Goodacre she and her father had occasionally encountered in the old days, visiting the sick of Paggleham. It was clear that he had not the faintest recollection of her; but, taking soundings as it were in these uncharted seas, his glances encountered something familiar—an ancient dark-blue blazer with "O. U. C. C." embroidered on the breast pocket.

"An Oxford man, I see," said the vicar, happily, as though this did away with any necessity for further identification.

"Balliol, sir," said Peter.

"Magdalen," returned Mr. Goodacre, unaware that, by merely saying "Keble," he could have shattered a reputation. He grasped Peter's hand and shook it again. "Bless me! Wimsey of Balliol. Now, what is it I—?"

"Cricket, perhaps," suggested Peter, helpfully.

"Yes," said the vicar, "ye—yes. Cricket and—Ah, Frank! Am I in your way?"

Crutchley, coming briskly in with a stepladder and a watering-pot, said, "No, sir, not at all," in the tone of voice which means, "Yes, sir, very much." The vicar dodged hastily.

"Won't you sit down, sir?" said Peter, uncovering a corner of the settee.

"Thank you, thank you," said Mr. Goodacre, as the stepladder was set down on the exact spot where he had been standing. "I really ought not to take up your time. Cricket, of course, and—"

"Getting into the veteran class, now, I'm afraid," said Peter, shaking his head. But the vicar was not to be diverted.

"Some other connection, I feel sure. Forgive me—I did not precisely catch what your manservant said. Not Lord *Peter* Wimsey?"

"An ill-favored title, but my own."

"Really!" cried Mr. Goodacre. "Of course, of course. Lord Peter Wimsey—cricket and crime! Dear me, this is an honor. My wife and I were reading a paragraph in the paper only the other day—most interesting—about your detective experiences—"

"Detective!" exclaimed Miss Twitterton in an agitated squeak.

"He's quite harmless, really," said Harriet.

"I hope," continued Mr. Goodacre, gently jocose, "you haven't come to detect anything in Paggleham."

"I sincerely hope not," said Peter. "As a matter of fact, we came here with the idea of passing a peaceful honeymoon."

"Indeed!" cried the vicar. "That is delightful. I hope I may say, God bless you and make you very happy."

Miss Twitterton, overcome by the thought of the chimneys and the bed-linen, sighed deeply, and then turned to frown at Frank Crutchley, who, from his point of vantage upon the stepladder, was indulging in what seemed to her to be an unbecoming kind of grimace over the heads of his employers. The young man instantly became unnaturally grave and gave his attention to mopping up the water which, in his momentary distraction, had overflowed the rim of the cactus-pot. Harriet earnestly assured the vicar that they were very happy, and Peter concurred, observing:

"We have been married nearly twenty-four hours, and are still married; which in these days may be considered a record. But then, you see, padre, we are old-fashioned, country-bred people. In fact, my wife used to be a neighbor of yours, so to speak."

The vicar, who had seemed doubtful whether to be amused or distressed by the first part of this remark, at once looked all eager interest, and Harriet hastened to explain who she was and what had brought them to Talboys. If Mr. Goodacre had ever heard or read anything of the murder trial, he showed no sign of such knowledge; he merely expressed the greatest delight at meeting Dr. Vane's daughter once more and at welcoming two new parishioners to his fold.

"And so you have bought the house! Dear me! I hope, Miss Twitterton, your uncle is not deserting us."

Miss Twitterton, who had scarcely known how to contain herself during this prolonged exchange of introductions and courtesies, broke out as though the words had released a spring:

"But you don't *understand*, Mr. Goodacre. It's *too* dreadful. Uncle never let me know a word about it. Not a *word*. He's gone off to Broxford or somewhere, and left the house like this!"

"But he's coming back, no doubt," said Mr. Goodacre.

"He told Frank he would be here today—didn't he, Frank?"

Crutchley, who had descended from the steps and appeared to be occupied in centralizing the radio cabinet with great precision beneath the hanging pot, replied:

"So he *said*, Miss Twitterton."

He folded his lips firmly, as though, in the vicar's presence, he preferred not to make the comments he might have made, and retired into the window with his watering-pot.

"But he isn't *here*," said Miss Twitterton. "It's all a terrible muddle. And poor Lord and Lady Peter—"

She embarked on an agitated description of the previous night's events, in which the keys, the chimneys, Crutchley's new garage, the bed-linen, the ten o'clock bus, and

Peter's intention of putting in an electric plant were jumbled into hopeless confusion. The vicar ejaculated from time to time and looked increasingly bewildered.

"Most trying, most trying," he said at length, when Miss Twitterton had talked herself breathless. "I am so sorry. If there is anything my wife and I can do, Lady Peter, I hope you will not hesitate to make use of us."

"It's awfully good of you," said Harriet. "But really, *we* are quite all right. It's rather fun, picnicking like this. Only, of course, Miss Twitterton is anxious about her uncle."

"No doubt he has been detained somewhere," said the vicar. "Or"—a bright thought occurred to him—"a letter may have gone wrong. Depend upon it, that is what has happened. The post office is a wonderful institution, but even Homer nods. I am sure you will find Mr. Noakes at Broxford safe and sound. Pray tell him I am sorry to have missed him. I had called to ask him for a subscription to the concert we are getting up in aid of the Church Music Fund—that explains my intrusion upon you. I fear we parsons are sad mendicants."

"Is the Choir still going strong?" inquired Harriet. "Do you remember once bringing it over to Great Pagford for a great combined Armistice Thanksgiving? I sat beside you at the Rectory tea, and we discussed Church music very seriously. Do you still do dear old Bunnett in F?"

She hummed the opening bars. Mr. Puffett, who all this time had remained discreetly withdrawn and was, at the moment, assisting Crutchley to sponge the aspidistra leaves, looked up, and joined in the melody with a powerful roar.

"Ah!" said Mr. Goodacre, gratified; "we have made a great deal of progress. We have advanced to Stanford in C. And last Harvest Festival we tackled the Hallelujah Chorus with great success."

"Hallelujah!" warbled Mr. Puffett, in stentorian tones. "Hallelujah! Hal-le-lu-jah!"

"Tom," said the vicar, apologetically, "is one of my most enthusiastic choirmen. And so is Frank."

Miss Twitterton glanced at Crutchley, as though to check him if he showed signs of bursting into riotous song. She was relieved to see that he had dissociated himself from Mr. Puffett, and was mounting the steps to wind the clock.

"And Miss Twitterton, of course," said Mr. Goodacre, "presides at the organ."

Miss Twitterton smiled faintly and looked at her fingers.

"But," pursued the vicar, "we sadly need new bellows. The old ones are patched past mending, and since we put in that new set of reeds they have become quite inadequate. The Hallelujah Chorus exposed our weaknesses sadly. In fact, the wind gave out altogether."

"So embarrassing," said Miss Twitterton. "I didn't know *what* to do."

"Miss Twitterton must be saved embarrassment at all costs," said Peter, producing his note-case.

"Oh, dear!" said the vicar. "I didn't mean. . . . Really, this is most generous. Too bad, your very first day in the parish. I—really—I am almost ashamed to—So very kind —so large a sum—Perhaps you would like to look at the program of the concert. Dear me!" His face lit up with a childlike pleasure. "Do you know, it is quite a long time since I handled a *proper* Bank of England note."

For the space of a moment, Harriet saw every person in that room struck into a kind of immobility by the magic of a piece of paper as it crackled between the vicar's fingers. Miss Twitterton awestruck and open-mouthed; Mr. Puffett suddenly pausing in mid-action, sponge in hand; Crutchley, on his way out of the room with the stepladder over his shoulder, jerking his head round to view the miracle; Mr. Goodacre himself smiling with excitement and delight; Peter amused and a little self-conscious, like a kind uncle presenting a teddy-bear to the nursery; they might have posed as they stood for the jacket-picture of a thriller: *Bank-Notes in the Parish*.

Then Peter said meaninglessly, "Oh, not at all." He picked up the concert program which the vicar had let fall in clutching at the note; and all the arrested motion flowed on again like a film. Miss Twitterton gave a small ladylike cough, Crutchley went out, Mr. Puffett dropped the sponge into the watering-can, and the vicar, putting the ten pound note carefully away in his pocket, inscribed the amount of the subscription in a little black notebook.

"It's going to be a grand concert," said Harriet, peering over her husband's shoulder. "When is it? Shall we be here?"

"October 27th," said Peter. "Of course we shall come to it. Rather."

"Of course," agreed Harriet; and smiled at the vicar.

Whatever fantastic pictures she had from time to time conjured up of married life with Peter, none of them had ever included attendance at village concerts. But of course they would go. She understood now why it was that with all his masking attitudes, all his cosmopolitan self-adaptations, all his odd spiritual reticences and escapes, he yet carried about with him that permanent atmosphere of security. He belonged to an ordered society, and this was it. More than any of the friends in her own world, he spoke the familiar language of her childhood. In London, anybody, at any moment, might do or become anything. But in a village—no matter what village—they were all immutably themselves; parson, organist, sweep, duke's son and doctor's daughter, moving like chessmen upon their alloted squares. She was curiously excited. She thought, "I have married England." Her fingers tightened on his arm.

England, serenely unaware of his symbolic importance, acknowledged the squeeze with a pressure of the elbow. "Splendid!" he said, heartily. "Piano solo, Miss Twitterton—we mustn't miss that, on any account. Song by the Reverend Simon Goodacre, 'Hybrias the Cretan'—strong, he-man stuff, padre. Folksongs and Sea-shanties by the Choir . . ."

(He took his wife's caress to indicate that she shared his

appreciation of the program. And, indeed, their minds were not far apart, for he was thinking: How these old boys run true to form! "Hybrias the Cretan"! When I was a kid, the curate used to sing it—"With my good sword I plough, I reap, I sow"—a gentle creature who wouldn't have harmed a fly . . . Merton, I think or was it Corpus? . . . with a baritone bigger than his whole body . . . he fell in love with our governess. . . .)

"Shenandoah," "Rio Grande," "Down in Demerara." He glanced round the dust-sheeted room. "That's exactly how we feel. That's the song for us, Harriet." He lifted his voice:

"Here we sit like birds in the wilderness—"

All mad together, thought Harriet, joining in:

"Birds in the wilderness—"

Mr. Puffett could not bear it and exploded with a roar:

"BIRDS in the wilderness—"

The vicar opened his mouth:

"Here we sit like birds in the wilderness,
Down in Demerara!"

Even Miss Twitterton added her chirp to the last line.

"Now this old man, he took and died-a-lum,
Took and died-a-lum,
Took and died-a-lum,
This old man, he took and died-a-lum,
Down in Demerara!"

(It was just like that poem by someone or other: "Everyone suddenly burst out singing.")

"So here we sit like birds in the wilderness,
Birds in the wilderness,
Birds in the wilderness!
Here we sit like birds in the wilderness,
Down in Demerara!"

"Bravo!" said Peter.

"Yes," said Mr. Goodacre, "we rendered that with great spirit."

"Ah!" said Mr. Puffett. "Nothing like a good song to take your mind off your troubles. Is there, me lord?"

"Nothing!" said Peter. "Begone, dull care! *Eructavit cor meum.*"

"Come, come," protested the vicar, "it's early days to talk about troubles, my dear young people."

"When a man's married," said Mr. Puffett, sententiously, "his troubles begin. Which they may take the form of a family. Or they may take the form of sut."

"Soot?" exclaimed the vicar, as though for the first time he was asking himself what Mr. Puffett was doing in the domestic chorus. "Why, yes, Tom—you do seem to be having a little trouble with Mr. Noakes's—I should say, Lord Peter's—chimney. What's the matter with it?"

"Something catastrophic, I gather," said the master of the house.

"Nothing like that," dissented Mr. Puffett, reprovingly. "Just sut. Corroded sut. Doo to neglect."

"I'm sure—" bleated Miss Twitterton.

"No call to blame present company," said Mr. Puffett. "I'm sorry for Miss Twitterton, and I'm sorry for his lordship. It's corroded that 'ard you can't get the rods through."

"That's bad, that's bad," ejaculated the vicar. He braced himself as a vicar should, to deal with this emergency occurring in his parish. "A friend of mine had sad trouble with corroded soot. But I was able to assist him with an old-fashioned remedy. I wonder now—I wonder—is Mrs. Ruddle here? the invaluable Mrs. Ruddle?"

Harriet, receiving no guidance from Peter's politely impassive expression, went to summon Mrs. Ruddle, of whom the vicar instantly took charge.

"Ah, good morning, Martha. Now, I wonder if you could borrow your son's old shotgun for us. The one he uses for scaring the birds."

"I could pop over and see, sir," said Mrs. Ruddle, dubiously.

"Let Crutchley go for you," suggested Peter. He turned abruptly as he spoke and began to fill his pipe. Harriet, studying his face, saw with apprehension that he was brimming over with an awful anticipatory glee. Whatever cataclysm impended, he would not put out a finger to stop it, he would let the heavens fall and tread the antic hay on the ruins.

"Well," conceded Mrs. Ruddle, "Frank's quicker on his feet nor what I am."

"Loaded, of course," cried the vicar after her, as she vanished through the door. "There's nothing," he explained to the world at large, "like one of those old duck-guns, discharged up the chimney, for clearing corroded soot. This friend of mine—"

"I don't 'old with that, sir," said Mr. Puffett, every bulge in his body expressing righteous resentment and a sturdy independence of judgment. "It's the power be'ind the rods as does it."

"I assure you, Tom," said Mr. Goodacre, "the shotgun cleared my friend's chimney instantly. A most obstinate case."

"That may be, sir," replied Mr. Puffett, "but it ain't a remedy as I should care to apply." He stalked gloomily to the spot where he had piled his cast-off sweaters and picked up the top one. "If the rods don't do it, then it's ladders you want, not 'igh explosive."

"But, Mr. Goodacre," exclaimed Miss Twitterton anxiously, "are you *sure* it's quite safe? I'm always very nervous about guns in the house. All these accidents—"

The vicar reassured her. Harriet, perceiving that the owners of the house, at any rate, were to be relieved of all responsibility for their own chimneys, nevertheless thought it well to placate the sweep.

"Don't desert us, Mr. Puffett," she pleaded. "One can't hurt Mr. Goodacre's feelings. But if anything happens—"

"Have a heart, Puffett," said Peter.

Mr. Puffett's little twinkling eyes looked into Peter's, which were like twin grey lakes of limpid clarity and wholly deceptive depth.

"Well," said Mr. Puffett, slowly, "anything to oblige. But don't say I didn't warn you, m'lord. It's a thing I don't 'old with."

"It won't bring the chimney down, will it?" inquired Harriet.

"Oh, it won't bring the *chimney* down," replied Mr. Puffett. "If you likes to 'umor the old gentleman, on your 'ead be it. In a manner of speaking, m'lady."

Peter had succeeded in getting his pipe to draw, and, with both hands in his trousers-pockets, was observing the actors in the drama with an air of pleased detachment. At the entrance of Crutchley and Mrs. Ruddle with the gun, however, he began to retreat, noiselessly and backwards, like a cat who has accidentally stepped in a pool of spilt perfume.

"My God!" he breathed delicately. "Waterloo year!"

"Splendid!" cried the vicar. "Thank you, thank you, Martha. Now we are equipped."

"You *have* been quick, Frank!" said Miss Twitterton. She eyed the weapon nervously. "You're *sure* it won't go off of its own accord?"

"Will an army mule go off of its own accord?" queried Peter, softly.

"I never like the idea of firearms," said Miss Twitterton.

"No, no," said the vicar. "Trust me, there will be no ill effects." He possessed himself of the gun and examined the lock and trigger mechanism with the air of one to whom the theory of ballistics was an open book.

"It's all loaded and ready, sir," said Mrs. Ruddle, proudly conscious of her Bert's efficiency.

Miss Twitterton gave a faint squeak, and the vicar, thoughtfully turning the muzzle of the gun away from her, found himself covering Bunter, who entered at that moment from the passage.

"Excuse me, my lord," said Bunter, with superb nonchalance but a wary eye; "there is a person at the door—"

"Just a moment, Bunter," broke in his master. "The fireworks are about to begin. The chimney is to be cleared by the natural expansion of gases."

"Very good, my lord," Bunter appeared to measure the respective forces of the weapon and the vicar. "Excuse me, sir. Had you not better permit me—?"

"No, no," cried Mr. Goodacre. "Thank you. I can manage it perfectly." Gun in hand, he plunged head and shoulders beneath the chimney-drape.

"Humph!" said Peter. "You're a better man than I am, Gunga Din."

He removed his pipe from his mouth and with his free hand gathered his wife to him. Miss Twitterton, having no husband to cling to, flung herself upon Crutchley for protection, uttering a plaintive cry:

"Oh, Frank! I know I shall scream at the noise."

"There's no occasion for alarm," said the vicar, popping out his head like a showman from behind the curtain. "Now—are we all ready?"

Mr. Puffett put on his bowler hat.

"*Ruat cœlum!*" said Peter; and the gun went off.

It exploded like the crack of doom, and it kicked (as Peter had well foreseen) like a carthorse. Gun and gunman rolled together upon the hearth, entangled inextricably in the folds of the drape. As Bunter leaped to the rescue, the loosened soot of centuries came plunging in a mad cascade down the chimney; it met the floor with a soft and deadly violence and mushroomed up in a Stygian cloud, while with it rushed, in a clattering shower, masonry and mortar, jackdaws' nests and the bones of bats and owls, sticks, bricks and metalwork, with fragments of tiles and potsherds. The shrill outcry of Mrs. Ruddle and Miss Twitterton was drowned by the eruptive rumble and boom that echoed from bend to bend of the forty-foot flue.

"Oh, rapture!" cried Peter, with his lady in his arms. "Oh, bountiful Jehovah! Oh, joy for all its former woes a thousandfold repaid!"

"There!" exclaimed Mr. Puffett, triumphantly. "You can't say as I didn't warn yer."

Peter opened his mouth to reply, when the sight of Bunter, snorting and blind, and black as any Nubian Venus, struck him speechless with ecstasy.

"Oh, dear!" cried Miss Twitterton. She fluttered round, making helpless little darts at the swaddled shape that was the vicar. "Oh, dear, dear, dear! Oh, Frank! Oh, goodness!"

"Peter!" panted Harriet.

"I knew it!" said Peter. "Whoop! I knew it! You blasphemed the aspidistra and something awful *has* come down that chimney."

"Peter! it's Mr. Goodacre in the sheet."

"Whoop!" said Peter again. He pulled himself together and joined Mr. Puffett in unwinding the clerical cocoon; while Mrs. Ruddle and Crutchley led away the unfortunate Bunter.

Mr. Goodacre emerged in some disorder.

"Not hurt, sir, I hope?" inquired Peter with grave concern.

"Not at all, not at all," replied the vicar, rubbing his shoulder. "A little arnica will soon put that to rights!" He smoothed his scanty hair with his hands and fumbled for his glasses. "I trust the ladies were not unduly alarmed by the explosion. It appears to have been effective."

"Remarkably so," said Peter. He pulled a pampas grass from the drainpipe and poked delicately among the débris, while Harriet, flicking soot from the vicar, was reminded of Alice dusting the White King. "It's surprising, the things you find in old chimneys."

"No dead bodies, I trust," said the vicar.

"Only ornithological specimens. And two skeleton bats. And eight feet or so of ancient chain, as formerly worn by the mayors of Paggleham."

"Ah!" said Mr. Goodacre, filled with antiquarian zeal, "an old pot-chain, very likely."

"That's what it'll be," concurred Mr. Puffett. " 'Ung up on one of them ledges, as like as not. See 'ere! 'Ere's a bit of one o' they roasting-jacks wot they used in the old days. Look, see! That's the cross-bar and the wheel wot the chain went over, like. My grannie had one, the dead spit of this."

"Well," said Peter, "we seem to have loosened things up a bit, anyhow. Think you can get your rods through the pot now?"

"If," said Mr. Puffett, darkly, "the pot's still there." He dived beneath the chimney breast, whither Peter followed him. "Mind your 'ead, me lord—there might be some more loose bricks. I will say as you can see the sky if you looks for it, which is more than you'd see this morning."

"Excuse me, my lord!"

"Hey?" said Peter. He crawled out and straightened his back, only to find himself nose to nose with Bunter, who appeared to have undergone a rough but effective cleansing. He looked his servitor up and down. "By God, Bunter, my Bunter, I'm revenged for the scullery pump."

The shadow of some powerful emotion passed over Bunter's face; but his training held good.

"The individual at the door, my lord, is inquiring for Mr. Noakes. I have informed him that he is not here, but he refuses to take my word for it."

"Did you ask if he would see Miss Twitterton? What does he want?"

"He says, my lord, that his business is urgent and personal."

Mr. Puffett, feeling his presence a little intrusive, whistled thoughtfully, and began to collect his rods together and secure them with string.

"What sort of an 'individual,' Bunter?"

Mr. Bunter lightly shrugged his shoulders and spread forth his palms.

"A financial individual, my lord, to judge by appearances."

"Ho!" said Mr. Puffett, *sotto voce*.

"Name of Moses?"

"Name of MacBride, my lord."

"A distinction without a difference. Well, Miss Twitterton, will you see this financial Scotsman?"

"Oh, Lord Peter, I really don't know *what* to say. I know *nothing* about Uncle William's business. I don't know if he'd *like* me to interfere. If only Uncle—"

"Would you rather I tackled the bloke?"

"It's too kind of you, Lord Peter. I'm sure I oughtn't to bother you. But with Uncle away and everything so awkward—and gentlemen always understand so much better about business, *don't* they, Lady Peter? Dear me!"

"My husband will be delighted," said Harriet. She was wickedly tempted to add, "He knows *everything* about business," but was fortunately forestalled by the gentleman himself.

"Nothing delights me more," pronounced his lordship, "than minding other people's business. Show him in. And, Bunter! Allow me to invest you with the Most Heroic Order of the Chimney, for attempting a rescue against overwhelming odds."

"Thank you, my lord," said Mr. Bunter, woodenly, stooping his neck to the chain and meekly receiving the roasting jack in his right hand. "I am much obliged. Will there be anything further?"

"Yes. Before you go—take up the bodies. But the soldiers may be excused from shooting. We have had enough of that for one morning."

Mr. Bunter bowed, collected the skeletons in the dustpan and departed. But as he passed behind the settle, Harriet saw him unwind the chain and drop it unobtrusively into the drainpipe, setting the roasting-jack upright against the wall. A gentleman might have his joke; but a gentleman's gentleman has his position to keep up. One could not face inquisitive Hebrews in the character of Mayor of Paggleham and Provincial Grand Master of the Most Heroic Order of the Chimney.

CHAPTER VI

BACK TO THE ARMY AGAIN

The days have slain the days
And the seasons have gone by,
And brought me the Summer again;
And here on the grass I lie
As erst I lay and was glad
Ere I meddled with right and with wrong.
—WILLIAM MORRIS, *THE HALF OF LIFE GONE*

Mr. MacBride turned out to be a brisk young man, bowler-hatted, with sharp black eyes that seemed to inventory everything they encountered, and a highly regrettable tie. He rapidly summed up the vicar and Mr. Puffett, dismissed them from his calculations, and made a beeline for the monocle.

" 'Morning," said Mr. MacBride. "Lord Peter Wimsey, I believe. Very sorry to trouble your lordship. Understand you're stopping here. Fact is, I have to see Mr. Noakes on a little matter of business."

"Just so," said Peter, easily. "Any fog in Town this morning?"

"Ow naow," replied Mr. MacBride. "Nice clear day."

"I thought so. I mean, I thought you must have come from Town. Bred an' bawn in a briarpatch, Brer Fox. But you might, of course, have been elsewhere since then, so I asked the question. You didn't send in your card, I fancy."

"Well, you see," explained Mr. MacBride, whose native accents were, indeed—apart from a trifling difficulty with his sibilants—pure Whitechapel, "my business is with Mr. Noakes. Personal and confidential."

At this point, Mr. Puffett, finding a long piece of twine on the floor, began to roll it up slowly and methodically, fixing his gaze upon the stranger's face in no very friendly manner.

"Well," resumed Peter, "I'm afraid you have had your journey for nothing. Mr. Noakes isn't here. I only wish he was. But you'll probably find him over at Broxford."

"Oh, no," said Mr. MacBride again. "That won't work. Not a bit of it." A step at the door made him swing round sharply, but it was only Crutchley, armed with a pail and a broom and shovel. Mr. MacBride laughed. "I've been over to Broxford, and *they* said I should find him here."

"Did they indeed?" said Peter. "That's right, Crutchley. Sweep up this mess and get these papers cleared. Said he was here, did they? Then they were mistaken. He's not here and we don't know where he is."

"But," cried Miss Twitterton, "it isn't possible! Not over at Broxford? Then where *can* he be? It's most worrying. Oh, dear, Mr. Goodacre, can't *you* suggest something?"

"Sorry to make such a dust," said Peter. "We have had a slight domestic accident with some soot. Excellent thing for the flowerbeds. Garden pests are said to dislike it. Yes. Well now, this is Mr. Noakes's niece, Miss Twitterton. Perhaps you can state your business to her."

"Sorry," said Mr. MacBride, "nothing doing. I've got to see the old gentleman personally. And it's no good trying to put me off, because I know all the dodges." He skipped nimbly over the broom that Crutchley was plying about his feet, and sat down, uninvited, on the settle.

"Young man," said Mr. Goodacre, rebukingly, "you had better keep a civil tongue in your head. Lord Peter Wimsey has given you his personal assurance that we do not know where to find Mr. Noakes. You do not suppose that his lordship would tell you an untruth."

His lordship, who had wandered over to a distant whatnot, and was hunting through a pile of his personal belongings placed there by Bunter, glanced at his wife and cocked a modest eyebrow.

"Oh, wouldn't he, though?" said Mr. MacBride. "There's nobody like the British aristocracy to tell you a good stiff lie without batting an eyelid. His lordship's face would be a fortune to him in the witnessbox."

"Where," added Peter, extricating a box of cigars from the pile and addressing it in confidence, "it is not unknown."

"So you see," said Mr. MacBride, "that cock won't fight."

He stretched his legs out negligently, to show that he intended to stay where he was. Mr. Puffett, groping about his feet, discovered a stray stub of pencil and put it in his pocket with a grunt.

"Mr. MacBride." Peter had returned, box in hand. "Have a cigar. Now then, who do you represent?"

He stared down at his visitor with an eye so shrewd and a mouth so humorous that Mr. MacBride, accepting the cigar and recognizing its quality, pulled himself together, sat up and acknowledged his intellectual equal with a conspiratorial wink.

"Macdonald & Abrahams," said Mr. MacBride. "Bedford Row."

"Ah, yes. That clannish old North British firm. Solicitors? I thought so. Something to Mr. Noakes's advantage? No doubt. Well, you want him and so do we. So does this lady here. . . ."

"Yes, indeed," said Miss Twitterton, "I'm very worried about Uncle. We haven't seen him since last Wednesday, and I'm sure—"

"But," pursued Peter, "you won't find him in my house."

"Your house?"

"My house. I have just purchased this house from Mr. Noakes."

"Whew!" exclaimed Mr. MacBride excitedly, blowing out a long jet of smoke, "so *that's* the nigger in the woodpile. Bought the house, eh? Paid for it?"

"Really, really!" cried the vicar, scandalized. Mr. Puffett, struggling into a sweater, remained with arms suspended.

"Naturally," said Peter, "I have paid for it."

"Skipped, by thunder!" exclaimed Mr. MacBride. His sudden gesture dislodged his bowler from his knee and sent it spinning and skipping to Mr. Puffett's feet. Crutchley dropped the heap of papers he had collected and stood staring.

"Skipped?" shrieked Miss Twitterton. "What do you mean by that? Oh, what *does* he mean, Lord Peter?"

"Oh, hush!" said Harriet. "He doesn't really know, any more than we do."

"Gone away," explained Mr. MacBride. "Vamoosed. Done a bunk. Skipped with the cash. Is that clear enough? If I've said it to Mr. Abrahams once, I've said it a thousand times. If you don't come down sharp on that fellow Noakes, he'll skip, I said. And he has skipped, ain't it?"

"It looks like it, certainly," said Peter.

"Skipped?" Crutchley was indignant. "It's easy for you to say skipped. What about my forty pound?"

"Oh, Frank!" cried Miss Twitterton.

"Ah, you're another of 'em, are you?" said Mr. MacBride, with condescending sympathy. "Forty pounds, eh? Well, what about us? What about our client's money?"

"But what money?" gasped Miss Twitterton in an agony of apprehension. "*Whose* money? I don't understand. What's it all got to do with Uncle William?"

"Peter," said Harriet, "don't you think—?"

"It's no good," said Wimsey. "It's got to come out."

"See this?" said Mr. MacBride. "That's a writ, that is. Little matter of nine hundred pound."

"Nine 'undred?" Crutchley made a snatch for the paper as though it were negotiable security for that amount.

"Nine hundred *pounds!*" Miss Twitterton's was the top note in the chorus. Peter shook his head.

"Capital and interest," said Mr. MacBride, calmly.

"Levy, Levy & Levy. Running five years. Can't wait for ever, you know."

"My uncle's business—" began Miss Twitterton. "Oh, there must be some *mistake*."

"Your uncle's business, miss," said Mr. MacBride, bluntly but not altogether unsympathetically, "hasn't got a leg to stand on. Mortgage on the shop and not a hundred pounds' worth of stock in the place—and I don't suppose *that's* paid for. Your uncle's broke, that's what it is. Broke."

"Broke?" exclaimed Crutchley, with passion. "And how about my forty quid what he made me put into his business?"

"Well, you won't see that again, Mr. Whoever-you-are," returned the clerk, coolly. "Not without we catch the old gentleman and make him cough up the cash. Even then—might I ask, my lord, what you paid for the house? No offense, but it does make a difference."

"Six-fifty," said Peter.

"Cheap," said Mr. MacBride, shortly.

"So we thought," replied his lordship. "It was valued at eight hundred for mortgage; but he took our offer for cash."

"Looking for a mortgage, was he?"

"I don't know. I took pains to make sure that there were, in fact, no encumbrances. Further, I did not inquire."

"Ha!" said Mr. MacBride. "Well, you got a bargain."

"It will need a good bit of money spent on it," said Peter. "As a matter of fact, we'd have paid what he wanted if he'd insisted, my wife had a fancy for the place. But he accepted our first offer; ours not to question why. Business is business."

"Hum!" said Mr. MacBride, with respect. "And some people think the aristocracy's a soft proposition. Then I gather you're not altogether surprised."

"Not in the least," said Peter.

Miss Twitterton looked bewildered.

"Well, it's all the worse for our client," said Mr. MacBride, frankly. "Six-fifty won't cover us, even if we get it; and now he's gone and beat it with the money."

"Given me the slip, the swindlin' old devil!" ejaculated Crutchley, in angry tones.

"Steady, steady, Crutchley," implored the vicar. "Remember where you are. Think of Miss Twitterton."

"There's the furniture," said Harriet. "That belongs to him."

"If it's paid for," said Mr. MacBride, summing up the contents of the room with a contemptuous eye.

"But it's dreadful!" cried Miss Twitterton. "I can't *believe* it! We always thought Uncle was so well off."

"So he is," said Mr. MacBride. "Well off out of this. About a thousand miles by this time. Not heard of since last Wednesday? Well, there you are. A nice job, I don't think. Fact is, with all these transport facilities, it's too easy nowadays for absconding debtors to clear out."

"See here!" cried Crutchley, losing all control of himself. "You mean to say, even if you find him, I shan't get my forty pounds? It's a damn disgrace, that's what it is—"

"Hold hard," said Mr. MacBride. "He didn't take you into partnership or anything, I suppose? No? Well, that's a bit of luck for you, anyway. We can't come on you for what's missing. You thank your stars you're out of it for your forty pounds. It's all experience, ain't it?"

"Curse you!" said Crutchley. "I'll 'ave my forty pounds out o' somebody. Here, you, Aggie Twitterton—you know he promised to pay me. I'll 'ave the law on you!—Crooked, swindlin'—"

"Come, come," interposed Mr. Goodacre again. "It's not Miss Twitterton's fault. You must not fly into a passion. We must all try to think calmly—"

"Quite," said Peter. "Definitely. Let us beget a temperance that may give it smoothness. And talking of temperance, how about a mild spot? Bunter!—Oh, there you are. *Have* we any drink in the house?"

"Certainly, my lord. Hock, sherry, whisky—"

Here Mr. Puffett thought well to intervene. Wines and spirits were scarcely in his line.

"Mr. Noakes," he observed, in a detached manner, "alway-kep' a good barrel of beer in the 'ouse. I will say that for him."

"Excellent. Strictly speaking, I suppose, Mr. MacBride, it's your client's beer. But if you have no objection—"

"Well," conceded Mr. MacBride, "a drop of beer's neither here nor there, is it now?"

"A jug of beer, then, Bunter, and the whisky. Oh, and sherry for the ladies."

Bunter departed on this mollifying errand, and the atmosphere seemed to grow calmer. Mr. Goodacre seized on the last words to introduce a less controversial topic:

"Sherry," he said, pleasantly, "has always appeared to me a most agreeable wine. I was so glad to read in the newspaper that it was coming into its own again. Madeira, too. They tell me that both sherry and madeira are returning to favor in London. And in the Universities. That is a very reassuring sign. I cannot think that these modern cocktails can be either healthful or palatable. Surely not. But I can see no objection to a glass of sound wine now and again—for the stomach's sake, as the Apostle says. It is undoubtedly restorative in moments of agitation, like the present. I am afraid, Miss Twitterton, this has been a sad shock to you."

"I couldn't have thought it of Uncle," said Miss Twitterton sadly. "He has always been so much looked-up to. I simply can't believe it."

"I can—easily," said Crutchley, in the sweep's ear.

"You never know," said Mr. Puffett, struggling into his topcoat. "I always thought Mr. Noakes was a warm man. Seems like he was 'ot stuff."

"Gone off with my forty quid!" Automatically, Crutchley picked up the papers from the floor. "And never paid me only 2 per cent, neither, the old thief! I never did like that wireless business."

"Ah!" said Mr. Puffett. He caught at a loose end of string dangling from among the papers and reeled it out on his fingers, so that they looked absurdly like a stout maiden lady and her companion engaged in winding knitting wool.

"Safe bind, safe find, Frank Crutchley. You can't be too careful where you puts your money. Pick it up where you finds it and put it away careful, same as I does this bit of twine, and there it is, 'andy when you wants it." He stowed the string away in a remote pocket.

To this piece of sententiousness, Crutchley returned no answer. He went out, giving place to Bunter, who, with an inscrutable face, was balancing upon a tin tray a black bottle, a bottle of whisky, an earthenware jug, the two tumblers of the night before, three cut-glass goblets (one with a chipped foot), a china mug with a handle and two pewter pots of different sizes.

"Good Lord!" said Peter. (Bunter's eyes lifted for a moment like those of a scolded spaniel.) "These must be the Baker Street Irregulars; the chief thing is that they all have a hole in the top. I am told that Mr. Woolworth sells a very good selection of glassware. In the meantime, Miss Twitterton, will you take sherry as a present from Margate or toss off your Haig in a tankard?"

"Oh!" said Miss Twitterton. "I'm sure there are some in the chiffonier—Oh, thank you so much, but at this time in the morning—and then they would need dusting, because Uncle didn't use them—Well, I really don't know—"

"It'll do you good."

"I think you need a little something," said Harriet.

"Oh, *do* you, Lady Peter? Well—if you insist—Only sherry, then, and only a *little* of that—Of course, it isn't really so early any longer, is it?—Oh, please, really, I'm sure you're giving me *far* too much!"

"I assure you," said Peter, "you will find it as mild as your own parsnip wine." He handed her the mug gravely, and poured a small quantity of sherry into a tumbler for his wife, who accepted it with the remark:

"You are a master of meiosis."

"Thank you, Harriet. What's your poison, padre?"

"Sherry, thank you, sherry. Your health, my dear young people." He clinked the tumbler solemnly against Miss

Twitterton's mug, taking her by surprise. "Take courage, Miss Twitterton. Things mayn't be as bad as they seem."

"Thank you," said Mr. MacBride, waving away the whisky. "I'll wait for the beer if it's all the same to you. No spirits in office hours is my motto. I'm sure it's no pleasure to me, bringing all this unfortunate disturbance into a family. But business is business, ain't it, your lordship? And we've got our clients to consider."

"You're not to blame," said Peter. "Miss Twitterton realizes that you are only doing your rather unpleasant duty. They also serve who only serve writs, you know."

"I'm sure," cried Miss Twitterton, "if we could only find Uncle, he would explain *everything*."

"*If* we could find him," agreed Mr. MacBride, meaningly.

"Yes," said Peter, "much virtue in if. If we could find Mr. Noakes—" The door opened, and he dismissed the question with an air of relief. "Ah! Beer, glorious beer!"

"Excuse me, my lord." Bunter stood on the threshold empty-handed. "I'm afraid we have found Mr. Noakes."

"*Afraid* you've found him?" Master and man stared at one another, and Harriet, reading the unspoken message in their eyes, came up to Peter and laid a hand on his arm.

"For God's sake, Bunter," said Wimsey, with a strained note in his voice, "don't say you've found—Where? Down the cellar?"

The voice of Mrs. Ruddle broke the tension like the wail of a banshee:

"Frank! Frank Crutchley! It's Mr. Noakes!"

"Yes, my lord," said Bunter.

Miss Twitterton, unexpectedly quick-witted, sprang to her feet. "He's dead! Uncle's dead!" The mug rolled from her hands to crash on the hearthstone.

"No, no," said Harriet, "they can't mean that."

"Oh, no, impossible," said Mr. Goodacre. He looked appealingly at Bunter, who bent his head.

"I am very much afraid so, sir."

Crutchley, thrusting him aside, burst in. "What's happened? What's Ma Ruddle shouting about? Where's—?"

"I knew it, I knew it!" shrieked Miss Twitterton, recklessly. "I knew something terrible had happened! Uncle's dead and all the money's gone!"

She burst into a fit of hiccupping laughter, made a dart towards Crutchley, who recoiled with a gasp, broke from the vicar's supporting hand and flung herself hysterically into Harriet's arms.

"Here!" said Mr. Puffett, "let's 'ave a look."

He made for the door, cannoning into Crutchley. Bunter profited by the confusion to fling the door to and set his back against it.

"Wait a minute," said Bunter. "Better not touch anything."

As if the words were a signal for which he had been waiting, Peter took up his cold pipe from the table, knocked it out on his palm and flung the crushed ashes upon the tray.

"Perhaps," said Mr. Goodacre, as one who hopes against hope, "he has only fainted." He rose eagerly. "We might be able to assist him—"

His voice trailed away.

"Dead some days," said Bunter, "from the looks of him, sir." His eye was still on Peter.

"Has he got the money on him?" inquired MacBride. The vicar, unheeding, flung another question, like a wave, against the stone wall of Bunter's impassivity:

"But how did it happen, my man? Did he fall down the stairs in a fit?"

"Cut his throat, more likely," said Mr. MacBride.

Bunter, still looking at Peter, said with emphasis: "It isn't *suicide*." Feeling the door thrust against his shoulder, he moved aside to admit Mrs. Ruddle.

"Oh, dear! oh, dear!" cried Mrs. Ruddle. Her eyes gleamed with a dismal triumph. " 'Is pore 'ead's bashed in something shocking!"

"Bunter!" said Wimsey, and spoke the word at last: "Are you trying to tell us that this is murder?"

Miss Twitterton slid from Harriet's arms to the floor.

"I couldn't say, my lord; but it looks most unpleasantly like it."

"Get me a glass of water, please," said Harriet.

"Yes, my lady. Mrs. Ruddle! Glass of water—sharp!"

"Very well," said Peter, mechanically pouring water into a goblet and giving it to the charwoman. "Leave everything as it is. Crutchley, you'd better go for the police."

"If," said Mrs. Ruddle, "if it's the perlice you're wanting, there's young Joe Sellen—that's the constable, a-standing at my gate this very minnit a-yarning with my Albert. I seen 'im not five minutes agone, and if I knows anything o' them boys when they gits talking—".

"The water," said Harriet. Peter stalked over to Crutchley, carrying with him a stiff peg of neat spirits.

"Take this and pull yourself together. Then run over to the cottage and get this chap Sellon or whatever his name is. Quick."

"Thank you, my lord." The young man jerked himself from his daze and swallowed the whisky at a gulp. "It's a bit of a shock."

He went out. Mr. Puffett followed him.

"I suppose," said Mr. Puffett, nudging Bunter gently in the ribs, "you didn't manage to get that beer up afore—eh? Oh, well—there's worse happens in war."

"She's better now, pore thing," said Mrs. Ruddle. "Come on, don't give way now, there's a dear. What you want is a nice lay-down and a cupper tea. Shall I take 'er upstairs, me lady?"

"Do," said Harriet. "I'll come in a moment."

She let them go and turned to Peter, who stood motionless, staring down at the table. Oh, my God! she thought, startled by his face, he's a middle-aged man—the half of life gone—he mustn't—

"Peter, my poor dear! And we came here for a quiet honeymoon!"

He turned at her touch and laughed ruefully.

"Damn!" he said. "And damn! Back to the old grind. *Rigor mortis* and who-saw-him-last, blood-prints, finger-prints, foot-prints, information received and it-is-my-dooty-to-warn-you. *Quelle scie, mon dieu, quelle scie!*"

"Now then," said Police-constable Sellon, "wot's all this?"

CHAPTER VII

LOTOS AND CACTUS

I know what is and what has been;
Not anything to me comes strange,
Who in so many years have seen
And lived through every kind of change.
I know when men are good or bad,
When well or ill, he slowly said;
When sad or glad, when sane or mad,
And when they sleep alive or dead. . . .

And while the black night nothing saw,
And till the cold morn came at last,
That old bed held the room in awe
With tales of its experience vast.
It thrilled the gloom; it told such tales
Of human sorrows and delights,
Of fever moans and infant wails,
Of births and deaths and bridal nights.

—JAMES THOMSON, *IN THE ROOM*

Harriet left Miss Twitterton tucked up on the nuptial couch with a hot-water bottle and an aspirin and, passing softly into the next room, discovered her lord in the act of pulling his shirt over his head. She waited for his face to reappear and then said, "Hullo!"

"Hullo! All serene?"

"Yes. Better now. What's happening downstairs?"

"Sellon's telephoned from the post-office and the

Super's coming over from Broxford with the police-surgeon. So I came up to put on a collar and tie."

Of course, thought Harriet, secretly entertained. Someone has died in our hour, so we put on a collar and tie. Nothing could be more obvious. How absurd men are! And how clever in devising protective armor for themselves! What kind of tie will it be? Black would surely be excessive. Dull purple or an unobtrusive spot? No. A regimental tie. Nothing could be more proper. Purely official and committing one to nothing. Completely silly and charming.

She smoothed the smile from her lips and watched the solemn transference of personal property from blazer pockets to appropriate situations about a coat and waistcoat.

"All this," observed Peter, "is a damned nuisance." He sat on the edge of the naked bedstead to exchange his slippers for a pair of brown shoes. "It's not worrying you too much, is it?" His voice was a little smothered with stooping to fasten the laces.

"No."

"One thing, it's nothing to do with us. That is, he wasn't killed for the money we paid him. He had it all in his pocket. In notes."

"Good heavens!"

"There's not much doubt he meant to make a bolt of it when somebody intervened. I can't say I feel any strong personal regret. Do you?"

"Far from it. Only—"

"M'm? . . . It *is* worrying you. Blast!"

"Not really. Only when I think of him, lying down there in the cellar all the time. I know it's perfectly idiotic of me—but I can't help wishing we hadn't slept in his bed."

"I was afraid you might feel like that." He got up and stood for a moment looking from the window over the sloping field and woodland that stretched away beyond the lane. "And yet, you know, that bed must be pretty nearly as old as the house—the original bits of it, anyhow. It could tell a good many tales of births and deaths and bridal-nights. One can't escape from these things—except by living in a brand-new villa and buying one's furniture in the Tottenham Court Road. . . . All the same, I wish to God it hadn't happened. I mean, if it's going to make you uncomfortable every time you think about—"

"Oh, Peter, no. I didn't mean that. It's not as though—It would be different if we had come here in another sort of way—"

"That's the point. Supposing I'd come here to disport myself with somebody who didn't matter twopence, I should be feeling a complete wart. Quite reasonably, I dare say, but I can be just as unreasonable as anyone else, if I put my mind to it. But as things are, no! Nothing that you or I have done is any insult to death—unless you think so, Harriet. I should say, if anything could sweeten the atmosphere that wretched old man left behind him, it would be the feeling we—the feeling I have for you, at any rate, and yours for me if you feel like that. I do assure you, so far as I am concerned, there's nothing trivial about it."

"I know that. You're absolutely right. I won't think about it that way any more. Peter—there weren't—there weren't *rats* in the cellar, were there?"

"No, dearest, no rats. And all quite dry. Just a perfectly good cellar."

"I'm glad. I was sort of imagining rats. Not that I suppose it matters very much after one's dead, but I don't seem to mind all the rest nearly so much if I don't have to think of rats. In fact, I don't mind at all, not now."

"We shall have to stick around till after the inquest, I'm afraid, but we could easily get put up somewhere else. That's one thing I was going to ask you about. There's probably a decent inn at Pagford or Broxford."

Harriet considered this.

"No. I don't care about that. I think I'd rather stay here."

"Are you sure?"

"Yes. It's our house. It never was his—not really. And I'm not going to let you think there's any difference between your feelings and mine. That would be worse than rats, even."

"My dear, I'm not proposing to make staying here a test of your affections. Not love, quoth he, but vanity, sets love a task like that. It's easy enough for me. I was begotten and born in the bed where twelve generations of my forefathers were born and wedded and died—and some of them made pretty poor ends from the parson's point of view—so I don't suffer much from hauntings of that kind. But there's no reason at all why you shouldn't feel rather differently."

"Don't say another word about it. We're going to stay here and exorcise the ghosts. I'd rather."

"Well, if you change your mind, tell me," he said, still uneasy.

"I shan't change my mind. We'd better go down now, if you're ready, because Miss Twitterton ought to get some sleep if she can. Now I come to think of it, *she* didn't ask for another bedroom, and it's her own uncle."

"Country people are very matter-of-fact about life and death. They live so close to reality."

"So do your sort of people. It's my sort that go all sanitary and civilized, and get married in hotels and do their births and deaths in nursing-homes where they give offense to nobody. I say, Peter, do we have to feed all these doctors and superintendents and people? And does Bunter carry on all by himself, or ought I to give him some orders?"

"Experience has taught me," said Peter, as they moved down the stair, "that no situation finds Bunter unprepared. That he should have procured *The Times* this morning by the simple expedient of asking the milkman to request the postmistress to telephone to Broxford and have it handed to the 'bus-conductor to be dropped at the post-office and brought up by the little girl who delivers the telegrams is a trifling example of his resourceful energy. But he would probably take it as a compliment if you were to refer the difficulty to him and congratulate him when he tells you that everything is provided for."

"I will."

In the short time that they had been upstairs, Mr. Puffett had evidently finished his chimney-sweeping, for the sitting-room had been cleared of dust-sheets and a fire kindled upon the hearth. A table had been drawn out into the center of the room; on it stood a tray filled with plates and cutlery. Passing through into the passage, Harriet was aware of a good deal of activity in progress. Before the shut door of the cellar stood the uniformed figure of P.C. Sellon, like young Harry with his beaver on, prepared to resist any interference with the execution of his duty. In the kitchen, Mrs. Ruddle was cutting sandwiches. In the scullery, Crutchley and Mr. Puffett were clearing a quantity of pots and pans and old flower-pots from a long deal dresser, preparatory (as appeared from the presence beside them of a steaming pail) to scrubbing it clean to receive the body of its late owner. In the back door stood Bunter, conducting some kind of financial transaction with two men who seemed to have arrived from nowhere in a motor van. Beyond them could be seen Mr. MacBride, strolling about the back-yard; he had the air of inventorying its contents with a view to assessing their value. And at that moment there came a heavy knock on the front door.

"That'll be the police," said Peter. He went to let them in, and at the same time Bunter finished paying the men, came in, and shut the back door sharply.

"Oh, Bunter," said Harriet, "I see you're giving us something to eat—?"

"Yes, my lady. I succeeded in intercepting the Home & Colonial and procuring some ham for sandwiches. There is also a portion of the foie gras and the Cheshire cheese which we brought from Town. The draft beer in the cellar being at the moment not readily available, I took the liberty of instructing Mrs. Ruddle to fetch a few bottles of Bass from the village. If anything further should be required, there is a jar of caviar in the hamper, but we have no lemons, I am sorry to say."

"Oh, I don't think caviar would strike the right note, Bunter, do you?"

"No, my lady. The heavy luggage has just arrived, per Carter Paterson; I instructed that it should be deposited in the oil-shed until we had leisure to attend to it."

"The luggage! I'd forgotten all about it."

"Very naturally, my lady, if I may say so. . . . The scullery," went on Bunter, with a touch of hesitation, "appeared a more suitable place than the kitchen for—ah—the medical gentleman to work in."

"Certainly," said Harriet, with emphasis.

"Yes, my lady. I inquired of his lordship whether, in view of all the circumstances, he would desire me to order in any coal. He said he would refer the matter to your ladyship."

"He has. You can order the coal."

"Very good, my lady. I fancy there will be time between lunch and dinner to effect a clearance of the kitchen chimney, provided there is no interference from the police. Would your ladyship wish me to instruct the sweep accordingly?"

"Yes, please. I don't know what we should do without your head for detail, Bunter."

"I am much obliged to your ladyship."

The police party had been taken into the sitting-room. Through the half-open door one could hear Peter's high, fluent voice giving a lucid account of the whole incredible business, with patient pauses for interrogation or to allow a deliberate constabulary pencil to catch up with him. Harriet sighed angrily.

"I do wish he hadn't to be worried like this! It's too bad."

"Yes, my lady." Bunter's face stirred, as though some human emotion were trying to break through. He made no further comment, but something which Harriet recognized as sympathy seemed to waft out of him. She said impulsively:

"I wonder. Do you think I'm right in ordering the coal?"

It was scarcely fair to push Bunter on to such delicate ground. He remained impassive:

"It is not for me to say, my lady."

She was determined not to be beaten.

"You have known him much longer than I have, Bunter. If his lordship had only himself to consider, do you suppose he would go or stay?"

"Under those circumstances, my lady, I fancy his lordship would decide to remain."

"That's what I wanted to know. You had better order enough coal for a month."

"Certainly, my lady."

The men were coming out of the sitting-room. They were introduced: Dr. Craven, Superintendent Kirk, Sergeant Blades. The cellar door was opened; somebody produced an electric torch and they all went down. Harriet, relegated to the woman's role of silence and waiting, went into the kitchen to help with the sandwiches. The role, though dull, was not a useless one, for Mrs. Ruddle, with a large knife in her hand, was standing at the scullery door as though prepared to carry out a butcherly kind of post-mortem upon whatever might be brought up from the cellar.

"Mrs. Ruddle!"

Mrs. Ruddle gave a violent start and dropped the knife. "Law, m'lady! You did give me a turn."

"You want to cut the bread thinner. And please shut that door."

A slow, heavy shuffling. Then voices. Mrs. Ruddle broke off in the middle of a spirited piece of narrative to listen.

"Yes, Mrs. Ruddle?"

"Yes, m'lady. So I says to him, 'You needn't think you're going to ketch me that way, Joe Sellon,' I says. 'Like to make out you're somebody, don't you,' I says. 'I wonder you 'as the face, seein' what a fool you made of yourself over Aggie Twitterton's 'ens. No,' I says, 'when a proper policeman comes, 'e can ask all the questions 'e likes. But don't you think you can go ordering me about,' I says, 'an' me old enough to be your grandma. You can put away that there notebook,' I says, 'go on,' I says, 'it'd make me old cat laugh ter see yer,' I says. 'I'll tell 'em all I knows,' I says, 'don't you fret yourself w'en the time comes.' 'You ain't no right,' 'e says, 'to obstruct an orficer of the law.' 'Law?' I says, 'call yerself the law? If you're the law,' I says, 'I don't think much of it.' 'E got that red. 'You'll 'ear about this,' 'e says. And I says, 'And you'll ear summink, too. None o' yer sauce,' I says, 'they'll be glad enough to 'ear what I 'as to tell 'em, I dessay, without you goin' an' twistin' it all up afore they gets it,' I says. So 'e says—"

There was a peculiar mixture of malice and triumph in Mrs. Ruddle's voice which Harriet felt the episode of the hens did not altogether account for. But at this moment Bunter came in by the passage door.

"His lordship's compliments, my lady; and Superintendent Kirk would be glad to see you for a moment in the sitting-room if you can spare the time."

Superintendent Kirk was a large man with a mild and ruminative expression. He seemed already to have obtained from Peter most of the information he needed, asking only a few questions to confirm such points as the time of the party's arrival at Talboys and the appearance of the sitting-room and kitchen when they came in. What he really wanted to get from Harriet was a description of the bedroom. All Mr. Noakes's clothes had been there? His toilet articles? No suitcases? No suggestion that he intended to leave the house at once? No? Well, that confirmed the idea that Mr. Noakes intended to get away, but was in no immediate hurry. Not, for example, particularly expecting any unpleasant interview that night. The Superintendent was much obliged to her ladyship; he should be sorry to disturb poor Miss Twitterton, and, after all, nothing much was to be gained by examining the bedroom at once, since its contents had already been disturbed. That applied, of course, to the other rooms as well. Unfortunate, but nobody could be blamed for that. They might be a bit further on when they had Dr. Craven's report. He would perhaps be able to tell them whether Noakes had been alive when he fell down the cellar steps or had been killed and thrown there afterwards. No bloodshed, that was the trouble, though the skull had been broken by the blow. And with so many people in and out of the house all night and morning, one could scarcely expect footprints or anything like that. At any rate, nothing had been seen to suggest a struggle? Nothing. Mr. Kirk was greatly obliged.

Harriet said, Not at all, and murmured something about lunch. The Superintendent said he saw no objection to that; he had finished with the sitting-room for the moment. He would just like a word with this fellow MacBride about the financial side of the business, but he would send him in as soon as he had done with him. He tactfully refused to join the party, but accepted the offer of a mouthful of bread-and-cheese in the kitchen. When the doctor had finished, he would finish the interrogation in the light of whatever the medical examination might reveal.

Years afterwards, Lady Peter Wimsey was accustomed say that the first few days of her honeymoon remained in her memory as a long series of assorted surprises, punctuated by the most incredible meals. Her husband's impressions were even less coherent; he said he had had, all the time, the sensation of being slightly drunk and tossed in a blanket. The freakish and arbitrary fates must have given the blanket an especially energetic tweak, to have tossed him, towards the end of that strange, embarrassed luncheon, so high over the top of the world. He stood at the window, whistling. Bunter, hovering about the room, handing sandwiches and straightening out the last traces of the disorder left after the sweep's departure, recognized the tune. It was the one he had heard the night before in the woodshed. Nothing could have been less suited to the occasion, nothing should more deeply have offended his inborn sense of propriety; yet, like the poet Wordsworth, he heard it and rejoiced.

"Another sandwich, Mr. MacBride?"

(The new-wedded lady doing the honors at her own table for the first time. Curious, but true.)

"No more, thanks; much obliged to you." Mr. MacBride swallowed the last drop of his beer and polished his mouth and fingers politely with his handkerchief. Bunter swept down upon the empty plate and glass.

"I hope you've had something to eat, Bunter?"

(One must consider the servants. Only two fixed points in the universe: death, and the servants' dinner; and here they both were.)

"Yes, thank you, my lady."

"I suppose they'll be wanting this room in a minute. Is the doctor still there?"

"I believe he has concluded his examination, my lady."

"Nice job, I don't think," said Mr. MacBride.

"*La caill', la tourterelle*
Et la joli' perdrix—
Auprès de ma blonde
Qu'il fait bon, fait bon, fait bon,
Auprès de ma blonde—"

Mr. MacBride looked around, scandalized. He had his own notions of propriety. Bunter darted hastily across the room and attracted the singer's wandering attention.

"Yes, Bunter?"

"Your lordship will excuse me. But in view of the melancholy occasion—"

"Eh, what? Oh, sorry. Was I making a noise?"

"My dear—" His swift, secret, reminiscent smile was a challenge; she beat it down, and achieved the right tone of wifely rebuke. "Poor Miss Twitterton's trying to get to sleep."

"Yes. Sorry. Dashed thoughtless of me. And in a house of bereavement and all that." His face darkened with a sudden odd impatience. "Though, if you ask me, I doubt whether anybody—I say, *anybody* feels particularly bereft."

"Except," said Mr. MacBride, "that chap Crutchley with his forty pounds. I fancy that grief's genuine."

"From that point of view," said his lordship, "you should be the chief mourner."

"It won't keep *me* awake at night," retorted Mr. MacBride. "It ain't my money, you see," he added frankly. He rose, opened the door and glanced out into the passage. "I only hope they're getting a move on out there. I've got to toddle back to Town and see Mr. Abrahams. Pity you ain't on the telephone." He paused. "If I was you, I wouldn't let it worry me. Seems to me, deceased was a dashed unpleasant old gink and well out of the way."

He went out, leaving the atmosphere clearer, as though by the removal of funeral flowers.

"I'm afraid it's true," said Harriet.

"Just as well, isn't it?" Wimsey's tone was studiously light. "When I'm investigating a murder, I hate to have too much sympathy with the corpse. Personal feelings cramp the style."

"But, Peter—need you investigate this? It's rather rotten for you."

Bunter, piling plates on a tray, made for the door. This, of course, was bound to happen. Let them fight it out for themselves. He had delivered his own warning.

"No, I needn't. But I expect I shall. Murders go to my head like drink. I simply can't keep them off."

"Not even now? They can't expect you, surely! You've got a right to your own life sometimes. And it's such a beastly little crime—sordid and horrible."

"That's just it," he broke out, with unexpected passion. "That's why I can't leave it alone. It's not picturesque. It's not exciting. It's no fun at all. Just dirty, brutal bashing, like a butcher with a pole-ax. It makes me sick. But who the hell am I, to pick and choose what I'll meddle in?"

"I see. But after all, this was just wished on us. It's not as though you'd been called in to help."

"How often am I 'called in,' I wonder," he demanded, rather bitterly. "I call myself in, half the time, out of sheer mischief and inquisitiveness. Lord Peter Wimsey the aristocratic sleuth—my God! The idle rich gentleman who dabbles in detection. That's what they say—isn't it?"

"Sometimes. I lost my temper with somebody who said that, once. Before we were engaged. It made me wonder if I wasn't getting rather fond of you."

"Did it? Then perhaps I'd better not justify that view of myself. What do such fellows as I, crawling between heaven and earth? I can't wash my hands of a thing, merely because it's inconvenient to my lordship, as Bunter says of the sweep. I hate violence! I loathe wars and slaughter, and men quarreling and fighting like beasts! Don't say it isn't my business. It's everybody's business."

"Of course it is, Peter. Go ahead. I was just being feminine, or something. I thought you looked as if you'd be better for a little peace and quiet. But you don't seem to shine as a lotos-eater."

"I can't eat lotos, even with you," he said, pathetically, "with murdered bodies popping up all over the place."

"You shan't, angel, you shan't. Have a nice mouthful of prickly cactus instead. And don't pay any attention to my imbecile efforts to strew your path with rose-leaves. It won't be the first time we've followed the footprints together. Only"—she faltered a moment, as another devastating matrimonial possibility loomed up like a nightmare—"whatever you do, you'll let me take a hand, won't you?"

To her relief, he laughed.

"All right, domina. I promise you that. Cactus for both or neither, and no lotos till we can share it. I won't play the good British husband—in spite of your alarming plunge into wifeliness. The Ethiopian shall stay black and leave the leopardess her spots."

He appeared satisfied, but Harriet cursed herself for a fool. This business of adjusting oneself was not so easy after all. Being preposterously fond of a person didn't prevent one from hurting him unintentionally. She had an uncomfortable feeling that his confidence had been shaken and that this was not the end of the misunderstanding. He wasn't the kind of man to whom you could say, "Darling, you're wonderful, and whatever you do is right"—whether you thought so or not. He would write you down a fool. Nor was he the sort who said, "I know what I'm doing and you must take my word for it." (Thank God for that, anyway!) He wanted you to agree with him intelligently or not at all. And her intelligence did agree with him. It was her own feelings that didn't seem to be quite pulling in double harness with her intelligence. But whether it was her feeling for Peter or her feeling for the deceased Mr. Noakes, butchered to make a busman's honeymoon for them, or a merely selfish feeling that she didn't want to be bothered at this moment with corpses and policemen, she was not sure.

"Cheer up, sweetheart," said Peter. "They may not want my kind assistance. Kirk may cut the Gordian knot by booting me out."

"Well, he'd be an idiot!" said Harriet, with prompt indignation.

Mr. Puffett entered suddenly without knocking.

"They're takin' Mr. Noakes away. Shall I be gettin' on with the kitchen chimney?" He walked across to the fireplace. "Draws beautiful now, don't she? I allus said there was nothing the matter with the flue. Ah! it's a good thing Mr. Noakes ain't alive to see all that 'eap of coal. That's a fire as does credit to any chimney."

"All right, Puffett," said Peter, absently. "Carry on."

Steps on the path, and a dismal little procession passing the window: a sergeant of police and another uniformed man, carrying a stretcher between them.

"Very good, me lord." Mr. Puffett glanced from the window and removed his bowler hat. "And where's all 'is cheeseparin' brought 'im now?" he demanded. "Nowhere."

He marched out.

"*De mortuis*," said Peter, "and then some."

"Yes, he seems to be getting a nice derangement of epitaphs, poor old creature."

Corpse and policemen—there they were, not to be got rid of, whatever one's feelings might be. Much better to accept the situation and do one's best. Superintendent Kirk came in, followed by Joe Sellon.

"Well, well," said Peter. "All ready for the third degree?"

" 'Tain't likely to come to that, my lord," replied Mr. Kirk, jovially. "You and your lady had something better to do last week than committing murders, I'll be bound. That's right, Joe, come along. Let's see what you can do with a bit o' shorthand. I'm sending my sergeant over to Broxford to pick up what he can there, so Joe can give me a hand with the statements. I'd like to use this room, if it's not inconvenient."

"Not at all." Seeing the Superintendent's eye fix modestly upon a spindly specimen of Edwardian craftsmanship, Peter promptly pushed forward a stout, high-backed chair with gouty arms and legs and an eruption of heavy scroll work about its head. "You'll find this about up to your weight, I fancy."

"Nice and imposing," said Harriet.

The village constable added his comment:

"That's old Noakes's chair, that was."

"So," said Peter, "Galahad will sit down in Merlin's seat."

Mr. Kirk, on the point of lowering his solid fifteen stone into the chair, jerked up abruptly.

"Alfred," he said, "Lord Tennyson."

"Got it in one," said Peter, mildly surprised. A glow of enthusiasm shone softly in the policeman's ox-like eyes. "You're a bit of a student, aren't you, Superintendent?"

"I like to do a bit o' reading in my off-duty," admitted Mr. Kirk, bashfully. "It mellows the mind." He sat down. "I often think as the rowtine of police dooty may tend to narrow a man and make him a bit hard, if you take my meaning. When I find that happening, I say to myself, what you need, Sam Kirk, is contact with a Great Mind or so, after supper. Reading maketh a full man—"

"Conference a ready man," said Harriet.

"And writing an exact man," said the Superintendent.

"Mind that, Joe Sellon, and see you let me have them notes so as they can be read to make sense."

"Francis Bacon," said Peter, a trifle belatedly. "Mr. Kirk, you're a man after my own heart."

"Thank you, my lord. Bacon. You'd call him a Great Mind, wouldn't you? And what's more, he came to be Lord Chancellor of England, so he's a bit in the legal way, too. Ah! well, I suppose we'll have to get down to business."

"As another great mind so happily put it, 'However entrancing it is to wander through a garden of bright images, are we not enticing your mind from another subject of almost equal importance?' "

"What's that?" said the Superintendent. "That's a new one on me. 'Garden of bright images,' eh? That's pretty, that is."

"*Kai-Lung,*" said Harriet.

"*Golden Hours of,*" said Peter. "Ernest Bramah."

"Make a note 'o that for me, will you, Joe? 'Bright images'—That's just what you get in poetry, isn't it? Pictures, as you might say. And in a garden too—what you'd call flowers of fancy, I dessay. Well, now—" He pulled himself together and turned to Peter. "As I was saying, we mustn't waste time with the fancy-work. About this money we found on the body. What did you say you paid him for the house?"

"Six-fifty, altogether. Fifty at the beginning of the negotiations and the six hundred at quarter-day."

"That's right. That accounts for the six hundred he had in his pocket. He'd just about have cashed it the day he was put away."

"The quarter-day was a Sunday. The check was actually dated and sent on the 28th. It would have reached him Monday."

"That's right. We'll check the payment at the bank, but it's not really necessary. Wonder what *they* thought of him taking it away in cash instead of paying it in. H'm. It's a pity it ain't the bank's business to give us the office when people do things that look like bolting. But it wouldn't do, naturally."

"He must have had it in his pocket when he told poor Crutchley he'd no money to pay him his forty pounds. He could have given it him then."

"Course he could, my lady, if he'd wanted to. He was a proper old dodger, was Mr. Noakes, a regular Artful Dodger."

"Charles Dickens!"

"That's right. There's an author what knew a bit about crooks, didn't he? A pretty rough place London must have been in those days, if you go by what he says. Fagin and all. But we wouldn't hang a man for being a pickpocket, not now. Well—and having sent the check, you just came on here the next week and left it to him?"

"Yes. Here's his letter, you see, saying he'd have everything ready. It's addressed to my agent. We really ought to have sent someone ahead to see to things, but the fact is, as I told you before, what with newspaper reporters and one thing and another—"

"They give us a lot of trouble, them fellows," said Mr. Kirk, sympathetically.

"When," said Harriet, "they gate-crash your flat and try to bribe your servants—"

"Fortunately, Bunter is sea-green incorruptible—"

"Carlyle," said Mr. Kirk, with approval. "*French Revolution*. Seems a good man, that Bunter. Head screwed on the right way."

"But we needn't have troubled," said Harriet. "We'll have them all on our backs now."

"Ah!" said Mr. Kirk. "That's what comes of being a public character. You can't escape the fierce light that beats upon—"

"Here!" said Peter, "that's not fair. You can't have Tennyson twice. Anyway, there it is and what's done—no, I may want Shakespeare later on. The ironical part of it is that we expressly told Mr. Noakes we were coming for peace and quiet and didn't want the whole thing broadcast about the neighborhood."

"Well, he saw to that all right," said the Superintendent. "By George, you were making it easy for him, weren't you? Easy as pie. Off he could go, and no inquiry. Don't suppose he meant to go quite so far as he did go, all the same."

"Meaning, there's no chance of it's being suicide?"

"Not likely, is it, with all that money on him? Besides, the doctor says there's not a chance of it. We'll come to that later. About them doors, now. You're sure they were both locked when you arrived?"

"Absolutely. The front we opened ourselves with the latch-key, and the back—let me see—"

"Bunter opened that, I think," said Harriet.

"Better have Bunter in," said Peter. "He'll know. He never forgets anything." He called Bunter, adding, "What we want here is a bell."

"And you saw no disturbance, except what you've mentioned. Eggshells and such. No marks no weapon? Nothing out of its place?"

"I'm sure I didn't notice anything," said Harriet. "But there wasn't much light, and of course, we weren't looking for anything. We didn't know there was anything to look for."

"Wait a bit," said Peter. "Wasn't there something struck me this morning? I—no, I don't know. It was all upset for the sweep, you see. I don't know what I thought I—If there was anything, it's gone now. . . . Oh, Bunter! Superintendent Kirk wants to know was the back door locked when we arrived last night."

"Locked and bolted, my lord, top and bottom."

"Did you notice anything funny about the place at all?"

"Apart," said Bunter, warmly, "from the absence of those conveniences that we were led to expect, such as lamps and coal and food and the key of the house and the beds made up and the chimneys swept, and allowing further for the soiled crockery in the kitchen and the presence of Mr. Noakes's personal impedimenta in the bedroom—no, my lord. The house presented no anomalies nor incongruities of any kind that I was able to observe. Except—"

"Yes?" sad Mr. Kirk, hopefully.

"I attached no significance to it at the time," said Bunter, slowly, as though he were admitting to a slight defection from duty, "but there were two candlesticks in this room, upon the sideboard. Both candles were burnt down to the socket. Burnt out."

"So they were," said Peter. "I remember seeing you clean out the wax with a pen-knife. Night's candles are burnt out."

The Superintendent, absorbed in the implications of Bunter's statement, neglected the challenge till Peter poked him in the ribs and repeated it, adding, "I knew I should want Shakespeare again!"

"Eh?" said the Superintendent. "Night's candles? *Romeo and Juliet*—not much o' that about this here. Burnt out? Yes. They must a-been alight when he was killed. After dark, that means."

"He died by candle-light. Sounds like the title of a high-brow thriller. One of yours, Harriet. When found, make a note of."

"Captain Cuttle," said Mr. Kirk, not to be caught napping again. "October 2nd—sun would be setting about half-past five. No, it was Summer Time. Say half-past six. I dunno as that gets us much further. You didn't see nothing lying about as might have been used for a weapon? No mallet or bludgeon, eh? Nothing in the way of a—"

"He's going to say it!" said Peter to Harriet, in a whisper.

"—in the way of a blunt instrument?"

"He's said it!"

"I've never really believed they did say it."

"Well, now you know."

"No," said Bunter, after a short meditation. "Nothing beyond the customary household utensils in their appropriate situations."

"Have we any idea," inquired his lordship, "what kind of a jolly old blunt instrument we are looking for? How big? What shape?"

"Pretty heavy, my lord, that's all I can say. With a smooth, blunt head. Meaning, the skull was cracked like an eggshell, but the skin hardly broken. So there's no blood to help us, and the worst of it is, we don't know, no more than Adam, whereabouts it all 'appened. You see, Dr. Craven says deceased—Here, Joe, where's that letter Doctor wrote out for me to send to the coroner? Read it out to his lordship. Maybe he'll be able to make it out, seein' he's had a bit of experience and more eddication than you or me. Beats me what doctors want to use them long words for. Mind you, it's educational; I don't say it isn't. I'll have a go at it with the dictionary afore I goes to bed and I'll know I'm learning something. But to tell you the truth, we don't have many murders and violent deaths hereabouts, so I don't get much practice in the technical part, as you might say."

"All right, Bunter," said Peter, seeing that the Superintendent had finished with him. "You can go."

Harriet thought Bunter seemed a little disappointed. He would doubtless have appreciated the doctor's educational vocabulary.

P.C. Sellon cleared his throat and began: " 'Dear Sir—It is my duty to notify—' "

"Not there," interrupted Kirk. "Where it begins about deceased."

P.C. Sellon found the place and cleared his throat again:

" 'I may state, as the result of a superficial examination' —is that it, sir?"

"That's it."

" 'That deceased appears to 'ave been struck with a 'eavy blunt instrument of some considerable superficies'—"

"Meaning, he said, by that," explained the Superintendent, "as it wasn't a little fiddlin' thing like the beak of a 'ammer."

" 'On the posterior part of the'—I can't rightly make this out, sir. Looks to me like 'onion,' and that make sense all right, only it don't sound like doctor's language."

"It couldn't be that, Joe."

"Nor it ain't 'geranium' neither—leastways, there's no tail to the G."

" 'Cranium,' perhaps," suggested Peter. "The back of the skull."

"That'll be it," said Kirk. "That's where it *is*, anyhow, never mind what the doctor calls it."

"Yes, sir. 'A little above and beyond the left ear, the apparent direction of the blow being from behind downwards. An extensive fracture'—"

"Hullo!" said Peter. "On the left, from behind downwards. That looks like another of our old friends."

"The left-handed criminal," said Harriet.

"Yes. It's surprising how often you get them in detective fiction. A sort of sinister twist running right through the character."

"It might be a back-handed blow."

"Not likely. Who goes about swatting people left-handed? Unless the local tennis-champion wanted to show off. Or a navvy mistook old Noakes for a pile that needed driving."

"A navvy'd have hit him plumb center. They always do. You think they're going to brain the man who holds the thing up, but it never happens. I've noticed that. But there's another thing. My recollection of Noakes is that he was awfully tall."

"Quite right," said Kirk, "so he was. Six foot four, only he stooped a bit. Call it six foot two or three."

"You'll want a pretty tall murderer," said Peter.

"Wouldn't a long-handled weapon do? Like a croquet-mallet? or a golf club?"

"Yes, or a cricket-bat. Or a beetle, of course—"

"Or a spade—the flat side—"

"Or a gun-stock. Possibly even a poker—"

"It'd have to be a long, heavy one with a thick knob. I

think there's one in the kitchen. Or even a broom, I suppose—"

"Don't think it's be heavy enough, though it's possible. How about an ax or a pick—"

"Not blunt enough. They've got square edges. What other long things are there? I've heard of a flail, but I've never seen one. A lead cosh, if it was long enough. Not a sand-bag—they bend."

"A lump of lead in an old stocking would be handy."

"Yes—but look here, Peter! Anything would do—even a rolling-pin, always supposing—"

"I've thought of that. He might have been sitting down."

"So it might be a stone or a paper-weight like that one on the window-sill there."

Mr. Kirk started.

"Strewth!" he observed, "you're quick, you two. Not much you miss, is there? And the lady's as smart as the gentleman."

"It's her job," said Peter. "She writes detective stories."

"Does she now?" said the Superintendent. "I can't say I reads a lot o' them, though Mrs. Kirk, she likes a good Edgar Wallace now and again. But I couldn't rightly call 'em a mellering influence to a man in my line. I read an American story once, and the way the police carried on—well, it didn't seem right to me. Here, Joe, hand me that there paper-weight, would you? Hi! Not that way! Ain't you ever heard of fingerprints?"

Sellon, his large hands clasped around the stone, stood awkwardly and scratched his head with his pencil. He was a big, fresh-faced young man, who looked as though he would be better at grappling with drunks than measuring prints and reconstructing the time-table of the crime. At length he opened his fingers and brought the paper-weight balanced on his open palm.

"That won't take fingerprints," said Peter. "It's too rough. Edinburgh granite, from the look of it."

"It might a-done the bashing, though," said Kirk, "leastways, the underneath part, or this here rounded end. Model of a building, ain't it?"

"Edinburgh Castle, I fancy. It shows no signs of skin or hair or anything about it. Just a minute." He picked it up by a convenient chimney, examined its surface with a lens, and said, definitely, "No."

"Humph. Well. That gets us nowhere. We'll have a look at the kitchen poker presently."

"You'll find lots of fingerprints on that. Bunter's and mine, and Mrs. Ruddle's—possibly Puffett's and Crutchley's."

"That's the devil of it," said the Superintendent, frankly. "But none the more for that, Joe, you keep your fingers off anything what looks like a weapon. If you sees any of them things what his lordship and her ladyship here mentioned laying about, you just leave 'em be and shout till I come. See?"

"Yes, sir."

"To go back," said Peter, "to the doctor's report. I take it Noakes can't have bashed the back of his own head falling down the steps? He was an oldish man, wasn't he?"

"Sixty-five, my lord. Sound as a bell, though, as far as you can judge now. Eh, Joe?"

"That's a fact, sir. Boasted of it, he did. Talked large as Doctor said 'e was good for another quarter of a century. You ask Frank Crutchley. 'E 'eard 'im. Over at Pagford, in the Pig and Whistle. And Mr. Roberts wot keeps the Crown in the village—he've heard him many a time."

"Ah! well, that's as may be. It ain't never safe to boast. The boast of heraldry—well, I take it that'd be more in your lordship's line, but it all leads to the grave as Gray's Elegy has it. Still, he wasn't killed falling down the stairs, because there's a bruise on his forehead where he went down and hit the bottom step—"

"Oh!" said Peter. "Then he was alive when he fell?"

"Yes," said Mr. Kirk, a little put out by being anticipated. "That's what I was leading up to. But there again, that don't prove nothing, because seemin'ly he didn't die straight off. Accordin' to what Dr. Craven makes out—"

"Shall I read that bit, sir?"

"Don't bother with it, Joe. It's only a lot of rigmarole. I can explain to his lordship without all your onions and geraniums. What it comes to is this. Somebody 'it him and bust his skull, and he'd likely tumble down and lose consciousness—concussed, as you might say. After a bit, he'd come to, like as not. But he'd never know what hit 'im. Wouldn't remember a thing about it."

"Nor he would," said Harriet, eagerly. She knew that bit—in fact she'd had to expound it in her latest detective novel but one. "There'd be complete forgetfulness of everything immediately preceding the blow. And he might even pick himself up and feel all right for some time."

"Except," put in Mr. Kirk, who liked a literal precision, "for a sore head. But, generally speaking, that's correct, according to Doctor. He might walk about and do quite a bit for himself—"

"Such as locking the door behind the murderer?"

"*Exactly*, there's the trouble."

"Then," pursued Harriet, "he'd get giddy and drowsy, wouldn't he? Wander off to get a drink or call for help and—"

Memory suddenly showed her the open cellar-door, yawning between the back-door and the scullery.

"And pitch down the cellar-steps and die there. That door was standing open when we arrived, I remember Mrs. Ruddle telling her Bert to shut it."

"Pity they didn't happen to look inside," grunted the Superintendent. "Not as it'd have done the deceased any good—he'd been dead long enough—but if you'd a-known you could have kept the house *in statu quo*, as they say."

"We *could*," said Peter, with emphasis, "but I don't mind telling you frankly that we were in no mood to."

"No," said Mr. Kirk, meditatively, "I don't suppose you were. No. All things considered, it would have been inconvenient, I see that. But it's a pity, all the same. Because, you see, we've got very little to go on and that's a fact. The poor old chap might a-been killed anywhere—upstairs, downstairs, in my lady's chamber—"

"No, no, Mother Goose," said Peter, hastily. "Not there, not there, my child, Felicia Hemans. Let us pass on. How long did he live after he was hit?"

"Doctor says," put in the constable, "from half an hour to one hour, judging by the—the—hem-something or other."

"Hemorrhage?" suggested Kirk, taking possession of the letter. "That's it. Hemorrhagic effusion into the cortex. That's a good one."

"Bleeding in the brain," said Peter. "Good Lord—he had plenty of time. He may have been coshed outside the house altogether."

"But when do you suppose it all happened?" demanded Harriet. She appreciated Peter's effort to exonerate the house from all share in the crime, and was annoyed with herself for having betrayed any sensibility on the subject. It was distracting for him. Her tone, in consequence, was determinedly off-hand and practical.

"That," said the Superintendent, "is what we've got to find out. Some time last Wednesday night, putting what the doctor says with the rest of the evidence. After dark, if them candles are anything to go by. And that means—H'm! We'd better have this chap Crutchley in. Seems like he might have been the last person to see deceased alive."

"Enter the obvious suspect," said Peter, lightly.

"The obvious suspect is always innocent," said Harriet in the same tone.

"In books, my lady," said Mr. Kirk, with a little indulgent bow towards her, as who should say, "The ladies. God bless them!"

"Come, come," said Peter, "we must not introduce our professional prejudices into the case. How about it, Superintendent? Shall we make ourselves scarce?"

"That's as you like, my lord. I'd be glad enough if you'd stay; you might give me a bit of help, seeing as you know the ropes, so to speak. Not but what it'll be a kind of busman's holiday for you," he finished up, rather dubiously.

"That's what I was thinking," said Harriet. "A busman's honeymoon. Butchered to make a—"

"Lord Byron!" cried Mr. Kirk, a little too promptly. "Butchered to make a busman's—No, that don't seem right somehow."

"Try Roman," said Peter. "All right, we'll do our best. No objection to smoking in court, I take it. Where the devil did I put the matches?"

"Here you are, my lord," said Sellon. He produced a box and struck a light. Peter eyed him curiously, and remarked:

"Hullo! You're left-handed."

"For some things, my lord. Not for writing."

"Only for striking matches—and handling Edinburgh rock?"

"Left-handed?" said Kirk. "Why, so you are, Joe. I hope you ain't this tall, left-handed murderer what we're looking out for?"

"No, sir," said the constable, briefly.

"A pretty thing that'ud be, wouldn't it?" said his superior, with a hearty guffaw. "We shouldn't never hear the last of that. Now, you hop out and get Crutchley. Nice lad he is," he went on, turning to Peter as Sellon left the room. " 'Ard working, but no Sherlock 'Olmes, if you follow me. Slow in the uptake. I sometimes think his heart ain't rightly in his work these days. Married too young, that's what it is, and started a family, which is a handicap to a young officer."

"Ah!" said Peter, "all this matrimony is a sad mistake."

He laid his hand on his wife's shoulder, while Mr. Kirk tactfully studied his notebook.

CHAPTER VIII

£ s. d.

Sailor: *Faith, Dick Reede, it is to little end:*
His conscience is too liberal, and he too niggardly
To part from anything may do thee good. . . .
Reede: *If prayers and fair entreaties will not serve,*
Or make no battery in his flinty breast,
I'll curse the carle, and see what that will do.

—ARDEN OF FEVERSHAM

The gardener walked up to the table with a slightly belligerent air, as though he had an idea that the police were there for the sole purpose of preventing him from exercising his lawful right to obtain payment of forty pounds. He admitted, briefly, when questioned, that his name was Frank Crutchley and that he was accustomed to attend to the garden one day a week at Talboys for a stipend of five shillings per diem, putting in the rest of his time doing odd jobs of lorry-driving and taxi-work for Mr. Hancock at the garage in Pagford.

"Saving up, I was," said Crutchley, with insistence, "to get a garridge of my own, only for that there forty pounds Mr. Noakes had off of me."

"Never mind that now," said the Superintendent. "That's gone west, that has, and it's no use crying over spilt milk."

Crutchley was about as much convinced by this assurance as were the Allies, on being informed by Mr. Keynes, after the conclusion of the Peace Treaty, that they might whistle for their indemnities, since the money was not there. It is impossible for human nature to believe that money is not there. It seems so much more likely that the money is there and only needs bawling for.

"He promised," affirmed Frank Crutchley, in a dogged effort to overcome Mr. Kirk's extraordinary obtuseness, "that he'd let me have it when I came today."

"Well," said Kirk, "I dare say he might have done, if somebody hadn't butted in and brained him. You ought to a-been smarter and got it out of him last week."

This could be nothing but stupidity, Crutchley explained patiently: "He hadn't got it then."

"Oh, hadn't he though?" said the Superintendent. "That's all you know about it."

This was a staggerer. Crutchley turned white.

"Cripes! you don't mean to tell me—"

"Oh, yes, he had," said Kirk. This information, if he knew anything about it, was going to loosen his witness's tongue for him and save a deal of trouble. Crutchley turned with a frantic look at the other members of the party. Peter confirmed Kirk's statement with a nod. Harriet, who had known days when the loss of forty pounds would have meant greater catastrophe than Peter could ever suffer by the loss of forty thousand, said sympathetically:

"Yes, Crutchley. I'm afraid he had the money on him all the time."

"What! He had the money? You found it on him?"

"Well, we did," admitted the Superintendent. "There's no call to make a secret of it." He waited for the witness to draw the obvious conclusion.

"Mean to say, if he hadn't been killed, I might have had my money?"

"If you could have got in before Mr. MacBride," said Harriet, with more honesty than consideration for Kirk's tactics. Crutchley, however, was not troubling his head about Mr. MacBride. The murderer was the man who had robbed him of his own, and he took no pains to conceal his feelings.

"God! I'll—I'll—I'll—I'd like to—"

"Yes, yes," said the Superintendent, "we quite understand that. And now's your opportunity. Any facts you can give us—"

"Facts! I've been done, that's what it is, and I—"

"Look here, Crutchley," said Peter. "We know you've had a rotten deal, but that can't be helped. The man who killed Mr. Noakes has done you a bad turn, and he's the man we're after. Use your wits and see if you can't help us to get even with him."

The quiet, incisive tone had its effect. A kind of illumination spread over Crutchley's features.

"Thank you, my lord," said Kirk. "That's about the size of it, and put very plain. Now, my lad, we're sorry about your money, but it's up to you to give us a hand. See?"

"Yes," said Crutchley, with an almost savage eagerness. "All right. What d'you want to know?"

"Well, first of all—when did you last see Mr. Noakes?"

"Wednesday evening, same as I said. I finished up my work just before six and come in here to do the pots; and when I'd done 'em he gave me five bob, same as usual, and that's when I started askin' him for my forty quid."

"Where was that? In here?"

"No, in the kitchen. He always sat in there. I come out of here with the steps in my 'and—"

"Steps? Why the steps?"

"Why, for that there cactus and the clock. I wind the clock every week—it's an eight-day. I can't reach either of 'em without the steps. I goes to the kitchen, like I was saying, to put the steps away, and there he was. He give me my money—'arf a crown, and a bob, and two tanners and sixpence in coppers, if you want to be perticler, all out of different pockets. He liked to make out he couldn't 'ardly lay 'and on a 'apenny, but I was used to that. And when he'd finished play-actin', I asks him for my forty pound. I want that money, I says—"

"Just so. You wanted the money for the garage. What did he say to that?"

"Promised he'd let me have it next time I come—that's today. I might a-known 'e never meant it. Wasn't the first time he'd promised, and then always 'ad some excuse. But he promised faithful, this time—the dirty old swine, and well he might, and he all set to skip with 'is pockets stuffed full of bank-notes, the bleeder."

"Come, come," said Kirk, reprovingly, with a deprecatory glance at her ladyship. "Mustn't use language. Was he alone in the kitchen when you went out?"

"Yes. He wasn't the sort people dropped in for a chat with. I went off then, and that's the last I see of him."

"You went off," repeated the Superintendent, while Joe Sellon's right hand traveled laboriously among the pothooks, "and left him sitting in the kitchen. Now, when—"

"No, I didn't say that. He followed me down the passage, talkin' about givin' me the money first thing in the morning, and then I 'eard 'im lock and bolt the door be'ind me."

"Which door?"

"The back door. He mostly used that. The front door was allus kep' locked."

"Ah! is that a spring lock?"

"No; mortise lock. He didn't believe in them Yale things. Don't take much to bust *them* off with a jemmy, he'd say."

"That's a fact," said Kirk. "So that means the front door could only be opened with a key—from inside or out."

"That's right. I should a-thought you'd a-seen that for yourself, if you'd looked."

Mr. Kirk, who had indeed examined the fastenings of both doors with some care, merely inquired: "Was the front-door key ever left in the lock?"

"No; he kept it on his bunch. It ain't a big one."

"It certainly wasn't in the lock last night," volunteered

Peter. "We got in that way with Miss Twitterton's key, and the lock was perfectly free."

"Just so," said the Superintendent. "Was there any other spare key that you know of?"

Crutchley shook his head.

"Mr. Noakes wouldn't go 'andin' out keys by the bushel. Somebody might a-got in, you see, and pinched something."

"Ah! Well now, to get back. You left the house last Wednesday night—what time?"

"Dunno," said Crutchley, thoughtfully. "Must a-been getting on for twenty-past, I reckon. Anyway, it was ten past when I wound that there clock. And it keeps good time."

"It's right now," said Kirk, glancing at his watch. Harriet's wrist-watch confirmed this, and so did Joe Sellon's. Peter, after a blank gaze at his own watch, said "Mine's stopped," in a tone which might have suggested that Newton's apple had been observed to fly upward or a B.B.C. announcer heard to use a bawdy expression.

"Perhaps," suggested Harriet, practically, "you forgot to wind it up."

"I never forget to wind it up," said her husband, indignantly. "You're quite right, though; I did. I must have been thinking of something else last night."

"Very natural, I'm sure, in all the excitement," said Kirk. "Can you remember whether that there clock was going when you arrived?"

The question distracted Peter from his own lapse of memory. He dropped his watch back into his pocket unwound and stared at the clock.

"Yes," he said, finally. "It was. I heard it ticking, when we were sitting here, it was the most comfortable thing in the house."

"It was right, too," said Harriet. "Because you said something about its being past midnight and I looked, and it said the same as my watch."

Peter said nothing, but whistled a couple of bars almost

inaudibly. Harriet remained imperturbable; twenty-four hours of matrimony had taught her that, if one was going to be disturbed by sly allusions to Greenland's coast or anything else, one might live in a state of perpetual confusion.

Crutchley said:

"Of course it was going. It's an eight-day, I tell you. And it was right enough this morning when I wound it. What's the odds, anyhow?"

"Well, well," said Kirk. "We'll take it then that you left here some time after 6:10 by that clock, which was right as near as makes no difference. What did you do next?"

"Went straight to choir practice. See here—"

"Choir practice, eh? Ought to be easy enough to check up on that. What time's practice?"

"Six-thirty. I was in good time—you can ask anybody."

"Quite so," agreed Kirk. "All this is rowtine, you know—getting the times straight and so on. You left the house not earlier than 6:10 and not later than—say 6:25, to let you get to the church at 6:30. Right. Now, *as* a matter of rowtine, what did you do after that?"

"Vicar asked me to drive his car over to Pagford for him. He don't like driving himself after lighting-up. He ain't so young as he was. I had me supper over there at the Pig and Whistle and had a look-on at the darts match. Tom Puffett can tell you. He was there. Vicar give him a lift over."

"Puffett a darts player?" inquired Peter, pleasantly.

"Ex-champion. And still throws a tidy dart."

"Ah! it's the power he puts behind it, no doubt. Black he stood as night, Fierce as ten furies, terrible as hell, And shook a dreadful dart."

"Ha, ha!" cried Kirk, taken unaware and immensely tickled. "That's good. Hear that, Joe? That's good, that is. Black? He was black enough last time I saw him, halfway up the kitchen chimney. And shook a dreadful dart—I must tell him that. Worst of it is, I don't suppose he ever heard of Milton. Fierce as—well, there, poor old Tom Puffett!"

The Superintendent waited to roll the jest over on his tongue before returning to his inquiry.

"We'll see Tom Puffett presently. Did you bring Mr. Goodacre back?"

"Yes," said Crutchley, impatiently; he was not interested in John Milton. "Half-past ten I got him home, or just after. Then I went back to Pagford on my bike. I got in just on eleven and went to bed."

"Where do you sleep? Hancock's garage?"

"That's right. Along of their other chap, Williams. He'll tell you."

Kirk was in the middle of extracting further particulars about Williams, when in through the door the sooty face of Mr. Puffett poked itself.

"Excuse me," said Mr. Puffett, "but I can't do nothing with this 'ere pot. Will you 'ave the reverend's gun, my lord? or shall I fetch the ladders afore it gets dark?"

Kirk opened his mouth to reprove the intruder, but was suddenly overcome. "Black he stood as night," he muttered, joyfully. This new way of applying quotations, not to edification, seemed to have caught his fancy.

"Oh, dear," said Harriet. She glanced at Peter. "I wonder if we'd better leave it till tomorrow?"

"I don't mind telling you, me lady," observed the sweep, "Mr. Bunter's fair put out, thinkin' he'll have to cook dinner on that there perishin' oil-stove."

"I'd better come and talk to Bunter," said Harriet. She felt she could not bear to see Bunter suffer any more. Besides, the men would probably get on better without her. As she went out, she heard Kirk call Puffett into the room.

"Just a moment," said Kirk. "Crutchley here says he was at choir practice last Wednesday night from half-past six on. Do you know anything about that?"

"That's right, Mr. Kirk. We was both there. 'Arf-past six to 'arf-past seven. 'Arvest anthem. 'For 'Is mercies still endure, Ever faithful, ever sure.' " Finding his notes less powerful than usual, Mr. Puffett cleared his throat. "Been swallowing of the sut, that's what I've been doing of. 'Ever faithful, ever sure.' That's quite correct."

"And you see me round at the Pig, too," said Crutchley.

" 'Course I did. I'm not blind. You dropped me there and took vicar on to the Parish 'All and come back not five minutes arter for your supper. Bread and cheese, you 'ad, and four and 'arf pints, 'cause I counted 'em. Drahnd yourself one o' these days, I reckon."

"Was Crutchley there all the time?" asked Kirk.

"Till closin'. Ten o'clock. Then we 'ad to go round and pick up Mr. Goodacre again. Whist-drive was over at 10, but we 'ad to wait gettin' on ten minutes while he 'ad a chat with old Miss Moody. 'Ow that woman do clack on, to be sure! Then 'e come back with us. That's right, ain't it, Frank?"

"That's right."

"And," pursued Mr. Puffett, with a large wink, "if it's me you've got your eye on, you can ask Jinny wot time I got 'ome. George, too. Real vexed, Jinny was, at me settin' down to tell George about the match. But there! She's expectin' 'er fourth and it makes 'er fratchetty-like. I tell her, it ain't no good blamin' her dad, but I reckon she gotter take it outer George somehow."

"Very good," said the Superintendent, "that's all I want to know."

"Right," said Mr. Puffett. "I'll be seein' about them ladders, then."

He retired promptly, and Kirk again turned to Crutchley.

"Well, that seems straight enough. You left—call it 6:20—and didn't come back that night. You left deceased alone in the house, with the back door locked and bolted and the front locked, so far as you know. How about the windows?"

"Shut and locked 'em all afore I went. Burglar-proof catches you can see they have. Mr. Noakes didn't set much store by fresh air."

"H'm!" said Peter. "He seems to have been a careful

bird. By the way, Superintendent, did you find the front-door key on the body?"

"Here's his bunch," said Kirk.

Peter pulled Miss Twitterton's key from his pocket, looked over the bunch, picked out its counterpart and said, "Yes; here you are." He laid the two side by side on his palm, examined them thoughtfully with a lens, and finally handed the whole thing over to Kirk, remarking, "Nothing there, so far as I can see."

Kirk scrutinized the keys silently and then asked Crutchley:

"Did you come back here any time during the week?"

"No. Wednesday's my day. Mr. 'Ancock gives me Wednesday from eleven o'clock on. And Sundays, of course. But I wasn't here Sunday. I went to London to see a young lady."

"Are you a London man?" asked Peter.

"No, my lord. But I worked there once and I got friends there."

Peter nodded.

"And you can't give us any further information? Can't think of anybody who might have come to see Mr. Noakes that night? Anybody who might have had a grudge against him?"

"I might think o' plenty o' *them*," said Crutchley, with emphasis. "But nobody what you might call special."

Kirk was about to make a gesture of dismissal, when Peter put in a question.

"Do you know anything about a note-case Mr. Noakes lost some time ago?"

Kirk, Crutchley and Sellon all stared at him. Peter grinned.

"No; I wasn't born with second sight. Mrs. Ruddle was eloquent on the subject. What can you tell us about that?"

"I know he made a hell of a fuss about it, that's all. Ten pound he had in it—or so he said. If 'e'd a-lost forty pound like me—"

"That'll do," said Kirk. "Have we any information about that, Joe?"

"No, sir. Except it wasn't found. We made out he must have dropped it out of his pocket in the road."

"All the same," put in Crutchley, "he had new locks put on the doors and the windows done too. Two years ago, that was. You ask Ma Ruddle about it."

"Two years ago," said Kirk. "Well—it don't seem to have much connection with this here."

"It explains, perhaps," said Peter, "why he was so careful about locking up."

"Oh, yes, of course," agreed the Superintendent. "Well, all right, Crutchley. That'll do for the moment. Stay about in case you're wanted."

"It's my day here," said Crutchley. "I'll be workin' in the garden."

Kirk watched the door close behind him.

"It don't seem as if it could be him. Him and Puffett are alibis for one another."

"Puffett? Puffett is his own best alibi. You've only got to look at him. The man of upright soul and humor placid needs no blunt instrument nor prussic acid. Horace; Wimsey's translation."

"Then Puffett's word is enough to let out Crutchley. Not but what he mightn't have done it later on. Doctor only says, 'Dead only a week.' Suppose Crutchley did it the next day—"

"Not very likely. When Mrs. Ruddle came in the morning she couldn't get in."

"That's true. We'll have to check up the alibi with this chap Williams at Pagford. He might have come back and done the job after eleven."

"He might. Only remember, Noakes hadn't gone to bed. How about earlier—say, 6 o'clock, before he left?"

"Don't fit in with the candles."

"I was forgetting them. But you know, you could light candles at six o'clock on purpose to create that alibi."

"I suppose you could," agreed Kirk, with deliberation.

He was apparently unused to dealing with criminals of so much subtlety as that would imply. He ruminated for a moment, and then suggested:

"But them eggs and that cocoa?"

"I've known even that done, too. I've known a murderer sleep in two beds and eat two breakfasts in order to lend verisimilitude to an otherwise unconvincing narrative."

"Gilbert and Sullivan," said the Superintendent, a little hopelessly.

"Mostly Gilbert, I fancy. It's more likely, if Crutchley did it, that it was done then, because I don't see old Noakes letting in Crutchley after dark. Why should he? Unless Crutchley *did* have a key after all."

"Ah!" said Kirk. He swiveled around heavily in his chair and looked Peter in the face:

"What was you looking for on them keys, my lord?"

"Traces of wax in the wards."

"Oh!" said Kirk.

"If a duplicate was made," went on Peter, "it was made within the last two years. Difficult to trace, but not impossible. Especially when people have friends in London."

Kirk scratched his head.

"That'll be a nice job," he said. "But see here. The way I look at it is this. If Crutchley did it, how did he come to miss all that money? That's the thing I can't get over. That don't look reasonable to me."

"You're quite right. It's the most puzzling thing about the case, whoever committed the murder. It almost looks as though it wasn't done for money. But it's not easy to see any other motive."

"That's the funny thing about it," said Kirk.

"By the way, if Mr. Noakes had had any money to leave, who would have come in for it?"

"Ah!" The Superintendent's face brightened. "We've got that. Found this bit of a will in that old desk in the kitchen." He produced the paper from his pocket and spread it out. " 'After payment of my just debts—' "

"Cynical blighter! A fine fat legacy to leave anyone."

" 'All I die possessed of to my niece and sole surviving relative, Agnes Twitterton.' That surprise you?"

"Not at all. Why should it?" But Kirk, slow as he seemed, had seen Peter's quick frown and now pressed home his advantage.

"When this Jew-bird, MacBride, started blowing the gaff, what did Miss Twitterton say?"

"Er—well!" said Peter, "she went off the deep end—naturally."

"Naturally. Seemed a bit of a blow to her, eh?"

"Not more than you might expect. Who witnessed the will, by the way?"

"Simon Goodacre and John Jellyfield. He's the doctor from Pagford. It's all in order. What did Miss Twitterton say when your man discovered the body?"

"Well, she shrieked a bit and so on, and went off into hysterics."

"Did she say anything particular, besides shrieking?"

Peter was conscious of a curious reluctance. Theoretically, he was quite as ready to hang a woman as a man, but the memory of Miss Twitterton, frenziedly clinging to Harriet, was disturbing to him. He was tempted to feel, with Kirk, that marriage was a handicap to a young officer.

"See here, my lord," said Kirk, his ox-eyes mild but implacable, "I've heard one or two things from these other people."

"Then," retorted Peter, "why don't you ask them?"

"I'm going to. Joe, ask Mr. MacBride to step here a minute. Now, my lord, you're a gentleman and you've got your feelings. I know all that, and it does you credit. But I'm a police-officer, and I can't afford to indulge in feelings. They're a privilege of the upper classes."

"Upper classes be damned!" said Peter. This stung him, all the more that he knew he deserved it.

"Now, MacBride," went on Kirk, cheerfully, "he's no class at all. If I asked you, you'd tell the truth, but it might 'urt you. Now I can get it out of MacBride, and it won't 'urt him in the least."

"I see," said Peter. "Painless extractions a specialty."

He walked up to the fire and kicked the logs moodily.

Mr. MacBride came in with great alacrity; his face expressed that the sooner all this was over, the sooner to Town. He had already given the police the details of the financial situation and was straining like a greyhound at the official leash.

"Oh, Mr. MacBride, there's just one other thing. Did you happen to notice what sort of effect the discovery of the body had upon the family and friends, so to speak?"

"Well," said Mr. MacBride, "they were upset. Who wouldn't be?" (A silly question to keep a man waiting about for.)

"Remember anything special said?"

"Oh, ah!" said Mr. MacBride. "I get you. Well, now, the gardener chap—he went as white as a sheet, he did—and the old gentleman was badly put about. The niece had hysterics—but *she* didn't seem as much surprised as the rest, did she?"

He appealed to Peter, who avoided his sharp eye by strolling over to the window and gazing out at the dahlias.

"What do you mean by that?"

"Well, when the servant came in and said they'd found Mr. Noakes, she yelled out at once, 'Oh! Uncle's dead!' "

"Did she now?" said Kirk.

Peter swung around on his heel.

"That's not quite fair, MacBride. Anybody could have told that from Bunter's manner. I know *I* could."

"Could you?" said MacBride. "You didn't seem in any hurry to believe it." He glanced at Kirk, who asked:

"Did Miss Twitterton say anything else?"

"She said, 'Uncle's dead and all the money's gone!' just like that. Then she had the jim-jams. Nothing like £ s. d. for going straight to the heart, is there?"

"Nothing," said Peter. "You, if I recollect rightly, asked whether they'd found any money on the corpse."

"Quite right," admitted MacBride. "He was no relation of mine, you see, was he?"

Peter, worsted at every thrust, lowered his weapon and admitted defeat.

"The legal profession," he said, "must present you with a comprehensive picture of Christian family life. What do you think of it?"

"Not much," replied Mr. MacBride, succinctly. He turned back to the table. "I say, Mr. Superintendent, are you going to want me any more? I've got to get back to Town."

"That's O.K. We've got your address. Good morning, Mr. MacBride, and thanks very much."

As the door shut behind him, Kirk transferred his glance to Peter. "That right, my lord?"

"Quite right."

"Ah! well, I think we'll have to see Miss Twitterton."

"I'll get my wife to fetch her down," said Peter, and escaped. Mr. Kirk sat back in Merlin's seat and rubbed his hands thoughtfully.

"That's a real nice gentleman, Joe," said Mr. Kirk. "Straight out o' the top drawer. Pleasant and easy as kiss-me-'and. Well eddicated, too. But he sees which way the wind's blowing, and he don't like it. Small blame to him."

"But," objected the constable, "he can't think Aggie Twitterton coshed old Noakes on the 'ead with a mallet. She's a little slip of a thing."

"You never know, me lad. The female of the species is deadlier than the male. That's Rudyard Kipling. He knows that, though it's agin his upbringing to say so. Not but what he'd a-made it sound a lot better if he *had* said it, instead of leaving it to MacBride. But there! he couldn't lay tongue to it, I suppose. Besides, he knew well enough I'd have it out of MacBride in the end."

"Well, he ain't done her much good, as I can see."

"Them sort of feelings," pronounced Mr. Kirk, "commonly don't do much good, except to complicate things. But they're pretty, and, if taken the right way, 'armless. You got to learn to get round 'em, when you're dealing with gentry. And remember this: what they *don't* say is more important than what they *do* say, especially when they've got good brains, like this here gentleman has. He sees well enough that if Noakes was killed for what he had to leave—"

"But he hadn't nothing to leave."

"I know that. But *she* didn't. Aggie Twitterton didn't know. And *if* he was murdered for what he had to *leave*, that 'ud explain why the £600 wasn't took off the body. Maybe she didn't know it was there, and if she did, she didn't have to take it, because it'ud all be hers in the end. Use your 'ead, Joe Sellon."

Peter in the meantime had caught Mr. MacBride on the doorstep.

"How do you get back?"

"Lord knows," said Mr. MacBride, frankly. "I *came* by train to Great Pagford and took the bus on. If there's no bus handy I'll have to get a lift. I wouldn't have believed there were places like this, within fifty mile of London. Beats me how people can live in 'em. But it's all a matter of taste, ain't it?"

"Bunter can take you in the car to Pagford," said Peter. "They won't want him again for a bit. Sorry you should have been dumped into all this."

Mr. MacBride was grateful, and said so. "It's all in the day's work," he added. "You're the ones that come off worst, in one way, you and her ladyship. I never saw much to fancy in these three-by-four villages myself. Think it's the little woman, do you? Well, you can't be sure; but in our way of business we do have to keep our eyes peeled when it comes to relations, particularly if there's money in it. There's some people won't ever make a will—say it's like signing their own death-warrant. And they ain't so far out. But look here! This chap Noakes was pretty well up against it, wasn't he? He may have been doing some funny stuff on the side. I've known men get bumped off for other things besides money. Well, so long. My respects to her ladyship, and much obliged."

Bunter brought around the car and he hopped in, waving a friendly gesture. Peter caught Harriet, and explained what was wanted.

"Poor little Twitters," said Harriet. "Are you going to be there?"

"No. I'm going out for a breath of air. I'll come back presently."

"What's the matter? Kirk hasn't been unpleasant, surely?"

"Oh, no. He handled me with kid gloves on. Showed all the proper consideration for my rank and refinement and other inferiorities. My own fault, I asked for it. Oh, golly, here's the vicar. What does he want?"

"They asked him to come back. Go on out the back way, Peter. I'll tackle him."

Kirk and Sellon, from the window, had watched Mr. MacBride's departure.

"Hadn't I ought to fetch Aggie Twitterton down myself?" suggested Sellon. "His lordship will maybe tell his wife to give her the tip."

"The trouble with you, Joe," replied the Superintendent, "is, you ain't got no pussychology, as they call it. They wouldn't do a thing like that, neither of them. They ain't compounding no felonies nor yet obstructing the law. All that's the matter is, *he* don't like 'urting women and *she* don't like 'urting him. But they won't either on 'em put out a finger to stop it, because that sort of thing ain't done. And when things ain't done, they won't do 'em—and that's the long and the short of it."

Having thus laid down the code of behavior for the nobility and gentry, Mr. Kirk blew his nose, and resumed his seat; whereupon the door opened to admit Harriet and Mr. Goodacre.

CHAPTER IX

TIMES AND SEASONS

—Dost thou know what reputation is?
I'll tell thee—to small purpose, since the instruction
Comes now too late. . . .
You have shook hands with Reputation,
And made him invisible.
—JOHN WEBSTER, *THE DUCHESS OF MALFI*

The Rev. Simon Goodacre blinked nervously when confronted by the two officers drawn up, as it were, in battle-array, and Harriet's brief announcement on her way upstairs that he had "something to say to you, Superintendent," did little to set him at ease.

"Dear me! Well. Yes. I came back to see if you wanted me for anything. As you suggested, you know, as you suggested. And to tell Miss Twitterton—but I see she is not here—Well, only that I had seen Lugg about the—er, dear me, the coffin. There must be a coffin, of course—I am not acquainted with the official procedure in such circumstances, but no doubt a coffin will have to be provided?"

"Certainly," said Kirk.

"Oh, yes, thank you. I had supposed so. I have referred Lugg to you, because I imagine the—the body is no longer in the house."

"It's over at the Crown," said the Superintendent. "The inquest will have to be held there."

"Oh, dear!" said Mr. Goodacre. "The inquest—oh, yes."

"The coroner's office will give all the usual facilities."

"Yes, thank you, thank you. Er—Crutchley spoke to me as I came up the path."

"What did he say?"

"Well—I think he thinks he might be suspected."

"What makes him think that?"

"Dear me!" said Mr. Goodacre. "I fear I am putting my foot in it. He didn't say he did think it. I only thought he might think it from what he said. But I assure you, Superintendent, that I can confirm his alibi in every particular. He was at choir practice from 6:30 to 7:30, and then he took me over to Pagford for the whist-drive and brought me back here at 10:30. So, you see—"

"That's all right, sir. If an alibi's wanted for them times, you and him's out of it."

"I'm out of it?" exclaimed Mr. Goodacre. "Bless my soul, Superintendent—"

"Only my joke, sir."

Mr. Goodacre seemed to find the joke in but poor taste. He replied, however, mildly:

"Yes, yes. Well, I hope I may assure Crutchley that it's all right. He's a young man of whom I have a very high opinion. So keen and industrious. You mustn't attach too much importance to his chagrin about the forty pounds. It's a considerable sum for a man in his position."

"Don't you worry about that, sir," said Kirk. "Very glad to have your confirmation of those times."

"Yes, yes. I thought I'd better mention it. Now, is there anything else I can do to help?"

"Thank you very much, sir; I don't know as there is. You spent Wednesday night at home, I take it, after 10:30?"

"Why, of course," said the vicar, not at all relishing this tendency to harp upon his movements. "My wife and my servant can substantiate my statement. But you scarcely suppose—"

"We ain't got to supposing things yet, sir. That comes later. This is all rowtine. You didn't call here at any time during the last week, by any chance?"

"Oh, no. Mr. Noakes was away."

"Oh! you knew he was away, did you, sir?"

"No, no. At least I supposed so. That is to say, yes. I called here on the Thursday morning, but got no answer, so I supposed he was away, as he sometimes was. In fact I fancy Mrs. Ruddle told me so. Yes, that was it."

"That the only time you called?"

"Dear me, yes. It was only a little matter of a subscription—in fact, that was what I came about today. I was passing by, and saw a notice on the gate asking for bread and milk to be delivered, so I supposed he had returned."

"Ah, yes. When you came on Thursday, you didn't notice anything funny about the house?"

"Goodness me, no. Nothing unusual at all. What would there be to notice?"

"Well—" began Kirk; but, after all, what could he expect this short-sighted old gentleman to notice? Signs of a struggle? Fingerprints on a door? Foot marks on the path? Scarcely. Mr. Goodacre would possibly have noticed a full-sized corpse, if he had happened to trip over it, but probably nothing smaller.

He accordingly thanked and dismissed the vicar, who, once more observing that he could fully account for Crutchley's movements and his own after half-past six, blundered vaguely out again, murmuring a series of agitated "Good afternoons" as he went.

"Well, well," said Kirk. He frowned. "What makes the old gentleman so sure those *are* the essential times. *We* don't know they are."

"No, sir," said Sellon.

"Seems very excited about it. It can't 'ardly be him, though, come to think of it, he's tall enough. He's taller nor what you are—pretty well as tall as Mr. Noakes was I reckon."

"I'm sure," said the constable, "it couldn't be vicar, sir."

"Isn't that just what I'm saying? I suppose Crutchley must a-got the idea of the times being important from us questioning him so close about them. It's a hard life," added Mr. Kirk, plaintively. "If you ask questions, you tell the witness what you're after; if you don't ask 'em, you can't find out anything. And just when you think you're getting on to something you come slap up against the Judges' Rules."

"Yes, sir," said Sellon, respectfully. He rose as Harriet led Miss Twitterton in, and brought forward another chair.

"Oh, please!" exclaimed Miss Twitterton, faintly. "Please don't leave me, Lady Peter."

"No, no," said Harriet. Mr. Kirk hastened to reassure the witness.

"Sit down, Miss Twitterton; there's nothing to be alarmed about. Now, first of all, I understand you know nothing about your uncle's arrangement with Lord Peter Wimsey—selling the house, I mean, and so on. No. Just so. Now, when had you seen him last?"

"Oh! not for—" Miss Twitterton paused and counted the fingers of both hands carefully—"not for about ten days. I looked in last Sunday after morning service. I mean, of course, last Sunday *week*. I came over you see, to play the organ for the dear vicar. It's a tiny church, of course, and *not* many people—nobody in Paggleham plays the organ, and of course I'm delighted to help in any way—and I called on Uncle then and he seemed *quite* as usual, and—and that's the—the last time I saw him. Oh, dear!"

"Were you aware that he was absent from home ever since last Wednesday?"

"But he wasn't absent!" exclaimed Miss Twitterton. "He was here all the time."

"Quite so," said the Superintendent. "Did you know he was here, and not absent?"

"Of course not. He often goes away. He usually tells—I meant, told me. But it was quite an ordinary thing for him to be at Broxford. I mean, if I had known, I shouldn't have thought anything of it. But I didn't know anything about it."

"Anything about what?"

"About anything. I mean, nobody told me he wasn't here, so I thought he was here—and so he was, of course."

"If you'd been told the house was shut up and Mrs. Ruddle couldn't get in, you wouldn't have been surprised or uneasy?"

"Oh, no. It often happened. I should have thought he was at Broxford."

"You have a key for the front door, haven't you?"

"Oh, yes. And the back door, too." Miss Twitterton fumbled in a capacious pocket of the old-fashioned sort. "But I never use the back-door key because it's always bolted—the door, I mean." She pulled out a large key-ring. "I gave them both to Lord Peter last night—off this bunch. I always keep them on the ring with my own. They *never* leave me. Except last night, of course, when Lord Peter had them."

"H'm!" said Kirk. He produced Peter's two keys. "Are these the ones?"

"Well, they must be, mustn't they, if Lord Peter gave them to you."

"You haven't ever lent the front-door key to anybody?"

"Oh, *dear*, no!" protested Miss Twitterton. "Not *anybody*. If Uncle was away and Frank Crutchley wanted to get in on Wednesday morning, he *always* came to me and I went over with him and unlocked the door for him. Uncle was *ever* so particular. And besides, I should want to go myself and see that the rooms were all right. In fact, if Uncle William was at Broxford I used to come over *most* days."

"But on this occasion, you didn't know he was away?"

"No, I didn't. That's what I keep on telling you. I didn't know. So of course I didn't come. And he *wasn't* away."

"Exactly. Now, you're sure you've never left these keys about where they might be pinched or borrowed?"

"No, never," replied Miss Twitterton, earnestly—as though, thought Harriet, she asked nothing better than to twist a rope for her own neck. Surely she must see that the key to the house was the key to the problem; was it possible for any innocent person to be quite as innocent as that?

The Superintendent plowed on with his questions unmoved.

"Where do you keep them at night?"

"*Always* in my bedroom. The keys, and dear Mother's silver tea-pot and Aunt Sophy's cruet that was a wedding-present to grandpa and grandma. I take them up with me *every* night and put them on the little table by my bed, with the dinner-bell handy in case of fire. And I'm *sure* nobody could come in when I was asleep, because I always put a deck-chair across the head of the staircase."

"You brought the dinner-bell down when you came to let us in," said Harriet, vaguely corroborative. Her attention was distracted by the sight of Peter's face, peering in through the diamond panes of the lattice. She waved him a friendly gesture. Presumably he had walked off his attack of self-consciousness and was getting interested again.

"A deck-chair?" Kirk was asking.

"To trip up a burglar," explained Miss Twitterton, very seriously. "It's a *splendid* thing. You see, while he was getting all tangled up and making a noise, I should hear him and ring the dinner-bell out of the window for the police."

"Dear me!" said Harriet. (Peter's face had vanished—perhaps he was coming in.) "How dreadfully ruthless of you, Miss Twitterton. The poor man might have fallen over it and broken his neck."

"What man?"

"The burglar."

"But, dear Lady Peter, I'm trying to explain—there never *was* a burglar."

"Well," said Kirk, "it doesn't look as if anybody else could have got at the keys. Now, Miss Twitterton—about these money difficulties of your uncle's—"

"Oh, dear, oh, dear!" broke in Miss Twitterton, with unfeigned emotion. "I know *nothing* about those. It's terrible. It gave me *such* a shock. I thought—we *all* thought—Uncle was ever so well off."

Peter had come in so quietly that only Harriet noticed him. He remained near the door, winding his watch and setting it by the clock on the wall. Obviously he had come back to normal, for his face expressed only an alert intelligence.

"Did he make a will, do you know?" Kirk dropped the question out casually; the tell-tale sheet of paper lay concealed under his notebook.

"Oh, yes," said Miss Twitterton. "I'm sure he made a will. Not that it would have mattered, I suppose, because I'm the only one of the family left. But I'm certain he told me he'd made one. He always said, when I was worried about things—of course I'm *not* very well off—he always said, Now, don't you be in a hurry, Aggie. I can't help you now, because it's all tied up in the business, but it'll come to you after I'm dead."

"I see. You never thought he might change his mind?"

"Why, no. Who else *should* he leave it to? I'm the only one. I suppose now there won't be anything?"

"I'm afraid it doesn't look like it."

"Oh, dear! Was that what he meant when he said it was tied up in the business? That there wasn't any?"

"That's what it very often does mean," said Harriet.

"Then that's what—" began Miss Twitterton, and stopped.

"That's what, what?" prompted the Superintendent.

"Nothing," said Miss Twitterton, miserably. "Only something I thought of. Something private. But he said once something about being short and people not paying their bills. . . . Oh, what *have* I done? How ever can I explain—?"

"What?" demanded Kirk again.

"Nothing," repeated Miss Twitterton, hastily. "Only it sounds so silly of me." Harriet received the impression that this was not what Miss Twitterton had originally meant to say. "He borrowed a little sum of me once—not much—but of course I hadn't *got* much. Oh, dear! I'm afraid it looks dreadful to be thinking about money just now, but . . . I *did* think I'd have a little for my old age . . . and times are so hard . . . and . . . and . . . there's the rent of my cottage . . . and . . ."

She quavered on the verge of tears. Harriet said, confusedly:

"Don't worry. I'm sure something will turn up."

Kirk could not resist it. "Mr. Micawber!" he said, with a sort of relief. A faint echo behind him drew his attention to Peter, and he glanced around. Miss Twitterton hunted wildly for a handkerchief amid a pocketful of bast, pencils and celluloid rings for chickens' legs, which came popping out in a small shower.

"I'd counted on it—rather specially," sobbed Miss Twitterton. "Oh, I'm sorry. Please don't pay any attention."

Kirk cleared his throat. Harriet, who was as a rule good at handkerchiefs, discovered to her annoyance that on this particular morning she had provided herself only with an elegant square of linen, suitable for receiving such rare and joyful drops as might be expected on one's honeymoon. Peter came to the rescue with what might have been a young flag of truce.

"It's quite clean," he said, cheerfully. "I always carry a spare."

(The devil you do, said Harriet to herself; you are too well trained by half.)

Miss Twitterton buried her face in the silk and snuffled in a dismal manner, while Joe Sellon studiously consulted the back pages of his shorthand notes. The situation threatened to prolong itself.

"Shall you want Miss Twitterton any more, Mr. Kirk?" Harriet ventured, at length. "Because I really think—"

"Er—well," said the Superintendent. "If Miss Twitterton wouldn't mind telling us—just as a matter of form, you understand —where she was last Wednesday evening."

Miss Twitterton came quite briskly out of the handkerchief.

"But Wednesday is *always* choir practice," she announced, with an air of astonishment that anyone could ask so simple a question.

"Ah, yes," agreed Kirk. "And I suppose you'd quite naturally pop in on your uncle when that was over?"

"Oh, no!" said Miss Twitterton. "Indeed I didn't. I went home to supper. Wednesday's my busy night, you know."

"That so?" said Kirk.

"Yes, of course—because of market on Thursday. Why, I had half a dozen fowls to kill and pluck before I went to bed. It made me ever so late. Mr. Goodacre—he's always so kind—he's often said he knew it was inconvenient having the practice on Wednesday, but it happens to suit some of the men better, and so you see—"

"Six to kill and pluck," said Kirk, thoughtfully, as though estimating the time that this would take. Harriet looked at the meek Miss Twitterton in consternation.

"You don't mean to say you kill them yourself?"

"Oh, yes," said Miss Twitterton, brightly. "It's *so* much easier than you would think, when you're used to it."

Kirk burst into a guffaw, and Peter—seeing that his wife was disposed to attach overmuch importance to the matter—said in an amused tone:

"My dear girl, wringing necks is only a knack. It doesn't need strength."

He twisted his hands in quick pantomime, and Kirk, either genuinely forgetting the errand he was on, or of malice prepense, added:

"That's right." He tightened an imaginary noose about his own bull neck. "Wring 'em or string 'em up—it's the sharp jerk does it."

His head flopped sideways suddenly, sickeningly. Miss Twitterton gave a squeak of alarm; for the first time, perhaps, she realized where all this had to end. Harriet was angry, and her face showed it. Men; when they got together they were all alike—even Peter. For a moment he and Kirk stood together on the far side of a chasm, and she hated them both.

"Steady on, Super," said Wimsey; "we're alarming the ladies."

"Dear, dear, that'll never do." Kirk was jovial; but the

brown ox-eyes were as watchful as the gray. "Well, thank you, Miss Twitterton. I think that's all for the moment."

"That's all right then." Harriet got up. "It's all over. Come along and see how Mr. Puffett is getting on with the kitchen chimney." She pulled Miss Twitterton to her feet and steered her out of the room. As Peter opened the door for them, she darted a reproachful glance at him, but, as with Lancelot and Guinevere, their eyes met and hers fell.

"Oh, and my lady!" said the Superintendent, unmoved, "would you be so kind as to tell Mrs. Ruddle she's wanted? We must get those times straightened out a bit," he went on, addressing himself to Sellon, who grunted and took out a knife to sharpen his pencil.

"Well," said Peter, in a tone almost of challenge, "she was quite frank about that."

"Yes, my lord. She knew about it all right. A little knowledge is a dangerous thing."

"Not knowledge—learning!" Peter corrected him peevishly. "A little *learning*—Alexander Pope."

"Is that so?" replied Mr. Kirk, not at all perturbed. "I must make a note of that. Ah! it don't look as though anybody else could have got hold of the keys, but you never know."

"I think she was telling the truth."

"Reckon there's several kinds of truth, my lord. There's truth as far as you knows it; and there's truth as far as you're asked for it. But they don't represent the whole truth—not necess*ar*ily. F'rinstance, I never asked that little lady if she locked up the house after someone else, did I? All I said was, When did you last see your fa—your uncle? See?"

"Yes, I see. Personally, I always prefer *not* to have a key to the house in which they've discovered the body."

"There's that about it," admitted Kirk. "But there's circumstances in which you might rather it was you than somebody else, if you take my meaning. And there's times when—What do you suppose she meant when she said, what had she done? Eh? Maybe it come to her then as she might have left them keys about, accidental on purpose. Or maybe—"

"That was about the money."

"So it was. And maybe she thought of something else she'd done as wasn't much use to her nor anybody, as it turned out. Something she was hiding there, if you ask me. If she'd been a man, I'd a-got it out of her fast enough—but women! They get howling and sniffing and you can't do nothing with them."

"True," said Peter; and felt in his turn a momentary resentment against the whole sex, including his wife. After all, hadn't she, more or less, ticked him off in the matter of neck-wringing? And the lady who now entered rubbing her hands on her apron and crying in self-important tones, "Did you want me, mister?"—there was nothing in *her* to thrill to music the silent string of chivalry. Kirk, however, knew where he was with the Mrs. Ruddles of this life and attacked the position confidently.

"Yes. We wanted to fix up a bit more exactly about the time of this murder. Now, Crutchley says he saw Mr. Noakes alive and well on Wednesday evening about twenty-past six. You'd gone home by then, I suppose?"

"Yes, I had. I only came to Mr. Noakes mornings. I wasn't in the 'ouse after dinner-time."

"And you came up next morning and found the place shut up?"

"That's right. I knocks 'ard on both doors—'im bein' a bit deaf I allus knocks 'ard, and then I gives a shout, like, under 'is bedroom winder, and then I knocks again and nothing come of it, and I says, Drat the man, I says, 'e's gone off to Broxford. Thinkin' he'd took the 10 o'clock bus the night before. There! I says, 'e might a-told me, and me not paid for last week, neither."

"What else did you do?"

"Nothing. There wasn't nothing *to* do. Only tell the baker and milkman not to call. And the noospaper. And leave word at the post-office to bring 'is letters down to me.

Only there wasn't no letters, only two, and they was bills, so I didn't send 'em on."

"Ah!" said Peter. "That's the right way with bills. There, as the poet ungrammatically observes, there let them lay, like the goose with the golden egg."

Mr. Kirk found this quotation confusing and refused to pursue it.

"Didn't you think of sending over to Miss Twitterton? She usually came down when Mr. Noakes was away. You must have been surprised not to see her."

"It ain't my place to go sendin' for people if they don't choose to come," said Mrs. Ruddle. "If Mr. Noakes 'ad wanted Aggie Twitterton, he could a-told her. Leastways, that's how I thought about it. 'Im bein' dead, I see now, o' course, he couldn't, but I wasn't to know that, was I? And I was inconvenienced enough, not 'avin' 'ad me money—you don't expect me to go sendin' two miles for people, as if I 'adn't enough to do without that. Nor wasting good stamps on 'em, neither. And what's more," said Mrs. Ruddle, with some energy, "I says to meself, if 'e ain't said nothing to me about goin', maybe 'e ain't told Aggie Twitterton, neither—and I ain't one to interfere in other folks' business, and don't you think it."

"Oh!" said Kirk. "Mean to say you thought he might have had some reason for wanting to leave the place quiet like?"

"Well, he might and he mightn't. That's the way I looked at it. See? Of course, there was my week's money—but there wasn't no 'urry for that. Aggie Twitterton 'ud a-paid me if I arst 'er."

"Of course," said Kirk. "I suppose you didn't think of asking her on Sunday when she came over to play the organ in church?"

"Me?" said Mrs. Ruddle, quite affronted. "I'm chapel. They're out and gone by the time we finish. Not but what I *'ave* been to church now and again, but there ain't nothing to show for it. Up and down, up and down, as if one's knees wasn't wore out with scrubbing on week-days, and a pore little bit of a sermon with no 'eart in it. Mr. Goodacre's a very kind gentleman and friendly to all, I ain't sayin' a word agin' 'im, but I'm chapel and always was, and that's the other end of the village, which by the time I was back here, they've all gone 'ome and Aggie Twitterton on 'er bicycle. So you see, I couldn't ketch 'er, not if I wanted ever so."

"Of course you couldn't," said Kirk. "All right. Well, you didn't try to let Miss Twitterton know. I suppose you mentioned in the village that Mr. Noakes was away?"

"I dare say I did," admitted Mrs. Ruddle. "It wasn't nothing out o' the way."

"You told us," put in Peter, "that he'd gone by the bus at 10 o'clock."

"So I thought 'e 'ad," said Mrs. Ruddle.

"And that would seem natural, so there would be no inquiries. Did anybody call for Mrs. Noakes during the week?"

"Only Mr. Goodacre. I see him on Thursday morning, poking about the place, and he sees me and hollers out, 'Is Mr. Noakes away?' 'That's right,' I says, 'gone over to Broxford,' I says. And he says, 'I'll call another day,' he says. I don't remember as nobody come after him."

"Then last night," resumed Kirk, "when you let this lady and gentleman in, did you find everything as usual?"

"That's right. Exceptin' 'is dirty supper things on the table where 'e'd left them. 'E allus 'ad 'is supper at ar-par-seven reg'lar. Then 'e'd set in the kitchen with the paper till 'e come in 'ere for the noos at 9:30. Very reg'lar 'e was, a very reg'lar sort of man."

Kirk beamed. This was the kind of information he was looking for.

"So he'd had his supper. But his bed hadn't been slept in?"

"No, it 'adn't. But of course I put on clean sheets for the lady and gentleman. I 'ope I knows what's proper. Them," explained Mrs. Ruddle, anxious to make things clear, "wos the week-before's sheets, wot wos all dried and ready

Wednesday, but I couldn't take 'em in, along of the 'ouse bein' shet up. So I 'ad them all put aside neat in me kitchen, and I didn't 'ave to do more than put them to the fire a minnit and there they wos, all aired and fit for the King and Queen of England."

"That helps us a lot," said Kirk. "Mr. Noakes ate his supper at 7:30, so presumably he was alive then." He glanced at Peter, but Peter was offering no further embarrassing suggestions about murderers who ate their victims' suppers, and the Superintendent was encouraged to proceed. "He didn't go to bed, so that gives us—When did he usually go to bed, Mrs. Ruddle, do you know?"

"Eleven o'clock, Mr. Kirk, reg'lar as clockwork, 'e'd switch off the wireless and I'd see 'is candle go upstairs to bed. I can see 'is bedroom from my back winder, plain enough."

"Ah! now, Mrs. Ruddle, just you cast your mind back to Wednesday night. Do you recollect seeing his candle go upstairs to bed?"

"Well, there!" exclaimed Mrs. Ruddle, "now you comes to mention of it, Mr. Kirk, I did not. Which I remember saying to my Bert only the next day, 'There,' I says, 'if I'd only kep' awake, I mighter known 'e'd gone off, alonger seein' 'is bedroom winder dark. But there!' I says, 'I was that wore out, I dropped off the moment me 'ead was on the piller.' "

"Oh, well," said Kirk, disappointed, "it don't really matter. Seeing as his bed wasn't slept in, it's likely he was downstairs when—"

(Thank God! thought Peter. Not in my lady's chamber.)

Mrs. Ruddle interrupted with a sharp screech.

"Oh, lor', Mr. Kirk! There now!"

"Have you thought of something?"

Mrs. Ruddle had, and her expression, as her eyes wandered from Kirk to Sellon and then to Peter, indicated that it was not only important but alarming.

"Why, of course. I dunno how it didn't come into me

'ead before, but I been that moithered with all these dretful things a-'appenin'. 'Course, come to think of it, if 'e wasn't off by the 'bus, then 'e must a-been dead afore 'ar-pas'-nine."

The constable's hand paused in its note-taking. Kirk said sharply:

"What makes you think that?"

"W'y, 'is wireless wasn't a-workin', and I says to Bert—"

"Just a minute. What's all this about the wireless?"

"W'y, Mr. Kirk, if Mr. Noakes 'ad been alive, 'e wouldn't a-missed the 9:30 noos, not if it wos ever so. 'E set great store by the last noos, poor soul—though wot good it done 'im I *don't* know. And I recollects sayin' to Bert last Wednesday night as ever was, 'Funny thing,' I says, 'Mr. Noakes ain't got 'is wireless goin' tonight. That ain't like 'im,' I says."

"But you couldn't hear his wireless from your cottage with all these doors and windows shut?"

Mrs. Ruddle licked her lips.

"Well, I won't deceive you, Mr. Kirk." She swallowed, and then went on as volubly as ever; her eye avoided the Superintendent's and fixed itself on Joe Sellon's pencil. "I did jest run over 'ere a few minutes after the 'arf-hour to borrer a drop of paraffin from 'is shed. And if the wireless 'ad bin on then I couldn't a-'elped 'earin' of it, for them walls at the back ain't only plaster, and 'e allus 'ad it a-roarin' powerful 'ard on account of bein' 'ard of 'earin'."

"I see," said Mr. Kirk.

"No 'arm," said Mrs. Ruddle, backing away from the table, "no 'arm in borrowin' a drop o' paraffin."

"Well," replied Kirk, cautiously, "that's neither here nor there. Nine-thirty news. That's on the National."

"That's right. He never troubled with the 6 o'clock."

Peter consulted Kirk with a glance, stepped over to the radio cabinet and raised the lid.

"The pointer," he observed, "is set to Regional."

"Well, if you ain't altered it since—" Peter shook his head, and Kirk continued. "Looks like he didn't have it on

—not for the 9:30. H'm. We're getting there, aren't we? Whittling the time down. Line upon line, line upon line, here a little and there a little—"

"Isaiah," said Peter, shutting down the lid. "Or is it, more appropriately, Jeremiah?"

"Isaiah, my lord—and no call for Lamentations that I can see. That's pretty satisfactory, that is. Dead or unconscious at 9:30—last seen alive about 6:20—ate his supper at—"

"Six-twenty?" cried Mrs. Ruddle. "Go on! He was alive and kicking at 9 o'clock."

"What! How do you know? Why didn't you say so before?"

"Well, I thought you knowed it. You didn't ask. And 'ow do I know? 'Cause I seen 'im, that's why. 'Ere! wotter you gettin' at? Tryin' to put summat on me? You knows as well as I do 'e was alive at nine. Joe Sellon 'ere was a-talkin' to 'im."

Kirk gaped dumbfounded. "Eh?" he said, staring at the constable.

"Yes," muttered Sellon, dully, "that's right."

" 'Course it is," said Mrs. Ruddle. Her small eyes gleamed with malicious triumph, behind which lurked an uneasy horror. "You don't catch me that way, Joe Sellon. I come in 9 o'clock from fetchin' a pail o' water, and I sees you plain as the nose on my face a-talkin' to him at this very winder. Ah! and I 'eard you, too. Usin' language—you did oughter be ashamed of yourself—not fit for a decent woman to listen to. I come up the yard—which you know where the pump is, and the only water fit to drink, bar you goes down to the village, Mr. Kirk, and always free permission to use the pump in the yard, without it's for washin', what I always uses rainwater on account of the woollens, and I 'ears you from the pump—yes, you may look! And I says to meself, 'Lor',' I ses, 'wotever is agoing on?' And I comes round the corner of the 'ouse and I sees you—*and* your 'elmet, so don't you go a-denying of it."

"All right, Ma," said Kirk, shaken, but sticking loyally

by his subordinate. "Much obliged. That brings us pretty near the time. Nine o'clock, you say it was?"

"Near as makes no difference. My clock said ten past, but it gains a bit. But you ask Joe Sellon. If yer want to know the time, ask a p'leeceman!"

"Very good," replied the Superintendent. "We just wanted a bit of confirmation on that there point. Two witnesses are better than one. That'll do. Now, just you run along and—see here—don't you get shooting your mouth off."

"I'm sure," said Mrs. Ruddle, bridling, "I ain't one to talk."

"Certainly not," said Peter. "That's the last thing anybody would accuse you of. But you see, you're a very important witness—you and Sellon here—and there might be all sorts of people, reporters and so on, trying to wheedle things out of you. So you must be very discreet—just like Sellon—and come down sharp on them. Otherwise, you might make things difficult for Mr. Kirk."

"Joe Sellon, indeed!" said Mrs. Ruddle, contemptuously. "I can do as well as 'im any day. I 'ope I knows better than to go talking to newspaper fellows. A nasty, vulgar lot."

"Most unpleasant people," said Peter. He made for the door, driving her gently before him like a straying hen. "We know we can rely on you, Mrs. Ruddle, thou foster-child of Silence and slow Time. Whatever you do," he added earnestly, as he propelled her over the threshold, "don't say anything to Bunter—he's the world's worst chatterbox."

"Certainly not, my lord," said Mrs. Ruddle. The door closed. Kirk drew himself up in the big chair; his subordinate sat huddled, waiting for the explosion.

"Now, Joe Sellon. What's the meaning of this?"

"Well, sir—"

"I'm disappointed in you, Joe," went on Kirk, with more distress than anger in his puzzled voice. "I'm astonished. Mean to say you was there at nine o'clock talking to Mr.

Noakes and you said nothin' about it. Ain't you got no sense of duty?"

"I'm sure I'm very sorry, sir."

Lord Peter Wimsey strolled over to the window. One does not interfere with another man ticking off his subordinate. All the same—

"*Sorry?* That's a nice word to use. You—a police-officer? With'oldin' important evidence? And say you're sorry?"

(Dereliction of duty. Yes—that was the first way it would strike one.)

"I didn't mean—" began Sellon. Then, furiously: "I didn't know that old cat had seen me."

"What the hell does it matter who saw you?" cried Kirk, with rising exasperation. "You ought to have told me first thing. . . . My God, Joe Sellon. I don't know what to make of you. Upon my word I don't. . . . You're *for* it, my lad."

The wretched Sellon sat twisting his hands together, finding no answer but a miserable mumble:

"I'm sorry."

"Now, look here," said Kirk, with a dangerous note in his voice. "What were you doing here, that you didn't want anybody to know about? . . . Speak up! . . . Wait a minute. Wait a minute." (He's seen it, thought Peter, and turned around.) "You're left-handed, ain't you?"

"Oh, my God, sir, my God! I never done it! I swear I never done it! 'Eaven knows I 'ad cause enough, but I never done it—I never laid a 'and on 'im—"

"Cause? What cause? . . . Come on, now. Out with it! What were you doing with Mr. Noakes?"

Sellon looked around wildly. At his shoulder stood Peter Wimsey with an inscrutable face.

"I never touched 'im. I never done nothing to 'im. If I was to die the next minute, sir, I'm innocent!"

Kirk shook his massive head, like a bull teased by gadflies.

"What were you doing up here at nine o'clock?"

"Nothin'," said Sellon, stubbornly. The excitement died out of him. "Only to pass the time of day."

"Time o' day!" echoed Kirk, with so much contempt and irritation that Peter nerved himself to interfere.

"Look here, Sellon," he said, in the voice that had induced many a troubled private to disclose his pitiful secrets. "You'd much better make a clean breast of it to Mr. Kirk. Whatever it is."

"This," growled Kirk, "is a nice thing, this is. A police-officer—"

"Go easy with him, Superintendent," said Peter. "He's only a youngster." He hesitated. Perhaps it would be easier for Sellon without an outside witness. "I'll push along into the garden," he said, reassuringly. Sellon turned in a flash.

"No, no! I'll come clean. Oh, my God, sir!—Don't go, my lord. Don't *you* go! . . . I've made a damn bloody fool of myself."

"We all do that at times," said Peter, softly.

"*You*'ll believe me, my lord. . . . Oh, God—this'll break me."

"I shouldn't wonder," said Kirk, grimly.

Peter glanced at the Superintendent, saw that he, too, recognized the appeal to an authority older than his own, and sat down on the edge of the table.

"Pull yourself together, Sellon. Mr. Kirk's not the man to be hard or unjust to anybody. Now, what was it all about?"

"Well . . . that there note-case of Mr. Noakes's—what he lost—"

"Two years ago—well, yes, what happened to it?"

"I found it . . . I—I—he'd dropped it in the road—ten pound it had in it. I—my wife was desperate bad after the baby—doctor said she ought to have special treatment—I hadn't saved nothing—and the pay's not much, nor the allowance—I been a damned fool—I meant to put it back right away. I thought he could spare it, being well off. I know we're supposed to be honest, but it's a dreadful temptation in a man's way."

"Yes," said Peter. "A generous country expects a lot of honesty for two or three pounds a week." Kirk seemed incapable of speech, so he went on:

"And what happened about it?"

"He found out, my lord. I dunno how, but he did. Threatened to report me. Well, of course, that'd have been the end of me. Out of a job, and who'd a-given me work after that? So I 'ad to pay him what he said, to stop his tongue."

"Pay him?"

"That's blackmail," said Kirk, coming out of his stupefaction with a pounce. He spoke the words as though they were, somehow, a solution of this incredible situation. "It's an indictable offense. Blackmail. And compounding a felony."

"Call it what you like, sir—it was life and death to me. Five bob a week he been bleeding me for these last two years."

"Good God!" said Peter, disgusted.

"And I tell you, my lord, when I came in this room this morning and 'eard as he was dead, it was like a breath of 'Eaven to me. . . . But I didn't kill him—I swear I didn't. You do believe me? My lord, *you* believe me. I didn't do it."

"I don't know that I could blame you if you had."

"But I didn't," said Sellon, eagerly. Peter's face was noncommittal and he turned to Kirk again. "It's all right, sir. I know I been a fool—and worse—and I'll take my medicine; but as sure as I stand here, I didn't kill Mr. Noakes."

"Well, Joe," said the Superintendent, heavily, "it's bad enough without that. You've been a fool and no mistake. We'll have to see about that later. You'd better tell us now what *did* happen."

"I came up to see him, to tell him I hadn't got the money that week. He laughed in my face, the old devil. I—"

"What time was this?"

"I came up here by the path and I looked in at that there window. The curtains wasn't drawn, and it was all dark. Only then I see him coming in from the kitchen with a candle in his hand. He holds the candle up to the clock there, and I see it was five minutes past nine."

Peter shifted his position and spoke quickly:

"You saw the clock from the window. You're sure?"

The witness failed to catch the note of warning, and said briefly: "Yes, my lord." He licked his lips nervously and went on:

"Then I taps on the window and he comes over and opens it. I tells him I ain't got the money and he laughs at me, nasty-like. 'All right,' he says, 'I'll report you in the morning.' So then I plucks up 'eart and says to him, 'You can't. It's blackmail. All this money you've been takin' off of me is blackmail, and I'll see you in the dock for it.' And he says, 'Money? you can't prove you ever paid me money. Where's your receipts? You got nothing on paper.' So I swears at him."

"No wonder," said Peter.

" 'Get out,' he says, and slams the window shut. I tried the doors, but they was locked. So I gets out, and that's the last I seen of him."

Kirk drew a long breath.

"You didn't go into the house?"

"No, sir."

"Are you telling all the truth?"

"Honest to God, I am, sir."

"Sellon, are you sure?"

This time, the warning was unmistakable.

"It's God's truth, my lord."

Peter's face changed. He got up and walked slowly over to the fireplace.

"H'm, well," said Kirk. "I don't rightly know *what* to say. See here, Joe; you better go straight away to Pagford and check up that alibi for Crutchley. See this man Williams at the garage and get a statement from him."

"Very good, sir," said Sellon in a subdued tone.

"I'll talk to you when you come back."

Sellon said again, "Very good, sir." He looked at Peter,

who was gazing down at the burning logs and made no movement. "I hope you won't be too hard on me, sir."

"That's as may be," said Kirk, not unkindly. The constable went out, his big shoulders drooping.

"Well," said the Superintendent, "and what do you think of that?"

"It sounded straight enough—so far as the note-case was concerned. So there's a motive for you—a nice new motive, all a-growing and a-blowing. Widens the field a bit, doesn't it? Blackmailers don't as a rule stop at a single victim."

Kirk scarcely noticed this ingenious attempt to divert him from his natural suspicions. It was the breach of duty by one of his own officers that hurt him. Theft and the concealment of evidence—! He hammered on at this wretched worry, the angrier because it was the kind of thing that need not ever have occurred.

"Why couldn't the young fool have come to his sergeant, if he was short—or to me? This is the devil and all. Beats me altogether. I wouldn't have believed it."

"There are more things in heaven and earth," said Peter, with a kind of melancholy amusement.

"That's so, my lord. There's a lot of truth in *Hamlet*."

"Hamlet?" Peter's bark of harsh laughter astonished the Superintendent. "By God, you're right. Village or hamlet of this merry land. Stir up the mud of the village pond and the stink will surprise you." He paced the room restlessly. The light thrown on Mr. Noakes's activities had only confirmed his own suspicions, and if there was one sort of criminal whom he would have been ready to strangle with his bare hands, it was the blackmailer. Five shillings a week for two years. He could not doubt that part of the story; no man would so pile up the evidence against himself unless he were telling the truth. All the same—He stopped abruptly at Kirk's side.

"Look here!" he said. "You've had no *official* information about that theft, have you? And the money's been paid back—twice over."

Kirk fixed him with a steady eye. "It's easy enough for *you* to be soft-'earted, my lord. It ain't your responsibility."

This time the kid gloves were off, and Peter took it on the chin.

"Coo!" added Kirk, reflectively. "That there Noakes he must have been a proper old twister."

"It's a damned ugly story. It's enough to make a man—"

But it was not. Nothing was enough for that. "Oh, hell!" said Peter, beaten and exasperated.

"What's up?"

"Superintendent, I'm sorry for that poor devil, but—curse it—I suppose I've got to say it—"

"Well?"

Kirk knew that something was coming and braced himself to meet it. Force Peter's sort to the wall, and they will tell the truth. He had said so, and now his words were to be proved upon him, and he had got to take the punishment.

"That story of his. It sounded all right. . . . But it wasn't. . . . One bit of it was a lie."

"A lie?"

"Yes. . . . He said he never came into the house. . . . He said he saw the clock from that window. . . ."

"Well?"

"Well, I tried to do the same thing just now, when I was out in the garden. I wanted to set my watch. Well . . . it can't be done, that's all. . . . That damned awful cactus is in the way."

"What!"

Kirk sprang to his feet.

"I say, that infernal bloody cactus is in the way. It covers the face of the clock. You can't see the time from that window."

"You can't?

Kirk darted towards the window, knowing only too well what he would find there.

"You can try it," said Peter, "from any point you like. It's absolutely and definitely impossible. You can *not* see the clock from that window."

CHAPTER X

FOUR-ALE BAR

"What should I have done?" I cried, with some heat. "Gone to the nearest public-house. That is the center of country gossip."
—ARTHUR CONAN DOYLE,
THE SOLITARY CYCLIST

The police were out of the house by tea-time. Indeed the unhappy Kirk, having ascertained that by no dodging, stooping or standing on tiptoe could anyone obtain a sight of the clock-face from the window, found himself with but little zest to prolong his inquiries. He made the half-hearted suggestion that Noakes might have temporarily removed the cactus from its pot after 6:20 and replaced it before 9:30; but he could offer himself no plausible explanation of any such aimless proceeding. There was, of course, only Crutchley's word for it that the plant had been there at 6:20—if there was even that; Crutchley had mentioned watering it—he might have taken it down and left it for Noakes to put back. One could ask—but even as he made a note of this intention, Kirk felt little hope of any result. He examined the bedrooms in a dispirited way, impounded a number of books and papers from a cupboard and again examined Mrs. Ruddle about Sellon's interview with Noakes.

The result of all this was not very satisfactory. A notebook was discovered, containing, among other entries, a list of weekly payments, five shillings at a time, under the initials "J.S." This corroborated a story that scarcely needed corroboration. It also suggested that Sellon's frankness might be less a virtue than a necessity, since, had he suspected the existence of such a document, he would have realized that it was better to confess before being confronted with it. Peter's comment was, Why, if Sellon were the murderer, had he not searched the house for compromising papers? With this consideration Kirk tried hard to comfort himself.

There was nothing else that could be interpreted as evidence of blackmailing payments from anybody, though plenty of testimony going to show that Noakes's affairs were in an even worse state of confusion than had hitherto appeared. An interesting item was a bundle of newspaper cuttings and jottings in Noakes's hand, concerning cheap cottages on the west coast of Scotland—a country in which it is notoriously difficult to proceed for the recovery of civil debts contracted elsewhere. That Noakes had been the "proper twister" Kirk had supposed him was clear enough; unhappily, it was not *his* misdoings that needed proof.

Mrs. Ruddle was unhelpful. She had heard Noakes slam the window shut and seen Sellon retreat in the direction of the front door. Supposing that the show was over, she had hastened home with her pail of water. She thought she had heard a knocking at the doors a few minutes later, and thought, "He's got some hopes!" Asked whether she had heard what the quarrel was about, she admitted with regret, that she had not, but (with a malicious grin) "supposed as Joe Sellon knew all about it." Sellon, she added, "often came up to see Mr. Noakes"—her own opinion, if Kirk wanted it, was that he was "a-trying to borrer money" and that Noakes had refused to lend any more. Mrs. Sellon was thriftless, everybody knew that. Kirk would have liked to ask her whether, having last seen Mr. Noakes engaged in a violent quarrel, she had had no qualms about his subsequent disappearance; but the question stuck in his throat. He would be saying in so many words that an officer of the law could be suspected of murder; without better evidence he could not bring himself to do it. His next dreary job was to question the Sellons, and he was not looking forward to that. In a mood of the blackest depression, he went off to interview the coroner.

In the meantime, Mr. Puffett, having cleared the kitchen chimney from above and assisted at the lighting of the fire, had taken his fee and gone home, uttering many expressions of sympathy and good will. Finally, Miss Twitterton, tearful but flattered, was conveyed to Pagford by Bunter in the car, with her bicycle perched "high and disposedly" upon the back seat. Harriet saw her off and returned to the sitting-room, where her lord and master was gloomily building a house of cards with a greasy old pack which he had unearthed from the whatnot.

"Well!" said Harriet, in unnaturally cheerful tones, "they've gone. At last we are alone!"

"That's a blessing," said he, glumly.

"Yes; I couldn't have stood much more. Could you?"

"Not any more. . . . And I can't stand it now."

The words were not said rudely; he sounded merely helpless and exhausted.

"I wasn't going to," said Harriet.

He made no reply, seeming absorbed in adding the fourth story to his structure. She watched him for a few moments, then decided he was best left alone and wandered upstairs to fetch pen and paper. She thought it might be a good thing to write a few lines to the Dowager Duchess.

Passing through Peter's dressing-room, she found that somebody had been at work there. The curtains had been hung, the rugs put down and the bed made up. She paused to wonder what might be the significance of this—if any. In her own room, the traces of Miss Twitterton's brief occupation had been removed—the eiderdown shaken, the pillows made smooth, the hot-water bottle taken away, the disorder of washstand and dressing-table set to rights. The doors and drawers left open by Kirk had been shut, and a bowl of chrysanthemums stood on the window-sill. Bunter, like a steam-roller, had passed over everything, flattening out all traces of upheaval. She got the things she needed and carried them down. The card house had reached the sixth story. At the sound of her step, Peter started, his hand shook, and the whole flimsy fabric dissolved into ruins. He muttered something and began doggedly to rebuild it.

Harriet glanced at the clock; it was nearly five, and she felt she could do with some tea. She had coerced Mrs. Ruddle into putting the kettle on and doing some work; it could not take very long now. She sat down on the settle and began her letter. The news was not exactly what the Duchess would expect to receive, but it was urgently necessary to write something that she might get before the headlines broke out in the London papers. Besides, there were things Harriet wanted to tell her—things she would have told her in any case. She finished the first page and looked up. Peter was frowning; the house, risen once again to the fourth story, was showing signs of imminent collapse. Without meaning to, she began to laugh.

"What's the joke?" said Peter. The tottering cards immediately slid apart, and he damned them fretfully. Then his face suddenly relaxed, and the familiar, sidelong smile lifted the corner of his mouth.

"I was seeing the funny side of it," said Harriet, apologetically. "This looks not like a nuptial."

"True, O God!" said he, ruefully. He got up and came over to her. "I rather think," he observed in a detached and dubious manner, "I am behaving like a lout."

"Do you? Then all I can say is, your notion of loutishness is exceedingly feeble and limited. You simply don't know how to begin."

He was not comforted by her mockery. "I didn't mean things to be like this," he said, lamely.

"My dear cuckoo—"

"I wanted it all to be wonderful for you."

She waited for him to find his own answer to this, which he did with disarming swiftness.

"That's vanity, I suppose. Take pen and ink and write it down. His lordship is in the enjoyment of very low spirits, owing to his inexplicable inability to bend Providence to his own designs."

"Shall I tell your mother so?"

"Are you writing to her? Good Lord, I never thought about it, but I'm dashed glad you did. Poor old Mater, she'll be horribly upset about it all. She's got it firmly into her head that to be married to her white-headed boy meant an untroubled elysium, world without end, amen. Strange, that one's own mother should know so little about one."

"Your mother is the most sensible woman I ever met. She has a much better grasp of the facts of life than you have."

"Has she?"

"Yes, of course. By the way, you don't insist on a husband's right to read his wife's letters?"

"Great heavens, no!" said Peter, horrified.

"I'm glad of that. It mightn't be good for you. Here's Bunter coming back; we may get some tea. Mrs. Ruddle is in such a state of excitement that she has probably boiled the milk and put the tea-leaves into the sandwiches. I ought to have stood over her till she'd finished."

"Blow Mrs. Ruddle!"

"By all means—but I expect Bunter is doing that already."

The precipitate entry of Mrs. Ruddle with the tea-tray gave weight to the supposition.

"Which," said Mrs. Ruddle, setting down her burden with a rattle on a small table before the fire, "I'd a-brought it before, if it wasn't the policeman from Broxford come a-busting in, jest as I was makin' of the toast. Me 'eart come into me mouth, thinkin' summink 'orrible 'ad 'appened. But it ain't only summingses from the coroner. Quite a bunch of 'em 'e 'ad in 'is 'and, and these 'ere is yours."

"Oh, yes," said Peter, breaking the seal. "They've been pretty quick. 'To wit—To Lord Peter Death Bredon Wimsey, By virtue of a Warrant under the Hand and Seal of John Perkins'—all right, Mrs. Ruddle, you needn't wait."

"Mr. Perkins the lawyer, that is," explained Mrs. Ruddle. "A very nice gentleman, so I'm told, though I ain't never seen 'im to speak to."

" '. . . one of His Majesty's coroners for the said county of Hertfordshire to be and appear before him on Thursday the tenth day of October' . . . you'll see him and hear him tomorrow all right, Mrs. Ruddle . . . 'at 11 o'clock in the forenoon precisely at the Coroner's Court at the Crown Inn situate in the parish of Paggleham in the said County; then and there to give Evidence and be examined on His Majesty's behalf, touching the death of William Noakes, and not to depart without leave.' "

"That's all very fine," observed Mrs. Ruddle, "but 'oo's to give my Bert 'is dinner? Twelve o'clock's 'is time, and I ain't a-goin' to see my Bert go 'ungry, not for King George nor nobody."

"Bert will have to get on without you, I'm afraid," said Peter, solemnly. "You see what it says: 'Herein fail not at your peril.' "

"Lor', now," said Mrs. Ruddle. "Peril of what, I should like to know?"

"Prison," said Peter, in an awful voice.

"Me go to prison?" cried Mrs. Ruddle, in great indignation. "That's a nice thing for a respectable woman."

"Surely you could get a friend to see to Bert's dinner," suggested Harriet.

"Well," said Mrs. Ruddle, dubiously, "maybe Mrs. 'Odges would oblige. But I'm thinkin' she'll want to come and 'ear wot's going on at the 'quest. But there! I dessay I could make a pie tonight and leave it out for Bert." She retreated thoughtfully to the door, returning to say, in a hoarse whisper:

"Will I 'ave to tell 'im about the paraffin?"

"I shouldn't think so."

"Oh!" said Mrs. Ruddle. "Not as there's anything wrong in borrowin' a drop of paraffin, w'en it's easy replaced. But them there pleecemen do twist a woman's words so."

"I shouldn't think you need worry," said Harriet. "Shut the door, please, as you go out."

"Yes, my lady," said Mrs. Ruddle; and vanished with unexpected docility.

"If I know anything about Kirk," said Peter, "they'll adjourn the inquest, so it shouldn't take very long."

"No. I'm glad John Perkins has been so prompt—we shan't get such a crowd of reporters and people."

"Shall you mind the reporters very much?"

"Not nearly as much as you will. Don't be so tragic about it, Peter. Make up your mind that the joke's on us, this time."

"It's that, right enough. Helen's going to make a grand cockadoodle over this."

"Well, let her. She doesn't look as though she got much fun out of life, poor woman. After all, she can't alter the facts. I mean, here I am, you know, pouring out tea for you —from a chipped spout, admittedly—but I'm here."

"I don't suppose she envies you that job. I'm not exactly Helen's cup of tea."

"She'd never enjoy any tea—she'd always be thinking about the chips."

"Helen doesn't allow chips."

"No—she'd insist on silver—even if the pot was empty. Have some more tea. I can't help its dribbling into the saucer. It's the sign of a generous nature, or an overflowing heart, or something."

Peter accepted the tea and drank it in silence. He was still dissatisfied with himself. It was as though he had invited the woman of his choice to sit down with him at the feast of life, only to discover that his table had not been reserved for him. Men, in these mortifying circumstances, commonly find fault with the waiter, grumble at the food and irritably reject every effort to restore pleasantness to the occasion. From the worst exhibitions of injured self-conceit, his good manners were sufficient to restrain him, but the mere fact that he knew himself to be in fault made it all the more difficult for him to recover spontaneity. Harriet watched his inner conflict sympathetically. If both of them had been ten years younger, the situation would have resolved itself in a row, tears and reconciling embraces; but for them, that path was plainly marked, NO EXIT. There was no help for it; he must get out of his sulks as best he could. Having inflicted her own savage moods upon him for a good five years, she was in no position to feel aggrieved; compared with herself, indeed, he was making a pretty good showing.

He pushed the tea-things aside and lit cigarettes for both of them. Then, rubbing fretfully upon the old sore, he said:

"You show commendable patience with my bad temper."

"Is that what you call it? *I've* seen tempers in comparison with which you'd call that a burst of heavenly harmony."

"Whatever it is, you are trying to flatter me out of it."

"Not at all." (Very well, he was asking for it; better use shock tactics and carry the place by assault.) "I'm only trying to tell you, in the nicest possible manner, that provided I were with you, I shouldn't *greatly* mind being deaf, dumb, halt, blind and imbecile, afflicted with shingles and whooping-cough, in an open boat without clothes or food, with a thunderstorm coming on. But you're being painfully stupid about it."

"Oh, my dear!" he said, desperately, and with a very red face, "what the devil am I to say to that? Except that I shouldn't mind anything either. Only I can't help feeling that it's I that have somehow been idiot enough to launch the infernal boat, call up the storm, strip you naked, jettison the cargo, strike you lame and senseless and infect you with whooping-cough and—what was the other thing?"

"Shingles," said Harriet, dryly; "and it isn't infectious."

"Crushed again." His eyes danced, and all of a sudden

his heart seemed to turn right over. "O ye gods! render me worthy of this noble wife. All the same, I have a strong suspicion that I am being managed. I should resent it very much, if I were not full of buttered toast and sentiment—two things which, as you may have noticed, tend to go together. And that reminds me—hadn't we better get the car out and run over to Broxford for dinner? There's sure to be some sort of pub there, and a little fresh air may help to blow the bats out of my belfry."

"That's rather a good idea. And can't we take Bunter? I don't believe he's had anything to eat for years."

"Still harping on my Bunter! I myself have suffered many things for love, very like this. You may have Bunter, but I draw the line at a *partie carrée*. Mrs. Ruddle shall not come tonight. I observe the Round Table rule—to love one only and cleave to her. One at a time, I mean, of course. I will not pretend that I have never been linked up before, but I absolutely refuse to be coupled in parallel."

"Mrs. Ruddle can go home to bake her pies. I'll just finish my letter and then we can post it in Broxford."

But Bunter respectfully requested to be omitted from the party—unless, of course, his lordship required his services. He would prefer, if permitted, to utilize the leisure so kindly placed at his disposal in a visit to the Crown. He should be interested to make the acquaintance of some of the local inhabitants, and, as for his supper, Mr. Puffett had been so good as to hint that there was pot luck waiting for him at his house whenever he might care to step in and partake of it.

"Which means," said Peter, interpreting the decision to Harriet, "that Bunter wants to get a side-line through the local gossip on the late Noakes and all his household. In addition, he would like to establish diplomatic relations with the publican, the coal-merchant, the man who grows the best vegetables, the farmer who happens to have cut down a tree and can oblige with logs, the butcher who hangs his meat longest, the village carpenter and the man who does a job about the drains. You'll have to put up with me. Nothing is ever gained by diverting Bunter from his own mysterious ends."

The bar of the Crown was remarkably full when Bunter made his way in. No doubt the unobtrusive presence of the late Mr. Noakes behind a locked door lent a special body to the mild and bitter. At the entrance of the stranger, the voices, which had been busy, fell silent, and glances, at first directed to the door, were swiftly averted and screened behind lifted tankards. This was fully in accordance with etiquette. Bunter saluted the company with a polite "Good evening," and asked for a pint of old ale and a packet of Players. Mr. Gudgeon the landlord fulfilled the order with a dignified leisure, observing, as he changed a ten-shilling note, that the day had been fine. Bunter assented to this proposition, saying further that the country air was agreeable after Town. Mr. Gudgeon remarked that a-many London gentlemen had been known to say the same thing, and inquired whether this was his customer's first visit to that part of the country. Bunter said that though he had frequently passed through the district he had never stayed there before, and that Paggleham seemed to be a pretty spot. He also volunteered the information that he was Kentish by birth. Mr. Gudgeon said, Indeed? they grew hops there, he believed. Bunter admitted that this was so. A very stout man with one eye intervened at this point to say that his wife's cousin lived in Kent and that it was all 'ops where he was. Bunter said there were hops where his mother lived; he himself knew little about hops, having been brought up in London from the age of five. A thin man with a lugubrious countenance said he supposed that there gallon of beer he'd had off Mr. Gudgeon last June came from Kent. This appeared to be a reference to some standing jest, for the bar laughed appreciatively, and much chaff was bandied about, till the thin man closed the discussion by saying, "All right, Jim; call it 'ops if it makes you feel any better."

During this exchange the customer from London had

quietly retired to a window-seat, taking his pint with him. The conversation turned upon football. At length, however, a plump woman (who was, in fact, no other than Mrs. Ruddle's friend, Mrs. Hodges) remarked, with that feminine impulsiveness which rushes in where the lords of creation fear to tread:

"You lost a customer, seemin'ly, Mr. Gudgeon."

"Ah!" said Mr. Gudgeon. He darted a look towards the window-seat, but it encountered only the back of the stranger's head. "Where one goes another comes, Mrs. Hodges. 'Tain't much I'll be losing on the beer."

"You're right," said Mrs. Hodges. "Nor anybody else, neither. But it is true as 'e was put away a-purpose?"

"That's as may be," replied Mr. Gudgeon, cautiously. "We'll be hearin' tomorrow."

"And *that* won't do no 'arm to the trade, I reckon," observed the one-eyed man.

"Dunno about that," retorted the landlord. "We'll 'ave to close the 'ouse till it's over. 'Tis only decent. And Mr. Kirk's particular."

A scrawny woman of uncertain age piped up suddenly:

"Wot's 'e look like, George? Can't you let us 'ave a peep at 'im?"

" 'Ark at Katie!" exclaimed the lugubrious man, as the landlord shook his head. "Can't let a man alone, dead or alive."

"Go on, Mr. Puddock!" said Katie; and the bar laughed again. "You're on the jury, ain't you? You gets a front seat free."

"We don't 'ave to view the body these days," Mr. Puddock corrected her. "Not without we ask to. 'Ere's George Lugg; you better ask 'im."

The undertaker came out of the inner room, and all eyes were turned to him.

"When's the funeral to be, George?"

"Friday," said Mr. Lugg. He ordered a tankard of bitter and added to a young man who now came out, locking the door behind him and handing the key to Mr. Gudgeon:

"You better get started, Harry. I'll be along in two licks. We'll want to close him down after the inquest. He'll go till then."

"Ay," said Harry. " 'Tis fine, sharp weather." He called for a half-pint, took it down briskly, and went out, saying, "See you presently, then, Dad."

The undertaker became the center of a small circle, ghoulishly intent upon descriptive detail. Presently the voice of the irrepressible Mrs. Hodges was raised:

"And by what Martha Ruddle says, them as didn't 'ave 'is custom 'ull lose least by 'im."

"Ah!" said a small man with a fringe of sandy hair and a shrewd eye. "I've 'ad me doubts. Too many irons in that fire, I reckon. Not as I've a lot to grumble at. I don't let no books run beyond the month, and I got me money—allus expectin' that there collar of bacon as 'e made trouble about. But it's like that there. 'Atry and these other big companies as goes bust—you puts money out o' one thing into another, till you don't rightly know wot you've got."

"That's right," said the one-eyed man. "Allus investin' in things, 'e wos. Too clever be 'alf."

"And a 'ard bargain 'e did drive," said Mrs. Hodges. "Dear, oh, dear! Remember when 'e lent my poor sister that bit o' money? Crool, it was, wot she 'ad to pay. And makin' 'er sign away all her furniture."

"Well, 'e never made much on the furniture," said the sandy man. "A soakin' wet day that was, w'en they come up for sale. Tom Dudden 'ad 'em over at Pagford, and there wasn't a soul there but the dealers."

An ancient man with long gray whiskers raised his voice for the first time:

"Ill-gotten goods never thrive. 'Tis in Scripture. Because he hath oppressed and forsaken the poor, because he hath violently taken away a house which he builded not—ah! and the furniture, too—therefore shall no man look for his goods. In the fullness of his sufficiency shall he be in straits —ain't that so, Mr. Gudgeon?—He shall flee from the iron weapon—ay—but there ain't no good fleein' when the 'and of the Lord is agin the wicked man. There's a curse upon 'im, and we 'ave lived to see it fulfilled. Wasn't there a gentleman came down from London this morning with a writ agin 'im? In the same pit that 'e digged for others is 'is foot taken. Let the extortioner consume all that he hath—'tis writ so—Ah! let 'is children be vagabonds and beg their bread—"

"There, there, Dad!" said the innkeeper, seeing that the old gentleman was becoming excited, " 'e ain't got no children, praise be."

"That's true," said the one-eyed man, "but 'e 'ave got a niece. It'll be a sad come-down for Aggie Twitterton. Wonderful set up, she allus wos, thinkin' there was money comin' to 'er."

"Well," said Mrs. Hodges, "them as gives themselves airs above other folks don't deserve nothin' but disappointments. 'Er dad wasn't only Ted Baker's cowman when all's said and done, and a dirty, noisy, foul-mouthed fellow in 'is drink, wot's more, as there ain't no call to be proud on."

"That's right," said the old man. "A very violent man. Beat 'is poor wife something crool, 'e did."

"If you treat a man like dirt," opined the one-eyed man, " 'e'll act dirty. Dick Twitterton was a decent sort enough till 'e tuk it into 'is 'ead to marry the schoolmistress, with 'er airs and lah-di-dah ways. 'Wipe yer boots on the mat,' she says to 'im, 'afore you comes into the parlor.' Wot's the good of a wife like that to a man w'en 'e comes in mucky from the beasts an' wantin' 'is supper?"

"Good-lookin' feller, too, wasn't he?" said Katie.

"Now, Katie!" said the lachrymose man, reprovingly. "Yes, 'e wos a well set-up man, wos Dick Twitterton. That's wot the schoolmistress fell for, you see. You be keerful o' that soft 'eart o' yours, or it'll get you into trouble."

More chaff followed upon this. Then the undertaker said:

"None the more for that, I'm sorry for Aggie Twitterton."

"Bah!" said the lachrymose man, "*she*'s all right. She've

got 'er 'ens an' the church organ, and she don't do so bad. Gettin' a bit long in the tooth now, but a man might go farther and fare wuss."

"Well, there, Mr. Puddock!" cried Mrs. Hodges. "Don't say as you're thinkin' o' makin' an offer."

" 'E's a one to talk, ain't he?" said Katie, delighted to get her own back. The old man chimed in solemnly:

"Now, do 'ee look where you're goin', Ted Puddock. There's bad blood o' both sides in Aggie Twitterton. 'Er mother was William Noakes's sister, don't 'ee forgit that; and Dick Twitterton, 'e was a violent, God-forsaking man, a swearer and a sabbath-breaker—"

The door opened to admit Frank Crutchley. He had a girl with him. Bunter, forgotten in his corner, summed her up as a lively young person, with an up-and-coming eye. The couple appeared to be on affectionate, not to say intimate terms, and Bunter gained the impression that Crutchley was seeking consolation for his losses in the linked arms of Bacchus and Aphrodite. He stood the young lady a large port (Bunter shuddered delicately) and submitted with good humor to a certain amount of chaff when he offered drinks all around.

"Come into a fortune, 'ave you, Frank?"

"Mr. Noakes 'ave left 'im 'is share of liabilities, that's what it is."

"Thought you said your speckilations 'ad gone wrong."

"Ah, that's the way wi' these 'ere capitalists. Every time they loses a million they orders a case o' champagne."

" 'Ere, Polly, don't you know better 'a to go about with a chap wot speckilates?"

"She thinks she'll learn 'im better w'en 'e's bringin' the money 'ome to 'er."

"And so I would," said Polly, with some vigor.

"Ah! thinkin' o' gettin' spliced, you two?"

"No charge for thinkin'," said Crutchley.

" 'Ow about the young lady in London, Frank?"

"Which one's that?" retorted Crutchley.

" 'Ark at 'im! 'E've got so many 'e don't know 'ow to keep count on 'em."

"You watch your step, Polly. Maybe 'e's married three times a'ready."

"I *should* worry," said the girl, with a toss of the head.

"Well, well, after buryin' comes a weddin'. Tell us w'en it's to be, Frank."

"I'll 'ave ter save up for the parson's fee," said Crutchley, good temperedly, "seein' me forty pounds gone west. But it was almost worth it, to see old Aggie Twitterton's face. 'Ow! Uncle's dead and the money's gone!' she said. 'Ow, and 'im that rich—'oo'd a-thought it?' Silly old cow!" Crutchley laughed contemptuously. " 'Urry up with your port, Polly, if you want us to get over in time for the big picture."

"So that's what you're after. Ain't goin' into no mourning for old Mr. Noakes, is yer, from the looks of it?"

" 'Im?" said Crutchley. "No fear, the dirty old twister. There'll be more pickings out o' me lord than ever there was out of *'im*. Pocket full o' bank-notes and a nose like a cheese-faced rabbit—"

"Hey!" said Mr. Gudgeon, with a warning glance.

"His lordship will be much obliged to you, Mr. Crutchley," said Bunter, emerging from the window-seat.

"Sorry," said Crutchley, "didn't see you was there. No offense meant. A joke's a joke. "What'll you take, Bunter?"

"I'll take no liberties from anyone," said that gentleman, with dignity. "Mr. Bunter to you, if you please. And by the way, Mr. Gudgeon, I was to ask you kindly to send up a fresh nine-gallon cask to Talboys, the one that's there being the property of the creditors, as we understand."

"Right you are," said the landlord, with alacrity. "When would you like it?"

"First thing tomorrow," replied Bunter, "and another dozen of Bass while it settles. . . . Ah, Mr. Puffett, good evening! I was just thinking of looking you up."

"You're welcome," said Mr. Puffett, heartily. "I jest

came along to fetch up the supper-ale, George being called out. There's a cold pie in the 'ouse and Jinny'll be glad to see you. Make it a quart, then, Mr. Gudgeon, if you please."

He handed a jug over the counter, which the landlord filled, saying as he did so to Bunter:

"That's all right, then. It'll be up at ten o'clock and I'll step round and tap it for you."

"I am much obliged to you, Mr. Gudgeon. I shall attend personally to its reception."

Crutchley had seized the opportunity to go out with his young woman. Mr. Puffett shook his head.

"Off to them pictures again. Wot I says is, they things are unsettlin' the girls' minds nowadays. Silk stockin's and all. You wouldn't a-seen that in my young days."

"Ah! come now," said Mrs. Hodges. "Polly hev' been walkin' out wi' Frank a good while now. 'Tis time 'twere settled between 'em. She's a good girl, for all she's saucy in her ways."

"Made up 'is mind, hev' he?" said Mr. Puffett. "Thought 'e was set on 'avin' a wife from London. But there! maybe 'e thinks she won't 'ave 'im, now 'e's lost 'is forty pound. Ketch 'em on the rebound, as they say—that's 'ow they makes marriages these days. A man may do all 'e likes, there's some lass gets 'im in the end, for all 'is runnin' and dodgin' like a pig in a lane. But I likes to see a bit o' money into the bargain—there's more to marriage, as they say, than four bare legs in a bed."

" 'Ark at 'im!" said Katie.

"Or legs in silk stockings, neither," said Mr. Puffett.

"Well, Tom," said Mrs. Hodges, comfortably, "you're a widow-man with a bit o' money, so there's a chance for some on us yet."

"Is there?" retorted Mr. Puffett. "Well, I give yer leave to try. Now, Mr. Bunter, if you're ready."

"Is Frank Crutchley a native of Paggleham?" inquired Bunter, as they walked away up the road, slowly, so as not to set the beer all of a froth.

"No," said Mr. Puffett. "He came here from London. Answered an advertisement of Mr. 'Ancock's. Been here six or seven year now. I don't fancy 'e's got no parents. But 'e's a pushin' young fellow, only all the girls is arter 'im, which makes it 'ard for 'im to settle. I'd a-thought 'e'd more sense than to take up with Polly Mason—serious-like, I mean. 'E was allus set to look for a wife as could bring 'im a bit. But there! Say what you like before'and, a man proposes and a woman disposes on i'm for good an' all, and then it's too late to be careful. Look at your good gentleman—I dessay, now, there was a-many rich young ladies arter 'im. And maybe he said he didn't want none on 'em. And 'ere 'e is on 'is 'oneymoon, and from what they was a-tellin' the Reverend, not a wealthy young lady neither."

"His lordship," said Mr. Bunter, "married for love."

"I thought as much," said Mr. Puffett, shifting the jug to his other hand. "Ah, well—he can afford it, I dessay."

At the conclusion of a pleasant and, on the whole, profitable evening, Mr. Bunter congratulated himself on a number of things attempted and done. He had ordered the beer; he had put (through Mr. Puffett's Jinny) a nice duck in hand for the following day, and Mr. Puffett knew a man who could send around three pound of late peas in the morning. He had also engaged Mr. Puffett's son-in-law to deal with the leak in the copper and mend two broken panes in the scullery. He had found out the name of a farmer who cured his own bacon and had written and posted to London an order about coffee, potted meats and preserved. Before leaving Talboys he had assisted Mrs. Ruddle's Bert to bring the luggage upstairs, and he now had his lordship's wardrobe arranged, as fittingly as might be, in the cupboards at his disposal. Mrs. Ruddle had made up a bed for him in one of the back rooms, and this, though of minor importance, brought with it a certain satisfaction. He went around stoking all the fires (observing with pleasure that Mrs. Ruddle's friend's husband, Mr. Hodges, had delivered the logs as requested). He laid out his lordship's pajamas, gave a stir to the bowl of lavender in her ladyship's bedroom, and straightened the trifling disorder which she had left on the toilet-table, whisking away a few grains of powder and putting the nail-scissors back in their case. He noticed, with approval, an absence of lipstick; his lordship had a particular dislike of pink-stained cigarette-ends. Nor, as he had before thankfully observed, did her ladyship enamel her nails to the likeness of blood-stained talons; a bottle of varnish there was, but it was barely tinted. Quite good style, thought Bunter, and gathered up a pair of stout shoes for cleaning. Down below, he heard the car draw up to the door and stand panting. He slipped out by the Privy Stair.

"Tired, Domina?"

"Rather tired—but much better for the run. Such a terrific lot seems to have happened lately, hasn't it?"

"Like a drink?"

"No, thanks. I think I'll go straight up."

"Right you are. I'm only going to put the car away."

Bunter, however, was already dealing with this. Peter walked around to the shed and listened to what he had to say.

"Yes; we saw Crutchley and his young woman in Broxford. When the heart of a man is oppressed with cares, and so on. Have you taken up the hot water?"

"Yes, my lord."

"Then cut along to bed. I can look after myself for once. The gray suit tomorrow, with your permission and approval."

"Entirely appropriate, my lord, if I may say so."

"And will you lock up? We must learn to be householders, Bunter. We will presently purchase a cat and put it out."

"Very good, my lord."

"That's all then. Good night, Bunter."

"Good night, my lord, and thank you."

• • • • •

When Peter knocked at the door, his wife was sitting by the fire, thoughtfully polishing her nails.

"I say, Harriet, would you rather sleep with me tonight?"

"Well—"

"I'm sorry; that sounded a little ambiguous. I mean, do you feel any preference for the other room? I won't make a nuisance of myself if you're feeling fagged. Or I'll change rooms with you if you'd rather."

"That's very sweet of you, Peter. But I don't think you ought to give way to me when I'm merely being foolish. Are you going to turn out one of these indulgent husbands?"

"Heaven forbid! Arbitrary and tyrannical to the last degree. But I have my softer moments—and my share of human folly."

Harriet rose up, extinguished the candles and came out to him, shutting the door behind her.

"Folly seems to be its own reward," said he. "Very well. Let us be foolish together."

CHAPTER XI

POLICEMAN'S LOT

Elbow: *What is't your worship's pleasure I shall do with this wicked caitiff?*
Escalus: *Truly, Officer, because he hath some offences in him that thou wouldest discover if thou couldst, let him continue in his courses till thou knowest what they are.*

—WILLIAM SHAKESPEARE,
MEASURE FOR MEASURE

The distressful Mr. Kirk had in the meantime spent a strenuous evening. He was a slow-thinking man and a kindly one, and it was with reluctance and expenditure of severe mental labor that he hammered out a procedure for himself in this unusual situation.

His sergeant having returned to drive him over to Broxford, he sank back in the passenger's seat, his hat pulled over his eyes and his thoughts revolving silently in this squirrel-cage of mystification. One thing he saw clearly: the coroner must be persuaded to take as little evidence as possible at the inquest and adjourn *sine die* pending further investigation. Fortunately, the law now provided for such a course, and if only Mr. Perkins would not be sticky, everything might pass off very well. The wretched Joe Sellon would have, of course, to speak of seeing Mr. Noakes alive at nine o'clock; but with luck he would not have to go into details about the conversation. Mrs. Ruddle was the stumbling-block: she liked to use her tongue—and then, there was that unfortunate business of Aggie Twitterton's hens, which had left her with a grudge against the police. Also, of course, there was the awkward fact that one or two people in the village had wagged their heads when Mr. Noakes lost his pocketbook, and had hinted that Martha Ruddle might know something about it; she would not readily forgive Joe Sellon for that misunderstanding. Could one, without actually uttering threats or using improper methods, suggest that over-informativeness in the witness-box might involve an inquiry into the matter of paraffin? Or was it safer merely to hint to the coroner that too much talk from Martha would tend to hamper the police in the execution of their duty?

("Half a mo', Blades," said the Superintendent, aloud, at this point in his meditations. "What's that chap doing, obstructing the traffic like that?—Here, you! don't you know better than to park that lorry of yours on a blind corner? If you want to change your wheel you must go further along and get her onto the verge. . . . All right my lad, that's quite enough of that. . . . Let's have a look at your license. . . .")

As for Joe Sellon . . . This business of parking on bends, now, he wouldn't have it. A dashed sight more dangerous than fast driving by a man who knew how to drive. The police liked to be fair; it was the magistrates who were obsessed by miles per hour. All corners should be approached dead slow—all right, because there might be some fool sitting in the middle of the road; but equally, nobody should sit in the middle of the road, because there might be some fool coming around the corner. The thing was fifty-fifty, and the blame should be distributed fifty-fifty; that was only just. In a routine matter like that, it was easy to see one's way. But Joe Sellon, now . . . Well, whatever happened, Joe must be taken off the Noakes case p.d.q. It wasn't proper to have him investigating it as things were. Why, come to think of it, Mrs. Kirk had been reading a book only the other day, in which one of the police in charge of the case turned out actually to have done the murder. He distinctly remembered laughing, and saying, "It's wonderful what these writer-fellows think of." That Lady Peter Wimsey, who wrote these books—she'd be ready enough to believe a tale like that. So, no doubt, would other people.

("Was that Bill Skipton getting over the stile, Blades? Seemed a bit anxious to avoid notice. Better keep your eye on him. Mr. Raikes had been complaining about his birds—shouldn't wonder if Bill was up to his old tricks again."

"Yes, sir.")

It all went to show that an officer couldn't take too much trouble about getting to know his men. A kindly inquiry—a word in season—and Sellon wouldn't have got himself into this jam. How much did Sergeant Foster know about Sellon? One must look into that. Rather a pity in a way, that Foster was a bachelor and a tee-totaller and belonged to a rather strict sect of Plymouth Brethren or something. A most trustworthy officer, but not very easy for a young fellow to confide in. Perhaps one ought to give more attention to these traits of character. Handling men was born in some people—this Lord Peter, for instance. Sellon had never seen him before, yet he was readier to explain himself to *him* than to his own superior officer. One couldn't resent that, of course; it was only natural. What was a gentleman for, except to take your difficulties to? Why, look at the old squire and his lady, when Kirk was a lad—everybody in and out of the big house all day with their troubles. That sort was dying out, more's the pity. Nobody could go to this new man that had the place now—for one thing, half the time he wasn't there, and for another, he'd always lived in a town and didn't understand the way things worked in the country. . . . But how Joe could be such a blamed fool as to tell his lordship a lie—which was the one thing that sort of gentleman would never overlook; you could see his face change when he heard it. You needed a pretty good reason for telling a lie to a gentleman that was taking an interest in you—and, well, the reason you might have didn't bear thinking of.

The car drew up before Mr. Perkins's house, and Kirk heaved himself out with a deep sigh. Maybe Joe was telling the truth after all; he must look into that. Meanwhile, do the thing that's nearest—was that Charles Kingsley or Longfellow?—and, dear, dear, it just showed you what happened when lame dogs were left to get over stiles on their own three legs.

The coroner proved amenable to the suggestion that, in view of investigations now proceeding, based on information received, the inquest should be kept as formal as possible. Kirk was glad Mr. Perkins was a lawyer; medical coroners sometimes took the oddest views of their own importance and legal powers. Not that the police were anxious for any curtailing of the coroner's privileges; there were times when an inquest came in very handy to elicit information which couldn't be got any other way. The silly public liked to make a fuss about the feelings of witnesses, but that was the public all over—always shouting they wanted to be protected and always getting in your way when you tried to do it for them. Wanting it both ways. No, there was no harm in coroners, only they ought to put themselves under police guidance, that was the way Kirk looked at it. Anyhow, Mr. Perkins didn't seem eager to cause trouble; he had a bad cold, too, and would be all the better pleased to keep things short. Well, that was that. Now about Joe Sellon. Better look in at the station first and see if there was anything special needed attending to.

The first thing handed to him when he got there was Joe Sellon's own report. He had interviewed the man Williams, who asserted positively that Crutchley had come in to the garage just before eleven and gone immediately to bed. The two men shared a room, and Williams's bed was between Crutchley's and the door. Williams said he didn't think he could have failed to wake up if Crutchley had gone out during the night, because the door squeaked badly on its hinges. He was a light sleeper. As a matter of fact he had woken up, about 1 o'clock, with a fellow blowing his horn and knocking at the garage door. Turned out to be a commercial vehicle with a leaking feed, called for repairs and petrol. Crutchley had been asleep then, because Williams saw him when he lit his candle and went down to deal with the vehicle. The window was a small dormer—nobody could get out and down that way, and there were no marks of anybody's having done so.

That seemed all right—but in any case, it didn't amount to anything, since Noakes *must* have been dead before 9:30, as it seemed. Unless Mrs. Ruddle was lying. And she had no cause to lie, so far as Kirk could see. She had gone out of her way to mention her presence in the paraffin-shed, and she wouldn't do that for nothing. Unless she was telling lies on purpose to get Sellon into trouble. Kirk shook his head: that would be a big assumption to make. Still, lies or no lies, it was a good thing to check all alibis as closely as possible, and this one appeared to be sound. Always supposing Joe Sellon wasn't lying again. Confound it! when it came to not being able to trust your own men. . . . No doubt about it, Joe must come off this case. And what was more, for form's sake he would have to get Williams's evidence checked again and confirmed—a nuisance, and a waste of time. He asked where Sellon was and learned that, having waited a little in the hope of seeing the Superintendent, he had gone off back to Paggleham about an hour ago. They must have missed him on the road, then, somehow. Why hadn't he come to Talboys?—oh, drat Joe Sellon!

Anything else? Nothing much. P.C. Jordan had been called on to deal with a customer at the Royal Oak, who had used insulting language and behavior to the landlord with conduct tending to provoke a breach of the peace; a woman had reported the loss of a handbag containing 9*s.* 4*d.*, the return half of a ticket, and a latch-key; the sanitary inspector had been in about a case of swine-fever at Datchett's farm; a child had fallen into the river off the Old Bridge, and been dexterously retrieved by Inspector Goudy, who happened to be passing at the time; P.C. Norman had been knocked off his bicycle by a Great Dane under insufficient control and had sprained his thumb; the Noakes affair had been reported by telephone to the Chief Constable, who was in bed with influenza, but wanted an immediate and detailed report in writing; instructions had come through from headquarters that the Essex County Constabulary wanted a sharp lookout kept for a tramping youth aged about seventeen (description) suspected of breaking and entering a house at Saffron Walden (particulars) and stealing a piece of cheese, an Ingersoll watch and a pair of garden-shears valued at three shillings and sixpence, and thought to be making his way through Herts; there was a summons wanted for a chimney afire in South Avenue; a householder had complained about a barking dog; two lads had been brought in for playing at crown and anchor on the steps of the Wesleyan Chapel, and Sergeant Jakes had very competently tracked down and brought to book the miscreant who had improperly rung the fire-alarm on Monday evening: a nice, quiet day. Mr. Kirk listened patiently, distributed sympathy and praise where they were due, and then rang up Pagford and asked for Sergeant Foster. He was out at Snettisley, about that little burglary. Yes, of course. Well, thought Kirk, as he appended his careful signature to a number of routine documents, Datchett's farm was in the Paggleham district; he'd put young Sellon on to that; he couldn't do himself much harm over swine-fever. He telephoned instructions that Sergeant Foster was to report to him as soon as he returned and then, feeling empty, went over to his own quarters to enjoy, as best he might, a supper of beefsteak pie, plum-cake and a pint of mild ale.

He was just finishing, and feeling a little better, when Sergeant Foster arrived, self-congratulatory about the progress of the burglary, righteously dutiful about being summoned to Broxford when he ought to have been partaking of his evening meal, and coldly critical of his superior's taste in liquor. Kirk never found it easy to get on with Foster. There was, to begin with, this air of teetotal virtue;

he disliked having his evening pint referred to as "alcohol." Then, Foster, though much subordinate to him in rank, was more refined in speech; he had been educated at a bad grammar-school instead of a good elementary school, and never misplaced his h's—though, as for reading good literature or quoting the poets, he couldn't do it and didn't want to. Thirdly, Foster was disappointed; he had, somehow, always missed the promotion he felt to be his due—an excellent officer, but just somehow lacking in something or the other, he could not understand his comparative failure, and suspected Kirk of having a down on him. And fourthly, Foster never did anything that was not absolutely correct; this, perhaps, was his real weakness, for it meant that he lacked imagination, both in his work and in handling the men under him.

Kirk, feeling oddly at a disadvantage, in spite of his age and position, waited till Foster had said all he had to say about the Snettisley burglary, and then laid before him the full details of the Talboys affair. The outline of it, Foster of course knew already, since Paggleham was in the Pagford district. In fact, Sellon's original report had come through to him, only ten minutes after the report from Snettisley. Being unable to be in two places at once, he had then rung up Broxford and asked for instructions. Kirk had told him to proceed to Snettisley; he (Kirk) would personally take charge of the murder. This was just the way Kirk was always standing between him and anything important. On his return to Pagford, he had found a curiously unsatisfactory report from Sellon—and no Sellon, nor any news of him. While he had been digesting this, Kirk had sent for him. Well, here he was: he was ready to listen to anything the Superintendent had to tell him. Indeed, it was really time he *was* told something.

He did not, however, like what he was told. And it seemed to him, as the disgraceful narrative boomed on, that he was being blamed—for what? For not acting as a wet-nurse to Joe Sellon's baby, apparently. That was very unfair. Did the Superintendent expect him personally to examine the household budget of every village constable in the Pagford area? He ought to have seen that this young man had "something on his mind"—well, he liked that. Constables were always getting things on their minds—mostly young women, if it wasn't professional jealousies. He had quite enough to do with the men at the Pagford police-station; when it came to married police-officers in small villages, they ought surely to be supposed capable of looking after themselves. If they couldn't keep themselves and their families on the very generous pay and allowance then they ought not to have families. He had seen Mrs. Sellon—a shiftless girl, he thought, pretty before she was married, and dressed in cheap finery. He distinctly remembered warning Sellon against wedding her. If, when Sellon got into financial difficulties he had come to him (as, he quite agreed, he should have done) he would have reminded Sellon that nothing else was to be expected when one flouted the advice of one's superior officer. He would also have pointed out that, by knocking off beer and tobacco, a considerable saving of money might be effected, in addition to the saving of one's soul—always supposing Sellon took any interest in that immortal part of himself. When he (Foster) had been a constable, he had put away a considerable sum of his pay every week.

"Kind hearts," Kirk was saying, "are more than coronets; him as said that lived to wear a coronet himself. Mind you, I ain't saying as you been any way neglectful of your dooty—but it do seem a pity as a young fellow should have his career broke, all for want of a bit of 'elp and guidance. Not to speak of this other suspicion which it's to be hoped won't come to anything."

This was more than Foster could stomach in silence. He explained that he had offered help and guidance at the time of Sellon's marriage; it had not been well received. "I told him he was doing a foolish thing and that that girl would be the ruin of him."

"Did you?" said Kirk, mildly. "Well, then, perhaps it's no wonder he didn't turn to you when he was in a fix. I dunno as I would myself in his place. You see, Foster, when a young fellow's made up his mind, it ain't no good calling the young woman names. You only alienate him and puts yourself in a position where you can't do no good. When I was courtin' Mrs. K.; you don't think I'd have 'eard a word agen her, not from the Chief Constable himself. Not likely. Just you put yourself in his place."

Sergeant Foster said briefly that he couldn't put himself in the place of making a fool of himself over a bit of skirt—still less could he understand taking other people's money, defection from duty and failure to make proper reports to one's superior officer.

"I couldn't make head or tail of the report Sellon sent in. He dropped it in, didn't seem able to give a proper account of himself to Davidson, who was on duty at the station, and now he's off somewhere and can't be found."

"What's that?"

"He's not been back home," said Sergeant Foster, "and he's neither rung up nor left a message. I shouldn't be surprised if he'd made tracks."

"He was over there, looking for me at 5 o'clock," said Kirk unhappily. "He brought a report from Pagford."

"He wrote that out in the station, I'm told," said Foster. "And he left a bunch of shorthand stuff; they're typing it now. Davidson says it doesn't seem to be complete. I suppose it breaks off at the point where—"

"What do you expect?" retorted Kirk. "You don't suppose he'd go on taking down his own confession, do you? Be reasonable. . . . What's worrying me is, that if he was here at five, we ought to have passed him between here and Paggleham, if he was a-going home. I hope he ain't rushed off to do something rash. That 'ud be a nice thing, wouldn't it? Maybe he took the 'bus—but if he did, where's his bike?"

"If he took the 'bus he didn't get home by it," said the Sergeant, grimly.

"His wife must be worrying. I think we'd better have a look-see into this. We don't want nothing of an unfort'nate nature to 'appen. Now—where could 'e a-got to? You take your bike—no, that won't do—takes too long, and you've had a pretty hard day. I'll send Hart on his motor-bike, to see if anybody's seen Sellon round Pillington way—it's all woods round there—and the river—"

"You don't really think—?"

"I don't know what to think. I'm going over to see his wife. Shall I give you a lift over? Your bike can be sent back tomorrow. You'll get the 'bus at Paggleham."

Sergeant Foster could find nothing to resent in this offer, though his voice sounded injured in accepting it. As far as he could see, there was going to be an unholy row about Joe Sellon, and Kirk, characteristically, was taking steps to see that whatever happened he, Foster, should get the blame. Kirk was relieved when they overtook the local omnibus just outside Paggleham; he could drop his austere companion at once, without suggesting that they should go to Sellon's place together.

He found Mrs. Sellon in what Mrs. Ruddle would have called "a state of mind." She looked ready to drop with fright when she opened the door to him, and had evidently been crying. She was fair, pretty in a helpless sort of way, and delicate looking; Kirk noticed, with irritation as well as sympathy, that there was another baby coming. She asked him in, apologizing for the state of the room, which was indeed somewhat disorderly. The two-year-old whose arrival in the world was the indirect cause of all Sellon's misfortunes, was ramping noisily about, dragging a wooden horse, whose wheels squeaked. The table was laid for a tea now long overdue.

"Joe not come in yet?" said Kirk, pleasantly enough.

"No," said Mrs. Sellon. "I don't know what's gone of him. Oh, be quiet, Arthur, do!—He's not been in all day and his supper's spoiling. . . . Oh, Mr. Kirk! Joe ain't in any trouble, is he? Martha Ruddle's been saying such things —Arthur! you bad boy—if you don't give over I'll take that horse away from you."

Kirk captured Arthur and stood him firmly between his own massive knees.

"Now, you be a good boy," he admonished him. "Grown a lot, ain't he? He'll be getting quite a handful for you. Well, now, Mrs. Sellon—I wanted to have a bit of a talk with you about Joe."

Kirk had the advantage of being a local man, having in fact been born at Great Pagford. He had not seen Mrs. Sellon more than twice or thrice before; but he was at least not completely strange and therefore not completely awe-inspiring. Mrs. Sellon was induced to pour out her fears and troubles. As Kirk had suspected, she knew about Mr. Noakes and his missing note-case. She had not been told of it at the time, naturally; but later, when the weekly payments to Noakes had begun to press heavily on the exchequer, she had "wormed it out of" Joe. She had gone about in a state of anxiety ever since, fearing that something dreadful would happen. And then, a week ago today, Joe had had to go and tell Mr. Noakes he couldn't pay that week, and came back "looking awful," and saying "they were done for now for good and all." He'd been "very queer in his ways" all the week, and now Mr. Noakes was dead and Joe was missing and Martha Ruddle told her there'd been a dreadful quarrel and, "oh, I dunno, Mr. Kirk, I'm that terrified he may have done something rash."

Kirk, as delicately as he could, asked whether Joe had said anything to his wife about his quarrel with Noakes. Well, no, not exactly. All he'd said was, that Mr. Noakes wouldn't listen to nothing and it was all up. He wouldn't answer no questions—seemed regular fed-up like. Then he'd suddenly said he thought the best thing would be to chuck everything and go out to his elder brother in Canada, and would she go with him? She'd said, Why goodness gracious, Joe, surely Mr. Noakes wasn't going to tell on him after all this long while—it'd be a wicked shame, and after he'd paid all that money! Joe had only said gloomily, Well, you'll see tomorrow. And then he'd sat with his head in his hands, and there wasn't nothing to be got out of him. Next day they heard that Mr. Noakes had gone away. She had been afraid he'd gone to Broxford to tell on Joe; but nothing happened, and Joe cheered up a bit. And then this morning, she heard Noakes was dead, and she was that thankful, you couldn't think. But now Joe had gone off somewhere and Martha Ruddle came in with her talk—and since Mr. Kirk had found out about the note-case, she supposed it had all come out, and oh, dear, what *was* she to do and where was Joe?

None of this was very comforting to Kirk. It would have cheered him up a good deal to learn that Sellon had spoken frankly to his wife about the quarrel. And he didn't at all like reference to the brother in Canada. If Sellon really had done away with Noakes, he would have had about as much chance of escaping to Canada as of being made king of the Cannibal Islands, and reflection must have told him so; but that his first blind impulse should have been to flee the country was unpleasantly significant. It occurred to Kirk, incidentally, that whoever did the murder must have been going through a pretty trying time. For it seemed very unlikely that he or she had thrown Noakes down the cellar steps—else why was the door left open? The murderer, having clubbed Noakes and left him for dead, would have expected—what? Well, if he had done it in the sitting-room or the kitchen or any room downstairs, the body might have been seen the next time anyone happened to look in at the windows—Mrs. Ruddle, or the postman, or an inquisitive lad from the village, or the vicar, on one of his visits. Or Aggie Twitterton might have come over to see her uncle. At any moment the discovery might have been made. Some poor devil (Kirk really felt a passing twinge of pity for the culprit) had been sitting for a whole week on the safety-valve, wondering! At any rate, the body *must* have been found the next Wednesday (that was today) because of Crutchley's weekly attendance. If, of course, the murderer knew about that, as he or she was bound to do; unless the crime could be traced to a passing tramp or somebody—and what a good thing if it could!

(While thinking this out, Kirk was talking soothingly in his slow speech, saying that something unexpected might have called Joe away; he had sent a man out to hunt him up; a constable in uniform couldn't very well get lost; it didn't do to imagine things.)

It was queer that Sellon . . .

Yes, by God, thought Kirk, that *was* queer; queerer than he cared to think about. He must take that away and chew it over. He couldn't think properly, with Mrs. Sellon's lamenting voice in his ear. . . . And the time didn't fit, because Crutchley had been over an hour in the house before the body was discovered. If Joe Sellon had been hanging around there at, say, eleven o'clock instead of past twelve. . . . Coincidence. He breathed again.

Mrs. Sellon was wailing on.

"We were that surprised when Willy Abbot come up with the milk this morning, to hear as a gentleman had taken Talboys. We didn't know rightly what to make of it. I said to Joe, 'Surely,' I said, 'Mr. Noakes wouldn't go away like that and let the house'—because, of course, we thought he'd let it like he often done before—'not without letting someone know,' I said. And Joe looked awful excited. I said, 'D'you suppose he's gone off somewhere,' I said, 'it looks queer to me,' I said, and he said, 'I don't know, but I'll soon find out.' And off he went. And he came in afterwards and wouldn't hardly swallow his breakfast, and he said, 'I can't hear nothing,' he said, 'only there's a lady and gentleman come and Noakes ain't turned up,' he said. And he went out again, and that's the last I see of him."

Well, thought Kirk, that puts the lid on. He'd forgotten the Wimseys, coming in and upsetting everything. Though he was not an imaginative man, he could see Sellon, startled by hearing that there was someone in the house, rushing out to learn the news, perplexed beyond expression by the fact that no body had been found, not daring to go and make open inquiries, but hovering around the house, manufacturing excuses for talking to Bert Ruddle—and he didn't like the Ruddles—waiting, waiting for the summons he knew must come, to him, to the only man with authority, hoping that the people in the house would leave it to him to examine the corpse, remove all evidences—

Kirk wiped his forehead, saying apologetically that he felt the room a little hot. He did not hear Mrs. Sellon's reply; he was imagining again.

What the murderer (better not call him Sellon), what the murderer found in that house was—not a helpless pair of London holiday-makers, not some vague artistic couple without practical common-sense, not some pleasant retired schoolmistress coming to the country to enjoy a few weeks of fresh air and fresh eggs, but—a duke's son who cared for no man and knew exactly where the local bobby got off, who had investigated more murders than Paggleham had known in four centuries, whose wife wrote detective stories, and whose manservant was here, there and everywhere on swift and silent feet. But supposing, just supposing, the first people who arrived had been Aggie Twitterton and Frank Crutchley—as in rights they ought to have been? Even a local bobby could do as he liked with them; take charge, turn them out of the house, arrange things as he chose—

Kirk's wits were slow-moving, but when they took hold of a thing they worked with an efficiency which dismayed their owner.

He was trying to make some sort of commonplace rejoinder to Mrs. Sellon, when there was the sound of a motorcycle drawing up at the gate. Looking out of the window, he saw it was Police-Sergeant Hart with Joe Sellon behind him, like two knights templars on one mount.

"Well!" said Kirk, with a cheerfulness he was far from feeling, "here's Joe back, anyhow, safe and sound."

But he didn't like the beaten, exhausted look on Sellon's face as Hart steered him up the little garden path. And he didn't look forward to questioning him.

CHAPTER XII

POT-LUCK

Why, how now, friends! what saucy mates are you
That know nor duty nor civility?
Are we a person fit to be your host;
Or is our house become your common inn
To beat our doors at pleasure? What such haste
Is yours, as that it cannot wait fit times?
Are you the masters of this commonwealth
And know no more discretion?

—JOHN FORD, *'TIS PITY SHE'S A WHORE*

Superintendent Kirk was spared the greater part of his ordeal; Sellon was in no fit state for undergoing a long interrogation. Sergeant Hart had picked up his trail in Pillington, where he had ridden through on his bicycle about half-past six. Then a girl was found who had seen a policeman following the field path on foot in the direction of Blackraven Wood—a favorite resort of ramblers and children during the summer months. She had particularly noticed him, because it was an unusual place in which to see a uniformed policeman. Following, as he said, this indication, Hart had found Sellon's bicycle propped against a hedge near the entrance to the path. He had hastened in pursuit—rather uneasy when he remembered that the little wood ran down to the bank of the Pagg. It was darkish by that time, and quite dark among the trees. With the aid of his torch, he had searched about for some time, calling as loudly as he could. After about three-quarters of an hour (he admitted that it had seemed a lot longer) he came upon Sellon, sitting on a fallen tree. He wasn't doing anything—just sitting. Seemed dazed-like. Hart asked him what on earth he thought he was about, but could get no sense out of him. He told him, pretty sharply, that he must come along at once—the Super was asking for him. Sellon offered no objection, but came without protest. Asked again what brought him there, he said he was "trying to think things out." Hart—who knew no details of the Paggleham affair—could make neither head nor tail of him; he didn't think he was fit to be trusted to ride back alone, and therefore took him up on the carrier and brought him straight home. Kirk said he couldn't have done better.

This explanation took place in the sitting room. Mrs. Sellon had got Joe into the kitchen and was trying to coax him into eating a bit of something. Kirk sent Hart back to Broxford, explaining that Sellon was unwell and in a spot of trouble, and warning him not to say too much about it to the other men. He then went in to tackle his black sheep.

He soon came to the conclusion that Sellon's chief trouble, beside worry, was sheer exhaustion and lack of food. (He remembered now that he had had practically no lunch, though ham sandwiches and bread-and-cheese had been liberally provided at Talboys.) Sellon's account of himself, when Kirk got it out of him, was that, after interviewing Williams and writing his report, he had gone straight over to Broxford, expecting to find Kirk already there. He hadn't liked to go back to Talboys, on account of what had happened—seemed to him he was better out of the way. He'd waited about half an hour for Kirk; but the men kept asking him about the murder, and what with one thing and another he couldn't stick it. So he'd left the station and gone down to the canal and walked about a bit by the gas-works, meaning to come back later. But then it "came over him" how he'd been and gone and done for himself, and even if he could clear himself of the murder charge there were no hopes for him. So he'd taken his bike again and gone off, he couldn't rightly remember where or why, because he couldn't get his mind clear, and he thought if he could just go and walk about somewhere, maybe he could think better. He remembered going through Pillington and walking over the fields. He didn't think he'd had any special reason for going to Blackraven Wood—he'd only wandered about. He might have fallen asleep. He had had a sort of notion about chucking himself into the river, but he was afraid it would upset his wife. And he was very sorry, sir, but he couldn't say no more than that, only that he didn't do the murder. But, he added, oddly, if his lordship didn't believe him, then nobody else would.

This didn't seem quite the moment for going into his lordship's reasons for disbelief. Kirk told Sellon he was a young fool to go rambling away like that, and that everybody was ready to believe him so long as he was telling the truth. And he'd better go to bed and try and wake up more sensible; he'd frightened his wife quite enough as it was, and here it was close on 10 o'clock (Crumbs! and the Chief Constable's report not written yet!); he would be over in the morning and would see him before the inquest.

"You'll have to give evidence, you know," said Kirk, "but I've seen the coroner and maybe he won't press you too hard, on account of the investigation being in progress."

Sellon only put his head in his hands, and Kirk, really feeling that there was little to be done with him in this state, left him. As he went out, he said what cheering things he could to Mrs. Sellon, and advised her not to fidget her husband with too many questions, but to let him rest and try to keep in good heart.

All the way back to Broxford, his mind was churning over his new ideas. He couldn't get out of his head that picture of Sellon, standing at Martha Ruddle's cottage door —waiting—

There was only one thing that gave him comfort—a

comfort altogether irrational: that one curious sentence, "If his lordship won't believe me, then nobody else will." There was no reason why Wimsey should believe Sellon, if it came to that—there was no sense in it at all—but it had sounded, well, genuine. He could hear again Sellon's desperate cry: "Don't *you* go, my lord! My lord, *you*'ll believe me!" Kirk, rummaging the filing-cabinet of his mind, found words which seemed to him apt. Thou hast appealed to Caesar; unto Caesar thou shalt go. But Caesar had disallowed the appeal.

Not till Kirk, weary and patient, was writing out his report to the Chief Constable did the great illumination come upon him. He stopped, pen in hand, staring at the wall. Something like an idea, that was. And he'd been on to it before, as near as nothing, only he hadn't properly followed it up. But of course, it explained everything. It explained Sellon's statement and exonerated him; it explained how he had seen the clock from the window; it explained how Noakes came to be killed behind locked doors; it explained why the body hadn't been robbed; and it explained the murder—explained it right away. Because, Kirk told himself with triumph, there had never been any murder!

Wait a bit, thought the Superintendent, figuring the thing out in his careful way; mustn't go too fast. There's a big snag at the start. How can we get over that, I wonder?

The snag was that, to make the theory work, one had to assume that the cactus had been removed from its place. Kirk had already dismissed this idea as silly; but he hadn't seen then what a lot it would explain. He had gone so far as to have a word with Crutchley, among the chrysanthemums, just as he left Talboys. He had managed the inquiry pretty well, he thought. He had been careful not to ask straight out: "Did you put the cactus back before you left?" That would have drawn attention to a point which was at present a secret between himself and his lordship. He didn't want any talk about that to get around to Sellon before he himself confronted him with it in his own way. So he had merely pretended to have misremembered what Crutchley had said about his final interview with Noakes. It took place in the kitchen? Yes. Had either of them gone back into the sitting-room after that? No. But he thought Crutchley said he was watering them plants at the time. No, he'd finished watering the plants and was putting back the steps? Oh! then Kirk had got that wrong. Sorry. He just really wanted to get at how long the altercation with Noakes had lasted. Had Noakes been there while Crutchley was seeing to the plants? No, he was in the kitchen. But didn't Crutchley take the plants out to the kitchen to water them? No, he watered them just where they were, and wound the clock and came out with the steps, and it wasn't till he'd done that that Noakes gave him his day's money and the argument started. It hadn't lasted more'n maybe ten minutes or so—not the argument. Well, possibly fifteen. Six o'clock was rightly Crutchley's time to stop work—he charged five bob for an eight-hour day, barrin' time off for lunch. Kirk apologized for his mistake: the step-ladder had confused him; he had thought Crutchley meant he needed the step-ladder to get the hanging plants out of their pots. No; the step-ladder was to get up to water them, same as he'd done this morning—they was above his head—and to wind the clock, like he said. That was all. It was quite ordinary, him using the step-ladder, he always did, and put it back in the kitchen afterwards. "You ain't tryin' to make out," added Crutchley, a little belligerently, "as I stood on them steps with a 'ammer to cosh the old bird over the 'ead?" That was an ingenious idea nobody had yet thought of. Kirk replied that he wasn't thinking anything particular; only trying to get the times clear in his head. He was glad to have given the impression that his suspicions were directed to the step-ladder.

Unfortunately, then, he couldn't begin by substantiating that the cactus had been out of its pot at 6:20. But now—suppose Noakes had taken it out himself for some purpose or the other. What purpose? Well, it was difficult to say. But suppose Noakes had seen something wrong with it —a spot of mildew, maybe, or whatever these ugly things suffered from. He might have taken it down to wipe it or— But he could have done that easy enough, standing on the steps or, as he was so tall, on a chair. Not good enough. What other things could happen to plants? Well, they might become pot-bound. Kirk didn't know whether that happened to cactuses (or was it cacti?), but suppose you wanted to look and see if its roots were growing out through the bottom of the pot. You'd have to take it out for that. Or to tap the pot to see if—no; it had been given water. But wait! Noakes hadn't *seen* Crutchley do that. He might have suspected Crutchley was neglecting it. Perhaps he felt at the top and it didn't seem wet enough, and then —Or, more likely, he thought it was being over-watered. These spiky cactus-affairs didn't like too much damp. Or did they? It was annoying not to know their habits; Kirk's own gardening was of the straightforward flowerbed-and-kitchen-stuff variety.

Anyhow, it wasn't outside the bounds of possibility that Noakes had removed the cactus for some purpose of his own. You couldn't prove he hadn't. Say he did. All right. Then, at 9 o'clock, up comes Sellon, and sees Noakes coming into the parlor. . . . Here Kirk paused to consider again. If Noakes was coming for the 9:30 News as usual, he was before his time. He came in (said Sellon) and looked at the clock: The dead man had worn no watch, and Kirk had taken it for granted that he had come in merely to see how near it was to news-bulletin time. But he might also have been meaning to put the cactus back and come in a bit early on that account. That was all right. He comes in. He thinks, Now, have I got time to fetch that there plant in from the scullery, or wherever it is, before the News comes on? He looks at the clock. Then Joe Sellon taps at the window and he comes over. They have their talk and Joe goes away. The old boy fetches in his plant and gets up on a chair or something to put it back. Or maybe he gets the steps. Then, while he's doing that, he sees it's getting on for half-past nine, and that flurries him a bit. He leans over too far, or the steps slip, or he ain't careful getting down, and over he goes backwards and gives his head a crack on the floor—or, better still, on the corner of the settle. He's knocked out. Then presently he comes to, puts away the chair or the steps or whatever it was and after that—well, after that, we know what happened to him. So there you are. Simple as pie. No cutting or stealing keys or hiding blunt instruments or telling lies—nothing at all but a plain accident and everybody telling the truth.

Kirk was as much overcome by the beauty, simplicity and economy of this solution as Copernicus must have been when he first thought of putting the sun in the center of the Solar System and saw all the planets, instead of describing complicated and ugly geometrical capers, move onward in orderly and dignified circles. He sat and contemplated it with affection for nearly ten minutes before venturing to examine it. He was afraid of knocking the bloom off it.

Still, a theory was only a theory; one had got to find evidence to support it. One must at any rate be sure there was no evidence against it. First of all, could a man kill himself like that, simply by falling off a pair of steps?

Side by side with half-crown editions of English poets and philosophers, flanked on the right by Bartlett's *Familiar Quotations* and on the left by that handy police publication which dissects and catalogues crimes according to the method of their commission, stood, tall and menacing, the two blue volumes of Taylor's *Medical Jurisprudence*, that canon of uncanonical practice and Baedeker of the back doors to death. Kirk had often studied it in a dutiful readiness for the unexpected. Now he took it down and turned the pages of Volume I, till he came to the running head: "Intercranial Hemorrhage—Violence or Disease." He was looking for the story of the gentleman who fell out of a chaise. Yes, here he was: he emerged with a kind of personality from the Report of Guy's Hospital for 1859:

A gentleman was thrown out of a chaise, and fell upon his head with such violence as to stun him. After a short time he recovered his senses, and felt so much better that he entered the chaise again, and was driven to his father's house by a companion. He attempted to pass off the accident as of a trivial nature, but he soon began to feel heavy and drowsy, so that he was obliged to go to bed. His symptoms became more alarming, and he died in about an hour from effusion of blood in the brain.

Excellent and unfortunate gentleman, his name unknown, his features a blank, his life a mystery; embalmed for ever in a fame outlasting the gilded monuments of princes! He lived in his father's house, so was presumably unmarried and young—a bit of a swell, perhaps, wearing the fashionable new Inverness cape and the luxuriant silky side-whiskers which were just coming into favor. How did he come to be thrown out of the chaise? Did the horse bolt with him? Had he looked on the wine when it was red? The vehicle, we observe, was undamaged, and his companion at any rate sober enough to drive him home. A courageous gentleman (since he was resolute to enter the chaise again), a considerate gentleman (since he made light of the accident in order to spare his parents anxiety); his premature death must have occasioned much lamentation among the crinolines. No one could have guessed that, nearly eighty years later, a police superintendent in a rural district would be reading his brief epitaph: "A gentleman was thrown out of a chaise. . . ."

Not that Superintendent Kirk troubled his head with these biographical conjectures. What exasperated him was that the book did not mention the height of the chaise from the ground or the rate at which the vehicle was proceeding. How would the fall compare in violence with that of an elderly man from a step-ladder on to an oak floor? The next case quoted was even less to the point: this was a youth of eighteen, who was hit on the head in a fight, went about his business for ten days, had a headache on the eleventh day and died in the night. Then came a drunken carter, aged fifty, who fell from the shafts of his cart and was killed. This seemed more hopeful; except that the wretched creature had fallen three or four times, the last time being thrown under the wheels of the cart by the bolting horse. Still, it did seem to show that a short fall would do quite a lot of damage. Kirk pondered a little, then went to the telephone.

Dr. Craven listened with patience to Kirk's theory, and agreed that it was an attractive one. "Only," he said, "if you want me to tell the coroner that the man fell on his back, I can't do it. There is no bruising whatever on the back, or on the left-hand side of the body. If you looked at my report to the coroner you must have seen that all the marks were on the right-hand side and in front, except the actual blow that caused death. I'll tell you again what they are. The right forearm and elbow show heavy bruises, with considerable extravasation from the surface vessels, showing that they were inflicted some time before death. I should say that when he was hit behind the left ear, he was flung over forwards on to his right side with the force of the blow. The only other marks are bruises and slight abrasions on the shins, hands and forehead. The hands and forehead are marked with dust, and this suggests, I think, that he got the injuries in falling forwards down the cellar steps. He died shortly after that, for there is very little extravasation from these injuries. I am, of course, excluding the hypostasis producing by his having lain a whole week face downwards in the cellar. That, naturally, is all in the front part of the body."

Kirk had forgotten the meaning of "hypostasis," which the doctor pronounced in a very unlikely way; but he gathered that it wasn't a thing that could be made to support the theory. He asked whether Noakes could have been killed by hitting his head in a fall.

"Oh, certainly," said Dr. Craven; "but you'll have to

explain how he hit the back of his head in falling and yet came down on his face."

With this Kirk had to be content. It looked rather as though a flaw might be developing in his beautiful rounded theory. It is the little rift within the lute, he thought, mournfully, that by and by will make the music mute. But he shook his head angrily. Tennyson or no Tennyson, he wasn't going to abandon the position without a struggle. He called to his assistance a more robust and comforting poet—one who held "we fall to rise, are baffled to fight better"—called to his wife that he was going out, and reached for his hat and overcoat. If only he could have another look at the sitting-room, he might be able to see how that fall could have come about.

At Talboys the sitting-room was dark, though a light still burned in the casement above it and in the kitchen. Kirk knocked at the door, which was presently opened by Bunter in his shirt-sleeves.

"I'm very sorry to disturb his lordship so late," began Kirk, only then realizing that it was past eleven.

"His lordship," said Bunter, "is in bed."

Kirk explained that, unexpectedly, a necessity had arisen to re-examine the sitting-room, and that he was anxious to get this done before the inquest. There was no need for his lordship to come down in person. Nothing was sought but permission to enter.

"We should be most unwilling," replied Bunter, "to obstruct the officers of the law in the execution of their duty; but you will permit me to point out that the hour is somewhat advanced and the available illumination inadequate. Besides that, the sitting-room is situated exactly underneath his lordship's—"

"Superintendent! Superintendent!" called a soft and mocking voice from the window above.

"My lord?" Mr. Kirk stepped out of the porch to get a view of the speaker.

"Merchant of Venice, Act V, Scene 1. Peace, ho! the moon sleeps with Endymion, and would not be awak'd."

"I beg your pardon, my lord," said Kirk, devoutly thankful that the mask of night was on his face. And the lady listening, too!

"Don't mention it. Is there anything I can do for you?"

"Only to let me take another look round downstairs," pleaded Kirk, apologetically.

"Had we but world enough and time that trifling request, Superintendent, were no crime. But take whatever you like. Only do, as the poet sings, come and go on lissome, clerical, printless toe. The first is Marvell and the second, Rupert Brooke."

"I'm very much obliged," said Mr. Kirk, generally, to cover the permission and the information. "The fact is, I got an idea."

"I only wish I had half your complaint. Do you want to unfold your tale now, or will it do in the morning?"

Mr. Kirk earnestly begged his lordship not to disturb himself.

"Well, good luck to it and good night."

Nevertheless, Peter hesitated. His natural inquisitiveness wrestled with a right and proper feeling that he should credit Kirk with intelligence enough to pursue his own inquiries. Proper feeling prevailed, but he remained for fifteen minutes perched on the window-sill, while soft scrapes and bumpings sounded from below. Then came the shutting of the front door and steps along the path.

"His shoulders are disappointed," said Peter aloud to his wife. "He has found a mare's-nest, full of cockatrice's eggs."

That was perfectly true. The rift in Kirk's theory had widened and with alarming rapidity silenced all that he could find to say for Joe Sellon. Not only was it extremely hard to visualize any way by which Noakes could have fallen so as to injure himself on both sides at once, but it was now plainly evident that the cactus had remained all the while solidly in its place.

Kirk had thought of two possibilities: the outer pot might have been unhooked from the chain, or the inner pot removed from the outer. On careful examination, he discounted the first alternative. The brass pot had a conical base, which would prevent it from standing upright when taken down; moreover, in order to relieve the strain on the hook, the ring which untied the three chains that rose from the sides of the pot itself had been secured to the first link above the hook by a sixfold twist of stout wire, the ends of which had been neatly turned in with the pliers. No one in his senses would have gone to the trouble of undoing that when he could more readily remove the inner pot. But here Kirk made a discovery which, while it did credit to his detective ability, destroyed all possibility of any such removal. Around the top of the shining brass pot ran a band of pierced work forming a complicated pattern, and within the openings the earthenware of the inner flower-pot was blackened with the unmistakable stain of brass-polish. If the flower-pot had been removed since the last cleaning, it was inconceivable that it should have been replaced with such mathematical exactness as to show no thin red line of earthenware at the edges of that band of open-work. Kirk, disappointed, called Bunter to give his opinion. Bunter, disapproving but correctly ready to assist, agreed absolutely. What was more, when they tried, together, to shift the inner pot in the outer, it proved to be an exceedingly tight fit. Nobody, unaided, could have turned it after wedging it in so as to make the pierced band coincide with the outlines stenciled on the earthenware—certainly not an elderly man in a hurry by the light of a distant candle. As a forlorn hope, Kirk asked:

"Did Crutchley polish the brass this morning?"

"I fancy not; he brought no brass-polish with him, nor did he use the materials contained in the kitchen cupboard. Will there by anything further tonight?"

Kirk gazed blankly about the room.

"I suppose," he suggested, despairingly, "the clock couldn't have been moved?"

"See for yourself," said Bunter.

But the plastered wall showed no trace of any hook or nail to which the clock might have been temporarily transferred. The nearest landmark to the east was the nail supporting "The Soul's Awakening" and that to the west, a fretwork bracket with a plaster image on it—both too light to take the clock and in the wrong line of sight from the window. Kirk gave it up.

"Well, that seems to settle it. Thanks very much."

"Thank *you*," retorted Bunter, austerely. Still dignified, in spite of his shirt-sleeves, he conducted the unwelcome guest to the door, as though ushering out a duchess.

Being human, Kirk could not but wish he had left his theory alone till after the inquest. All that he had done was to rule it definitely out of court, so that he could not now, in honesty, even hint at such a possibility.

CHAPTER XIII

THIS WAY AND THAT WAY

"Serpent, I say again!" repeated the Pigeon . . . and added with a kind of sob, "I've tried every way, and nothing seems to suit them!"

"I haven't the least idea what you're talking about," said Alice.

"I've tried the roots of trees, and I've tried banks, and I've tried hedges," the Pigeon went on without attending to her; "but those serpents! There's no pleasing them!"

—LEWIS CARROLL, *ALICE IN WONDERLAND*

"And what," inquired Lord Peter Wimsey of Bunter the following morning, "did the Superintendent want last night?"

"He wished to ascertain, my lord, whether the hanging cactus could have been removed from its containing pot during the events of last week."

"What, again? I thought he'd realized that it couldn't. The marks of the brass polish should have told him that with half an eye. No need to get the step-ladder and bump around at midnight like a bumble-bee in a bottle."

"Quite so, my lord. But I thought it better not to intervene, and your lordship wished him to have every facility."

"Oh, quite. His brain works like the mills of God. But he has some other divine qualities; I know him to be magnanimous and suspect him of being merciful. He is trying hard to exonerate Sellon. That's natural enough. But he's attacking the strong side instead of the weak side of the case against him."

"What do you think about Sellon yourself, Peter?"

They had breakfast upstairs. Harriet was dressed, smoking a cigarette in the window. Peter, in the half-way dressing-gown stage, was warming the back of his legs at the fire. The ginger cat had arrived to pay its morning compliment, and had taken up a position on his shoulder.

"I don't know what to think. The fact is, we've got dashed little material for thinking with. It's probably too early for thinking."

"Sellon doesn't look like a murderer."

"They very often don't, you know. He didn't look, either, like the sort of man who would tell me a thundering great lie, except for a very good reason. But people do tell lies when they're frightened."

"I suppose he didn't notice till after he'd said that about the clock that it implied having been inside the house."

"No. You've got to be a very sharp-witted person to see ahead when you're telling half-truths. A story that's a lie from beginning to end will be consistent. And since he obviously hadn't meant to tell the story of the quarrel at all, he had to make up his mind on the spur of the moment. The thing that's bothering me is, how did Sellon get into the house?"

"Noakes must have left him in."

"Just so. Here's an elderly man, locked up alone in a house. Up comes a young man, big and strong and in a murderous rage, and quarrels with him, using strong language and possibly threats. The old man tells him to be off, and bangs the window shut. The young man goes on knocking at the doors and trying to get in. The old man has nothing to gain by admitting him; yet he does it, and obligingly turns his back to him, on purpose that the angry young man may attack him with a blunt instrument. It is possible, but, as Aristotle might say, it is an improbable-possible."

"Suppose Sellon said he *had* got the money after all, and Noakes let him in and sat down to write a—No, he wouldn't write a receipt, of course. Nothing on paper. Unless Sellon threatened him."

"If Sellon had the money, Noakes could have told him to hand it in through the window."

"Well, suppose he did hand it in—or said he was going to. Then, when Noakes opened the window, Sellon could have climbed in himself. Or could he? Those mullions are pretty narrow."

"You can have no idea," said Peter, irrelevantly, "how refreshing it is to talk to somebody who has a grasp of method. The police are excellent fellows, but the only principle of detection they have really grasped is that wretched phrase, *Cui bono?* They *will* hare off after motive, which is a matter for psychologists. Juries are just the same. If they can see a motive they tend to convict, however often the judge may tell them that there's no need to prove motive, and that motive by itself will never make a case. You've got to show how the thing was done, and then, if you like, bring in motive to back up your proof. If a thing could only have been done one way, and if only one person could have done it that way, then you've got your criminal, motive or no motive. There's How, When, Where, Why and Who—and when you've got How, you've got Who. Thus spake Zarathustra."

"I seem to have married my only intelligent reader. That's the way you construct it from the other end, of course. Artistically, it's absolutely right."

"I have noticed that what's right in art is usually right in practice. In fact, nature is a confirmed plagiarist of art, as somebody has observed. Go on with your theory—only do remember that to guess how a job *might* have been done isn't the same thing as proving that it *was* done that way. If you will allow me to say so, that is a distinction which people of your profession are very liable to overlook. They will confuse moral certainty with legal proof."

"I shall throw something at you in a minute. . . . I say,

do you think something might have been *thrown* at Noakes? Through the window? Bother! now I've got two theories at once. No—wait! . . . Sellon gets Noakes to open the window and then starts to climb in. You didn't answer about those mullions."

"I think I could climb in through them; but then I'm rather narrow in the shoulders compared with Sellon. But on the principle that where your head can go your body can follow I dare say he could manage it. Not very quickly, and not without giving Noakes plenty of warning of his intentions."

"That's where the throwing comes in. Suppose Sellon started to climb and Noakes got alarmed and made for the door. Then Sellon might snatch up something—"

"What?"

"That's true. He would scarcely have brought a stone or anything on purpose. He might have picked one up in the garden before he came back to the window. Or—I know! That paperweight on the sill. He could have snatched that up, and chucked it at Noakes's retreating back. Would that work? I'm not good at trajectories and things."

"Very likely it would. I'd have to go and look."

"Well, then. Oh, yes. Then he'd only have to finish scrambling in, pick up the paperweight and put it back and go out through the window again."

"Really?"

"Of course not; it was locked inside. No. He'd shut and lock the window, get Noakes's keys from his pocket, open the front door, put back the keys and—Well, then he'd have to go out leaving the door unlocked. And when Noakes came to, he obligingly locked it behind him. We've got to allow for that possibility, whoever did the murder."

"That's really brilliant, Harriet. It's very difficult to find a flaw in it. And I'll tell you another thing. Sellon was the only person who could, with comparative safety, leave the door unlocked. In fact, it would be an advantage."

"You've got ahead of me there. Why?"

"Why, because he was the village policeman. Look what

happens next. In the middle of the night, he takes it into his head to go on a round of inspection. His attention, as he would put it in his report, is directed to the house by the circumstance of the candles being still alight in the sitting-room. That's why he left them burning, which no other murderer would be likely to do. He tries the door and finds it open. He goes in, sees that everything looks nice and natural, and then hurries out to call up the neighbors with the announcement that some tramp or other has been in and knocked Mr. Noakes on the head. It's a nuisance to be the last man to see the deceased alive, but it's a hell of a good wheeze to be the first to discover the body. It must have been a nasty shock to find that door locked after all."

"Yes. I suppose that would make him give up his idea. Especially if he looked in through the window and saw that Noakes wasn't lying where he'd left him. The curtains weren't drawn, were they? No—I remember—they were open when we arrived. What *would* he think?"

"He'd think Noakes wasn't killed after all, and would wait for the morning, wondering when—and how—"

"Poor man!—And then, when nothing happened after all, and Noakes didn't turn up—why, it was enough to drive him dotty."

"If it happened that way."

"And then we came and—I suppose he was hanging about here all morning, waiting to hear the worst. He was right on the spot when the body was found, wasn't he? . . . I say, Peter, all this is a bit grim."

"It's only a theory, after all. We haven't proved a word of it. That's the worst of you mystery-mongers. Anything's a solution so long as it holds together. Let's make a theory about somebody else. Whom shall we have? How about Mrs. Ruddle? She's a tough old lady and not an altogether sympathetic character."

"Why on earth should Mrs. Ruddle—?"

"Never mind Why. Why never gets you anywhere. Mrs. Ruddle came to borrow a drop of paraffin. Noakes was sniffing round and heard her. He invited her to step in and explain herself. He said he had often had doubts of her honesty. She said he owed her a week's money. High words passed. He made for her. She snatched up the poker. He ran away and she threw the poker at him and caught him on the back of the head. That's Why enough, when people lose their tempers. Unless you prefer to believe that Noakes made improper advances to Mrs. Ruddle and she dotted him one accordingly."

"Idiot!"

"Well, I don't know. Look at old James Fleming and Jessie MacPherson. I shouldn't fancy Mrs. Ruddle myself, but then, my standard is high. Very well. Mrs. Ruddle knocks Noakes on the head, and—Wait a minute; this is coming rather pretty. She runs over to the cottage in a terrible stew, crying, 'Bert! Bert! I've killed Mr. Noakes!' Bert says, 'Oh, nonsense,' and they come back to the house together, just in time to see Noakes go tumbling down the cellar steps. Bert goes down—"

"Leaving no footprints?"

"He'd taken off his boots for the night and ran over in his slippers—it's all grass over the field to the cottage. Bert says, 'He's dead this time, all right.' Then Mrs. Ruddle goes to fetch a ladder, while Bert locks the door and puts the key back in the dead man's pocket. He goes upstairs, through the trapdoor on to the roof, and Mrs. Ruddle holds the ladder while he gets down."

"Do you mean that seriously, Peter?"

"I can't mean it seriously till I've had a look at the roof. But there's one thing they remember afterwards—Bert has left the cellar-door open—hoping it will look as though Noakes had had an accident. But when we arrive, they are a bit put out. We were not the people who were intended to discover the body. That was to be Miss Twitterton's job. They know *she's* easily hoodwinked, but they know nothing about *us*. First of all, Mrs. Ruddle isn't keen to have us here at all—but when we insist on getting the key and coming in, she makes the best of it. *Only*—she calls out to Bert, 'Shut the cellar-door, Bert! It's perishing cold.'

Thinking to postpone matters a little, you see, and take stock of us first. And by the way, we've only got Mrs. Ruddle's word for it that Noakes died at that particular time, or that he didn't go to bed, or anything. It might all have happened much later at night, or, better still when she came in the morning; because then he'd be ready dressed, and she'd only have to make the bed again."

"What? In the morning? All that business on the roof? Suppose anybody came by?"

"Bert on a ladder, cleaning out the gutters. No 'arm in cleaning out a gutter."

"Gutter? . . . What does that? . . . gutter—guttered—the candles! Don't they prove it happened at night?"

"They don't prove it; they suggest it. We don't know how long the candles were to start with. Noakes may have sat listening to the wireless till they burnt themselves out in the sockets. Thrift, thrift, Horatio. It was Mrs. Ruddle who said the wireless wasn't going—who put the time at between 9 and 9:30—just after Sellon and Noakes had been quarreling. It's not awfully like Mrs. Ruddle to have gone away without hearing the end of the row, when you come to think of it. If you look at the thing in a prejudiced way, all her actions seem odd. And she had it in for Sellon, and sprang it on him beautifully."

"Yes," said Harriet, thoughtfully. "And, you know, she kept on sort of hinting things to me when we were doing the sandwiches for lunch. And she was very artful about refusing to answer Sellon's questions before the Superintendent came. But, honestly, Peter, do you think she and Bert have brains enough between them to work out that business with the keys? And would they have had the sense and self-restraint to keep their hands off the money?"

"Now you're asking something. But one thing I do know. Yesterday afternoon, Bert fetched a long ladder from the outhouse and went up on the roof with Puffett."

"Oh, Peter! so he did!"

"Another good clue gone west. We do at least know

there was a ladder, but how are we to tell now what marks were made when?"

"The trapdoor."

Peter laughed ruefully.

"Puffett informed me when I met them fetching the ladder that Bert had just been up to the roof that way, to see if there was a 'sut-lid' anywhere in the chimney for cleaning the flue. He went up by the Privy Stair and through your bedroom when Miss Twitterton was being questioned down here. Didn't you hear him? You brought Miss Twitterton down, and up he nipped, pronto."

Harriet lit a fresh cigarette.

"Now let's hear the case against Crutchley and the vicar."

"Well—they're a bit more difficult, because of the alibi. Unless one of them was in league with Mrs. Ruddle, we've got to explain away the silence of the wireless. Take Crutchley first. If he did it, we can't very well make up a story about his climbing in at the window, because he couldn't have got there till after Noakes was in bed. He deposited the vicar at the parsonage at 10:30 and was back in Pagford before eleven. There'd be no time for long parleyings at windows and clever business with keys. I'm assuming, of course, that Crutchley's times at the garage have been confirmed; if he's guilty, of course, they will be, because they're part of the plan. If it was Crutchley, it must have been premeditated—which means that he might somehow have stolen a key or had one cut. Very early in the morning is Crutchley's time, I fancy—taking out a taxi for a non-existent customer or something of that kind. He leaves the car somewhere, walks up to the house and lets himself in—um! yes, it's awkward after that. Noakes would be upstairs, undressed and in bed. I can't see the point of it. If he attacked him, it would be to rob him—and he didn't rob him."

"Now it's you who are asking Why. But suppose Crutchley came to rob the house, and was rummaging in a bureau or something—in the kitchen, where the will was found—and Noakes heard him and came downstairs—"

"Stopping to put on his collar and tie, and carefully taking all his precious bank-notes with him?"

"Of course not. In his night-things. He interrupts Crutchley, who goes for him. He runs away, Crutchley hits him, thinks he's dead, gets the wind up and runs off, locking the door after him from outside. Then Noakes comes to, wonders what he's doing down there, goes back to his room, dresses, feels queer, goes towards the back door, meaning to fetch Mrs. Ruddle, and falls down the stairs."

"Excellent. But who made the bed?"

"Oh, bother! Yes—and we haven't explained about the wireless."

"No. My idea was that Crutchley had put the wireless out of action, meaning to establish his alibi for the night before the murder. I meant it to be a murder—but you put me off with your theory about robbing a bureau."

"I'm sorry. I was starting two hares at once. The Crutchley red herring does seem to be rather a mild one. Is the wireless working now, by the way?"

"We'll find out. Supposing it isn't, does that prove anything?"

"Not unless it looks as though it had been deliberately put out of order. I suppose it works from batteries. Nothing's easier than to loosen a terminal in an accidental-looking manner."

"Old Noakes could easily put a thing like that right for himself."

"So he could. Shall I run down and see whether it's working now or not?"

"Ask Bunter. He'll know."

Harriet called down the stairs to Bunter, and returned to say:

"Working perfectly. Bunter tried it yesterday evening after we'd gone."

"Ah! Then that proves nothing, one way or the other. Noakes may have tried to turn it on, failed to spot the trouble till the news-bulletin was over, put it right and left it at that."

"He may have done that in any case."

"And so the time-scheme goes west again."

"This is very discouraging."

"Isn't it? It now leaves the way open for a murderous attack by the vicar, between 10:30 and 11 o'clock."

"Why should the—? Sorry! I keep on asking why."

"There's an awful strain of inquisitiveness on both sides of the family. You'd better reconsider those children, Harriet; they'll be intolerable pests from the cradle."

"So they will. Frightful. All the same, I do think it looks neater to have a comprehensible motive. Murder for the fun of it breaks all the rules of detective fiction."

"All right. Well, then. Mr. Goodacre shall have a motive. I'll think of one presently. He walks over from the vicarage at about 10:35 and knocks at the door. Noakes lets him in—there's no reason why he shouldn't let in the vicar, who has always appeared mild and friendly. But the vicar, underneath his professional austerity, conceals one of those dreadful repressions so common among clergymen as depicted by our realistic novelists. So, of course, does Noakes. The vicar, under cover of a purity campaign, accuses Noakes of corrupting the village maiden whom subconsciously he wants for himself."

"Of course!" said Harriet, cheerfully. "How silly of me not to think of it. Nothing could be more obvious. They have one of those squalid senile rows—and the vicar ends up with a brainstorm and imagines he's the hammer of God, like the parson in Chesterton's story. He lays Noakes out with the poker and departs. Noakes recovers his senses —and we go on from there. That accounts beautifully for the money's having been left on the body; Mr. Goodacre wouldn't want that."

"Exactly. And the reason why the vicar is so pleasant and innocent about it all now, is that the brainstorm has passed, and he has forgotten the whole thing."

"Dissociated personality. I think that's our best effort

yet. We only need now to put a name to the village maiden."

"It need not even be that. The vicar may have had a morbid fancy for something else—a passion *à la* Plato for an aspidistra, or a strange, covetous longing for a cactus. He's a great gardener, you know, and these vegetable and mineral loves can be very sinister indeed. Remember the man in the Eden Philpotts story who set his heart on an iron pineapple and brained a fellow with it? Believe me or believe me not, the vicar came prowling round for no good, and when old Noakes flung himself on his knees, crying, 'Take my life but spare the honor of my cactus!' he upped with the aspidistra-pot—"

"It's all very well, Peter—but the poor old thing was really killed."

"My heart, I know it. But until we find out *how*, one theory's as fanciful as another. We've got to laugh or break our hearts in this damnable world. It makes me sick to think that I didn't go down into the cellar the night we came. We might have made a job of it then, with the place left just as it was, no clues disturbed, no Ruddles and Puffetts and Wimseys tramping round and upsetting everything—My God! that was the worst night's work I ever put in!"

If he had been wanting to make her laugh, this time he succeeded beyond hope or desire.

"It's no good," said Harriet, when she had recovered. "Never, never, never shall we do anything like other people. We shall always laugh when we ought to cry and love when we ought to work, and make ourselves a scandal and a hissing. Don't do that! What ever will Bunter say if he sees you with your hair full of ashes? You'd better finish dressing and face the situation." She wandered back to the window. "Look! there are two men coming up the path, one of them with a camera."

"Hell!"

"I'll go and entertain them."

"Not alone," said Peter, chivalrously; and followed her down.

Bunter, in the doorway, was fighting a desperate verbal battle. "It's no good," said Peter. "Murder will in. Hullo! it's you, Sally, is it? Well, well! Are you sober?"

"Unfortunately," said Mr. Salcombe Hardy, who was a personal friend, "I am. Have you got anything in the place, old man? You owe us something, after the way we were treated on Tuesday."

"Whisky for these gentlemen, Bunter; and put some laudanum in it. Now, children, make it snappy, because the inquest's at eleven and I can't turn up in a dressing-gown. What are you after? Romance in High Life? Or mysterious Death in Honeymoon House?"

"Both," said Mr. Hardy, with a grin. "I suppose we'd better begin by offering our mingled congratulations and condolences. Do we mention that you are both in a state of collapse? Or is the message to the Great British Public that you are marvelously happy in spite of this untoward occurrence?"

"Be original, Sally. Say we are fighting like cat and dog, and only relieved from irritable boredom by the prospect of a little detective occupation."

"That would make a grand story," said Salcombe Hardy, with a regretful shake of the head. "You're conducting an investigation in double harness, I take it?"

"Not at all; the police are doing that. Say when."

"Thanks very much. Well, cheerio! The police, of course, officially. But, dash it all, you must have some personal angle on the thing. Come on, Wimsey, look at it from our point of view. It's the story of the century. Famous amateur sleuth weds mystery-writer, finds corpse on bridal night."

"We didn't. That's the snag."

"Ah! Why, now?"

"Because we had the sweep in next morning and all the clues got destroyed in the muddle," said Harriet. "We'd better tell you, I suppose."

She glanced at Peter, who nodded. "Better we than Mrs. Ruddle," was in both their minds. They told the story as briefly as possible.

"Can I say you've got a theory of the crime?"

"Yes," said Peter.

"Fine!" said Salcombe Hardy.

"My theory is that you put the corpse there yourself, Sally, to make a good headline."

"I only wish I'd thought of it. Nothing else?"

"I tell you," said Peter, "the evidence is destroyed. You can't have a theory without evidence to go on."

"The fact is," said Harriet, "he's completely baffled."

"As baffled as a bathroom geyser," agreed her husband. "My wife's baffled too. It's the only point on which we are at one. When we're tired of heaving crockery about we sit and sneer at one another's bafflement. The police are baffled too. Or else they confidently expect to make an arrest. One or other. You can take your choice."

"Well," said Sally, "it's a devil of a nuisance for you, and I'm a nuisance too, but I can't help myself. D'you mind if we take a photograph? Quaint Tudor farmhouse with genuine rafters—bride delightfully workmanlike in tweed costume and bridegroom in full Sherlock Holmes rig-out—you ought to have a pipe and an ounce of shag."

"Or a fiddle and cocaine? Be quick, Sally, and get it over. And see here, old man—I suppose you've got to earn your living, but for God's sake use a little tact."

Salcombe Hardy, his violet eyes luminous with sincerity, promised that he would. But Harriet felt that the interview had left both her and Peter badly mauled, and that, of the two, Peter had come off the worse. He had picked his words carefully, and his light tone rang brittle as glass. There was going to be more of this—much more. With sudden determination she followed the pressmen out of the room and shut the door.

"Mr. Hardy—listen! I know one's absolutely helpless. One has to put up with what newspapers choose to say. I've reason to know it. I've had it before. But if you put in anything sickening about Peter and me—you know what I mean—any of the sort of things that make one writhe and wish one was dead, it'll be pretty rotten for us and pretty rotten of you. Peter—isn't exactly a rhinoceros, you know."

"My dear Miss Vane—I'm sorry—Lady Peter. . . . Oh, and by the way, I forgot to ask, do you intend to go on writing now you are married?"

"Yes, of course."

"Under the same name?"

"Naturally."

"Can I say that?"

"Oh, yes, you can say that. You can say *anything* except all that awful matrimonial tripe about 'said he with a laughing glance at his brand new wife,' and the rest of the romantic bilge water. I mean, it's all quite trying enough; do leave us a little human dignity, if you possibly can. Look here! If you'll be reasonably restrained, and try to keep the other reporters reasonable, you've much more chance of getting stories out of us. After all, we're both News—and it's no good offending News, is it? Peter's been very decent; he's given you all the facts he can. Don't make his life a burden to him."

"Honestly," said Sally, "I'll try not. But editors are editors—"

"Editors are ghouls and cannibals."

"They are. But I'll really do my best. About this writing story—can you give me anything exclusive on that? Your husband eager you should continue your professional career—that kind of thing? Doesn't think women should be confined to domestic interests? You look forward to getting hints from his experience for use in your detective novels?"

"Oh, damn!" said Harriet. "Must you have the personal angle on everything? Well, I'm certainly going on writing, and he certainly doesn't object—in fact, I think he entirely approves. But don't make him say it with a proud and tender look, or anything sick-making, will you?"

"No, no. Are you writing anything now?"

"No—I've only just finished a book. But I've got a new one in my head. In fact, it's just come there."

"Good!" said Salcombe Hardy.

"It's about the murder of a journalist—and the title is, *Curiosity Killed the Cat.*"

"Fine!" said Sally, quite unperturbed.

"And," said Harriet, as they passed along the path between the chrysanthemums, "we told you that I knew this place when I was a child, but we didn't mention that a dear old couple lived here who used to ask me in and give me seedy-cake and strawberries. That's very pretty and human, and they're dead, so it can't hurt them."

"Splendid!"

"And all the ugly furniture and aspidistras were put there by Noakes, so don't blame us for them. And he was a grasping sort of man, who sold the Tudor chimney-pots to make sundials." Harriet opened the gate and Sally and the photographer walked meekly through.

"And *that,*" continued Harriet, triumphantly, "is somebody's ginger cat. He has adopted us. He sits on Peter's shoulder at breakfast. Everybody likes an animal story. You can have the ginger cat."

She shut the gate and smiled over it at them.

Salcombe Hardy reflected that Peter Wimsey's wife was almost handsome when she was excited. He sympathized with her anxiety about Peter's feelings. He really thought she must be fond of the old blighter. He was deeply moved, for the whisky had been generously measured. He determined to do all he could to keep the human story dignified.

Half way down the lane, he remembered that he had somehow omitted to interview the servants. He looked back; but Harriet was still leaning over the gate.

Mr. Hector Puncheon of the *Morning Star* was less lucky. He arrived five minutes after Salcombe Hardy's departure, and found Lady Peter Wimsey still leaning over the gate. Since he could scarcely force his way past her, he was obliged to take his story then and there, as she chose to give it to him. Half way through, he felt something blow warmly upon his neck, and turned round with a start.

"It's only a bull," said Harriet, sweetly.

Mr. Puncheon, who was town-bred, turned pale. The bull was accompanied by six cows, all inquisitive. Had he known it, their presence was the best guarantee of the bull's good conduct; but to him they were all, equally, large beasts with horns. He could not with courtesy drive them away, because Lady Peter was thoughtfully scratching the bull's forehead while contributing some interesting and exclusive details about her own early life at Great Pagford. Manfully—for a reporter must accept all risks in the execution of his duty—he stuck to his post, listening with (he could not help it) a divided attention. "You are fond of animals?" he inquired. "Oh, very," said Harriet; "you must tell your readers that; it's a sympathetic trait, isn't it?" "Sure thing," replied Hector Puncheon. All very well; but the bull was on his side of the gate and she was on the other. A friendly cow all red and white licked his ear—he was astonished to find its tongue so rough.

"You'll excuse my not opening the gate," said Harriet, with an engaging smile. "I love cows—but not in the garden." To his embarrassment, she climbed over and escorted him with a firm hand to his car. The interview was over, and he had had very little opportunity of getting a personal angle on the murder. The cows scattered, with lowered heads, from before his moving wheels.

By a remarkable coincidence, no sooner had he gone than the invisible guardian of the cattle rose up from nowhere and began to collect the herd. On seeing Harriet, he grinned and touched his cap. She strolled back to the house, and before she had got there the cows were gathered round the gate again. At the open kitchen window stood Bunter, polishing glasses.

"Rather convenient," said Harriet, "all those cows in the lane."

"Yes, my lady," agreed Bunter demurely. "They graze

upon the grass verge, I understand. A very satisfactory arrangement if I may say so."

Harriet opened her mouth, and shut it again as a thought struck her. She went down the passage and opened the back door. She was not really surprised to see an extraordinarily ugly bull-mastiff tied by a rope to the scraper. Bunter came out of the kitchen and padded softly into the scullery.

"Is that our dog, Bunter?"

"The owner brought him this morning, my lady, to inquire whether his lordship might desire to purchase an animal of that description. I understand he is an excellent watchdog. I suggested that he should be left here to await his lordship's convenience."

Harriet looked at Bunter, who returned her gaze unmoved.

"Have you thought of airplanes, Bunter? We might put a swan on the roof."

"I have not been able to hear of a swan, my lady. But there is a person who owns a goat. . . ."

"Mr. Hardy was rather fortunate."

"The cattle driver," said Bunter, with sudden wrath, "was late. His instructions were perfectly clear. The lost time will be deducted from his remuneration. We must not be paltered with. His lordship is not accustomed to it. Excuse me, my lady—the goat is just arriving, and I fear there may be a little difficulty with the dog on the doorstep."

Harriet left him to it.

CHAPTER XIV

CROWNER'S QUEST

Love? Do I love? I walk
Within the brilliance of another's thought,
As in a glory. I was dark before,
As Venus' chapel in the black of night:
But there was something holy in the darkness,
Softer and not so thick as other where;
And as rich moonlight may be to the blind,
Unconsciously consoling. Then love came,
Like the out-bursting of a trodden star.

—THOMAS LOVELL BEDDOES,
THE SECOND BROTHER

The coroner did not, after all, confine himself to taking evidence of identity; but he showed a laudable discretion in handling his witnesses. Miss Twitterton, in a brand-new black frock, a perky little close-fitting hat and a black coat of old-fashioned cut, clearly resurrected for the occasion, testified, with sniffs, that the body was that of her uncle, William Noakes, and that she had not seen him since the last Sunday week. She explained her uncle's habit of dividing his time between Broxford and Paggleham, and about the two sets of keys. Her endeavors to explain also about the sale of the house and the astonishing financial situation disclosed were kindly but firmly cut short, and Lord Peter Wimsey, in act more graceful, took her place and gave a brief and rather nonchalant *résumé* of his surprising wedding-night experiences. He handed the coroner various papers concerning the purchase of the house and sat down amid a murmur of sympathetic comment. Then came an accountant from Broxford, with a statement about the moribund condition of the wireless business, as revealed by a preliminary examination of the books. Mervyn Bunter, in well-chosen language, recounted the visit of the sweep and the subsequent discovery of the body. Dr. Craven spoke to the cause and probable time of death, described the injuries, and gave it as his opinion that they could not have been self-inflicted or produced by an accidental fall.

Next came Joe Sellon, very white in the face, but in official control of himself. He said he had been summoned to see the dead body, and described how it lay in the cellar.

"You are the village constable?"

"Yes, sir."

"When did you last see the deceased alive?"

"On the Wednesday night, sir, at five minutes past nine."

"Will you tell us about that?"

"Yes, sir. I had a certain matter of a private nature to discuss with the deceased. I proceeded to the house and spoke to him at the sitting-room window for about ten minutes."

"Did he then seem just as usual?"

"Yes, sir; except that words passed between us and he was a little excited. When we had finished our conversation he shut and bolted the window. I tried both doors and found them locked. I then went away."

"You did not enter the house?"

"No, sir."

"And you left him at 9:15 p.m., alive and well?"

"Yes, sir."

"Very well."

Joe Sellon turned to go; but the lugubrious man whom Bunter had met in the pub rose up from among the jury and said:

"We should like to ask the witness, Mr. Perkins, what he had words with the deceased about."

"You hear," said the coroner, slightly put out. "The jury wish to know the cause of your dispute with the deceased."

"Yes, sir. The deceased threatened to report me for a breach of duty."

"Ah!" said the coroner. "Well, we are not here to examine into your official conduct. It was he that threatened you, not you that threatened him?"

"That's right, sir; though I admit I was annoyed and spoke a bit sharp to him."

"I see. You did not return to the house that night?"

"No, sir."

"Very well; that will do. Superintendent Kirk."

The little stir of excitement aroused by Sellon's evidence died down before the enormous impassivity of Mr. Kirk, who described, very slowly and at considerable length, the arrangement of the rooms in the house, the nature of the fastenings on the doors and windows and the difficulty of ascertaining the facts due to the (quite fortuitous though very unfortunate) disturbance caused by the arrival of the new occupiers. The next witness was Martha Ruddle. She was in a great state of excitement, and almost excessively ready to assist the law. It was, indeed, her own readiness that undid her.

". . . that taken aback," said Mrs. Ruddle, "you could a-knocked me down with a feather. Driving up to the door in the middle of the night as you might say, in sech a big motorcar as I never did see in all my born days, not without it was on the picturs—Lord what? I says, not believing him, which I'm sure, sir, it ain't surprising, more like filmstars I says, begging your pardon, and of course I were mistook, but that there car being so big and the lady in a fur coat and the gentleman with a glass in his eye jest like Ralph Lynn, which was all I could see in the—"

Peter turned the monocle on the witness with so outraged an astonishment that the giggles turned to loud laughter.

"Kindly keep to the question," said Mr. Perkins, vexed; "you were surprised to hear that the house was sold. Very well. We have heard how you got in. Will you please describe the condition of the house as you observed it."

From a tangle of irrelevancies, the coroner disengaged the facts that the bed had not been slept in, that the supper things were on the table, and that the cellar-door had been found open. With a weary sigh (for his cold was a severe one and he wanted to finish and get home), he took the witness back to the events of the preceding Wednesday.

"Yes," said Mrs. Ruddle, "I did see Joe Sellon, and a nice sorter pleeceman 'e is, usin' language not fit for a respectable woman to listen to, I don't wonder Mr. Noakes shet the window in 'is face. . . ."

"You saw him do that?"

"Plain as the nose on your face, I see 'im. Standin' there 'e was with the candlestick in 'is 'and, same as I couldn't miss seein' 'im, and laffin' fit to bust, and well 'e might, 'earin' Joe Sellon carryin' on that ridiculous. Well, I says to meself, a nice pleeceman you are, Joe Sellon, and I oughter know it, seein' you 'ad ter come ter me to find out 'oo took them 'ens of Miss Twitterton's. . . ."

"We are not inquiring into that," began the coroner, when the lugubrious man again rose up and said:

"The jury would like to know whether the witness heard what the quarrel was about."

"Yes, I did," said the witness, without waiting for the coroner. "They was quarrellin' about 'is wife, that's what they was quarrellin' about, and I say it's a—"

"Whose wife?" asked the coroner; while the whole room rustled with expectation.

"Joe's wife, o'course," said Mrs. Ruddle. "What 'ave you done wi' my wife, you old villain, 'e says, usin' names wot I wouldn't put me tongue to."

Joe Sellon sprang to his feet.

"That's a lie, sir!"

"Now, Joe," said Kirk.

"We'll hear you in a moment," said Mr. Perkins. "Now, Mrs. Ruddle. You're sure you heard those words?"

"The bad words, sir?"

"The words, 'What have you done with my wife'?"

"Oh, yes, sir—I heard that, sir."

"Did any threats pass?"

"N'no, sir," admitted Mrs. Ruddle, regretfully, "only sayin' as Mr. Noakes was bound for the bad place, sir."

"Quite so. No suggestions about how he was likely to get there?"

"Sir?"

"No mention of killing or murder?"

"Not as I 'eard, sir, but I wouldn't be surprised if 'e did offer to kill Mr. Noakes. Not a bit, I wouldn't."

"But actually you heard nothing of the sort?"

"Well, I couldn't rightly say I did, sir."

"And Mr. Noakes was alive and well when he shut the window?"

"Yes, sir."

Kirk leaned across the table and spoke to the coroner, who asked:

"Did you hear anything further?"

"I didn't *want* to 'ear nothing further, sir. All I 'eard was that Joe Sellon a-'ammerin' on the door."

"Did you hear Mr. Noakes let him in?"

"Let 'im in?" cried Mrs. Ruddle. "Wot 'ud Mr. Noakes want ter be lettin' 'im in for? Mr. Noakes wouldn't let nobody in wot used language to 'im like wot Joe used. 'E was a terrible timid man, was Mr. Noakes."

"I see. And the next morning you came to the house and got no answer?"

"That's right. And I says, lor', I says, Mr. Noakes must a-gone over to Broxford. . . ."

"Yes; you told us that before. And although you had heard all this terrible quarrel the night before, it never occurred to you that anything might have happened to Mr. Noakes?"

"Well, no, I didn't. I thought 'e'd gone off to Broxford, same as 'e often did. . . ."

"Quite. In fact, until Mr. Noakes was found dead, you thought nothing of this quarrel and attached no importance to it?"

"Well," said Mrs. Ruddle, "only w'en I knowed as 'e must a-died afore 'ar-pas'-nine."

"How did you know that?"

Mrs. Ruddle, with many circumlocutions, embarked upon the story of the wireless. Peter Wimsey wrote a few lines on a scrap of paper, which he folded and passed to Kirk. The Superintendent nodded, and passed it on to the coroner, who, at the conclusion of the story, asked:

"Wireless was Mr. Noakes's business?"

"Oh, yes, sir."

"If anything had gone wrong with the set, could he have put it right?"

"Oh, yes, sir. 'E was very clever with them things."

"But he only cared to listen to the news-bulletin?"

"That's right, sir."

"What time did he usually go to bed?"

"Eleven o'clock, sir. Reg'lar as clockwork 'e was, supper at 'ar-pas'-seven, Noos at 'ar-pas'-nine, bed at eleven, w'en 'e wos at 'ome, that is."

"Quite. How did you come to be near enough at half past nine to know whether the wireless was on?"

Mrs. Ruddle hesitated.

"I jest stepped over to the shed, sir."

"Yes?"

"Jest ter fetch something, sir."

"Yes?"

"Only a mite o' paraffin, sir," said Mrs. Ruddle, "which I'd a-put it back faithful in the morning, sir."

"Ah, yes. Well, that's none of our business. Thank you. Now, Joseph Sellon—you want to make a further statement?"

"Yes, sir. Only this, sir. Them words about Mrs. Sellon wasn't never mentioned at all. I might a-said, 'Now, don't you report me, sir, or I'll be in trouble, and what'll become of my wife?' That's all, sir."

"The deceased never interfered with your wife in any way?"

"No, sir. Certainly not, sir."

"I think I had better ask you whether the last witness bears you any grudge, to your knowledge."

"Well, sir, about them 'ens o' Miss Twitterton's. In the execution of my duty I 'ad to interrogate 'er son Albert, and I think she took it amiss, sir."

"I see. I think that's—Yes, Superintendent?"

Mr. Kirk had just received another message from his noble colleague. It appeared to perplex him; but he faithfully put the question.

"Well," said Mr. Perkins, "I should have thought you could have asked him yourself. However. The Superintendent wishes to know the length of the candle deceased had in his hand when he came to the window."

Joe Sellon stared.

"I don't know, sir," he said, finally. "I never noticed. I don't think it was special one way or the other."

The coroner turned interrogatively to Kirk, who, not knowing what was behind the question, shook his head.

Mr. Perkins, blowing his nose irritably, dismissed the witness and turned to the jury.

"Well, gentlemen, I don't see that we can finish this inquiry today. You see that it is impossible to fix the exact moment when deceased met his death, since he may have been prevented from hearing the news bulletin by a temporary defect in the wireless apparatus, which he may have subsequently repaired. You have heard that the police are in a considerable difficulty as regards the collecting of evidence, since (by a most unfortunate accident for which nobody is at all to blame) various possible clues were destroyed. I understand that the police would like an adjournment—is that so?"

Kirk said that it was so; and the coroner adjourned the

inquiry to that day fortnight, thus putting a tame end to a very promising affair.

As the audience scrambled from the little court, Kirk caught Peter.

"That old catamaran!" he said, angrily. "Mr. Perkins came down pretty sharp on her, but if he'd listened to me, he wouldn't have taken any evidence, only to identity."

"You think that would have been wise? To let her put her story all round the village, and everybody saying you didn't dare to let it come out at the inquest? He did at least give her the opportunity for an open display of spite. I think he's done better for you than you realize."

"Maybe you're right, my lord. I didn't see it that way. What was the point about that candle?"

"I wondered how much he really did remember. If he's not sure about the candle, he may only have imagined the clock."

"That's so," said Kirk, slowly. He was not sure about the implications of this. Nor, to tell the truth, was Wimsey.

"He might," Harriet suggested softly in her husband's ear, "have lied about the time."

"So he might. The queer thing is that he didn't. Mrs. Ruddle's clock said the same."

"Hawkshaw the Detective, in *Who Put Back the Clock?*"

"Here!" said Kirk, exasperated; "look at that!"

Peter looked. Mrs. Ruddle, on the doorstep, was holding a kind of court among the reporters.

"Goodness!" said Harriet. "Peter, can't you take them away? Who was the chap who leapt into the gulf?"

"Rome prizes most her citizens—"

"But every Englishman loves a lord. That's the idea."

"My wife," said Peter mournfully, "would cheerfully throw me to the lions, if required. *Moriturus*—very well, we'll try."

He advanced resolutely on the group. Mr. Puncheon, seeing this noble prey at his mercy, unprotected by fat bulls of Basan, flung himself upon him with a gleeful cry. The other hounds closed in about them.

"I say," said a grumbling voice close by, "I ought to 'ave given evidence. The law ought to know about them forty quid. Trying to 'ush it up, that's what they are."

"I don't suppose it seems so important to them, Frank."

"It's important to me. 'Sides, didn't 'e tell me as 'e was goin' to pay me on Wednesday? I reckon the coroner ought to a-been told about it."

Salcombe Hardy, having had his chance with Peter, had not abandoned his hold on Mrs. Ruddle. Mischievously, Harriet determined to pry him loose.

"Mr. Hardy—if you want an inside story, you'd better get hold of the gardener, Frank Crutchley. There he is, over there, talking to Miss Twitterton. He wasn't called at the inquest, so the others may not realize he's got anything to tell them."

Sally bubbled over with gratitude.

"If you make it worth his while," said Harriet, with serpent malice, "he *might* keep it exclusive."

"Thanks very much," said Sally, "for the tip."

"That's part of our bargain," said Harriet, beaming upon him. Mr. Hardy was rapidly coming to the conclusion that Peter had married a most fascinating woman. He made a rapid dart at Crutchley and in a few moments was seen to depart with him in the direction of the Four-Ale bar. Mrs. Ruddle, suddenly deserted, gazed indignantly about her.

"Oh, *there* you are, Mrs. Ruddle! Where's Bunter? We'd better let him drive us home and come back for his lordship, or we shall get no lunch. I'm simply starving. What an impertinent, tiresome lot these newspaper men are!"

"That's right, m'lady," said Mrs. Ruddle. "I wouldn't talk to the likes of them!"

She tossed her head, setting some curious jet ornaments on her bonnet jingling, and followed her mistress to the car. Sitting up in all that grandeur she would feel just like a film star herself. Reporters, indeed!

As they drove away, six cameras clicked.

"There now," said Harriet. "You'll be in all the papers."

"Well, to be sure!" said Mrs. Ruddle.

• • • • •

"Peter."

"Madam?"

"Funny, after what we said, that suggestion cropping up about Mrs. Sellon."

"Village matron instead of village maiden. Yes; very odd."

"There can't be anything in it?"

"You never know."

"You didn't think so when you said it?"

"I am always trying to say something too silly to be believed; but I never manage it. Have another cutlet?"

"Thanks, I will. Bunter cooks like an angel in the house. I thought Sellon got through his examination surprisingly well."

"Nothing like telling the exact official truth and no more. Kirk must have coached him pretty thoroughly. I wonder if Kirk—No, dash it! I won't wonder. I won't be bothered with all these people. We seem curiously unable to get any time to ourselves this honeymoon. And that reminds me—the vicar wants us to go round to his place this evening for a sherry-party."

"A sherry-party? Good heavens!"

"We provide the party and he provides the sherry. His wife will be so delighted to see us, and will we excuse her not calling first, as she has a Women's Institute this afternoon."

"Must we?"

"I think we must. Our example has encouraged him to start a sherry-fashion in these parts, and he has sent for a bottle on purpose."

Harried gazed at him in dismay.

"Where from?"

"From the best hotel in Pagford. . . . I accepted with pleasure for both of us. Was that wrong?"

"Peter, you're not *normal*. You have a social conscience far in advance of your sex. Public-house sherry at the vicarage! Ordinary, decent men shuffle and lie till their wives drag them out by the ears. There must be *something* you'll jib at. Will you refuse to put on a boiled shirt?"

"Do you think a boiled shirt would please them? I suppose it would. Besides, you've got a new frock you want to show me."

"You're definitely too good to live. . . . Of course we'll go and drink their sherry, if we die of it. But couldn't we just be selfish and naughty this afternoon?"

"As how?"

"Go off somewhere by ourselves."

"By God, we will! . . . Is that really your notion of happiness?"

"To that depth have I fallen. I admit it. Don't dance on a woman when she's down. Have some of this—I don't know what it is—this thing Bunter's made. It looks absolutely marvelous."

"Just how naughty and selfish may I be? . . . May I drive fast? . . . I mean, really fast?"

Harriet repressed a shudder. She liked to drive, and even liked being driven, but anything over seventy miles an hour made her feel hollow inside. Still, married people cannot have everything their own way.

"Yes, really fast—if you feel like that."

"Definitely too good to live!"

"I should say, definitely too good to die. . . . But really fast means the main road."

"So it does. Well, we'll do the main road really fast and get rid of it."

The ordeal lasted only as far as Great Pagford. Happily they encountered none of Superintendent Kirk's black sheep parked on bends, though, just outside, they shot past Frank Crutchley driving a taxi and were rewarded by his astonished and admiring stare. Passing the police station at a demure legal thirty, they turned out westward and took to the sideroads. Harriet, who could not distinctly recollect having breathed at all since they left Paggleham, filled her lungs and observed in resolutely steady tones that it was a lovely day for a run.

"Isn't it? Do you approve of this road?"

"It's beautiful," said Harriet, fervently. "*All* corners!" He laughed.

"*Prière de ne pas brutaliser la machine*. I ought to know better—God knows I'm frightened of enough things myself. I must have a streak of my father in me. He was one of the old school—you either faced a fence of your own accord or were walloped over and no nonsense. It worked—after a fashion. One learned to pretend one wasn't a coward, and take out the change in bad dreams."

"You certainly don't show any signs of it."

"One of these days you'll find me out, I expect. I don't happen to be afraid of speed—that's why I like to show off. But I give you my word I won't do it again, this trip."

He let the needle drop back to twenty-five and they dawdled on through the lanes in silence, with no particular direction. About the mid afternoon, they found themselves in a village some thirty miles from home—an old village with a new church and a pond flanking a trim central green, all clustered at the base of a little rise. On a side opposite the church, a narrow and rather ill-made lane appeared to rise towards the brow of the hill.

"Let's go up there," said Harriet, appealed to for instructions. "It looks as though we should get a good view."

The car swung into the lane and wound its way up with lazy ease between low hedges already touched with autumn. Below and to their left was spread the pleasant English country, green and russet with well-wooded fields sloping to a stream that twinkled placidly in the October sunshine. Here and there the pale glint of stubble showed amid the pasture; or the blue smoke drifted above the trees from the red chimneys of a farm. On their right, at a bend of the road, they came upon a ruined church, only the porch and a portion of the chancel arch left standing. The other stone-work had doubtless been carried away to build the new church in the center of the village; but the abandoned graves with their ancient headstones had been trimly kept, and just within the open gate a space had been leveled and made into a kind of garden plot with flower beds and a sundial and a wooden seat on which visitors could rest to view the distant prospect. Peter gave an exclamation, and let the car slide to a standstill on the grass verge.

"May I lose my last dollar," he said, "if that isn't one of our chimney-pots!"

"I believe you're right," said Harriet, staring at the sundial, whose column did indeed bear a remarkable resemblance to a "Tooder pot." She followed Peter out of the car and through the gate. Seen close to, the sundial revealed itself as a miscellany; the dial and gnomon were ancient; the base was a millstone; the column, when sharply tapped, sounded hollow.

"I will have my pot back," said Peter in determined tones, "if I die for it. We will present the village with a handsome stone pillar in its place. Jack shall have Jill, Nought shall go ill, the man shall have his mare again and all go well. This suggests a new variation of the time-honored sport of pot-hunting. We will track down our bartered chimneys from end to end of the county, as the Roman legions sought the lost eagles of Varus. I think the luck went out of the house with the chimney-pots, and it's our job to bring it back."

"That will be fun. I counted this morning: there are only four of them missing. This looks exactly like the three that are left."

"I'm positive it is ours. Something tells me so. Let us register our claim to it by a trifling act of vandalism which the first rain will blot out." He solemnly took out a pencil and inscribed upon the pot: "Talboys, *Suam quisque homo rem meminit*. Peter Wimsey." He handed the pencil to his wife, who added, "Harriet Wimsey," with the date below.

"First time of writing it?"

"Yes. It looks a little drunk, but that's because I had to squat down to it."

"No matter—it's an occasion. Let's occupy this handsome seat and contemplate the landscape. The car's well off the road if anybody wants to get up the lane."

The seat was solid and comfortable. Harriet pulled off her hat and sat down, pleased to feel the soft wind stir her hair. Her gaze wandered idly over the sunlit valley. Peter hung his hat on the extended hand of a stout eighteenth-century cherub engaged in perusing a lichenous book on an adjacent tombstone, sat down on the other end of the seat and stared reflectively at his companion.

His spirits were in a state of confusion, into which the discovery of the murder and the problem of Joe Sellon and the clock had introduced only a subsidiary set of disturbing factors. These he dismissed from his mind, and set himself to reduce the chaos of his personal emotions to some sort of order.

He had got what he wanted. For nearly six years he directed his resolution stubbornly to a single end. Up to the very moment of achievement he had not paused to consider what might be the results of his victory. The last two days had given him little time for thought. He only knew that he was faced with an entirely strange situation, which was doing something quite extraordinary to his feelings.

He forced himself to examine his wife with detachment. Her face had character, but no one would ever think of calling it beautiful, and he had always—carelessly and condescendingly—demanded beauty as a prerequisite. She was long-limbed and sturdily made, with a kind of loosely-knit freedom of movement that might, with a more controlled assurance, grow into grace; yet he could have named—and if he had chosen might have had—a score of women far lovelier in form and motion. Her speaking voice was deep and attractive; yet, after all, he had once owned the finest lyric soprano in Europe. Otherwise, what?—A skin like pale honey and a mind of a curious, tough quality that stimulated his own. Yet no woman had ever so stirred his blood; she had only to look or speak to make the very bones shake in his body.

He knew now that she could render back passion for passion with an eagerness beyond all expectation—and also with a kind of astonished gratitude that told him more than she knew. While a mannerly reticence forbade that the name of her dead lover should ever be mentioned between them, Peter, interpreting phenomena in the light of expert knowledge, found himself mentally applying to that unhappy young man quite a number of epithets, among which "clumsy lout" and "egotistical puppy" were the kindest. But the passionate exchange of felicity was no new experience: what was new was the enormous importance of the whole relationship. It was not merely that the present bond could not be sundered without scandal and expense and the troublesome interference of lawyers. It was that, for the first time in his experience, it really mattered to him what his relations with a lover were. He had somehow vaguely imagined that, the end of desire attained, soul and sense would lie down together like the lion and the lamb; but they did nothing of the sort. With orb and scepter thrust into his hands, he was afraid to take hold on power and call his empire his own.

He remembered having said to his uncle (with a solemn dogmatism better befitting a much younger man): "Surely it is possible to love with the head as well as the heart." Mr. Delagardie had replied, somewhat drily: "No doubt; so long as you do not end by thinking with your entrails instead of your brain." This, he felt, was precisely what was happening to him. As soon as he tried to think, a soft, inexorable clutch seemed to fasten itself upon his bowels. He had become vulnerable in the very point where always, until now, he had been most triumphantly sure of himself. His wife's serene face told him that she had somehow gained all the confidence he had lost. Before their marriage, he had never seen her look like that.

"Harriet," he said, suddenly, "what do you think about life? I mean, do you find it good on the whole. Worth living?"

(He could, at any rate, trust her not to protest, archly: "That's a nice thing to ask on one's honeymoon!")

She turned to him with a quick readiness, as though here was the opportunity to say something she had been wanting to say for a long time:

"Yes! I've always felt absolutely certain it was good—if only one could get it straightened out. I've hated almost everything that ever happened to me, but I *knew* all the time it was just things that were wrong, not everything. Even when I felt most awful I never thought of killing myself or wanting to die—only of somehow getting out of the mess and starting again."

"That's rather admirable. With me it's always been the other way round. I can enjoy practically everything that comes along—while it's happening. Only I have to keep on doing things, because, if I once stop, it all seems a lot of rot and I don't care a damn if I go west tomorrow. At least, that's what I should have said. Now—I don't know. I'm beginning to think there may be something in it after all . . . Harriet—"

"It sounds like Jack Sprat and his wife."

"If there was any possible chance of straightening it out for *you*. . . . We've begun well, haven't we, with this awful bloody mess? When once we get clear of it, I'd give anything. But there you are, you see, it's the same thing over again."

"But that's what I'm trying to tell you. It ought to be, but it isn't. Things have come straight. I always knew they would if one hung on long enough, waiting for a miracle."

"Honestly, Harriet?"

"Well, it *seems* like a miracle to be able to look forward—to—to see all the minutes in front of one come hopping along with something marvelous in them, instead of just saying, Well, that one didn't actually hurt and the next may be quite bearable if only something beastly doesn't come pouncing out—"

"As bad as that?"

"No, not really, because one got used to it—to being

everlastingly tightened up to face things, you see. But when one doesn't have to any more, it's different—I can't tell you what a difference it makes. You—you—you—Oh, damn and blast you, Peter, you *know* you're making me feel exactly like Heaven, so what's the sense of trying to spare your feelings?"

"I don't know it and I can't believe it, but come here and I'll try. That's better." His chin was pressed upon her head when the sword came back from the sea. "No, you are not too heavy—you needn't insult me. Listen, dear, if that's true or even half true, I shall begin to be afraid of death. At my age it's rather disturbing. All right—you needn't apologize. I like new sensations."

Women had found paradise in his arms before now—and told him so, with considerable emphasis and eloquence. He had accepted the assurance cheerfully, because he had not really cared whether they found paradise or only the Champs Elysées, so long as the place was a pleasant one. He was as much troubled and confused now as though somebody had credited him with the possession of a soul. In strict logic, of course, he would have had to admit that he had as much right to a soul as anybody else, but the mocking analogy of the camel and the needle's eye was enough to make that claim stick in his throat as a silly piece of presumption. Of such was not the kingdom of heaven. He had the kingdoms of the earth, and they should be enough for him: though nowadays it was in better taste to pretend neither to desire nor deserve them. But he was filled with a curious misgiving, as though he had meddled in matters too high for him; as though he were being forced, body and bones, through some enormous wringer that was squeezing out of him something undifferentiated till now, and even now excessively nebulous and inapprehensible. *Vagula, blandula,* he thought—pleasantly erratic and surely of no consequence—it couldn't possibly turn into something that had to be reckoned with. He made the mental gesture of waving away an intrusive moth, and tightened his bodily hold on his wife as though to remind himself of the palpable presence of the flesh. She responded with a small contented sound like a snort—an absurd sound that seemed to lift the sealing stone and release some well-spring of laughter deep down within him. It came bubbling and leaping up in the most tremendous hurry to reach the sunlight, so that all his blood danced with it and his lungs were stifled with the rush and surge of this extraordinary fountain of delight. He felt himself at once ridiculous and omnipotent. He was exultant. He wanted to shout.

Actually, he neither moved nor spoke. He sat still, letting the mysterious rapture have its way with him. Whatever it was, it was something that had been suddenly liberated and was intoxicated by its new freedom. It was behaving very foolishly and its folly enchanted him.

"Peter?"

"What is it, lady?"

"Have I got any money?"

The preposterous irrelevance of the question made the fountain shoot sky-high.

"My darling, fool, yes, of course you have. We spent a whole morning signing papers."

"Yes, I know, but where is it? I mean, can I draw a check on it? I was thinking, I'd never paid my secretary her salary and at the moment I haven't got a penny in the world except what's yours."

"It isn't mine, it's your own. Settled on you. Murbles explained all that, though I don't suppose you were listening. But I know what you mean, and yes, it's there, and yes, you can draw a check on it straight away. Why this state of sudden destitution?"

"Because, Mr. Rochester, I wasn't going to be married in grey alpaca. And I spent every blessed thing I had to do you proud, and then some. I left poor Miss Bracey lamenting *and* borrowed ten bob of her at the last minute for enough petrol to get me to Oxford. That's right, laugh! I did kill my pride—but, oh, Peter! it had a lovely death."

"Full sacrificial rites. Harriet, I really believe you love

me. You couldn't do anything so unutterably and divinely right by accident. *Quelle folie—mais quel geste!*"

"I thought it would amuse you. That's why I told you instead of borrowing a stamp from Bunter and writing a formal inquiry to the bank."

"Meaning that you don't grudge me my victory. Generous woman! While you're about it, tell me something else. How the blazes, with all the other things, did you manage to afford the Donne autograph?"

"That was a special effort. Three five-thousand-word shorts at forty guineas each for the *Thrill Magazine*."

"What? the story about the young man who murdered his aunt with a boomerang?"

"Yes; and the unpleasant stockbroker who was found in the curate's front parlor with his head bashed in, like old Noakes—Oh, dear! I was forgetting all about poor Mr. Noakes."

"Damn old Noakes! At least, perhaps I'd better not say that. It might be true. I remember the curate. What was the third? The cook who put prussic acid in the almond icing?"

"Yes. Where did you get hold of that exceedingly low class rag? Does Bunter pore over it in his leisure moments?"

"No; he reads photographic journals. But there are such things as press cutting agencies."

"Are there, indeed? How long have you been collecting cuttings?"

"Nearly six years, isn't it, by now? They lead a shamefaced existence in a locked drawer, and Bunter pretends to know nothing about them. When some impertinent beast of a boneheaded reviewer has turned me dyspeptic with fury, he politely attributes my ill-temper to the inclement season. Your turn to laugh. I had to be maudlin over something, curse it, and you didn't overwhelm me with material. I once lived three weeks on a belated notice in *Punch*. Brute, fiend, devil-woman—you might say you're sorry."

"I can't be sorry for anything. I've forgotten how."

He was silent. The fountain had become a stream that

ran chuckling and glittering through his consciousness, spreading as it went into a wide river that swept him up and drowned him in itself. To speak of it was impossible; he could only have taken refuge in inanities. His wife looked at him, thoughtfully drew her feet up on to the seat so as to take her weight from his knees and settled herself into acquiescence with his mood.

Whether, left to themselves, they would have succeeded in emerging from this speechless trance, and might not, in the manner of Donne's ecstatic couple, have remained like sepulchral statues in the same posture and saying nothing until nightfall, is uncertain. Three quarters of an hour later an elderly bearded person came creaking up the lane with a horse and wagon. He looked at them with ruminative eyes, showing no particular curiosity; but the spell was broken. Harriet swung herself hurriedly off her husband's knees and stood up; Peter, who in London would rather have been seen dead than embracing anybody in public, astonishingly showed no embarrassment, but cried out a cordial greeting to the carter.

"Is my bus in your way?"

"No, sir, thank 'ee. Don't disturb yourself."

"Lovely day it's been." He strolled down to the gate, and the man checked his horse.

"That it has. A real lovely day."

"Pleasant little spot, this. Who put up the seat?"

"That's squire done that, sir; Mr. Trevor over at the big house. He done it along of the women as likes to come up Sunday arternoons with their flowers and such. The new church ain't only been built five year, and there's a sight of folks likes to 'tend to the graves in the old churchyard. It's closed for buryings now, of course, but squire says, why not make it pleasant and comfor'ble-like. It's a stiffish pull up the lane and weariful to the children and the old people. So that's what he done."

"We are very much beholden to him. Was the sundial here before that?"

The carter chuckled.

"Lord love you, no, sir. She's a regular job, is that there sundial. Vicar, he found the top of her put away in the rubbish-'ole when they was clearing away the old church, and Bill Muggins he says, 'There's the stone outer the old mill 'ud make a beautiful base for 'er, if so be we 'ad a bit of a drainpipe or summat to put between 'em.' And Jim Hawtrey, *he* says, 'I know a man,' he says, 'over at Paggleham wot 'as 'arf-a-dozen of them ancient old chimbley-pots for sale. What's the matter with that?' So they tells vicar and he tells squire and they gets the bits together and Joe Dudden and 'Arry Gates, they puts 'em up with a lick o' mortar in their spare time, vicar puttin' the top on with 'is watch in 'is 'and a little book so she'll tell the time correct. You'll find 'er middlin' right now, sir, if you look. 'Course, in summer she's an hour out, her keepin' to God's time and us 'aving to go by Gov'ment time. It's a cur'ous thing you askin' about that there sundial, because why? The very man wot sold vicar the chimbley-pot, 'e wos found dead in his own 'ouse only yesterday, and they do say it was murder."

"You don't say so. It's a queer world, isn't it? What's the name of this village? Lopsley? Thanks very much. Get yourself a drink. . . . By the way, you know you've got a loose shoe on your near hind?"

The carter said he had not noticed it and thanked the observant gentleman for his information. The horse lolloped on.

"Time we were getting back," said Peter, with a reluctant note in his voice, "if we're to change in time for the vicar's sherry. We'll call on the squire, though, before we're many days older. I'm determined to have that pot."

CHAPTER XV

SHERRY—AND BITTERS

Fool, hypocrite, villain—man! Thou canst not call me that.

—GEORGE LILLO, *TRAGEDY OF GEORGE BARNWELL*

Harriet was glad they had taken the trouble to dress. The vicar's wife (whom she vaguely remembered to have seen in the old days at bazaars and flower shows, perpetually stout, amiable and a little red in the face) had done honor to the occasion with a black lace dress and a daring little bridge coat in flowered chiffon velvet. She advanced with a beaming face to meet them.

"You poor things! What an upset for you! It is so nice of you to come and see us. I hope Simon apologized for my not calling, but what with my house and the parish work and the Women's Institute I was quite busy all day. Do come and sit down by the fire. *You*, of course, are an old friend, my dear, though I don't suppose you remember me. Let my husband help you off with your coat. *What* a pretty frock! Such a lovely color. I hope you don't mind my saying so. I do so love to see bright colors and bright faces about me. Come and sit on the sofa, against this green cushion—you'll make quite a picture. . . . No, no, Lord Peter, don't sit on that! It's a rocking-chair; it always takes people by surprise. Most men like *this* one, it's nice and deep. Now, Simon, where did you put those cigarettes?"

"Here they are, here they are. I hope they're the kind you like. I'm a pipe-smoker myself and not very knowledgeable, I fear. Oh, thank you, thank you, no—not a pipe just before dinner. I will try a cigarette, just for a change. Now, my dear, will you join us in this little dissipation?"

"Well, I don't *usually*," said Mrs. Goodacre, "because of the parish, you know. It's very absurd, but one has to set an example."

"These particular parishoners," said Peter, striking a match persuasively, "are corrupted already beyond hope of repentance."

"Very well, then, I will," said the vicar's lady.

"Bravo!" said Mr. Goodacre. "That really makes it quite a gay party. Now! It is my prerogative to distribute the sherry. I believe I am right in saying that sherry is the only wine with which the goddess Nicotina does not quarrel."

"Quite right, padre."

"Ah! You confirm that opinion. I am very glad—very glad indeed to hear you say so. And here—ah, yes! Will you have some of these little biscuits? Dear me, what a remarkable variety! Quite an *embarras de richesses!*"

"They come assorted in boxes," said Mrs. Goodacre, simply. "Cocktail biscuits, they call them. We had them at the last whist drive."

"Of course, of course! Now which is the kind that has cheese inside it?"

"These, I think," said Harriet, from a plenitude of experience, "and those long ones."

"So they are! How clever of you to know. I shall look to you to guide me through this delectable maze. I must say, I think a little social gathering like this before dinner is a most excellent idea."

"You are sure you would not like to stay and dine with us?" said Mrs. Goodacre, anxiously. "Or to spend the night? Our spare room is always ready. Are you *really* comfortable at Talboys, after all this terrible business? I told my husband to tell you that if there was anything at all we could do—"

"He faithfully delivered your kind message," said Harriet. "It's ever so good of you. But really and truly we're quite all right."

"Well," said the vicar's wife, "I expect you would rather be alone, so I won't be an officious old busybody. In our position one's always interfering with people for their good, you know. I'm sure it's a bad habit. By the way, Simon, poor little Mrs. Sellon's very much upset. She was taken quite ill this morning, and we had to send for the district nurse."

"Oh, dear, dear!" said the vicar. "Poor woman! That was a very extraordinary suggestion Martha Ruddle made at the inquest. There can't, surely, be anything in it."

"Certainly not. Nonsense. Martha likes to make herself important. She's a spiteful old thing. Though I can't help saying, even now he's dead, that William Noakes was a nasty old creature."

"Not in *that* way, surely, my dear?"

"You never know. But I meant, I couldn't blame Martha Ruddle for disliking him. It's all very well for you, Simon. You always think charitably of everyone. And besides, you never talked to him about anything except gardening. Though as a matter of fact, Frank Crutchley did all the work."

"Frank is a very clever gardener, indeed," said the vicar. "In fact he is clever all round. He found the defect in my motorcar engine immediately. I'm sure he will go far."

"He's going a little too far with that girl Polly, if you ask me," retorted his wife. "It's about time they asked you to put up the banns. Her mother came up to see me the other day. Well, Mrs. Mason, I said, you know what girls are, and I admit it's very difficult to control them these days. If I were you, I should speak to Frank and ask him what his intentions are. However, we mustn't begin talking about parish matters."

"I should be sorry," said the vicar, "to think ill of Frank Crutchley. Or of poor William Noakes, either. I expect there is nothing in it but talk. Dear me! To think that when I called at the house last Thursday morning, he was lying there dead! I particularly wanted to see him, I remember. I had a small offering of a *Teesdalia nudicaulis* for his rock-garden—he was fond of rock-plants. I felt very melancholy when I planted it here, myself, this morning."

"You are even fonder of plants than he was," said Harriet, glancing round the shabby room, which was filled with pot-plants on stands and tables.

"I am afraid I must admit the soft impeachment. Gardening is an indulgence of mine. My wife tells me it runs away with too much money, and I dare say she is right."

"I said he ought to get himself a new cassock," said Mrs. Goodacre, laughing. "But if he prefers rock-plants, that's his business."

"I wonder," said the vicar, wistfully, "what will become of William Noakes's plants. I suppose they will belong to Aggie Twitterton."

"I don't know," said Peter. "The whole thing may have to be sold, I suppose, for the benefit of the creditors."

"Dear, dear!" exclaimed the vicar. "Oh, I do hope they will be properly looked after. Especially the cacti. They are delicate creatures, and it is getting rather late in the year. I remember peeping in at the window last Thursday and thinking it was hardly safe for them to be left in that room without a fire. It's time they were put under glass for the winter. Particularly the big one in the hanging pot and that new variety he's got in the window. Of course, *you* will be keeping up good fires."

"We shall, indeed," said Harriet. "Now that we have got the chimneys clear, with your assistance. I hope your shoulder isn't still painful."

"I can feel it, I can feel it a little. But nothing to speak of. Just a slight bruise, that is all. . . . If there is to be a sale, I shall hope to make an offer for the cacti—if Aggie Twitterton doesn't want to buy them in for herself. And with your permission, my dear, of course."

"Frankly, Simon, I think them detestably hideous

things. But I'm quite ready to offer a home to them. I know you've been coveting those cacti for years."

"Not coveting, I hope," said the vicar. "But I fear I must confess to a great weakness for cacti."

"It's a morbid passion," said his wife.

"Really, my dear, really—you shouldn't use such exaggerated language. Come, Lady Peter—another glass of sherry. Indeed, you mustn't refuse!"

"Shall I put them peas on, Mr. Bunter?"

Bunter paused in his occupation of tidying the sitting-room and strode with some haste to the door.

"*I* will see to the peas, Mrs. Ruddle, at the proper time." He looked up at the clock, which marked five minutes past six. "His lordship is very particular about peas."

"Is he now?" Mrs. Ruddle seemed to take this as a signal for conversation, for she appeared on the threshold. "That's jest like my Bert. 'Ma,' 'e allus says, 'I 'ates peas 'ard.' Funny, 'ow often they *is* 'ard. Or biled right away outer their shells. One or other."

Bunter offered no comment, and she tried again. " 'Ere's them things you arst me to polish. Come up lovely, ain't they?"

She offered for inspection a brass toasting-fork and the fragment of a roasting-jack that had so unexpectedly made its appearance from the chimney.

"Thank you," said Bunter. He hung the toasting-fork on a nail by the fireplace and, after a little consideration, set the other specimen upright on the what-not.

"Funny" pursued Mrs. Ruddle, "the way the gentry is about them old bits o' things. Curios! Rubbish, if you ask me."

"This is a very old piece," replied Bunter, gravely, stepping back to admire the effect.

Mrs. Ruddle sniffed. "Reckon them as shoved it up the chimbley knew wot they wos doin'. Give me a nice gas-oven any day. Ah! I'd like that—same as my sister's wot lives in Biggleswade."

"People have been found dead in gas-ovens before now," said Bunter, grimly. He took up his master's blazer, shook it, appeared to estimate its contents by their weight, and removed a pipe, a tobacco-pouch and three boxes of matches from one pocket.

"Lor' now, Mr. Bunter, don't you talk like that! Ain't we 'ad enough corpusses about the 'ouse already? 'Ow they can go on livin' 'ere I *don't* know!"

"Speaking for his lordship and myself, we are accustomed to corpses." He extracted several more matchboxes and, at the bottom of the nest, discovered a sparking-plug and a corkscrew.

"Ah!" said Mrs. Ruddle, with a deep, sentimental sigh. "And we're *'e's* 'appy, *she's* 'appy. Ah! It's easy to see she worships the ground 'e treads on."

Bunter drew out two handkerchiefs, male and female, from another pocket and compared them indulgently. "That is a very proper sentiment in a young married woman."

" 'Appy days! But it's early days yet, Mr. Bunter. A man's a man w'en all's said and done. Ruddle, now—'e useter knock me about something shocking w'en 'e'd 'ad a drop—though a good 'usband, and bringin' the money 'ome reg'lar."

"I beg," said Bunter, distributing matchboxes about the room, "you will not institute these comparisons, Mrs. Ruddle. I have served his lordship twenty years, and a sweeter-tempered gentleman you could not wish to find."

"You ain't married to 'im, Mr. Bunter. *You* can give 'im a munce warning any day."

"I hope I know when I am well situated, Mrs. Ruddle. Twenty years' service, and never a harsh word nor an unjust action in all my knowledge of him." A tinge of emotion crept into his tone. He laid a powder-compact aside on the what-not; then folded the blazer together with loving care and hung it over his arm.

"You're lucky," said Mrs. Ruddle. "I couldn't rightly say the same of pore Mr. Noakes, which though he's dead and gone I will say 'e wos a sour-tempered, close-fisted, suspicious brute, pore old gentleman."

"Gentleman, Mrs. Ruddle, is what I should designate as an elastic term. His lordship—"

"There now!" interrupted Mrs. Ruddle. "If there ain't love's young dream a-comin' up the path."

Bunter's brows beetled awfully. "To *whom* might you be referring, Mrs. Ruddle?" he demanded in a voice like Jupiter Tonans.

"W'y, that Frank Crutchley, to be sure."

"Oh!" Jupiter was appeased. "Crutchley? Is he your choice for a second?"

"Go along with you, Mr. Bunter! Me? No fear! No—Aggie Twitterton. Runs after 'im like an old cat with one kitten."

"Indeed?"

"At *'er* age! Mutton dressed as lamb. Makes me fair sick. If she knowed wot I knows—but there!"

This interesting revelation was cut short by the entrance of Crutchley himself.

" 'Evenin'," said he, generally, to the company. "Any special orders tonight? I ran over, thinkin' there might be. Mr. 'Ancock don't want me for an hour or two."

"His lordship gave instructions that the car was to be cleaned; but now it's out again."

"Ah!" said Crutchley, apparently taking this as an intimation that gossip might proceed unchecked. "Well, they've got a nice day for it."

He made a tentative motion to seat himself, but caught Bunter's eye and compromised by leaning negligently against the end of the settle.

" 'Ave you 'eard when they've fixed for the funeral?" inquired Mrs. Ruddle.

" 'Leven-thirty termorrer."

"And 'igh time too—with 'im layin' there a week or more. There won't be many wet eyes, neither, if you ask me. There's one or two couldn't abide Mr. Noakes, not countin' i'm wot did away with 'im."

"They didn't get much forrader at the inquest, seems to me," observed Crutchley.

Bunter opened the what-not, and began to select wine-glasses from among its miscellaneous contents.

" 'Ushin' it up," said Mrs. Ruddle, "that's wot they wos. Tryin' to make out there wasn't nothing atween Joe Sellon and 'im. That Kirk, 'is face was a treat w'en Ted Puddock got askin' all them questions."

"Seemed to me they went a bit quick over all that part of it."

"Didn't want nobody to think as a bobby might a-been mixed up in it. See 'ow the crowner shut me up w'en I started to tell 'im? Ah! But them noospaper men wos on to it sharp enough."

"Did you communicate your opinion to them, may I ask?"

"I might a-done, or I might not, Mr. Bunter, only jest at that instant minnit, out comes me lord, and they wos all on to 'im like wopses round a jam-pot. 'Im and 'is lady'll be in all the papers termorrer. They took a photer o' me too, with 'er ladyship. It's nice to see your friends in the papers, ain't it now?"

"The laceration of his lordship's most intimate feelings can afford no satisfaction to me," said Bunter, reprovingly.

"Ah! if I'd telled 'em all I thinks about Joe Sellon they'd 'ave me on the front page. I wonder they lets that young feller go about at large. We might all be murdered in our beds. The moment I see pore Mr. Noakes's body, I says to myself, 'Now, wot's Joe Sellon doin' in this 'ere—'im bein' the last to see the pore man alive?' "

"Then you were already aware that the crime had been committed on the Wednesday night?"

"Well, o'course I—No, I didn't, not then—See 'ere, Mr. Bunter, don't you go a-puttin' words in a woman's mouth —I—"

"I think," said Bunter, "you had better be careful."

"That's right, Ma," agreed Crutchley. "You go on

imaginin' things, you'll land yourself in Queer Street one o' these days."

"Well," retorted Mrs. Ruddle, backing out of the door, "*I* didn't bear no pertickler grudge against Mr. Noakes. Not like some as I could name—with their forty poundses."

Crutchley stared at her retreating form.

"Gawdamighty, wot a tongue! I wonder 'er own spit didn't poison 'er. I wouldn't 'ang a dog on '*er* evidence. Mangy old poll-parrot!"

Bunter voiced no opinion, but picked up Peter's blazer and a few other scattered garments and walked upstairs. Crutchley, relieved of his vigilant eye and stern regard for the social proprieties, strolled quietly over to the hearth.

"Ho!" said Mrs. Ruddle. She brought in a lighted lamp, set it on a table on the far side of the room and turned on Crutchley with a witchlike smile. "Waitin' for kisses in the gloamin'?"

"Wotcher gettin' at?" demanded Crutchley, morosely.

"Aggie Twitterton's a-comin' down the 'ill on 'er bicycle."

"Gawd!" The young man shot a quick look through the window. "It's 'er all right." He rubbed the back of his head and swore softly.

"Wot it is to be the answer to the maiden's prayer!" said Mrs. Ruddle.

"Now, see 'ere, Ma. Polly's my girl. You know that. There ain't never been nothin' atween me and Aggie Twitterton."

"Not between you and 'er—but there might be atween 'er and you," replied Mrs. Ruddle, epigrammatically, and went out before he could reply. Bunter, coming downstairs, found Crutchley thoughtfully picking up the poker.

"May I ask why you are loitering about here? Your work is outside. If you want to wait for his lordship, you can do so in the garage."

"See 'ere, Mr. Bunter," said Crutchley, earnestly. "Let me bide in here for a bit. Aggie Twitterton's on the prowl, and if she was to catch sight o' me—you get me? She's a bit—"

He touched his forehead significantly.

"H'm!" said Bunter. He went across to the window and saw Miss Twitterton descend from her bicycle at the gate. She straightened her hat and began to fumble in the basket attached to the handlebars. Bunter drew the curtains rather sharply. "Well, you can't stop here long. His lordship and her ladyship may be back any minute now. What is it now, Mrs. Ruddle?"

"I've put out the plates like you said, Mr. Bunter," announced that lady with meek self-righteousness. Bunter frowned. She had something rolled in the corner of her apron and was rubbing at it as she spoke. He felt that it would take a long time to teach Mrs. Ruddle a good servant's-hall manner.

"And I've found the other vegetable-dish—only it's broke."

"Very good. You can take these glasses out and wash them. There don't seem to be any decanters."

"Never you mind that, Mr. Bunter. I'll soon 'ave them bottles clean."

"Bottles?" said Bunter. "What bottles?" A frightful suspicion shot through his brain. "What have you got there?"

"Why," said Mrs. Ruddle, "one o' them dirty old bottles you brought along with you." She displayed her booty in triumph. "Sech a state as they're in. All over whitewash."

Bunter's world reeled about him and he clutched at the corner of the settle.

"My God!"

"You couldn't put a thing like that on the table, could you now?"

"Woman!" cried Bunter, and snatched the bottle from her, "that's the Cockburn '96!"

"Ow, is it?" said Mrs. Ruddle, mystified. "There now! I thought it was summink to drink."

Bunter controlled himself with difficulty. The cases had been left in the pantry for safety. The police were in and out of the cellar, but by all the laws of England, a man's pantry was his own. He said in a trembling voice:

"You have not, I trust, handled any of the other bottles?"

"Only to unpack 'em and set 'em right side up," Mrs. Ruddle assured him cheerfully. "Them cases'll come in 'andy for kindling."

"Gawdstrewth!" cried Bunter. The mask came off him all in one piece, and nature, red in tooth and claw, leapt like a tiger from ambush. "Gawdstrewth, would you believe it? All his lordship's vintage port!" He lifted shaking hands to heaven. "You lousy old nosey-parking bitch! You ignorant, interfering old bizzom! Who told you to go poking your long nose into my pantry?"

"Really, Mr. Bunter!" said Mrs. Ruddle.

"Go it," said Crutchley, with relish. " 'Ere's someone at the front door."

" 'Op it out of here!" stormed Bunter, unheeding, "before I take the skin off you!"

"Well, I'm sure! 'Ow was I to know?"

"Get out!"

Mrs. Ruddle retired, but with dignity.

"Sech manners!"

"Put yer flat foot right into it that time, Ma," observed Crutchley. He grinned. Mrs. Ruddle turned in the doorway.

"People can do their own dirty work after this," she remarked, witheringly, and departed.

Bunter took up the violated bottle of port and cradled it mournfully in his arm.

"All the port! all the port! Two and a half dozen, all shook up to blazes! And his lordship bringing it down in the back of the car, driving as tender and careful as if it was a baby in arms."

"Well," said Crutchley, "that's a miracle, judgin' by the way he went into Pagford this afternoon. Nearly blew me and the old taxi off the road."

"Not a drop fit to drink for a fortnight!—And him looking forward to his glass after dinner!"

"Well," said Crutchley again, with the philosophy we keep for other men's misfortunes, "he's unlucky, that's all."

Bunter uttered a Cassandra-like cry:

"There's a curse upon this house!"

As he turned, the door was flung violently open to admit Miss Twitterton, who shrank back with a small scream, on receiving this blast of eloquence full in the face.

" 'Ere's Miss Twitterton," said Mrs. Ruddle, unnecessarily, and banged out.

"Oh, dear!" gasped the poor lady. "I beg your pardon. Er . . . is Lady Peter at home? . . . I've just brought her a . . . Oh, I suppose they are out. . . . Mrs. Ruddle is so stupid. . . . Perhaps . . ." She looked appealingly from one man to the other. Bunter, pulling himself together, recaptured his mask, and this stony metamorphosis put the finishing touch to Miss Twitterton's discomfort.

"If it isn't troubling you too much, Mr. Bunter, would you be so kind as to tell Lady Peter that I've brought her a few eggs from my own hens?"

"Certainly, Miss Twitterton." The social solecism had been committed and could not now be redeemed. He received the basket with the condescending kindness due from my lord's butler to a humble dependent of the house.

"The Buff Orpingtons," explained Miss Twitterton. "They—they lay such pretty brown eggs, don't they? And I thought, perhaps—"

"Her ladyship will greatly appreciate the attention. Would you care to wait?"

"Oh, thank you. . . . I hardly know . . ."

"I am expecting them back very shortly. From the vicarage."

"Oh!" said Miss Twitterton. "Yes." She sat down rather helplessly on the proffered chair. "I meant just to hand the basket to Mrs. Ruddle, but she seems very much put about."

Crutchley gave a short laugh. He had made one or two attempts at escape; but Bunter and Miss Twitterton were between him and the door, and now he appeared to resign himself. Bunter seemed glad of the opportunity for an explanation.

"*I* have been very much put about, Miss Twitterton. Mrs. Ruddle has violently agitated all his lordship's vintage port, just as it was settling down nicely after the journey."

"Oh, how dreadful!" cried Miss Twitterton, her sympathetic mind grasping that the disaster, however incomprehensible, was of the first magnitude. "Is it all spoiled? I believe they have some very good port wine at the Pig and Whistle—only it's rather expensive—4*s*. 6*d*. a bottle and nothing on the empties."

"I fear," said Bunter, "that would scarcely meet the case."

"Or if they would like some of my parsnip wine I should be delighted to—"

"Huh!" said Crutchley. He jerked his thumb at the bottle in Bunter's arm. "What does that stand his nibs in for?"

Bunter could bear no more. He turned to go.

"Two hundred and four shillings the dozen!"

"Cripes!" said Crutchley. Miss Twitterton could not believe her ears.

"The dozen *what?*"

"Bottles!" said Bunter. He went out shattered, with drooping shoulders, and shut the door decisively. Miss Twitterton, reckoning rapidly on her fingers, turned in dismay to Crutchley, who stood with a derisive smile, making no further effort to avoid the interview.

"Two hundred and four—seventeen shillings a bottle! Oh, it's impossible! It's . . . it's wicked!"

"Yes. Cut above you and me, ain't it? Bah! there's a chap could give away forty pound out of his pocket and never miss it. But does he? No!"

He strolled over to the hearth and spat eloquently into the fire.

"Oh, Frank! You mustn't be so bitter. You couldn't expect Lord Peter—"

" 'Lord Peter!'—who're you to be calling him by his pet name? Think you're somebody, don't you?"

"That is the correct way to speak of him," said Miss Twitterton, drawing herself up a little. "I know quite well how to address people of rank."

"Oh, yes!" replied the gardener, sarcastically, "I deesay. And you say 'Mister' to his blasted valet. Come off of it, my girl. It's 'me lord' for you, same as for the rest of us. . . . I know your mother was a schoolteacher, all right. *And* your father was old ted Baker's cow-man. If she married beneath 'er, it ain't nothing to be stuck up about."

"I'm sure," Miss Twitterton's voice trembled—"*you're* the last person that ought to say such a thing to me."

Crutchley's face lowered.

"That's it, is it? Tryin' to make out you been lowerin' yourself by associating with me, eh? All right! You go and hobnob with the gentry. *Lord* Peter!"

He thrust his hands deep down in his pockets and strode irritably towards the window. His determination to work up a quarrel was so evident that even Miss Twitterton could not mistake it. It could have only one explanation. With fatal archness, she wagged a reproving finger.

"Why, Frank, you silly old thing! I believe you're jealous!"

"Jealous!" he looked at her and began to laugh. It was not a pleasant laugh, though it showed all his teeth. "That's good! that's rich, that is! What's the idea? Startin' to make eyes at his lordship now?"

"Frank! He's a married man. How can you say such things?"

"Oh, he's married all right. Tied up good and proper. 'Ead well in the noose. 'Yes, darling!' 'No, darling!' 'Cuddle me quick, darling.' Pretty, ain't it?"

Miss Twitterton thought it *was* pretty, and said so.

"I'm sure it's beautiful to see two people so devoted to one another."

"Quite a ro-mance in 'igh life. Like to be in '*er* shoes, wouldn't you?"

"You don't really think I'd want to change places with anybody?" cried Miss Twitterton. "But, oh, Frank! If only you and I could get married at once—"

"Ah, yes!" said Crutchley, with a kind of satisfaction. "Your Uncle Noakes has put a bit of spoke in that wheel, ain't 'e?"

"Oh!—I've been trying all day to see you and talk over what we were to do."

"What *we're* going to do?"

"It isn't for myself, Frank. I'd work my fingers to the bone for you."

"And a fat lot 'o good that 'ud do. 'Ow about my garridge? If it 'adn't a-been for your soft soap I'd a-got my forty quid out o' the old devil months ago."

Miss Twitterton quailed before his angry eyes.

"Oh, please don't be so angry with me. We couldn't either of us know. And oh!—there's another terrible thing—"

"What's up now?"

"I—I—I'd been saving up a little bit—just a little here and there, you know—and I'd got close on £50 put away in the savings bank—"

"Fifty pounds, eh?" said Crutchley, his tone softening a little. "Well, that's a tidy little bit. . . ."

"I meant it for the garage. It was to be a surprise for you—"

"Well, and what's gone wrong with it?" The sight of her imploring eyes and twitching, bony hands brought back his irritation. "Post office gone bust?"

"I—I—I lent it to Uncle. He said he was short—people hadn't paid their bills—"

"Well," said Crutchley with impatience, "you got a receipt for it, I suppose." Excitement seized him. "That's *your* money. They can't get at that. You 'ave it out o' them—you got a receipt for it. You give me the receipt and I'll settle with that MacBride. That'll cover my forty quid, anyhow."

"But I never thought to ask Uncle for a *receipt*. Not between relations. How could I?"

"You never thought—? Nothing on paper—? Of all the blasted fools—!"

"Oh, Frank dear, I'm so sorry. Everything seems to have gone wrong. But you know, you never dreamt, any more than I did—"

"No; or I'd 'ave acted a bit different, I can tell you."

He ground his teeth savagely and struck a log on the hearth with his heel so that the sparks flew. Miss Twitterton watched him miserably. Then a new hope came to sustain her.

"Frank, listen! Perhaps Lord Peter might *lend* you the money to start the garage. He's ever so rich."

Crutchley considered this. Born rich and born soft were to him the same thing. It was possible, if he made a good impression—though it did mean truckling to a blasted title.

"That's a fact," he admitted. "He might."

In a rosy flush, Miss Twitterton saw the possibility as an accomplished fact. Her eager wishes flew ahead into a brilliant future.

"I'm sure he would. We could get married at once, and have that little corner cottage—you know—on the main road, where you said—and there'd be ever so many cars stopping there. And I could help quite a lot with my Buff Orpingtons!"

"You and your Buff Orpingtons!"

"And I could give piano lessons again. I know I could get pupils. There's the stationmaster's little Elsie—"

"Little Elsie's bottom! Now, see here, Aggie, it's time we got down to brass tacks. You and me getting spliced with the idea of coming into your uncle's money—that was one thing, see! That's business. But if there's no money from you, it's off. You get that?"

Miss Twitterton uttered a faint bleat. He went on, brutally:

"A man that's starting in life wants a wife, see? A nice little bit to come 'ome to. Some'un he can cuddle—not a skinny old hen with a brood o' Buff Orpingtons."

"How can you speak like that?"

He caught her roughly by the shoulder and twisted her round to face the mirror with the painted roses.

"Look at yourself in the glass, you old fool! Talk about a man marrying his grandmother—"

She shrank back and he pushed her from him.

"Coming the schoolmarm over me, with yer 'Mind yer manners, Frank,' and 'mind yer aitches,' and bum-sucking round to his lordship—'Frank's so clever'—t'sha! making me look a blasted fool."

"I only wanted to help you get on."

"Yes—showing me off, like as if I was your belongings. You'd like to take me up to bed like the silver teapot—and a silver teapot 'ud be about as much use to you, I reckon."

Miss Twitterton put her hands over her ears. "I won't listen to you—you're mad—you're—"

"Thought you'd bought me with yer uncle's money, didn't you? Well—where is it?"

"How can you be so cruel?—after all I've done for you?"

"You've done for me, all right. Made me a laughingstock and got me into a blasted mess. I suppose you've been blabbing about all over the place as we was only waitin' for vicar to put up the banns—"

"I've never said a word—truly, truly I never have."

"Oh, ain't you? Well, you should a-heard old Ruddle talk."

"And if I had," cried Miss Twitterton with a last, desperate burst of spirit, "why shouldn't I? You've told me over and over again you were fond of me—you said you were—you said you were—"

"Oh, can that row!"

"But you did say so. Oh, you can't, you can't be so cruel! You don't know—you don't know—Frank, please! Dear Frank—I know it's been a dreadful disappointment—but you can't mean this—you can't! I—I—I—oh, do be kind to me, Frank—I love you so—"

In frantic appeal, she flung herself into his arms; and the contact with her damp cheeks and stringy body drove him to an ugly fury.

"Damn you, get off! Take your blasted claws out of my neck. Shut up! I'm sick and tired of the sight of you."

He wrenched her loose and flung her heavily upon the settle, bruising her, and knocking her hat grotesquely over one ear. As he looked at her with a sort of delight in her helpless absurdity and her snuffling humiliation, the deep roar of the Daimler's exhaust zoomed up to the gate and stopped. The latch clicked and steps came along the path. Miss Twitterton sobbed and gulped, hunting savagely for her handkerchief.

"Hell's bells!" said Crutchley, "they're comin' in."

Above the creak of the gravel came the sound of two voices singing together softly.

"*Et ma joli' colombe*
Qui chante jour et nuit,
Et ma joli' colombe
Qui chante jour et nuit,
Qui chante pour les filles
Qui n'ont pas de mari—
Auprès de ma blonde
Qu'il fait bon, fait bon, fait bon,
Auprès de ma blonde
Qu'il fait bon dormi."

"Get up, you fool!" said Crutchley, hunting in a hurry for his cap.

"Qui chante pour les filles
Qui n'ont pas de mari,
Qui chante pour les filles
Qui n'ont pas de mari—"

He found the cap on the windowsill and pulled it on with a jerk. "You'd better clear out, sharp. I'm off."

The woman's voice rang out, alone and exultant:

"Pour moi ne chante guère
Car j'en ai un joli—"

The tune, if not the words, stabbed Miss Twitterton into a consciousness of that insolent triumph, and she stirred wretchedly on the hard settle as the duet was joined again:

"Auprès de ma blonde
Qu'il fait bon, fait bon, fait bon,
Auprès de ma blonde
Qu'il fait bon dormi."

She lifted a blotched and woebegone face; but Crutchley was gone—and the words of the song came back to her. Her mother, the school mistress, had had it in that little book of French songs—though, of course, it was not a thing one could teach the school children. There were voices in the passage outside.

"Oh, Crutchley!" casual and commanding. "You can put the car away."

And Crutchley's, colorless and respectful, as though it did not know how to use cruel words:

"Very good, my lord."

Which way out? Miss Twitterton dabbed the tears from her face. Not into that passage, among them all—with Frank there—and Bunter perhaps coming out of the kitchen—and what would Lord Peter think?

"Anything further tonight, my lord?"

"No, thanks. That's all. Good night."

The doorknob moved under his hand. Then her ladyship's voice—warm and friendly:

"Good night, Crutchley."

"Good night, my lord. Good night, my lady."

Seized with panic, Miss Twitterton fled blindly up the bedroom stairs as the door opened.

CHAPTER XVI

CROWN MATRIMONIAL

Norbert: *Explain not: let this be!*
This is life's height.
Constance: *Yours, yours, yours!*
Norbert: *You and I—*
Why care by what meanders we are here
I' the centre of the labyrinth! Men have died
Trying to find this place, which we have found.

—ROBERT BROWNING, *IN A BALCONY*

"Well, well, well!" said Peter. "Here we are again." He lifted his wife's cloak from her shoulders and gently saluted the nape of her neck.

"In the proud consciousness of duty done."

His eyes followed her as she crossed the room. "Wonderfully inspiring thing, doing one's duty. Gives one a sort of exalted sensation. I feel quite lightheaded."

She dropped on to the couch, laying lazy arms along its back.

"I'm feeling slightly intoxicated, too. It couldn't possibly be the vicar's sherry?"

"No," he said firmly, "not possibly. Though I fancy I have drunk worse. Not much, and not more than once. No—it's just the stimulating effects of well doing—or perhaps it's the country air—or something."

"Rather giddy-making, but nice."

"Oh, definitely." He unwound the scarf from his neck, hung it with the cloak over the settle and drifted irresolutely to a position behind the couch. "I mean to say—yes, definitely. Like champagne. Almost like being in love. But I don't think it could be that, do you?"

She tilted her face to smile at him, so that he saw it oddly and intriguingly inverted.

"Oh, surely not." She caught his roving hands, held them, dumbly protesting, away from her breast, brought them up under her chin and imprisoned them there.

"I thought not. Because, after all, we are married. Or aren't we? One can't be married *and* in love. Not with the same person, I mean. It isn't done."

"Absolutely not."

"Pity. Because I'm feeling rather youthful and foolish tonight. Tender and twining, like a very young pea. Positively romantic."

"That, my lord, is disgraceful in a gentleman of your condition."

"My mental condition is simply appalling. I want the violins to strike up in the orchestra and discourse soft music while the limelight merchant turns up the moon. . . ."

"And the crooners are crooning in tune!"

"Damn it, why not? I *will* have my soft music! Unhand me, girl! Let's see what the B.B.C. can do for us."

She released him; and her eyes, in their turn, followed him to the radio cabinet.

"Stand there a moment, Peter. No—don't turn round."

"Why?" he said, standing obediently. "Has my unfortunate face begun to get on your nerves?"

"No—I was just admiring your spine, that's all. It has a kind of sort of springy line about it that pleases me. Completely enslaving."

"Really? I can't see it. But I must tell my tailor. He always gives me to understand that he invented my back for me."

"Does he also imagine he invented your ears and the back of your skull and the bridge of your nose?"

"No flattery can be too gross for my miserable sex. I am purring like a coffee-mill. But you might have picked a more responsive set of features. It's difficult to express devotion with the back of one's head."

"That's just it. I want the luxury of a hopeless passion. There, I can say to myself, there is the back of his adorable head, and nothing I can say will soften it."

"I'm not so sure of that. However, I'll try to live up to your requirements—my true love hath my heart, but my bones are my own. Just at the moment, though, the immortal bones obey control of dying flesh and dying soul. What the devil did I come over here for?"

"Soft music."

"So it was. Now my little minstrels of Portland Place! Strike, you myrtle-crownèd boys, ivied maidens, strike together!"

"Arrch!" said the loud speaker, ". . . and the beds should be carefully made up beforehand with good, well-rotted horse manure or . . ."

"Help!"

"That," said Peter, switching off, "is quite enough of that."

"The man has a dirty mind."

"Disgusting. I shall write a stiff letter to Sir John Reith. Isn't it an extraordinary thing that just when a fellow's bubbling over with the purest and most sacred emotions—when he's feeling like Galahad and Alexander and Clark Gable all rolled into one—when he so to speak bestrides the clouds and sits upon the bosom of the air—"

"Dearest! are you sure it's not the sherry?"

"Sherry!" His rocketing mood burst in a shower of spangles. "Lady, by yonder blessèd moon I swear . . ." He halted, gesturing into the shadows. "Hullo! they've put the moon on the wrong side."

"Very careless of the limelight merchant."

"Drunk again, drunk again. . . . Perhaps you're right about the sherry. . . . Curse this moon, it leaks. O more than moon, Draw not up seas to drown me in thy sphere!" He wrapped his handkerchief about the stem of the lamp, brought it across from the table and set it beside her, so that the red-orange of her dress shone in the pool of light like an oriflamme. "That's better. Now we begin all over again. Lady, by yonder blessèd moon I swear. That tips with silver all these fruit-tree tops. . . . Observe the fruit-trees. *Malus aspidistriensis*. Specially imported by the management at colossal expense. . . ."

The voices came faintly to Aggie Twitterton, crouched shiveringly in the room overhead. She had meant to escape by the back stair; but at the bottom of it stood Mrs. Ruddle, engaged in a long expostulation with Bunter, whose replies from the kitchen were inaudible. Apparently on the point of departure, she kept on coming back to make some fresh remark. Any minute she might take herself off, and then—

Bunter came out so silently that Miss Twitterton did not hear him till his voice boomed suddenly from just below her:

"I have nothing more to say, Mrs. Ruddle. Good night to you."

The back door shut sharply and there was the noise of the drawing of bolts. One could not now escape unheard. In another moment, feet began to ascend the stair. Miss Twitterton withdrew hastily into Harriet's bedroom. The feet came on; they passed the branching of the stair; they were coming in. Miss Twitterton retired still further, shocked to find herself trapped in a gentleman's bedroom that smelt faintly of bay rum and Harris tweed. Next door she heard the crackle of a kindled fire, the rattle of curtain rings upon the rods, a subdued clink, the pouring of fresh water into the ewer. Then the door-latch lifted, and she fled breathless back into the darkness of the stairs.

". . . Romeo was a green fool, and all his trees had green apples. Sit there, Aholibah, and play the queen, with a vineleaf crown and a scepter of pampas-grass. Lend me your cloak, and I will be the kings and all their horsemen. Speak the speech, I pray you, trippingly on the tongue. Speak it! My snow-white horses foam and fret—sorry, I've got into the wrong poem, but I'm pawing the ground like anything. Say on, lady of the golden voice. 'I am the Queen Aholibah—' "

She laughed; and let the magnificent nonsense roll out organ-mouthed:

"*My lips kissed dumb the word of Ah*
Sighed on strange lips grown sick thereby.
God wrought to me my royal bed;
The inner work thereof was red,
The outer work was ivory.
My mouth's heat was the heat of flame
With lust towards the kings that came
With horsemen riding royally—

Peter, you'll break that chair. You *are* a lunatic!"

"My dearest, I've got to be." He flung the cloak aside and stood before her. "When I try to be serious, I make such a bloody fool of myself. It's idiotic." His voice wavered with uncertain overtones. "Think of it—laugh at it—a well-fed, well-groomed, well-off Englishman of forty-five in a boiled shirt and an eyeglass going down on his knees to his wife—to his own wife, which makes it so much funnier—and saying to her—and saying—"

"Tell me, Peter."

"I can't. I daren't."

She lifted his head between her hands, and what she saw in his face stopped her heart.

"Oh, my dear, don't. . . . Not all that. . . . It's terrifying to be so happy."

"Ah, no, it's not," he said quickly, taking courage from her fear.

"*All other things to their destruction draw,*
Only our love hath no decay;
This no tomorrow hath, nor yesterday;
Running it never runs from us away
But truly keeps his first, last, everlasting day."

"Peter—"

He shook his head, vexed at his own impotence.

"How can *I* find words? Poets have taken them all, and left me with nothing to say or do—"

"Except to teach me for the first time what they meant."

He found it hard to believe.

"Have I done that?"

"Oh, Peter—" Somehow she must make him believe it, because it mattered so much that he should. "All my life I have been wandering in the dark—but now I have found your heart—and am satisfied."

"And what do all the great words come to in the end, but that?—I love you—I am at rest with you—I have come home."

There was such a stillness in the room that Miss Twitterton thought it must be empty. She crept down softly, stair by stair, afraid lest Bunter should heard her. The door was ajar and she pushed it open inch by inch. The lamp had been moved, so that she found herself in darkness—but the room was not empty, after all. On the far side, framed in the glowing circle of the lamplight, the two figures were bright and motionless as a picture—the dark woman in a dress like flame, with her arms locked about the man's bowed shoulders and his golden head in her lap. They were so quiet that even the great ruby on her left hand shone steadily without a twinkle.

Miss Twitterton, turned to stone, dared neither advance nor retreat.

"Dear." The word was no more than a whisper, spoken without a movement. "My heart's heart. My own dear lover and husband." The locked hands must have tightened their hold, for the red stone flashed sudden fire. "You are mine, you are mine, all mine."

The head came up at that and his voice caught the triumph and sent it back in a mounting wave:

"Yours. Such as I am, yours. With all my faults, all my follies, yours utterly and for ever. While this poor, passionate, mountebank body has hands to hold you and lips to say, I love you—"

"Oh!" cried Miss Twitterton, with a great strangling sob, "I can't bear it! I can't bear it!"

The little scene broke like a bubble. The chief actor leapt to his feet and said very distinctly:

"Damn and blast!"

Harriet got up. The sudden shattering of her ecstatic mood and a swift, defensive anger for Peter's sake made her tone sharper than she knew:

"Who is it? What are you doing there?" She stepped out of the pool of light and peered into the dusk. *"Miss Twitterton?"*

Miss Twitterton, incapable of speech and terrified beyond conception, went on choking hysterically. A voice from the direction of the fireplace said grimly:

"I knew I should make a bloody fool of myself."

"Something's happened," said Harriet, more gently, putting out a reassuring hand. Miss Twitterton found her voice:

"Oh, forgive me—I didn't know—I never meant—" The remembrance of her own misery got the upper hand of her alarm. "Oh, I'm so dreadfully unhappy."

"I think," said Peter, "I had better see about decanting the port."

He retreated quickly and quietly, without waiting to shut the door. But the ominous words had penetrated to Miss Twitterton's consciousness. A new terror checked her tears in midflow.

"Oh, dear, oh, dear! The port wine! Now he'll be angry again."

"Good heavens!" exclaimed Harriet, completely bewildered. "What has gone wrong? What is it all about?"

Miss Twitterton shuddered. A cry of "Bunter!" in the passage warned her that the crisis was imminent.

"Mrs. Ruddle has done something *dreadful* to the port wine."

"Oh, my poor Peter!" said Harriet. She listened anxiously. Bunter's voice now, subdued to a long, explanatory mumble. "Oh, dear, oh, dear, oh, dear!" moaned Miss Twitterton.

"But what *can* the woman have done?"

Miss Twitterton really was not sure.

"I *believe* she's shaken the bottle," she faltered. "Oh!"

A loud yelp of anguish rent the air within. Peter's voice lifted to a wail:

"What! *all* my pretty chickens and their dam?"

The last word sounded to Miss Twitterton painfully like an oath.

"O-o-oh! I do *hope* he won't be violent."

"Violent?" said Harriet, half amused and half angry. "Oh, I shouldn't think so."

But alarm is infectious . . . and much-tried men have been known to vent their exasperation upon their servants. The two women clung together, waiting for the explosion.

"Well," said the distant voice, "all I can say is, Bunter, don't let it happen again. . . . All right. . . . Good God, man, you needn't tell me that . . . of course you didn't. . . . We'd better go and view the bodies."

The sounds died away, and the women breathed more freely. The dreadful menace of male violence lifted its shadow from the house.

"Well!" said Harriet, "that wasn't so bad after all. . . . My dear Miss Twitterton, what *is* the matter? You're trembling all over. . . . Surely, *surely* you didn't really think Peter was going to—to throw things about or anything, did you? Come and sit down by the fire. Your hands are like ice."

Miss Twitterton allowed herself to be led to the settle.

"I'm sorry—it was silly of me. But . . . I'm always so terrified of . . . gentlemen being angry . . . and . . . and . . . after all, they're all men, aren't they? . . . and men are so horrible!"

The end of the sentence came out in a shuddering burst. Harriet realized that there was more here than poor Uncle William or a couple of dozen of port.

"Dear Miss Twitterton, what is the trouble? Can I help? Has somebody been horrible to you?"

Sympathy was too much for Miss Twitterton. She clutched at the kindly hands.

"Oh, my lady, my lady—I'm ashamed to tell you. He said such dreadful things to me. Oh, please forgive me!"

"Who did?" asked Harriet, sitting down beside her.

"Frank. Terrible things. . . . And I know I'm a little older than he is—and I suppose I've been very foolish—but he *did* say he was fond of me."

"Frank Crutchley?"

"Yes—and it wasn't my fault about Uncle's money. We were going to be married—only we were waiting for the forty pounds and my own little savings that Uncle borrowed. And they're all gone now and no money to come from Uncle—and now he says he hates the sight of me, and—and I *do* love him so!"

"I *am* so sorry," said Harriet, helplessly. What else was there to be said? The thing was ludicrous and abominable.

"He—he—he called me an old hen!" That was the almost unspeakable thing; and when it was out Miss Twitterton went on more easily. "He was so angry about my savings—but I never thought of asking Uncle for a receipt."

"Oh, my dear!"

"I was so happy—thinking we were going to be married as soon as he could get the garage started—only we didn't tell anybody, because, you see, I *was* a little bit older than him, though of course I was in a better position. But he was working up and making himself quite superior—"

How fatal, thought Harriet, how fatal! Aloud she said: "My dear, if he treats you like that he's not superior at all. He's not fit to clean your shoes."

Peter was singing:

"*Que donneriez-vous, belle,*
Pour avoir votre ami?

Que donneriez-vous, belle,
Pour avoir votre ami?"

(He seems to have got over it, thought Harriet.)

"And he's so *handsome*. . . . We used to meet in the churchyard—there's a nice seat there. . . . Nobody comes that way in the evenings. . . . I let him kiss me. . . ."

"Je donnerais Versailles,
Paris et saint Denis!"

". . . and now he hates me. . . . I don't know what to do. . . . I shall go and drown myself. . . . Nobody *knows* what I've done for Frank. . . ."

"Auprès de ma blonde
Qu'il fait bon, fait bon, fait bon,
Auprès de ma blonde
Qu'il fait bon dormi!"

"Oh, *Peter!*" said Harriet in an exasperated undertone. She rose and shut the door upon this heartless exhibition. Miss Twitterton, exhausted by her own emotions, sat weeping quietly in a corner of the settle. Harriet was conscious of a whole series of emotions, arranged in layers like a Neapolitan ice.

What on earth am I to do with her? . . .
He is singing songs in the French language. . . .
And it must be nearly dinner-time. . . .
Somebody called Polly. . . .
Mrs. Ruddle will drive those men distracted. . . .
Bonté d'âme. . . .
Old Noakes dead in our cellar. . . .
(Eructavit cor meum!) . . .
Poor Bunter! . . .
Sellon? . . .

(Qu'il fait bon dormi). . . .
If you know How, you know Who. . . .
This house. . . .
My *true love hath my heart and I have his*. . . .

She came back and stood by the settle. "Listen! Don't cry so terribly. He isn't worth it. Honestly, he couldn't be. There isn't a man in ten million that's worth breaking your heart over." (No good to tell people that.) "Try to forget him. I know it sounds difficult. . . ."

Miss Twitterton looked up.

"*You* wouldn't find it so easy?"

"To forget Peter?" (No; nor other things.) "Well, of course, Peter. . . ."

"Yes," said Miss Twitterton, without rancor. "You're one of the lucky ones. I'm sure you deserve it."

"I'm quite sure I don't." (God's bodikins, man, much better. . . . Every man after his desert?)

"And *what* you must have thought of me!" cried Miss Twitterton, suddenly restored to a sense of the actual. "I hope he isn't too terribly angry. You see, I heard you coming in—just outside the door—and I simply couldn't face anybody—so I ran upstairs—and then I didn't hear anything so I thought you'd gone and came down—and seeing you so happy together. . . ."

"It doesn't matter the very least bit," said Harriet, hastily. "*Please* don't think any more about it. He knows it was quite an accident. Now—don't cry any more."

"I must be going." Miss Twitterton made vague efforts to straighten her disordered hair and the jaunty little hat. "I'm afraid I look a sight."

"No, not a bit. Just a touch of powder's all you want. Where's my—oh! I left it in Peter's pocket. No, here it is on the what-not. That's Bunter. He always clears up after us. Poor Bunter and the port—it must have been a blow to him."

Miss Twitterton stood patiently to be tidied up, like a

small child in the hands of a brisk nurse. "There—you look *quite* all right. See! No one would notice anything."

The mirror! Miss Twitterton shrank at the thought of it, but curiosity spurred her on. This was her own face, then—how strange!

"I've never had powder on before. It—it makes me feel quite fast."

She stared, fascinated.

"Well," said Harriet, cheerfully, "it's helpful sometimes. Let me tuck up this little curl behind—"

Her own dark, glowing face came into the mirror behind Miss Twitterton's and she saw with a shock that the trail of vine-leaves was still in her hair. "Goodness! how absurd I look! We were playing silly games—"

"You look lovely," said Miss Twitterton. "Oh, dear—I hope nobody will think—"

"Nobody will think anything. Now, promise me you won't make yourself miserable any more."

"No," said Miss Twitterton, mournfully. "I'll try not." Two large, lingering tears rolled slowly into her eyes, but she remembered the powder and removed them carefully. "You *have* been so kind. Now I *must* run."

"Good night." The opening of the door revealed Bunter, hovering with a tray in the background.

"I *hope* I haven't kept you from your supper."

"Not a bit," said Harriet, "it isn't time for it yet. Now goodbye and don't worry. Bunter, please show Miss Twitterton out."

She stood absently, gazing at her own face in the mirror, the vine-wreath trailing from her hand.

"Poor little soul!"

CHAPTER XVII

CROWN IMPERIAL

One cried, "God bless us!" and "Amen" the other, As they had seen me with these hangman's hands.

—WILLIAM SHAKESPEARE, MACBETH

Peter came in cautiously, carrying a decanter.

"It's all right," said Harriet. "She's gone."

He put down the wine at a carefully calculated distance from the fire and observed, in a conversational tone:

"We found some decanters, after all."

"Yes—I see you did."

"My God, Harriet—what was I saying?"

"It's all right, darling. You were only quoting Donne."

"Is that all? I rather fancied I had put in one or two little bits of my own. . . . Oh, well, what's it matter? I love you and I don't care who knows it."

"Bless you."

"All the same," he went on, determined to put the embarrassing topic in its place for good and all, "this house is making me jumpy. Skeletons in the chimney, corpses in the cellar, elderly females hiding behind the doors—I shall look under the bed tonight—Ough!"

He started nervously, as Bunter came in carrying a standard lamp; and covered his confusion by stooping, unnecessarily, to feel the decanter again.

"Is that the port, after all?"

"No, claret. It's a youngish but pleasant Hermitage, with only a very light sediment. It seems to have travelled all right—it's quite clear."

Bunter, setting the lamp near the hearth, cast a look of mute anguish at the decanter and retired with hushed footsteps.

"I'm not the only sufferer," said his master, with a shake of the head. "Bunter's nerves are very much affected. He feels this Ruddle muddle acutely—coming on top of everything else. I enjoy a little bustle and movement myself, but Bunter has his standards."

"Yes—and though he's charming to me, our marriage must have been an awful blow to him."

"More in the nature of an emotional strain, I think. And he's a little worried about this case. He fancies I'm not giving my mind to it. This afternoon, for instance—"

"I'm afraid so, Peter, yes. The woman tempted you—"

"O *felix culpa!*"

"Frittering away your time among the tombstones, instead of following up the clues. But there aren't any clues."

"If there ever were any, Bunter probably cleared them away with his own hands—he and Ruddle, his partner in crime. Remorse is eating his soul like a caterpillar in a cabbage. . . . But he's quite right; because all I've done so far is to throw suspicion on that wretched boy, Sellon—when I might just as well have thrown it on someone else, as far as I can see."

"On Mr. Goodacre, for instance. He *has* got a morbid passion for cacti."

"Or on the infernal Ruddles. I *could* climb through that window, by the way. I tried after lunch."

"Did you? And did you find out whether Sellon might have altered Mrs. Ruddle's clock?"

"Ah! . . . you took that point. Trust a detective novelist to go hot-foot for a clock problem. You're looking like the cat that's swallowed the canary. Out with it—what have you discovered?"

"It couldn't have been altered more than about ten minutes either way."

"Indeed? And how does Mrs. Ruddle come to have a clock with quarter-chimes?"

"It was a wedding-present."

"It would be. Yes, I see. You could put it forward, but you couldn't put it right again. And you couldn't put it back at all. Not more than ten minutes or so. Ten minutes might be valuable. Sellon said it was five past nine. Then, by all the rules, he should need an alibi for—Harriet, no! that makes no sense. It's no use having an alibi for the moment of the murder unless you take pains to *fix* the moment of the murder. If a ten minute alibi is to work, the time must be fixed within ten minutes. And it's only fixed within twenty-five—and even then, we can't be *sure* about the wireless. Can't *you* do something with the wireless? That's the mystery-monger's white-headed boy."

"No, I can't. A clock and a wireless ought to add up to something, but they don't. I've thought and thought—"

"Well, you know, we only started yesterday. It seems longer, but that's all it is. Hang it! We've not been married fifty-five hours."

"It feels like a lifetime—no, I don't mean that. I mean, it feels as if we'd always been married."

"So we have—from the foundation of the world—Confound you, Bunter, what do you want?"

"The menu, my lord."

"Oh! Thanks. Turtle soup . . . That's a little citified for Paggleham—a trifle out of key. Never mind. Roast duck and green peas are better. Local produce? Good. Mushrooms on toast—"

"From the field behind the cottage, my lord."

"From the—? Good God, I hope they *are* mushrooms—we don't want a poison-mystery as well."

"No poison, my lord, no. I consumed a quantity myself to make sure."

"Did you? Devoted Valet Risks Life for Master. Very

well, Bunter. Oh! and, by the way, was it you playing hide-and-seek with Miss Twitterton on our stairs?"

"My lord?"

"All right, Bunter," said Harriet, quickly.

Bunter took the hint and vanished, murmuring, "Very good."

"She was hiding from us, Peter, because she'd been crying when we came in and she didn't want to be caught."

"Oh, I see," said Peter. The explanation satisfied him, and he turned his attention to the wine.

"Crutchley's been behaving like a perfect beast to her."

"Has he, by jove?" He gave the decanter a half-turn.

"He's been making love to the poor little wretch."

As though to prove himself a man and no angel, his lordship gave utterance to a faintly derisive hoot.

"Peter—it isn't funny."

"I beg your pardon, my dear. You're quite right. It's not." He straightened himself suddenly and said, with some emphasis: "It's anything but funny. Is she fond of the blighter?"

"My dear, pathetically. And they were going to be married and start the new garage—with the forty pounds and her little savings—only they're gone, too. And now he finds she won't come into any money from her uncle. . . . What are you looking at me like that for?"

"Harriet, I don't like this at all." He was gazing at her with an expression of growing consternation.

"Of course, he's chucked her over now—the brute!"

"Yes, yes—but don't you see what you're telling me? She'd have given him the money, of course? Done anything in the world for him?"

"She said nobody knew what she *had* done for him—Oh, Peter! You can't mean *that!* It *couldn't* be the little Twitterton!"

"Why not?"

He flung the words out like a challenge; and she faced it squarely, standing up to him with her hands on his shoulders, so that their eyes met level.

"It's a motive—I see it's a motive. But you didn't want to hear about motive."

"But you're cracking my ear-drums with it," he cried, almost angrily. "Motive won't make a case. But once you've got the How, the Why drives it home."

"All right, then." He should fight on his own ground. "*How?* You made no case against her."

"There was no need. Her How is child's play. She had the key of the house, and no alibi after 7:30. Killing hens is no alibi for killing a man."

"But to smash in a man's head with a blow like that—she's tiny, and he was a big man. I couldn't break your head open like that, though I'm nearly as tall as you are."

"You're about the one person who could. You're my wife. You could take me unawares—as a loving niece might her uncle. I can't see Noakes sitting down and letting Crutchley or Sellon go pussy-footing about behind him. But a woman one knows and trusts—that's different."

He sat down at the table, with his back towards her, and picked up a fork.

"Look! Here I am, writing a letter or doing my accounts. . . . You're fidgeting round somewhere in the background. . . . I take no notice; I'm used to it. . . . You take up the poker quietly . . . don't be afraid, you know I'm slightly deaf. . . . Come up on the left, remember; my head leans over a little to the side of the pen. . . . Now . . . two quick steps and a brisk rap on the skull—you needn't hit too hard—and you're an exceedingly wealthy widow."

Harriet put the poker down rather hastily.

"Niece—Widow's a hateful word; so weedy—let's stick to niece."

"I slump down, and the chair slips away, so that I bruise my right side against the table in falling. You remove any fingerprints from the weapon—"

"Yes—and then just let myself out with my own key and lock the door behind me. Quite simple. And you, I suppose, when you come to, obligingly tidy away whatever you were writing—"

"And tidy myself into the cellar. That's the idea."

"I suppose you've seen this all along."

"I have. But I was irrational enough to tell myself that the motive was insufficient. I couldn't see the Twitterton doing murder for money to extend her hen runs. Serve me right for being weak-minded. The moral is, Stick to How, and somebody will hand you the Why on a silver salver."

He read remonstrance in her eyes, and added earnestly: "It's a whacking great motive, Harriet. A middle-aged woman's last bid for love—and the money to make the bid."

"It was Crutchley's motive, too. Couldn't she have let him in? Or lent him the key, not knowing what he wanted it for?"

"Crutchley's times are all wrong. Though he may have been an accomplice. If so, he's got damned good reason for giving her the chuck now. In fact, it's the best move he can possibly make, even if he only *suspects* she did it."

His voice was like flint. It jarred on Harriet.

"It's all very well, Peter, but where's your proof?"

"Nowhere."

"What did you say yourself? It's no good showing how it *might* have been done. Anybody *might* have done it—Sellon, Crutchley, Miss Twitterton, you, I, the vicar or Superintendent Kirk. But you haven't proved how it *was* done."

"Good God, don't I know that? We want proofs. We want facts. How? how? how?" He sprang up and struck at the air passionately with his hands. "This house would tell us, if roof and walls could but speak. All men are liars! Send me a dumb witness that cannot lie!"

"The house? . . . we've silenced the house ourselves, Peter. Gagged and bound it. If we'd asked it on Tuesday night—but it's hopeless now."

"That's what's biting me. I hate fooling about with maybe and might-have-been. And Kirk isn't likely to examine the thing too closely. He'll be so damned thankful to get a likelier suspect than Sellon that he'll hare off after the Crutchley-Twitterton motive—"

"But, Peter—"

"And then, as like as not," he went on, absorbed in the technical aspect of the thing, "he'll fall down on it in court for lack of direct proof. If only—"

"But, Peter—you're not going to tell Kirk about Crutchley and Miss Twitterton!"

"He'll have to know, of course. It's a fact, as far as it goes. The point is, will he see—"

"Peter—no! You can't do that! That poor little woman and her pathetic love-affair. You can't be so cruel as to tell the police—the police, good heavens!"

For the first time he seemed to realize what she was saying. "Oh!" he said, softly, and turned away towards the fire. "I was afraid it might come to this." Then, over his shoulder:

"One can't suppress evidence, Harriet. You said to me, 'Carry on.' "

"We didn't *know* these people then. She told me in confidence. She—she was grateful to me. She trusted me. You can't take people's trust and make it into a rope for their necks. Peter—"

He stood staring down into the flames. "It's abominable!" cried Harriet, in a sort of consternation. Her excitement broke against his rigidity like water against a stone. "It's—it's brutal."

"Murder is brutal."

"I know—but—"

"You have seen what murdered men look like. Well, I saw this old man's body." He swung round and faced her. "It's a pity the dead are so quiet; it makes us ready to forget them."

"The dead—are dead. We've got to be decent to the living."

"I'm thinking of the living. Till we get at the truth, every soul in this village is suspect. Do you want Sellon broken and hanged, because we wouldn't speak? Must

Crutchley be left under suspicion because the crime was never brought home to anybody else? Are they all to go about in fear, knowing there's an undiscovered murderer among them?"

"But there's no proof—no proof!"

"It's evidence. We can't pick and choose. Whoever suffers, we *must* have the truth. Nothing else matters a damn."

She could not deny it. In desperation, she broke through to the real issue:

"But must it be *your* hands—?"

"Ah!" he said, in a changed voice. "Yes. I have given you the right to ask me that. You married into trouble when you married my work and me."

He spread out his hands as though challenging her to look at them. It seemed strange that they should be the same hands that only last night . . . Their smooth strength fascinated her. License my roving hands and let them go before, behind, between—His hands, so curiously gentle and experienced. . . . With what sort of experience?

"These hangman's hands," he said, watching her. "You knew that, though, didn't you?"

Of course she had known it, but—She burst out with the truth:

"I wasn't married to you then!"

"No. . . . That makes the difference, doesn't it? . . . Well, Harriet, we are married now. We are bound. I'm afraid the moment has come when something will have to give away—you, or I—or the bond."

(So soon? . . . Yours, utterly and forever—He was hers, or else all faith was mockery.)

"No—no! . . . Oh, my dear, what is happening to us? What has become of our peace?"

"Broken," he said. "That's what violence does. Once it starts, there's no stopping it. It catches us all, sooner or later."

"But . . . it mustn't. Can't we escape?"

"Only by running away." He dropped his hands in a hopeless gesture. "Perhaps it would be better for us to run. I have no right to drag any woman into this mess—least of all, my wife. Forgive me. I have been my own master so long—I think I have forgotten the meaning of an obligation." The stricken whiteness of her face startled him. "Oh, my dear—don't upset yourself like this. Say the word, and we'll go right away. We'll leave this miserable business and never meddle again."

"Do you really mean that?" she said, incredulously.

"Of course I mean it. I have said it."

His voice was the voice of a beaten man. She was appalled, seeing what she had done.

"Peter, you're mad. Never dare to suggest such a thing. Whatever marriage is, it isn't that."

"Isn't what, Harriet?"

"Letting your affection corrupt your judgment. What kind of life could we have if I knew that you had become less than yourself by marrying me?"

He turned away again, and when he spoke, it was in a queerly shaken tone:

"My dear girl, most women would consider it a triumph."

"I know, I've heard them." Her own scorn lashed herself—the self she had only just seen. "They boast of it—'My husband would do *anything* for me. . . .' It's degrading. No human being ought to have such power over another."

"It's a very real power, Harriet."

"Then," she flung back passionately, "we won't use it. If we disagree, we'll fight it out like gentlemen. We won't stand for matrimonial blackmail."

He was silent for a moment, leaning back against the chimney-breast. Then he said, with a lightness that betrayed him:

"Harriet, you have no sense of dramatic values. Do you mean to say we are to play out our domestic comedy without the great bedroom scene?"

"Certainly. We'll have nothing so vulgar."

"Well—thank God for that!"

His strained face broke suddenly into the familiar mischievous smile. But she had been too much frightened to be able to smile back—yet.

"Bunter isn't the only person with standards. You *must* do what you think right. Promise me that. What I think doesn't matter. I swear it shall never make a difference."

He took her hand and kissed it gravely.

"Thank you, Harriet. That is love with honor."

They stood so for a moment, both conscious that something had been achieved that was of enormous—of overmastering importance. Then Harriet said, practically:

"In any case, you were right, and I was wrong. The thing has got to be done. By any means, so long as we get to the bottom of it. That's your job, and it's worth doing."

"Always provided I can do it. I don't feel very brilliant at the moment."

"You'll get there in the end. It's all *right*, Peter."

He laughed—and Bunter came in with the soup.

"I regret that dinner is a little late, my lady."

Harriet looked at the clock. It seemed to her that she had lived through interminable ages of emotion. But the hands stood at a quarter past eight. Only an hour and a half had gone by since they had entered the house.

CHAPTER XVIII

STRAWS IN THE HAIR

Follow the knave; and take this drab away.
—WILLIAM SHAKESPEARE, *II HENRY VI.II.I*

"The really essential thing," said Peter, executing a sketch on the table-cloth with the handle of his soup-spoon, "is to put in a workable hot-water system and build out a bathroom over the scullery. We can make the furnace-house *here*, so as to get a straight fall from the cistern *there*. And that will give us a direct outfall for the bath to the sewer—if I may dignify it by that name. I think there'd be room to make another little bed-room near the bathroom; and when we want more space, we can convert the attics. The electric plant can live in the stable."

Harriet agreed and offered her own contribution:

"Bunter speaks none too kindly of the kitchen range. He says he would designate it as a period piece, my lady, but, if I will permit him to say so, of an inferior period. I think it's mid-Victorian."

"We will take it a few periods back and have it Tudor. I propose to install an open fire and roasting-spit and live in the baronial manner."

"With a scullion to turn the spit? Or one of those bandy-legged period dogs?"

"Well—no; I was going to compromise about that, and have the spit turned by electricity. And an electric cooker for the days when we didn't feel so period. I like the best of both worlds—I'm quite ready to be picturesque but I draw the line at inconvenience and hard work. I'm sure it would be hard work training a modern dog to turn a spit."

"Talking of dogs—are we keeping that terrific bull-mastiff?"

"We've only hired him till after the funeral. Unless you feel a fancy for him. He is almost embarrassingly affectionate and demonstrative; but he'd do to play with the children. The goat, on the other hand, I have sent home. It got loose while we were out and ate a row of cabbages and Mrs. Ruddle's apron."

"Are you sure you don't want to keep it to provide milk for the nursery tea?"

"Quite sure. It's a billy-goat."

"Oh! well, that's very smelly and useless. I'm glad he's gone. Are we going to keep things?"

"What should you like to keep? Peacocks?"

"Peacocks need a terrace. I was thinking of pigs. They're comfortable; and when you feel dreamy and indolent you can go and scratch their backs like Mr. Baldwin. And ducks make a pleasant noise. But I don't care much for hens."

"Hens have peevish faces. By the way, I'm not sure you weren't right before dinner. On principle, it's the proper thing to give Kirk information, but I wish one knew how he was going to use it. If once he gets a fixed idea—"

"There's someone at the door. If that's Kirk, we'll have to make up our minds."

Bunter entered, bringing with him the fragrance—but only the fragrance—of sage and onion.

"My lord, there is an individual—"

"Oh, send him away. I can't stand any more individuals."

"My lord—"

"We're at dinner. Send him away. Tell him to call again later."

There was the noise of swift footsteps on the gravel

outside; and at the same moment a stout, elderly Hebrew burst into the room.

"Very thorry to intrude," said this gentleman, in a breathless and hasty manner. "No wish to cause inconvenience. I," he added helpfully, "am Moss & Isaacs—"

"You were wrong, Bunter. It's not an individual—it's a company."

"—and here in my hand I have—"

"Bunter, take the company's hat."

"Very thorry," said the company, whose failure to uncover seemed due rather to oblivion than to want of natural courtesy. "No intention to offend. But I have here a bill of thale on the furniture in this house, and I have run—"

A thunderous knocking on the door caused him to fling up despairing hands. Bunter hurried out.

"A bill of sale?" cried Harriet.

The intruder turned eagerly to her:

"For a debt of theventy-three, thickthteen, thickth," he said, emotion choking his speech—"and I have run all the way from the buth-thtop—all the way—and there ith a man—"

He was right; there was a man. He pushed his way past Bunter, crying out in reproachful tones:

"Mr. Solomons, Mr. Solomons! that's not fair. Everything in this house is the property of my clients, and the executrix has agreed—"

"Good evening, Mr. MacBride," said the master of the house, politely.

"I can't help that," said Mr. Solomons, his voice drowning Mr. MacBride's reply. He mopped his forehead with his handkerchief. "We hold a bill of sale on the furniture—look at the date on this document—"

Mr. MacBride said firmly:

"Ours has been running five years."

"I don't care," retorted Mr. Solomons, "if it's been running as long as Charley's Aunt!"

"Gentlemen, gentlemen!" said Peter, in conciliatory accents, "cannot this matter be amicably arranged?"

"Our van," said Mr. Solomons, "will call for the goods tomorrow."

"Our clients' van," replied Mr. MacBride, "is on the way now."

Mr. Solomons uttered a loud expostulatory howl, and Peter tried again:

"I implore you, gentlemen, have some consideration for my wife, if not for me. We are in the middle of dinner, and you propose to remove the table and chairs. We have to sleep—will you not leave us so much as a bed to lie on? We also, if it comes to that, have some claim upon the furniture, since we hired it. Pray do not be so precipitate. . . . Mr. MacBride, you have known us long and (I hope) loved us well—you will, I am sure, have compassion on our nerves and feelings, and not turn us out dinnerless to sleep under the nearest haystack."

"My lord," said Mr. MacBride, somewhat moved by this appeal, but conscious of his duty, "in the interests of our clients—"

"In the interests of our firm," said Mr. Solomons.

"In all our interests," said Peter, "will you not sit down and share our roast duck with apple sauce and sage and onion stuffing? You, Mr. Solomons, have run fast and far—your strength needs sustaining. You, Mr. MacBride, spoke feelingly yesterday morning about our English family life—will you not for once consent to see it at its best? Do not break up the happy home! Over a slice of the breast and a glass of the best any little differences may be adjusted."

"Yes, indeed," said Harriet. "Do join us. Bunter will break his heart if the bird gets dried up in the oven."

Mr. MacBride hesitated.

"It's very good of you," began Mr. Solomons, wistfully. "If your ladyship—"

"No, no, Solly," said Mr. MacBride, "it ain't fair."

"My dear," said Peter, with a polite inclination, "you know very well that it is a husband's incurable habit to invite his business friends to dine under any circumstances and on the shortest possible notice. Without that habit, home life would not be what it is. Therefore I make no apology."

"Of course not," said Harriet. "Bunter, these gentlemen will dine with us."

"Very good, my lady." He laid dexterous hands on Mr. Solomons and relieved him of his overcoat. "Allow me." Mr. MacBride, without further argument, valeted himself and then helped Peter to bring two more chairs to the table, observing as he did so: "I don't know what you advanced on these, Solly, but they weren't worth it."

"So far as we are concerned," said Peter, "you may have the whole lot tomorrow and welcome. Now—are we all quite comfortable? Mr. Solomons on the right—Mr. MacBride on the left. Bunter—the claret!"

Mr. Solomons and Mr. MacBride, mellow with Hermitage and cigars, departed fraternally at a quarter to ten, having previously made a brief tour of the house, so as to check their inventories together. Peter, who had accompanied them in order to establish his right to his own belongings, returned, bearing in his hand one of the little straw wig-wams in which wine-bottles are housed while traveling.

"What's that for, Peter?"

"Me," said his lordship. He detached the straws methodically, one by one, and began to thread them through his hair. He had succeeded in making a very passable bird's-nest of himself when Superintendent Kirk was announced.

"Good evening, Mr. Kirk," said Harriet, with as much warmth of welcome as she could put into words.

"Good evening," said the Superintendent. "I'm afraid I'm intruding." He looked at Peter, who made a horrible face at him. "It's a bit late for a call."

"This," said Peter, wildly, "is the foul fiend Flibbertigibbet: he begins at Curfew and walks till the first cock. Have a straw, Superintendent. You'll need one before you've finished."

"Have nothing of the sort," said Harriet. "You look tired. Have a glass of beer or some whiskey or something and don't mind my husband. He sometimes gets taken that way."

The Superintendent thanked her absent-mindedly; he seemed to be in travail with an idea. He slowly opened his mouth, and looked at Peter again.

"Sit down, sit down," said the latter, hospitably. "I'll talk a word with this same learned Theban."

"Got it!" cried Mr. Kirk. "King Lear! Though their injunction be to bar my doors And let this tyrannous night take hold upon you, Yet have I ventur'd to come seek you out."

"You're very nearly right about that," said Harriet. "We really thought we were going to be turned out into the tyrannous night. Hence the distraction and the straws."

Mr. Kirk inquired how this might be.

"Well," said Harriet, installing him on one of the settles, "there's a Mr. Solomons of Moss & Isaacs, who holds a bill of sale on the furniture, and your old friend Mr. MacBride, who wants to distrain on the furniture for his writ, and they both came in together to take the furniture away. But we gave them dinner and they went peaceably."

"You may ask," added Peter, "why they rather choose to have a weight of carrion flesh than to receive three thousand ducats—I cannot tell you, but so it was."

Mr. Kirk paused so long this time that both Peter and Harriet thought he must have become stricken with aphasia; but at last, and with a wide smile of triumph, he gave tongue:

"He is well paid that is well satisfied! Merchant of Venice!"

"A Daniel come to judgment! Harriet, the Superintendent has caught the hang of our half-witted manner of conversation. He is a man, take him for all in all, we shall not look upon his like again. Give him his drink—he has deserved it. Say when. Shall I make spirits fetch me what I please, Resolve me of all ambiguities?"

"Thank you," said the Superintendent, "not too stiff, my lord, if you don't mind. We'll have it gentle and the elements so mixed—"

"That a spoon might stand up in it," suggested Peter.

"No," said Mr. Kirk. "That bit doesn't seem to finish up quite right. But thanks all the same. Here's health."

"And what have you been doing all afternoon?" inquired Peter, bringing a stool to the fire and seating himself on it between his wife and Kirk.

"Well, my lord," said Kirk. "I've been up to London."

"To London?" said Harriet. "That's right, Peter. Come a little further this way and let me take the straws out. *Il m'aime—un peu—beaucoup—*"

"But not to see the Queen," pursued the Superintendent. "I went to see Frank Crutchley's young woman. In Clerkenwell."

"Has he got one there?"

"*Passionément—à la folie—*"

"He *had,*" said Kirk.

"*Pas du tout. Il m'aime—*"

"I got the address from that chap Williams over at Hancock's. Seems she's a good-looking young woman—"

"*Un peu—beaucoup—*"

"With a bit of money—"

"*Passionément—*"

"Lived with 'er dad and seemed dead struck on Frank Crutchley. But there—"

"A *la folie—*"

"You know what girls are. Some other fellow turned up—"

Harriet paused, with the twelfth straw in her fingers.

"And the long and the short of it is, she married the other bloke three months back."

"*Pas du tout!*" said Harriet; and flung the straws into the fire.

"The devil she did!" said Peter. He caught Harriet's eye.

"But what got me all worked up," said Kirk, "was finding out what 'er father was."

"It was a robber's daughter, and her name was Alice Brown. Her father was the terror of a small Italian town."

"Not a bit of it. He's a—There!" said Mr. Kirk, arresting his glass half way to his mouth, "of all the trades and professions open to a man, what should you say he was?"

"From your air," replied Peter, "of having, so to speak, found the key that cuts the Gordian knot—"

"I can't imagine," said Harriet, hastily. "We give it up."

"Well," announced Kirk, eyeing Peter a little dubiously, "if you give it up, then I'll tell you. 'Er father is an ironmonger and locksmith as cuts keys when wanted."

"Good God, you don't say so!"

Kirk, putting down a mouthful, nodded emphatically.

"And what's more," he went on, setting the glass down on the table with a smack, "what's more, none so long ago —six months more or less—young Crutchley comes along, bright as you please, and asks him to cut a key for him."

"Six months ago! Well, well!"

"Six months. But," resumed the Superintendent, "now this I'm going to tell you *will* surprise you. I don't mind saying it surprised me. . . . Thank you, I don't mind if I do. . . . Well—the old boy didn't make no secret of the key. Seems there'd a-been a bit of a tiff between the young people before they parted brass-rags. Anyhow, he didn't seem to feel no special call to speak up for Frank Crutchley. So when I asked the question, he answered straight off, and what's more, he took me round to his workshop. He's a methodical old bird, and when he makes a new key, he keeps a cast of it. Says people often lose their keys, and it comes in 'andy to have a record. I dunno. Shouldn't wonder if he'd had official inquiries round there before. But that's neether here nor there. He took me round and he showed me the cast what he'd made of the key. And what do you think that key was like?"

Peter, having been once rebuked, did not this time venture on so much as a veiled guess. But Harriet felt that some sort of reply was called for. Mustering up all the astonishment the human voice is capable of expressing, she said:

"You *can't* mean it was the key to one of the doors in his house?"

Mr. Kirk smote his thigh with a large hand.

"Aha!" he cried. "What did I say? I knew I should catch you there! No—it was not, and nothing like, neether. Now! What do you think of that?"

Peter picked up the remains of the bottle-straw and began to weave himself a fresh headdress. Harriet felt that her effort had gone even better than she had intended.

"How astonishing!"

"Nothing like it," repeated the Superintendent. "A huge great thing it was, more like a church key."

"Was it," asked Peter, his fingers working rapidly among the straws, "made from a key or from a wax mold?"

"From a key. He brought it along with him. Said it was the key to a barn he'd hired to keep some stuff in. Said the key belonged to the owner and he wanted another for himself."

"I should have thought it was the owner's business to supply a key for the tenant," said Harriet.

"So should I. Crutchley explained he'd had one once and lost it. And mind you, that might be true. Anyhow, that's the only key the old man had cut for him—or so he said, and I don't think he was lying, neether. So away I come, by the evening train, no wiser. But after I'd had me bit o' supper, I says to myself, Well, I says, it's a line—never leave a line, I says, till you've followed it up. So out I goes to Pagford to look for our young friend. Well, he wasn't in the garage, but Williams said he'd seen him go out on his bike along the road to Ambledon Overbrook—you may know it—about a mile and a half out o' Pagford on the Lopsley road."

"We came through it this afternoon. Pretty little church with a brooch spire."

"Yes, it's got a spire. Well, I thought I'd have a look for my gentleman, so I pushed along and—do you remember seeing a big old barn with a tiled roof about three quarters to a mile out of Pagford?"

"I noticed it," said Harriet. "It stands all by itself in a field."

"That's right. Well, going past there, I see a light, as it might be a bicycle-lamp, going across that field, and it came to me all of a sudden that about six months ago, Crutchley did a bit of work on a tractor for Mr. Moffatt as owns that barn. See? I just put them things together in my mind. So I gets out of the car, and I follows the bicycle light across the field. He wasn't going fast—just walking with it—and I went pretty quick, and when he was about half way across, he must aheard me coming, because he stopped. So I come up and then I see who it was."

The Superintendent paused again.

"Go on," said Peter. "We'll buy it this time. It wasn't Crutchley. It was Mr. Goodacre or the landlord of the Crown."

"Caught you again," said Kirk, jovially. "Crutchley it was, all right. I asked him what he was doing there, and he said that was his business and we argued a bit, and I said I'd like to know what he was doing with a key to Mr. Moffatt's barn, and he wanted to know what I meant by that and—anyhow, the long and the short was, I said I was going to see what there was in the barn and he was damn well going to come with me. So we went along, and he sounded pretty sulky, but he says: 'You're barking up the wrong tree,' and I says, 'We'll see about that.' So we got to the door and I says, 'Give me that key,' and he says, 'I tell you I ain't got no key,' and I says, 'Then what do you want in this field, because it don't lead nowhere, and anyhow,' I says, 'I'm going to see.' So I puts me 'and on the door and it come open as easy as winking. And what do you think was inside that barn?"

Peter contemplated his plait of straw and twisted the ends together to form a crown.

"At a guess," he replied, "I should say—Polly Mason."

"Well, there!" exclaimed the Superintendent. "Just as I

was all set to catch you again! Polly Mason it was, and she wasn't half scared to see me, neether. 'Now, my girl,' I said to her, 'I don't like to see you here,' I says. 'What's all this?' And Crutchley says, 'No business of yours, you stupid cop. She's over the age of consent.' 'Maybe,' I said, 'but she's got a mother,' I said, "as brought her up decent; and what's more,' I said, 'it's breaking and entering, and that's a civil trespass, and Mr. Moffatt'll have something to say about it.' So there was more words passed, and I said to the girl, 'You 'and over that key, which you ain't got no right to, and if you've got any sense or feeling,' I said, 'you'll come along home with me.' And the end of it was, I brought her back —and a lot of sauce she gave me, the young piece. As for me lord, I left him to twiddle his thumbs—I beg your pardon, my lord—no offense intended."

Peter finished his crown and put it on.

"It's an odd thing," he observed, "that men like Crutchley, with quantities of large white teeth, are practically always gay Lotharios."

"Not frivolously gay, either," said Harriet. "Two strings to the bow for use and one for pleasure."

"Frank Crutchley," said Kirk, "has got too much o' what the cat cleans 'er paws with. Stupid cop, indeed—I'll cop 'im, the cheeky 'ound, one o' these days."

"There is a certain lack of the finer feelings," said Peter. "Euphelia serves to grace my measure but Chloe is my real flame, no doubt. But to get Euphelia's father to cut the key for Chloe is—tactless."

" 'Tain't my business to run a Sunday school," said the Superintendent, "but that Polly Mason's asking for trouble. 'The banns is going up next Sunday,' says she, bold as brass. 'Are they?' says I. 'Well, if I was you, my girl, I'd run round to parson with 'em myself, straight away, before your young man changes his mind. If you and him's walking out in a proper way, there's no need to have keys to other folks' barns.' I didn't say anything about the young lady in London, because that's over and done with, but where there's one there might be two."

"There were two," said Harriet resolutely; "and the other one was here, in Pagford."

"What's that?" said Kirk.

Harriet told her story for the second time that evening.

"Well, I'm bothered!" exclaimed Mr. Kirk, laughing heartily. "Poor old Aggie Twitterton! Kissing Frank Crutchley in the churchyard. That's a good 'un!"

Neither of the other two made any comment. Presently, Kirk's mirth subsided and he showed signs of being once more in a state of mental gestation. His eyes became fixed and his lips moved silently. "'Alf a moment, 'alf a moment," said Kirk while they watched him breathlessly; "Aggie Twitterton, eh? And young Crutchley? Now, that's made me think of something, that has. . . . Now, don't you tell me. . . . There! I knew I'd get it!"

"I thought you would," said Peter, only half aloud.

"Twelfth Night!" cried Mr. Kirk, exultantly. "Orsino, that's it! 'Too old, by heaven, Let still the woman take An elder than herself'—I knew there was something in Shakespeare." He fell silent again. "Hullo!" he said, in a changed tone, "that's all right, but see here! If Aggie Twitterton wanted the money for Frank Crutchley and had the keys to the house, what was to prevent her—eh?"

"Nothing whatever," said Peter. "Only you've got to prove it, you know."

"I've had my eye on Aggie Twitterton all along," said the Superintendent. "After all, you can't get over them things she said. And her knowing about the will and all. And, come to look at it, whoever did it had to get into the house, now, hadn't they?"

"Why?" demanded Peter. "How do you know Noakes didn't come out and get killed in the garden?"

"No," said Kirk, "that's the one thing he couldn't, and you know that as well as I do; and for why? There wasn't no earth nor gravel on his shoes nor yet on his coat where he fell on it. And this time of the year, and with the rain we had last week there would a-been. No, my lord, springs to catch woodcocks! You don't catch me that way."

"Hamlet," said Peter, meekly. "Very well. Now we'd better tell you all the ways we've thought of for getting into the house."

After nearly an hour, the Superintendent was shaken, but not convinced.

"See here, my lord," he said at last. "I see your point, and you're quite right. It's no good saying, He might or She might, because there'd always be a clever counsel to say, might ain't necess*ar*ily right. And I see I been a bit hasty, overlooking that window and the trap-door and about something having been thrown at deceased. Better late than never. I'll be round again in the morning, and we'll go into all them points. And here's another thing. I'll bring Joe Sellon with me, and you can try for yourself about him gettin' through them—mullions, d'you call them? Because, not to put too fine a point upon it, he'd make two of you, my lord—and what's more, it's my belief *you* could get through pretty well almost anything, including a judge and jury, if you'll pardon me saying so. . . . No, don't you mistake me. I ain't out to put nothing on Aggie Twitterton —I'm out to find who killed deceased, and prove it. And I *will* prove it, if I have to go through the place with a toothcomb."

"Then," said Peter, "you have to be up pretty early in the morning, to stop our London friends from carrying away the furniture, lock, stock and barrel."

"I'll see they don't take the trapdoor," retorted the Superintendent. "Nor yet the door and windows. And now I'll be getting off home, and I'm very sorry for keeping you and her ladyship up like this."

"Not at all," said Peter. "Parting is such sweet sorrow— We've had quite a Shakespearean evening, haven't we?"

"Well," said Harriet, as her lord returned from seeing the Superintendent to the door, "he wasn't unreasonable, after all. But oh! I do hope there won't be any more people tonight."

"*Nous menons une vie assez mouvementée*. I've never

known such a day. Bunter looks quite haggard—I have sent him to bed. As for me, I don't feel like the same person I was before breakfast."

"I don't even feel the same person I was before dinner. Peter—about that. It's frightened me rather. I've always so loathed and dreaded any sort of possessiveness. You know how I've always run away from it."

"I've reason to know it." He made a wry face. "You ran like the Red Queen."

"I know I did. And now—I start it, of all people! I simply can't think what came over me. It's frightful. Is that sort of thing always going to happen to me?"

"I don't know," he said, lightly. "I can't imagine. In an experience of women extending, like the good Dr. Watson's, over many nations, and three separate continents—"

"Why separate? Do ordinary continents come blended, like teas?"

"I don't know. That's what it says in the book. Three separate continents. In all my experience, you are completely unprecedented. I never met anybody like you."

"Why? Possessiveness isn't unprecedented."

"On the contrary—it's as common as mud. But to recognize it in one's self and chuck it overboard is—unusual. If you want to be a normal person, my girl, you should let it rip and give yourself and everybody else hell with it. And you should call it something else—devotion or self-sacrifice and that sort of thing. If you go on behaving with all this reason and generosity, everybody will think we don't give a damn for one another."

"Well—if ever I do anything like that again, for heaven's sake don't give in . . . you wouldn't have, really?"

"If it had come to the point—yes, I should. I couldn't live in a wrangle. Not with you, anyway."

"I wouldn't have believed you could be so weak. As if a possessive person is *ever* going to be satisfied. If you gave in once, you'd have to do it again and again. Like Danegeld."

"Don't be harsh with me, Domina. If it happens again,

I'll take a stick to you. I promise. But I wasn't sure what I was up against—*la femme jalouse de l'oeuvre*, or a perfectly reasonable objection, or just marriage as such. I can't expect being married to be just like not being married, can I? I thought I might be heading the wrong way. I thought if I show you where the hitch was—I don't know what I thought. It doesn't matter. I only know what you said, and that it took my breath away."

"I only know that I started to behave like a pig and thought better of it. Peter—it hasn't upset the—the things you said before? It hasn't spoilt anything?"

"To know that I can trust you better than myself? What do you think? . . . But listen, dear—for God's sake let's take that word 'possess' and put a brick round its neck and drown it. I will not use it or hear it used—not even in the crudest physical sense. It's meaningless. We can't possess one another. We can only give and hazard all we have—Shakespeare, as Kirk would say. . . . I don't know what's the matter with me tonight. Something seems to have got off the chain. I've said things I didn't think I could say if I lived to be a hundred—by which time most of them wouldn't be worth saying."

"It seems to be that kind of day. I've said things too. I think I've said everything, except—"

"That's true. You never have said it. You've always found some other phrase for it. *Un peu d'audace, que diable!* . . . Well?"

"I love you."

"Bravely said—though I had to screw it out of you like a cork out of a bottle. Why should that phrase be so difficult? I—personal pronoun, subjective case; L-O-V-E, love, verb active, meaning—Well, on Mr. Squeer's principle, go to bed and work it out."

The window was still open; for October, the air was strangely mild and still. From somewhere close at hand a cat—probably the ginger tom—lifted its voice in a long-drawn wail of unappeasable yearning. Peter's right hand searched the sill, and closed upon the granite paperweight. But even in the act, he changed his mind, released his grip and with the other hand drew the casement to and fastened it.

"Who am I," said he aloud, "to cast stones at my fellow-mortal?"

He lit his candle, extinguished the lamps and made his way upstairs.

Two minutes later, Bunter, prompted by God knows what savage libido, flung a boot from the back bedroom; and on the mere the wailing died away.

CHAPTER XIX

PRICKLY PEAR

This is the dead land
This is cactus land
Here the stone images
Are raised, here they receive
The supplication of a dead man's hand
Under the twinkle of a fading star. . . .

Between the idea
And the reality
Between the motion
And the act
Falls the Shadow.

—T. S. ELIOT, *THE HOLLOW MEN*

Peter, what were you dreaming about early this morning? It sounded pretty awful."

He looked vexed.

"Oh, my God, have I started that again? I thought I'd learnt to keep my dreams to myself. Did I say things? Tell me the worst."

"I couldn't make out what you said. But it sounded as though—to put it mildly—you had something on your mind."

"What an agreeable companion I must be," he said, bitterly. "I know. I've been told about it before. The perfect bedfellow—so long as I keep awake. I'd no business to risk it; but one always hopes one's going to come right again sometime. In future I'll remove myself."

"Don't be an idiot, Peter. You stopped dreaming as soon as I got hold of you."

"So I did. It comes back to me now. . . . Fifteen of us marching across a prickly desert, and we were all chained together. There was something I had forgotten—to do or tell somebody—but I couldn't stop, because of the chain. . . . Our mouths were full of sand, and there were flies and things. . . . We were in dark blue uniforms, and we had to go on. . . ."

He broke off. "I don't know why blue uniforms—it's usually something to do with the War. And telling one's dreams is the last word in egotism."

"I want to hear it; it sounds perfectly foul."

"Well, it was, in a way. . . . Our boots were broken with the march. . . . When I looked down, I saw the bones of my own feet, and they were black, because we'd been hanged in chains a long time ago and were beginning to come to pieces."

"*Mais priez dieu que tous nous veuille absoudre*."

"Yes, that's it. Very like the Ballade des Pendus. Only it was hot, with a sky like brass—and we knew that the end of the journey would be worse than the beginning. And it was all my fault, because I'd forgotten—whatever it was."

"What was the end of it?"

"It didn't end. It changed when you touched me—something about rain and a bunch of chrysanthemums. . . . Oh, it was only the old responsibility-dream, and a mild one at that. The funny thing is that I know there *is* something I've forgotten. I woke up with it on the tip of my tongue—but it's gone."

"It'll come back if you don't worry it."

"I wish it would; and then I shouldn't feel so guilty about it. . . . Hullo, Bunter, what's that? The post? Heaven above, man, what have you got there?"

"Our silk hat, my lord."

"Silk hat? Don't be ridiculous, Bunter. We don't want that in the country."

"The funeral is this morning, my lord. I thought it possible your lordship might desire to attend it. The prayer-books are in the other parcel with the black suit."

"But surely to goodness I can go to a village funeral without a mourning suit and a top-hat!"

"The conventional marks of esteem are highly appreciated in rural communities, my lord. But it is as your lordship wishes. Two vans have arrived to take the furniture, my lord, and Superintendent Kirk is below with Mr. MacBride and Mr. Solomons. With your lordship's permission, I will suggest that I should take the car over to Broxford and order a few temporary necessities—such as a couple of camp-beds and a kettle."

"Peter," said Harriet, looking up from her correspondence, "there's a letter from your mother. She says she is going down to the Dower House this morning. The shooting-party at the Hall has broken up, and Gerald and Helen are going for the weekend to Lord Attenbury's. She wonders whether we should like to join her for a day or two. She thinks we may need rest and change—not from one another, she is careful to explain, but from what she calls housekeeping."

"My mother is a very remarkable woman. Her faculty for hitting the right nail on the head is almost miraculous —especially as all her blows have the air of being delivered at random. Housekeeping! The house is about all we're likely to keep, by the looks of it."

"What do you think of her idea?"

"It's rather for you to say. We've got to go somewhere or other, unless you really prefer the kettle and the camp-bedstead to which Bunter so feelingly alludes. But it is said to be unwise to introduce the mother-in-law complication too early on."

"There are mothers-in-law and mothers-in-law."

"True; and you wouldn't be bothered with the others-in-law, which makes a difference. We once talked about seeing the old place when we could do it on our own."

"I'd like to go, Peter."

"Very well, then, you shall. Bunter, send Her Grace a wire to say we're coming down tonight."

"Very good, my lord."

"Heartfelt satisfaction," said Peter, as Bunter left them. "He will be sorry to abandon the investigation, but the camp-beds and the kettle would break even Bunter's spirit. In a way I feel rather thankful to Mr. Solomons for precipitating matters. We haven't run away; we've received the order to retreat and can march out with all the honors of war."

"You really feel that?"

"I think so. Yes, I do."

Harriet looked at him and felt depressed, as one frequently does when one gets what one fancied one wanted.

"You'll never want to come back to this house again."

He shifted uneasily. "Oh, I don't know. I could be bounded in a nutshell . . . were it not that I have bad dreams."

But he would always have bad dreams in that house while the shadow of failure lay on it. . . . He pushed the subject aside by asking:

"Any other news from the Mater?"

"Not news, exactly. Of course, she's awfully sorry we've been tr-r-roubled by all this. She thinks she has found us a very suitable pair of housemaids, to come in November. The chandelier is up, and every drop has been separately silenced so as not to jingle; she had the piano-tuner playing the piano at it for an hour on end, and it didn't let out a single ting-a-ling. Ahasuerus caught a mouse on Tuesday night and put it in Franklin's bedroom slipper. Your nephew Jerry had a little difference of opinion with a policeman, but explained that he had been marrying off his uncle and escaped with a fine and a caution. That's all. The rest is—well, it more or less amounts to saying she's glad I can give you a good chit and it may not be a bad thing to begin with a little adversity."

"Perhaps she's right. I'm thankful it was a good chit, anyhow. Meanwhile, here's a note for you from Uncle Pandarus—I mean, Uncle Paul—enclosed in a letter to me in which he has the impertinence to hope that my addiction of late years to what he calls 'intemperate orgies of virtue' have not left me too much out of practice for my *métier d'époux*. He recommends *une vie réglée* and begs I will not allow myself to become *trop émotionné*, since emotion tends to impair *les forces vitales*. I do not know anybody who can cram more cynical indelicacy into a letter of good advice than my Uncle Pandarus."

"Mine's good advice, too; but it isn't exactly cynical."

(Mr. Delagardie had, in fact, written:

> MY DEAR NIECE—I hope that my absurd, but on the whole agreeable nephew is contriving to fill your cup with the wine of life. May an old man who knows him well remind you that what is wine to you is bread to him. You are too sensible to be offended by *cette franchise*. My nephew is not sensible at all—il n'est que sensible et passablement sensuel. Il a plus besoin de vous que vous de lui; soyez généreuse—c'est une nature qu'on ne saurait gâter. Il sent le besoin de se donner—de s'épancher; vous ne lui refuserez certes pas ce modeste plaisir. La froideur, la coquetterie même, le tuent; il ne sait pas s'imposer; la lutte lui répugne. Tout cela, vous le savez déjà—Pardon! je vous trouve extrèmement sympathique, et je crois que son bien-être nous est cher à tous deux. Avec cela, il est marchand du bonheur à qui en veut; j'espère que vous trouverez en lui ce qui pourra vous plaire. Pour le rendre heureux, vous n'avez qu'à être heureuse; il supporte mal les souffrances d'autrui. Recevez, ma chère nièce, mes voeux les plus sincères.)

Peter grinned.

"I won't ask what it is. The least said about Uncle Paul's good advice, the soonest mended. He is a most regrettable old man, and his judgment is disgustingly sound. According to him I suffer from a romantic heart, which plays the cat-and-banjo with my realistic mind."

(Mr. Delagardie had, in fact, written:

> . . . Cette femme te sera un point d'appui. Elle n'a connu jusqu'ici que les chagrins de l'amour; tu lui en apprendra les délices. Elle trouvera en toi des délicatesses imprévues, et qu'elle saura apprécier. Mais surtout, mon ami, pas de faiblesse! Ce n'est pas une jeune fille niaise et étourdie; c'est une intelligence forte, qui aime à résoudre les problèmes par la tête. Il ne faut pas être trop soumis; elle ne t'en saura pas gré. Il faut encore moins l'enjôler; elle pourra se raviser. Il faut convaincre; je suis persuadé qu'elle se montrera magnanime. Tâche de comprimer les élans d'un coeur chaleureux—ou plutôt réserve-les pour ces moments d'intimité conjugale où ils ne seront pas déplacés et pourront te servir à quelque chose. Dans toutes les autres circonstances, fais valoir cet esprit raissoneur dont tu n'es pas entièrement dépourvu. A vos âges, il est nécessaire de préciser; on ne vient plus à bout d'une situation en se livrant à des étreintes effrénées et en poussant des cris déchirants. Raidistoi, afin d'inspirer le respect à ta femme; en lui tenant tête tu lui fourniras le meilleur moyen de ne pas s'ennuyer. . . .)

Peter folded this epistle away with a grimace, and inquired:

"Do you mean to go to the funeral?"

"I don't think so. I've got no black frock to do your top-hat credit, and I'd better stay here to keep an eye on the Solomons-MacBride outfit."

"Bunter can do that."

"Oh, no—he's panting to attend the obsequies. I've just seen him brushing his best bowler. Are you coming down?"

"Not for a moment. There's a letter from my agent I've simply got to attend to. I thought I'd cleared everything up nicely, but one of the tenants has chosen this moment to create a tiresomeness. And Jerry has got himself into a jam with a woman and is really frightfully sorry to bother me, but the husband has turned up with the light of blackmail in his eye and what on earth is he to do?"

"Great heavens! That boy again?"

"What I shall *not* do is to send him a check. As it happens, I know all about the lady and gentleman in question, and all that is required is a firm letter and the address of my solicitor, who knows all about them too. But I can't write downstairs, with Kirk oiling in and out of the windows and brokers' men wrangling over the what-not."

"Of course you can't. I'll go and see to things. Be busy and good. . . . And I used to think you were God's own idler, without a responsibility in the world!"

"Property won't run itself, worse luck! Nor yet nephews. Aha! Uncle Pandarus likes giving avuncular advice, does he? Trust *me* to distribute a little avuncular advice in the quarter where it will do most good. Every dog has his day. . . . *C'est bien, embrasse-moi. . . . Ah, non! voyons, tu me dépeignes. . . . Allons, hop! il faut être sérieux.*"

Peter, having dealt with his correspondence and been persuaded, fretfully protesting, into a black suit and a stiff collar, came downstairs and found Superintendent Kirk about to take his leave, and Mr. MacBride just issuing victor from a heated three-cornered argument between himself, Mr. Solomons and a dusty-looking professional person who explained that he represented the executrix. What precise business arrangement had been come to, Peter did not ask and never discovered. The upshot seemed to be that the furniture was to go, Harriet (on Peter's behalf) having waived all claim to it on the grounds (a) that they had so far paid nothing for the use of it, (b) that they would not have it if it were given away with a pound of tea and (c) that they were going away for the weekend and (d) would be glad to have it out of the house as soon as possible to make room for their own goods.

This point having been settled, Mr. MacBride appealed to the Superintendent for leave to carry on. Kirk nodded gloomily.

"No luck?" asked Peter.

"Not a ha'porth," said Kirk. "It's as you said. Puffett and Bert Ruddle have left their marks all over the place upstairs, but there's no telling if some of them wasn't made last week. There's no dint on this floor, as there might be if a stone had been thrown down—but *on* the other 'and, this old oak is that 'ard, you couldn't make any impression on it if you heaved rocks at it for a week. I dunno, I'm sure. I never see such a case. There don't seem to be nothing you can lay your fingers on, like."

"Have you tried squeezing Sellon through the window?"

"Joe Sellon?" Kirk snorted. "If you was to go down to the village, you'd see Joe Sellon. Coo! Talk of a traffic jam! I never see nothing like it in all my born days. There's 'alf Pagford here and pretty well the 'ole of Broxford, and all them newspapermen from London, and the *Broxford and Pagford Gazette* and the *North-Herts Advertiser* and a chap with one of them moving-picture cameras, and cars that thick in front of the Crown nobody can't get in, and such a mob around the bar, they can't get served when they are in. Joe's got more'n he can do. I've left my sergeant down there to lend 'im a hand. And," said the Superintendent, indignantly, "jest as we'd got about twenty cars parked neat and tidy in the lane by Mr. Giddy's field, up comes a kid and squeaks, 'Oh, please, mister—can't you let me by? I've brought the cow to bull'—and we 'ad to move 'em all out again. Aggravating ain't the word. But there! It can't last forever, that's a comfort; and I'll bring Joe up here when the funeral's over and out of the way."

• • • • •

Mr. MacBride's men worked expertly. Harriet, watching the swift disintegration of her honeymoon house into a dusty desert of straw and packing-cases, rolled-up curtains and spidery pictures spreading their loose wires like springs, wondered whether the whole of her married life would have the same kaleidoscopic quality. Character is destiny: probably there was something in her and Peter that doomed them never to carry any adventure to its close without preposterous interruptions and abrupt changes of fortune. She laughed, as she assisted matters by tying a bunch of fire-irons together, and remembered what a married friend had once confided to her about her own honeymoon.

"Jim wanted a peaceful place, so we went to a tiny fishing village in Brittany. It was lovely, of course, but it rained a good deal, and I think it was rather a mistake we had so little to do. We were very much in love, I don't mean we weren't—but there were a great many hours to get through, and it didn't seem somehow quite the right thing just to sit down quietly and read a book. There's something to be said, after all, for the sightseeing kind of honeymoon—it does give one a program."

Well; things did not always go according to program. Harriet looked up from the fire-irons and with some surprise observed Frank Crutchley.

"Were you wanting any help, my lady?"

"Well, Crutchley, I don't know. Are you free this morning?"

Crutchley explained that he had brought a party over from Great Pagford for the funeral; but they were going to lunch at the Crown and would not be wanting him again till later on.

"But don't you want to go to the funeral? You're in the Paggleham choir, aren't you? And the vicar said something about a choral service."

Crutchley shook his head.

"I've had words with Mrs. Goodacre—leastways, she 'ad words with me. That Kirk . . . interfering. It ain't no business of Vicar's wife about me and Polly Mason. I went up about 'aving the banns published, and Mrs. Goodacre set on me."

"Oh!" said Harriet. She was not very well pleased with Crutchley herself; but since he obviously had no idea that Miss Twitterton had made her troubles public, it seemed better not to refer to the subject. By this time, Miss Twitterton was probably regretting that she had spoken. And to take the matter up with Crutchley would only emphasize the poor little woman's humiliation by giving it importance. Besides, one of the removalmen was kneeling in the window, laying the bronze horsemen and other objects of art tenderly away in a packing-case, while another, on the stepladder, had relieved the walls of the painted mirror and was contemplating an attack on the clock.

"Very well, Crutchley. You can give the men a hand if they need it."

"Yes, my lady. Shall I get some of this stuff out?"

"Well—no, not for the moment." She turned to the man in the window, who had just placed the last atrocity in the case and was putting the lid on.

"Do you mind leaving the rest of this room to the last? My husband will be coming back here after the funeral and may have one or two people with him. We shall need some chairs to sit on."

"Right you are, lady. Could we do a bit upstairs?"

"Yes; certainly. And we shan't want this room very long."

"O.K., lady. Come along, Bill, this way."

Bill, a thin man with an apologetic mustache, came obediently down from the steps.

"Right-ho, George. It'll take us a bit o'time to take down them four-posters."

"Can this man give you any help? He's the gardener here."

George eyed Crutchley, who had taken the steps and brought them back to the center of the room. "There's them plants in the green'us," said George. "We ain't got no special instructions about them, but we was told to take everything."

"Yes, the plants will have to go, and the ones in here as well. But these will do later. Go and see to the greenhouse, Crutchley."

"And there's a sight o'things in the outhouse," said George. "Jack's out there; he'd be glad of a hand with them."

Crutchley put the steps back against the wall and went out. George and Bill departed upstairs. Harriet remembered that Peter's tobacco and cigars were in the what-not and collected them. Then, smitten by a sudden pang, she hastened out into the pantry. It was already stripped. With the Furies at her heels, she bounded down the cellar steps, not even pausing to remember what had once lain at the foot of them. The place was dark as Egypt, but she struck a match, and breathed again. All was well. The two-and-a-half dozen of port lay carefully ranged upon the racks; and in front of them was tacked a notice in large letters: HIS LORDSHIP'S PROPERTY. DO NOT TOUCH. Coming up again into the light, she encountered Crutchley entering by the back door. He started at seeing her.

"I went to see if the wine was all right. I see Bunter has put up a notice. But please tell the men specially that they mustn't on any account lay a finger on those bottles."

Crutchley broke into a wide smile that showed Harriet how attractive his face could be and threw light on the indiscretions of Miss Twitterton and Polly Mason.

"They ain't likely to forget, my lady. Mr. Bunter, he spoke to them himself—very solemn. He sets great store by that wine, seemin'ly. If you could a-heard him yesterday ticking off Martha Ruddle—"

Harriet wished she had heard it, and was greatly tempted to ask for an eye-witness account of the scene, but considered that Crutchley's forwardness of manner scarcely called for encouragement; besides, whether he knew it or not, he was in her bad books. She said, repressively:

"Well, take care they don't forget it."

"Very good. They can't take the barrel, I suppose."

"Oh, yes—that doesn't belong to us. Only the bottled beer."

"Very good, my lady."

Crutchley went out again, without taking whatever it was he had come for, and Harriet returned to the sitting-room. With a kind of tolerant pity, she lifted the aspidistras from their containing pots and gathered them into a melancholy little group on the floor, together with a repellent little cactus like an over-stuffed pincushion and a young rubber-plant. She had seldom seen plants she could care less for, but they were faintly hallowed by sentimental association: Peter had laughed at them. She reflected she must be completely besotted about Peter, if his laughter could hallow an aspidistra.

"Very well," said Harriet aloud to herself, "I will *be* besotted." She selected the largest aspidistra and kissed one of its impassive shining surfaces. "But," she added cheerfully to the cactus, "I won't kiss *you* till you've shaved." A head came suddenly through the window and startled her.

"Excuse me, lady," said the head. "Is that there perambulator in the outhouse yourn?"

"What? Oh, dear, no," said Harriet, with a vivid and sympathetic appreciation of Peter's feelings the evening before. (*I knew I should make a bloody fool of myself*—they both seemed to be fated that way.) "It must be something the late owner picked up in a sale."

"Right you are, lady," said the head—Jack's, presumably—and disappeared whistling.

Her own clothes were packed. Bunter had come up shortly after breakfast—while Peter was writing letters—and had discovered her struggling with the orange frock. After watching her thoughtfully for a few moments he had offered his assistance, and it had been accepted with relief. The more intimate parts of the business had, after all, been effected previously—though, when Harriet saw her underwear unpacked later on, she could not remember having used so much tissue paper and was surprised to know herself such a neat packer.

Anyhow; it was all done.

Crutchley came into the sitting-room, with a number of glasses on a tray.

"Thought you might be needing these, my lady."

"Oh, thank you, Crutchley. How very sensible of you. Yes, we probably shall. Just put them down over there, would you?"

"Yes, my lady." He seemed disposed to linger.

"That fellow Jack," he said suddenly, after a pause, "wants to know what he's to do with some of that tinned and bottled stuff."

"Tell him to leave it in the pantry."

"He don't know which is yours, my lady."

"Everything with a Fortnum-&-Mason label. If there's anything else, it probably belongs to the house."

"Very good, my lady. . . . Shall you and his lordship be coming back here again, later on, if I might ask?"

"Oh, yes, Crutchley—I'm sure we shall. Were you thinking about your job here? Of course. We may be going away for a time while alterations are done, but we should like you to keep the garden in order."

"Thank you, my lady. Very good." There was a slightly embarrassed silence. Then:

"Excuse me, my lady. I was wonderin'—" He had his cap in his hands, twisting it rather awkwardly . . . "—seein' as me and Polly Mason is goin' to get married, whether his lordship . . . We was meanin' to start that garridge, only me 'avin' lost that forty pound . . . If it might be a loan, my lady, we'd pay it back faithful—"

"Oh, I see. Well, Crutchley, I can't say anything about that. You must speak to his lordship yourself."

"Yes, my lady . . . If you was to put in a word for me, maybe . . ."

"I'll think about it."

For the life of her, she could not infuse any genuine warmth into her tone; she wanted so much to say, "Are we to advance you the amount of Miss Twitterton's savings, too?" On the other hand, there was nothing unreasonable about the request, since Crutchley could not know how much she knew. The interview was ended, but the young man lingered, so that she was relieved to hear the car at the gate.

"They're coming back. They haven't been very long."

"No, my lady; it don't take long."

Crutchley hesitated for a second, and went out.

It was quite a large party that entered—if they had all come in the Daimler they must have looked like an undertakers' bean feast; but no! the vicar was there, and he might have brought some of them in his own little car. He came in, wearing his cassock, with his surplice and Oxford hood over one arm while with the other he gave fatherly support to Miss Twitterton. She, Harriet saw at a glance, was in a much more resilient mood than she had been the evening before. Though her eyes were red with funerary tears, and she clutched a handkerchief with a sable border in her black-kid-gloved hand, the excitement of being chief mourner behind so important a hearse had evidently restored all her lost self-importance. Mrs. Ruddle followed. Her mantle, of strange and ancient cut, glittered with black beads, and the jet ornaments on her bonnet danced even more gaily than they had done at the inquest. Her face was beaming. Bunter, following upon her heels, and burdened with a pile of prayer-books and a severe-looking bowler, might, by contrast, have been the deceased's nearest and dearest relative, so determined was his countenance in an appropriate gloom. After Bunter came, rather unexpectedly, Mr. Puffett, in a curious greenish-black cutaway coat of incredible age, buttoned perilously across his sweaters over his working trousers. Harriet felt sure he must have been married in that coat. His bowler was not the bowler of Wednesday morning, but of the mashing curly-brimmed pattern affected by young bloods of the 'nineties.

"Well!" said Harriet, "here you all are!"

She hastened forward to greet Miss Twitterton, but was

arrested mid-way by the entrance of her husband, who had stopped to put a rug over the radiator. He came in now with a touch of bravura, probably induced by self-consciousness. The effect of his somber suit and scarf, rigidly tailored black overcoat, and tightly furled silk umbrella was slightly marred by the irresponsible tilt of his tophat.

"Hullo-ullo-ullo," said his lordship, genially. He grounded the umbrella, smiled diffidently, and removed the topper with a flourish.

"Do come and sit down," said Harriet, recovering herself, and leading Miss Twitterton to a chair. She took the black-kid hand and squeezed it comfortingly.

"Jerusalem, my happy home!" His lordship surveyed his domain and apostrophized it with some emotion. "Is this the city that men call the perfection of beauty? Woe to the spoiler—the chariots of Israel and the horsemen thereof!"

He appeared to be in that rather unreliable mood which is apt to follow upon attendance at funerals and other solemn functions. Harriet said severely, "Peter, behave yourself," and turned quickly to ask Mr. Goodacre:

"Were there many people at the funeral?"

"A very large attendance," replied the vicar. "Really a remarkable attendance."

"It's *most* gratifying," cried Miss Twitterton, "—all this respect for Uncle." A pink flush spread over her cheeks—she looked almost pretty. "Such a *mass* of flowers! Sixteen wreaths—including your *beautiful* tribute, dear Lady Peter."

"Sixteen!" said Harriet. "Just fancy!" She felt as though she had received a sharp jolt over the solar plexus.

"And fully choral!" continued Miss Twitterton. "Such *touching* hymns. And *dear* Mr. Goodacre—"

"The Reverend's words," pronounced Mr. Puffett, "if I may say so, sir, went right to the 'eart."

He pulled out a large red cotton handkerchief with white spots and trumpeted into it briskly.

"Ow," agreed Mrs. Ruddle, "it was all just beautiful. I never seen a funeral to touch it, and I been to every buryin' in Paggleham these forty year and more."

She appealed to Mr. Puffett for confirmation, and Harriet seized the opportunity to question Peter:

"Peter—*did* we send a wreath?"

"God knows. Bunter—*did* we send a wreath?"

"Yes, my lord. Hothouse lilies and white hyacinths."

"How very chaste and appropriate!"

Bunter said he was much obliged.

"*Everybody* was there," said Miss Twitterton, "Dr. Craven came over, and old Mr. and Mrs. Sowerton, and the Jenkinses from Broxford and that rather odd young man who came to tell us about Uncle William's misfortunes, and Miss Grant had all the schoolchildren carrying flowers—"

"And Fleet Street in full force," said Peter. "Bunter, I see glasses on the radio cabinet. We could do with some drinks."

"Very good, my lord."

"I'm afraid they've commandeered the beer-barrel," said Harriet, with a glance at Mr. Puffett.

"That's awkward," said Peter. He stripped off his overcoat, and with it his last vestige of sobriety. "Well, Puffett, I dare say you can make do for once with the bottled variety. First discovered, so they say, by Izaak Walton, who while fishing one day—"

Into the middle of this harangue there descended unexpectedly from the stairs Bill and George, carrying, the one a dressing mirror and a wash-basin, and the other, a ewer and a small bouquet of bedroom utensils. They seemed pleased to see the room so full of company, and George advanced gleefully upon Peter.

"Excuse me, guv'nor," said George, flourishing the utensils vaguely in the direction of Miss Twitterton, who was sitting near the staircase. "All them razors and silver-mounted brushes up there—"

"Tush!" said his lordship, gravely, "nothing is gained by coarseness." He draped his coat modestly over the offending crockery, added his scarf, crowned the ewer with his top-hat, and completed the effect by hanging his umbrella over George's extended arm. "Trip it featly here and there through the other door and ask my man to come up presently and tell you which things are what."

"Right-oh, guv'nor," said George, ambling away a trifle awkwardly—for the topper showed a tendency to overbalance. The vicar, surprisingly, relieved the general embarrassment by observing with a reminiscent smile:

"Now, you might not believe it, but when I was up at Oxford I once put one on the Martyr's Memorial."

"Did you?" said Peter. "I was one of the party that tied an open umbrella over each of the Caesars. They were the Fellows' umbrellas. Ah! here come the drinks."

"Thank you," said Miss Twitterton. She shook her head sadly at the glass. "And to think that last time we partook of Lord Peter's sherry—"

"Dear me, dear me!" said Mr. Goodacre. "Thank you. Ah! yes, indeed."

He turned the wine musingly upon his tongue and appeared to compare its flavor favorably with that of the best sherry in Pagford.

"Bunter—you've got some beer in the kitchen for Puffett."

"Yes, my lord."

Mr. Puffett, reminded that he was, in a manner of speaking, in the wrong place, picked up his curly bowler and said heartily:

"That's very kind of your lordship. Come along, Martha. Get off your bonnet and shawl and we'll give these lads a 'and outside."

"Yes," said Harriet. "Bunter will be wanting you, Mrs. Ruddle, to see about getting some lunch of some sort. Will you stay and have something with us, Miss Twitterton?"

"Oh, no, really. I must be getting home. It's so good of you—"

"But you mustn't hurry," said Harriet, as Puffett and Mrs. Ruddle vanished. "I only said that because Mrs. Ruddle—though an excellent servant in her way—sometimes needs a reminder. Mr. Goodacre, won't you have a drop more sherry?"

"No, really—I must be moving homewards."

"Not without your plants," said Peter. "Mr. Goodacre has prevailed on Mr. MacBride, Harriet, to let the cacti go to a good home."

"For a consideration, no doubt?"

"Of course, of course," said the vicar. "I paid him for them. That was only right. He has to consider his clients. The other person—Solomons, I think his name is—made a slight difficulty, but we managed to get over that."

"How did you manage?"

"Well," admitted the vicar, "I paid him too. But it was a small sum. Quite a small sum, really. Less than the plants are worth. I did not like to think of their going to a warehouse with no one to care for them. Crutchley has always looked after them so well. He is very knowledgeable with cacti."

"Indeed?" said Miss Twitterton, so sharply that the vicar stared at her in mild astonishment. "I am *glad* to hear that Frank Crutchley fulfilled *some* of his obligations."

"Well, padre," said Peter, "rather you than me. I don't like the things."

"They are not to everybody's taste, perhaps. But this one, for instance—you must acknowledge that it is a superb specimen of its kind."

He shuffled his shortsighted way towards the hanging cactus and peered at it with an anticipatory pride of possession.

"Uncle William," said Miss Twitterton in a quavering voice, "always took great pride in that cactus."

Her eyes filled with tears, and the vicar turned quickly towards her.

"I know. Indeed, Miss Twitterton, it will be quite happy and safe with me."

Miss Twitterton nodded, speechlessly; but any further demonstration was cut short by the entrance of Bunter, who said, coming up to her:

"Excuse me. The furniture removers are about to clear the attics and have desired me to inquire what is to be done with the various trunks and articles labelled 'Twitterton.' "

"Oh! dear me! Yes, of course. Oh, dear—yes, please tell them I think I had better come and see to that myself. . . . You see—dear me!—however did I come to forget?—there are quite a lot of my things here." She fluttered towards Harriet. "I *hope* you won't mind—I *won't* trespass on your time—but I'd *better* just see what's mine and what isn't. You see, my cottage is so very *small*, and Uncle very kindly let me store my little belongings—some of dear Mother's things—"

"But of course," said Harriet. "Do go anywhere you like, and if you want any help—"

"Oh, thank you so much. Oh, Mr. Goodacre, thank you."

The vicar, politely holding open the staircase door, extended his hand.

"As I shall be going in a very few minutes, I'll say goodbye now. Just for the moment. I shall of course come and see you. And now, you mustn't allow yourself to brood, you know. In fact, I'm going to ask you to be very brave and sensible and come and play the organ for us on Sunday as usual. Now, will you? We've all come to rely on you so much."

"Oh, yes—on Sunday. Of course, dear Mr. Goodacre, if you wish it, I'll do my best—"

"Oh, thank you. I—you—everybody's so good to me."

Miss Twitterton vanished upstairs in a little whirl of gratitude and confusion.

"Poor little woman! poor little soul!" said the vicar. "It's most distressing. This unsolved mystery hanging over us—"

"Yes," said Peter, absently; "not too good."

It gave Harriet a shock to see his eyes, coldly reflective, still turned towards the door by which Miss Twitterton had gone out. She thought of the trapdoor in the attic—and the boxes. Had Kirk searched those boxes, she wondered. If not—well, then, what? Could there be anything in a box? A blunt instrument, with perhaps a little skin and hair on it? It seemed to her that they had all been standing silent a very long time, when Mr. Goodacre, who had resumed his doting contemplation of the cactus, suddenly said:

"Now, this is very strange—very strange indeed!"

She saw Peter start as it were out of a trance and cross the room to see the strange thing. The vicar was staring up into the nightmare vegetable above his head with a deeply puzzled expression. Peter stared too; but since the bottom of the pot was three or four inches over his head, he could see very little.

"Look at that!" said Mr. Goodacre, in a voice that positively shook. "Do you see what that is?"

He fumbled in his pocket for a pencil, with which he pointed excitedly to something in the center of the cactus.

"From here," said Peter, stepping back, "it looks like a spot of mildew, though I can't see very well from this distance. But perhaps in a cactus that's merely the bloom of a healthy complexion."

"It *is* mildew," said the vicar, grimly. Harriet, feeling that intelligent sympathy was called for, climbed on the settle, so that she could look at the plant on a level.

"There's some more of it on the upper side of the leaves —if they are leaves, and not stalks."

"Somebody," said Mr. Goodacre, "has been giving it too much water." He looked accusingly from husband to wife.

"We haven't any of us touched it," said Harriet. She stopped, remembering that Kirk and Bunter had handled it. But they were scarcely likely to have watered it.

"I'm a humane man," began Peter, "and though I don't *like* the prickly brute—"

Then he, too, broke off; and Harriet saw his face change. It frightened her. It became the kind of face that might have belonged to that agonized dreamer of the morning hours.

"What is it, Peter?"

He said in a half whisper:

"Here we go round the prickly pear, the prickly pear, the prickly pear—"

"Once the summer is over," pursued the vicar, "you must administer water very sparingly, very sparingly indeed."

"Surely," said Harriet, "it couldn't have been the knowledgeable Crutchley."

"I think it was," said Peter, as though returning to them from a long journey. "Harriet—you heard Crutchley tell Kirk how he watered it last Wednesday week and wound the clock before collecting his wages from old Noakes."

"Yes."

"And the day before yesterday you saw him water it again."

"Of course; we all saw him."

Mr. Goodacre was aghast.

"But, my dear Lady Peter, he couldn't have done that. The cactus is a desert plant. It only requires watering about once a month in the cooler weather."

Peter, having emerged to clear up this minor mystery, seemed to be back on his nightmare trail. He muttered: "I can't remember—" But the vicar took no notice.

"*Somebody* has touched it lately," he said. "I see you've put it on a longer chain."

Peter's gasp was like a sob.

"That's it. The chain. We were all chained together."

The struggle passed from his face, leaving it empty as a mask. "What's that about a chain, padre?"

CHAPTER XX

WHEN YOU KNOW HOW, YOU KNOW WHO

And here an engine fit for my proceeding!
—WILLIAM SHAKESPEARE, *TWO GENTLEMEN OF VERONA*

To be interrupted at a crisis had become so much a feature of daily life at Talboys that Harriet felt no surprise to see Bunter enter upon these words, as upon a cue. Behind him hovered the forms of Puffett and Crutchley.

"If it will not inconvenience your lordship, the men are anxious to get these pieces of furniture out."

"You see," added Mr. Puffett, stepping forward, "they works on contract. Now, if we could jest slip some of these 'ere things out to them—" He waved a fat hand persuasively towards the sideboard, which was a massive dresser, made all in one piece and extremely heavy.

"All right," said Peter, "but be quick. Take them and go."

Bunter and Puffett seized upon the near end of the dresser, which came staggering away from the wall, its back festooned with cobwebs. Crutchley seized the far end and backed with it to the door.

"Yes," continued Mr. Goodacre, whose mind, once it

fastened on anything, clung to it with the soft tenacity of a sea-anemone. "Yes, I suppose the old chain had become unsafe. This is an improvement. You get a much better idea of the cactus now."

The sideboard was moving slowly across the threshold; but the amateurs were not making too good a job of it, and it stuck. Peter, with sudden impatience, pulled off his coat.

"How he hates," thought Harriet, "to see anything bungled."

"Easy does it," said Mr. Puffett.

Whether by good luck or superior management, no sooner had Peter set his hand to it than the topheavy monstrosity abandoned the position and went sweetly through.

"That's done it!" said Peter. He shut the door and stood before it, his face slightly flushed with exertion. "Yes, padre —you were saying about the chain. It used to be shorter?"

"Why, yes. I'm positive it was. Quite positive. Let me see—the bottom of the pot used to come about here."

He raised his hand slightly above the level of his own tall head.

Peter came down to him.

"About four inches higher. You're sure?"

"Oh, yes, quite. Yes—and the—"

Through the unguarded door came Bunter once more, armed with a clothes-brush. He made for Peter, seized him from behind and began to brush the dust from his trousers. Mr. Goodacre, much interested, watched the process.

"Ah!" he said, dodging out of the way as Puffett and Crutchley came in to remove the settle nearest the window —"that's the worst of those heavy old sideboards. It's so difficult to clean behind them. My wife always complains about ours."

"That'll do, Bunter. Can't I be dusty if I like?"

Bunter smiled gently and began on the other leg.

"I am afraid," went on the vicar, "I should give your excellent man many hours of distress if I were his employer. I am always being scolded for my untidiness." Out of the tail of his eye he saw the door shut behind the other two men, and his mind, lagging behind his vision, made a sudden bound to catch up with it. "Wasn't that Crutchley? We ought to have asked him—"

"Bunter," said Peter, "you heard what I said. If Mr. Goodacre likes, you can brush him. I will *not* be brushed. I refuse."

He spoke with more sharpness, under his light tone, than Harriet had ever heard him use. She thought: "For the first time since we were married he has forgotten my existence." She went over to the coat he had thrown off and began to search it for cigarettes; but she did not miss Bunter's quick upward glance or the almost imperceptible jerk of Peter's head.

Bunter, without a word, went to brush the vicar, and Peter, released, walked straight up to the fireplace. Here he stopped, and his eye searched the room.

"Well, really," said Mr. Goodacre, with a refreshing delight in novelty. "Being valeted is quite a new experience for me."

"The chain," said Peter. "Now, where—?"

"Oh, yes." Mr. Goodacre took up his thread again. "I was about to say, that is certainly a new chain. The old one was of brass to match the pot, whereas this—"

"Peter!" said Harriet, involuntarily.

"Yes," he said, "I know now." He seized upon the ornamental drain-pipe, tossed the pampas-grasses out of it and tilted it up, just as Crutchley came in—this time with the man Bill—and advanced upon the other settle.

"If you don't mind, guv'nor."

Peter jerked the pipe swiftly back and sat on it.

"No," he said. "We haven't finished here. Take yourself off. We must have something to sit on. I'll make it right with your employer."

"Oh!" said Bill. "Well—right y'are, guv'nor. But mind you, this job's got to be done today."

"It will be," said Peter.

George might have stood out; but Bill evidently possessed a more sensitively balanced temperament or a livelier eye to the main chance. He said submissively, "Right-ho, guv'nor," and went out, taking Crutchley with him.

As the door shut, Peter lifted the drain-pipe. At the bottom of it lay a brass chain, curled together like a sleeping serpent.

Harriet said: "The chain that came down the chimney."

Peter's glance swept over her as though she had been a stranger.

"A new chain was fixed up and the other one hidden up the chimney. Why?" He lifted the chain and looked at the cactus as it hung centered over the radio cabinet. Mr. Goodacre was deeply intrigued.

"Now, that," he said, taking the end of the chain in his hand, "looks remarkably like the original chain. See. It is darkened with soot, but it's quite bright when you rub it."

Peter dropped his end of the chain, leaving it dangling in the vicar's hand. He picked out Harriet from the rest and said to her, as though propounding a problem to the brightest-looking of a not-too-hopeful class:

"When Crutchley had watered the cactus, which he had watered the week before and which should only be watered once a month—"

"—*in* the colder weather," said Mr. Goodacre.

"—he was on the steps here. He wiped the pot. He got down. He put back the steps over here by the clock. He came back here to the cabinet. Can you remember what he did next?"

Harriet shut her eyes, once more seeing the room as it had been on that strange morning.

"I believe—"

She opened them again. Peter laid his hands gently, one on each side of the cabinet.

"Yes—he did. I know he did. He pulled the cabinet forward to bring it centrally under the pot. I was sitting quite close to him at the end of the settle—that's why I noticed."

"I noticed it too. That's the thing I couldn't remember."

He pushed the cabinet gently back, moving forward

with it so that the pot now hung directly over his head and about three inches above it.

"Dear me," said Mr. Goodacre, surprised to discover that something of importance was apparently going on, "this is all very mysterious."

Peter made no reply, but stood gently lifting and letting fall the lid of the radio cabinet. "Like this," he said, softly. "Like this . . . This is London calling."

"I'm afraid I'm being very stupid," ventured the vicar again.

This time Peter looked up and smiled at him.

"Look!" he said. He put up his hand and lightly touched the pot, setting it gently swinging at the end of its eight-foot chain. "It's possible," he said. "My God! it's possible. Mr. Noakes was about your height, wasn't he, padre?"

"Just about. Just about. I may have had the advantage of him by an inch, but not more."

"If I'd had more inches," said Peter, regretfully (for his height was a sensitive point with him), "I might have had more brains. Better late than never." His eye roamed the room, passed over Harriet and the vicar and rested on Bunter. "You see," he said, "we've got the first and last terms of the progression—if we could fill in the middle terms."

"Yes, my lord," agreed Bunter, in a colorless voice. His heart had leapt within him. Not the new wife this time, but the old familiar companion of a hundred cases—the appeal had been to him. He coughed. "If I might make a suggestion, it would be as well to verify the difference in the chains before we proceed."

"Quite right, Bunter. Clear as you go. Get the steps."

Harriet watched Bunter as he mounted and took the brass chain that the vicar mechanically handed to him. But it was Peter who heard the steps on the stair. Before Miss Twitterton was in the room he was half-way across it, and when she turned from shutting the door after her, he stood at her elbow.

"So *that's* all seen to," said Miss Twitterton, brightly.

"Oh, Mr. Goodacre—I didn't think I should see you again. It *is* nice to think you're having Uncle William's cactus."

"Bunter's just coping with it," said Peter. He stood between her and the steps and his five-foot nine was an effectual screen to her four-foot eight. "Miss Twitterton, if you've really finished, I wonder if you would do something for me?"

"But of *course*—if I *can!*"

"I think I must have dropped my fountain-pen somewhere in the bedroom, and I'm rather afraid one of those fellows up there may put his foot on it. If I might trouble you—"

"Why, with pleasure!" cried Miss Twitterton, delighted that the task was not beyond her powers. "I'll run up and look for it at once. I always say I'm *remarkably* good at finding things."

"It's extraordinarily kind of you," said Peter. He maneuvered her gently to the door, opened it for her, and shut it after her. Harriet said nothing. She knew where Peter's pen was, for she had seen it in the inner breast pocket of his coat when she was looking for cigarettes, and she felt a cold weight at the pit of her stomach. Bunter, who had slipped quickly down from the steps, stood, chain in hand, as though ready to put the gyves on a felon when he heard the word. Peter came back with urgency in his step.

"Four inches difference, my lord."

His master nodded.

"Bunter—no, I shall want you." He saw Harriet and spoke to her as though she had been his footman. "Here, you, go and fasten the door at the top of the back stair. Don't let her hear you if you can help it. Here are the house-keys. Lock the doors, front and back. Make sure that Ruddle and Puffett and Crutchley are all inside. If anyone says anything, those are my orders. Then bring the keys back—do you understand? . . . Bunter, take the steps and see if you can find anything in the way of a hook or a nail in the wall or ceiling on that side of the chimney-place."

Harriet was out of the room, and tiptoeing along the

passage. Voices in the kitchen and a subdued clinking told her that lunch was being got ready—and probably eaten. Through the open door she glimpsed the back of Crutchley's head—he was tilting a mug to his lips. Beyond him stood Mr. Puffett, his wide jaws moving slowly on a large mouthful. She could not see Mrs. Ruddle, but in a moment her voice came through from the scullery. ". . . See it was there that Joe, plain as the nose on 'is face, and goodness knows that's big enough, but there! 'e's too much taken up with 'is good lady . . ." Somebody laughed. Harriet thought it was George. She scurried past the kitchen, ran up the privy as she went and found herself panting, more with excitement than haste, at the door of her own room. The key was on the inside. She turned the handle softly and crept in. Nothing was there but her own boxes, packed and waiting, and the component parts of what had been the bed, stacked ready for removal. In the next room she could hear little scuffling sounds, and then Miss Twitterton chirping agitatedly to herself (like the White Rabbit, thought Harriet): "Oh, dear, oh, dear! what has become of it?" (or was it, "What will become of me?") For a flash of time Harriet stood, her hand already on the key. If she were to go in and say, "Miss Twitterton, *he knows* who killed your uncle, and . . ." Like the White Rabbit—a white rabbit in a cage. . . .

Then she was out and locking the door behind her.

Back in the passage now . . . and quietly past that open door. Nobody seemed to take any notice. She locked the front door, and the house was fast, as it had been on the night of the murder.

She returned to the sitting-room, and found she had been so quick that Bunter was still on the steps by the fireplace, searching the dark beams with a pocket-torch.

"A cup-hook, my lord, painted black and screwed into the beam."

"Ah!" Peter measured the distance with his eye, from the hook to the cabinet and back again. Harriet held out the keys to him and he pocketed them absentmindedly without so much as a nod.

"Proof," he said. "Proof of something at last. But where is the—?"

The vicar, who seemed to have been putting two and two carefully together in his mind, cleared his throat:

"Do I understand," he said, "that you have discovered a —what they call a *clue* to the mystery?"

"No," said Peter. "We're looking for that. The clue. Ariadne's clue of thread—the little ball of twine to thread the labyrinth—th—Yes, twine. Who said twine? Puffett, by Jove! He's our man!"

"Tom Puffett!" exclaimed the vicar. "Oh, I should not like to think that Puffett—"

"Fetch him here," said Peter.

Bunter was off the steps before he spoke. "Yes, my lord," he said, and was gone like lightning. Harriet's eye fell on the chain, which lay, where Bunter had left it, on top of the cabinet. She picked it up and the clink of the links caught Peter's ear.

"Best get rid of that," he said. "Give it me." He scanned the room for a hiding-place—then, with a sort of chuckle, made for the chimney.

"We'll put it back where it came from," he said, as he dived under the cowl. "Safe bind, safe find, as Puffett is fond of observing." He emerged again, dusting his hands.

"There's a ledge, I suppose," said Harriet.

"Yes. The gun dislodged the chain. If Noakes had kept his chimneys swept, his murderer might have been safe. What's that, padre, about doing evil that good may come?"

Mr. Goodacre was spared discussion of this doctrinal point by the arrival of Mr. Puffett with Bunter at his elbow.

"Did you want me, my lord?"

"Yes, Puffett. When you were cleaning up this room on Wednesday morning after we'd loosened the soot, do you remember picking up a bit of string from the floor?"

"String?" said Mr. Puffett. "If it's string you're looking for, I reckon you've come to the right place for it. When I sees a bit o' string, my lord, I picks it up and puts it away, 'andy when wanted." He pulled up his sweaters with a grunt and began to produce rolls of string from his pockets as a conjurer produces colored paper. "There's all sorts 'ere, you can take your choice. As I says to Frank Crutchley, safe bind, safe find, I says. . . ."

"That was about a piece of string, wasn't it?"

"That's right," said Mr. Puffett, extracting with some difficulty a thick piece of small-cord. "I picks up a piece of string off this very floor, and I says to him—alloodin' to that there forty pound of his—I says to him—"

"I thought I saw you pick some up. I suppose you can't tell by this time *which* piece it was?"

"Oh!" said Mr. Puffett, enlightened. "I get you now, me lord. You was wantin' that pertickler bit o' string. Well, now, I dunno as I could rightly say which was that identical piece of strong. Not the *string*, I couldn't. Not but what it was a good bit of string, too—a good thick piece, reckon it might be a yard long without knots. But whether it was *this* piece now, or *that* piece I wouldn't pretend to say."

"A yard long?" said Peter. "It must have been more than that."

"No," said Mr. Puffett. "Not the string—well, it might a-been four foot, not more. There was a rare good bit o' black fishin'-line, mebbe twenty feet or so—But it's string you're lookin' for."

"I made a mistake," said Peter. "I ought, of course, to have said fishing-line. Naturally, it would be fishing-line. And black. It had to be. Have you got that on you?"

"Oh!" said Mr. Puffett, "if it's fishin'-line you're after, w'y didn't you say so? Safe bind—"

"Thank you," said Peter. He whipped the roll of black line deftly from the sweep's slow fingers. "Yes. That's it. That would hold a twenty-pound salmon. And I'll bet you there's a sinker at each end. I thought so—yes."

He threaded one end of the line through one of the rings at the lip of the pot, brought the two ends with their sinkers together and handed them to Bunter, who took them without a word, mounted the steps and passed the double line over the hook in the ceiling.

"Oh!" said Harriet. "I see now. Peter, how horrible!"

"Haul up," said Peter, unheeding. "Take care you don't foul the line."

Bunter hauled on the line, grunting a little as it cut into his fingers. The pot, steadied from below by Peter's outstretched hand, stirred, lifted, moved up and away out of reach, rising in a great semicircle at the end of the iron chain.

"It's all right," said Peter. "The plant won't fall out. It's a dead tight fit—as *you* know. Haul steady."

He went to take the slack of the line as it came down over the hook. The pot now lay level, strung out flat below the rafters, the cactus emerging sideways, so that it looked in the dimness like a monstrous hermit crab clawing out greedily from its shell.

The vicar, peering up at it, ventured a remonstrance.

"Pray, be careful, my man. If that thing was to slip and come down it might easily kill somebody."

"Very easily," said Peter. "That's what I was thinking." He walked backwards towards the radio cabinet, keeping the double string taut in his hand.

"It must weigh getting on for fourteen pound," said Bunter.

"I can feel it," said Peter, grimly. "How did you come not to notice its weight when you and Kirk were examining it? It's been loaded with something—lead shot from the feel of it. This must have been planned some time ago."

"So that," said Harriet, "is how a woman could have broken a tall man's head. A woman with strong hands."

"Or anybody," said Peter, "who didn't happen to be there at the time. Anyone with a cast-iron alibi. God makes power, padre, and man makes engines."

He brought the two ends of the line to the edge of the cabinet, to which they reached exactly. He lifted the lid and slipped them under; then brought the lid down upon them. The spring catch stood up to the strain, and the sinkers held firm against the flange, though Harriet noticed that the pull of the heavy pot had raised the near side of the cabinet slightly from the ground. But it could not lift far; since its feet were jammed close against the end of the settle, over which the thin black line stretched taut and nearly invisible to the hook in the beam.

A sharp knock at the window made them all start. Kirk and Sellon stood outside, beckoning excitedly. Peter walked quickly across and opened the lattice, while Bunter came down from the steps, folded them and set them quietly back against the wall.

"Yes?" said Peter.

"My lord!" Sellon's voice was quick and eager. "My lord, I never told you no lie. You *can* see the clock from the window. Mr. Kirk, he's just told me—"

"That's right," said Kirk. "Half-past twelve, plain as a pike-staff. . . . Hullo!" he added, able to see better now that the window was open—"they've took the cactus down."

"No, they haven't," said Peter. "The cactus is still there. You'd better come along in. The front door's locked. Take the keys and lock it again behind you. . . . It's all right," he added, speaking into Kirk's ear. "But come in quietly—you may have to make an arrest."

The two policemen vanished with surprising speed.

Mr. Puffett, who had been scratching his head in a contemplative manner, accosted Peter.

"That's an orkerd-looking arrangement of yours, me lord. Are you dead sure it won't come down?"

As some safeguard against this possibility, he clapped on his bowler.

"Not unless somebody opens the cabinet for the 12:30 gramophone orgy. . . . For God's sake, padre, stand away from that lid!"

The vicar, who had advanced towards the cabinet, started away guiltily at the peremptory tone.

"I was only looking more closely at the string," he explained. "You can't see it at all against the paneling, you know. Most remarkable. It's being so black and so fine, I suppose."

"That," said Peter, "is the idea of fishing-line. I'm sorry I shouted, but do keep back in case of accident. Do you realize you're the one person in this room who isn't safe?"

The vicar retired into a corner to work this out. The door was flung open, and Mrs. Ruddle, uncalled and unwanted, announced in loud tones:

" 'Ere's the p'leece!"

"There!" said Mr. Puffett. He tried to urge her out, but Mrs. Ruddle was determined to know what all this long conference was about. She planted herself firmly beside the door with arms akimbo.

Kirk's ox-like eyes went to Peter and then followed his glance up to the ceiling, where they encountered the astonishing phenomenon of the cactus, floating Houdini-fashion, without visible means of support.

"Yes," said Peter. "That's where it is. But don't touch that cabinet, or I won't answer for the consequences. I fancy that's where that cactus was at 9:30 P.M. last Wednesday week, and that's why Sellon was able to see the clock. This is what's called reconstructing the crime."

"The crime, eh?" said Kirk.

"You wanted a blunt instrument that could strike a tall man from behind and above. There it is. That would break the skull of an ox—with the power we've put behind it."

Kirk looked at the pot again.

"H'm," he said slowly. "Pretty—but I'd like a bit o' proof. There weren't no blood nor 'air on that there pot we'en I last see it."

"Of course not!" cried Harriet. "It was wiped."

"When and how?" said Peter, slewing around on her sharply.

"Why, not till last Wednesday morning. The day before yesterday. You reminded us only just now. On Wednesday morning, under our very eyes, while we all sat around and watched. That's How, Peter, that's How!"

"Yes," he said, smiling at her excitement. "That's How. And now we know How, we know Who."

"Thank God, we know something at last," said Harriet. At the moment she cared little for How or Who. Her jubilee was for the alert cock of Peter's head, as he stood and smiled at her, balancing himself lightly and swaying a little on his toes. A job finished—and after all, no failure—no more frustrated dreams about chained and defeated men seeking a lost memory among hot deserts horrid with prickly cactus.

But the vicar, not being Peter's wife, took the thing otherwise.

"You mean," he said, in a shocked voice, "that when Frank Crutchley watered the cactus and wiped the pot—oh! but that is a dreadful conclusion to come to! Frank Crutchley—one of my own choirmen!"

Kirk was better satisfied.

"Crutchley?" said he. "Ah! *now* we're getting at it. He had his grudge about the forty pound—and 'e thought he'd get even with the old man and marry the heiress—two birds with one blunt instrument, eh?"

"The heiress?" exclaimed the vicar, in fresh bewilderment. "But he's marrying Polly Mason—he came round about the banns this morning."

"That's rather a sad story, Mr. Goodacre," said Harriet. "He was secretly engaged to Miss Twitterton and he—hush!"

"D'you think they were in it together?" began Kirk—and then suddenly woke up to the fact that Miss Twitterton was in the room with them.

"I couldn't find your fountain-pen *anywhere*," said Miss Twitterton, earnest and apologetic. "I do hope—" She became aware of something odd and strained in the atmosphere, and of Joe Sellon, who was stupidly gaping in the one direction that everybody else was avoiding.

"Good gracious!" said Miss Twitterton. "*What* an extraordinary thing! How ever did Uncle's cactus get up there?"

She made a bee-line for the cabinet. Peter caught her and pulled her back.

"I don't think so," he said, cryptically to Kirk over his shoulder; and led Miss Twitterton away to where the vicar still stood petrified with astonishment.

"Now," said Kirk, "let's get this clear. How exactly do you make out he worked it?"

"If that trap was set like that on the night of the murder when Crutchley left at 6:20"—Miss Twitterton uttered a faint squeak—"then, when Noakes came in, as he always did at half-past nine, to turn on the wireless for the news-bulletin—"

"Which he did," said Mrs. Ruddle, "reg'lar as clock-work—"

"Why, then—"

But Harriet had thought of an objection, and whatever Peter thought of her she must put in.

"But, Peter—could anybody—even by candlelight, walk right up to that cabinet without noticing that the cactus wasn't there?"

"I think—" said Peter.

The door opened so quickly that it caught Mrs. Ruddle sharply on the elbow—and Crutchley walked in. In one hand he carried the standard lamp, and had apparently come in to fetch something on his way to the van outside, for he called back to some invisible person behind him:

"All right—I'll get it and lock it up for you."

He was abreast of the cabinet before Peter could say:

"What do you want, Crutchley?"

His tone made Crutchley turn his head.

"Key o' the radio, my lord," he said briefly and, still looking at Peter, lifted the lid.

For the millionth part of a second, the world stood still. Then the heavy pot threshed down like a flail. It flashed as it came. It skimmed within an inch over Crutchley's head, striking white terror into his face with its passing, and shattered the globe of the lamp into a thousand tinkling fragments.

Then, and only then, Harriet realized that they had all cried out, and she among them. And after that, there was silence for several seconds, while the great pendulum swung over them in a gleaming arc.

Peter spoke, warningly:

"Stand back, padre."

His voice broke the tension. Crutchley turned on him with a face like the face of a beast.

"You devil! you damned cunning devil! How did you Curse you—how did you know I done it? I'll have the throat out of you!"

He leapt, and Harriet saw Peter brace himself; but Kirk and Sellon caught him as he sprang from under the death-swing of the pot. He wrestled with them, panting and snarling.

"Let me go, blast you! Let me get at him! So you set a trap for me, did you? Well, I killed him. The old brute cheated me. So did you, Aggie Twitterton, blast you! I been done out o' my rights. I killed him, I tell you, and all for nothing."

Bunter went quietly up, caught the pot as it swung and brought it to a standstill.

Kirk was saying:

"Frank Crutchley, I arrest you. . . ."

The rest of the words were lost in the prisoner's frenzied shouting. Harriet went over and stood by the window. Peter had not moved. He left Bunter and Puffett to help the police. Even with this assistance, they had their work cut out to drag Crutchley from the room.

"Dear me!" said Mr. Goodacre. "This is a most shocking thing." He picked up his surplice and stole.

"Keep him off!" shrieked Miss Twitterton, as the struggling group surged past her. "How horrible! Keep him off! To think that I ever let him come near me!" Her small face was distorted with fury. She ran after them, shaking her clenched fists and crying out grotesquely: "Beast! beast! how dare you kill poor Uncle!"

The vicar turned to Harriet.

"Forgive me, Lady Peter. My duty is with that unhappy young man."

She nodded, and he followed the rest out of the room. Mrs. Ruddle, arrested on her way to the door by the sight of the fishing-line dangling from the pot, was illuminated with sudden understanding.

"Why, there!" she cried, triumphantly. "That's a funny thing, that is. That's the way it was when I come in 'ere Wednesday morning to clear for the sweep. I took it off meself and throwed it down on the floor."

She looked about her for approbation, but Harriet was past all power of comment and Peter still stood unmoving. Gradually, Mrs. Ruddle realized that the moment for applause had gone by, and shuffled out. Then from the group in the doorway Sellon detached himself and came back, his helmet askew and his tunic torn open at the throat.

"My lord—I don't rightly know how to thank you. This clears me."

"All right, Sellon. That'll do. Buzz off now like a good chap."

Sellon went out; and there was a pause.

"Peter," said Harriet.

He looked around, in time to see Crutchley hauled past the window, still struggling in the four men's hands.

"Come and hold my hand," he said. "This part of the business always gets me down."

EPITHALAMION

CHAPTER I

LONDON: AMENDE HONORABLE

Verges: *You have always been called a merciful man, partner.*
Dogberry: *Truly, I would not hang a dog by my will, much more than a man.*

—WILLIAM SHAKESPEARE, *MUCH ADO ABOUT NOTHING*

Miss Harriet Vane, in those admirable detective novels with which she was accustomed to delight the hearts of murder-fans (see blurb), usually made a point of finishing off on a top-note. Mr. Robert Templeton, that famous though eccentric sleuth, would unmask his murderer with a flourish of *panache* in the last chapter and retire promptly from the stage amid a thunder of applause, leaving somebody else to cope with the trivial details of putting the case together.

What happened in real life, she discovered, was that the famous sleuth, after cramming down a hasty lunch of bread and cheese, which he was almost too preoccupied to eat, spent the rest of the afternoon at the police-station, making an interminable statement. The sleuth's wife and servant also made statements, and all three were then bundled unceremoniously out while statements were taken from the sweep, the charwoman and the vicar; after which, the police were prepared, if the going looked good, to sit up all night taking a statement from the prisoner. A further agreeable feature was a warning that neither the sleuth nor any of his belongings was to leave the country, or indeed go anywhere, without previously informing the police, since the next part of the procedure might take the form of a batch of summonses to appear before the magistrates. Returning home from the police-station, the sleuth family found the house occupied by a couple of constables taking photographs and measurements, preparatory to removing the wireless cabinet, the brass chain, the hook and the cactus to figure as Exhibits A to D. These were by now the only portable objects left in the house, other than the owner's personal property; since George and Bill had finished the job and left with their van. There had been difficulty and delay in persuading them to leave without the wireless set; but here the arm of the law at length prevailed. At last the police went away and left them alone.

Harriet looked around the empty sitting-room with a curiously blank sensation. There was nothing to sit on except the window-sill, so she sat on that. Bunter was upstairs, locking trunks and suitcases. Peter walked aimlessly up and down the room.

"I'm going up to Town," he said abruptly. He looked vaguely at Harriet. "I don't know what you'd care to do."

This was disconcerting, because she could not tell from his tone whether he wanted her in London or not. She asked:

"Shall you be staying the night in Town?"

"I don't think so, but I must see Impey Biggs."

So that was the difficulty. Sir Impey Biggs had been her own counsel when she had stood her trial, and Peter was wondering how she would take the mention of his name.

"Do they want him for the prosecution?"

"No; I want him for the defense."

Naturally—what a stupid question.

"Crutchley must be defended, of course," pursued Peter, "though at the moment he's in no state to discuss anything. But they've persuaded him to let a solicitor act for him. I've seen the man and offered to get Biggy for them. Crutchley needn't know we've had anything to do with it. He probably won't ask."

"Must you see Sir Impey today?"

"I'd rather. I rang him up from Broxford. He's in the House tonight, but he can see me if I go round after the debate on some Bill or other he's concerned in. That will make it rather late for you, I'm afraid."

"Well," said Harriet, resolved to be reasonable whatever happened, "I think you had better run me up to Town. Then we can sleep at a hotel, if you like, or in your mother's house, if the servants are there; or if you'd rather stay at your club, there's a friend I can always ring up; or I can get out my own car and run down to Denver ahead of you."

"Resourceful woman! We'll go to Town, then, and wait upon the event."

He seemed relieved by her readiness to accommodate herself, and presently went out to do something or other to the car. Bunter came down, looking worried.

"My lady, what would you wish to have done with the heavy luggage?"

"I don't know, Bunter. We can't very well take it to the Dower House, and if we take it to Town, there's nowhere much to put it, except the new house—and I don't suppose we shall be going there, yet awhile. And I don't care to leave it here, with no one to see to it, since we can't possibly come back for some time. Even if his lordship— That is to say, we should have to get some furniture in."

"Precisely, my lady."

"I suppose you have no idea what his lordship is likely to decide?"

"No, my lady, I regret to say I have not."

For nearly twenty years, Bunter had known no plans which did not include the Piccadilly flat; and he was for once at a loss.

"I'll tell you what," said Harriet. "Go up to the vicarage and ask Mrs. Goodacre for me whether we may leave it with her for a few days till we have made our plans. She can then send it on, carriage forward. Make some excuse for my not going myself. Or find me a piece of paper and I will write a note. I would rather his lordship could find me here when he wants me."

"I understand perfectly, my lady. If I may say so, I think that will be an excellent arrangement."

One felt rather shabby, perhaps, for not going to say *au revoir* to the Goodacres. But, quite apart from what Peter might or might not want, the thought of Mrs. Goodacre's questions and Mr. Goodacre's lamentations was a daunting one. When Bunter returned, bringing a cordial note of assent from the vicar's wife, he reported that Miss Twitterton was also at the parsonage, and Harriet was more than ever thankful to have escaped.

Mrs. Ruddle seemed to have disappeared. (She and Bert were, indeed, having a sumptuous six o'clock tea with Mrs. Hodges and a few neighbors, eager to have their news served up piping hot.) The only person who lingered to bid them farewell was Mr. Puffett. He did not intrude; only, as the car moved out into the lane, he popped into ken from the top of a neighboring gate, where he seemed to have been enjoying a peaceful smoke.

"Jest," said Mr. Puffett, "to wish you luck, me lord and me lady, and 'ope as we shall be seein' you 'ere again afore long. You ain't 'ad things so comfortable as you might 'ave 'oped, but there's more than one 'ud be sorry if you wos to take a misliking to Paggleham on that account. And if you'd like them chimneys given a thorough over'aul, or any other little job in the sweepin' or buildin' line, you've only to mention it and I'd be 'appy to oblige."

Harriet thanked him very much.

"There's on thing," said Peter. "Over at Lopsley there's a sun-dial in the old churchyard, made from one of our chimney-pots. I'm writing to the squire to offer him a new sun-dial in exchange. May I tell him that you will call for the old one and see to getting it put back?"

"I'll do that and welcome," said Mr. Puffett.

"And if you know where any of the others have gone, you might let me know."

Mr. Puffett promised readily that he would. They shook hand with him, and left him standing in the middle of the lane, cheerfully waving his bowler till the car had turned the corner.

They drove for five miles or so in silence. Then Peter said:

"There's a little architect who would make a good job of that bathroom extension. His name's Thipps. He's a common little blighter, but he has very real feeling for period stuff. He did the church at Duke's Denver, and he and I got really friendly about thirteen years ago, when he was troubled with a corpse in his bathroom. I think I'll send him a line."

"He sounds just right. . . . You haven't taken what Puffett calls a misliking to Talboys, then? I was afraid you might want to get rid of it."

"While I live," he said, "no owner but ourselves shall ever set foot in it."

She was satisfied and said no more. They ran into London in time for dinner.

Sir Impey Biggs extricated himself from his debate about midnight. He greeted Harriet with a cheerful friendliness, Peter as the lifelong friend and connection that he was, and both with all proper congratulations on their marriage. Although there had been no further discussion of the subject, it had somehow been taken for granted that there was now no more question of Harriet's going to sleep with a friend or driving to Denver alone. After dinner, Peter had merely said, "It's no good going down to the House yet," and they had turned into a news-cinema and seen a Mickey Mouse and an educational film about the iron and steel industry.

"Well, well," said Sir Impey. "So you want me to tackle a defense for you. This business down in Hertfordshire, I suppose."

"Yes. I warn you beforehand you haven't a very good case."

"Never mind. We've tackled some pretty hopeless jobs before now. With you on our side I know we can put up a good fight."

"I'm not, Biggy. I'm a witness for the prosecution."

The K.C. whistled.

"The devil you are. Then why are you briefing counsel for the prisoner? Conscience-money?"

"More or less. It's rather a rotten show altogether, and we'd like to do our best for the man. I mean to say, don't you know—that we were, just married and everything pleasant about us. And then this happens, and the local bobbies can make nothing of it. And we horn in, looking all silklined, and fasten the crime on a poor devil who hasn't got a bean in the world and hasn't done *us* any harm except dig the garden—Well, anyway, we'd like you to defend him."

"You'd better begin at the beginning."

Peter began at the beginning, and went on, interrupted only by the older man's shrewd questions, to the end. It took a long time.

"Well, Peter, you're handing me a nice pup. Including the criminal's own confession."

"He didn't give that on oath. Shock—nerves—frightened into it by my unfair trick with the pot."

"Suppose he's made it again to the police?"

"Badgered into it by questions. Surely you're not going to be worried by a little thing like that."

"There's the chain and the hook and the lead in the pot."

"Who's to say Crutchley put them there? They may have been part of one of old Noakes's little games."

"And the watering of the cactus and wiping of the pot?"

"*Bagatelles!* We've only the vicar's opinion about the metabolism of cacti."

"Can you dispose of the motive, too?"

"Motive doesn't make a case."

"It does, for nine juries out of ten."

"Very well—several other people had motives."

"Your Twitterton woman, for instance. Had I better try to hint that she might have done it?"

"If you fancy she'd have the wits to realize that a pendulum must always pass directly beneath its point of suspension."

"H'm!—by the way, supposing you people hadn't turned up, what would have been the murderer's next step? What did he think would happen?"

"If Crutchley was the murderer?"

"Well, yes. He must have expected that the body would be found lying on the sitting-room floor by the next person who entered the house."

"I've thought this out. The next person to enter would, in the ordinary way, have been Miss Twitterton, who had the key. She was completely under his thumb. Remember, they used to meet in the evenings in Great Pagford churchyard. He'd have no difficulty in finding out whether she intended to go over at any time during the week to see her uncle. If she'd announced any such intention, he'd have taken steps—asked for an hour off from the garage on private business and contrived to run across Miss Twitterton on her way to the house. If Mrs. Ruddle had thought to tell Miss Twitterton that old Noakes had disappeared, it would have been easier still. The first person to be consulted would have been dear Frank, who knew all about everything. Best of all would have been what nearly happened—that Mrs. Ruddle should have taken the situation for granted and said nothing to anyone. Then Crutchley would have arrived at Talboys as usual on the Wednesday morning, found (to his surprise) he couldn't get in, gone to fetch the key from Miss Twitterton and discovered the body for himself. In any case, he'd have been first on the scene, with or without Miss Twitterton. If he was alone, very good. If not, he'd have dispatched her on her bicycle to fetch the police and taken the opportunity while her back was turned to rescue the string, polish the pot, remove the other chain from the chimney and generally see that the whole place presented an innocent appearance. I don't know why the chain was put up the chimney in the first instance; but I imagine old Noakes came in on him unexpectedly, just as he'd made the exchange, and he had to get rid of it quickly. Probably he thought it would be safe enough there, and didn't bother too much."

"And suppose Noakes had come into the sitting-room between 6:20 and 9 o'clock?"

"That was the risk. But old Noakes was 'reg'lar as clock-work.' He had his supper at 7:30. The sun set at 6:38 and the room is low-windowed and darkish. At any time after 7 the chances were that he would notice nothing. But make what play you like with that."

"He must have had a disagreeable morning the day you arrived," said Sir Impey. "Always supposing, of course, that this prosecution is justified. I wonder he made no efforts, after the crime was discovered, to get the chain removed."

"He did," said Harriet. "He came in three times while the furniture-movers were there; and made a quite determined effort to get me out of the room to investigate some tinned goods. I did go out once, and met him in the passage, making for the sitting-room."

"Ah!" said Sir Impey. "And you'd be prepared to go into the box and swear to that. You don't leave me much chance between you. If you'd had any consideration for me, Peter, you'd have married a less intelligent woman."

"I'm afraid I've been selfish about that. But you'll take the case, Biggy, and do your best?"

"To please you, I will. I shall enjoy cross-examining you. If you think of any awkward questions to put to yourself, let me know. Now be off with you. I'm getting old, and bed's the place for me."

"So that's that," said Peter. They stood on the pavement, shivering a little. It was nearly three in the morning and the air was sharp. "What now? Do we seek a hotel?"

(What was the right answer to that? He looked at once

tired and restless—a state of body in which almost any answer is the wrong one. She decided to risk a bold shot.)

"How far is it to Duke's Denver?"

"Just over ninety miles—say ninety-five. Would you like to drive straight down? We could pick up the car and be out of Town by half-past three. I'd promise not to drive fast—and you might be able to get a bit of sleep on the way."

Miraculously, the answer has been the right one. She said, "Yes; let's do that." They found a taxi. Peter gave it the address of the garage where they had left the car and they trundled away through the silent streets.

"Where's Bunter?"

"He's gone on down by train, with a message to say we might be a little late."

"Will your mother mind?"

"No. She's known me forty-five years."

CHAPTER II

DENVER DUCIS: THE POWER AND THE GLORY

"And the moral of that is," said the Duchess. . . .
—LEWIS CARROLL, *ALICE IN WONDERLAND*

The Great North Road again, mile upon mile, through Hatfield, Stevenage, Baldock, Biggleswade, north and east to the Hertfordshire border—the same road they had traveled four days earlier, with Bunter sitting behind and two-and-a-half dozen of port stowed under his feet in an eiderdown. Harriet found herself dozing. Once, Peter's touch on her arm roused her to hear him say, "That's the turn for Pagford. . . ." Huntingdon, Chatteris, March—still north and east, with the wind blowing keener over the wide flats from the bitter northern sea, and the grayness that heralds the dawn lifting coldly into the sky ahead.

"Where are we now?"

"Coming into Downham Market. We've just passed through Denver—the original Denver. Duke's Denver is about fifteen miles further on."

The car swung through the little down and turned due east.

"What time is it?"

"Just upon six. I've only averaged thirty-five."

The fen lay behind them now, and the country was growing more wooded. As the sun rose, they slipped into a tiny village with a church from whose tower a clock struck the quarter.

"Denver Ducis," said Peter. He let the car dawdle down the narrow street. In the cottages, lighted windows showed where men and women were rising to go early to work. A man came out from a gate, stared at the car and touched his hat. Peter acknowledged the salute. Now they were out of the village, and running along beside a low wall, with high forest trees hanging over it.

"The Dower House is on the other side," said Peter. "It'll save time to go through the park." They swung into a tall gateway, with a lodge beside it. The growing light showed the stone beasts crouched upon the posts, holding each a shield of arms. At the noise of the horn, a man hurried out of the lodge in his shirt-sleeves and the gates swung back.

"Morning, Jenkins," said Peter, and let the car stop. "Sorry to bring you out so early."

"No call to be sorry, my lord." The lodge-keeper turned to call over his shoulder. "Mother! here's his lordship!" He was an elderly man, and spoke with the familiarity of long service. "We were expecting you any time, and the sooner the better for us. Will this be her new ladyship?"

"Got it in one, Jenkins."

A woman appeared wrapping a shawl about her and curtsying. Harriet shook hands with the pair of them.

"This is no way to bring your bride home, my lord," said Jenkins, reprovingly. "We had the bells rung for you o' Tuesday, and we were meaning to give you a good welcome when you came."

"I know, I know," said Peter, "but I never could do anything right from a boy, could I? Talking of that, are the boys all well?"

"Doing first-rate, my lord, thank you. Bill's got his sergeant's stripes last week."

"Good luck to it," said Peter heartily. He let the clutch in, and they moved on up a wide avenue of beeches.

"I suppose it's a mile from your gate to the front door?"

"Just about."

"And do you keep deer in the park?"

"We do."

"And peacocks on the terrace?"

"I'm afraid so. All the story-book things."

At the far end of the avenue, the great house loomed gray against the sunlight—a long Palladian front, its windows still asleep, and behind it the chimneys and turrets of rambling wings and odd, fantastic sprouts of architectural fancy.

"It's not very old," said Peter, apologetically, as they turned away, leaving the house on their left. "Nothing before Queen Elizabeth. No donjon keep. No moat. The castle fell down a good many years ago, I'm thankful to say. But we've got specimens of all the bad periods since then and one or two of the good ones. And the Dower House is impeccable Inigo Jones."

Harriet, stumbling sleepily up the impeccable Inigo Jones staircase in the wake of a tall footman, was aware of a scurry of high heels on the landing and a cry of delight. The footman flattened himself swiftly against the wall as the Dowager Duchess shot past him in a rose pink dressing-gown, her white plaits flying and Ahasuerus clinging for dear life to her shoulder.

"My darlings, how lovely to see you!—Morton, go and get Franklin out of bed and send her to her ladyship immediately—You must be tired and famished—How dreadful about the poor young man!—Your hands are frozen, my dear—I do hope Peter hasn't been driving at a hundred miles an hour this horrid cold morning—Morton, you silly man, can't you see Ahasuerus is scratching me? Take him off at once—I've put you in the Tapestry Room, it's warmer —Dear me! I feel as though I hadn't seen either of you for a month—Morton, tell them to bring breakfast up here instantly—and what *you* want, Peter, is a hot bath."

"Baths," said Peter, "real baths are definitely a good idea." They walked along a wide landing, with aquatints along the wall, and two or three tables in Queen Anne Chinoiserie, with Famille Rose jars upon them. At the door of the Tapestry Room was Bunter—who must either have got up very early or never gone to bed, for he was dressed with an impeccability worthy of Inigo Jones. Franklin, also impeccable, but slightly flurried in her manner, arrived almost at the same moment. The grateful sound of running water broke refreshingly upon the ear. The Duchess kissed them both, announcing that they were to do exactly as they liked and that she wasn't going to bother them; and before the door shut they heard her energetically scolding Morton for not having gone to see the dentist and threatening him with gumboils, pyorrhea, septic poisoning, indigestion and a complete set of false teeth if he persisted in behaving like a baby.

"This," said Peter, "is one of the presentable Wimseys—Lord Roger; he was a friend of Sidney's and wrote poetry and died young of a wasting fever, and all that kind of thing. That, as you see, is Queen Elizabeth; she slept here in the usual way and nearly bust the family bank. The portrait is said to be by Zucchero, but it's not. The contemporary duke, on the other hand, really is by Antonio Moro, and that's the best thing about it. He was one of the tedious Wimseys, and greed was his leading characteristic. This old harridan was his sister, Lady Stavesacre, who slapped Francis Bacon's face. She's no business to be here, but the Stavesacres are hard up, so we bought her in. . . ."

The afternoon sun slanted in through the long windows of the gallery, picking out here a blue Garter ribbon, there a scarlet uniform, lighting up a pair of slender hands by Van Dyck, playing among the powdered curls of a Gainsborough, or throwing into sudden startling brilliance some harsh white face set in a somber black periwig.

"That awful ill-tempered-looking brute is the—I forget which duke, but his name was Thomas and he died about 1775—his son made a sad, imprudent marriage with a hosier's widow—here she is, looking rather fed-up about it. And there's the prodigal son—rather a look of Jerry about him, don't you think?"

"Yes, it's very like him. Who's this one? He's got a queer, visionary sort of face, rather nice."

"That's their younger son, Mortimer; he was as mad as a hatter and founded a new religion with himself as its only follower. That's Dr. Gervase Wimsey, Dean of St. Paul's; he was a martyr under Queen Mary. This is his brother, Henry—he raised the standard for Queen Mary in Norfolk at her accession. Our family's always been very good at having a foot in both camps. That's my father, like Gerald, but much better looking. . . . That's a Sargent, which is about its only excuse for existence."

"How old were you then, Peter?"

"Twenty-one; full of illusions and trying hard to look sophisticated. Sargent saw through that, damn the fellow! Here is Gerald, with a horse, by Furse; and downstairs in the horrible room he calls his study, you will find a picture of a horse, with Gerald, by Munnings. Here's my mother, by Laszlo—a first-class portrait of her, a good many years ago, of course. Not that anything but a very rapidly moving picture could really convey her quality."

"She fills me with delight. When I came down just before lunch I found her in the hall, putting iodine on Bunter's nose, where Ahasuerus had scratched him."

"That cat scratches everybody. I saw Bunter—he was very self-conscious about it. 'I am thankful to say, my lord, that the color of the application is exceedingly transient.' My mother is rather wasted upon a small household. She was at her best with the staff at the Hall, who all went in mortal terror of her. There is a legend that she personally ironed our old butler's back for lumbago; but she says it wasn't a flatiron but a mustard-plaster. Have you seen enough of this Chamber of Horrors?"

"I like looking at them, though they make me feel sympathetic to the hosier's widow. And I'd like to hear some more about their histories."

"You'll have to get hold of Mrs. Sweetapple. She's the housekeeper and knows them all by heart. I'd better show you the library, though it isn't what it ought to be. It's full of the most appalling rubbish and the good stuff isn't properly catalogued. Neither my father nor my grandfather did anything about it, and Gerald's hopeless. We've got an old bird muddling round there now—he's my third cousin, not the one who's potty and lives at Nice, his younger brother. He hasn't got a bean, so it quite suits him to toddle about down here; and he does his best, and really knows quite a bit of antiquarian stuff, only he has very short sight and no method, and never can keep to one subject at a time. This is the great ballroom—it's rather fine, really, if you don't object to pomp on principle. You get a good view from here over the terraces down to the water-garden, which would look much more impressive if the fountains were turned on. That silly-looking thing among the trees there is one of Sir William Chambers's pagodas, and you can just see the roof of the orangery. . . . Oh, look! there you are—you insisted on peacocks; don't say we didn't provide them for you."

"You're right, Peter—it *is* a story-book place."

They went down the great staircase and across a hall chilly with statuary and thence by way of a long cloister to another hall. A footman came up with them as they paused before a door ornamented with classical pilasters and a carved cornice.

"Here's the library," said Peter. "Yes, Bates, what is it?"

"Mr. Leggatt, my lord. He wanted to see His Grace urgently. I told him he was away, but that your lordship was here, and he asked, could you spare him a moment?"

"It's about that mortgage, I expect—but *I* can't do anything about it. He must see my brother."

"He seems very anxious to speak to your lordship."

"Oh—very well, I'll see him. Do you mind, Harriet?—I

won't be long. Have a look round the library—you may find Cousin Matthew there, but he's quite harmless, only very shy and slightly deaf."

The library, with its tall bays and overhanging gallery, looked east and was already rather dark. Harriet found it restful. She wandered along, pulling out here and there a calf-bound volume at random, sniffing the sweet, musty odor of ancient books, smiling at a carved panel over one of the fireplaces, on which the Wimsey mice had escaped from the coat of arms and played in and out of a heavily undercut swag of flowers and wheat-ears. A large table, littered deep in books and papers, she judged to belong to Cousin Matthew—a half-written sheet in an elderly man's rather tremulous writing appeared to be part of a family chronicle; propped open on a stand beside it was a fat manuscript book, containing a list of household expenses for the year 1587. She pored over it for a few moments, making out such items as "to i paire quysshons of redd sarsnet for my lady Joans chambere" and "to ii li tenter-hooks, and iii li nayles for the same," and then continued to explore, till rounding the corner of the bookshelves into the end bay, she was quite startled to come upon an elderly gentleman, in a dressing-gown. He was standing by the window, with a book in his hand, and the family features were so clearly marked on him—especially the nose—that she could have no doubt of his identity.

"Oh!" said Harriet, "I didn't know anyone was here. Are you—" Cousin Matthew must have a surname, of course; the potty cousin at Nice was the next heir, she remembered, after Gerald's and Peter's lines, so they must be Wimseys—"are you Mr. Wimsey?" (Though, of course, he might quite well be Colonel Wimsey, or Sir Matthew Wimsey, or even Lord Somebody.) "I'm Peter's wife," she added, by way of explaining her presence.

The elderly gentleman smiled very pleasantly and bowed, with a slight wave of the hand as though to say, "Make yourself at home." He was slightly bald, and his gray hair was cropped very closely above his ears and over the temples. She judged him to be sixty-five or so. Having thus made her free of the place, he returned to his book, and Harriet, seeing that he seemed disinclined for conversation, and remembering that he was deaf and shy, decided not to worry him. Five minutes later, she glanced up from examining a number of miniatures displayed in a glass case, and saw that he had made his escape and was, in fact, gazing down at her from a little stair that ran up to the gallery. He bowed again and the flowered skirts of the dressing-gown went whisking up out of sight, just as somebody clicked on the lights at the inner end of the room.

"All in the dark, lady? I'm sorry to have been so long. Come and have tea. That bloke kept me talking. I can't stop Gerald if he wants to foreclose—as a matter of fact, I advised him to. The Mater's come over, by the way; and there's tea going in the Blue Room. She wants you to look at some china there. She's rather keen on china."

With the Duchess in the Blue Room was a slight, oldish man, rather stooping, dressed neatly in an old-fashioned knickerbocker suit, and wearing spectacles and a thin gray beard like a goat's. As Harriet entered, he rose from his chair and came forward with extended hand, uttering a faint nervous bleat.

"Oh, hullo, Cousin Matthew!" cried Peter, heartily, clapping the old gentleman smartly on the shoulder. "Come and be introduced to my wife. This is my cousin, Mr. Matthew Wimsey, who keeps Gerald's books from falling to pieces with age and neglect. He's writing the history of the family from Charlemagne downwards, and has just about got to the Battle of Roncevaux."

"How do you do?" said Cousin Matthew. "I—I hope you had a pleasant journey. The wind's rather chilly today. Peter, my dear boy, how are you?"

"All the better for seeing you. Have you got a new chapter to show me?"

"Not a *chapter*," said Cousin Matthew. "No. A few more pages. I'm afraid I got rather led away upon a sideline of research. I *think* I have got upon the track of the elusive

Simon—the twin, you know, who disappeared and was supposed to have turned pirate."

"Have you, by Jove? Sound work. Are these muffins? Harriet, I hope you share my passion for muffins. I meant to find out before I married you, but the opportunity never arose."

Harriet accepted the muffin, and said, turning to Cousin Matthew:

"I made a silly mistake just now. I met somebody in the library and thought it must be you, and addressed him as Mr. Wimsey."

"Eh?" said Cousin Matthew. "What's that? Somebody in the library?"

"I thought everybody was away," said Peter.

"Perhaps Mr. Liddell came in to look up the *County Histories*," suggested the Duchess. "Why didn't he ask them to give him tea?"

"I think it was someone living in the house," said Harriet, "because he was in his dressing-gown. He's sixty-ish and a little bald on top, with the rest of his hair very short, and he's rather like you, Peter—side-face, anyhow."

"Oh, dear me," said the Duchess; "it must have been Old Gregory."

"Good lord! so it must," agreed Peter, with his mouth full of muffin. "Well, really now, I take that very kind of Old Gregory. He doesn't usually venture out so early in the day—not for a visitor, at any rate. It's a compliment to you, Harriet. Very decent of the old boy."

"Who is Old Gregory?"

"Let me see—he was some sort of cousin of the eighth—ninth—which duke was it, Cousin Matthew?—the William-and-Mary one, anyway. He didn't speak, I suppose? . . . No, he never does, but we always hope that one day he'll make up his mind to."

"I quite thought he was going to, last Monday evening," said Mr. Wimsey. "He was standing up against the shelves in the fourth bay, and I was positively obliged to disturb him to get at the Bredon Letters. I say, 'Pray excuse me, just for one moment,' and he smiled and nodded and seemed about to say something. But he thought better of it, and vanished. I was afraid I might have offended him, but he reappeared in a minute or two in the politest way, just in front of the fireplace, to show there was no ill feeling."

"You must waste quite a lot of time bowing and apologizing to the family spooks," said Peter. "You should just walk slap through them as Gerald does. It's much simpler, and doesn't seem to do either party any harm."

"*You* needn't talk, Peter," said the Duchess. "I distinctly saw you raise your hat to Lady Susan one day on the terrace."

"Oh, come, Mother! That's pure invention. Why on earth should I be wearing a hat on the terrace?"

Had it been possible to imagine either Peter or his mother capable of discourtesy, Harriet would have suspected an elaborate leg-pull. She said tentatively:

"This sounds almost too story-book."

"Not really," said Peter, "because it's all so pointless. They never foretell deaths or find hidden treasures or reveal anything or alarm anybody. Why, even the servants don't mind them. Some people can't see them at all—Helen, for example."

"There!" said the Duchess, "I knew there was something I meant to tell you. Would you believe it?—Helen's insisted on making a new guests' bedroom in the west wing, right in the middle of where Uncle Roger always walks. So stupid and thoughtless. Because, however well one knows they're not solid, it *is* disconcerting for anyone like Mrs. Ambrose to see a captain of the guard step out of the towel-cupboard when she's in no state either to receive him or retreat into the passage. Besides, I can't think that all that damp heat is good for his vibrations, or whatever they call them—last time I saw him he looked quite foggy, poor thing!"

"Helen is sometimes a trifle tactless," said Mr. Wimsey. "The bathroom was certainly needed, but she could quite well have put it further along and given Uncle Roger the housemaid's pantry."

"That's what I told her," said the Duchess; and the conversation took another turn.

Well, no! thought Harriet, sipping her second cup of tea; the idea of being haunted by old Noakes was not likely to worry Peter much.

". . . because, if I'm interfering, you know," said the Duchess, "I had much better be put in a lethal chamber at once, like poor Agag—not in the Bible, of course, but the one before Ahasuerus, he was a blue Persian—and why everybody shouldn't be if they feel like it, I don't know, when they get old and sick and a nuisance to themselves—but I was afraid you might find it a little worrying the first time it happened, so I mentioned it . . . though being married may make a difference and it may not happen at all. . . . Yes, that's Rockingham—one of the good designs—most of it is too two-pence-colored, but this is one of Brameld's landscapes. . . . You wouldn't think anyone who talked so much could be so inaccessible, really, but I always tell myself it's that absurd pretense that one hasn't got any weaknesses—so silly, because we all have, only my husband never would hear of it. . . . Now isn't this bowl amusing? . . . You can see it's Derby by the glaze, but the painting was done by Lady Sarah Wimsey, who married into the Severn-and-Thameses—it's a group of her and her brother and their little dog, and you can recognize the funny little temple, it's the one down by the lake. . . . They used to sell the white china, you know, to amateur artists, and then it went back to be fired in the factory. It's sensitive work, isn't it? Wimseys are either very sensitive, or not sensitive at all, to things like painting and music."

She put her head on one side and looked up at Harriet over the rim of the bowl with bright brown eyes like a bird's.

"I thought it might be rather like that," said Harriet, going back to what the Duchess had really said. "I remember one time, when he'd just finished up a case, he came out to dinner and really seemed quite ill."

"He doesn't like responsibility, you know," said the Duchess, "and the War and one thing and another was bad for people that way. . . . There were eighteen months . . . not that I suppose he'll ever tell you about that, at least, if he does, then you'll know he's cured. . . . I don't mean he went out of his mind or anything, and he was always perfectly sweet about it, only he was so dreadfully afraid to go to sleep . . . and he couldn't give an order, not even to the servants, which made it really very miserable for him, poor lamb! . . . I suppose if you've been giving orders for nearly four years to people to go and get blown to pieces it gives you a—what does one call it nowadays?—an inhibition or an exhibition, or something, of nerves. . . . You needn't sit holding that tea pot, my dear, I'm so sorry—give it to me, I'll put it back. . . . Though really I'm chattering away quite in the dark, because I don't *know* how he takes these things now, and I shouldn't think anybody did, except Bunter—and considering how much we owe Bunter, Ahasuerus should have known better than to scratch him like that. I do hope Bunter isn't being difficult or anything."

"He's a marvel—and quite amazingly tactful."

"Well, that's nice of the man," said the Duchess, frankly, "because sometimes these attached people *are* rather difficult . . . and seeing that if anybody can be said to have pulled Peter round again it was Bunter, one might have to make allowances."

Harriet asked to be told about Bunter.

"Well," said the Duchess, "he was a footman at Sir John Sanderton's before the War and he was in Peter's unit . . . sergeant or something eventually . . . but they were in some—what's that American word for a tight place?—jam, isn't it?—yes, some jam or other together, and took a fancy to one another . . . so Peter promised Bunter that, if they both came out of the War alive, Bunter should come to him. . . . Well, in January 1919, I think it was—yes, it was, because I remember it was a dreadfully cold day—Bunter turned up here, saying he'd wrangled himself out. . . ."

"Bunter never said that, Duchess!"

"No, dear, that's my vulgar way of putting it. He said he had succeeded in obtaining his demobilization, and had come immediately to take up the situation Peter had promised him. Well, my dear, it happened to be one of Peter's very worst days, when he couldn't do anything but just sit and shiver. . . . I liked the look of the man, so I said, 'Well, you can try—but I don't suppose he'll be able to make up his mind one way or the other." So I took Bunter in, and it was quite dark, because I suppose Peter hadn't had the strength of mind to switch the lights on . . . so he had to ask who it was. Bunter said, 'Sergeant Bunter, my lord, come to enter your lordship's service as arranged'—and he turned on the lights and drew the curtains and took charge from that moment. I believe he managed so that for months Peter never had to give an order about so much as a soda-siphon. . . . He found that flat and took Peter up to Town and did everything. . . . I remember . . . I hope I'm not boring you with Bunter, my dear, but it really was rather touching . . . . I'd come up to Town one morning early and looked in at the flat. Bunter was just taking in Peter's breakfast . . . he used to get up very late in those days, sleeping so badly . . . and Bunter came out with a plate in his hand and said, 'Oh, your Grace! His lordship has told me to take away these damned eggs and bring him a sausage.' . . . He was so much overcome that he put down the hot plate on the sitting-room table and took all the polish off. . . . From those sausages," concluded the Duchess, triumphantly, "I don't think Peter ever looked back!"

Harriet thanked her mother-in-law for these particulars. "If there is a crisis," she said, "when the Assizes come on, I'll take Bunter's advice. Anyway, I'm very grateful to you for warning me. I'll promise not to be wifely and solicitous—that would probably put the lid on."

• • • • •

"By the way," said Peter, the following morning, "I'm terribly sorry and all that, but could you possibly bear being hauled off to church? . . . I mean, it'll be kind of well-thought-of if we turn up in the family pew . . . gives people something to talk about and all that sort of thing. Not, of course, if it makes you feel *absolutely* like Saint Thingummy on the gridiron—all hot and beginning to curl at the corners—only if it's a comparatively mild martyrdom, like the little-ease or the stocks."

"Of course I'll come to church."

It felt a little odd, all the same, to stand virtuously in the hall with Peter, waiting for a parent to come and shepherd one away to Morning Service. It took, for one thing, so many years off one's age. The Duchess came down, putting on her gloves, just as one's mother had always done, and saying, "Don't forget, dear, there's a collection today," as she handed her prayer-book to her son to carry.

"And oh!" said the Duchess, "the vicar sent up a message that his asthma's rather bad and the curate away; so as Gerald isn't here he'd be very grateful if you'd read the Lessons."

Peter said amiably that he would, but hoped it wouldn't be anything about Jacob, whose personality irritated him.

"No, dear. It's a nice gloomy piece out of Jeremiah. You'll do it so much better than Mr. Jones, because I was always very careful about adenoids, making you breathe through the nose. We'll pick up Cousin Matthew on the way. . . ."

The small church was packed. "Good house," said Peter, surveying the congregation from the porch. "The peppermint season has begun, I notice." He removed his hat and followed his female belongings up the aisle with preternatural decorum.

". . . world without end, amen."

The congregation sat down with a creak and a shuffle, and disposed itself to listen with approval to his lordship's rendering of Jewish prophecy. Peter, handling the heavy red-silk markers, glanced around the building, collected the attention of the back pews, clasped the brass eagle firmly by either wing, opened his mouth, and then paused, to direct his eyeglass awfully upon a small boy sitting just beneath the lectern.

"Is that Willy Blodgett?"

Willy Blodgett became petrified.

"Now, don't you pinch your sister again. It's not cricket."

"There," said Willy Blodgett's mother in an audible whisper, "sit still! I declare I'm ashamed of you."

"Here beginneth the Fifth Chapter of the Book of Prophet Jeremiah.

"Run ye to and fro through the streets of Jerusalem, and see now, and know, and seek in the broad places thereof, if ye can find a man, if there be any that executeth judgment. . . ."

(Yes, indeed. Frank Crutchley in the local jail—was he listening to execution and judgment? Or didn't you have to attend Divine Service until after you were tried and sentenced?)

"Wherefore a lion out of the forest shall slay them, and a wolf of the evenings shall spoil them, a leopard shall watch over their cities. . . ."

(Peter seemed to be rather enjoying the zoo. Harriet noticed that the family pew had crouching cats in place of the ordinary poppy-heads, in compliment no doubt to the Wimsey crest. There was a chantry at the east end of the south aisle, with canopied tombs. Wimseys again, she supposed.)

"Hear now this, O foolish people, and without understanding; which have eyes and see not . . ."

(To think how they had looked on while that pot was wiped clean. . . . The reader, untroubled by this association of ideas, had passed happily on into the next verse—the exciting one, about waves tossing and roaring.)

"For among my people are found wicked men: they lay

wait, as he that setteth snares; they set a trap, they catch men."

(Harriet looked up. Had she fancied that slight check in the voice? Peter's eyes were steadily fixed on the page.)

". . . and my people love to have it so: and what will ye do in the end thereof?

"Here endeth the First Lesson."

"Very well read," said Mr. Wimsey, leaning across Harriet, "excellent; I can always hear everything you say."

Peter said in Harriet's ear:

"You ought to hear old Gerald, when he gets in among the Hivites and the Perizzites and the Girgashites."

As the Te Deum started, Harriet again thought of Pagglehem, and wondered whether Miss Twitterton had found courage to preside at the organ.

CHAPTER III

TALBOYS: CROWN CELESTIAL

So here I'll watch the night and wait
To see the morning shine
When he will hear the stroke of eight
And now the stroke of nine.

—A. E. HOUSMAN,
A SHROPSHIRE LAD

After the magistrates' court they were free until the Assizes. So they finished their honeymoon in Spain, after all.

The Dowager Duchess wrote that the furniture had been sent up to Talboys from the Hall and that the painting and plastering were done. It would be better to leave work on the new bathroom until the frosts were over. But the house was habitable.

And Harriet wrote back that they were coming home in time for the trial, and that no marriage had ever been so happy as theirs—only, Peter was dreaming again.

Sir Impey Biggs, cross-examining:

"And you expect the jury to believe that this remarkable piece of mechanism went unnoticed by the deceased from 6:20 to 9 o'clock?"

"I expect nothing. I have described the mechanism as we constructed it."

Then the judge:

"The witness can only speak to his knowledge of the facts, Sir Impey."

"Quite so, m'lud."

The point made. The suggestion implanted that the witness was a little unreasonable. . . .

"Now, this booby-trap you set for the prisoner. . . ."

"I understood the witness to say that the trap was set by way of experiment, and that the prisoner arrived unexpectedly and sprang it before he could be warned."

"That is so, my lord."

"I am obliged to your lordship. . . . What effect did the accidental springing of this booby-trap have upon the prisoner?"

"He seemed very much frightened."

"We may easily believe that. And astonished?"

"Yes."

"When suffering under this very natural surprise and alarm, was he able to speak coolly and collectedly?"

"He was anything but cool and collected."

"Did you think he was aware of what he was saying?"

"I can scarcely be a judge of that. He was agitated."

"Would you go so far as to call his manner frenzied?"

"Yes; that word describes it very well."

"He was out of his mind with terror?"

"I am not qualified to say so."

"Now, Lord Peter. You have explained very clearly that this engine of destruction at the lowest point of its swing was not less than six feet from the ground?"

"That is so."

"Anybody less than six feet in height would be perfectly safe from it?"

"Exactly."

"We have heard that the prisoner's height is five feet and ten inches. He was, therefore, not at any time in danger from it?"

"Not in the slightest."

"If the prisoner himself had arranged the pot and chain as the prosecution suggest, he would know better than anybody else that it could not even touch him?"

"In that case, certainly he must have known it."

"Yet he was very much alarmed?"

"Very much alarmed indeed."

An exact and noncommittal witness.

Agnes Twitterton, an excited and spiteful witness, whose very obvious resentment against the prisoner did him if anything more good than harm. Dr. James Craven, a highly technical witness. Martha Ruddle, a talkative and circumlocutory witness. Thomas Puffett, a deliberate and sententious witness. The Rev. Simon Goodacre, a reluctant witness. Lady Peter Wimsey, a very quiet witness. Mervyn Bunter, a deferential witness. P.C. Joseph Sellon, a witness of few words. Superintendent Kirk, an officially impartial witness. A strange iron-monger from Clerkenwell, who had sold the prisoner a quantity of lead shot and an iron chain, a damaging witness.

Then, the prisoner himself, witness in his own defense: a very bad witness indeed, sullen and impudent by turns.

Sir Impey Biggs, eloquent on behalf of the prisoner—"this industrious and ambitious young man"; hinting at prejudice—"a lady who may have some cause to fancy herself ill-used"; indulgently skeptical about "the instrument of destruction so picturesquely constructed by a gentleman whose ingenuity is notorious"; virtuously indignant at the construction placed upon "words uttered at random by a terrorized man"; astonished to discover in the case for the Prosecution "not a scintilla of direct proof"; passionately moving in his appeal to the jury not to sacrifice a young and valuable life on evidence so flimsily put together.

Counsel for the Prosecution, gathering up the threads of proof that Sir Impey had tossed into disorder, weaving them into a rope as thick as a cable.

The Judge, undoing the twist again to show the jury exactly what was the strength of each separate strand, and handling the materials back to them, neatly assorted.

The Jury, absent for an hour.

Sir Impey Biggs came over. "If they hesitate all this time, they may acquit him in spite of himself."

"You ought to have kept him out of the box."

"We advised him to stay out. I think he got swollen head."

"Here they come."

"Members of the jury, are you agreed upon your verdict?"

"We are."

"Do you find the prisoner guilty or not guilty of the murder of William Noakes?"

"Guilty."

"You say he is guilty and that is the verdict of you all?"

"Yes."

"Prisoner at the bar, you have been arraigned upon a charge of murder, and have placed yourself upon your country. That country has now found you guilty. Have you anything to say why judgment of death should not be pronounced upon you according to law?"

"I say I don't care a damn for the lot of you. You've proved nothing against me. His lordship's a rich man and he had a down on me—him and Aggie Twitterton."

"Prisoner at the bar, the jury, after a careful and patient hearing, have found you guilty of murder. In that verdict I entirely concur. The sentence of the court upon you is that you be taken from hence to the place from which you came, and thence to a place of execution, and you be there hanged by the neck until you be dead and your body buried in the precincts of the prison in which you shall last have been confined, and may the Lord have mercy upon your soul."

"Amen."

. . . . .

One of the most admirable features of the English criminal law is said to be its dispatch. You are tried as soon as possible after your arrest, the trial takes three or four days at most, and after your conviction (unless, of course, you appeal), you are executed within three weeks.

Crutchley refused to appeal, preferring to announce that he done it, that he'd do it again, and let them get on with it, it made no odds to him.

Harriet, in consequence, was left to form the opinion that three weeks was quite the worst period of waiting in the world. A prisoner should be executed the morning after his conviction, as after a court-martial, so that one could get all the misery over in a lump and have done with it. Or the business should be left to drag on for months and years, as in America, till one was so weary of it as to have exhausted all emotion.

The worst feature, she thought, about those three weeks, was Peter's determined courtesy and cheerfulness. Whenever he was not over at the county jail, patiently inquiring whether there was anything he could do for the prisoner, he was at Talboys, being considerate, admiring the arrangement of the house and furniture, or putting himself at his wife's disposal to tour the country in search of missing chimney-pots or other objects of interest. This heart-breaking courtesy was punctuated by fits of exigent and exhausting passion, which alarmed her not only by their reckless abandonment, but by being apparently automatic and almost impersonal. She welcomed them, because he would sleep afterwards as though stunned. But every day found him more firmly entrenched behind some kind of protective fortification, and herself becoming less and less a person to him. In his present mood, she felt unhappily, almost any woman would have done.

She was unspeakably grateful to the Duchess, who had forewarned and so, to some extent, fore-armed her. She wondered whether her own decision "not to be wifely and solicitous" had been a wise one. She wrote, asking for counsel. The Duchess's reply, ranging over a variety of subjects, amounted to saying, "Let him find his own way out." A postscript added: "One thing, my dear—*he is still there*, and that's encouraging. It's so easy for a man to be somewhere else."

About a week before the execution, Mrs. Goodacre turned up in a state of considerable agitation. "That wretched man Crutchley!" she said. "I *knew* he would get Polly Mason into trouble, and he *has!* And now what's to be done? Even supposing he could get leave to marry her and wanted to do it—and I don't suppose he cares a rap for the girl—is it better for the child to have no father or one who's been hanged for murder? I'm sure *I* don't know! Even Simon doesn't know—though naturally he says he ought to marry her. I don't see why he shouldn't—it won't make the least difference to him. But now the girl doesn't want him to, either—says she doesn't want to be married to a murderer, and I'm sure I can't blame her. Her mother's in a great way, of course. She should have kept Polly at home or sent her into good service—I told her she was much too young to go into that drapery shop at Pagford, and *not* really steady, but it's too late to say that now."

Peter asked whether Crutchley knew anything about this development.

"The girl says not. . . . And goodness me!" said Mrs. Goodacre, suddenly waking up to a whole series of possibilities, "suppose old Mr. Noakes hadn't lost his money and Crutchley hadn't been found out, what would have happened to Polly? He meant to have that money by hook or by crook . . . if you ask me, my dear Lady Peter, Polly's had a narrower escape than she thought for."

"Oh, it mightn't have come to that," said Harriet.

"Perhaps not; but one undiscovered murder makes many. However, that isn't the point. The point is what we're to do about this baby that's on the way."

Peter said he thought Crutchley ought at least to be told about it. He thought it was only fair that the man should be given the chance to do what he could. He offered to take Mrs. Mason over to see the governor of the prison. Mrs. Goodacre said it was very good of him.

Harriet, escorting Mrs. Goodacre down the path to the gate, said it would do her husband good to have something definite to do about Crutchley; he worried a good deal.

"Very likely he does," said Mrs. Goodacre. "You can see he's that sort. Simon's just the same if he has had to be severe with anybody. But that's men all over. They want the thing done and then, of course, they don't like the consequences. Poor dears, they can't help it. They haven't got logical minds."

Peter reported in the evening that Crutchley had been very angry and refused categorically to have anything further to do with Polly or any more blasted women. He had, in fact, refused to see either Mrs. Mason or Peter or anybody else, and had told the governor to damn well leave him alone. Peter then began to worry about what ought to be done for the girl. Harriet let him wrestle with this problem (which had at least the merit of being a practical one) and then said:

"Couldn't you put Mrs. Climpson on to it? With all her High-Church connections she ought to be able to hear of some job that would do. I've been to see the girl, and she doesn't seem to be a bad sort, really. And you could help with money and that sort of thing."

He looked at her as though seeing her for the first time for a fortnight.

"Why, of course. I think my brain must have gone mushy. Miss Climpson is the obvious person. I'll write to her at once."

He got pen and paper, wrote the address and "Dear Miss Climpson," and sat blankly, pen in hand.

"Look here—I think you could write this better than I could. You've been to see the girl. You can explain. . . . Oh, God! I'm so tired."

It was the first crack in the defenses.

• • • • •

He made his last effort to see Crutchley on the night before the execution. He was armed with a letter from Miss Climpson containing the outline of some very excellent and sensible arrangements for Polly Mason.

"I don't know when I shall be back," he said. "Don't wait up for me."

"Oh, Peter—"

"I say, for God's sake don't wait up for me."

"Very well, Peter."

Harriet went to look for Bunter, and found him running over the Daimler from bonnet to back axle.

"Is his lordship taking you with him?"

"I couldn't say, my lady. I have had no instructions."

"Try and go with him."

"I will do my best, my lady."

"Bunter . . . what usually happens?"

"It depends, my lady. If the condemned man is able to display a friendly spirit, the reaction is less painful for all concerned. On the other hand, I have known us take the next boat or airplane to a foreign country at a considerable distance. But the circumstances have, of course, been different."

"Yes, Bunter, his lordship has particularly said he does not wish me to sit up for him. But if he should return tonight, and he doesn't . . . if he should be very restless . . ." That sentence did not seem to be ending properly. Harriet began again. "I shall go upstairs, but I don't see how one could possibly sleep. I shall sit by the fire in my room."

"Very good, my lady."

Their eyes met with perfect understanding.

The car was brought around to the door.

"All right, Bunter. That will do."

"Your lordship does not require my services?"

"Obviously not. You can't leave her ladyship alone in the house."

"Her ladyship has been good enough to give me permission to go."

"Oh!"

A pause during which Harriet, standing in the porch, had time to think: Suppose he asks me whether I imagine he needs a keeper!

Then Bunter's voice, with exactly the right note of dignified inquiry:

"I had anticipated that your lordship would wish me to accompany you as usual."

"I see. Very well. Hop in."

The old house was Harriet's companion in her vigil. It waited with her, its evil spirit cast out, itself swept and garnished, ready for the visit of devil or angel.

It was past two o'clock when she heard the car return. There were steps on the gravel, the opening and shutting of the door, a brief murmur of voices—then silence. Then, unheralded by so much as a shuffle on the stair, came Bunter's soft tap at the little door.

"Well, Bunter?"

"Everything has been done that could be done, my lady." They spoke in hushed tones, as though the doomed man lay already dead. "It was some considerable time before he would consent to see his lordship. At length the governor persuaded him, and his lordship was able to deliver the message and acquaint him with the arrangements made for the young woman's future. I understand that he seemed to take very little interest in the matter; they told me there that he continued to be a sullen and intractable prisoner. His lordship came away very much distressed. It is his custom under such circumstances to ask the condemned man's forgiveness. From his demeanor, I do not think he had it."

"Did you come straight back?"

"No, my lady. On leaving the prison at midnight, his lordship drove away in a westerly direction, very fast, for about fifty miles. That is not unusual; I have frequently known him drive all night. Then he stopped the car suddenly at a crossroads, waiting for a few minutes as though he were endeavoring to make up his mind, turned around and came straight back here, driving even faster. He was shivering very much when we came in, but refused to eat or drink anything. He said he could not sleep, so I made up a good fire in the sitting-room. I left him seated on the settle. I came up by the back way, my lady, because I think he might not wish to feel that you were in any anxiety about him."

"Quite right, Bunter—I'm glad you did that. Where are you going to be?"

"I shall remain in the kitchen, my lady, within call. His lordship is not likely to require me, but if he should do so, he will find me at hand, making myself a little supper."

"That's an excellent plan. I expect his lordship will prefer to be left to himself, but if he should ask for me—not on any account unless or until he does—will you tell him—"

"Yes, my lady?"

"Tell him there is still a light in my room, and that you think I am very much concerned about Crutchley."

"Very good, my lady. Would your ladyship like me to bring you a cup of tea?"

"Oh, Bunter, thank you. Yes, I should."

When the tea came, she drank it thirstily, and then sat listening. Everything was silent, except the church clock chiming out the quarters; but when she went into the next room she could hear faintly the beat of restless feet on the floor below.

She went back and waited. She could think only one thing, and that over and over again. I must not go to him; he must come to me. If he does not want me, I have failed altogether, and that failure will be with us all our lives. But the decision must be his and not mine. I have got to accept it. I have got to be patient. Whatever happens, I must not go to him.

It was four by the church clock when she heard the

sound she had been waiting for: the door at the bottom of the stair creaked. For a few minutes nothing followed, and she thought he had changed his mind. She held her breath till she heard his footsteps mount slowly and reluctantly and enter the next room. She feared they might stop there, but this time he came straight on and pushed open the door which she had left ajar.

"Harriet. . . ."

"Come in, dear."

He came over and stood close beside her, mute and shivering. She put her hand out to him and he took it eagerly, laying his other hand in a fumbling gesture on her shoulder.

"You're cold, Peter. Come nearer the fire."

"It's not cold," he said, half-angrily, "it's my rotten nerves. I can't help it. I suppose I've never been really right since the War. I hate behaving like this. I tried to stick it out by myself."

"But why should you?"

"It's this damned waiting about till they've finished. . . ."

"I know. I couldn't sleep either."

He stood holding out his hands mechanically to the fire till he could control the chattering of his teeth.

"It's damnable for you too. I'm sorry. I'd forgotten. That sounds idiotic. But I've always been alone."

"Yes, of course. I'm like that, too. I like to crawl away and hide in a corner."

"Well," he said, with a transitory gleam of himself, "you're my corner and I've come to hide."

"Yes, my dearest."

(And the trumpets sounded for her on the other side.)

"It's not as bad as it might be. The worst times are when they haven't admitted it, and one goes over the evidence and wonders if one wasn't wrong, after all. . . . And sometimes they're so damned decent . . ."

"What was Crutchley like?"

"He doesn't seem to care for anybody or regret anything except that he didn't pull it off. He hates old Noakes just as much as the day he killed him. He wasn't interested in Polly—only said she was a fool and a bitch, and I was a bigger fool to waste time and money on her. And Aggie Twitterton could go and rot with the whole pack of us, and the sooner the better."

"Peter, how horrible!"

"If there *is* a God or a judgment—what next? What have we done?"

"I don't know. But I don't suppose anything we could do would prejudice the defense."

"I suppose not. I wish we knew more about it."

Five o'clock. He got up and looked out into the darkness, which as yet showed no sign of day's coming.

"Three hours more. . . . They give them something to make them sleep. . . . It's a merciful death compared with most natural ones. . . . It's only the waiting and knowing beforehand. . . . And the ugliness. . . . Old Johnson was right; the procession to Tyburn was kinder. . . . 'The hangman with his gardener's gloves comes through the padded door.' . . . I got permission to see a hanging once. . . . I thought I'd better know . . . but it hasn't cured me of meddling."

"If you hadn't meddled, it might have been Joe Sellon or Aggie Twitterton."

"I know that. I keep telling myself that."

"If you hadn't meddled six years ago, it would almost certainly have been me."

That stopped him in his caged pacing to and fro.

"If you had had to live through that night, Harriet, knowing what was coming to you, I would have lived it through in the same knowledge. Death would have been nothing, though you were little to me then compared with what you are now. . . . What the devil am I doing, to remind you of that horror?"

"If it hadn't been for that, we shouldn't be here—we

should never have seen one another. If Philip hadn't been murdered, we shouldn't be here. If I'd never lived with Philip, I shouldn't be married to you. Everything wrong and wretched—and out of it all I've somehow got *you*. What can one make of that?"

"Nothing. There seems to be no sense in it at all."

He flung the problem away from him and began his restless walk again.

Presently he said:

"My gracious silence—who called his wife that?"

"Coriolanus."

"Another tormented devil. . . . I'm grateful, Harriet—No, that's not quite right; you're not being kind, you're being yourself. Aren't you horribly tired?"

"Not the least bit."

She found it difficult to think of Crutchley, baring his teeth at death like a trapped rat. She could see his agony only at second-hand through the mind that it dominated. And through the mind's distress and her own there broke uncontrollably the assurance that was like the distant note of a trumpet.

"They hate executions, you know. It upsets the other prisoners. They bang on the doors and make nuisances of themselves. Everybody's nervous. . . . Caged like beasts, separately. . . . That's the hell of it . . . we're all in separate cells. . . . I can't get out, said the starling. . . . If one could only get out for one moment, or go to sleep, or stop thinking. . . . Oh, damn that cursed clock! . . . Harriet, for God's sake, hold on to me . . . get me out of this . . . break down the door. . . ."

"Hush, dearest. I'm here. We'll see it out together."

Through the eastern side of the casement, the sky grew pale with the forerunners of the dawn.

"Don't let me go."

The light grew stronger as they waited.

Quite suddenly, he said, "Oh, damn!" and began to cry

—in an awkward, unpracticed way at first, and then more easily. So she held him, crouched at her knees, against her breast, huddling his head in her arms that he might not hear eight o'clock strike.

Now, as in Tullia's tomb one lamp burnt clear
  Unchanged for fifteen hundred year,
  May these love-lamps we here enshrine,
In warmth, light, lasting, equal the divine.
  Fire ever doth aspire,
And makes all like itself, turns all to fire,
But ends in ashes; which these cannot do,
For none of these is fuel, but fire too.
This is joy's bonfire, then, where love's strong arts
Make of so noble individual parts
One fire of four inflaming eyes, and of two loving
  hearts.

—JOHN DONNE, *ECLOGUE FOR THE MARRIAGE OF THE EARL OF SOMERSET*